For Bernie, the loveliest of women, the kindest of friends.
So missed by all those who loved you and knew you.
Forever in our hearts.

For Mark and all his family.

For Arline and Charlie, my friends in Bronxville, New York.
Big thanks. See you at Bill's, PJ's, Covent Garden.

And a special thank you to Amanda Ridout at Headline,
she knows what for.

FACELESS

Martina Cole

HEADLINE

I'll Never Fall In Love Again
Words by Hal David. Music by Burt Bacharach.
© Copyright 1968 New Hidden Valley Music Company/Casa David Music
Incorporated, USA. Universal/MCA Music Limited, Elsinore House,
77 Fulham Palace Road, London W6 8JA (50%)/Windswept Music (London)
Limited, Hope House, 40 St. Peter's Road, London W6 9BD (50%).
Used by Permission of Music Sales Ltd. All Rights Reserved.
International Copyright Secured.

Pusher Man
Words and Music by Curtis Mayfield.
© 1975 Warner–Tamerlane Music Publishing Corp, USA.
Warner/Chappell Music Ltd, London W6 8BS.
Lyrics reproduced by permission of IMP Ltd. All rights reserved.

First published in 2001 by
HEADLINE BOOK PUBLISHING

10 9 8 7 6 5 4 3 2 1

British Library Cataloguing in Publication Data

Cole, Martina
  Faceless
  1.Women ex-convicts - England - London - Fiction
  2.Revenge - Fiction 3.Suspense fiction
  I.Title
  823.9'14[F]

  ISBN 0 7472 1836 6 (hardback)
  ISBN 0 7472 7753 2 (trade paperback)

Typeset by Letterpart Limited, Reigate, Surrey
Printed and bound in Great Britain by
Mackays of Chatham PLC, Chatham, Kent

HEADLINE BOOK PUBLISHING
A division of Hodder Headline
338 Euston Road
LONDON NW1 3BH

www.headline.co.uk
www.hodderheadline.com

Introduction

People often ask me about the titles of my books. The idea for this new one came to me while I was researching. I was interviewing a very nice woman whom I had known for a good few years. She'd been a prostitute for most of her life and was always kind enough to keep me up to date on the pavement jargon and with anecdotes about her working life. Anyway, the two of us were talking over a bottle of wine when she said something I shall never forget.

She had been, in her day, 'a well-paid brass' as she put it herself. By then, though, she was older and on the slippery slope that age invariably brings to women who sell themselves for profit.

Laughing, she said, 'We are faceless women, Tina, living faceless lives. Our punters are faceless. If I took a bloke on and he came back ten minutes later I wouldn't even recognise him. If we met again in the supermarket we wouldn't know one another.'

Well, she gave me the title of this book.

Since then her phone has been cut off and I can't seem to track her down. I heard she'd died of AIDS. I hope she is happy wherever she is. She was a good laugh and a good mate.

You know who you are. If you read this, give me a call and let me know you are OK. This one's for you and for all the laughs we have had over the years.

Book One

'What do you get when you fall in love?
A guy with the pin to burst your bubble.
That's what you get, for all your trouble.
I'll never fall in love again' –

Hal David and Burt Bacharach

'Mutual Forgiveness of each vice,
Such are the Gates of Paradise.'

William Blake (1757-1827)

Prologue

She heard the grille open and kept her eyes closed. She knew it would be Walker, a good PO as POs went, but she wasn't in the mood for talk just yet.

She breathed in heavily, feeling the close, heavy scent of the cell, letting it wash over her one last time. After twelve years and ten months on remand she was finally being released. She didn't think of it as going home because she had no home. She had no friends, no family, nothing that other women took for granted. Her children were lost to her; her mother had given up on her. The few friends she'd had, and they were *few*, had all dropped away over the years. But that was understandable. She was a convicted murderess. A double murderess. A woman who had killed two friends, no less, so it wasn't surprising that the few others she'd had were wary of continuing the acquaintance.

Inside she had kept herself to herself and the other women had respected that. One good thing about a big lump of a sentence, people left you alone.

She smiled gently and the action changed her face completely. The permanent frown was gone, revealing smooth unwrinkled skin. Her high cheekbones, the envy of more than a few screws and prisoners over the years, gave her face a Nordic beauty. Full, curving lips made her face look enigmatic, interesting. Her cool blue eyes were softer than usual, with the look of the girl she had been twelve years earlier when she had walked into a prison cell, more aware than anyone realised that she was away for what should have been the best, most productive years of her life.

She had kissed her children goodbye, and in effect kissed her life goodbye. But it was her own doing, she knew that. The judge had called her a callous and disturbed individual. He had been right. From her teens on, her whole life had been lived through a drug- and alcohol-induced haze. From petty thief to prostitute in two easy steps, she thought, a faraway look in her eyes.

Her mother had been right. Her favourite saying had always been: 'You will never amount to nothing.'

And her mother would know better than anyone. After all, it was a family trait.

The door rattled and she frowned, aware that she should have been up and dressed by now and ready to go. But she had been incarcerated for so long she wasn't sure if she could cope with the outside world again. It had never been kind to her.

Her eyes travelled around her cell. It was like a refuge to her today. It felt safe and homely. It felt *right*.

She pushed the thought away, knowing it was a natural feeling. Telling herself over and over that once she walked out of the gates and was free, her life would start again.

She was counting on it.

The first thing she'd do, after twelve years without a glimpse of them, was see her kids.

She sat upright, looking around her with the eyes of a woman about to be freed. Eyes that could bore into people's souls and see them as they really were. Eyes that were desperate for a glimpse of her children, greedily contemplating her first sight of them in all their glory. Not as distant memories that were hard to place because she had been out of it for so much of their young lives, but seeing the people they had become and hoping against hope that they didn't hold it all against her. That they would understand she had had no control over what had happened to them. That she wasn't really capable of motherhood then, any more than she was now.

Children were unlucky really. They were born without any say in things whatsoever. It was a lottery for them in some respects, what kind of mother they would acquire once out of the warmth of a snug and comfortable womb. A loving caring individual who would rush to fulfil their every whim? Or a selfish one who resented their intrusion into her otherwise orderly life? Children were a shock to the system for most women. The idea of a baby was wonderful; the reality of a toddler devastating. They drained you, made you realise you would never again be your own person. They kept you up half the night and ran around all the day. They needed feeding, training, time, effort, sweat and tears.

She had been fifteen when Tiffany had been born and seventeen when she had had Jason. Two different kids with radically different fathers. One black, one white. Her sister had joked she should go

4

on Race Relations Board outings. But it had not been funny really.

She had been twenty-one, pretty in a make-up and tits kind of way, when she had beaten to death two other prostitutes in a squat in Kensington.

She closed her eyes at the unwanted image: waking up to the blood. Blood everywhere. On the walls, door, even the ceiling. She had been covered in their blood; it was in her eyes, her hair, her skin.

She felt the familiar rise of bile at the image and the crashing of her heart as it pumped her own blood through her body at a rate that made her feel light-headed. It was a reminder, every time her heart beat like this, just what she had robbed her friends of. And they had been friends, that was the strangest thing of all.

Why had she done it?

Why could she never remember what it had been over?

Why the fuck had she pumped herself so full of narcotics she'd successfully blotted out whole days of her life, never to be recalled?

All she could remember was drugs and drink and man after man. How had she lived that life for so long? After twelve years clean, more or less, she saw the world through different eyes. Saw the world as a straight person saw it. Didn't need to blot it out any more. Didn't need to get so out of it she could vomit and not know anything about it until she awoke to the familiar sour smell.

But she also knew she was institutionalised, living in an artificial environment. No bills to pay, and warmth, food and drink provided for her at regular intervals. She had not turned off a light switch in over twelve years. Had been bedded down by seven-thirty most nights, and escaped into books through the absence of television as a stimulus.

She turned towards the door, hearing the screw's approach.

'Come on, girl, up and out of it. Have you forgotten what day this is?'

She didn't answer, but made an effort to look busy. She was already packed, in fact, had been for a week. What she owned was so minimal she could put it all into a carrier bag. In over twelve years she had had not one visitor, not one letter.

She washed her face in cold water, then dressed quickly, silently. She sat on the bed with her small bag and waited for the breakfast she wouldn't even eat, though the bitter coffee would be welcome.

One half of her could not wait to get out of the door, get a new life, join society this time as a productive member. The other half was frightened witless at the thought of being out in the real world, talking and interacting with real people. People who knew nothing about her or, worse, people who did.

She put her face in her hands and sighed. Her Bible was on the bed beside her and she picked it up, whispering over and over, 'God forgive me, God forgive me, God forgive me.'

And in her mind's eye she saw Caroline and Bethany again, lying mangled and dead as she finally realised what she had done to them.

Caroline her friend; Bethany her best friend.

She had reduced them to bloody pulp with a baseball bat and a torque wrench. But why? That was the question she asked herself a hundred times a day.

Why?

For nearly thirteen years, she had not been able to find an answer.

She finally walked out of Cookham Wood Prison into a light rain. She stood for a few moments, savouring the feeling of the moisture on her face. It was cold, the kind of misty rain that soaked through clothes and skin, the kind of rain other people hated, but for her it was proof she was alive and well.

She trudged to the bus stop, aware that her clothes left a lot to be desired, in her pocket the address of a halfway house. She fingered the money beside it. It felt dirty and used, crumpled as it lay in her palm.

It felt like her.

Two young girls walked past her, their clothes and hairstyles looking completely alien. They stared at her rudely and she ignored them, remembering a time when she would have faced up to them. Would have frightened them with her language and her aggression. Instead she walked on, oblivious to their stares and muttered comments.

She breathed in the misty air, sucked it deep into her chest. Enjoyed the feeling of being outside yet alone. Wanted the comfort of the anonymous room she would occupy tonight. She wanted desperately to be alone, properly alone again. Wanted the opportunity to think in peace.

Instead she found herself on a train. She didn't want to think about where she was going. It would hurt too much.

She drank in the scenes that rushed by as she stared out of the window. A woman sat opposite her with a young boy. He was handsome, well-behaved. She couldn't help staring into his face as if she could read his mind with her eyes alone.

What were her own children doing at this minute? Did anyone keep in contact with them? She had signed the papers for them to go into long-term care and that had been that. The social workers would tell her nothing except that her kids were well cared for. Told her to forget about them, get her head down and do her time.

Well, she had done all that and the pain of parting from them was as real today as it had been all those years ago. Why did you have to lose something before you could fully appreciate it?

She stepped down from the train and jumped into a cab. The familiar streets made her nervous. She strained to see a face she recognised, a shop she might have frequented. Most of the pubs were gone. It was all different. This upset her more than she'd thought possible.

She paid the cab and walked up the narrow path to her childhood home, feeling sick with apprehension. She forced herself to knock on the door, watching through the glass as a woman bowled up the hallway, her bleached blonde hair like a magnet to the visitor's eyes.

The door opened and her mother stood there speechless, the smile of welcome dying on her face.

They stared at one another for long seconds.

'Hello, Mum . . .'

The other woman held up her arm as if warding off evil, hatred plain upon her face.

'Fuck off, Marie – and don't you ever come here again. We don't want you, we never did. You're trouble. Nothing but bloody trouble.'

The door was slammed shut in her face.

She wavered on the doorstep and seemed to sink down. She was sitting on the step, her tears mingling with the rain which was heavier now. A roll of thunder above her head made her shiver with fright, but she sat there and cried as she hadn't cried in years: deep sobs, wrenched from her bowels. The sound was as lonely as it was heart-breaking. As loud as it was terrifying. But the door didn't open again.

She knew it never would.

Chapter One

Louise Carter lit a cigarette and stared at her husband with anger and disgust. She smashed the kettle down on to the worktop and plugged it in with a venom he had not seen in years.

'Fucking cheek of her, coming round here after the trouble she caused!' He noticed her hand was shaking as she puffed deeply on her Embassy cigarette. 'I can't believe she had the fucking nerve . . .'

Kevin Carter stood up and pulled his tiny wife into his arms.

'Calm down, we knew it would happen one day.'

He hated to see her like this. Over the years they had resumed a semblance of normal life again. Their daughter Marie's aberration had been forgotten, or at least it had on the surface anyway. Friends stopped mentioning her and life had just about returned to normal. But it had been hard on Lou, bloody hard. It had broken her as the tablets she constantly popped proved.

'How did she look?'

Louise pulled herself from his arms. She stared into his face as if he had gone mad before her eyes, like their child had done all those years ago when she had killed her two friends.

'What kind of fucking question is that? She looked alive, which is more than the two girls she battered to death bloody look!'

'Calm down, Lou, for fuck's sake. I was only asking. I mean, would you recognise her, like? Remember her? Know who she was?'

She swiped her tongue across her lips and nodded.

'I'd know that bastard anywhere, but she was slimmer, prettier than ever. Waste on her, that was. Bloody whore! Always a bloody whore from a kid . . .'

Kevin shut out his wife's words. He had heard them too many times over the years for them to have any real effect. He wanted to go outside and see his daughter but knew that if he did, it would cause too much trouble.

Louise had never got over it all. In fact, none of them had, though he would still like to know if Marie was OK. Instead he made his wife a cup of tea and gave her one of her tablets.

But the thought of his Marie so close, and he unable to talk to her, hurt him inside. Whatever she had done she was still his daughter. Nothing his wife said could change the tie of blood, and Marie was his blood.

Still, Louise was his priority at the moment. Her breakdown had split the family, made everything so difficult. Marshall's suicide on top of everything else had finished her. Oh yes, his daughter Marie had a lot to answer for. He closed his eyes because tears were threatening.

Kevin Carter was a big man. At over six foot, he weighed in at seventeen and a half stone. In his younger days he had fought bare-knuckled to get himself a stake and now he had a small building business.

The Carters were *respectable*. The thought made him smile. Or they had been once, anyway. And over the years they had fought to get that much back at least. They would never get their son back. He was dead and buried this long time, but Louise visited his grave every day. It was Marshall's putting a gun into his mouth and blowing his head off that had tipped her over the edge once and for all. In a way it had seemed more of an act of violence than Marie's killings because Marshall had killed himself while he was sober and straight whereas Marie had been so out of it on drugs she at least could argue she had not known what she was doing.

A son and a daughter, gone in weeks. A family ripped apart in the time it took other families to have a holiday, come back, and go to work. It was all such a bloody waste, and now she was back, his Marie was back, and he wondered what trouble would follow her this time. Because trouble had followed her from the day she could talk and walk.

The front door opened and they both turned towards it fearfully. It was Lucy.

'What's the matter with you two, sitting in the dark?'

Their other daughter's keen eyes registered tension in the room. 'She's gone then?'

Louise's voice was heavy with dread.

'Who? Who's gone?' queried Lucy.

'Marie.'

At the sound of her sister's name Lucy's face screwed up into a

10

mask of disgust and she pulled her lips back over her teeth until she looked almost feral in her hatred.

'That's all we need! Mickey popped the question this lunchtime and I said yes. I suppose I can kiss him goodbye now, can't I?'

Louise stirred herself.

'Don't be so silly. I fucked her off out of it. We won't be seeing her again, love.'

Lucy slung her leather bag over her shoulder and walked towards the stairs. She didn't answer her mother, but the sound of her heavy footfalls on the stairs said all they needed to hear. Her bedroom door slammed and it was like a death knell.

'What made her come back here, Kev?'

He sighed.

'I don't know, love. Blood, I expect. We are her parents, after all.'

Louise stood up and smashed her mug into the sink. It was a satisfying feeling, smashing something. She had learned that over the years.

'You, Kevin Carter, can speak for your fucking self. She is nothing to me – nothing.'

He was getting angry now.

'Well, whatever you say, Lou. That's how it's always been in this fucking house so why change the habit of a lifetime, eh?'

He dragged his jacket from the back of a kitchen chair and stormed out. He walked slowly to the pub, eyes and ears peeled for any sign of his Marie. But she was gone.

Half of him was glad, the other half desperate just for a glimpse of her. Just to know she had survived and was OK.

In the pub he sipped his pint slowly. He had a lot to think about.

Amanda Stirling smiled easily at the woman before her.

'I've put you through here, OK?'

Marie followed her along a dimly lit corridor. It was freshly painted but still had the feel of decay about it. The coving was cracked and aged, the thin carpet bare in places. Marie closed her mind to it.

She walked into a room that was not much larger than her cell had been. It had a single bed, a bureau and a wardrobe. The walls were painted white, and a dark blue carpet graced the floor. The bedspread was like a throwback to the sixties, orange and blue circles on a green background.

She smiled her thanks tentatively.

Amanda shrugged.

'Not much, I know, but it's clean and it's yours.'

'It's fine, really.'

Amanda was aware that this woman was trying to make her feel better and decided she liked her. Considering what she knew about her, that was quite a surprise. Marie seemed to understand and smiled again.

'There's tea- and coffee-making facilities in the bureau, but as you know there is a large rec room if you feel up to mixing with the others.'

Marie smiled again and turned away. Amanda took this as her cue to leave.

'If you need anything I'm in my office.'

Alone, Marie let the mask slip and sank down on the bed. It groaned under her weight and she put her arms out as if she was going to fall.

It all felt surreal.

She looked at her carrier bag and sighed. Twelve years and ten months and she had nothing.

Nothing.

She busied herself making a cup of tea and tried to block out the thoughts that were crowding her head. Twenty-five minutes later she was in bed, a book in her hands and the curtains closed. She felt safe at last. Snug and safe. But she didn't feel free, and wondered if she ever really would.

Patrick Connor was black. Black, handsome and rich. He was a body builder with enormous biceps, a wide grin and, strangest of all, deep blue eyes. His Irish grandfather's namesake, he loved the shock people felt on first meeting him. Those blue eyes gave him the edge, no doubt about it.

He pulled out a Tesco bag stuffed with grass and shoved it unceremoniously into his gym bag. He was dropping it off as a favour, but he also had a mission in mind. He locked the door to his flat and skipped towards the lift. As he drove away in his brand-new BMW he let his mind wander.

He had a new bird, Corinne. She was half-caste and she was pretty, but she was also heavily into crack. Just what he was looking for, in fact. He was going to visit her later and see if she fancied a job. He had a feeling she'd jump at the opportunity. Crackheads would sleep with a Siberian tiger for a rock. That's what he liked about them.

His mobile rang and he answered it, his deep brown voice full of confidence as he shouted, 'Yo!'

A moment later his face paled and he pulled his car over, screeching to a halt to the consternation of the driver behind him.

'Are you sure?'

His street accent had reverted to Queen's English in a matter of seconds. He snapped the phone off and closed his eyes. Marie was out. She was out and about. She'd be looking for him and, Christ forgive him, he had nothing to tell her. Or nothing she would want to hear anyway.

He turned the car around and drove towards Silvertown. He needed some answers and he needed them now.

Lucy opened the front door.

'You took your fucking time.'

Patrick walked into the small terraced house, his huge bulk blocking out the light.

'Don't worry, they're out. Me dad's took her over her mum's. She was really in a state. Marie actually came here and knocked on our door.'

They stood in the kitchen facing one another.

Lucy was like Marie, you could see they were sisters, but she was a watered-down version. She didn't have the same thick blonde hair or piercing blue eyes. She was pretty enough until Marie stood beside her, and then she paled into insignificance. She also had an unfortunate way about her. Seemed to be constantly looking down her nose at people. She had always put his back up and she was enjoying doing it now.

'Fuck! Fuck!'

Patrick's voice was deep, low.

'She'll want to know where the kids are. What are you going to tell her?' Lucy goaded him.

He shrugged but didn't answer her.

'They might tell her, Patrick. Social Services. Now she's out they might think she has a right to know. They are her kids, after all.'

The sarcasm was not lost on him, but still he didn't answer her.

'Do you actually know where your son is?'

He finally met her eyes but didn't answer her.

'How did you get my mobile number?'

13

Lucy looked up at the ceiling.

'Is that all you can fucking say? That mad bitch is home, and she *will* come looking for us all. I know her better than anyone. She's going to cause trouble, she can't help it, Patrick. It's what she *does*.'

'Do you lot know where they are?'

She shook her head.

'Of course not. My mum made sure of that. I ain't so sure about me dad, though. Marie was always his pet.'

The bitterness in her voice was not lost on Patrick. He grinned.

'I kept meaning to ring, like, but I just never got round to it,' he said sheepishly.

Lucy looked at him, her face serious.

'She'll come looking for you, I guarantee it. And you know what she's like if she wants something.'

He laughed.

'Twelve years' bird will have knocked all that out of her. Take it from me, I know. She'll have changed. Anyway, she might not want to see the kids.'

His voice held a note of hope and Lucy turned her eyes to the ceiling once more.

'You are a fucking twat, do you know that? As bad as she was, she loved them kids. Even I have to give her that one.'

Patrick didn't answer for a few seconds then said thoughtfully, 'Well, she had a funny way of showing it, that's all I can say. Leaving them on their own for hours on end. Pissed up and shooting up in front of them. Oh yeah, she adored them.'

'You put her on the drugs, Patrick, and you put her on the game. The least you could do after you fucked up her head was look out for your own son.'

He laughed again, this time with genuine amusement.

'Hark at you! If he is really my son he'll be able to take care of himself. I had to and I ain't done too bad.'

'That, Patrick, is a matter of opinion. But I felt you should be warned. I mean, supposing she decides to pay back a few old debts, eh? Who'll be first in line?'

Lucy let the words hang in the air for a few seconds. Then she too laughed.

'Baseball bats and torque wrenches are still on sale locally, I should imagine.'

She was laughing as he stormed from the house.

14

★ ★ ★

Carole Halter heard the doorbell and looked at the clock beside her bed. It was twenty past nine in the morning. She snuggled into the warmth of her bed once more and closed her eyes.

The doorbell rang again and then a hammering on her front door caused her to leap from the bed naked and storm through the flat. She opened her front door wide, displaying a body that had seen its fair share of wear and tear. The obscenity she was about to scream died on her lips when she saw who was standing there.

'Marie? Marie Carter?'

Marie smiled at her.

'Can I come in, Carole?'

She walked into the flat and was instantly assailed by once familiar smells: sweat, fried food, perfume and damp. It brought her back to reality. It was years since she had breathed in a similar foetid odour, only then she had not really noticed it. Everyone she knew then had the same sour smell in their home, like old farts and alcohol mixed together. It was disgusting.

Carole saw her wrinkling her nose up. For a split second she felt the old antagonism return. Then she reminded herself why she had not seen this particular friend for so long and swallowed down the retort.

'Coffee?'

She made her voice light, but it took an effort.

Marie smiled.

'Please. If it's not too much trouble. Late night?'

Carole picked up a T-shirt off the worn sofa and pulled it over her head. It just covered her bum and heavy thighs.

'I was working last night. I'm in a club now. It's better money.'

As she put the kettle on she was eyeing Marie. The years had been kinder to her old friend than she would have expected.

'You look well, Marie.'

'Thanks, so do you.'

It was a kindly lie, but well meant. Carole looked dreadful, all dark rings under the eyes, wrinkles and dry skin. She looked fifteen years older than her actual thirty-five. Marie realised that she was aware of the fact herself and tried to change the subject.

'How are the kids?'

Carole shrugged.

'Bernice is duffed by some coon from Romford, she's just

seventeen, and LaToyah is in Borstal. They caught her skanking in Oxford Street. She beat up the arresting officer.'

Carole grinned.

'Always a lairy bitch, her. Broke the geezer's nose and split his eye. She got bird, bless her. Her baby lives with foster parents and I visit every fortnight. Nice people, good house and that. I wish they could keep the little fucker – and her Shaquille is a fucker with a capital Fuck!'

She laughed at her own wit.

'Got a mouth like a sewer and she's only three.'

'Like her mother then. I remember LaToyah was a swearer.'

Carole placed two mugs on the cluttered table.

'She certainly was. Remember when she called your Tiffany a cunt and Tiffany jobbed her?'

She laughed again.

'Like you, Tiff. Deep waters, her.'

The laughter was suddenly gone from Carole's voice.

'I'm not supposed to be here. I'm on licence, like. So keep this under your hat, eh?' Marie told her.

Carole nodded as she lit a cigarette.

''Course. You'll be on licence for life. I mean, that's what happens after a murder stretch, ain't it?'

Marie nodded but didn't answer.

'You do look well, though. You've hardly changed.'

Marie had heard enough compliments. She got to the point.

'Where's Patrick, and what's he doing now?'

Carole had been expecting the question.

'Ain't you heard from him?' Her voice was incredulous. 'The black bastard! Are you telling me in all these years that ponce never kept in touch?'

Marie smiled now, a real grin.

'What do you think? You never wrote or visited. No one did.'

Carole drew deeply on her cigarette. Silence hung in the air like the smoke.

'I understand, Carole. It was all a long time ago. And, I mean, it ain't like I was in for shoplifting, is it? I had a fucking big lump and I accept it all now. I have done me time and don't want any more trouble. I just want to see me kids.'

'Ain't they told you where they are then?'

Marie shook her head.

'I ain't asked and they ain't offered. Enough said. Tiffany is just

16

nineteen and Jason is seventeen. All I want to know is that they're OK. But I don't want everyone knowing what I'm about. I'll see them in me own time.'

'If *they* want to see *you*, you mean.'

'In a nutshell. So where is Patrick these days?'

'Gone right up in the world, him. Still runs women but with drugs as a sideline. He owns a gym and a wine bar, too. All blonde birds and BMW these days. Thinks he's the dog's gonads.'

Marie grinned.

'No change there then?'

Carole laughed with her, felt herself relaxing at last.

'Nah. No change there, girl. But I don't think he sees anything of Jason. Last I heard the kids were in a home in Wales. I saw your mum a few years back.'

'How was she?'

Carole shrugged.

'Same as usual, acting like her shit didn't stink. Do you know something, Marie? That is one bastard of a woman.'

Marie didn't answer her.

'Where's the gym?'

'Spitalfields, you can't miss it. There's a dirty great big sign saying "Pat's Gym". Real nineties stuff. Glass windows so they can train and show off all at the same time.'

Marie smiled.

'Why am I not surprised?'

Carole gripped her hand tightly.

'It's done my heart good to see you, love. We'll have to get out one night. Tie one on like the old days.'

Marie removed her hand and shook her head sadly.

'I couldn't cope with all that now. Those days are gone and I want to leave them like that.'

Carole's face creased into a frown of concern.

'Well, how are you going to live?'

Marie sipped at her coffee to give herself time to think before she answered.

'They're going to help me get a job and eventually a place to live.'

Carole lit another cigarette and blew out smoke noisily.

'Are you telling me you're going to go and work in a factory for a couple of ton a week when you could earn that and more in a night?'

17

Marie nodded.

'I done a degree inside. I also did computer studies, IT. I'll get by without flashing me clout.'

She tried to make it sound like a joke but it fell flat. She knew Carole was in complete and utter shock.

'You! You did a degree? What in, for fuck's sake – blow jobs?'

Marie closed her eyes tightly before answering.

'No, actually, it was in English literature. And I did a certificate after that. I could teach if I wanted to.'

Carole grinned.

'I know they're crying out for teachers in this day and age but I expect even sink estates would think twice about a double murderer, don't you?'

Marie didn't answer, just stared at her with dark blue eyes that seemed to look into Carole's very soul.

'I'm sorry, that was out of order,' she said nervously.

Marie stood up.

'It was true, and even I can't argue with the truth. But I'll keep me head down and see what happens. I'll be in touch, eh?'

Carole nodded.

'If you need anything, Marie, you only have to ask.'

'I know, mate. Thanks.'

As she walked away from the flat she was aware of her friend's eyes boring into her back. Marie knew she had made a mistake. Carole had always had a loose lip and now word of Marie's visit would be all over Silvertown within hours. But she had not known where else to go for information.

Seeing Carole had reminded her of a life she wanted to forget. She could still smell the odour of decay on her clothes as she stepped on to the bus.

Amanda looked at Marie as she sat down in the office of the halfway house. As duty probation officer Amanda had seen her fair share of murderers come and go but there was something different about Marie Carter.

She was self-contained, but then a long stretch did that to a body. This was different in that the woman before her seemed to have stopped living. She was just going through the motions and it showed. It was almost painful to watch her.

'How was the Job Centre?'

'OK.'

18

Amanda had long since realised that it was like pulling teeth, getting any reaction from Marie, so she took a deep breath and commented, 'You were a long time.'

'I was walking. It's so long since I could wander around, look in shops . . .'

Marie's voice trailed off.

'I understand. How are you adjusting?'

'OK. It's early days.'

Amanda nodded reassuringly.

'It gets easier.'

Marie didn't answer her.

'Is there anything specific you want to ask me?'

'My children?'

It was out before Marie knew what she was saying.

Amanda had been expecting the question. Had been surprised not to be asked immediately. She smiled again, uneasily this time.

'They have been approached and both have declined to see you. I'm sorry . . .'

Marie nodded. She had expected as much. Standing up, she picked up her bag.

'I think I'll go out and walk again, if that's all right? Try and get used to the area.'

'Certainly. Grab a coffee and get your bearings. Don't forget you have a curfew – six-thirty.'

Marie didn't turn back to face or answer her. Instead she walked from the office and closed the door quietly behind her.

Out in the street tears slid down her face and she wiped them away angrily. It was what she had expected, but it didn't make it any easier. They had blanked her. Her own kids had blanked her.

And who could blame them?

Lucy walked out of work and made her way to the bus stop. A red car pulled up beside her and she looked down into the face of Mickey Watson, her boyfriend.

'Have I done anything wrong, Luce?'

His voice was heavy with fear and she felt a moment's sorrow for the way she had treated him. She got into the car and smiled gently at him.

'It's me, Mickey. Something happened and I've been worried about it.'

19

'What's wrong, mate? You can tell me.'

She looked into his big moon face. He might not have the looks but he was a decent, kind man and that was what she wanted. When she was with him she was a nice person – he made her nice. Made her feel nice inside. Since childhood Lucy had had a nasty streak in her. It all stemmed from her jealousy of her sister. She knew that, but it didn't help. In fact it just made it worse because she couldn't control the urge to hate, and hate deeply, unequivocally.

'Marie's out.'

She saw his change of expression.

'Your mum won't like that, Mickey, will she? The murderer's loose again.'

He didn't answer her.

'Is she living back home then?'

Mikey was terrified of his mother's reaction and it showed.

'Don't be so bloody wet! Of course not.'

'Where is she then?'

'How the fuck should I know where's she's living? Why would I *want* to know. I'm telling you before someone else does, that's all.'

'All right! Calm down, Luce, for fuck's sake.'

'I hate her, Mickey. She ruins all our lives and then thinks she can just waltz back in as if nothing happened.'

'Well, I can't see your mum giving her house room, can you? It'll be a nine-days wonder and then everyone will forget about it.'

She could hear the hope and desperation in his voice.

'Do you think so?'

He nodded vigorously.

'It's nothing to do with me and you, is it?'

She shook her head.

'I suppose not. But your mum . . .'

'Well, we'll cross that bridge when we come to it.'

He kissed her on the lips.

'Stop worrying. What can she do to us?'

Lucy didn't answer. She knew exactly what her sister was capable of, especially when she found out about her kids, and she would find out. She had always been a sifter, had Marie. She sifted information and calculated what it meant to her. The fact she had come to their front door spoke volumes. She was out . . . and out for revenge if Lucy knew anything about it. She herself would be, in

20

her sister's place, Oh yes, she would settle a few old scores if she was in Marie's shoes.

But she didn't voice her opinion. As Mickey said, they'd cross the bridges as they came to them.

They had no other choice.

Chapter Two

Marie answered the loud knocking at her door, frowning to see a woman standing there. She had dark back-combed hair and heavy black eyeliner. She smiled at Marie, her false teeth too big for her mouth.

'Marie Carter?'

It was a statement more than a question.

Marie nodded.

The woman held out her hand in a friendly manner.

'Sally Potter. I'm next door.'

Marie shook hands, saying nothing.

'You can call me Sal,' her visitor said encouragingly.

'Thank you.'

The woman grinned.

'I done a lump, love, murder like yourself. Been out nearly eight months. 'Course, I topped me old man, and give his bird something to think about and all. I thought I would introduce meself, that's all. I ain't trying to pry or nothing. If you fancy a bit of company give me a knock, OK? It takes a few weeks to acclimatise, like.'

She smiled again and walked off.

Marie shut the door, her heart hammering in her chest. She sat on the bed and listened as the radio blared through the thin wall. Closing her eyes, she sighed heavily. She wanted out of this place and she wanted out soon. Everyone wanted to pry into her business, everyone wanted something from her and she had nothing to give.

She felt dry, empty.

Even friendship frightened her these days and yet once, friends had been everything to her. She closed her eyes and saw once more the two bloodied bodies, saw the carnage her drink- and drug-fuelled rage had caused, and felt the familiar bile rise into her throat.

Friends were not an option any more. She was much safer alone. *Everyone* was safer if Marie could just stay alone.

Carole Halter sat in the club alone. It was early, most of the girls wouldn't be in till later, but she liked to have a few drinks under her belt before she started her night's work.

The bouncer, a young blond body builder called Declan, looked her over and obviously found her wanting.

'Had your look?'

She challenged him from habit, neither of them really caring about the other's opinion. He put himself above her and she saw herself as beneath him. It worked for them both.

'Have you seen anything of Tiffany?' Carole asked.

He shook his head. Didn't even bother to answer properly.

'Why the fuck would I want to see her anyway?'

'I was only asking!'

Carole's voice was loud and aggressive now.

She carried on sipping her drink, eyes prowling the club in case a punter had crept past her. A small good-looking blonde girl came in. Though heavy-breasted she was otherwise practically anorexic in build. Long bleached hair hung like a curtain across her face. She pushed it away with one slim hand, violet-painted nails looking dangerously long.

Carole smiled at her.

'All right, Tiff?'

The girl stared at her for a few seconds.

'It's OK, Carole, I know. I was told earlier.'

She carried on walking to the cloakroom that also doubled as the strippers' changing room and Carole followed her.

'What are you going to do?'

The girl pushed the door open with surprising force and shrugged.

'Do? What am I supposed to do?'

'Well, she is your mother.'

Tiffany grinned into the dirty mirror above the sinks.

'So I hear.'

Carole was alarmed at the girl's attitude and it showed.

'I don't think you quite realise the strength of her, Tiff. She is strong, not just physically – and we all know the truth of that. But mentally she's like man mountain Dean. If that fucker wants to see you bad enough, she will.'

24

Tiffany shrugged.

'Yeah, so? Shall I practise my curtsey now then?'

Carole shook her head sadly.

'Listen to me. She is still your mother, love. No matter what. She loved you in her own way . . .'

Tiffany waved her hands angrily.

'Oh, yeah? Left us for hours on end by ourselves, drugged out of her fucking brain! Well, Carole, that kind of mother love I can do without, OK? Now if you don't mind I have to get undressed.'

'But I've had her round my gaff, Tiffany . . . She won't give up. Especially if she finds out 'bout little Anastasia.'

The girl rolled her eyes in exasperation.

'Yeah? So? If I don't want to see her, then I won't. Now piss off!'

Her voice was hard, uncaring, and Carole knew better than to push it. She left the room quietly, her heart heavy at the thought that her one-time friend's daughter wanted nothing to do with her. And if Marie found out that Carole actually worked with Tiffany and had not said so, what would be the upshot? It was this that worried Carole more than anything.

Tiffany stared into the cracked mirror and then began to apply a thick layer of foundation to hide the acne scars in her skin. As she brushed on her blusher she knew she was just putting on an act for everyone. In fact she was frightened of what her mother might stir up. As Carole said, if Marie wanted to see her she would.

Tiffany's eyes registered her grimy surroundings and she shuddered. What would Marie make of her daughter's life and job? 'History repeating itself' was how Pat described it, saying she was just like her mother at the same age.

Well, fuck her mother! She had in effect dumped Tiffany when she was a baby so she had no right to any respect now. And if pushed, Tiffany would tell her that.

Oh yeah, she would tell her that to her face.

The girl remembered her mother as a force to be reckoned with. The neighbours had all been terrified of her. Marie could make even men nervous when she was out of it. There was an air of violence about her that people picked up on pretty quickly. Pat had regaled her with stories of her mother's marathon temper bouts and drinking and drug binges. Tiffany knew enough about Marie to realise she didn't want her anywhere near her own child. A double murderess was hardly the kind of person she wanted around her Anastasia, thank you very much. But inside she wondered exactly what can of worms would be opened by her mother's release into society.

Ten minutes later Tiffany was ready for her first act. Stripping was lucrative and Pat had promised to get her into a lap dancing club where the money would be even better. It was her ambition in life to buy a little place of her own, and she was determined to do it. Her daughter deserved the best, and she would see that Anastasia got it.

Tiffany cut herself a line of coke to give herself an edge. As she went through the ritual of cutting, cleaning and snorting it, she felt more relaxed inside.

Unlike her mother she used drugs, and not vice versa. All she needed was a little lift now and then, just a lift to give her an edge.

And after the revelations of today, she needed that lift more than ever.

Louise Carter listened to her daughter's mother-in-law-to-be, gritting her teeth. Mary Watson was a busybody, a two-faced, interfering bastard of a woman.

'I hear she walked up to the front door, large as life and twice as pretty . . .' The last was a jibe at her son's girlfriend and they all knew it. 'But then she was always a good-looking girl, you can't take that away from her. Fair's fair in that respect. Marie was a looker.'

'For all the good it did her. Now if you don't mind, Mary, I would rather we dropped the subject.'

Louise's voice was dangerously low and Mary suppressed a small triumphant smile.

Lucy stood up abruptly and said in a false bright voice, 'Shall I make more tea?'

She left the room and Mickey followed her.

Louise stared at the woman before her, took in the brown rat-like eyes and tightly pursed mouth, and wondered how her daughter could want to join a family with this vicious old bitch at its head. It never occurred to Louise that she was looking at another version of herself. The two women hated one another because, as Mickey had pointed out on many occasions, they were too alike to get on.

Though no one had yet had the guts to say that to either of them.

'So, I suppose it will all be dragged up again, won't it? The violent murders. The drink, drugs, whoring . . . It will give this lot round here grist to their mills for a while.'

Louise didn't answer the taunt. She dropped her eyes and concentrated on a small stain on the carpet, fighting an urge to swing back her arm and fell the woman sitting on her sofa. Instead she plastered on a smile and said gaily, 'The wedding will likely take the edge off the gossip anyway. You know, the murderess's sister marrying your only son.'

She saw the barb had hit home. Mickey was a mummy's boy and everyone knew it. But Lucy was well able for him and his mother once the marriage was a fact. They both fell silent, but the animosity in the room was almost tangible.

Marie watched the activity in the Spitalfields gym. It was eight-thirty in the morning and people were already there working up a sweat. She observed them from a small café opposite and marvelled at the women working so industriously to keep their bodies in shape for men. It was the same in prison; most women were only in there because of a man yet their one aim in life was to get out and get another as soon as possible. It had amazed her.

Marie was happy to be alone. She was an expert in it nowadays. As she sipped her coffee she kept an eye out for Pat Connor. The thought of facing him scared her, but she knew she had to. He owed her, owed her big time, and although she was wary of him there was no real fear of him any more. There was nothing he could do to her now, say to her now, that she hadn't done or said to herself.

One thing about prison, it made you mentally strong if nothing else.

He arrived at nine-thirty-five in a black BMW convertible. He looked good, but the old feelings she'd harboured for him were long gone. Once his body had drawn her like a beacon. He looked better these days, toned, well-dressed, but she knew what he really was now and he no longer attracted her.

She paid her bill, gasped at the thought that three cups of coffee had cost nearly six pounds, and as she crossed the road to the gym told herself she would have to walk back to the hostel because she was skint.

Marie gathered a few admiring glances despite her old clothes. She was a good-looking woman even without make-up or expensively styled hair. But she ignored them. She was on a mission and she was going to complete it. She was smiling as she walked into Pat's Gym.

Patrick Connor was sipping herbal tea and totting up his night's takings when Wednesday, his young secretary, told him a woman was outside insisting she wanted to see him.

'What's she like?'

The girl shrugged.

'Blonde, not bad-looking but scruffy . . .'

Before she could finish Marie had walked into the room.

'Hello, Pat. Long time no see, eh?'

She enjoyed seeing the fear in his eyes, and the greyness that was appearing underneath his chocolate-brown skin.

Wednesday looked from one to the other with obvious interest.

Pat sat down behind his executive desk. His legs felt weak.

'Goodbye, Wednesday.'

His voice had a note she had never heard in it before. She had seen her boss deal with violent drug dealers and bona fide faces. This woman was intriguing. Who was she that she could rattle Patrick Connor?

'Shall I bring through some coffee?'

The girl was smiling at Marie as she said it, evading Pat's eye.

Marie nodded in a friendly way.

'That would be lovely, thank you.'

Alone she and Pat looked at one another for long moments. He broke the silence as Marie knew he would. It was a knack she had developed in prison. Quietness scared people, she'd found. If you waited long enough they would speak first and it gave you the upper hand. And with Pat, you needed that edge. He would lie about what he'd had for breakfast, couldn't help it, it was part of his make-up.

'You look well, Marie. How's things?'

It was lame, they both knew it was lame, and it made Marie smile. That changed her face and she saw him relax.

'How do you think I am, Pat? I'm confused, scared, but most importantly, keen to know about me kids.'

Pat stared at her. She knew his mind was crunching like a 1950s gearbox.

'Have you seen them at all? Have you kept in contact with our son? That's all I want to know, Pat.'

He was biting his top lip, a nervous action she remembered from years gone by. Then his mobile rang. It was a loud tune, Bob Marley's 'No Woman, No Cry'. It seemed appropriate to them both and he stared at it, then at Marie, who grinned.

'Clever. Never seen one close up before. One of the women on my wing had one, a PO smuggled it in for her, but I never actually saw it meself. They turned her cell over and that was that. Four days on the block for wanting to phone her daughter. But then, unlike me, she had a number for her, an address. She actually saw her child.'

Pat wiped one large hand across his face.

'What you want, Marie?'

'Don't try your Jamaican accent on me! You never left London all your life. I heard through the grapevine you was finding your roots – well, save it for the silly little birds who are interested in it. Where's me kids?'

'How the fucking hell would I know that?'

She looked into his piercing blue eyes and sighed.

'You never bothered with your own son, is that what you're telling me?'

He couldn't look her in the eye but stared at his hands instead. He was ashamed and they both knew it. Annoyed, Pat tried to justify himself.

'I didn't need this shit, Marie. I was having enough trouble keeping meself . . .'

She sat quietly staring at him as he attempted to dismiss twelve years of neglect. With that accusing stare levelled on him he tried, unsuccessfully, to excuse what he had done.

'What good would I have been to him, eh? Think about it. I wouldn't have been able to take care of him, would I? I mean, think about it, what would I do with a kid?'

She was shaking her head in despair.

'So he didn't have either of us then. What about Tiffany, have you seen her?'

Patrick was quiet for a moment.

'No. Why would I? She wasn't mine, was she?' he said at length.

It was what she'd expected.

He opened the desk drawer and took out a bundle of money, twenties and tens, all rolled up with an elastic band around them.

'Here you are, girl. I was gonna give you something anyway, get you on your feet, like.'

Wednesday came in with the tray of coffee. Marie brushed past her and walked from the room. Pat's mobile rang again and the tune brought back more painful memories. It made her think of blues in Brixton, walking along the Railton Road looking for a dealer. Standing around half-naked in the freezing cold, staring into car windows and smiling at strange men. Brought back the salty smell of sex and the uncomfortable feeling of being fucked unceremoniously in the back seat of cars. New cars, old cars. Cars that had kids' toys in the back, or a briefcase. Cars that said so much about their owners' lives, if they only knew it.

It made her aware once more of the wasted years she had spent in prison until in a strange way they brought her salvation.

She still wanted to cry for her little boy, left without a father and a mother. Unlike her daughter Jason had known who his father was, had had a sort of relationship with him. He must have been terrified going into care, being alone with no one to look out for him. And you read such stories in the papers . . . kids being abused, left unloved, starved, beaten.

'Are you all right, love?'

Marie looked into the old lady's face and nodded.

She realised she was standing in the middle of the street oblivious to passers-by and traffic. The pain in her heart was tangible. It felt like a hand was gripping it tightly. She thought she was going to faint.

She could still see the kids' faces looking at her with big expressive eyes on that last day in court. Could still smell their hair as she'd hugged them close. A year on remand had cleaned her up, made her realise what she was missing out on all those years she was drugged out of her brains.

It had been too late then and it was too late now.

She began the long walk back to the hostel, the cold air cutting into her lungs. She didn't want anything from Pat, especially not money he had made off young girls and women. That money was tainted with tragedy and shame. She could do without it.

'Who was she then, Pat?'

Wednesday's nasal voice was getting on his nerves.

'Why don't you mind your own fucking business for once?'

Wednesday was miffed and it showed.

'I was only asking!'

She stormed from the room, her tight little ass wiggling for all it was worth. Pat was oblivious. He knew that Marie was going to bring trouble, big trouble, and wasn't sure how he could stop it. If she knew the full SP, would she kill him?

30

He had a feeling she was capable of it for all her newfound calm. She was always a funny one, was Marie. Could pick an argument with her own fingernails if the mood was on her.

And he had tucked her up big time.

He realised that much, just wondered how long it would be before she got wind of the whole situation and what would be the upshot then.

Tiffany smiled at her daughter's little face. Anastasia really was a very pretty child, all wide eyes and crinkly black hair. She was light-skinned, very light-skinned. If her hair was relaxed she could pass for Greek or Italian.

Tiffany loved her with a passion that had surprised her. She wondered if her own mother had ever felt like that about her, but doubted it.

Tiffany would kill for her child. Her mother had killed for a fix.

A knock at the front door sent her leaping from her chair. She was smiling widely as she opened it.

'All right, mate?'

Patrick smiled into the girl's eyes. She was just how he liked them: skinny, adoring and malleable. He wondered if the fact that she was Marie's daughter added to her attraction. Sometimes she frowned and it was like looking at Marie again. Tiffany didn't have her mother's stunning looks, or her lush body at the same age, but she had the look of her.

That innocent look that belied the fact they would fuck anything for a few quid. Well, Tiffany wasn't that bad yet, but he was working on it.

'I talked to me mate. He says you can audition for him tomorrow night. It's the Aida Club by Tobacco Dock. Wear a schoolgirl's uniform, he's a right fucking perve.'

'It *is* a lap dancing club, ain't it?'

Tiffany's voice was heavy with sarcasm.

'Of course it is, but the girls always come out in costume like, then someone pays for it to be removed. It's good money, Tiff, I promise.'

Anastasia put her hands on Patrick's trousers and he jumped as if he had been burnt. The little girl was upset and Tiffany picked her up gently.

'For crying out loud, Pat, she was only touching you.'

'These trousers cost me over three hundred quid and I'm not

31

about to have them covered in her old crap.'

He could see the confusion on Tiffany's face as she stared at him and it reminded him of her mother's expression when she had sat in his office earlier that day. Anastasia looked from one to the other, her face a picture of puzzled innocence as she felt the tension between them.

Tiffany felt the familiar sinking of her heart as she watched father and daughter survey one another.

'She is your child, Pat . . .'

He took a deep breath and sighed.

'Look, Tiff, I have seven kids to my knowledge and I love them all, your brother included. But I ain't the hands-on type, you know that. I give you money and I see you both all right but I have never connected with any of them.'

Tiffany knew he was telling her the truth but all the same it galled her. He was the only man she had ever been with and he had pursued her. Christ, had he pursued her. Always taking her out, giving her things, and then she was pregnant. Like her mother before her she soon found out that Patrick Connor was not only unreliable but downright cold and callous. At six months old Anastasia had been taken to hospital and Tiffany had rung and rung his mobile to no avail.

She knew he was with someone else and it hurt her, hurt her so much she had felt an actual physical pain, but there was something about him that held her to him though she didn't know for the life of her what that was. But once his arms went around her she was his. No matter what he had done.

He was Pat, and he was a law unto himself, and if you wanted to keep within his orbit you learned that lesson fast.

He had arrived home a few days after Anastasia was discharged, made a fuss of Tiffany and the baby, and she had forgiven him.

But it had hurt, hurt her deeply.

Now she was aware that her days with him were numbered. He was into youth, extreme youth. He needed little girls with no brain and no idea about the real world. She was getting into the lap dancing club because she knew deep inside that soon she would be the sole breadwinner for her daughter, and also that what she wanted for her child was going to take money, real money, to achieve. Anastasia would have the life she had wanted for herself, all those lonely nights spent in the children's home and later in foster care.

Anastasia was going to get everything, Tiffany was going to see to it personally. She might look a bit like her own mother but that was where the similarity ended. Her child was her world and she would do anything for her.

It was a promise she was to keep but the price was to be far higher than she'd expected.

Patrick was already walking towards the door. She watched him sadly. He was annoyed and it showed. Now he would walk out on her for a few days because she had had the nerve to make a remark.

'Have you seen me mum yet?'

Even as she said it she was telling herself to shut up, not to antagonise him further, but she couldn't help it.

'She's been round to Carole's so she's obviously on the prowl.'

Patrick looked at her coldly.

'If I see her I'll offer her her old job back. I like to keep things in the family – or haven't you noticed that yet?'

As the front door slammed behind him Anastasia whimpered and Tiffany felt the old longing for him return. She felt an urge to run to the door and beg him not to leave her for days on end as he usually did, but she fought it. Instead she hugged her little daughter close and wondered if her school uniform was still in the top cupboard in the bedroom. Once she was financially secure she would feel better able to cope with Patrick Connor and his mood swings.

But at times like this she felt so very, very lonely. He was all the family she had ever really known.

As Pat pulled up outside Sonny Lee's flat he was fuming inside. Tiffany had the knack of making him feel guilty; her mother had had the same way about her. Anastasia meant literally nothing to him. Oh, he liked showing her off to his mates when she was dressed up and looking cute, but the actual everyday care of kids, especially little kids, pissed him off.

Sometimes he wondered why he let women have his babies, it changed them inside. A lot of them changed on the outside as well – stretch marks and flab being just a few of the things he hated about some of his exes. Still, the punters didn't give a toss and that was the main thing. All his kids' mothers were on the game, and soon he knew Tiff would be just like them. She had a shock coming to her at that club and he was intrigued to see how she would handle it.

Before he rang the buzzer of Sonny's flat he checked inside his sports bag. He had two hand guns and a large bag of cocaine. Pat liked Sonny; he was an earner and was also sound. Would keep his mouth shut if he was caught and do his time without too much trouble. Young men today opened their traps to their briefs before they were even charged. It was laughable. Big men on the streets and little boys in the filth shop if they thought they had a good capture.

Winning Patrick's trust took time and effort and Sonny had come up trumps for him more than once. As he buzzed for entry Pat was smiling again.

Sonny's flat was smart, all black leather and cream walls, completely at odds with his appearance. He looked like a walking flag of Ethiopia, Jamaican through and through. In fact Sonny was a Brixton boy, had never even been to Jamaica, but that didn't bother him too much. His mother was white, a school teacher, his father an African businessman with the gift of the gab. Sonny had never met him, nor had his mother seen him again after their three-week fling.

Now Sonny was playing with his dreadlocks and smoking a large joint. His permanent grin was in place and he gave off the sweet odour of grass and sweat. He was a plastic Rasta, Jamaican when it suited him, like Connor.

'That fucking skunk stinks!'

Pat was waving his hands in front of his face in mock horror.

'It's the plants in the bedroom. Fuck me, the electric bill is like the National Debt!'

Both men laughed.

'Can you smell it outside, Patrick?'

He shook his head.

'Nah. Are they nearly ready?'

'A few days, that's all, then we can harvest. Have you got the stuff?'

Pat nodded as he was given an ice-cold Bud.

'Tell Devlin if he fucking shoots anyone with that gun it's a serious drink, right? He knows that, don't he?'

Sonny nodded, his grin wider than usual.

'I think he wants to shoot Dicky Tranter with it. I know they've had a fucking big tear up over money. Dicky is a cunt to himself. He always has to have a touch, it's in his nature.'

Pat sighed and dropped on to the black leather sofa.

'Dicky has been asking for a serious word for a while. He was the same at school, a prat to himself. Have you got me money?'

Sonny was weighing a gun in his hand and smiling.

'You ever shot anyone, Patrick?'

His voice was genuinely interested.

Patrick laughed.

'As I said to Old Bill not six weeks ago, Sonny, that's for me to know and you to find out!'

'You're a bad man and no mistake. How's that little woman of yours?'

Sonny realised he had said the wrong thing from Patrick's expression but pressed on.

'Still giving you hag? Listen, you ain't had hag till you lived with my old woman. Liselle could aggravate Jah himself when she gets going.'

'Where is she?'

'Over Lakeside with her sister. I thank God every day for that place. It is the easiest place for shoplifting in the country, she reckons – and she should know, she's done them all.'

'She still skanking?'

'It's in her blood, innit? She can't help it.'

Pat laughed.

'Usual rates for the guns and the sniff. There's a good few cuts in there so you should do a nice bit on top for yourself, OK?'

Sonny nodded.

'Can you deliver some rocks for Irie?' he asked. 'He's selling out like mad. I had to chase him for the money. I think he smokes most of them himself.'

'Jimmy has a new cook and I'm going to try him out. But tell Irie that if I hear any more about him then he is rowed out once and for all, right? Tell him he'll disappear like Wilson and I will see to it personally, OK?' Patrick still looked calm and relaxed. Sonny wasn't smiling now.

It was the first time that Pat had ever given an inkling that he knew what had happened to Tony Wilson, and it shocked Sonny. Word on the street had put Patrick's face in the frame and so did Old Bill, but so far it had only been speculation. Patrick Connor was harder than most people realised. Sonny knew that, had always known it.

If he was branching out again Sonny wanted part of it, but not if it meant a large lump of bird. He had already done one stretch and wasn't inclined to do another, especially not for Patrick Connor.

'You largeing it up, Pat?'
Sonny's voice was jocular.
Patrick looked at him with piercing blue eyes.
'You'll have to wait and see, won't you, Sonny?'

Chapter Three

Lucy was at work. She hated her job but she liked the money. The other girls were all a good laugh and she enjoyed her days there. But her new supervisor, Karen Black, was giving her grief. As luck would have it she was a cousin of Bethany Jones, the same Bethany Jones who had been beaten to death by Marie. Unlike Lucy's own family, Karen hadn't had a problem with her cousin being on the game. In fact, she always pointed out that Bethany had sold her arse for her kids, making her cousin sound almost saint-like in her maternal devotion, though in fairness to Bethany she had been a good mother to all intents and purposes.

Now Marie was out and it was common knowledge, old enmities had flared back into life and going to work was almost a torture.

Lucy had liked Bethany, she had been a naturally up person, always joking and laughing. Marie had loved her.

But then Marie had also killed her.

As Lucy placed her coat in her locker, Karen was waiting as usual these days. She was big all over, all double chins and flabby belly. As she walked her legs seemed to meet at the knees from the weight and she looked as if she was going to drop to the floor at any moment. Her hair was permed, badly, and her teeth were yellowing. She always had a smell about her, a mixture of cigarettes and cats. As she leant on the lockers she looked like a grotesque parody of a good-time girl, though considering her cousin's sad demise Lucy felt it might not be diplomatic to mention this fact.

Puffing deep on a Raffles cigarette, Karen blew the smoke into Lucy's face. It was a heavy stream, blown with gusto, and she closed her eyes tightly at the onslaught.

'Seen your sister lately?'

Lucy sighed heavily.

'No. And before you ask, Karen, I won't be seeing her. I *loathe* her, can't you understand that? I know what she did, and I hate her for it. I *liked* Bethany. So why you keep wanting to hassle me, I really don't know. But if makes you feel better then go for it.'

As she went to pass Karen a heavy push knocked her backwards. Lucy was shocked by the force of the attack and it showed on her face. The hand holding the cigarette was raised and for a split second Lucy thought Karen was going to stub it out on her face; she was capable of it. Instead she poked it towards her victim menacingly as she spoke.

'You tell your sister I am going to smash her fucking face in, right? Tell your mum and your dad, too, and make sure Marie gets the message. I ain't scared of her. I ain't scared of no one. You remember that. Bethany's kids are without her while your sister is walking round with normal people, having a life. Well, I will see that she pays properly for what she did.'

Lucy could feel terror welling up inside her.

'I hope you do find her, Karen. If I find out where she is, I'll let you know, OK?'

Karen smiled then.

'But you *can* find out where she is, can't you? Being her sister, like.'

Lucy realised then exactly what Karen wanted. She wanted to set her sister up for a beating, and knowing Karen, a serious one.

'How am I supposed to do that?'

'You ring the parole board, probation, whatever, and tell them you want to meet her. I'll take it from there.'

'You want me to set Marie up? Blatantly set her up?' Lucy's voice was incredulous. 'That's a nicking for the lot of us, you included.'

Karen saw the logic of what she was saying.

'I suppose I can find out where she is and let you know without setting up any meeting. What you do after that is your business,' Lucy said slowly.

Karen grinned.

'Fancy a cuppa?'

Her fierce expression was changing by the second. Now she had what she wanted she was her old amiable self again. As they walked to the canteen Karen grabbed Lucy tightly in a head lock. The stench was overpowering. It was a jokey gesture outwardly but was Karen's way of letting her know who was the stronger. The message was heard loud and clear.

Lucy would happily set her sister up for a bit of righteous retribution if it kept Karen Black off her own back for the foreseeable future.

Mrs Harper was a trial but Kevin felt he was well able for her. He was building a small extension on to her kitchen and it felt like he was undertaking the construction of the Sistine Chapel. Her Irish accent grated on him now. This was the longest job in recorded history. Or at least it felt like it anyway.

'Do you think I should move the sink at all?'

Kevin sighed.

'The sink is better off at the window. Give you a bit of a view when you're washing up, eh?'

He smiled as he looked out over her twenty-three-foot garden and into the home that backed on to it.

'But won't I have the dishwasher?'

Kevin looked at the ceiling and took a deep breath.

'You will still use the sink, though, won't you?'

Silently he cursed her, as he cursed his wife and everyone he could think of. It was nearly time to go home and he couldn't wait. It was Thursday and that meant steak and eggs, his favourite meal of the week. With thick bread and butter it slipped down a treat.

But along with the food he would have Louise's whining and never-ending saga of Marie and what she might do, could already have done or might be considering doing in the future. It was driving him mad. As much as he loved his daughter and he did, though he could only admit that in the privacy of his own thoughts, her release had opened up a real can of worms. But for all the upset, he was glad she was out.

The thought of her locked up all those years had preyed on his mind. Every Christmas had been like a knife in his ribs as he wondered what she was doing, if she was enjoying herself. As they had sat down to dinner he had wondered what she was eating. Did she get any cards, gifts, whatever?

Although what she had done was terrible, she was still a person, still his daughter, and she had been a drug addict. That was something everyone conveniently forgot. Marie was so out of it in those days she didn't know the day of the week most of the time. He remembered how she would prowl the streets looking for a dealer. It was an illness, whatever people wanted to think. But it was a self-inflicted illness.

He began to get his tools together and heard a theatrical sigh from Mrs Harper. Well, she could go and boil her shite. He had had enough for one day. Ten minutes later he was sinking a large brandy in the pub.

Cissy Wellbeck walked over to him and he forced himself to smile. She was all right, was Cissy, but he wasn't in the mood for her at the moment.

'Can I have a word in private, like?'

He nodded, had no choice. If Cissy wanted to talk to him she would.

'Marie was down the market today.'

The words had the effect of a bucket of cold water thrown over him. At least Cissy had dropped her voice. Usually she sounded like a fog horn.

'So?'

He didn't know what else to say to her. Louise would have been well able with a put-down, but it wasn't his style.

Cissy poked her large moon face at him.

'Look, Kev, I ain't trying to add to your burdens but Marie is not exactly flavour of the month round here. You know that without me having to spell it out. All I'm saying is, have a word with her. There are still a lot of people who feel she ain't paid the right price for what she did. Personally I think they were all as bad as one another. Accidents waiting to happen, the three of them. But she's taking a big risk showing her boatrace round the market. Caroline's mother still has a stall there and if she sees her . . .'

Cissy left the rest of the sentence unspoken.

'What do you want me to do?'

'Have a word.'

He smiled grimly.

'I can't have a word, as you put it. We fucked her off out of it. We don't even know where she is.'

Cissy shrugged.

'Fair enough. I'll keep it to meself, but others must have recognised her too.'

'Well, if they did that's their problem, ain't it?'

Cissy looked into his eyes and felt sad for the man before her. She could see the misery inside him. Knew that Marie had been his favourite. She had been a good kid, old Marie. But the drugs had taken their toll, as drugs and drink are wont to do. Whether alcohol or smack, eventually it destroys whoever is involved with it.

'It's no good getting the fuck with me, Kevin. I'm only trying to avert a disaster. I knew it was pointless talking to Lou about it, so I

40

thought I would mention it to you.'

He gripped her arm gently.

'I'm sorry, Cissy. But since she's been released it's brought it all back, you know?'

She nodded.

'I know, mate. I know. But if she wants lynching, she's come to the right place. Too many long memories here. You know that as well as I do.'

He watched her walk away. She wasn't a bad old stick really. Lou hated her even though she spoke to her. But if Marie was back in the area his wife was going to go berserk. Maybe he should visit his daughter. Put her wise, like. Without Louise knowing, of course.

It was a good idea. It would give him a bona fide reason to see Marie, and if Lou found out he could always say he went to see Marie for *her*. To stop Lou getting grief. To stop Marie going to the market and stirring up trouble.

He knew he was a coward, but with Lou being like she was it was the only way he could see his child.

And he wanted to see her desperately.

Marie listened with half an ear to the woman at the Job Centre. She had heard it all before, she knew better than anyone that the chances of her getting a real job were nil, but she went through with the charade anyway.

It had taken her four years to go from A-category, lockup, to D-category, open prison, and then another year before she had been able to hit the pavement. Her life had been decided by a panel of police and probation officers and social workers. People she knew would be looking over her shoulder for the rest of her life. If she changed jobs, they had to know. If she moved, they had to be told. If she shat more than twice in one day . . . She could not even get into an argument like normal people. If she caused any kind of disturbance she was back inside and forced to finish her sentence. Even an unpaid parking ticket could get her locked up for years.

She forced the thoughts from her mind but it was wearing, this constant vigilance. Keeping your natural reactions under close check. She daren't even argue with anyone because then she could be straight back inside, and maybe that wasn't such a bad thing.

Now she was out she could see that her real climb back to normal living was going to be harder than anything she had ever accomplished before. But she listened politely because it made life easier.

That was the first thing she had learned twelve years ago. Listen, and listen, and listen. Whether it was to a screw, the Governor, or another prisoner. Keep a still tongue and smile or frown as required. It made life much easier in the long run.

She was brought back to the present by the bombshell dropped by the woman sitting opposite her.

'Mr Jarvis is willing to give you a go. He knows your history, remembers reading about it, and he knows also that he is getting you and your skills cheap. But beggars can't be choosers, eh?'

Marie forced herself to smile politely, but the urge to tell this woman what to do with her job and her condescending attitude was almost overwhelming.

The woman handed her a piece of paper with an address in East London.

'He wants someone to do the wages and generally run his office for him. I think you will be more than up to it but he won't pay you very well. Five pounds an hour max.'

Five minutes later Marie was walking along a busy road and pondering what the woman had said.

It was a job and she needed one. Needed something to fill in the time which was lying heavy on her hands. It was in an office, which she wanted. Factory work was too personal. People in factories knew each other's lives intimately, and camaraderie and back biting didn't really appeal to her. No, a small office would do for her, and Mr Jarvis had a small office by all accounts.

As Marie jumped on a bus she felt lighter than she had for a long while, for all she knew she could earn more in a few hours back in her old life than she would in a week with Mr Jarvis.

But that was in the past, when money had been the be-all and end-all of her existence. Money for skag, brown, shit, whatever epithet you wanted to put on heroin. She was assailed once more with fractured memories of strange men, strange cars, and the sickly smell of unwashed male bodies. She went quiet inside as she had taught herself to do when such memories flooded her being.

That was the past. What she needed to get herself was a future.

Tiffany was dressed and ready to go when the doorbell rang. It was Carole Halter and her sidekick Mary Bragg. She let them in and made them a quick coffee.

'Where's Anastasia?'

'Me mate's got her till the morning. I'm off on a job interview.'

The two women looked at her in the skimpy school uniform and smiled.

'You look about twelve in that!'

Tiffany grinned.

'I ain't got me make-up on yet, and I will have to blow soon. What do you want?'

Carole blew out her lips, making a raspberry sound.

'Could you borrow me a ton? Just till the weekend, like.'

'Look, Carole, if I had it I'd give it to you, but I really ain't got it.'

Carole looked deflated, all her good humour leaving her in an instant. She shook her head sorrowfully.

'All I done for you . . .'

Tiffany had heard it before, but she didn't interrupt the woman.

'I didn't tell your mum where you were. I *lied* for you. Lied through me teeth to me oldest mate for you. Told her no one knew where you were. I lied to a *murderer* for you, and you can't see your way clear to lending me a few quid.'

The whine in the older woman's voice was annoying and unnecessary.

'I ain't got it . . .'

Carole stood up as if to leave.

'Well, if you ain't got it . . .'

'I can let you have thirty quid, but that's all I've got. I'll leave meself short.'

As she said it Tiffany cursed herself. She would have to get the fucking bus in a school uniform now. Or try and borrow some dosh herself.

But Carole was her only link with the past and she needed that sometimes. Though why, she wasn't sure. Maybe it was true, the old saying that blood was thicker than water. She still wanted to feel that her mother was close by even if she didn't actually want to see her in the flesh, and over the years Marie's old pal Carole had provided that contact with the past Tiffany seemed to crave. As she handed over the money she knew she wouldn't see Carole for a few weeks. She never did when she was owed money. Carole was scum with a capital S. But she had been there for Tiffany when she was younger and she owed her for that much at least.

When they had gone she went into Anastasia's room and opened the little girl's piggy bank. As she emptied it she felt shame wash over her like a blanket of sweaty heat.

43

But she would replace it, she would, and if she got this job it would be back before the weekend.

At least that's what she told herself.

Alan Jarvis surveyed the woman in front of him with a smile.

'Coffee . . . tea?'

Marie was so nervous she could hear her heartbeat.

'No, thank you.'

She sat down when he offered her a chair; noticed that he watched as she crossed her legs.

He was a good-looking man in his early fifties, tall and well-built if inclined to fat. She guessed he ate properly to stop himself piling it on. He had nice eyes, but was full-lipped which made him look as if he had sex on his mind constantly. Years ago she would have booked him as a good punter.

The thought made her tremble.

He *could*, to all intents and purposes, have *been* a punter.

That bothered her more now she was out than it had when she had been inside. To acknowledge that there had been a time in her life when the filthiest of old men would have been worth a trick to get a few quid preyed on her mind.

She had that same feeling now she had hated then. Receiving that once-over look men had always given her made her feel she was still the old Marie, the one who would do anything for money.

His office was a Portakabin full of pornographic calendars and the usual crap collected by men who had no real understanding of the female mind, let alone body. He was sad and he knew it and she knew.

The old Marie would have overlooked it all, done whatever he wanted for the cash. Not the new one. The new improved version, like the washing-powder adverts claimed, was stain-free these days. But it took just one look to bring all the shame and humiliation right back.

'I understand you want the wages and PAYE doing. What else is in the job description?'

He smiled again, a lascivious smile that made him look ridiculous.

'What else do you want to do, love?'

She stared at him with cold blue eyes. Quiet again, she knew that eventually she would unnerve him. She carried on staring at him and saw confusion first and then embarrassment in his eyes again.

'Let's start again, shall we?'

She didn't answer him, just raised one eyebrow a fraction.

He pretended to read her CV this time.

'I see you have a degree in English literature.'

He glanced up at her as he spoke and she nodded.

'For all the good it will do me. But it made the time pass. Reading is a big hobby in prison, as I am sure you appreciate.'

Mentioning prison first was a good gambit for her and she realised it immediately.

'Long time, I understand?'

'Nearly thirteen years including remand. I was cat-A, locked up, and eventually went down cats until I was allowed out. Now here I am, in your office, looking for a job. Time is a funny thing, Mr Jarvis. You think it will never pass but it does. And the next thing you know, a whole new life is opening up before you.'

It was the right thing to say.

He looked ashamed and also relieved that she had put her cards on the table. She knew it had suddenly occurred to him that he was trying to banter with a woman who had already killed twice.

She smiled and the expression completely changed her face.

'Look, Mr Jarvis, you know what I was imprisoned for – it was a nine-days wonder at the time. But if you give me this job I will work hard for you and can promise I will do whatever is necessary to keep this office running smoothly. I am over-qualified for this job, but as the woman at the Job Centre pointed out, beggars can't be choosers.'

'Do you know *anything* about the scrap metal business?'

Marie grinned.

'No, sir. But I am willing to learn.'

He looked into her open face, remembering the photos of her in the papers. The *Sun* had said she was a murderer with the face of an angel, and they were right for once. She had the blonde good looks that many women envied. She had a good bone structure and with the right clothes could be a stunner.

He knew that her novelty value would go a long way in his line of work. Most of the people who needed his services were faces, villains, etc. He had a feeling she would fit right in once she got over her nerves.

'When can you start?'

'How about tomorrow?'

She looked around the scruffy little room and then gazed at him in a friendly way. 'I'll bring cleaning stuff, shall I?'

He nodded, amazed to find that he actually liked her. She was far stronger than most people would be in her position.

Yes, he liked her a lot – and that was not something he'd ever have expected to say of a murderess.

Joey Carr was big, fat and ugly. His mother had once remarked that at his birth the midwife had slapped his face instead of his arse. Joey had thought this hilarious and repeated the story to friends and enemies alike.

He was a self-made man with no scruples, no feelings and no morals. His clubs were seedy dives for seedy people and he understood that fact and revelled in it. He drove a gold Rolls-Royce, had enough diamond rings on his pudgy fingers to keep a family in luxury for a year, and wasn't the greatest at personal hygiene.

He took one look at Tiffany in her school uniform and thick make-up and grinned widely. She was just his cup of tea: young, scared and desperate to make some money.

'Tiffany, ain't it?'

He had a gravelly voice from the fat Churchill cigars he smoked constantly. They had made his teeth brown and his breath stink. Again, not things that bothered him. He bought company and knew that if the price was right he could buy any female company he wanted.

This girl was about to put out for a job even if she didn't realise it yet.

'Show me your tits, love.'

'Eh?'

Tiffany was shocked at the barefaced cheek of the remark.

'Show me your tits. I need to see what the punters will see, don't I?'

She undid her blouse slowly.

'Pop them out of the bra. You'll be naked round the pole, love, so I need to see the goods properly. If you have stretch marks we have professional cover-up you can buy at trade price, OK? I know you have a kiddie.'

He was so matter-of-fact it made Tiffany relax a bit. He was only doing his job. Eventually she was naked before him. His office was cold and her whole body was shivering as she stood there.

He walked around her as if she was a horse he was going to buy. She half expected him to look at her teeth. She put her mind on

46

auto-pilot and concentrated on the office around her. It was lovely, all mahogany desk and thick pile carpet. He obviously liked his comforts.

As his hands squeezed her breasts she closed her eyes.

'You'll do. A bit on the scrawny side, but the older men like that. You *are* over sixteen?'

'Of course!'

'Well, that cunt Patrick brings me babes in arms sometimes. Fucking jail bait!'

She ignored what he was saying. She really didn't want to know. He sat at his desk and surveyed her.

'You could earn in excess of three hundred a night dancing from seven-thirty till two-thirty in the morning. You *can* earn more. I take twenty per cent and for that the bouncers keep the beady on you in case you have hag, whatever. As the drink flows, the abuse grows. One of the girls coined that phrase and it's true. So be prepared. Now then, do you want the job?'

She nodded hesitantly and smiled. Over a grand a week! What she couldn't do with that.

He started to undo his trousers and she watched him in amazement. He was already erect. She looked into his little piggy eyes.

'Well, come on then, it's fucking freezing in here. You do this as and when I request it as part of the deal, OK? It gets you the front tables, the real earning tables, so get your laughing gear round that and stop playing the wilting fucking virgin.'

Tiffany hesitated and he began to replace his member in his pants.

'Fair enough, love. But in excess of a grand a week is sitting here and you should think long and hard about that.'

She walked over to him and dropped down on to her knees. She just prayed she wouldn't throw up all over his nice carpet.

This was for her daughter, for her child.

It was the same thing her mother had told herself many years before, though Tiffany didn't know that.

Ten minutes later he gave her a glass of brandy. The burning sensation was worth it. Someone had once told her that alcohol was like bleach, it killed bugs and germs. She hoped it was true.

Tiffany couldn't bring herself to kiss her daughter for days afterwards, but it was for a thousand quid a week. It was worth it in the long run.

At least, that's what she repeatedly told herself.

47

Marie answered the knock on her door warily. It was Amanda Stirling. She carried a half-bottle of white wine and two glasses. She also held a large brown paper bag.

'Congratulations. You got a job!'

She was genuinely pleased the first big hurdle was over and it showed. She unscrewed the wine and poured it out. As she passed a glass to Marie she saw the confusion in her face.

'I ain't had alcohol for years. Even inside I never bothered with the home-made.' She didn't take the glass. 'Do you mind if I pass on this? I was an addict and that means I'm addicted to any kind of stimulant or drug. Especially alcohol.'

Amanda felt bad to have put her on the spot but she smiled.

'Sure. I brought these for you.'

She placed the brown paper bag on the bed. Inside were two black tailored suits. They were newish and smart. Marie was overwhelmed.

'Just what I needed. I was wondering what the hell I was supposed to wear to work. I guessed I would need new stuff.'

'Well, I hope they fit. I put them aside when they came in as I thought they'd be ideal for you.'

Marie was overcome with emotion. The kind act made her feel like breaking down and sobbing her heart out. It was so long since anyone had thought of her expressly it overwhelmed her.

'I can't thank you enough.'

'You'll have to get shoes, of course, but I think we have enough in the kitty to provide them. A couple of blouses and some tights and you should be OK for a while.'

'I was going to go to Romford when I got paid and look round. I need a coat, a proper coat.'

'A bit of make-up and you'll look a million dollars.'

'I don't need make-up.'

'True. What I wouldn't give for your skin and eyes.'

Marie was shaking her head in embarrassment.

'I didn't mean it that way . . .'

Amanda laughed gently.

'I know! I was only joking. But you are a very attractive woman.'

'For all the good it's ever done me.'

The two women looked at each other for long moments.

'This is a new life, Marie, and you have to embrace it. Leave the past right where it is – in the past.'

'I'm trying but it's hard.'

A little while later Marie was wearing one of the suits. It fitted like a glove and she knew she looked good in it. Her eyes strayed to the glass of wine Amanda had left on the bedside table. She picked it up and smelled it.

The aroma was tart. It was cheap wine and she remembered drinking stuff just like this as a forerunner to going out when she was a girl. Carole and she would drink a litre of cheap Liebfraumilch to get them in the mood for the night's events. They had to be out of their heads to enjoy themselves then. Drink made them lose their inhibitions, made them relax. She remembered the feeling as if it was yesterday.

The temptation to take a sip of wine was strong. But she knew that one sip would lead to one glass and that in turn would lead to one bottle. She poured it down the sink and washed the glass out, then she went back and tried on the other suit.

She felt good about herself. Better than she had in a long time. She could handle Alan Jarvis. She would keep the job and get a life. For the first time that seemed a possibility.

When she finally went to bed she slept like a baby. The usual dreams and worries were put on hold for a while.

She had made a start. Now she would take one step at a time.

Tiffany was drunker than she had ever been in her life and she knew it. She had tracked Pat down to the gym and now he was looking at her as if he didn't know her.

The gym was closed, they were in his office. She started to strip off and he stopped her.

'Leave it out, Tiff. I'm knackered. I have an appointment in a while anyway.'

'You bastard! Who you going to see this time of night? A fucking bird, that's who.'

'So what if I am?' In a parody of a black woman's voice, holding up his hand he cried, 'I don't see no ring on my finger, baby.'

Tiffany knew she was defeated, inside her drink-fuddled mind she knew it, but reason was tossed aside.

'If you go to another bird then we are finished, right?'

It sounded childish even in her own ears.

'Fair enough. Goodbye, Tiff.'

He was hard, so hard, and he loved it.

'Give me some money.'

'Bollocks! You want to be Miss Independent, you get your own money.'

'I need a cab. I need to get home to our child.'

Pat laughed.

'You make me fucking die. You really think you are something else, don't you? Why do you think I got you that job, Tiff? It was to get shot of you, my love. I knew you were just like your mother, that you'd blow that fat cunt for the money. It's in the blood, love. Enjoy it, did you?'

Somehow Tiffany had believed Patrick would never find out what she had done. It had never occurred to her that he could have set her up for the night's events. She felt suddenly sick, her stomach rebelling at the alcohol and the unpalatable truth. She walked unsteadily from the room.

Outside in the street the cold hit her and she pulled her coat tighter around her. Then the tears came, maudlin tears because she felt so sorry for herself. A little later she heard Pat's BMW. He passed her by without a second glance.

As drunk as she was, she'd learned a valuable lesson. She was alone with her daughter, and would always be alone. It was a sobering thought. She had crossed a boundary tonight and she knew it. But it was a boundary she would have to cross frequently to keep her head above water and give her child all the things she herself had never had.

Carole had once said that Pat had brought her mother to ruin. Finally it occurred to Tiffany that she might have been right about that. Because if he had treated her mother as he had just treated her, then it must be right.

Tiffany threw up in the gutter and it made her feel physically better at least. But the mental wounds would take a lot longer to heal.

Chapter Four

Alan Jarvis was pleased with Marie. The office looked so different. It was clean and he could find anything he wanted. The VAT man would be happy about that too. He had even taken down the more lurid calendars though Marie had never said a word about them. It felt odd coming in in the mornings. There was fresh milk for his coffee and now the place didn't have that unkempt odour that used to cling to his clothes and hair.

He kept his sidelines private so Marie had no knowledge of what went on here late at night, and that suited them both. Alan was in over his head there and he knew it. But the money was phenomenal.

Marie had the computer up and running and also had everything but his private business on disk. It was great to come in and see her sitting there in her black suit. She was easy to be around. Unlike most of the women of his acquaintance, she didn't feel the urge to talk all the time. His ex-wife Beverley could talk for the Olympics and get the gold. It was one of the things he had eventually hated about her.

He liked the way Marie was quiet, in her voice and demeanour. He was pleased he had employed her. He only hoped he could pass over all the legal stuff to her soon and then he could get on with his other businesses in peace. This place was a good front and he knew it.

'You had a few parcels turn up.'

He nodded.

'I've been expecting them, Marie. Where are they?'

'I put them in the back office. I know it's none of my business but they have "Medical Supplies" written on them.'

Alan frowned. 'Do they?'

He walked into the back office and cursed his associate in France who was so thick he thought he could get away with that scam in a scrapyard.

'Leave it with me, Marie. I'll sort it out. Now have you mastered the overseas stuff yet? Africa is one of our biggest money spinners and I have a batch of fridges to go there in the next few days.'

He shook his head sagely.

'Amazing, really. All our old crap is recycled out there. Makes you think, don't it? In a few months that scrap will be up and running again and people will be buying it hand over fist. All the shit we dump, they love. There's money in rubbish, love. Big money.'

Marie smiled.

'It's certainly been an eye opener for me.'

She was always polite to him. He liked that about her. She called people 'sir' when they called, and she had a deep sexy voice that sounded great over the phone. Two men he had dealt with for years wanted to know where the hell he had found her and were convinced he was shagging her. He let them think it. He wasn't about to lose her to more money.

The strange thing was, where her past should hinder her, in his game it was a help. Everyone he dealt with had had their collar felt or had done real time so she was just like one of the lads. Except for those great big tits, of course, but he wasn't looking at them now as often as he had been and felt that was an advance in itself.

'I'm putting your money up from next month, Marie. Seven-fifty an hour. You've earned it, love.'

She just smiled and looked at him.

'Thank you. I really need to get myself sorted. I might be able to get a flat in another few months if I start saving.'

He cleared his throat noisily. When she talked about what she might be able to do it always made him feel bad. He couldn't for the life of him imagine what it must be like to have to watch yourself twenty-four hours a day. It had occurred to him that her presence might lead to Old Bill poking about, but he didn't have so much as a parking ticket outstanding so that wasn't a real worry. He knew that any checks on her would have been done by now and the fact that he had heard nothing spoke volumes. Anyway he enjoyed sailing close to the wind, it was in his nature.

'Me mate rents out places. I'll see what I can do, OK?'

She was saved from answering by the door opening. A short copper-blonde woman came bursting into the confined space.

'Hello, love, all right?'

She smiled at Marie in a friendly fashion, all Elizabeth Arden and expensive perfume.

'You must be the new girl. I'm Beverley – you can call me Bev. I'll be on the phone a lot so it's best we're mates, eh?'

She laughed loudly and Marie saw that for the first time her boss was not his usual jovial self.

'If he shakes your hand count your bleeding fingers and check your rings, right? He's about as trustworthy as a fucking starving yeti.'

Bev turned on her ex-husband then.

'Where's me money? The kids' school fees are due and that bleeding nun is giving me grief.'

He grinned good-naturedly.

'Oh Beverley, light of my life. Been to evening classes again, have we? How to make the best of a limited personality?'

Beverley laughed.

'One thing I will give you, Al, you are a crack. Now, money or your nuts ripped off. It's your choice, sweetie.'

Alan shook his head and tried not to laugh.

'Cheque book it is then.'

'You know it makes sense.' She turned to Marie. 'How do you stand it here with him? Miserable fucker he is. Mind you, it smells better. Still bring your little tarts here of a night, do you, Al? He keeps the slag population in leggings and home perms, don't you, darling?'

Alan ignored her and Marie watched, fascinated by a woman with so much confidence she didn't care what she said or who she said it to.

'Christ, but he has had some rough ones! Don't let him sweet talk you, my love. He'd shag a fence in the right light.'

'All right, Beverley, give it a rest now. Remember what the judge said.'

She took the cheque.

'He said if I didn't keep quiet he would have me removed from court. But that was when you was up for trying to get out of your maintenance payments, darling. Nothing to do with the divorce, was it?'

She kissed the piece of paper in her hand.

'Jessica needs a new horse as well. I'll send you the bill, OK? And don't forget to pick them up on Saturday early. I've got a date with a man.'

'Where did you find him then, Bev? Rent a Coma dating agency?'

She laughed again.

53

'I'll chalk one up to you this time, Al.' She turned to Marie. 'Ta-ra, love. Remember what I said.'

Then she was gone and the office seemed very small and quiet after she'd left.

'Sorry about that.'

Marie started to laugh. It was a high-pitched sound that was almost hysterical in its intensity. She laughed for a full five minutes. Alan watched as she wiped her eyes with a tissue. Tears were streaming down her face.

'I'm so sorry, but she is a scream.'

Alan laughed with her. He realised this was the first time she had really laughed in years and for once was glad of Beverley's big trap.

When Marie had finished laughing she looked different somehow. Looser.

'You want to try living with her,' Alan growled. 'Do you know what she done once? I was seeing a little bird from Romford. Nice she was . . . thick as two short planks but nice. Beverley only went round her mum and dad's. She was waiting there when I dropped the girl off. I nearly died.'

Marie started laughing again.

'There I was in their living room with their only daughter, and me wife chatting away like she was a long-lost relative. But that's Bev. What you see is what you get.'

'I liked her, Alan.'

He smiled ruefully.

'So did I, once. In fact I loved her. But she couldn't cope with me and me philandering ways, as she put it so succinctly to the divorce court. Her constant talking drove me fucking mental and all. Now she calls me Cheque Book Charlie to me face.'

Marie made them both a coffee.

'Thanks for giving me a chance with the job, Mr Jarvis.'

Even her voice sounded brighter than before.

'You are an asset, Marie. If you can cope with Beverley, you can cope with anything. But there is one thing. Can you call me Alan? Every time you say "Mr Jarvis" I think me dad's outside.'

Marie didn't answer. She wasn't sure how to answer. It was so long since she had practised the niceties of everyday living it was hard to know what to say.

But Beverley Jarvis had been like a breath of fresh air and Marie would be grateful to her till she died for breaking the ice like she had and making her laugh out loud. It had felt strange, odd, to be laughing again. But she had enjoyed it. That was the great thing, she had really enjoyed it.

Kevin stood nervously outside the halfway house. As women walked in and out he felt they were all staring at him. He moved along the road so he could watch the doorway unobserved. His nervousness was caused mostly by the thought that his wife would launch him into outer space if she knew where he was.

As Marie walked along the pavement his breath caught in his chest. She looked beautiful. There was no mistaking her. She had that proud bearing. Even drugged out of her brains she still seemed to be looking down her nose at the world.

Her long legs were shown off to advantage by the black pencil skirt of the suit she wore, which was fitted and made her look almost school-marmish in its severity. But Marie was a big sexy woman and nothing she did could ever really hide that fact. His mother had once said, 'Men will love her or hate her, and the same with women.'

Marie was too good-looking for her own good.

He blamed himself for the way she had turned out. Himself and his wife. He had loved his eldest daughter too much, her mother had loved her too little.

As he walked towards her he raised his hand in greeting. He saw the look on his daughter's face turn from confusion to joy and was glad he had come. It was the look she had given him as a child when he came in from work and stood up for her against her mother. A look of joy tinged with relief.

'Dad?'

Her voice was different, quieter.

'Marie. You look well, love.'

It was the right thing to say.

'How did you find me?'

They stared at each other for long moments.

'I rang Old Bill. They told me where you were, being your father, like . . .'

The cold was cutting into her bones but she didn't know where to take him. It was after six and she had to be in by six-thirty. For the first time this irked her. Suddenly she wanted to go out for the evening. Catch up on old times. Be herself.

'Come in with me and we'll have a coffee, eh?'

Kevin nodded.

'That would be lovely.'

He hugged her then. It was a spontaneous gesture and she hugged him back, awkwardly at first until she relaxed. They laughed together. She felt the tears then and swallowed them down. After thirteen years, close human contact seemed at odds with what she had become accustomed to and tears burned her eyes.

'Oh Dad, it's so good to see you.'

As they walked into the building they were so wrapped up in one another that neither of them saw Lucy standing across the road, a look of complete revulsion on her face.

Anastasia had the demons in her. She had cried literally all day and nothing was right for her. At thirteen months she was at a stroppy age and Tiffany was tired after her night on drink and drugs. She'd wanted to obliterate that scene with her new boss. Now she was paying the price.

As the child picked up a cup of cold coffee and poured it on to the carpet Tiffany lashed out. It was a hard smack and caught the little girl unawares. She screamed with fright and pain. Immediately, Tiffany was cuddling her.

'Mummy's sorry. Mummy's sorry,' she repeated over and over again.

Anastasia clung to her, hot tears pouring down her face and making her hair damp. Tiffany had never felt so bad in her life but the day had been so long. Every time she thought of what she had done last night she felt sick inside.

She cradled the child in her arms, whispering to her and trying to make the little girl feel better. Eventually Anastasia went to sleep, still giving occasional little hiccoughing cries. As her mother laid her gently in her cot she realised the full extent of her responsibilities. The thought that her temper had got the better of her like that and made her hurt her own child filled her with such guilt and self-loathing she wanted to die.

The flat was quiet. Too quiet.

Normally Pat would have been round by now and Tiffany realised she had come to rely on seeing him. She had no real friends, her years in care had seen to that. Any friends she had made then she didn't mix with now. Didn't want to be reminded of what her early life had been like. So it was a lonely existence for her. Carole would have been welcome, because she had known Carole all her life and didn't have to pretend to be something she wasn't with her. But she knew she wouldn't see her mother's old friend for a while.

Tiffany rolled herself a joint and smoked it until she felt calmer. The babysitter would be coming soon and she had to get ready for her first night's work. The thought of leaving the child after smacking her made her feel even guiltier. But she got ready anyway.

She wanted to really earn tonight to prove to herself that she was doing the right thing. Had done the right thing the night before.

She gently stroked her daughter's brow and then went and got ready.

An hour later she was sitting on the bus in a heavy coat, dressed like a schoolgirl underneath and feeling ridiculous. But the money was uppermost in her mind. She suppressed every other emotion. Especially the guilt and the shame.

Louise dished up in her usual haphazard fashion. As Kevin sipped a scalding hot cup of tea he glanced over at Lucy and caught the look she was giving him.

'All right, love?'

His voice was concerned.

'Why shouldn't I be?'

She sounded sullen.

'Who you talking to?' Louise's voice was sharp and she stopped serving to look daggers at her youngest daughter.

Lucy stared at her mother in confusion. She wanted to blow her father right out of the water but knew she couldn't. Not yet. Not until she had done her dirty deed for Karen Black.

'I'm tired.'

It sounded lame even in her own ears.

Louise slammed the saucepan on to the table.

'We're all bleeding tired! What makes you think you're any more tired than me or your father? He's out by six most mornings.'

'Since that bitch was paroled this house has been like a bloody morgue. She ain't even in it but we're all paying the price anyway.'

Lucy looked at her father as she spoke and he averted his eyes.

Louise, however, thought her daughter was now the fountain of wisdom.

'I know what you mean. I was at Marshall's grave yesterday and I saw Maeve Cavendish. She walked right past me. I know why and all. Everyone knows *she's* out and about so it will all start again, you mark my words, the phone calls, the threats . . . It will all start again, I know it will.'

57

'We should have moved away before. When it all happened.'

Kevin's voice was loud in the confined kitchen and Louise rounded on him.

'Oh, that's right. Run away. That's you all over, you spineless git. Well, no one is forcing me from my home and that's that.'

He sighed heavily.

'In that case, you'll have to put up with the hag then, won't you?'

Lucy watched her mother and father in fascination. He'd never, ever stopped her before when she was going off about Marie.

Already her sister was working her magic. Like all men, her father was automatically on her side, no matter what she had done.

Louise looked at her husband as if she had never seen him before and he had just appeared to her as an apparition. She slung the spoon she had been using to serve the dinner into the sink and turned on him.

'Who's rattled your fucking cage? First *she* comes in with the hump and now I have you and all. I am plagued by the pair of you.'

She stormed from the kitchen and banged heavily up the stairs.

Lucy laughed nastily.

'Pity Marie's not here to see her handiwork. Even from miles away she can still cause a row in this house, can't she?'

Kevin had had enough.

'She didn't need to with you here, Lucy. I seem to remember most of the rows were caused by jealousy, yours and your mother's, and you can tell her that from me if you like. I am off down the fucking pub for a pint and a pie.'

Lucy was shocked by her father's words. The fact they had the ring of truth about them didn't help in any way. She stared at the debris of her mother's efforts and felt a flicker of hatred once more for the sister who even as a murderess could still get her father to defend her.

As the door shut on him, her mother came down the stairs. She looked old suddenly. Old and haggard. Lucy felt ashamed of what she had caused.

'Sit down, Mum, I'll dish up, shall I?'

Her voice was small, like a little girl's.

Louise surveyed the tepid food and shook her head.

'Bin it, Lucy. I ain't hungry now. He gone to the pub?'

Lucy nodded.

'No surprise there then.'

Louise lit a cigarette and smoked in silence as her daughter cleared away. Her whole life was crumbling around her as it had once before. And the same person was responsible.

If only she had had an abortion all those years ago, how different her life would have been today.

How much easier it would all have been.

Patrick stood at the back of the club and watched Tiffany at her first night's work. She stood out from the other girls because of her extreme thinness and was in high demand because she was new.

He saw her dancing provocatively before a table of middle-aged men. They would be her prime market and she was sensible enough to know it. Her legs were long for her height and she was narrow-waisted. If she'd only had her mother's build she'd have been worth a fortune in no time.

When she went for her break he shot round to the dressing room. It was full of the smell of deodorant and fresh sweat. Girls sat around smoking, snorting and laughing.

He saw Tiffany's eyes widen at the sight of him.

'All right, Tiff? Thought I'd bring you a little gift.'

He placed the gram of cocaine into her palm.

'A little gift of a little lift!' He laughed at his own wit.

Tiffany was so pleased to see him she felt the urge to cry. She had missed him so much. Other than Anastasia he was her only source of affection. All the girls were looking at him. Some seemed to know him. Tiffany deliberately overlooked that fact, telling herself he was a dealer so of course some of them knew him. How well she didn't care to dwell on too much.

As she cut herself a line and snorted it she felt all her inhibitions and fears melt away. After drinking down a large gin and tonic, she felt much happier.

'You needed that, didn't you, darling?'

She nodded.

'You coming round later?'

Pat smiled at her.

'I might. But I have to see a bloke. I'll pick you up about two-ish and you and me can do my bit of business first, eh?'

She nodded, ecstatically happy now. She was high and she was friends with Pat again.

Life was looking up at last.

★ ★ ★

59

Marie lay in her bed and for the first time in years felt restless. It was a strange feeling. Half of her was scared shitless at the thought of seeing her family again, the other half desperate for a glimpse of her kids.

Her father was going to try and find out their addresses so she could at least look at them from a distance, even though it would be hard not to go up to them, talk to them. But she would have to be satisfied with what she got. That was something that would be true of the rest of her life, and she knew it.

She was finally glad she was released.

She had a job and she had had contact with her father. God love him, she knew the trouble it would cause if her mother ever learned he had come to see her. So the fact he had done it was all the more important to her.

She tried again to picture her children. She hoped they were happy, living good lives surrounded by nice people. It was important to her that her children were leading happy, fulfilled lives. Clean lives where they could look others in the face and know they were good people.

Marie smiled in the darkness.

If she could just look at them once more she would be happy.

Her father said that Jason had been with the same family for years. They had informally adopted him and that pleased her. She hoped her daughter had fallen on her feet as well.

If only she had listened to her mother all those years ago!

But Louise had not offered advice, she had demanded things of her daughter, and being the type of girl she was, that had made Marie worse. Each fresh shocking thing she had done had given her a feeling of satisfaction. Each time her mother went ballistic she had felt she had achieved something. Each time her mother called her a whore she had made sure she fully lived up to the epithet.

She had been such a fool! If only she had known then what she knew now. But then, as a friend in prison had once pointed out, eventually you regretted the things you hadn't done as much as the things you had.

That was very true.

Every time she had picked up a drink or taken a drug she had felt better inside. She had needed to obliterate the present. Now she wanted to obliterate the past.

But she couldn't.

All she could do was take the little things life gave her and be grateful for them. Seeing her kids, even if only from a distance, would be the start of real life for her. She could put her mind at rest about them once and for all.

Or at least she hoped she could.

Tiffany didn't like Sol Medlock. He was a man in his fifties with a heavy belly and a distinct shortage of hair and teeth. She knew he was also a number one dealer and that Patrick needed him. That had been explained to her over and over in the car on their way to his flat.

'So be nice to him, OK, Tiff? Just for me, eh?'

She smiled confidently at him.

'Of course I will. Stop worrying.'

She was high as a kite. Patrick had given her a pipe to smoke and the buzz was astronomical. She felt invincible inside. It was a fantastic feeling.

'Your eyes look fucking sexy, girl. You want to see them.'

She was buzzing. The car window was open and icy cold hit her face and it felt great. As they pulled up outside Sol's flat, Patrick handed her another pipe.

'Have a quick blast before we go in, babe.'

She was happy to oblige.

Ten minutes later she was sipping a vodka and Red Bull and could hear Patrick arguing with Sol in the state-of-the-art kitchen. The flat blew her mind. All steel units and polished wood floors, it was like a magazine picture. She wanted a place like this one day and was determined to get it.

Patrick came back into the lounge and sat beside her.

'All right, mate?'

She nodded.

'Can we go soon? I have to take the babes to playschool in the morning so I can have a few hours' kip.'

Patrick looked at her with his deep blue eyes.

'I need a favour, Tiff.'

She knew what he was going to say before he asked but still she told herself not to be so silly. That Patrick wouldn't do this to the mother of his baby girl.

'What do you want, Pat?'

He grinned, displaying his even white teeth.

'Could you be nice to Sol for me, babe? Just for a while. I have to go and call in a debt otherwise he is going to cause me right grief.'

She was already shaking her head.

He gripped her arm tightly.

'The thing is, Tiff, I ain't asking as such. Know what I mean? He said if you put out for him he would give me the time I needed, see.'

Tiffany knew that she was being asked to perform a function Patrick would normally have required from one of his working girls. The confusion on her face was heartbreaking to see. Yet he just stared at her as if she was the one who was in the wrong. He could do that, make you feel you should be doing what he wanted instead of what you knew you should be doing.

'Don't do this to me, Pat. Please.'

Her voice was low, barely a whisper, and she realised he was not going to listen to her. Instead he prepared another pipe.

He was speaking in a singsong tone as if to a recalcitrant child.

'Get that down you, nice and deep, Tiff. Then just do what the fuck you are told. You know I will not be crossed. If I say something, I expect it to be done. All my women know this, Tiffany.'

She took the pipe gratefully and drew deeply. The crack hit her brain in nanoseconds and she felt the overwhelming rush of euphoria.

Then Patrick smiled at her. A real smile.

'Whatever he wants, OK? And I'll give you a couple of ton for your trouble, baby, OK?'

As he left the flat Tiffany saw that Sol had been observing them from the kitchen doorway. He was smiling at her. She felt her heart sink down to her expensive sexy boots. She was caught in a nightmare and it was of her own making. She knew she should have walked out but she hadn't.

What was it with her? Why did she roll over every time Patrick told her to? Even when she knew that what she was doing was wrong? Even the new rush of crack wasn't enough to blot out the horror of exactly what she had agreed to do.

There was a ringing in her ears and she found herself feeling sick. As Sol put his hand on her shoulder she forced herself to relax.

It was how it had always been. Patrick spoke and she responded by doing whatever he wanted. As she walked to the bedroom with Sol she felt as if she was in a dream. She had learned to tune out the real world in care, and that stood her in good stead now.

★ ★ ★

62

Patrick was collecting from his girls. He pulled up beside them and smiled his endearing smile. Then he complimented each one of them before holding out his hand and letting them stuff it full of cash.

One girl, Bonita, a beautiful black girl with wide eyes and terrific legs, didn't give him the money straight off.

'Hey, Patrick. Channy Baker has been round the Cross – he took money from Camelia and Joely. I saw it with my own eyes, man. He wants in.'

Patrick kept on smiling.

Ten minutes later he had picked up two men from a bar and was inside the Hound Club in King's Cross, a private drinking den that was fraternised by whores and pimps. Channy took the kicking of a lifetime as Pat watched. Then he took the man's money and his weapons before personally kicking him in the face.

So it took him longer than usual to get back to Sol's place.

He let himself in and poured himself a drink, but they were still out of sight. It wouldn't be long, he decided, before he had Tiffany exactly where he wanted her. On her back with whoever he wanted, when he wanted, for money or for crack.

He opened the bedroom door and watched his girlfriend, the mother of another of his children, performing for him with a disgusting man.

It was a sight that gladdened his heart.

All women were the same. He had proved his own theory time and time again.

Chapter Five

Tiffany opened her eyes with difficulty. She could hear a hammering noise and it took a few seconds before she realised it was at her front door. As she dragged herself from the bed she saw that it was nearly twelve o'clock and her heart started beating erratically as she realised she had overslept. What the hell was Anastasia doing?

She rushed semi-naked into the child's room. The little girl was sitting in her cot. Her soaking nappy was on the floor and she had been crying, that much was obvious.

'Mummy . . .'

Her face creased with pleasure and Tiffany picked her up and hugged her tightly. The hammering on the door was still very much in evidence.

'All right, I'm coming.'

Her voice was harsh and Anastasia started to whimper.

'Did I make you jump, sweetie?'

Tiffany hugged her again as she opened the door.

'Package for Tiffany Carter.'

She signed for it awkwardly and the boy placed it in her hallway, trying his hardest to sneak a peek at her tits. She ignored him. Putting the child down, she opened the package.

It was a game she had ordered for her daughter and Anastasia was soon clapping her hands with glee. She left the child playing and pulled on a dressing gown. In the bathroom she squatted to pee and saw her reflection in the mirror tiles around the bath. She looked terrible. Her eyes were dark hollows and her skin was grey. She had lost hours sleeping. Normally she was up and about for her daughter, getting her breakfast and making sure she was dressed beautifully for playgroup. The thought of what could have happened frightened her.

She remembered that her dope and cigarette lighter were on the table in the lounge. If Anastasia had got out of the cot . . . Fear made her sweat. In future she would set the alarm on high. This must never happen again. The acrid smell of her own body reminded her of the night before and gradually she pieced the evening together as she showered. The heat of shame engulfed her once more, but she put it firmly out of her mind.

As Anastasia tucked into her Weetabix Tiffany dragged her handbag out from under the table and opened it. She counted out four hundred pounds and some loose change.

The feel of the money in her hands was fantastic. She was going to go out and blow it all on her and the babes. After all, there was plenty more where that came from. She smiled then, a real smile that made her look like the young girl she was.

Like her mother before her, money was her god.

As she put the notes back in her bag she saw the crack pipe. Patrick must have put it there. It was made from a piece of ebony, a beautiful little thing. Her first instinct was to throw it in the bin and she nearly did. But something stopped her. Instead she placed it in the zipped compartment where she kept her make-up.

Putting it out of her mind, she concentrated on getting her daughter dressed. She would take her to McDonald's for lunch as a treat to make up for being such a useless mother. She was determined it would never happen again.

Anastasia was happy. Her belly was full and Mummy was smiling. What more could a little girl want?

Louise was going through the washing. The smell of her husband's socks emanating from the washing basket made her smile. It was only from his work boots, she knew, but his feet were a family joke. Suddenly she was assailed by a memory.

She had just had Marie and her husband had picked her up from the hospital. They had driven straight to his mother's with the new baby and her mother-in-law had always insisted everyone remove their shoes before they came into her house. Kevin's feet had been ripe that day and they had all laughed like drains as he had been despatched up the stairs with a bar of soap and stern orders to 'scrub them buggers till they smell like everyone else's'.

She could remember looking down at her newborn daughter's face and wondering when the rush of love that was supposedly the norm was going to occur.

It never did, not with either of the girls, only with her Marshall.

Now he had made her heart sing from the moment she had set eyes on him. She felt the familiar sting of tears as she thought of him. His little hands, perfectly formed. She always thought of his hands, she didn't know why that was. Sometimes she couldn't remember his face. She found herself panicking in the middle of the night, trying to remember what her son had looked like. Trying to picture him. Then she would get out of bed and come down to the lounge where photographs of him stood everywhere.

She would light a cigarette and stare at them until the panic subsided and she could find solace in sleep once more.

Every time she thought of him putting that gun into his mouth she felt a wave of nausea. That someone could actually do that to themselves was beyond her comprehension. And for someone who'd had the whole world at their feet to do it made her wonder if there was any justice in the world at all.

Yet her daughter, the cause of every ill that had befallen the family, was walking round as large as life and still breathing. Mixing with normal folk, people who didn't know what she was. What she had done.

Louise sat at the table and lit a cigarette, drawing the smoke deep into her lungs. If only there was some way she could pay Marie back she would feel better. The hatred she felt for her own child always amazed her. Even when her elder daughter had been a toddler Louise had disliked her, resented her and the intrusion she had made into their lives. Yet she knew her daughter looked like her. Was the living image of her at the same age. People were supposed to love their kids because they were part of them, surely? It was an inverted form of self-love. Or at least that was what she'd always thought.

But for herself, she had never wanted any part of her elder daughter. In fact, if she had found Marie with her head blown off she would have felt only relief. A weight would have been lifted off her mind.

Marie had always been trouble. At school she had spent her whole time bunking off, getting drunk. At thirteen she was already on the pill. Louise could remember finding it in her daughter's school bag: Ovranette. Years later it was supposed to have been a big killer, caused blood clots or something, but not for her daughter. Didn't stop her getting pregnant either. Fourteen and a belly full of arms and legs. Fifteen she was pushing a pram. No shame about it either. Bold as brass, walking round with the child.

Another little slut brought into the world because of a quick fumble. No love, nothing. Couldn't even name the father properly. Everyone knew it could have been literally anyone.

The shame at the time was almost unbearable. But Kevin had said if she wanted the baby, let her have it. If she was big enough to get pregnant, she was big enough to look after it. In fairness to him he had thought it might calm her down, but the reverse was true. It made her worse.

Louise lit another cigarette and made herself a coffee. She wondered briefly what Tiffany was doing with herself. She was so like her mother it was unbelievable. Same looks and demeanour. Even had the same temper, banging her head on the floor when she couldn't get her own way. Marie just laughed at her. When the council had given her daughter a flat Louise had felt that, just for once, God was being good to her. The day Marie had walked out of the house she had felt such relief.

Then she had had the other one, the boy. Black as the ace of spades and that bitch didn't give a toss. Flaunted him. Thought she was so clever. Marshall had been like a man demented over it. Called her every name he could lay his tongue round. He was right and all. Having a baby again, another fatherless one, was bad enough – but to have one by Patrick Connor! Drug dealer, whore master . . . and that was just what the nice people said about him. It was going too far. It was a deliberate slap in the face for them all.

But by then Marie had been on the game and on drugs. So people just shook their heads and winked knowingly when they saw her. The waste of her daughter's life would always be a sore spot. Marie had had the looks to be anything she wanted. She could have had anyone she wanted. Men were lining up for her then. But in the end they were getting it from her for free or for a small price so her mystique shot out the window with the last of her morals.

She'd been a slut then and she still was. You couldn't write off all those men, no matter what. It was like a smell that clung to her, making her different from everyone else. How they had held their heads up Louise didn't know. Then the murders.

Finally, that bitch had been found out. She had been taken away and locked up and it was the happiest day of her mother's life when it had happened. It was a relief to see the back of her. To know that once the shock wore off they could get on with their lives. Their decent lives. Yet she knew Kevin had missed his daughter. He had always had a soft spot for her. Always wanted to be near her. All over her, he was. That's why she was like it. She'd learned early that male company was an earner.

He was always giving her money, getting her things. It never occurred to him to get her to work for a living like everyone else. That's why she went on the game. Easy money as far as she was concerned. Getting paid for something she did naturally anyway, that was Marie's logic. She was the talk of her block of flats, always fighting and drinking, turning up here in the middle of the night with her vicious mouth and her drunken ramblings.

If Marie was in front of her now her mother would beat her, beat her like she should have when she was a girl. Let her know exactly what she thought of her.

Louise wiped a hand across her face.

She felt ill again and took another anti-depressant. It was all Marie's fault, coming home after all these years and causing more trouble.

Well, if she came back here again Louise knew what she would do this time. What she should have done years ago. What she should have done when Marie knocked on the door not six weeks ago.

She would kill her.

Alan opened the packages that he had hidden at the back of the scrapyard. They contained cocaine which would be cooked in a microwave and sold as crack. He knew this and was not that happy about it, but he needed the money badly.

He was a gambler. It was his one passion in life and that fact had broken Beverley when she'd found out. His womanising she had laughed off. It had become almost a game between them. While he gave her what she wanted for herself and their three daughters she was cool about it. It was the gambling that had finally brought her to her knees.

She believed that he was cured now. That the psychiatrist had cured his compulsion to bet on anything and everything.

When he had got into debt with Mikey Devlin he had honestly believed he was just having a run of bad luck and that soon it would be over. Instead he got himself in deeper and deeper. The worst thing was, before Mikey, he had rung up loan companies and mortgaged the house and business to the hilt as well. He was a desperate man and desperate men were exactly what Mikey was always looking for. Especially desperate men with a scrapyard and no previous convictions.

At first it had seemed like the answer to all Alan's prayers. He was out of debt in no time and the money was rolling in. Then the fright set in. One night the Old Bill arrived and he had literally shat himself with fright at the thought of getting his collar well and truly felt. It turned out they were looking for two youngsters who had broken into a warehouse nearby, but it had been enough to take the gleam off what he was doing. It was Alan's wake-up call and he knew that he had needed it badly.

Now he was still making a mint but wanted out before he was locked up somewhere and the judge threw away the key.

But it just wasn't that easy telling Mikey he didn't want to do it any more. Mikey had once facially scalped a bloke he'd thought was going to grass him up. When their little disagreement was finally resolved and the man was deemed innocent, Mikey had apologised profusely and given him a rather large drink. About ten grand. But did that make up for the fact he looked like a reject from the space shuttle crash? Not as far as Alan was concerned.

So he was in a quandary. He knew he was on borrowed time; deep inside he knew a capture was on the cards. If scams went on too long it was inevitable. Most people got a lump through sheer greed. They kept up a scam even though it was getting shaky and more and more people were getting involved. The more people in the game, the greater the likelihood of a grass being among them. It was common sense really. Someone gets banged up for one offence and talks their head off to get out of doing bird. Consequently, whoever they were ducking and diving with gets the full bifta of the law while they get a quick eighteen months. Old Bill have a field day and everyone's happy. Except that Alan knew that if it ever went off over the scrapyard he would be the one getting twenty-five years, not eighteen months.

It was his yard, his premises and his money that was supposedly backing this lot. Mikey was out of the frame through pure and unadulterated fear. No one would dare finger him. Any grassing was going to bring the knock straight to Alan's front door.

As if these thoughts had conjured him up, Mikey's car pulled up in the yard. Alan saw the headlights and walked out of the shed to greet him.

'You locked that bleeding dog up?'

Carlos the Rottweiler was a bone of contention between them. The dog hated Mikey who normally fancied himself a dog lover. Normally the wilder ones loved him but Carlos would rip anyone apart, it was in his nature. So Mikey had drawn a blank where he was concerned and now he hated the animal.

'He's in me office, having his tea.'

Mikey walked into the yard. He wasn't a big man but he was heavy. His bald head and big gut made him look fatherly, until he opened his mouth. Then he was a loud and obnoxious individual with a wicked temper. He was chauvinist and racist with the tattoos to prove it.

In his hand-made suit he looked what he was, a diamond geezer, and proud of it.

'Has it arrived?'

He walked back into the shed with Alan as he spoke.

'They put fucking "Hospital Supplies" on the package. Is he fucking stupid or what?'

Mikey grinned.

'He is a cunt but I'll talk to him, OK? Help me load it in the car and then we have to do a drop at Thurrock services for about midnight. Jimmy Baxby is a partner now and we are supplying him and all, so the parcels should start coming thicker and faster.'

Alan forced a smile on to his face. He was getting in deeper and deeper and there was nothing he could do about it.

'Put a few bets on with what you'll be getting, eh, Al?'

Mikey was actually being friendly to him and that worried Alan Jarvis more than anything.

Karen Black was waiting in the car park. As Lucy approached her she considered her own position and decided she might as well get what she could out of it.

Everyone knew that the factory was losing stuff hand over fist, and everyone also knew that it was Karen Black and her partner Gregory the supervisor who were the main dealers. The factory made paper products: kitchen rolls, loo rolls, serviettes and such like. It was a rival to Bowater Scott, and the workforce all received monthly 'goodie bags', free stuff that the firm supplied ostensibly to stop thieving. Instead it increased it as people sold stuff on and then wanted a bigger profit.

Karen and Gregory supplied restaurants, cafes, even some local shops. They also sold off market stalls all over the smoke so it was a big earner for them. Now Lucy decided that she wanted in. If she was getting married then she'd need some extra cash and what better way to get it?

71

She was smiling amiably as she walked over to the woman who was the cause of so much heartache in the firm. But as she was also the union rep she got away with murder.

'I have the address here.'

She handed Karen an envelope with the details scrawled on it.

'Good stuff.' Karen grinned. 'Glad you ain't my sister.'

The barb hit home. If Marie had been *her* sister Karen would have taken on the world for her, she implied. The Blacks didn't care that their relative had been on the streets and a druggie. That didn't bother them. The blood tie did. Bethany had been family and that was that. Unlike Lucy's own family who believed that what the neighbours thought was more important than whether you were having a nice time, or a good life. The neighbours were her mother's yardstick for everything.

When the Patels had moved in her mother had had a blue fit. The thought of Indians in the street had done her head in. That was until she found out Mr Patel's son was a pharmacist, and that he owned the pharmacy in the little block of shops nearby. He had assumed saintly proportions then.

In fact, her mother would cheerfully have had the whole population of Asia in her street rather than the next new arrivals, the McDuffs, a crowd of swearing, screaming Irish. But they had bought the house and that was that. If their Friday night cabaret annoyed everyone else, it sent her mother demented: the night out at Bingo and then the pub and the fight afterwards in the street.

Mrs McDuff could give as good as she got so the couple were evenly matched and her husband often came off the worst. Their son was in prison for armed robbery, and so Mrs McDuff saw herself and Louise as kindred spirits, which did not go down well at all.

'Marie is going to regret ever leaving prison, you realise that, don't you?' Karen gloated.

Lucy shrugged.

'Big deal. Can I have an in on the paper scam then?'

Karen laughed.

'No! What would we want you in on it for? How could we trust you for a start?'

'What do you mean? Of course you can trust me.'

Karen looked her over and obviously found her wanting.

'You just grassed your own sister up. I wouldn't trust you as far as I could throw you now, love.'

She saw the look of confusion on Lucy's face.

'You just don't get it, do you?'

Lucy shook her head. 'Get what?'

'You're scum, Lucy. Whatever Marie did she's still your sister. I'd have her any day of the week over you, love. She was out of her nut when she topped everyone. But you are as sober as a judge and you still want to tuck her up. I'd have had more respect for you if you'd told me where to get off.'

'If she's so great then why do you want to give her a hiding?'

Karen sighed heavily.

'You really are that thick, ain't you? It's family, ain't it? Family loyalty. Bethany was me cousin and she was topped so I have to have something to say about that, don't I? My mum took her kids in so they didn't go into care. It's what you do, isn't it?'

Lucy didn't answer.

'Your mother should have took Marie's kids – people would have thought more of her if she had. Stuck-up bitch she is! You can tell her that from me. She is really disliked round these parts. She should have looked after them kids and made some sense out of it all. They hadn't done anything wrong, had they?'

Lucy felt as if she was getting an education in life in double quick time. All those years they'd thought everyone had admired the stand they had taken when in fact it was the opposite.

But her mother had not wanted the kids, especially the boy. He was half-caste but too dark for her to cope with, and the girl was Marie all over again. Big trap as well as stroppy.

If her mother knew what people really thought it would kill her. She set such stock on what others thought of her. How she was perceived.

That was the trouble, they all did, Lucy included. For all the good it had done her. As Karen walked away she felt the urge to cry.

Tiffany listened with half an ear to the girl beside her. She was wittering on about how much money there was to be made in Manchester. Her sister had gone up there and was now the proud owner of a convertible and a big black pimp who was the dog's gonads.

'I was telling Pat Connor about it last night and he's going to look into it.'

She had Tiffany's undivided attention now.

'You saw Pat last night?'

The girl, Lauren, nodded craftily.

'Went to a party near Praed Street with him. Had a right laugh.'

The girl's long blonde hair was tossed back as she spoke. Tiffany knew she was trying to wind her up and smiled evenly.

'I hope you used a condom, love, he's got the big syph.'

She saw the girl's face pale.

'It's them Russian birds, see. All dosed up to the eyebrows, ain't they? He's been buying them from Jimmy the Greek to work the black rooms.'

Tiffany was smiling sweetly now.

'Looks like you better get your arse down the Old London and have a check up, eh?'

The girl screwed her eyes up and laughed.

'You're a fucking wind-up!'

Tiffany opened her eyes wide and said innocently, 'Am I?'

Then she walked from the room.

In the toilet she pressed her forehead to the cold tiles and sighed. He was a bastard if he was pulling from her own workplace. But inside she knew that was what Pat did. He put a girl in then moved in on the action. It kept the girls fighting and made sure he got all the gossip. Prostitutes grassed one another up without a second's thought. It was in their nature.

She felt the familiar sickness inside her and made herself walk back into the girls' changing room. She picked up her bag nonchalantly and went back to the toilets. As amenable as the club owners were about grass and cocaine, crack was strictly off limits. It was a fighting drug, even more so than coke or speed. Previously mousy girls had turned into demons after a smoke. It was the downside. The euphoria was so short-lived it was over in a moment and then the craving was twice as bad as before.

In the few weeks since she had been introduced to it Tiffany knew it had taken a grip on her. She also knew that was exactly what Pat wanted. But the need for it was too great now. It was put above everything else.

As she inhaled the little rock she felt only blinding pleasure and all else was conveniently forgotten.

Even Anastasia.

Marie got off the train and walked wearily out of the station into the cold night air. It was just after six and dark as hell. The street lighting was bad, but she knew the route well now as she had been walking it for so long. She was looking forward to a bath and an early night. It was Friday and while everyone else would be getting ready for a night on the town, she was still under a six-thirty curfew.

It didn't bother her, though, not tonight. She was tired out and tomorrow she was going to see her father. He would have news of the kids, she hoped.

As she turned the corner, she felt someone behind her. She'd half turned to see who it was when something hit her heavily on the side of her face.

She crumpled to the pavement.

She knew that feet and instruments were raining blows all over her, but was powerless to stop them. She curled up into a ball and covered her face. It was all she could do.

People watched but did nothing to help her. They just hurried on their way. After what seemed like hours she was pulled to her feet.

Karen Black looked into her face nastily.

'This is for Caroline and Bethany, you murdering cunt!'

Her fist encased in a knuckle-duster hit Marie square between the eyes. She slumped to the ground then, losing consciousness.

Karen and her two sisters carried on the beating for another five minutes. Finally, spent and sweating, they spat on the prostrate form before running off. They knew they were in the clear. No one was going to call Old Bill. Not until they were well and truly off the scene. It was the law of the street and as far as they were concerned, it was a good law.

A Hindu woman and her daughter finally got an ambulance. They stayed with the unconscious woman until help arrived and then disappeared.

Kevin had just finished his dinner when the phone rang. He picked it up casually and said hello. Louise stood watching as his face turned paler and paler.

'Where is she?'

She saw him nodding. Then he put the phone down and went to get his coat.

'What's wrong? Is it Lucy?'

He shook his head sadly.

'No. What you on about, woman? It was one of the workmen. Mrs Harper's kitchen's flooded and she's doing her crust. I have to go round there now.'

He rushed out of the door and into his van, Louise's eyes

75

following him distrustfully. If he was seeing another woman again that would be it. He thought she didn't know about his other life but she did. He was like all men – his cock was both god and brain to him. Well, he had a short sharp shock coming to him if he thought he was going to start all that crap again. If this one was another screamer, he'd be looking for someone with a bollock donor card before the week was out.

She dialled 1471. Number withheld. Well, that told her all she needed to know.

She poured herself a large medicinal port and sat down to await his homecoming. Her eyes strayed to her son's photographs. If only Marshall had lived, how different it would all have been.

Marie opened her eyes painfully and then closed them immediately. Her whole body was screaming and she felt sick. She tried to open her eyes again but all she saw was the starkness of the white ceiling above her.

'How are you, love?'

Her father's voice was quiet. She tried to smile but it was too painful. Instead she squeezed his hand and drifted off to sleep again.

'Are you sure she was mugged?' he asked.

Kevin's voice was controlled now, the edge of fear gone since he had seen her for himself.

'Well, her bag's not gone for a start. She probably fought for it.'

Amanda Stirling stared into his face.

'Do you think it's not a mugging then?' she asked. 'Only if it was something else it could get her locked up again, you see.'

He stared at her in complete incomprehension.

Amanda looked earnestly back at him.

'If it was, say, a beating because she had done something, or was involved in something, then that something would have to be illegal, wouldn't it? And if she's involved in anything illegal at all then she goes back inside.'

He realised then the enormous burden his daughter carried in order to enjoy her new 'normal' life.

Amanda continued, 'She can go back inside just for associating with her old friends, or anyone with a criminal record. She has to be on her guard twenty-four hours a day. The police are treating this as a mugging but if you think it's something different then you have to tell them.'

Kevin carefully made his face a blank.

'Nah. It was a mugging, of course it was. Why would anyone want to do her? She ain't even seen anyone, I know that much.'

The probation officer nodded sadly.

'She's a nice woman. I think she's paid the price and deserves to be left alone now.'

He didn't answer her but knew she still thought there was more to it than met the eye, as he did. Well, his daughter could do nothing about it but he could. He had been handy in his day and would ask about, see how the land lay. See who he could find who might have some news for him.

It was a world he had left years ago but it was a world he was willing to enter once more if it would help his daughter, lying battered and bruised in her hospital bed. Louise might have made them respectable but old habits died hard.

Whoever had done this had better watch out. Kevin Carter was going to get them.

Karen Black was in the pub. Her face was flushed with excitement and her breath was coming in short shallow bursts. It had gone like a dream and she was the Queen of the Friday night fight. Everyone knew what she had done because she had told them all about it. Drinks were being bought for her and the backslapping was phenomenal. Her husband was proud of her, her brothers were proud of her, and the regulars and friends in the pub were all toasting her.

'Fucking whore got what she deserved! When I think of Caroline and Bethany . . . Now she'll know what it feels like, won't she?'

She was so high on adrenaline and hate, she was euphoric.

'Yeah, she'll know what it's like to have a baseball bat round the head. I hope she fucking dies in the Old London, I really do.'

She didn't really, not deep down. She would rather die herself than be banged up for a big lump but it was all part of the act. Part of the persona.

'I've done me bit for British justice so who's going to have a drink with me then?'

Karen was shaking from her taste of violence. Real violence. It was heady stuff.

Her brother Luke, a large skinhead with tattoos, grinned as he passed her a vodka and Red Bull.

'I wonder what Pat Connor will have to say, Kal? Gonna take him on and all?'

He was laughing at her and she knew it. Trust Luke to piss on everyone's fireworks.

'He can fuck off and all. I did it for this family, mate. For justice.'

Her niece Tamara smiled sadly.

'Me mum would have been over the moon, I'm sure.'

Karen was non-plussed.

'I did it for you, Tams, for what you lost.'

Tamara sighed heavily.

'What did I lose, eh? A skaghead mother. And what did I gain? You lot. Thanks a fucking bunch.'

Karen watched her walk from the pub.

'Ungrateful little bastard!'

Luke laughed again.

'Runs in the family.'

'Bollocks to the lot of you!'

Luke's laughter followed her out of the pub.

Chapter Six

Alan Jarvis opened the door to the Portakabin with a flourish. The girl with him tripped over the step and practically skidded into the room. They were both drunk and laughing.

'Got any drink here?'

Her voice was heavy with booze and amphetamines. She was already shrugging off her Romford Market shaggy coat to reveal a plump overheated body.

'I have some Scotch.'

'That'll do. Why do you bring girls here – are you married?'

Her voice had the dulcet tones of a South London council estate. She was rough even for him.

He nodded. It was easier that way. He couldn't say that the last time he had brought back a bird to his flat she had robbed him the next day. But he blamed himself for leaving her sleeping. He should have routed her when he left.

'What's your wife like?'

Her voice was genuinely interested which meant she saw herself as a contender. He felt the urge to laugh again.

He frowned instead.

'She's big, aggressive. Lairy bitch she is. She beat up me last bird.'

He watched as the girl digested this bit of information.

'Came right in this office she did, with her brothers.'

Alan was warming to his theme.

The girl was looking wary and he turned away to pour himself another drink. Steady on, he told himself, you don't want her doing a runner till you've finished the night's work. But the truth was, he didn't want to fuck her. Not here anyway. Where Marie worked. Where he sometimes brought his kids when he had to work on a Saturday.

He sighed. If he wasn't careful he was in danger of becoming a clean-living man. He knew it was mostly the thought of Marie that was making him hesitant. She had got under his skin. Little birds with no brains and no morals were losing their allure suddenly. He wouldn't even weigh out for a cheap hotel. They weren't worth the fucking hag half the time.

She was snorting a line of amphetamine and afterwards hawked deep in her throat. The noise made him shudder. She was far rougher than his usual birds. The knowledge made him sad.

He thought of Marie in hospital, her body broken by muggers, and suddenly any urge to fornicate left him completely.

What was he doing? Fifty odd years old with a young girl who would shag anyone if they supplied her with enough narcotics.

He sighed heavily and caught sight of himself in the mirror above the sink. He looked what he was, a silly old fucker, still chasing skirt at this advanced stage in his life. It was laughable.

'Chanel . . .'

'It's Chantel, Alan, I keep telling you that!'

Her voice was hard now, as were her eyes. He knew she would tap him soon for some money, dressing it up as cab fare. First, though, he had to give her one and at this moment in time he wasn't sure if Charles Atlas himself could lift it.

Usually by now his cock had had enough of the inane chatter and wanted to get the main business out of the way. But tonight it was dead. He was dead. If he could have anyone he wanted it would only be Marie.

The knowledge threw him completely. He turned back to Chantel.

'Hurry up, Alan, I want to get home!'

Her lipstick was smudged and her face was glistening with sweat. She was speeding out of her nut. Her little tits were heaving where she was getting the rushes. He knew that sexually she would get nothing out of any encounter she had tonight. She was too far gone. Now she was kneeling in front of him, trying to unzip his jeans.

He smiled down at her as she tried desperately to make him hard. Suddenly it was all too much and he started to laugh. But it wasn't happy laughter; it was a deep, sad sound which soon turned to tears until he was crying like a baby.

The whole of his life rose up before him, all the failures. His marriage. His gambling. His business. On top of all that he knew he was heading for a twenty-year stretch if it all fell out of bed. And he also knew without a shadow of a doubt that he wouldn't cope with it like Marie had. It would break him, tear him apart. He would top himself rather than do that much bird. He cried harder, snot running from his nose and his eyes aching with tears waiting for release.

Chantel was terrified. Whatever else she had expected from tonight it wasn't this. He was supposed to be a face, a hard man. A lunatic, more like.

He was sobbing, really sobbing.

Ten minutes later she had a ton in fivers and a cab coming to pick her up. She stood out in the freezing cold, waiting for it. Anything was better than listening to him crying his bleeding eyes out.

Fucking blokes! None of them was worth a wank.

Tiffany was at home. Her babysitter was ill and she had had to cry off from the club. Anastasia was asleep and she looked down at her daughter lovingly. She really was a beautiful child.

Closing the door quietly behind her, she went into the lounge and turned on the TV. She was feeling ill a lot lately. Her eyes felt heavy, itched constantly. Getting up quickly, she went into the kitchen and poured herself a glass of wine; she drank it down in one gulp. It helped relax her. Deep inside she knew what she needed was a pull on her little pipe. She wondered if she should ring Pat and get him to drop off a rock or two, but dismissed the idea out of hand. Anyone would think she was addicted.

The thought made her smile, but as the evening wore on the idea kept coming back into her mind. Eventually, she took a Mogadon and went to bed. It was ten-fifteen.

She was soon sweating. Slipping on her dressing gown, she got up again. She glanced at the clock. It was only ten-twenty. The evening was crawling by and sleep, she knew, was a long way off.

She put on Sade, poured herself more wine and settled on the leather sofa once more. The words of 'Somebody Already Broke My Heart' seemed poignant tonight. She felt a great well of loneliness. Patrick hadn't been in touch for days. She felt the sting of tears again.

Anastasia cried out in her sleep and Tiffany leapt off the sofa and went to the child's room. She was settled again, one little chubby arm flung over her eyes, legs spread-eagled, the picture of restful sleep.

Tiffany wiped a damp hand across her face. Even her skin felt wrong. Itchy, unreal. She picked up the phone and dialled Patrick's number.

It rang and rang in her ear, as she knew it would. She wondered briefly who he was with. She dialled again. Her friend Rosie would get her what she needed, she was good like that. One little pull and she would sleep, her nerves would be sorted and her mind would shut down.

It was only for one night. She just needed a little something to expel the demons that stopped her relaxing properly. Rosie needed the money up front but she would do the good deed.

As soon as Tiffany knew the rock was on its way she felt herself start to relax. She smiled. She had done the right thing, already she felt better.

In future, she told herself, it might be worth keeping a little stash for her own use. She already knew she couldn't rely on Pat to supply her all the time and it wasn't really that cheap, but she consoled herself with the fact that she was in the money now and could afford whatever treats she wanted. For her daughter and for herself.

She wondered what she would have done if she had not got hold of Rosie. It had crossed her mind, only briefly, to maybe leave her baby sleeping while she jumped in a cab and scored a rock.

The knowledge scared her even as the thought of the crack arriving cheered her.

She put it out of her mind; she would *never* have done it, *never*. She had not seriously considered doing it anyway. It had just been a thought that had crossed her mind. That was her mother's little game, and she wasn't like her mother. She was *nothing* like her mother at all.

She was just down in the dumps, that was all. A bit depressed.

It didn't occur to her that the depression was a direct result of her love of crack. Like her mother before her Tiffany had a very selective memory and it stood her in good stead.

She stood at the window looking out for Rosie's cab. She seemed very young and very vulnerable and very agitated.

And of course she was all three.

Marie had been in hospital for four days. She smiled when she saw Alan Jarvis walking towards her with a large bunch of flowers. He looked sheepish.

Unlike most women of his acquaintance Marie didn't worry about the damage to her face. She'd made no attempt to hide the marks with make-up. The look of her broke his heart.

'Are you in pain?' His voice was gentle.

'Nothing I can't handle.'

Her voice was small now, as if she had just realised what a sight she must look.

'The flowers are lovely but you shouldn't have, you know.'

He grinned.

'That's me, ain't it? All flamboyant gestures. I thought you might need cheering up.'

Two plainclothes officers arrived in Marie's side room then and Alan instinctively recognised them. He was immediately nervous. She picked up on this and made his escape easy for him.

'Thanks so much for coming, Mr Jarvis. I should be back at work next week.'

'When you're ready, mate. See you later then. 'Bye.'

He was out of the room as fast as his legs would carry him, sweat running down his back. Outside he took deep breaths to calm himself.

DI Smith grinned at Marie.

'How you feeling?'

She shrugged.

'Sore. What can I do for you now?'

Her voice was low, full of sleep.

Smith left it a beat before he spoke again, concentrating on her face and arms which were black and blue.

'We don't think this was a simple mugging.'

Marie already knew that much.

'Nothing was taken, was it?' the police officer observed.

'I told you over and over, I kept hold of me bag. Why I don't know, there was fuck all in it.'

'So you say. Now, knowing your past history, we think this might have been some kind of revenge attack.'

She shrugged again. Her slim shoulders made her look very vulnerable and Smith was sorry for her despite himself.

'Well, if it was, they didn't say anything to me.'

Smith knew her well enough already to know that she was very economical with words.

'You wouldn't tell us anyway, would you?'

The voice of DC Snetterton was high and childlike, completely at odds with his large and lumbering frame.

Marie stared at him for a few seconds before answering.

'That's where you're wrong. I would have told you because I don't ever want to feel or look like this again.'

It was the right answer. They left soon afterwards. But the fear was inside her again like a cancer. She could be taken back into prison in an instant and she knew that. All she wanted was to get out of hospital, back to her job, and then she wanted to see her children. Both of them.

That was her priority at the moment. Nothing else mattered.

Kevin rolled over in bed. He felt great. Inside he was buzzing. He turned back and kissed the woman beside him.

'I needed that.'

Susan Tranter smiled. 'So did I. Fancy a cup of tea?'

She slipped on a dressing gown and padded downstairs to put the kettle on. Kevin lay back and surveyed the bedroom. It was, as usual, like a tip. That was part of Susan's charm. She was seriously untidy yet the bedding was clean, her cups were clean, *she* was clean.

The house, though, was like a pigsty. But he relaxed there like he had never relaxed at home. Susan was so easygoing it was unbelievable. Even his feet, and *they* were legendary, didn't faze her.

He knew that if Lou had an inkling where he was there would be creations of Olympic proportions but at this moment in time he didn't give a flying fuck. He had needed someone and Susan was someone who liked to be needed. It worked well for them.

She loved sex, adored it. She settled down for a session and put her whole heart into it. That alone was a touch as far as he was concerned. Plus he could have a cuppa, get dressed and go on his merry way without any recriminations whatsoever.

Yet he knew she loved him. Loved him deeply. He could feel it from her, feel it wrapping around him, and in his heart he loved her back though he had never told her. They talked about everything, but they had no need to talk about themselves or their feelings.

She brought up the tea and climbed into bed with him.

'How is Marie?'

He sipped the scalding liquid.

'I don't know, I really don't. She puts on this front to the world and it's impossible to get behind it.'

Susan sighed.

'Well, that's understandable really. All she wants is a bit of peace. From what you've said she's a changed woman. She would be – twelve years' bird would change anyone. Give her time to acclimatise herself to being home.'

Kevin nodded.

'But she's not home, is she? She's in a hostel.'

Susan was a fatalist. If it was going to happen, it happened. That was her philosophy in life.

'Not for ever. Soon she'll be out of there and doing what we all do: surviving. One day she will have good times, another day bad times. It's called real life and she will have to get used to it.'

Kevin hugged her.

'You are better than a tonic, girl, do you know that?'

'I have me moments. Have you told her you know where Tiffany is yet?'

He shook his head.

'I'll wait until she gets over this lot first.'

'Bastards, that family are. Especially that Karen. Fat whore she is.'

Kevin felt his temper rising again.

'They will get their comeuppance, don't you worry about that.'

He gulped at his tea. He was going to see to it that whoever had hurt his daughter would know what pain felt like themselves. It didn't occur to him that retaliation would only exacerbate an already explosive situation. He was out for revenge.

Patrick was smiling; it was a real smile that made him look younger and more handsome. Louella Vidon liked the look of the big black man chatting her up and let him know it by smiling provocatively back.

Jimmy Dickinson watched as his bird eyed the coon. He was not a happy bunny.

'Go and get us another drink, Louella.'

She jumped up to do his bidding. Louella Vidon knew exactly what side her bread was buttered, and she knew better than to ignore a direct order.

As she went to the kitchen Jimmy grinned.

'Like what you see, do you, Pat?'

He shrugged good-naturedly.

'Give us a break, Jim. With them tits, who wouldn't?'

Even Jimmy laughed at the answer.

'Show me what stock you got, mate, I have another appointment,' Patrick prompted him.

Louella came back with the beers and the men retired to the cellar of the house to do their business. As they walked down the steep staircase Jimmy kept up a running commentary.

'Most of the guns are old, I keep them for the divs. But they're a very lucrative earner. The main money, though, is in semi-automatics. I rent them out, see, but the penalty if they're used for a murder is big. I mean, the gun's a fuck then, ain't it? Old Bill have it profiled and want the fucker. Stands to reason. I borrowed out to Jerry the Ponce; he shot his fucking brother and got caught. Never got me dough or me fucking gun. Ponce by name, eh?'

Both men laughed.

Patrick took in all the hardware at once, pricing it in his head. He could see the look of pride in his cache on Jimmy's face and smiled at him.

Louella's voice came down the stairs.

'There's some geezers here for you, Jim. Mickey Samms and Nobby Brewer.'

Pat saw a fleeting expression of fear cross Jimmy's face.

'This anything to do with you, Pat?'

Patrick grinned.

''Course it is, Jimmy. I want what you've got, my son.'

He called out loudly, 'Down here, boys.'

Jimmy was gutted.

'You black fucking cunt . . .'

Patrick laughed good-naturedly.

'You always take everything so personally, Jimmy. This is just business, mate.'

Mickey and Nobby were smiling from the stairwell. Nobby opened his coat and from a long pocket inside took out a pump-action shot gun. He threw it to Patrick who cocked it and aimed it at Jimmy's face without a second's thought.

''Bye-bye, Jimmy.'

He pulled the trigger and took the boy's head off. Louella came screaming down the stairs. He caught her just above her enormous breasts and the report threw her back into the hallway.

Nobby and Mickey had been forced to duck as he fired and were annoyed.

'Fuck you, Pat, you mad bastard!' Nobby yelled indignantly.

He laughed.

'Clear this place while I look around. We're OK for a while, Jimmy had it all soundproofed last year.'

He stepped over the boy's body without glancing at it. At the top of the stairs Louella was still breathing loudly, a wet sound from the blood seeping into her lungs. He looked into her eyes as he passed her by and smiled.

'Not long now, Louella, and you'll be reunited with your boyfriend.'

As he ran upstairs he wondered where Jimmy kept his jewellery. He had a few nice diamond rings that Pat had always admired, and a blinding necklace. He was whistling between his teeth as he opened drawers and cupboards.

He heard another shot and guessed that someone had put Louella out of her misery. He heard the others laughing as he began to tear the place apart.

On the dressing table stood a photo of Jimmy's two young sons. He picked it up and dropped it into the bin. He was still smiling as he ransacked the house.

Tiffany was feeling better. She had given her baby breakfast and drawn on a little rock to get her head together. When she opened the front door to Carole Halter she was smiling.

'Hello, mate.'

Carole followed her into the lounge.

'That kid is so good-looking!'

She produced a tube of Smarties and Anastasia squealed with delight. In the kitchen Tiffany put the kettle on and looked out over the grey building opposite.

'You ain't heard then, Tiff?'

'Heard what?'

'About your mum?'

She rolled her eyes.

'What's she done now?'

Carole shook her head.

'Karen Black and her sisters give her a kicking. She's in hospital.'

Tiffany let the news sink in.

'Is she bad then?'

Her voice sounded as if she didn't care one iota.

'Very bad by all accounts.'

Tiffany sighed.

'It was on the cards, I suppose. Karen Black wasn't going to let it go, was she? And who can blame her?'

'I suppose you're right but I wish I could go and see her.'

Tiffany didn't answer.

'She was a good mate to me, old Marie.'

The girl poured scalding water into the cups.

'You've changed your fucking tune!'

Carole was instantly on the defensive.

'Marie was a rip, I don't dispute that. But she could be a good mate when she wanted to.'

Tiffany shook her head at the hypocrisy of the woman before her. You never got the truth out of Carole Halter, she would lie about anything. If you asked her what she'd had for breakfast she would add a sausage.

'Anyway, what are you telling me for? It's nothing to do with me.'

'She is your mother. I thought you had a right to know, that's all.'

Tiffany sighed heavily, her baby face looking cross.

'My mother? According to you and Patrick she didn't give a fucking toss about me or me brother, so how come you want me to feel sorry for her now?'

Carole shook her head.

'She's still your mother, love.'

Then she eyed the crack pipe on the table.

'Whose is that?'

Tiffany didn't answer her but her face had paled.

'You stupid little whore! That's a mug's game and you of all people should know. It's more addictive than a twelve-inch cock!'

Tiffany threw the mug of scalding tea into the sink, anger making two bright red spots appear on her cheeks.

'I am not addicted. It's recreational, that's all . . .'

Her voice trailed off as she saw the genuine concern on Carole's face.

Tiffany lowered her voice.

'I am not addicted, Cal, honestly.'

Carole stared at the girl in front of her for long seconds.

'You are your mother's daughter all right. That's what she used to say and all.'

Tiffany's face twisted with anger at her words.

'Why don't you fuck off, Cal, and leave me alone?'

The other woman's natural aggression was to the fore now and she said nastily, 'Who d'you think you're talking to, eh? I ain't a fucking ice cream you can cunt at will, girl. I'll slap your face for you if you keep that attitude up, you lairy little bitch. All I've done for you over the years . . .'

She seemed genuinely aggrieved, but Tiffany was having none of it.

'What the fuck have you ever done for me, eh, except ponce me few quid and slag off me mother? The mother you now want me to go and visit because you are shit scared she'll find out how you've slagged her off in the past. Now piss off home, Carole, before I really lose me rag.'

Carole's arm shot out and she caught Tiffany a stinging blow to the face; her half-sovereign ring split the girl's eyebrow in seconds. Shock brought tears to Tiffany's eyes. She put her hand up to her face and saw the blood.

'What you done to me? I have to work tonight!'

Carole's face was a mask of shame.

'I'm sorry, Tiff. Christ, I am so sorry. I wouldn't hurt you for the world.'

As Tiffany pushed a wet dishcloth to her eyes the baby started crying. Carole rushed to her and picked her up. The little girl's body was shaking.

They heard a key in the lock and Carole felt her heart sink down to her boots. Patrick took one look at the two women and his child then his fist shot out and caught Carole full in the face. Her nose crunched under the blow and Anastasia screamed in terror.

How Carole stayed on her feet was a miracle, but the feel of the child in her arms gave her added strength.

'Stop it, Pat! It was my fault, I started it,' Tiffany insisted.

She dragged the screaming child from Carole's arms.

'How you going to fucking work with an eye like that, eh? I had a private for you tonight and now it's all fucked up, ain't it?'

He was bellowing in anger and Anastasia was even more terrified.

'Get out, you fat whore, and don't you let me see you round here ever again.'

Pat's eyes were manic with anger and drugs. Carole staggered from the room with blood pouring down her face.

Patrick took Anastasia from her mother none too gently and put her into her cot then he shut the door on the distressed child and walked back into the kitchen. He slapped Tiffany across the face hard and her crying stopped.

'I don't fucking believe this. I come home and what do I find, eh? You fighting, and not even fucking winning at that.'

He was dragging the ice tray from the fridge and making a compress with a tea towel.

'You'd better look good tonight. I promised you to Leroy

McBane and you'd better be good, girl, you had better be fucking good.'

Tiffany listened to the man she had loved like a father and a brother and a lover all rolled into one, and now the effect of the crack had worn off she was seeing her life and what it had become with stunning clarity.

Her eye was burning with pain and her daughter was still screaming in fright. But she didn't go to the child. She knew better than to antagonise the man before her when he was like this.

The only consolation she had was that he had called her little flat home. Only now he had finally said the magic word she wasn't sure she wanted to hear it.

'It's broken, Miss Halter.'

'I guessed that much meself.'

As the nurse set about patching her face up Carole relaxed against the pillow and tried to get comfortable.

Patrick Connor was not an enemy she wanted or needed, but she knew he wouldn't forgive her for many a long day. She sighed and her whole body shuddered. If Tiffany told him why they had argued she would be in for another hiding, a real one this time.

She closed her eyes once more in distress.

When the nurse had finished Carole made her way to the canteen and ordered a cup of sweet tea. As she sat down to drink it she noticed Karen Black at another table. She watched Karen who was sitting with a large dark-haired woman, possibly her sister, and talking animatedly.

They were obviously up to something.

Another woman joined the table. She was dressed in the distinctive pink overalls of the hospital cleaning squad.

Marie was in this hospital and Carole knew she was witnessing the planning of another attack.

Leaving her tea, she made her way to reception and got Marie's ward and room number. As she walked up the stairs she felt an overwhelming tiredness assail her but carried on to Marie's room regardless. She saw the two plainclothes officers and slipped into the day room to keep an eye out for their departure. Whatever she had said about Marie in the past, she was out and she was hurt. Also, Carole might need her old friend's help at some point now she was in the shit with Patrick and probably with Tiffany as well.

When the coast was clear she walked towards the side room. Her face was screaming and her eyes nearly shut. She should be at home in bed. But that could wait. She was a streetwalker. Pain was something she had learned to suppress many years before.

Trying to smile so as not to frighten the woman in the bed she walked sedately into Marie's room.

Chapter Seven

Louise tidied up the lounge and as usual cleaned the glass on all her son's photographs with a soft cloth. Each one was duly polished and gazed at, tears never far from her eyes.

Kevin watched her silently as she performed the ritual. Years ago the sight of her as she was now, looking vulnerable and sad, had broken his heart. Nowadays, it irritated him. Marshall was dead, they had two daughters living. One she tolerated, and that was the only word he could use about her relationship with Lucy, and the other daughter might as well be dead as far as her mother was concerned. In fact sometimes he thought it would have been better for all concerned if Marie had died.

Turning reproachful eyes towards him his wife said sadly, 'I miss him so much, Kev. I still expect to hear his cheery voice in the morning. See his little face smiling at me. Sometimes it all seems too much to bear.'

She didn't expect an answer, she had said the same thing twice a day since the boy died.

'You have a grandson, another boy. Maybe you should have taken him in.'

Kevin walked into the kitchen and his wife followed him angrily.

'Who the fuck's rattled your cage?'

She was upset and for a few seconds he was contrite. Then he took a deep breath.

'No one has rattled my cage, Lou, you just aggravate me at times talking about Marshall. You make him out to be a saint and he wasn't, love. He wasn't.'

Louise looked at him as if he was a complete stranger she had encountered in her kitchen. Her eyes were screwed up with hurt.

'He was the best of the bunch. He could have been anything he wanted. And he wanted the best, for me and for him.'

Her words were uttered with a vehemence that startled her

husband. They also annoyed him.

'He wanted the best for *you*? Like I didn't, is that what you're saying? He would have provided you with whatever you wanted, is that it? I AM JUST THE USELESS PONCE WHO PAYS THE BILLS AND PUTS THE FOOD ON THE TABLE! But Saint bloody Marshall would have given you greater riches and made you proud, is that what this is all about? Is that why you had no time for your two girls, eh? They weren't going to give you any reflected glory, were they? You make me sick.'

Louise picked up the canister that held the tea bags, and as she lifted it high he cried, 'Don't even think about it, Lou. I will slap you till your ears ring if you throw that fucking thing and I take oath on that. I hate this bloody house. Sitting in the front room is like sitting in a mausoleum – that boy's face everywhere you look. No photos of the girls, though, eh, or your grandchildren. Only him, Saint Marshall. Well, you'd better listen to me and listen good. I am *sick* of hearing about him.'

'You was always jealous of him. All of you were. That boy was everything to me and you all knew it. Well, I am keeping his memory alive whether you like it or not. He is with me every moment of the day. I think about him as soon as I open my eyes in the morning . . .'

'This marriage would be a lot better if you opened your fucking legs every morning.'

Louise started to laugh then, a painful sound in the quiet of the house.

'Oh, so that's what this is all about really. Well, mister, you have no chance now. I've put up with you pawing me for years. Not any more. You disgust me, at our age and all. We should be winding down now . . .'

He bellowed in her face, 'We *should* have our fucking grand-children round us, we *should* have a happy family, we *should* have had a lot of things except you stopped all that as usual. It's all what *you* fucking want. Well, *I* want things as well.' He stabbed himself in the chest with his thumb. 'Companionship for a start. Friendship. A bit of fun and me leg over now and again. What about me, Lou, eh? What about me?'

She stared into his anguished face. Inside her head a little voice was telling her to tread warily. Build a few bridges. But her natural antagonism cancelled the voices out.

'Fuck you, Kev. Fuck you and what *you* want. I want Marshall back, and that's *all* I want. I don't want any of *you*, do you hear me? Not you, not Lucy, and especially not Marie or the fucking animals she bred. So now you know, don't you, eh? Now you fucking well know.'

It had gone too far and they both knew it.

Kevin's voice was quiet when he next spoke.

'I know all right, Lou. Now I know.'

He turned and walked from the house, leaving his wife alone in the kitchen in a crashing silence broken only by her sobs.

Marie looked at Carole for long moments before she spoke.

'I didn't recognise you for a second.'

Carole tried to grin but failed.

'I could say the same about you, love!' She settled herself into a chair by the bed. 'How you feeling, Marie?'

'How do you think? What happened to your boat then?'

Marie knew her old pal wanted something or was after some kind of information and she was naturally wary.

Carole sat in the chair looking defeated. It was all in her body language. Her shoulders slumped, her battered face drooped. One half of her wanted to tell Marie about the Blacks and what they were planning, but she suddenly wanted revenge. Revenge against Pat for what he had done. Against Tiffany for what she had said. But she dressed it up in her mind as wanting to help her friend, wanting Marie to know what was happening to her daughter and grandchild. She was a good person, she was trying to help. In less than eight seconds she had decided to act the concerned friend to both this woman and her daughter. She could tell her the other news about the Blacks if Marie didn't look like she was going to do anything. Save it for last.

'Patrick did it. He smashed me one because I slapped Tiffany.'

Marie pulled herself up on to her elbows and said loudly, 'I beg your pardon?'

'I slapped your Tiff. Honestly, Marie, that is one fucker of a girl . . .'

Marie interrupted her.

'What has Patrick got to do with her? How is he involved with her?'

Carole could see the fear in Marie's eyes and wished now she had not been the bearer of such bad news. But she persevered.

'He has her on the bash. You know what he's like.'

95

Marie slumped back into the bed. Her blackened eyes felt hot with the dryness anger can bring.

Slowly and painfully Carole explained the situation. As Marie listened, the new world that had never felt stable crumbled even further about her ears.

'And you knew this? You knew this when I came to your flat after my release? You knew and you didn't tell me . . . is that what you're saying?'

Carole nodded.

'My God, Carole, you are one piece of shit! My own mate. What else do you know that you haven't told me, eh?'

Carole couldn't look at her.

'How could I tell you, Marie? You know what he's like. And her! She is more stubborn than you are. You know how he can be when he wants something, all sweetness and fucking light. She was all over him like a fucking rash. Now he's being his usual arsehole self and she is having problems. Bad problems.'

'The rotten bastard! How did he get to her, Carole, how did he find her? What about my Jason, is he dealing crack yet?'

Carole shook her head; she had introduced Patrick back into Tiffany's life though she wasn't going to admit that to Marie Carter.

'Jason is adopted, you know that. Pat isn't interested in him. Never liked boys, did he? Young girls was always his gig.'

'My poor little Tiff . . .'

'Don't know about the "poor little" bit, Marie. She is a cow. She's on crack, Tiffany is. Out of her fucking box on it most days. Little Anastasia was everything to her, still is, but we both know once the old Persians kick in that will all go out the window. Fucking drugs, what's wrong with a good old-fashioned drink?'

Marie listened to her old friend and her mind was screaming at her. She had listened to women in prison talking about daughters in other prisons, about how they were living their mothers' lives all over again. Even Carole Halter had one daughter who was living her life; she was in prison and had kids in care. Now it was happening to Marie's Tiff. Her little Tiffany who she'd thought wanted nothing to do with her because she was having a good life. Was living a clean life. Now all Marie's nightmares were reality and she had to try and do something about them. She pulled herself painfully from the bed.

'What you doing?' Carole's voice was high.

'What's it look like?' Marie said. 'I'm discharging meself. I need to see her and you had better tell me everything you know, Cal, or I'll brain you and I mean that, OK?'

Carole nodded.

She knew better than to argue with Marie. Look what had happened when her other friends had argued with her. That fact was never far from Carole's mind.

She would edit out her own part in Tiffany's downfall, put all the blame on Patrick. Let him deal with her because one thing she knew, everyone was wary of Marie. Even Karen Black had only dared take her mob-handed, though by the looks of Marie's face she had done a good job. Let Marie sort out Pat Connor. Let her give him what he needed.

Carole Halter hoped that Marie killed him. Someone was going to do it one day and, unlike Marie, she herself didn't have the guts.

Fifteen minutes later they were in a taxi and Carole was sweating with fear. Patrick would eat her face and smile while he did it if he found out what she'd done. And what would Tiffany's reaction be to her mother turning up unannounced on her doorstep?

Lucy was at work. As she sipped coffee during a break, she saw her father storming through the workshop. Being a paper factory it was large and noisy; they made everything from Hoover bags to large industrial rolls of paper. She assumed her father was looking for her and left the glass-walled Portakabin used for breaks with her coffee mug still in her hands.

As she walked towards him she saw him stop and look around as if searching for someone, and suddenly she knew exactly what was going to happen.

She dropped her mug and rushed through the machines to where she knew Karen Black was working. She was too late. She saw her father dragging the woman from the building by her hair. The fear in Lucy's chest was so great she lost the power to breathe and had to concentrate on expelling air from her lungs.

She felt faint with fright.

What the hell was he doing?

Didn't he realise the Blacks were a force unto themselves? A family so feared even the police visited them in groups of four? Karen would take her by the throat and throttle her for this.

As she burst out into the cold air she saw Karen Black take a swing at her father, but he blocked it easily. Then, dragging the struggling woman, he threw her unceremoniously on to the ground.

'You ever touch me or mine again, Black, and I will kill you. Marie won't be in it when I get through. Do you understand what I'm saying?'

Karen seemed to understand that he was over the edge. She nodded, barely moving her head. Kevin's eyes were manic, his whole face screwed up with hatred. For the first time in her life she was on the receiving end of violence. Like most bullies she was basically a coward. She picked on the weak, or made sure she had a crowd with her. Now she was alone, as most of her victims had been, and she was terrified.

Kevin kicked her three times in the back and stomach.

'I should have brought a wrench with me, I understand from my daughter they do a much better job. You tell your brothers to look out because they will be seeing me, OK? They will be seeing me sooner than you think.'

With that he walked away, or ambled would be a better description because he wasn't even breathing heavily after all his exertions.

Kevin slid his hands into his pockets and strolled out of the car park without a care in the world. He felt his manhood returning. He felt for the first time in years that he was taking control again, of his life and his children's.

People who had witnessed the attack were standing quietly by the entrance. No one said a word. The shop steward went back to his office. He had no intention of getting involved in all that. Black was an accident waiting to happen and like most of her workmates he had enjoyed seeing her get for once what she had dished out so often.

Karen Black pulled herself painfully to her feet. The fat had cushioned the blows to her body but it would be a long time before she could cope with the blow to her self-esteem. She was humiliated and it showed. A large chunk of her hair had been pulled out and was hanging on the shoulders of the tracksuit she always wore to work. It was a reminder of what had happened to her and as she saw it blowing in the wind she felt the tears begin. In front of everyone she cried, and walked past Lucy without a word.

Pat had gone and Tiffany was giving her daughter a boiled egg when she heard the doorbell. She picked Anastasia up and went to answer it.

Emotionally she was still fragile. It had been a fraught few hours. When she saw her mother on the doorstep it was like a hallucination. This scruffy battered woman was like something from her worst nightmares. For a few moments she thought it was a side effect of the crack. But this woman was real, she was flesh and blood. She was Tiffany's flesh and blood.

The girl's eyes bored into Carole Halter's. The other woman was standing nervously behind Marie.

'You rotten bitch . . .'

Anastasia watched them with wide eyes. On one level Marie wanted to take her grandchild into her arms and embrace her, but the knowledge of who her father was made that impossible. She looked like him, and like her Jason at the same age, only lighter-skinned.

Marie walked into the flat and shut the door quietly behind her. She saw the conflicting emotions on her daughter's face, resisted the urge to take her too into her arms and embrace her. She saw the shock turn to pain and felt a physical ache in her own heart at the sight. The little girl she had pictured all these years was a woman, a grown woman, with the same fears and the same problems she had encountered herself.

Tiffany stared at her mother and in her head registered the recent bruises, the pain reflected in her shadowed eyes, and the slim supple body that was at odds with the woman she remembered.

How many times had she cried out for her over the years? Cries that were useless because her mother was incarcerated, gone from her when she most needed her. Now Marie was standing as bold as brass in her hallway, bringing the stench of prison and memories of old loneliness with her.

'Hello, Tiff.'

It was the sound of her mother's voice that undid her. That deep husky voice she remembered making her laugh and also telling her to get lost. The voice that she'd conjured up at night in the home, wishing her mother would come and get her. The voice she had longed for yet hated all her life.

'Long time no see, eh?'

Marie felt such a rush of emotion at the sight of her daughter she nearly forgot why she was there. She saw that hair, the soft blonde hair she had loved, the doe eyes and the skinny woman's body that belied a little girl in disguise.

'Get out, Mum. You ain't welcome here.'

Marie laughed gently.

'I ain't welcome anywhere, sweetie, but it never stopped me going somewhere if I really wanted to, did it?'

The words were softly spoken but hid a threat and they all knew it. Marie was not going anywhere. Not yet. She was using the fear that had been her only weapon all those years before and the knowledge was painful to her.

She walked through to the kitchen and looked around her. She knew from Carole that the place was usually spotlessly clean. Today it had the grimy look of a drughead's place. Once drugs took hold it was all you thought about, all you wanted. Your priorities changed. She knew that better than anyone.

Carole watched the little tableau: mother, daughter and grand-daughter.

Tiffany put her daughter back into her high chair and Anastasia resumed eating her egg. As long as no one shouted she was OK. She had heard too much shouting in her short life and was already aware of what it could lead to. Did lead to.

Marie looked at her daughter for long moments.

'Pat Connor of all people.'

The disgust in her voice was unmistakable.

'What's the matter, Tiff, couldn't you live without making my mistakes? Couldn't you learn to make new ones for yourself?'

Tiffany couldn't answer for a while. It was surreal seeing her mother in her own home. It was the weirdest thing that had ever happened to her. Marie was acting like a proper mother, too, trying to help her. What the fuck had brought her here today of all days? But she knew. Carole had opened her big trap. Well, Pat would put paid to her when he found out.

'He loves me, which is more than you ever fucking did.'

'Is that right? Well, sweetie, he loved me once, gave me a child as well. Jason, your brother. He also gave me my first fix and set me on the road to destruction. Got me my first trick as well. Him and his best mate did. He is such a generous bloke he even gave me my first black eye and knocked out a few of me teeth. But, hey, we all know how good he can be as well, don't we? What a nice bloke he is deep down.'

'He's good enough for me. Unlike you, I can handle him. I got me money, got a job. I don't spunk it all up on meself, like you did.'

'Does Patrick know you're playing happy families? You stupid little mare!'

100

Marie shook her head.

'Get a fucking grip, Tiffany. Didn't you learn anything from the fucking abortion that was my so-called life? He's scum, and he'll make you scum, you and this little mite. It's what he *does*. What he's good at. And if you don't sort yourself out soon you will let history repeat itself once more. Christ, for someone who hates me so much you like my life well enough to walk in the same fucking shoes. Are you a bit stupid or something?'

She picked up the crack pipe from the table.

'I saw plenty of these in nick, Tiff, saw what they did to people there. I know what drugs can do. I can't ever make up for my life, what I did, but I can try and stop you going the same way.'

Tiffany lit herself a cigarette. She needed it, needed the kick of nicotine because she daren't get the kick of crack. Not in front of her mother. She looked at Marie with cold eyes but didn't answer her.

Marie tried to talk more gently, hoping her daughter would listen. But Carole butted in first. 'Listen to her, Tiffany . . .'

It was Carole's voice that seemed to set the girl off.

That Carole, who had brought her into contact with Pat and had served her up on a plate to him in her own grubby little flat, could now bring the past to her home sent her into a rage so acute she could almost taste its bitterness.

'You wait till I tell Patrick about this, he'll kill you both. He told me all about you two. The way you would fuck for a fix until in the end he had to drum you out of everything. He knew you were nothing but pieces of crap. Told me about coming home and finding me and little Jason alone, no food in the house, nothing. You gone for days on end with her, Mum. She told me all about it as well. Your so-called mate. It's too late for the concerned mother act, twelve years too fucking late. Now go away from me. Leave me alone. I couldn't care less if you died, OK? I feel nothing but contempt for you. He takes care of me in the only way I have ever known, so pat yourself on the back, Mum. You bred another whore.'

'Look at your face, Tiff.'

'Look at yours, and hers for that matter. It's happened, deal with it.'

Marie shook her head again.

'This is what living with violence leads to. I took a hammering because of what I did thirteen years ago. I deserved this in a way, though violence solves no problems. That's why wars flare up over and over again. You are bringing up a small child in this atmosphere of sexual tension and violence. If you won't learn by my mistakes, please don't learn by your own or one day you will be saying all this to your own kid there. Believe me, I know what I am talking about.'

Marie's voice broke, tears so close she had to turn from her daughter and gather herself together.

'That's right, turn your back on me. You were always good at that. Me and Jason were always secondary to you and what you wanted. We still are. You could have found us if you'd really wanted to. You just never did. Now you're jealous because you know about me and Pat. Well, tough shit!'

'Listen to her, Tiffany, she means well.'

The girl wiped a hand across her nose.

'Get stuffed, Carole. You two-faced fucking witch!'

Anastasia had stopped eating and was watching them all warily.

Marie found it painful to look at the child who was so like Jason and yet equally like Patrick. It was Patrick's eyes that looked out at her, but without the hatred. Though that would come with the years, if the child's father had anything to do with it.

'I love you so much, Tiff . . .'

It was the wrong thing to say, completely the wrong thing to say.

Tiffany took Carole roughly by her arm and marched her to the front door. Marie followed.

The girl opened the door.

'Get out, and stay out. Fucking preaching to me! You have some nerve, the two of you. "Murdering whore" is how me granny referred to you once, and she told me that what was bred in the blood came out in the bone. And she was right, except I am going to be someone. My child will not be used and abused. I will make money and then use it to make my life better. So keep all your old shit to yourself, you need it much more than I do.'

Marie stared into cold eyes, full of hatred of her, and felt the futility of her own life and the hopelessness of Tiffany's.

This was all her fault. If she had been a better person all those years ago her daughter would be a good clean-living girl now with proper boyfriends and a decent job. Instead it was like looking in a mirror.

Marie saw a pad and pen on the hall table and scribbled down her address and phone number.

'If you need me, call me. I'll be there for you, Tiff, I promise. I've been clean twelve years. I'm a different person from the one you remember. I can be there for you, if you'll let me.'

'Piss off.'

The door was slammed in her face.

Tiffany looked through the spy hole at her mother's tears and hardened her heart. Marie was all talk; she had always been all talk. Promises and crap, that was her mother. She was not like Tiffany; *she* was in charge of her own life and always would be. The words sounded hollow but she said them again and again like a mantra.

She went to her bag and took out her little tin.

She needed a hit more than anything; it had been such a stressful day. As she burned the crack and inhaled it she felt the tensions disappear. Felt her shoulders relax. Felt her mind clear.

As she inhaled she saw her daughter watching her with big brown eyes. Anastasia pointed at the little crack pipe and said clearly, proudly, 'Mummy's pipe.'

Tiffany had held a memory for many years. She remembered the dark living room of her mother's flat. The curtains were always closed even on the hottest summer day. Marie had slept late as usual and Tiff had picked up her mother's fix case. She was pretending to inject herself when her mother walked into the room. She could still feel the sting of her mother's hand across her face and behind. Could remember running terrified on fat little legs into her bedroom, her tears loud and noisy.

Suddenly she knew why her mother had been so upset.

Like her mother, she had somehow convinced herself that her lifestyle would not affect her daughter. But of course it had, as Marie's own disintegration had affected her. She pushed the thought from her mind as she pushed away anything she didn't want to think about. But Anastasia's words haunted her all day.

Patrick looked at the girl and shook his head.

'She's ugly, Jonny. How can I earn off her?'

Jonny laughed, his fat face quivering with mirth.

'Show him your tits, love.'

The girl dutifully lifted her baggy top. She had a squint and prominent teeth, but she also had large firm breasts that would be her fortune until they drooped.

'She can hardly walk round with her tits out on display, can she? She's still a cheap shag.'

'Granted, granted, Pat. But she has a couple of lethal weapons up her sleeve. Anyway the older blokes like the ugly birds.'

'Not the older blokes I know. They like to look at the mantel-piece, know what I mean? I charge dear for half-decent shags.'

Jonny smiled gamely.

'I hear you have your fingers in so many pies you need a few transplants to keep up with them all.'

Patrick's expression froze, the amiable façade gone.

'And where do you hear that from then?'

Jonny knew he had dropped a clanger and tried to make amends.

'Leave it out, Pat, you can't go around shooting up half of fucking Brixton and expect it to be kept quiet. You are a face now, a real one. Carlton Margolis wants a meet with you, and they don't come much heavier than that.'

'If he wants to cut a deal, I'm listening. You tell him that from me.'

Jonny nodded his head so hard it nearly rocked from his shoulders.

Pat smiled. He liked the notoriety he was earning. He liked the fact that everyone was talking about him even though he knew that it could eventually lead to his downfall. It was what he had always craved. All his life he had wanted to be somebody. Had wanted to be known, had wanted to be respected. From a child, when he had first found out what it was like to be ignored, to be looked down on because of who you were before people even knew you personally, it had been his dream. Now he was realising it.

He got it through fear and through violence, but he was sensible enough to know this was the only way he was ever going to achieve his aims.

As he saw the fear he instilled in Jonny he felt a sense of achievement. It was the same when he dumped on women. He loved dumping on women. Loved to hurt them, physically and emotionally. They were all whores, and he liked to prove this to himself and to them. He made them all see themselves as they really were. As he would the poor child in front of him, who'd been unlucky enough to meet up with Jonny and even unluckier that Jonny was selling her on to him.

They did the deal quickly and it wasn't until Jonny was leaving that Patrick asked what her name was.

Jonny grinned as he answered, 'Her name is Shayla but she answers to Pig.'

He was still laughing as he walked out of the door.

Shayla didn't react to any of it. But once they were alone she smiled timidly at Patrick. He admitted she had a certain childishness about her that some of his weirder clients would appreciate. The gang bangers would love her.

'What you smiling at, Pig? You smile when I tell you to smile, OK? Don't even think of taking anything on yourself, girl. If I tell you to shit, you shit. If I tell you to fuck, you fuck. And that's the end of it. Do you understand me?'

Shayla nodded, her face and eyes devoid of expression.

Patrick felt like the main man again. He revelled in the strength he possessed because of his spitefulness and innate hatred of other human beings.

He felt good about himself once more.

Now all he had to do was pick up his daughter's mother and her humiliation would be complete. All in all it had been a good day's work.

Chapter Eight

Anastasia was crying and getting on her mother's nerves. It was bad enough that Tiffany had to go to a man tonight, that she was out of crack and had experienced the weirdest day of her life. Her mother turning up at her home had blown her away. On top of it all Anastasia was playing up and Tiffany knew that Pat would be annoyed with her. He liked his daughter like a little lamb around him. As long as she smiled and treated him like a god he was happy. If she cried or played up his answer was to leave or to give her grief.

As she tried to put her mother and her old life out of her mind, memories invaded Tiffany's senses. Smells, pictures, sounds.

When she looked into the mirror to apply her shadow she saw her mother's eyes looking back at her, the same shape and colour; saw the same bone structure. Saw her mother as a girl, a girl like her, with two kids and Pat Connor hanging round her neck. But her mother had been a fighter, she wasn't. Unlike her mother, though, she was getting it together. It was all for the money and for her daughter. Unlike her mother she would own her own home, send her kid to a good school, feed her regularly and love her above all else.

She would keep by Patrick Connor until he finally pushed her away. She could never push him away, he wouldn't let her. When Patrick had had enough of her he would drop out of her life, she knew that. But while he was still in it she would take the goodies on offer and make her money work for her. She had her lap dancing, she would make a career out of that. As for Pat, her eyes were being opened on a daily basis. The love for him was fast disappearing, but the need for him was still strong. She needed him to protect her and her child from the outside world. In her chosen profession, predators were rife. Tiffany was convinced she was better off with the devil she knew, one who would provide her with a few rocks and a few good times. She was as hooked on him as she was on the crack, and deep inside she knew it.

107

Anastasia's voice broke into her reverie and she turned to look down at the child. She was holding up a video she had destroyed and when Tiffany realised it was one of Patrick's she felt a rush of anger so acute it took all her will-power not to knock her daughter on her arse.

It was one of Pat's blueys. Unlike most men, Pat's videos had him as the star attraction. He liked to video himself with girls on their first outing. He had one of her that he showed to friends and 'colleagues'. She realised now that he showed them to prospective clients, men who were looking for that little bit extra. And in Patrick's vids that little bit extra was mandatory.

She took the video from her daughter's hands, snatched it roughly, and the child's eyes filled with tears. Tiffany picked her up and hugged her tightly, something she remembered her own mother doing to her. Marie was always either kicking or kissing her. Either giving her the earth or telling her in no uncertain terms to fuck off out of it – that expression had been her favourite. Then she would be remorseful and want to love Tiffany all over again. It was a pattern she'd known all her life. Now it was being repeated in her relationship with her own child, and with Pat. The knowledge grieved her. She looked at the clock and panicked. He would be here soon and the babysitter hadn't even arrived.

She took Anastasia through to the lounge and put on a Disney video then rushed back to the bedroom and resumed getting ready. She knew that what she was going to do tonight would mean crossing another line, and she also knew she had to do it. In a part of her she knew that Patrick would leave her over it and that itself in some ways made what she was about to do easier. He was a better pimp than a lover, and she was realising that. But, oh God, she loved him. She loved the man he had been at first when she first knew him. The man who had swept her off her feet and taken her to heights of passion she never knew existed. But she realised that for the sake of her child – her child, not his – she had to get off the roundabout once and for all. Tonight was the beginning of the end. Soon he would be her pimp, and that was all. He would mercy fuck her now and again but she would not have to live with the pressure she had now, the constant fear of what he was going to do or say.

The fact she had finally admitted she was going to go on the game full-time took a load off her. She saw herself doing the lap dancing and the extras for five years, in which time she would accrue enough money to start a business herself.

108

Her mind was so muddled she drank a glass of white rum down neat to try and give herself some confidence. If she thought about it all too much she knew she would freak herself out and that was the worst thing that could happen to her tonight. Because even if she wanted to back out, she knew she couldn't do it. Pat wouldn't let her. He owned her.

There was a knock at the door. She heard the loud calling of her friend Beatrice and as she answered the door slapped a smile on her face.

Keep smiling, Tiff, she told herself over and over. Just keep smiling and taking the money, it's all just a means to an end.

How else was a girl like her ever going to get her hands on real money anyway? She had no qualifications, nothing. It was work in a factory for a pittance or make a career out of sex. She'd chosen the latter and busily convinced herself that what she was doing was for the best.

Leroy McBane was ugly. He was extremely thin, almost emaciated, and he was also dangerous. His trade was drug dealing, but his hobby was women. Young women, old women, he didn't care as long as they did what they were told. And if they didn't want to do it, so much the better.

As he set up the video camera he was whistling through his teeth and his live-in girlfriend was getting ready to go out with her friends.

Sarah was obese, a huge bleached blonde with a very pretty face and a lively personality. Leroy kept her like a pet. She made him laugh and was the only woman ever to understand him and his needs. As long as he took care of her she didn't mind what he did. She had produced two children, both looked after by her mother though she visited them every day. He saw them for a few hours on a Sunday. The arrangement suited them all.

Sarah for her part enjoyed her association with him. When she had met him five years earlier she had found something good in him that baffled her, her mother, and even Leroy. She made him feel good about himself. She was also a scream and that was part of her charm. She was from a white middle-class family which again strongly appealed to Leroy. She could talk well when she needed to and he liked that. It was a strange relationship that worked on many levels.

As she jumped around the room to Aswad he smiled at her.

'Where you going?'

109

'Ministry of Sound with a few girls. It's Candace's birthday so it'll be a late one.'

She was telling him what he wanted to know. She wasn't going to come home and interrupt his evening.

He smiled at her.

'Have a good time.'

'I will, you know me. Do you want me to make you any sandwiches or anything before I go?'

He shook his head. Taking a wad of money from his pocket, he pushed it into her hand.

She grinned. Her white teeth were even and perfect; he had always liked her teeth.

'Thanks. See you later then.'

She kissed him and left the house. He turned off the stereo and savoured the quiet. Sarah was a good girl, but she was noisy.

Alan Jarvis was worried. He had sixteen kilos of cocaine in his yard and no one had turned up to collect it. He had rung everyone concerned in the transaction and no one was answering. Every time he heard a car he expected it to be Old Bill.

He lit another cigarette and then saw one still smoking in the ash tray. He stubbed them both out and poured another large Scotch. As he stood at the window of the Portakabin a white Transit van pulled into the yard. A large black man got out and Alan walked outside to meet him.

'Can I help you, mate?'

'You Alan Jarvis?'

He nodded, wary suddenly.

'Who wants to know?'

As he spoke the back of the Transit opened and three other men got out. All black, all big. He felt nausea assail him as he realised what was going down.

'Who are you?'

His voice sounded much more aggressive than he felt. He was a coward, and he knew it.

'We come to pick up some gear, ain't we?'

The man smiled. He had gold teeth and Alan's eyes were drawn to them.

'What gear?'

The man grinned again. 'What gear? Are you a fucking comedian by any chance? We're after the two beams for Freddie Jackson. We

110

got lost on the M25 – else we would have been here ages ago.'

Alan felt the tension escape his body. He had forgotten all about the two steel beams. Had forgotten that Freddie wanted them today.

'Oh, right, follow me.'

They followed him across the yard and he showed them the beams.

'Measure up yourself, I have to get back for a call, OK?'

'Are you all right, mate?'

'Yeah, bit pissed is all.'

The men watched him. He knew he was acting strangely. He saw the first man shrug at his colleagues and warned himself to calm down. But his nerves were shot. He went back into the office and poured himself more Scotch. The sooner he was out of this the better.

He poured another shot and went through all the numbers again. No one was answering.

Patrick was cross and consequently Tiffany was quiet. As they drove to Leroy's he kept staring at her face intently. She had put on a lot of make-up and knew she looked OK. This had pacified him a little.

But what had happened earlier had rattled her. If he knew her mother had been to the house he would go ballistic. This was her life: lying, cheating, never letting on about things. She had learned that from her mother as a child and it had served her in good stead ever since.

He smiled at her and she felt her heart lift. He was still the man she had given herself to and had a child with. This Patrick she loved. It was the other Patrick, the one who was going to take her to a strange man's house and leave her there, that she hated. She smiled back, her heart lighter. At least he wasn't cross with her any more.

Inside she knew she should get out of the car and run. But she had no chance on her own. She was in too deep. She had to keep this up and take the money and wait until he tired of her.

It was the thought of the money that kept her going.

The thing about Patrick was, he could be so loving, so kind, that he brought tears to her eyes. That man she was seeing less and less of. But the memory of him was still fresh and he could still break her heart with a casual smile or look.

He stopped the car in a layby and took her into his arms.

'I love you, Tiff. You are the only one I love. You know that, don't you?'

She nodded sadly.

'You make me get cross with you by being a cunt. I have all my businesses to run and I don't need added hag, love. I really don't. You, of all people, should know that.'

'I'm sorry, Pat.'

She was sorry and the fact amazed her. He had the knack of making you feel everything that happened was your own fault.

He squeezed her to him, feeling her delicate ribs through the crop top she was wearing.

'You're a good kid, Tiff. And a good little mum as well.'

She basked in his attention, all her earlier doubts out of the window now. He was her man again and he was making her feel good.

He prepared a pipe for her.

'Have a whiff, girl, let the good feelings roll.'

He was laughing as she inhaled the crack. It was a large rock, more than she had ever had before, and she felt her body relax. It felt as if her bones were melting and she could disappear into a small space if she needed to. The high didn't last long but the good feelings were still around her. She leant her head back against the seat and exhaled slowly. Patrick covered her mouth with his, his tongue exploring her until she tingled. This was what she wanted, what she liked. What she needed.

She felt safe again, safe with her man.

As bad as he was, Patrick would take care of her, she was sure of that now. She just had to accept him as he was.

When she was stoned, she saw him as a different man. He was the person who gave her the means to get out of her head. She loved the feeling that crack gave her. Loved the feeling of being part of the world around her without actually having to join in. She felt fluid, relaxed and able to cope with life. As she let the good feelings roll she knew that, no matter what happened to her, crack would always be a part of her life. It was wonderful to leave the world behind and just chill out.

Anastasia was far from her mind now, as were her mother and brother. She was into the moment, and, like all drug addicts, for her the moment never lasted quite long enough.

Patrick watched her. Her eyes were closed and she was in her secret place. He loved the power this gave him. He had made her into what she was and she was his. All the time he had a few rocks she was his. A few more weeks and she would do anything for a rock; she was nearly there now. Soon she would have to perform to get the rock, and that was when he would really earn from her. He'd get her on to the street, earning exclusively for him.

He was smiling as he pulled out of the layby. The stripping and the lap dancing had broken down her reserves. Next step was getting her out on the pavement and teaching her to take care of herself once she hit the street. Then he could concentrate on his new girls and Tiffany would be just another earning machine, someone he saw twice a day to give her drugs and collect her money. It was too easy really. It was all too easy.

He dropped her off at Leroy's and drove away without a backward glance. He knew what she was in for but it didn't cross his mind to warn her so she knew what to expect, she was so out of it she would just go with the flow.

He was already on to the next deal and the next girl. Tiffany was nothing to him now, damaged goods. Already used by others and himself.

Marie and Carole Halter sat in the pub nursing drinks. Marie was looking at a large gin and tonic and resisting the urge to drink it. She was off alcohol, had been for years, but seeing her daughter had brought back the urge to obliterate everything as she used to all those years ago.

'Drink it, Marie, one bleeding drink won't hurt,' urged Carole.

'I should be back at the hostel. If they knew I'd discharged myself . . .'

'Fuck them. How they going to know?'

Marie sipped the drink and the acid taste hit her, making her eyes water.

'To see her like that, Cal . . . I'd convinced myself she was a regular person. That she was having a normal life. Boyfriends, the usual. I never dreamt she was involved with him. That he was dragging her down like he did me.'

Marie finished the drink in two gulps. Her hands were shaking and her head felt as if it was going to explode. She looked at the clock. It was after eight-thirty. She stood up. She knew that another drink would be the end of her. She would go on it for the night.

'I have to go, Cal. I have to get back to the hostel and hope against hope that they don't report me. I'll be in touch tomorrow

113

and then I want you to tell me everything you know, OK?'

There was a hidden threat in the words and Carole stared down into her glass. She couldn't look her old friend in the face.

'Before you go, Marie, Karen Black is still out for you. I saw her and her mates at the hospital, they were brewing something. You know what she's like. Watch yourself.'

Marie laughed gently.

'I've been watching my back for twelve years, it's kind of a habit now.'

She walked from the pub and hailed a cab.

Leroy liked the look of Tiffany. Her thinness appealed to him, being so thin himself, and her eyes with the pupils so dilated looked dreamy. He realised immediately she was out of her head and gave her a large glass of white wine laced with Rohypnol. He had already set up the camera in the bedroom. All he had to do now was wait for the drug to take effect and then he could play with her for hours and she wouldn't make a sound.

He smiled at her as she sipped the wine. It was sweet and cold. Tiffany gulped at it, hoping that the alcohol would blot out tonight.

Then she smiled back at him.

Teddy Prendergrass was on the CD and the soft sounds penetrated her mind. She wanted to relax, could feel her body going fluid once more. As Leroy led her into the bedroom she stumbled, but her mind registered the array of tools laid out on the bed before she lost control of her bodily functions.

Leroy stripped her off as he hummed along to 'Turn Off the Lights'. It was one of Teddy's best tracks and he played it at least once a day. As he looked down at the girl he squeezed her breast hard, but she didn't cry out. She wasn't capable. Positioning her for the camera, he went to work.

In a few days it would all start to come back to her. He wished he could see her face when that happened.

It would add to the excitement.

Patrick's sister Busby was a huge woman, much taken with African head-dresses and bright printed clothes. She was religious to the point of mania, being a gospel singer. Her brother was like her child. She was twenty years older than him and believed he was a good man leading a good life. No one had yet had the guts to tell her differently. It wasn't just Patrick's reputation that stopped people, it was her kindness. Busby would give the bread out of her mouth to anyone in need. She believed everyone to be as good, kind and decent as she was.

When she heard her brother's voice she called out to him loudly. He was everything to her. Always had been.

'Hello, baby. I was just thinking about you.'

He hugged her hard and kissed her. He acted loud and jovial, everything she wanted him to be. He was also far more West Indian when he was with her.

'You're looking good, girl! Can I use your dining room for a chat with a friend? You know Maxie? He has a problem, and we need somewhere quiet to talk it over.'

''Course you can. Take him through and I'll bring you some chicken and rice and a cold drink.'

Patrick hugged her again.

'Thank you. I knew I could rely on you.'

He walked through to the dining room with its picture of the Last Supper and the large wooden crucifix above the doorway. Shutting the door, he sat at the table with his friend Maxie James.

'This place is giving me the creeps, Pat.'

He laughed.

'Don't let it get to you, it's the safest place in the smoke. I use it when I want to talk freely. She's a soul sister, man, you know that. Remember Easton, the husband! They good people. He died and now she lives for me and the church. So chill out and eat, she makes the best chicken and rice in the country.'

Maxie had no choice but to do as he was told. He needed this meet with Patrick to sort a few things out. At least he was safe here and admitted to himself that he didn't always feel safe lately when he was with Patrick Connor. No one did any more, it was like he had become a different person overnight. He had always been a lad, a bad boy. Now, though, he was a bona fide lunatic and that was worrying in itself. Especially if you were a partner in a deal with him.

Busby brought in plates of food and cold drinks, bread and collard beans. Soon Maxie was eating with gusto and Patrick saw him visibly relax. He smiled, his most engaging smile.

'See, this is a treat, man, as well as a business meeting.'

Maxie grinned back. Pushing his locks over his shoulder he shovelled in more food.

115

'So what's this new deal then?'

Patrick sipped at his Diet Coke then, grimacing, took out a small bottle of white rum and topped up both glasses.

'I want to expand, that's all. I've seen opportunities for big deals all over. I have two new suppliers on hold, one in Holland and one in Brussels. We can piss the market and rake in the dough. Easy.'

Maxie stopped chewing.

'We big already. We get bigger then we become too noticeable, you know that. The filth's all over us as it is. How you gonna work this in with everything else, man? Be reasonable, Patrick. We got enough.'

He was expecting this.

'I don't think you understand me, Maxie. I ain't asking you, man, I telling you. It's already set up, all you got to do is recruit, innit?'

Maxie was miffed and it showed.

'What you fucking telling me for after you made arrangements, Patrick? This is always happening lately. What you want me in for if you gonna run it all yourself? Fucking . . .'

He slammed his fork on to the plate and it made a loud scraping noise. Maxie was clearly upset.

'I am sick of this, Patrick. We been partners all these years and now you treat me like a fucking boy. Like I am your boy. People are noticing as well, man. Even Yvonne say she notice it.'

Patrick sighed.

'Fuck Yvonne. She is a loud-mouthed, white-haired cunt, and if you listen to her no wonder you in a state with yourself. I told you before, your ambition white bird then get the ones that toe the fucking line. She don't want to get in my face, you tell her that, or I'll blast her off the face of the earth.'

'You are dissing me, Pat, and you know it. You got no respect for me or mine. Yvonne is my wife and I love her. She looks out for me and my kids and that is a result as far as I am concerned. I take the flak. If I get banged up she will be waiting for me no matter how long I get. You can't say that about anyone, let alone your women. Of course she want me out of this now. We got the money, we got the lifestyle, we can get along without bringing in all sorts of new faces and eventually the filth. We have had a good long run, let's not push it, eh?'

Patrick stared at his friend long and hard. They had been mates since schooldays and though they largely kept out of each other's private life these days Maxie was still the oldest friend he had. But he was also becoming a liability. Businesses had to expand to survive, Patrick knew that. He had legitimate businesses as well as his illegal ones. His women, his drugs, his clubs. He bought and sold guns, oversaw most of what went on in his manor, and was feared and respected all over the smoke.

He firmly believed if he got enough money he would be immune from the law. A couple of barristers he had used in the past were now judges, and he knew that if he did get a capture he could buy a short sentence. But it was all about extremes, and extreme amounts of money made you untouchable. That and extreme fear. He knew how to instil fear, it came naturally to him.

'Are you in or out, Maxie? I need to know.'

Maxie shrugged. His huge head with its thick dreadlocks made him look like an African Aslan.

'I suppose I'm in, whether I want it or not.'

He sounded as if he had been forced into the decision, as he had been. But neither of them mentioned the fact.

'Eat up and we can grab a quick drink before I drop you home, OK?'

Their business was finished and Maxie knew his friend wouldn't discuss it any more, no matter what.

That was Pat all over.

He ate.

Amanda Stirling opened the door and her look of surprise told Marie all she needed to know.

'I discharged meself, I hated it in there. It was like being back in nick.'

'Oh, my God, come in and sit down.'

Amanda ushered her through to her office and waited till she was seated before she spoke. 'What's happened? This is more than the mugging, isn't it? You look positively haunted.'

Marie looked at the kindly woman before her and felt an overwhelming tiredness. The gin and tonic had knocked her for six and she really wasn't sure she was up to a long talk about her life at this moment in time.

'Look, Miss Stirling, I took a beating and I am sore and tired. I just want to sleep. Sleep and sleep and sleep.'

Amanda knew in her heart that something was going on. After all the years she had worked with lifers she could read them like books. They came out to nothing, most of them. Came out into a world that was so changed even buying a newspaper was traumatic. This woman before her had lost everything – her children, her family – everything. Amanda should really inform the police because she was convinced Marie was involved with someone or something detrimental. But she wanted to give her the benefit of the doubt. She actually liked her. Didn't want to see her dragged back to prison. Wanted to see her get on with what was left of her life.

'If you want to talk, I'm always here, you know.'

Marie smiled.

'I know that, Amanda, thank you. But I'm just sore and tired, that's all.'

Marie didn't know how the hell she was sounding so reasonable. All she wanted to do was go to her child and try and undo some of the damage she had inflicted on Tiffany all those years ago with her lifestyle and her drugs.

Her eyes filled with tears.

'You're worn out. Let me walk you up to your room.'

Ten minutes later she was tucked up in bed in the dark. She was a friend of the dark. You could think, hide and scheme in the dark.

But tonight she couldn't settle. Her daughter was out there with Patrick Connor, who had been the cause of every bad thing that had ever befallen Marie. Jason's little face came into her mind. His beautiful eyes and soft curly hair. His hot little body as he slept in her arms. After his birth she had started to get herself together. It had forced her to take a look at her life. She had told Patrick she was giving up the drugs and going to rehab.

He had laughed at her.

She could see him now, in his rude boy suit. Being the big man.

'You ain't going nowhere, Marie. You just shaking your tail for me, baby.'

His perfect teeth and flawless skin, shining with good health, were an affront to her. She herself was pasty-faced and ill from heroin abuse. It was Jason's having to be weaned off it after his birth that had frightened her so much. That she had made her unborn child an addict had really brought home to her what her life had become.

Patrick was doing his American pimp talk again, he knew how it wound her up.

'Stop that talk! You know you've never been out of East London in your life. You've never even been to Jamaica on holiday so stop the stupid talk. You think you're fucking Desmond Decker – 007, eat your heart out. You look a prat and sound like one.'

She remembered that beating from him. Every blow, every kick. She had insulted him and what he wanted to be. The strange thing was she had felt so sorry for him. She had always felt sorry for him. His desperate need to be someone had made him vulnerable and he knew she sensed that. He saw kindness as weakness. Now her little daughter, who had grown into a lovely young woman and a mother herself, was hooked on him as Marie had been. Maybe it was in the genes. Maybe it was socialisation as she had been taught.

Whatever it was, it was her fault, she knew that much.

She had never gone to rehab, she had been back on the street within three weeks of her son's birth. When she thought about it now, she wondered who that person had been. How had that happened to her, Marie Carter, the prettiest girl in her school? The most desired friend, and of course the hardest nut in the whole area. What had she been looking for all those years? What was her daughter looking for in Patrick Connor?

Every time she thought of that child, that little child Anastasia, who was her uncle's sister, she felt sick inside. That she was her flesh and blood made her feel sick. That her daughter could have had a child with the man who was her brother's father was beyond belief. But then, Marie knew just how persuasive Patrick Connor could be. He probably saw it as funny, a big joke.

Yes, that would have appealed to him. He'd had the mother, now he had the daughter. He would have got off on that and she knew his sexual preferences. Knew what he was all about, what he was capable of. The thought of him doing that to her child, the girl who had once called him Daddy, aroused a rage in her so acute she felt she could kill him with her bare hands.

Well, that's what she would do if she had to.

She would kill him.

It was the least she could do for her daughter. Christ Himself knew she had done little enough up to now.

The thought took hold. As Marie went over everything in her mind, she decided that if there was nothing else for it then that was what she would do. A decision reached, she felt better. Finally she slept.

Chapter Nine

Tiffany awoke in the dimness of a strange bedroom. She was hurting, really hurting, and when she tried to bring her hands up to her face she realised that she couldn't move. They were tied behind her back.

She had no knowledge of where she was, or how she had got there. Her head felt as if it was full of cotton wool and her mouth was so dry her tongue was sticking to the roof of it. Terror made a scream spiral through her body, but no sound came out of her mouth. She was assailed with smells, faeces and blood being the strongest. As tears slid down her face she heard the door open and footsteps coming across the room towards her.

Tiffany squeezed her eyes tight shut.

'Here, let me help you, mate,' a gentle voice said.

She felt her hands being released and the pain in her shoulders was so acute she did cry out then.

The girl put a hand over her mouth.

'Shhh! Don't wake him up.'

Tiffany felt her arms being massaged and was aware that the strong fingers knew exactly what they were doing. The girl helped her to sit up properly.

'I've run you a bath, OK? It's got Dettol in it so it might sting at first.'

Tiffany allowed the girl to help her to the bathroom. She still felt groggy, and still had no knowledge of what had happened to her or how she had arrived at this place. All she could remember was drinking a glass of wine, and having a pipe with Patrick.

'Who are you?'

Tiffany's voice felt as if it had not been used for years, it was croaky and it hurt her to speak.

The girl smiled in a friendly manner.

'I'm Sarah. And you?'

121

'Tiffany – Tiffany Carter. What am I doing here? Have I had an accident?'

She sounded childlike, she was still so disorientated. Sarah didn't reply but started to wash the blood and faeces off Tiffany's body. The hot water made her feel more alive. As she woke properly, she saw the wounds all over her. The Dettol did sting, it was making her body feel that it was on fire, especially between her legs and in her anus. She started to cry, little sobs of pain.

'What happened to me, Sarah? What the fuck happened to me?'

Sarah saw the shallow knife wounds, and knew that Leroy had gone over the top again. She also worried that Patrick Connor was not going to be happy about the state of his girl. He had a kid with this one, she knew, but then he had kids all over the place.

Sarah had flicked through last night's video and what she had seen had made her feel squeamish so fuck knew what this girl would be like when she started to remember – and she would remember. That was the thing with Rohypnol. You got your memory back in bits and pieces over weeks, sometimes months. Sarah hoped the girl *didn't* remember what had happened to her.

Leroy had never done it to her, only to the girls he bought, and normally when he had them here he didn't use the drug on them. She assumed he had used it on this girl because of Patrick.

It was the Patrick Connor connection that was bothering Sarah. He sometimes passed girls on to Leroy, she knew, they bought and sold between them. But she had heard about this one, this Tiffany. Her mother had just come out from a double lifer, and Tiffany was also supposed to be Patrick's daughter. Now if *that* bit of gossip was true then she had a child by her own father. Sarah shook her head. That was one barrier even Leroy wouldn't cross.

The knife wounds all over Tiffany were scabbed over, but some had started to bleed again because of the washing. She had evacuated all over herself and the bed so the stench was overpowering. Sarah would dump the sheets, not bother to try and wash them. As she was cleaning Tiffany's hair Leroy walked into the bathroom and urinated into the toilet. He ignored them both.

Tiffany looked at him. Suddenly she didn't want Sarah to tell her anything. She had a feeling she didn't want to know. But she didn't say anything, just kept her head down and made sure she didn't make eye contact.

'Get her a cab and get her out.'

His voice was gruff, uncaring, and Sarah nodded at him without speaking. When he was in one of his moods it was the only way to deal with him. Twenty minutes later Tiffany was dressed and on her way home. She was still unable to walk without help and her whole body was aching.

She was amazed to see Patrick in her flat giving Anastasia her breakfast. He had cooked her an egg and made her toast. She also had a beaker of milk and some fresh fruit. He helped Tiffany into a chair and gave her a strong cup of coffee with plenty of sugar and cream. She sipped it as Anastasia gabbled to her. She found it in herself to smile at the child and stroke her hair.

Patrick chatted as if this was all perfectly normal. The mere fact that he was waiting on her was enough to disorientate her, without all this kindness and playing the perfect father. She was coming round now and watched him warily as he played with his daughter and made her laugh.

He kissed Tiffany gently on the mouth. 'All right, babe?'

His voice was soft, gentle; he looked genuinely concerned.

'He hurt me, Pat.'

Her voice was so quiet he had to bring his head forward to catch what she said. He knelt in front of her and wiped away the tears with his fingers.

'I know, darling.'

He was undoing her clothes and looking at the marks on her body. He kissed her shoulders and breasts as he buttoned her back up. She was starting to sob at his kindness. When he put his arms around her and hugged her close she really started to cry. And as she cried he rubbed her back and kissed her face and hair, murmuring endearments all the time. He looked so forlorn, so sorry for her, that she felt herself respond to him. She needed this now, a strong man to tell her everything was going to be OK.

Then he pulled her face up to his and kissed her nose. She stared into his eyes as he stared into hers. She saw the love in his eyes and felt a lifting of her heart as he smiled at her.

He carefully prepared her a pipe, holding it for her as he urged her to breathe deeply and take in all the crack in one go.

'Come on, Tiff, this will make you feel better. Breathe it in, sweetheart.'

She took it in quickly, needing the release the crack would give her, desperate as she was to feel better again, to forget her pain and discomfort.

He smiled as he saw her body relaxing. He laid her carefully back in the chair, watched as her eyes glazed over and the lines disappeared from her brow.

Then he said seriously, 'Don't worry about last night, Tiff. You'll get used to it.'

Kevin sipped at his tea and ate his toast. He had had to make his breakfast himself which spoke volumes. Louise was one of those women who felt that no one could do anything as well as her. She made all meals, all drinks, and nine times out of ten complained all the time she was doing it because she had no help and had to do everything herself.

Today she watched him as he opened the *Sun* and started to read. She hated him, she realised now. All her natural animosity was focused on him and what he had done.

'Do you realise the trouble you caused our Lucy yesterday with your stupid heroics?' she snapped at him.

He shrugged.

'Do I look like I give a fuck, Lou?'

He didn't even raise his eyes from the newspaper.

'We'll have the Blacks after us now. You know what they're like . . .'

Kevin was enjoying her discomfort, he realised. A small part of him was ashamed of that but, after all the years spent listening to her go on and on about Marshall when they still had two daughters and grandchildren that needed them, it was sweet revenge.

'Like I say, Lou, do I look like I give a fuck? We are harder than they think. I am not sitting back and letting the likes of them dictate to me and mine. I have kept me trap shut and me head down too long. That goes for you and all.'

Louise felt like she was about to explode. She stood up and pointed a finger at him. Her voice quivering with rage she said, 'How dare you speak to me like that? All I do for you . . .'

He started to laugh at her.

'Listen to yourself. What do you do then? A bit of washing and ironing, a bit of cooking? Millions of women do that and they don't go on and on about it. Shut the fuck up until you have something to say! Get off your fat arse and do something constructive with your life. In fact, I will rephrase that – Get A Fucking Life. Because I intend to.'

'What's that supposed to mean?'

He could hear the fear in her voice, the uncertainty creeping in.

'What it says. You made your intentions perfectly clear to me yesterday. Well, in my book that means I have to get me conjugal rights somewhere else, don't it? And I will, Lou. I can't live like a fucking monk. If I got a habit you'd have me out monking for a few quid, wouldn't you? Money mad you are. Well, in future, I pay the bills and that's it. You want a few quid to go to Bingo, you better get a job, girl. This house is changing and you had better learn to change with it. There's a new order here and it's mine.'

He finished his tea. Picking up his car keys, he strolled from the kitchen. He didn't even slam the front door, though he wanted to. Oh, how he wanted to.

Louise stood in the kitchen staring at the door for long moments. Then Lucy came into the room and said nonchalantly, 'You caused all this. What's the next step for him, Mum, eh? What's he going to do next?'

Louise couldn't answer her.

She was still in shock at her husband's words. He meant them. She realised he meant every word he'd said. And he would do exactly what he'd said. That was one thing you could guarantee with Kevin Carter: if he said he was going to do something it was done. The thought of all her friends and neighbours knowing he was out and about almost gave her a coronary with embarrassment. She had managed to live down what Marie had done. Looking people in the face as she gave them a piece of her mind. Making them understand that her daughter was nothing to her. Nothing. In the end they had managed to make a life of sorts. But it was still there, underneath the surface. She knew her daughter was a legend in some respects. A double murderess, a whore who had drugged and drunk herself into oblivion. But she had made people respect her, she had forced them to give her what she saw as her due. Now Kevin was making it hard for them again. He was going to wreck the little bit of respectability she had left. She would be a laughing stock.

It was Marie's fault. Since she had been let out of prison Kevin had changed. She was working her evil magic again like she always had. Like all men, he would do what she wanted.

Well, Louise would see them all get their comeuppance. If it was the last thing she did, she would sort that bitch out once and for all.

As she watched Lucy making a pot of tea she started planning, and the act of working out her revenge calmed her down. She would get even, not mad, that would become her motto from now on.

125

★ ★ ★

Marie had been brought tea and toast in bed by Amanda, who remarked that she looked better. Marie had smiled at the kindly woman. She had eaten the toast and drunk the tea as the woman chatted to her. It was true what Amanda had told her, she did look much better, yet how that could be she didn't know with the knowledge she had inside her head.

The swelling in her face had gone down considerably and she knew that skilfully applied make-up would hide the worst of it. But nothing would cheer her up. Seeing the nightmare that had been her own life re-enacted in her daughter's had brought her to an all-time low. Even at her lowest ebb in prison she had never felt this badly about anything.

How many times had she lain awake trying to remember the night her friends had died so horrifically? How many nights had she tossed and turned trying to fathom what had made her capable of such an act? She had always come to the same conclusion: it had been the drugs and the booze. She had had so many blackouts by the time of the deaths that it had become normal for her not to remember days at a time. She would forget to feed her children, forget everything but the constant urge to obliterate her demons. She had fought punters as well, and started fights in pubs and clubs until she was notorious for being trouble. For being a druggie. An addict. A lunatic.

Yet the act of burning heroin made her calm; the knowledge it would take her out of the ball game gave her strength. As she injected it, the feeling of the drug taking over was preferable to any other feeling she had ever experienced. It made her euphoric for a few moments, made everything seem beautiful for a while. It calmed her and made her happy.

But that feeling had lasted for shorter and shorter spaces of time. In the end she was chasing the dragon and chasing the feelings because they were overtaken by her addiction. But whacked out of her brains was still the only time she felt entirely safe. Heroin was her friend, her only consolation. She didn't want people, she didn't need people, all she had needed was the skag.

Prison had been her wake-up call. The drugs in there had been so badly cut they couldn't get a cat high, let alone a full-grown woman. She had realised then she had lost everything and had gradually come off drugs. Nights spent sweating and heaving had become rarer, and then she was seeing the world as an adult instead of a junkie.

Her children's faces had haunted her; the fact she had left them behind and would never get the chance to make it up to them had been a stick she had beat herself with constantly. But she had consoled herself with the thought that they would be taken care of. Finally be part of real families, see normal life and learn from that. Instead they had been parcelled out and Tiffany had become just like her mother without even realising it. Patrick's fault. He was clever and devious, she knew that better than anyone.

Now she must find Jason and see what had happened to him. He was still only a boy – please God let him be a good one, she prayed. A happy, well-adjusted boy. Don't let any part of his father be replicated in him, or any part of herself for that matter. Don't let the drugs have taken him too.

She had murdered while high. Everything bad in her life had happened to her while she was high. Now she was going to kill again, but this time she would be stone cold sober and if she got a capture afterwards it would be worth it.

She would willingly never see the light of day again if it gave her daughter the chance to break free from Patrick Connor and his evil influence. He was like a devil, waiting his chance to wreck people's lives. He had no conscience and no real feelings. Pat was out for number one and number one only.

It was down to Marie to stop him, and she would. If it was the last thing she did, she would take him out of the ball park and watch him die. Inside herself, she was almost looking forward to it. This fact frightened her more than anything.

Alan nearly fainted when he saw Marie cleaning up the office. Her movements were stiff, but she looked much better.

'What are you doing here, Marie?'

She looked at him and smiled.

'I had to be doing something. It's strange, but in prison I was always busy. It was how I coped. Now I guess it's a habit. Most of my injuries are just bruises, so as long as I'm careful I'm fine.'

'Your boat still looks sore.'

His sympathy cheered her. He cared, and after so many years of no one caring it was nice.

'Shall I make us a cup of tea?'

He nodded and watched as she moved about the little Porta-kabin. Already it looked better. Women were a touch at cleaning. It only took Marie ten minutes and the place was tidy. When he tried it took all day and still looked grubby.

His mind was on the cocaine in his yard. He was getting seriously worried now. He could contact no one. All mobiles were off and no one was getting in touch with him. He had to get rid of it, and soon. If someone had had a capture, and that seemed likely, eventually one of them would give him up in exchange for a shorter sentence. He would hold no animosity, it was something he would do himself. He didn't want a lump either. Especially since he didn't even want to be in the business any more.

The phone rang and he answered it.

Marie sighed as she heard him put three grand on the two-thirty at Kempton. Alan was a gambler, and always would be a gambler. Addiction took so many forms that she wondered at times whether it was genetic.

'I bought a greyhound, Marie. I was wondering, when you feel better, do you fancy a trip up to Peterborough to see it run? It's a lovely dog. Been bumped a few times coming out the traps but if it gets a clean run it goes like the wind.'

'Peterborough? Why not Walthamstow or Romford?'

'It can't run on SIS tracks, see. Not yet. But once we get it sorted it will.'

Marie felt like laughing again. He was so bent it was impossible for him to do anything like normal people.

As they sipped their tea she said nonchalantly, 'Do you know a black bloke called Patrick Connor? He has blue eyes which makes him noticeable.'

She had trouble keeping her voice level.

Alan looked at her for long moments.

'I thought *you* knew him very well. He ain't exactly hard to trace, love, is he?'

His voice had gone cold on her and she mentally kicked herself for underestimating the man before her. She swallowed hard and the sound was loud in the silence.

'I'll rephrase that, shall I? What do you know about him and his dealings these days?'

'Dealings being the operative word with him, eh? I probably know as much as you. He's a face now. Always was a bit of a wide boy, but he's worked hard and now he's emerging as one of the main dealers. Have I told you anything you don't know?'

Sarcasm was evident in his voice and demeanour. Marie was sorry to have vexed him. Alan was a nice man and had been good to her.

128

Giving her a chance when no one else would have. He was a good man despite his obvious faults. He was kind, decent enough by his own lights, and didn't deserve her giving him grief or involving him in things he had no business getting into or even knowing about.

She decided on the truth. He deserved that much at least.

'I'm sorry, Alan, but I suppose you know he's in a relationship with my daughter? I was worried about her, that's all.'

'Have you seen your kids then?'

She nodded.

'Only Tiffany. I'm seeing my son at the weekend.'

She didn't add that she was going to look at him from afar, not actually speak to him. Her father was getting the address from Social Services though she understood from Carole Halter that Tiffany had contact with Jason. If her father had no joy she would get the address from Tiff. She was determined to see him. If Tiff knew where he was, then Patrick Connor knew as well. That was what worried Marie.

'Oh. How is your daughter? I bet she was pleased to see you?'

Alan was being nice again and she felt the sting of tears as she answered.

'Oh, she was over the moon. Over the fucking moon.'

It was the first time he had heard her swear. She went down in his estimation and that saddened him. For all he knew about her life and her troubles, her not swearing and being so ladylike had appealed to him.

They finished the tea in silence. Finally Alan spoke.

'One thing I have learned over the years, Marie. Nothing is ever how you want it to be. People are rarely what you thought they were. The best way to cope is to take one day at a time.'

She looked into his face and felt an urge to kiss him. He was such a kind man despite his faults – and they were legion as his wife had pointed out to them both.

'I know that, Alan. But sometimes it's hard to do it. Especially when every day seems to bring a new problem, a new trouble. In prison it's a controlled environment. You don't pay bills, and everything is done for you. I never turned a light switch off or on in over twelve years. All I bought was toothpaste and sundries, a packet of biscuits or a Mars Bar. Now I have to try and fit in with the world, have to try and help my kids, and do you know the worst thing of all? I ain't sure I can even help myself.'

Alan shrugged.

'Who can? I have trouble getting dressed in the mornings, that's how fucked up I am. But you just have to keep at it, girl. It's what you do. Just keep trying, day by day, to sort everything out.'

His words were heartfelt and Marie appreciated the sadness behind them. He was absolutely right, though. You just had to keep going, day by day. Prison had taught her that if it had taught her nothing else.

Louise was at the graveyard, her favourite place. She was kneeling down to pull errant tufts of grass and weed from Marshall's grave and watering the small garden she had planted there. As she worked she talked to him, telling him all about her life and how much she missed him. Choice bits of gossip about how well his old friends were doing and how they all still missed him. She wouldn't admit that she liked the vicious gossip better, like when she had heard that Marshall's old school-friend Brendan had been given nineteen years for drug dealing. She had enjoyed that one. Brendan's mother had always looked down on her and now she would know what it was like to lose a son.

She could still remember Tracy saying to her all those years ago: 'Nothing will bring Marshall back. Move on, Lou.'

She smirked to herself. God paid back debts without money, and Tracy had been paid back tenfold for her remark. All the years they had been friends and she could say that to Louise, as if Marshall was a pet dog or cat! Something to be replaced. Well, Louise had blanked her after that pearl of wisdom and hadn't spoken to her for years. Now she would find out what it was like to be without a child, a favoured child. But then, she reflected, at least Tracy could see her son, talk to him. Hold him even, on visits. Louise had heard that prisoners could ring home now. That had been a revelation to her. They were locked up because they were bad, and yet they had the privilege of using a phone. The world, as far as she was concerned, had gone mad.

Tracy's son could ring home, a drug-dealing bastard was still in touch with his mother, whereas her son, her good, kind boy, was in the ground and she could not touch him again until her own time came. And that couldn't come quick enough for her. She would welcome death because it would reunite her with her son once more. The thought brought a smile to her face.

The weather was warming up, May would soon be upon them and then she could spend hours in this place. She would bring her lunch and read, sitting comfortably by her son's remains.

And she could think here, plan how she was going to put a spoke into her daughter's relationship with *her* husband.

Kevin was Louise's husband, after all, only Marie's father. Louise had given birth to a viper who used everyone around her. The trouble she had caused over the years, and still he wanted contact with her. Wanted to see her. Sometimes Louise had seen him staring into space and had known instinctively that he was thinking about his daughter. That Marie was in his mind as she had been from the day she was born. It had been hard on him, having to come to terms with the fact that his favourite child was a drug-taking whore, and Louise had allowed for that. She had at first expected him to disown the girl as she had, but had realised early on that if it wasn't for her own strength of mind he would have stood by Marie. Fool that he was, he would have stood by her. Louise had put paid to that all right. She had forced him to abandon Marie and let them get a life of sorts without her running everything. But the hold she had over her father was strong and of long standing. Now she was threatening once more to take him from Louise. She would take her own mother's husband without a second's thought. That was what Louise had bred and the knowledge had nearly broken her.

But she would fight Marie, and she would fight him. She would finally prove to Kevin what a whore his daughter was. How she used her body to get what she wanted. She had slept with everyone: friends of the family, teachers, anyone who could help her get what she wanted. And still Kevin had forgiven her. She probably let him touch her like she did everyone else. Louise's mind forced the thought away. She knew in her heart that her husband was not like that. But, she reasoned, Marie was capable of making him do whatever she wanted. She could as a child. He had always been besotted with her. Since her birth, he had been all over her like a rash. It was something Marie had inside her, for all the badness. It was something that attracted men to her.

Even her school-teachers had fallen victim to her charms. The humiliation of being told that her daughter had to leave the school because she had been caught out with the Maths teacher still smarted. She had charged the boys at school five cigarettes for sex, apparently. That was another story that had gone the rounds like wildfire. Friends would look at Louise with pity as Marie had yet another sexual escapade that was the talk of the district. No matter what her mother did, beat her, grounded her, put her in care, Marie wouldn't change, wouldn't toe the line. Sometimes Louise had thought she enjoyed the trouble she caused because it made her the centre of attention.

She shook her head at the malice of a child who had set out every day of her life to vex her mother in any way she could. It had been a war between them, a war she had won. The day her child had been put into prison Louise had felt relieved because at last her troublesome daughter was somewhere safe and somewhere she couldn't harm anyone ever again.

She had celebrated that night. Alone she had drunk a toast to Marshall and told him that she loved him and his sister was paying for his death as she should. Marie had finally got what she deserved. Not just because of Bethany and Caroline – they were whores like her – but for the death of Louise's beloved son who had been unable to live with what his sister had done. A decent, kind boy had died because of Marie and her lifestyle.

Her daughter should have been hung for what she did. For the lives she had ruined, Louise's included. Her marriage had died the day her daughter was sentenced, because Kevin had never forgiven his wife for being a witness for the prosecution. But what could she do? She *had* seen her that day with Bethany and Caroline. She *had* seen them arguing. She had had to tell the truth, she couldn't lie about something like murder, no matter what her husband thought. This wasn't one of Marie's usual escapades, this was deadly serious. Someone had had to stop her once and for all, and that person had been Louise. Who better to bring her to justice than her own mother, the woman who had given birth to her and had tried to make her change her lifestyle? Yes, she had been forced to tell the truth. It was the only decent thing to do.

Now Lucy, at thirty years old, was marrying that bloody prat Mickey because she was convinced no one else would ever want her. Marie had a lot to answer for, by Christ. Well, it was up to her to stop her daughter once more and she would. As God was her witness, she would stop her once and for all.

Whatever she had to do.

She didn't notice Karen Black watching her, she didn't notice the priest watching them both. She was with her Marshall and that was all that mattered. That was all that had ever mattered to her. When she was near him she felt her life was easier, that she had someone close by who understood her.

Father Boyd stood over her and Louise looked up at him and smiled. 'Afternoon, Father.'

'The grave looks gorgeous. I wish more people remembered their dead.'

He looked at the neglect around him and sighed.

'It's the least I can do for him, Father. He was a good son.'

As usual she was near to tears talking about her child. Father Boyd wiped a hand across his bald head and smiled gently.

'He was that. Always the good boy, Marshall. A fine altar boy as well.'

He saw Louise Carter almost swell physically with joy at this praise of her son and prayed to God that the poor woman would finally be given ease from her grief. It consumed her like a fire and eventually would burn her out.

She looked like a mad woman with her fiery eyes and grim expression. Marie, God love her, had always been a troubled child and a lot of that trouble had stemmed from this good Christian woman standing in front of him. One who, God Himself knew, would give to strangers yet demolish her own family without a second's thought. Who saw only trouble in her girls and only goodness in her son, the lad who'd known how to smile and tell her everything she wanted to hear. Louise caused so much of her own unhappiness, was so determined to find the bad in everyone around her, including her own daughters.

He had always liked the girls, though Lucy had too much of her mother in her ever to be happy. She had inherited the same jealousy that was the blight of the woman before him.

Marie now had been a great child altogether when she wasn't around this woman, full of fun and laughter, a good little girl who had been a joy to be around and had clearly loved her father. The priest had seen the jealousy her mother had tried to stifle as she observed father and daughter together. Though Kevin Carter had loved all his children, he had given Marie extra attention because this woman, her own mother, had not found it in her heart to give the little girl anything but verbal abuse and put-downs.

Marie had been so pretty, a beautiful child who had grown into a beautiful girl. But she had been troubled all her young life, and no matter what she was supposed to have done he still prayed for her soul and for her peace of mind. Especially her peace of mind.

'Would you not come and have a nice cup of coffee with me, Lou? I could do with the company.'

She gathered her things together and walked proudly with the priest to the vestry. She complained about everyone and everything as they walked and he listened politely as he always did. He would talk once more to Kevin Carter, he privately decided. This woman needed psychiatric treatment and she needed it soon. It was like listening to a lunatic as she droned on and on about how terrible it was that other boys were living while her son was dead.

He half guessed that Marshall Carter wished he could rest in peace and didn't have to listen to this one every day of his mother's life. Sure, the ground was cold, he knew that himself. But Marshall's soul was gone to a better place and he deserved a bit of peace now until this one finally wore herself out and joined him.

Father Boyd sighed heavily and listened to her, his face devoid of expression but his heart heavy with her sadness. He lit a cigarette even though he was supposed to be giving up. He always needed a crutch when this woman was around, and nicotine was as good a crutch as any though, if he was honest, he would much prefer a large Scotch.

He looked out of the window and saw that Karen Black was gone at last. There was trouble brewing there and he had a feeling that nothing he or anyone else did could stop it.

Chapter Ten

I n the last week Marie had felt she was finally getting to grips with her life and her past. Work was a priority for her, it kept her sane, though it seemed that Alan Jarvis was having problems of his own. He hadn't said anything but she could feel his nervousness. It helped take her mind off her own problems.

Her father too had been a great comfort to her. Now, as they sat together in an Italian restaurant, she felt herself relax a little. They ate slowly. Marie enjoyed her food lately, even if she was eating too much of it. After years of prison stodge and the occasional treat, food was now a great comforter. They ate together in companionable silence, both aware that they had much to talk about but plenty of time to discuss things.

That was another of the things prison had taught her. Time really was a great healer. In fact, time was something she had learned to appreciate because when you spent so many years waiting for it to pass, you realised that time wasn't the enemy: you were the enemy of time. It was there to be used because time past could never be regained. And time did pass, excruciatingly slowly at times but it *did* pass, and you could let it pass you by or use it to your own benefit.

The time spent without her children could never be brought back. What she had to do now was give them something to hold on to. Give herself something to hold on to. In prison she'd had no letters to write, no visits, so she was completely self-contained. She had had to be. Now it stood her in good stead.

'What are you going to do, Marie? I'm sorry I couldn't get the address but the social worker was a real hard nut.'

She shrugged.

'Tiffany knows where Jason is. I'll go and see her again. Want to come?'

She'd asked him as an afterthought and they both knew that. But Kevin thought before answering.

'From what you've said, Marie, if I go there I'll just cause trouble. You know me, love, the proverbial bull at a gate.'

She didn't answer. She remembered him coming after her years before. Looking for her in squats and grubby flats. Fighting anyone who stood in the way of his getting to his daughter. He had wasted so much time and energy on her.

She closed her eyes against the memories. She couldn't change those times and she knew better than to dwell on them. She had to concentrate on now. On her kids, on getting a semblance of a decent life around her.

'She sounds so much like you, Marie,' her father said wistfully.

His voice was sad and she felt sorry for him. Knew the disappointment she had been to both her parents.

'I expect she knows it all, eh? Been there, done that. You have to step back and let her get on with it otherwise it will drive you mad, love. I had to let you go in the end, as harsh as that sounds. Your mother couldn't take any more, and frankly neither could I.'

Marie looked at her plate, tears gathering in her eyes at the futility of her father's words. He was still confused about what had made her like she was. Still felt guilty as if it was directly his fault. She knew he still lay in bed trying to work out what he could have done to make it all different. Her heart went out to him and the guilt made her feel almost nauseous it was so acute.

She grasped his hand.

'I'm sorry, Dad. Sorry for everything. I think about Caroline and Bethany every day. I know they would be walking around now, enjoying life, if I hadn't been such a mess. I still don't remember anything. In a way that's probably a good thing, don't you think? At least I only see them dead. I don't see them cowering and begging for their lives so that's a touch, I suppose.'

She swallowed deeply.

'I still don't understand how it all happened, Dad. How I could end up killing me mates and leaving me kids. And doing thirteen years in prison. Sitting day after day feeling like my life was on hold and trying to stop thinking about my babies . . . the babies I didn't give two fucks about once because I wanted to be permanently high. The kids I loved and nevertheless abused because I thought they would always be there. I'm frightened of seeing Jason, Dad. I'm frightened he will turn his back on me like Tiffany did. I know I deserve it, but I'm not sure I could cope with it if it happened. Patrick dumped him just after I did. He must know that. His sister has a child by his father. My grandchild and my son are brother and sister. I fucked them up, Dad, I fucked us all up. Me, you, Mum, Lucy, all of us, but especially my kids. My poor kids.'

She was openly crying now and other people in the restaurant were watching her, fascinated.

'How am I supposed to cope with all this, Dad? They didn't even give me weekend release, I was just dumped into the outside world – a place I left when people still wore glitter boots and twenty fags cost a quid. Everything is alien to me, everything. I just don't know what to do, where to turn. I'm lost, Dad, as lost as I was when I was pumping myself full of heroin.'

Kevin listened to his daughter with sympathy but also with pride. She was facing up to her life and that could only be a good thing. She had no false expectations, made no demands. She had faced up to life, faced up to what she had done. If anyone deserved his help it was Marie. He would trace her son and see him for her. Pave the way. Make it easier for her if possible.

Yes, she had done a terrible thing, but she had paid the price. More than paid the price.

He held her until she stopped crying, and then he ordered her a large dessert. Comfort was what she needed now and this was as good a place as any to start.

'Listen, you have paid your debt to society, OK? You have a job and a new life just starting for you. The past is the past, leave it there. Concentrate on the future. You're still a young woman, a beautiful woman, and unlike most people you have learned by your mistakes. You just need to resolve some unfinished business.

'We'll sort things out with your boy, I promise you. But whatever happens, you have to move on, right? We all do, it's what life is all about. Moving on and making the best of bad situations. I should know, I've been married to your fucking mother for years, that's a life sentence in itself. If I'd topped her years ago I'd be out now and wouldn't have to look at those accusing eyes every day of me life.

'I chose to stay with her and I regret it, Marie. She is one bastard of a woman as you know. She made you what you were, like she made Marshall what he was. She bowls through life, destroying everyone around her, can't help it, and Lucy, poor whore, takes after her. They both live joyless existences where they try and control everyone around them. You rebelled, that's all, in the only way you could. By getting out of your nut. And that black ponce didn't help, putting you on drugs, making you graft on the streets for him. If you hadn't met him, most of the trouble would never have happened. I believe that. I have *always* believed that. Now eat that apple pie and cream, and let's say no more about any of it until we both feel calmer.'

Marie listened to him, shocked by such plain speaking. She didn't believe any of it, but she was grateful to have him as an ally. He had always taken her part and had paid for that over the years with her mother. Marie knew that better than anyone.

Louise sat in her lounge with pictures of Marshall all around her. She sipped at a cup of tea and smoked a king-size Embassy slowly, savouring the quiet and her time alone with her son.

The priest always made her feel so much better. There was a man who knew what he was talking about, and how to stay quiet to show he agreed with her. She wished she had visited him again today but she'd felt under the weather.

It never occurred to her that the priest was only humouring her by listening to her and that his silence did not mean he agreed with her. Louise put her own connotation on everything. In her mind he was a great man; anyone who agreed with her was a great person. A decent person. She felt so lonely at times, it was refreshing to find a kindred spirit. Someone who understood the pieces of shit that had to be dealt with on a daily basis while her son, her golden child, was dead to her.

She closed her eyes and pictured Marshall as a little boy: his hair curly and silky soft, his blue eyes forever smiling at her. He had been exquisite, like a little doll, while the girls had been great lumps of children. Heavy on the hip and miserable to boot, especially that Marie, all blue eyes and heavy limbs. Even as a small child she would show off, singing and dancing for people, saying nursery rhymes that were risqué. That was her father's doing, of course. People always made a fuss of her. 'She'll be a film star with them looks.' How many times had Louise heard that one? 'She'll be a model, look at that figure.' All breasts and make-up by the time she was twelve. Whoring was in her blood. At least Louise had made a point of keeping Lucy under wraps. At least *she* had not shown the family up.

She closed her eyes against the scenes in her mind. Her husband . . . another useless ponce as far as she was concerned . . . walking the streets looking for their daughter at all hours of the day and night. He cared more about her than any of them. Hardly noticed his son. Poor Marshall had had to fight against that big-titted slut for attention. They all did. Even her, his wife. Kevin would sit there on the sofa with Marie, cuddling her and laughing and joking with her. Ignoring the other kids.

Louise conveniently forgot that she herself had had no interest in her daughters, though out of the two she'd preferred Lucy because she at least toed the line.

Marie had sussed her mother out at a young age. There had been no respect from her ever. The girl would look at her with those ancient eyes and Louise knew she was laughing at her, behind her back and to her face. Her sleeping around was meant as a personal affront to her mother. Marie had done it to get back at her. That was what galled Louise more than anything, that her daughter could so demean herself to score points.

The cigarette had burned down until it was nearly touching her fingers. She stubbed it out and immediately lit another.

Marshall smiled at her from his photographs and she felt at peace once more. How she loved him still, her baby. She lay back in the chair and pushed the bad thoughts from her mind. All she wanted to do was think about her son. She forced herself to relax in peace and sighed heavily with contentment.

This was what she did. She pretended Marshall was still alive and invented a life for him of academic success and happiness. He earned a fortune and the neighbours were all impressed and suitably humble in his presence. He was a god who adored his mother and did everything for her.

It was balm to her tortured soul, these dreams of what might have been, of her son's success reflecting on her. It took away the bad taste of her daughter's decline into drugs and debauchery.

These dreams made her happy. Were what made sleep come easier, and kept her going from day to day.

As she pictured him achieving yet another academic feat she was smiling happily.

The petrol bomb came through the front window at speed. As it shattered against the wall, flames engulfed Louise as she sat in her chair. The nylon overall she wore to do her housework was melting but she didn't notice. She was trying to pick up Marshall's photos and save them from destruction. She could smell her own hair burning.

The shock had set in quickly and the pain was not yet evident. She was running on pure adrenaline. Instead of racing from the house she kept on trying to collect Marshall's memorabilia. His school swimming certificates. His Sunday School Bible. All the little things that meant so much to her. The curtains were in flames, shreds of black charred material floating round the room and causing further fires. But Louise wasn't interested. She *had* to remove all her son's things, couldn't let them be taken by the fire.

The smoke was making her eyes water. With her arms full, she finally pulled open the door. The whole room seemed to explode before her eyes with the rush of air. Flames were licking across the carpet and rushing down the hallway towards the front door. That was when she realised the hallway too was on fire. The front door was ablaze, petrol fumes everywhere.

She tried to make her way to the kitchen, arms laden with memorabilia. Then she collapsed, and before she lost consciousness shielded her most precious possessions with her body to try and save them from the flames.

Her last thought, as usual, was of Marshall.

Patrick and Tiffany were in bed. He was holding her close and whispering how much he loved her. It was a tonic that she needed. Like this, being held and loved, she felt that her life was worth all the upset. In the last few days he had tried to repair the damage he had done to her. She listened out with half an ear for Anastasia, who had fallen asleep happily after an eventful day.

Patrick knew what she was doing and as he was in a good mood it didn't annoy him like it sometimes did.

'You're a good little mum, Tiff. One of the best mums I have ever seen.'

She basked in his praise.

'I try. I love her so much.'

'Not as much as me, I hope?'

It was said as a joke, but a serious question nevertheless. She smiled and buried her face in his chest so she didn't have to answer him. He pulled her face up to his. Her eyes were wary now and one part of him hated what he was doing while another part wouldn't let him stop.

Like Marie, she made him feel guilty. Marie had had a knack of doing that and it took away from the enjoyment he garnered from destroying them. Tiff's mother had had a mouth on her and she would use it.

'My kids mean more to me than you ever will, Patrick bloody

Connor. I only want you when you can fix me, you prat.'

The words echoed in his mind as he looked down at Marie's little daughter in his arms. She had meant every word as well, so he would hold back the gear then watch her beg. But no matter how much she'd needed a fix Marie would never say she loved him more than the kids. In the end she would score for herself if he didn't come through. In the end Marie would fuck anyone for a fix. Eventually she would fuck for whatever she needed. She had even fucked the fat old git in the off licence for a hundred fags. He closed his eyes in disgust. No wonder these women needed a pimp, they'd give themselves away for nix otherwise.

Tiffany watched the fleeting expressions on his face and, satisfied she was out of the shit, relaxed against him once more.

He pulled himself roughly from the bed, knocking her flying.

'I'm going.'

The curt words were almost barked at her. She sat up in the bed and pulled the clothes around her.

'Why do you do this, Pat?' Her voice was a plea, she was desperate and they both knew it.

'Do what?'

He was nonchalantly pulling on his clothes, his face set and angry. He couldn't get one trainer on and threw it at the wall. It crashed down on to the dressing table, sending all her little bits and pieces flying.

She stared at him with her mother's eyes and suddenly she had had enough.

'Fuck you, Patrick. I'm sick of all this. Jealous of your own daughter now.' She picked up her cigarettes and lit one, her hands visibly shaking. 'Why do you have to wreck everything, eh? I am trying to get a home around me for our child, for little Anastasia and what do you do? Break everything. Well, you can fuck off, I have had enough.'

He was staring at her now. She finally had his full attention.

'What did you say?' His voice was incredulous. 'Run that by me again, bitch.'

She was losing her nerve.

'You heard.'

Her voice was smaller now, scared. How it should be as far as he was concerned. He moved suddenly, and then he was dragging her naked from the bed by her hair. He dragged her through the flat then, opening the front door, threw her out on to the landing. She was trying to scramble to her feet, aware that she was naked and that any minute now the neighbours would be looking through their spy holes to see what was going on. But he had her again, then she heard the door shut behind them and fought to get on her feet.

'The baby's in there and we're locked out!'

He dropped her to the ground and, turning from her, kicked the door in. The child's cries could be heard all over the flats now.

Then he grabbed Tiffany again and carried on dragging her down the stairwell. He threw her through the lobby doors and out into the street. Her humiliation was complete. As she lay on the pavement, her whole body screaming with pain, he kicked her in the ribs then said in a normal-sounding voice: 'Be ready at seven. You're working tonight.'

He pulled out his car keys and unlocked the BMW. He drove off at speed without looking back.

Melanie Drover, a neighbour, helped Tiffany to her feet. She put a dressing gown around her shoulders and held her as she stumbled back up to her flat. Anastasia was being comforted by Melanie's eldest daughter, a painfully thin thirteen year old with acne and overlarge hips.

'He'll kill you one of these days,' the girl said.

Even at her young age she was aware of what went on in the world of adults.

Tiffany didn't answer her. She just took the baby and hugged her tight as they cried together.

Her life was a mess. She wanted the neighbours to go so she could have a hit on her pipe. It was the de-stresser she needed daily now. In fact, two or three times a day. And as Patrick had taken the crack with him she was working out in her mind where to score even as she cuddled her baby daughter in her arms.

Lucy listened to her mother's breathing, loud in the confines of the ICU. The police had already filled her in on the events of the day. Every time she thought of what had happened she felt sick inside.

Someone had not only thrown a petrol bomb at the house but simultaneously poured petrol through the letter box at the front and set fire to the large wheelie bin by the back door. Louise had been trapped inside alone.

She had suffered seventy per cent burns and no one would say what her chances were. She was to be moved to Billericay burns unit the next morning, but Lucy had a feeling that she would not be alive by then and that frightened her. As bad as her mother was, she was still the only ally Lucy had ever had in her life. The house had been completely destroyed by the fire and she was in effect homeless. No one had been able to locate her father as his mobile was switched off. He did that a lot lately, switched off his phone and disappeared for hours on end.

Mickey Watson watched his intended as she wiped her eyes again. He felt useless, but that was nothing new so he didn't dwell on it too much. He knew as well as she did who had done the evil deed and like Lucy he would not tell the Old Bill. No way were they going to get any comebacks. Her father should have left well alone where the Blacks were concerned.

Kevin should never have pushed Karen so far. She was a complete lunatic, as this had shown. Kevin had committed the cardinal sin, he had shown her up, and that was tantamount to a death sentence in the world of the East End hard nut families. The Blacks were a by-word for lunacy and being a law unto themselves. Now this was the upshot.

He looked at Louise. She was covered in tubes and had one for breathing coming out of her chest. It made a regular clunking sound, horrendous to listen to, but he had to keep Lucy company. At least until his dinner was ready. His mother was already being very vocal about the incident and he knew he was going to get it in the neck as soon as he walked in the door.

Fucking Marie! Wherever she was trouble soon followed. She was a magnet for upset and aggravation. Always had been, even as a girl. Men fought over her. She seemed to bring out the worst in people. Made them go against the grain, do things they wouldn't normally do. Look how she had affected her own brother. Nearly sent him mad, she did, with her escapades.

Now she was inadvertently the cause of her mother being fired like a Walker's crisp, and him getting it like billyo from his own mother for the next six months.

Fucking women. They were more hag than they were worth.

Still, he reasoned, if Louise breathed her last at least that would be one less cross to bear when he married. Pity no one had decided to do his mother and all. That could have been classed as a mercy killing.

He looked once more at the woman's burned face and hands. She was bald, and as she had never been a Brahma to start off with, he had a feeling she was going to look like something from a Hammer Horror after this little lot.

And if she did survive, who was going to get lumbered with her? That's what he would like to know before he was much older. In a way he wished he had left the engagement for a few more months. As his mother had already pointed out, Louise would need nursing and who was there to do it? Fucking silly Lucy, that's who.

Well, not if he had anything to do with it.

'Drink your tea, love, before it gets cold.'

His voice was its usual whisper and Lucy smiled for the first time that night. He was a good man, she was so lucky to have him and his support. She smiled again and sipped at the lukewarm tea.

He squeezed her shoulder and she rested her cheek gently against the warmth of his hand.

'I love you, Mickey.'

He squeezed her shoulder once more.

'I know, Luce. I know, love.'

Patrick walked the street without fear. People hailed him and he either waved or ignored them completely, depending on who they were. As he went into the club he was buzzing with excitement and adrenaline.

It was situated near Praed Street and was strictly Rasta, bad Rasta, frequented solely by drug dealers, pimps, or people who were a mixture of the two. It had a peculiar smell of white rum and grass mixed with cheap perfume from the women who popped in and out to weigh out money to their minders.

Patrick had loved this place from the first time he had stepped foot in it. He owned it now, though none of the patrons realised this.

Jacksy Gower, the original owner, ran it for him, took a cut and was happy to do without all the aggravation. Patrick made sure it ran on top form and that was good enough for him. Jacksy was going back to the Big J as soon as he could and he was going to retire with a good few quid, a nice white bird and a new apartment complex just south of Montego Bay, far enough from the shanties to make people think they were safe.

He put a vodka and Red Bull on the counter as soon as he saw Pat and, nodding discreetly, let him know they had important visitors sitting in the corner.

Patrick glanced over as he sipped his drink and even he was impressed with who he saw sitting there.

Malcolm Derby was six foot six inches of Rasta bulk and

temperament. He was one of the new breed of Rastamen who had taken hold in the nineties. Primarily businessmen, their only concessions to their Rasta roots were in their hair and the fact that they didn't eat pork or shellfish. Other than that they were pure capitalists, out to make a mint and live the life. But Malcolm also traded with the Yardies. He was the face of Yardie in London and anyone who was anyone knew that. He procured passports and he provided addresses, safe houses for his Jamaican friends. He was a dangerous man and he loved it. He had taken over clubs with a gun and a smile, had routed local bully boys and either destroyed them, shot them dead, or made them work for him. He was also untouchable. In fact he was so dangerous even the police gave him a wide berth. He was an advocate of black on black killings. Saw it as business, nothing more. As long as they killed each other he knew the heat wouldn't be too bad.

Malcolm was rich as Croesus and used his money wisely. He lived with a beautiful black woman, pure Jamaican, listened to Bob Marley and no one else, and smoked the old-style twists. He also had a nice white wife, a good-looking, educated, middle-class social worker who allowed him free rein. He always wore, summer or winter, a big black sheepskin coat, and he dragged out his British passport every time he had a drink.

Patrick could hear him now, shouting about the Bosnians and how they were a drain on society and how we British should not get involved in other people's wars.

'They take the money out of the mouths of the children – they don't work, not even a good scam, just live off the land.' His voice was disgusted.

No one answered him and no one would ever dare disagree. That was how it was when Malcolm was around.

He saw Patrick and waved him over.

'It's the main man, Mr P.'

Malcolm's mouth opened wide, displaying gold teeth set off by a large diamond that glinted in the subdued light. Patrick walked over nonchalantly and sat down. His hand disappeared into an enormous paw that was displaying its own strength as it shook Patrick's whole body, spilling the drink from his glass.

'You looking good, Bwana.'

'You look pretty good yourself, Malcolm. How's tricks?'

'You haven't heard?' His voice was scandalised and incredulous all at once. Malcolm was a real drama merchant and Patrick knew he had to go with it. He shook his head.

'Someone killed me blood kin. Shot him face off two days ago.' He watched Patrick's expression as he said it and then added in broad South London, 'The cunt is dead, Pat, and you know where I can find him. A little bird warned him but he will get his hand slapped at a later date. I just want Leroy tonight.'

'What you talking about?'

Malcolm looked scandalised once more. His broad face framed by three-inch thick dreads looked almost hurt as he shouted, voice growing higher and higher as he got more irate, 'What am I talking about? You taking the piss? Leroy McBane, that's who I am referring to, the black bastard. He shot me wife's brother, ain't you got no ear on the street, boy? *How* the fuck you do your business if you don't know fuck all about nothing?'

'All right, Mal, relax! I ain't heard a fucking dicky bird.'

Malcolm stared at him as if he was an errant child.

'That's not Leroy's style. He ain't a shooter. What's it all over?' Patrick asked.

'Someone shot me boy, one of me gun boys. Took his stuff. My brother-in-law was sniffing round, see what he could gather, and he gets topped at a party Saturday night in Peckham. Shot in the boat five times.'

He broke off and wiped his hand across his mouth. Patrick could see the animosity coming off him in waves. The man was demented with anger. His boys were usually safe as houses, as no one in their right mind would cross this man. Not deliberately anyway.

'It's no coincidence, Patrick. He was topped for a reason. That reason being I was after the cunt who took me boy out. Now I heard from Maxie James, *your mate*, that it was Leroy who scrounged me guns. And Leroy is on the missing list. *Big coincidence* again, don't you think. So he must have put the finger on me boy, didn't he? Fucking scumbag! I'll pop his bastard eyes out and eat them for breakfast.'

He sat back and waited for Patrick to digest this information, his expression almost feral. Patrick felt the first tendril of fear creep down his spine.

'Who was the gun boy?'

'Jimmy Dickinson.'

He had known what Malcolm was going to say before he said it. He hadn't realised that Jimmy was in such big company. Patrick forced himself to stay calm. He took another sip of his drink.

'How long was he one of your boys then?'

'Long enough to make me mad.'

'You dealing with the white boys these days?'

Patrick sounded just surprised enough to get away with what he'd said.

'I deal with anyone who got what I want, Patrick. Even fucking *pimps.*'

The barb hit home.

'No one is so big they can bypass me. Remember that in future, won't you?'

It was a clear warning.

Malcolm opened his sheepskin and Patrick saw a large machete in a specially made pocket.

'This is Jamaican justice, Patrick. Leroy is getting a permanent fucking parting in his hair, and so is anyone who holds back information on me. So, I ask you once and for all, where the fuck is he?'

Patrick swallowed down his drink and signalled for another round.

'I'll take you there meself, OK? He has a little place in Swiss Cottage near his mum's where he hides out. He's a piece of shit perve. Done one of me birds really bad, cut her and everything. I owe him a slap meself. It will be a privilege to see him get done over.'

Malcolm grinned widely.

'You ever seen Jamaican retribution?'

Patrick shook his head.

'Good. Give you something to look forward to, won't it?'

Kevin was crying. His shoulders shook from the ferocity of the sobs. As he looked at the devastation caused by the fire he felt sick. Everything was gone, everything destroyed. The house was still smoking in places and as he looked at the blackened shell he thought of all the mementoes that had gone up in flames.

Someone put a hot mug of sweet tea, laced with Scotch, into his hand and he drank it gratefully. He sat on the kerb crying until someone pulled him up and helped him into their house. It was the Indian couple, the doctors, and he allowed himself to be settled down and ministered to.

As they poured him yet another large Scotch it occurred to him that this was the first time he had ever been in their home. He and

Louise had been invited many times but she had always refused the invitations.

The man's voice was gentle and kind as he gave Kevin the drink.

'My wife works at the hospital, Mr Carter. Your wife is very bad, you know.'

'Me wife?'

The shock was still setting in. Suddenly he realised that neither Lou nor his daughter were at the scene. He had assumed they were safe somewhere.

'How's me daughter Lucy?'

'She's fine. But your wife was in the house when they threw the petrol bomb and she is very badly burned. Let me take you to the hospital in my car. The police have been looking for you everywhere.'

Kevin had turned his phone off. He always did when he saw Marie. While they had been eating and chatting, someone had firebombed his home. And he knew who had done it as well. He knew exactly who had done it.

He knocked back the drink in one gulp.

'Is she bad then?'

His voice was so low, Mr Patel had to strain to hear him.

'Very bad. I was there when they attended to her in the ambulance. I went to the hospital with her.'

'That was very good of you.'

The man nodded a dismissal. He would have done the same for anyone.

'I will take you to the hospital.'

Kevin shook his head and stood up.

'No, that's OK. I'm not ready yet to face Lou. This is all my fault, you see.'

He was rambling and Mr Patel shrugged at his wife.

'Mr Carter, you don't understand. Your wife is dying.'

'Dying?'

Kevin sat back down. He felt as if the breath had been knocked from his body.

'What – Lou, you mean?'

The man nodded again, his expressive brown eyes full of sympathy for the shattered man before him. They left the house minutes later but Kevin did not speak another word.

Chapter Eleven

Malcolm and his cronies pulled up at the bottom of Leroy's road in Swiss Cottage. They had followed Patrick's BMW and now they were tooling up in case Leroy had a posse with him. He was capable of it, according to Patrick. The plan was for Pat to go in cold and see how the land lay. Leroy would not suspect him.

Before they had left the club Patrick had nipped into his office and grabbed a small cosh. He fingered the cold steel now as he walked up to Leroy's flat and buzzed the intercom.

'It's me, Lee. Let me in, mate, it's cold out here.'

Leroy answered him angrily.

'Just the man I want to see.'

As he walked into Leroy's flat Patrick received the full force of the other man's displeasure.

'You fucking tosser! You tucked me right up. *Everyone* knows you done Dickinson, and now, thanks to you, people think it's me. I never touched Malcolm's blood. I ain't a fucking mental case.'

Patrick waited.

In a way he understood the man's predicament. Who was he more frightened of, Patrick himself or Malcolm? It was hard on him and Patrick sympathised. But such was the life they lived and Leroy should have understood as much. If he had, he wouldn't find himself in the position he was in now.

Now Patrick grinned, his face looking amiable, friendly even.

'But, you see, *he* thinks you did. Now I think it was me who shot his boy's face off, but I ain't gonna say that, am I? So it looks like you have to be the fall guy, don't it?'

He sounded so reasonable, so honest, that it was a shock when he removed the cosh from his pocket and crashed it into the other man's face, breaking open his nose and mouth.

Leroy fell to the floor.

Patrick watched gleefully as Leroy tried to make his way to his desk where he had either a gun or some other weapon. He followed him, enjoying the other man's helplessness. Then he cracked him over the head a few times, bursting the skull, but leaving Leroy just alive enough to keep Malcolm and his machete happy.

He trashed the place, made it look like there'd been a fight. Then he searched to make sure there was nothing he wanted before phoning Malcolm on his mobile and telling him the boy was ready to receive him.

There was no way Leroy was going to get up at any point, or be able to speak, so Patrick felt safe enough as he let them into the flat and told them how Leroy had attacked him when he'd remonstrated with him over what he had done to Malcolm.

He was the hero of the hour, and as Malcolm brought the machete down on his friend's head Patrick wondered where he could purchase a really good one for his own use. He decided he liked Jamaican retribution, it was dramatic and bloody. The perfect weapon of fear.

He could also use this death to get back into Tiffany's good books. He would tell her that Leroy had died for what he had done to her. Patrick felt she was getting too feisty by half. He used fear to control her but he also used psychology. A bit of guilt thrown in wouldn't do her any harm either.

Nice then nasty. It worked with whores every time.

Kevin grasped Lucy's hand but she shrugged him off.

'Bit bloody late for all that now, Dad.'

Her voice had the same whine that her mother had perfected over the years and he closed his eyes against it. It grated on him.

'Calm down, Luce . . .'

She shook her head in amazement.

'Calm down? You want *me* to calm down? *My* mother is dying, *my* home is destroyed, and you want *me* to calm down?'

Kevin stared into his daughter's face. It was tight with anger and like her mother before her showed no real interest in anyone but herself. Me, me, me, me. It was all he had ever heard. Along with I want, I think, I will.

Lucy watched his face, the changing expressions on it, and laughed nastily.

'You really are a piece of work, do you know that? This is all your fault, Dad. Being the big I am for Marie by sorting out Karen Black has brought this on us. You would do anything for Marie, wouldn't you? Even put me and me mother up for trouble. But as long as she's all right . . .'

'The Blacks kicked the shit out of her . . .'

Lucy held her hand up as if warding off a blow.

'They had reason to, Dad. She battered one of their family to death. It's called taking care of your own. They've brought up Bethany's kids, taken care of their family, see? You should try it some time.'

Kevin had had enough.

'Like your mother and you took care of Marie's kids, you mean?'

Lucy narrowed her eyes. Trust him to bring all that up again. As if anyone would want anything that had come from *her* body.

'That's different and you know it.'

Kevin looked into his daughter's face. It just missed being pretty because of the expression on it. She always looked hard done by and she really believed she was. That was the saddest part of it all. She could never enjoy anything because she was too frightened someone else was enjoying themselves a bit more than she was. Had a better car, house, cardigan, whatever.

'How is it different, explain that to me? How was turning our backs on two defenceless little kids the right thing to do? What had they to do with what their mother had done? Tell me, come on, know all. Like your mother you can't answer that question, can you? Like her, deep inside, you knew it was wrong. I knew, and I did nothing about it. But I wish I had. I should have put your fucking mother out the front door and brought those kids into *my* home where they belonged. But I did what she wanted because she is such a difficult woman. I opted for a quiet life as usual.

'I wish I had fucked off years ago and left her. Any other man would have, and if you ain't careful, Lucy, Mickey will leave you because you're just like her. You have the same vindictive streak and the same jealous way she has. Your whole life will be a mixture of hatred and pain, just like hers. It's what people like you two do to yourselves.'

One part of Lucy knew that her father was talking sense. But it hurt, the truth always hurt, and no one knew that like Lucy Carter.

She was also incensed that this thoughtless man, her own father, could destroy them all. See his wife badly burned and still feel in the right enough to talk badly of her. Coupled with her natural jealousy of her sister, she felt rage take her over. She shook her head sagely.

'Well, now we know what you think, don't we? I hope Mum *does*

151

die so you can finally be shot of her. But you'll always know you were the cause of her death, won't you? Enjoy yourself, Dad, with your darling Marie. Everything has to be paid for in the end, remember that.'

Kevin stared at his daughter sadly.

'You are your mother's daughter all right, Lucy, no doubt about that. For all Marie's done she is still basically a good person. A better person than you or your mother could ever be. *You* remember that.'

He turned back to the bed and saw that Louise's eyes were open. She was listening to everything that was being said. Even in the midst of her pain she had the strength to look at him with a hatred so acute it was almost tangible.

'Oh, Mum!'

Lucy looked at her mother and felt such sorrow for her that the tears flowed freely. For her to hear all that now was terrible. Lucy, not for the first time, wished she could keep her big mouth shut.

Kevin walked out of the room quickly. He couldn't look at those accusing eyes any longer because it wasn't fair. None of it was. He took the flak for everything and in trying to help had only made things worse. Well, this was just the catalyst he'd needed to take a stroll, and he would. He was out of it all now. Let them get on with it.

As he left the hospital he knew in his heart that Louise would survive. On sheer will-power she would survive, and in surviving would make sure she destroyed them all. Especially her first-born child, her eldest daughter. She hated Marie with a vengeance that was unnatural.

One thing he knew for sure: no matter what happened now, this marriage was over. Pity might have kept him in it this long, but not any more. Lou being Lou, she would make him pay somehow. And if that was the case, he would pay happily as long as he never had to look at her again.

Mickey Watson had followed him outside. As Kevin unlocked his van he saw his daughter's fiancé standing nearby, looking embarrassed.

'What can I do for you, Mickey?'

'What's going to happen with Lou?'

Mickey's big moon face was inscrutable.

Kevin shrugged. 'Looks like your wife-to-be has already made up her mind about that. She's just lumbered herself with her. Ask *her* what's happening. Like her mother before her she knows everything so she should be able to answer that question.'

Mickey stood his ground.

'She's *your* wife.'

Kevin laughed gently.

'That's true, but there is such a thing as divorce, you know.'

'You'd divorce Lou, the state she's in?'

Mickey sounded amazed. In their circles you stood by your own through thick and thin or other people had something to say about it.

'Like a fucking shot! Your wife-to-be saw to that. I have had the pair of them up to my back teeth. Now this, and I'm blamed as usual. Well, I have had enough. A bit of advice for you, Mickey, look long and hard at Louise because the old saying is true where her and Lucy are concerned. Lucy is her mother all over again, and God help her, she will never know a day's real happiness. Consequently neither will you.'

Mickey watched him drive off. Half of him felt sorry for Louise, being left like that in the condition she was in. But another part of him knew that he would have done the same thing. She was a bastard of a woman.

Lou had taken Kevin and all but destroyed him over the years. Used him as a provider, a crutch for her ego, and the source of a wedding band to show off to the neighbours. In his heart of hearts Mickey didn't blame him for taking the easy way out now. But he resented the fact that it left his fiancée, and that meant him as well, with Louise. Fit and well she was a handful, but if she survived this she was going to be a nightmare. He needed to consider his own position in this. As his mother said, the sins of the fathers and all that.

He wasn't going to tie himself to someone who had to be at her mother's beck and call for the rest of their married life. No, he needed to think long and hard about what he was going to do now. He wasn't about to exchange one miserable mother for another. No way was that happening to him. Out of the two, he'd have his own any day of the week. And he had his own life to lead.

Karen Black was packing. They were all going to the caravan in Margate. She felt euphoric at her antics of earlier in the day. She would love to see the Carters' faces when they saw what she had done to their house!

153

That would teach Kevin not to fuck with people. He thought he was hard? Well, she would like to see him now. See him foraging for a few quid and a roof over his head.

She laughed delightedly.

She was away to Margate until the heat died down. It was the natural thing to do. Once the nine-days wonder was over she would slip back, a heroine and a meter-out of justice. This was important to her. She needed to feel that people respected her, and respect was best earned by threats and the ability to carry them out.

Kevin Carter would think twice before he messed with her again. The recollection of what he had done to her still rankled. Her workmates had seen her at her lowest ebb, humiliated and unable to fight back for once in her life. But she had paid him back one hundredfold for his little tantrum, and she knew that anyone with half a brain would swallow it and let things lie. After all, the next step from a fire bombing was actual physical harm. Kevin Carter knew that and would keep his head down and his mouth shut.

She only wished she could stay long enough to hear the talk in her local pub. She would be the topic of conversation for a long while after this little lot. Karen was shrewd enough to understand not all the talk would be praise, but she knew that her name would become synonymous with what she had done, what she had achieved, and others would treat her accordingly.

She would be able to say what she wanted to people, would enjoy drinks that she had not paid for and would also bask in the knowledge that everyone thought she was a bona fide nut case. Someone to be wary of, to watch closely in case you inadvertently brought her wrath down on your head.

Karen shivered with excitement.

Every time she thought of the flames licking their way around the Carters' house, thought of the heat, the destruction and havoc they had wrought, she felt an almost sexual thrill that encompassed her whole body.

The photos curling up, burning from the outside in. Flames searing faces wreathed in smiles; long-dead relatives forgotten for ever once their images had disappeared. Carpets melting, curtain material smoking and eventually bursting aflame. The smell of plastic and rubber. Black smoke that could choke anyone, even firemen in breathing apparatus.

She grinned again, feeling she had really achieved something phenomenal. Then her husband Petey came into the room. He was short, bull-necked and stank of BO. Karen looked at him with her usual mixture of derision and affection. He could be a laugh and that was all that mattered in the end.

'What's up with you?'

Her voice was quivering with the excitement of what she had done, but her natural belligerence was still evident.

Petey had dead blue eyes that seemed heedless of anything but hid a mind that worked faster than a computer.

'What you done, Kal?'

She heard the fear in his voice and an icy hand gripped her heart. Were Old Bill at the door? Had she been grassed?

'What you on about?'

Before he could answer she heard her mother bellowing as she pounded up the uncarpeted stairs. 'Where is she?'

Her footsteps on the bare wood sounded loud and angry. The bedroom door burst open and Rita Black rushed into the room, her eyes demented.

'Trust you, you stupid bloody cow!'

Karen felt the fear rising in her, spiralling towards her head.

'What's the matter, Mum?'

Her voice was unsteady. She knew she wasn't going to like this. Her brother Luke stood behind his mother and he was looking at Karen as if he was ready to kill her.

His voice was trembling as he answered her.

'Did you check the house was empty before you torched it?'

Karen felt the breath leave her body. She sat down on the unmade bed, the case digging into her back painfully. Her eyes were wide, her blood thundering in her ears as she waited for him to tell her the bad news.

'You did the front and back, didn't you? Left no escape route.'

It was her mother talking now, low-voiced, sounding almost normal as she looked at her daughter in disgust.

'You stupid bloody woman! Louise Carter was in there . . .'

Karen shook her head wildly.

'She wasn't! She goes to the graveyard every day. No one was in there.'

Her mother's hand connected with Karen's face and the pain was welcome. She needed it to prove this was really happening.

'She was in there, in the house.'

'No. You're wrong, I tell you. She goes to the graveyard every day. I've been watching her. Who told you this? They're fucking liars.'

155

Luke punched the bedroom door, tearing a hole in it. His temper was up now and he was in danger of losing it big time.

'It was on the fucking news, you stupid fat cunt. She is being moved to Billericay burns unit tomorrow. If she dies it's a murder charge. If she survives you're looking at a twelve at least.'

Karen was licking her lips. Her whole mouth was dry with fear. Her eyes were like saucers as the awful truth of what she had done finally sank in.

'Oh, Mum.'

'I'll give you, "Oh, Mum". Why couldn't you leave it alone? Tams is like a lunatic downstairs. She never wanted any of this. It was all about you as usual, Mrs fucking Big. Well, you are on your Jacksy this time, girl. You got yourself into this and you can get yourself out of it. Because I tell you now, Kal, no one will cover up for you after this little lot. People *want* shot of you. Like all bullies you're better off out of it. So think on that one as you travel down to Margate.'

'Please, Mum . . .'

'Piss off, Kal. If you want to do something about this, put your hand up and take the flak. At least that way you'll come out of it with a bit of respect. You're just like your father – all talk and no fucking trousers. I visited him for years because I had no choice. He was a bigger nutter than you could ever hope to be. I was so pleased when he died, I was over the fucking moon to get shot. So now you know.'

'Leave it out, Mum.'

Luke was upset. His father had been his idol.

'No. I am finally having my say. I hate my life and I hate the lot of you. Bethany on the game, you lot like animals . . . what have I got to brag about, eh? What have I got to show for all my kids and all my life, eh? Nothing. No fucking thing.'

Rita started to cry then and this shocked her children more than anything else she could have done. This wasn't the strong woman who had fought the schools, the police, the courts, and anyone else who dared to criticise her kids. Who had visited them in care, Borstal or prison. This was a woman who was ashamed of and embarrassed by her own family, and this knowledge was both shocking and humiliating to the people in that room with her.

'Louise Carter was all right. A pain in the arse but that was her prerogative. She had every right to live her life how the fuck she wanted. Who are *you* to take her home and destroy it? She had a nice home, a *clean*, decent home. Unlike me. I never could have anything like that because *you* lot wrecked it, took pride in living like animals. Well, you can all get fucked now. I want you out and I want me place to meself. Just for once I want peace and quiet and you lot gone from me. Tams can stay, but the rest of you can fuck off. And remember, whatever Louise was, she never deserved that. Especially not that.'

'It's all coming out tonight, ain't it?'

Luke was hurt and his anger was mounting.

'Looks like it, son. I should have said this years ago.'

He clenched his fists and his mother looked at him with derision.

'Temper, temper. What you gonna do then, turn *me* into a pork scratching as well? Burn me out, eh? Your answer to everything, ain't it? Violence. Well, you do what you must, but you're all gone from here tonight. When the filth come knocking, and they will, I want to be able to say I don't know where you are. Any of you.'

Karen was silently crying on the bed, her face awash with tears. Her mother shook her head in amazement.

'It's crying.'

She laughed at her daughter's distress.

'Look at it crying.'

'Of course she's crying after what you just said, Muvver.'

She turned to her son, her face devoid of expression.

'She's crying because she'll get caught for what she done. She knows she'll go down and for a long time. She should have cried it off days ago and left the matches at home then she wouldn't be in the state she's in now, would she? She gave Marie a hammering, wasn't that enough? But like you all, she just doesn't know when to stop.'

She pushed her way out of the room and walked sedately down the stairs. Her cumbersome body felt lighter than it had for years. She was going to get rid of them all and that knowledge made her feel twenty years younger. In the lounge she took her grand-daughter Tamara in her arms.

'Me and you now, kid. So at least something good came out of all this shit.'

A car pulled up and a blue light flashed around the walls of the lounge. Taking a deep breath, Rita went to open the front door.

The police were wary, knowing the trouble the Black family was

157

capable of. Normally the mother was like a raving lunatic when they arrived on her doorstep. But this time she just looked at them sadly and said, 'She's upstairs, officer.'

Marie sat in her room alone. News of the fire had baffled her. She felt responsible but couldn't understand why her mother and family had been brought into the equation after all this time.

It could only be the Blacks. No one else.

She wondered why she wasn't crying. Wasn't feeling anything other than shock and dismay. But then her mother had killed any feelings she'd had for her many years before.

But the pain . . . the pain of being burned was terrible. She had seen it first hand in prison, and that had only been a scalding. One of her fellow prisoners had been convicted of killing her own child. She had had a bucket of scalding water thrown in her face to show what the others thought of her. It was the smell Marie remembered, and the screaming. Like a trapped animal's. It had taken the POs ages to get to her because the other women had formed a cordon and would not let them through. In the end they had had to resort to riot batons to get to the screaming victim. Marie closed her eyes but the image was still there. The woman had only been young, about twenty-five, and quite pretty before the attack. She had confided in Marie that on the day of her child's death she had been higher than Concorde on drink and drugs.

Marie started to retch again but there was nothing to bring up. She had emptied her stomach already.

It was guilt and she knew it. This was all her fault. She should have gone far away and left it at that. But she had needed to see her kids. Had been determined to see them. And if Jason was anything like his sister now, it had all been for nothing.

She wondered how Lucy was coping. How her father was coping. Everything bad that had happened to her family had inadvertently been caused by her. Would Dad turn away from her now? If he did she wouldn't blame him, how could she?

The walls were coming in on her again like they used to do inside so she started counting. In prison she had counted everything. It had kept her sane.

Numbers took your mind off thoughts, off words, off images.

Karen Black would be feeling euphoric at what she had done. Marie had met many others like her in prison; women who had violent personalities and were proud of that fact. Women who needed the kudos of a reputation for savagery to feel they were someone others respected.

Kilty, also a double murderess, was out. Marie knew that if she went to see her Kilty would make sure Karen Black got what she deserved. Kilty was a mate but so far Marie had avoided her though she knew she should have got in touch.

Kilty had made her life easier in prison by befriending her. And the strange thing was, she had been a likeable woman. When they were alone she had been different, softer, less brash than she was when they were in the rec room or the workplace. Her public persona was her armour against the world. Basically she was a good person. Deep inside she had a soft heart and a pleasant personality. Yet she had murdered her husband and her pimp on the same night. Brothers, they had both used and abused her over a period of years until finally she had snapped.

She and Marie were kindred spirits in some ways, two women who were victims of their own weakness as opposed to inherently bad people. There was a big difference.

Marie opened her bag and took out a small bottle of Valium. Alan had left them in his office and she had binned them before reconsidering and pocketing them. They were five milligrams each and she shook two on to the palm of her hand and stared at them.

Small yellow happiness givers. They would at least let her sleep. But she knew that, like drink, if she took them she would enjoy the buzz before she crashed out, and there would lie the danger.

She swallowed them dry.

As she lay down and waited for the magic to work she felt one rogue tear slip from her eye. Her poor mother. The pain she must be in, and the terrible way she must look. And her poor father – what must he be thinking? How would he cope with Louise in the state she was in? The news had said that she was badly burned and would be in hospital for months. That she had over seventy per cent burns, mainly to her face, arms and back. That her hair was gone and her clothes had melted on to her body.

Why did all these bad things happen to their family?

It was her. She was a Jonah, a pariah.

No one she was involved with in any way was safe.

Suddenly Marie felt the lift. The heaviness of the drug taking control. It was like lying on a thick mattress and sinking into it. Her limbs felt heavy and her mind was fogged. She remembered this feeling. Had looked forward to it once. Needed it in fact. Now she was glad of it all over again. She craved oblivion once more. The guilt was too much for her to bear.

She wondered if she might be better off, if everyone might be better off, if she just ended everything once and for all?

Everything she touched went bad. Everyone she was involved with had trouble. It was her. Something bad was inside her and consequently she brought nothing but heartache to those near her.

She was trapped in this room, night after night, like a schoolgirl. Her whole life was open to scrutiny by everyone and anyone. She couldn't move but she had to explain herself to someone. What kind of half-life was that for anybody? She had been better off inside where at least she could cause no harm.

She had even been the cause of her daughter's problems. If she had not brought Patrick Connor into Tiffany's life she might have had a chance. Her daughter might be working in Woolworth's or as a secretary now. Be normal.

Yes, Marie was bad. She stank of badness and she attracted bad people. Always had done, always would do. Evil had taken root in her heart and it had grown until now she had nothing else to offer anyone, least of all herself.

Her last thought before the drugs sent her to sleep was of her mother and the pain she must be in.

Susan Tranter had heard the news and when her doorbell rang had half been expecting it. Now Kevin was in her lounge and looking like a man demented. His opening words had thrown her and she was unsure what exactly he wanted from her.

'I've left her, Sue. It's finally over.'

Susan pushed her heavy blonde hair back from her face.

'What do you mean, you've left her?'

'What I said.'

'But she needs you now, Kev.'

The censure in her voice made him wince.

'That's too bad. I was tortured by her over the years. I turned me back on me daughter and me grandchildren because of Lou and her big mouth. I should have done it years ago. Now Lucy is giving me grief and, quite frankly, I ain't putting up with it any more. I know who was responsible and I will take action on that. But as far as Lou is concerned . . .'

He couldn't finish his sentence. Instead he sat on the edge of her settee, his hands dangling down before him, looking like an errant schoolboy.

'You don't half pick your time, don't you?'

He shrugged.

'I was dying inside and I knew it. Marie coming home made me realise how bad things had got. I pussy-footed round Lou, always had done. It made life so much easier. But seeing my daughter coping with all that happened to her without a letter, a card, or anything from me or her sister, made me see them all for what they were. Especially Lou. Since Marshall killed himself she's changed, got worse. She blamed me for all of it. Said I was the cause of Marie's problems because I stuck up for her all the time. She wanted nothing from me except money and respectability. Her idea of sexual contact was if I accidentally brushed against her in bed. We had nothing to keep us close any more.'

He wiped a hand across his face as if washing it.

'The truth is, Sue, I feel nothing for her except pity, and that ain't enough to keep us together. Maybe if I hadn't met you I might have carried on living in my shell of a marriage, I don't know. But I can't take care of her, I can't. I just don't want to. I couldn't bear to talk to her again, let alone touch her.'

He looked at her with anguished eyes, pleading for understanding.

'When I was told she might die I felt nothing but relief. I know that's a terrible thing to say but it's true. I realised then that I wanted to get as far away from her as possible. Then Lucy . . . her words, her bitterness, were her mother all over again. I knew I would have to deal with two of them, both full of hatred and jealousy of poor Marie whose only real crime was to take as much shit as possible so as to forget that her mother hated her and her own father wasn't strong enough to protect her.'

Susan listened in fascination as he unburdened himself to her. It was a revelation all right. He was low but he was in his right mind, he *meant* what he was saying. This wasn't just anger talking. This was from the heart.

She loved this man with a passion so strong it made her dizzy just to look at him. He might not be every woman's dream lover but he certainly rang her bells. Always had done. Now she knew that if she wanted, she could have him full-time and the prospect was making her feel hot with longing. But it was at the expense of a woman at her lowest ebb. Who was hurt, in pain, and probably wondering who it was that her husband was going to run to. Because Louise

161

Carter was shrewd enough to know that he was going to someone. He wouldn't have the strength to do anything like this on his own. He would need a rock, a support. Perhaps she thought it would be his daughter? That he would go to Marie.

Whatever, Sue knew she was going to take what he was offering and damn the consequences. It would be a nine-days wonder locally but she didn't care about that. If it meant having Kevin she would walk over hot coals and cook for the devil himself.

When his hand came out to take hers she had to stop herself from snatching it off, such was her longing for him. She pulled him to his feet and dragged him to her bed. Then she allowed him to bury himself so far inside her he forgot everything for that short time. And as he moaned and ground himself into her, she thanked God for what had happened because it had given her tonight the only man she had ever wanted.

Louise Carter was a fool of a woman. The only man she'd wanted was dead and buried this long time. If she had transferred that love on to her husband she could have been the happiest woman alive.

As Sue kissed Kevin's sweaty face and stroked his strong body she knew that she would keep him by her side, no matter what she had to do.

Louise Carter had lost everything in one day. That was how other people would see it anyway. First her home, then her health, then her husband. They would have to face up to hostility and ridicule, but having Kevin by her side would be worth it. Worth everything that was going to come hurtling at them.

Wrapping her arms around him Sue held him until he slept. She was still awake as the sun crept through the curtains and she was still looking at him when he opened his eyes and smiled to find himself there with her.

'I love you, Sue.'

She smiled happily. She had waited to hear those words for such a long, long time.

Chapter Twelve

M arie listened to Amanda Stirling, her face devoid of expression. She knew the probation officer meant well, she was a kind and caring individual, but Marie wasn't in the mood for any of it.

The policeman was kind as well. He had a rough angular face that looked as if it had been slept in by a *Big Issue* seller, topped with iron-grey hair that seemed to have a life of its own. She instinctively felt he was a man she could trust.

But Karen Black's confinement to prison meant little to Marie. She had been in prison herself, knew that Karen would soon find a niche in there and consequently would not really be that put out. In fact, she would see it as just another layer in her own invincible hardness. But she kept these thoughts to herself.

'You see, Miss Carter, we believe that the attack on you was carried out by Black. She has been very vocal about seeking revenge for her cousin . . .'

Marie shook her head and interrupted him.

'I was mugged. I know Karen Black and she wasn't there. If they'd been teaching me a lesson of any kind they would have told me. I know the etiquette of such things. Probably better than you.'

DI Dawson looked into her eyes. He had noticed their dead expression, as if she had ceased living a long time ago and now merely existed. He had seen eyes like those many times over the years, but his heart went out to this woman and he didn't know why. She was big, tall, strong-boned. A voluptuous woman in some respects. But she also had a vulnerability that appealed to him. He guessed, correctly, that it was this part of her that had got her into so much trouble with men.

'She has admitted her part in the arson attack on your parents' home, but we urge you to be extra-vigilant. That is a big family she comes from and they are known for their violence.'

Marie smiled at him warmly and the effect on him was electric.

'Thank you, Mr Dawson, but I have lived with violence for the best part of my life and I learned how to avoid it in prison. I appreciate your concern but I have to live my life as best I can, don't I? Otherwise Karen Black has won.'

He didn't answer her. Amanda was staring with apparent interest at a jotter in front of her on her desk.

'I did a terrible thing and have had to live with that for many years. This seems petty in comparison. I just wish I had been the recipient of her hatred instead of my mother, though why she picked on my family I really don't know. My mother hates me more than Karen Black ever will. She wouldn't even take in my poor children, though in fairness to the Blacks they took in Bethany's.'

No one spoke.

'Black insists that she thought your mother was at the graveyard and she only meant to burn down the house.'

Marie looked him full in the face.

'I can believe that. Strangely enough, I'm sure I never intended to kill either Bethany or Caroline. Frighten them maybe, for whatever reason, so I believe her when she says that. But things get out of hand and before you know it you're in deep, over your head. One rash act causes a landslide you have to cope with the rest of your life. You only have to look at me to see that. I want to know why I killed them both yet another part of me is frightened of finding out why I did it. It might be worse to know the reason.'

She looked as if she had gone into a world of her own again. When she spoke once more her voice was laden with sorrow. Who it was for no one in the room could even guess.

'Are they doing her for conspiracy as well as attempted murder?'

Dawson nodded.

Marie shrugged.

'It's in the hands of the CPS then, isn't it? I just hope they're as thorough with her as they were with me.'

Dawson didn't know what to say and it showed. His face flushed a deep red and he spent a few seconds clearing his throat.

Two minutes after that they all went about their daily business. It was only later in the morning that Amanda Stirling saw she had written over and over on the pad on her desk: Poor woman. Poor woman.

Marie Carter affected her like that. Made her feel that she wanted to protect her. And considering what Marie had done all those years before, that fact amazed her.

164

'Have you heard, Tiff? Your granny is like a pork scratching.' Patrick Connor was roaring with laughter. 'Best fucking news I've heard in years that is. Pity Lucy was out, I'd have liked to have seen her burnt to a fucking crisp and all. Another mouthy prat, that is.'

Tiffany carried on washing Anastasia. She knew Pat didn't expect an answer and she was tired and wired out. All she wanted was a rock and she knew that if she did what he wanted she would get one. The little girl was soaped up and slippery, her laughing face subdued now her father was also in the bathroom.

'Hello, darling! Who's Daddy's best girl then?' Pat bellowed at the child, a big grin on his face. Anastasia's little face crumpled and she burst into tears. He rolled his eyes at the ceiling as the child's screams reached a crescendo.

'One miserable whore, that kid is. Like her granny. Stick her under the grill, that will shut her up.'

Tiffany turned on him.

'That's not funny, Pat. Don't say things like that.'

He grinned and took a small package from his pocket.

'I have a present for you and all so you better be nice to me.'

He waved the small sweetie packet full of rocks at her temptingly. He saw the need on Tiffany's face and moved slowly backwards out of the bathroom.

'Come to Daddy, Tiff.'

She put the crying child back into the bathwater and went to get up. He barked his orders at her.

'On your knees, Tiffany. Come to Daddy on your knees.'

On one level she knew she was a fool, but the lure of the crack was too strong. She did as he wanted.

Anastasia had picked up a Tweenie bath toy and was chewing it, her big eyes watching the antics of her mummy and daddy.

Tiffany shuffled around the flat as he moved away from her, the bag rustling noisily and offering her the oblivion she craved. Each time she grabbed for it he moved it quickly away, laughing all the while. He was enjoying watching her beg. Seeing her haggard face turn animated because the thing she craved so much was in front of her, within reach.

As he held the bag out for a second too long she snatched it from him. Her face was almost animal-like and he watched her in satisfaction as she rummaged through it for the biggest rock, shaking his head with pride.

165

She looked terrible. Her mouth had the beginnings of cold sores, her skin was flaking and her eyes had deep black bags underneath them. Her long blonde hair looked dirty, sovereign-coloured from lack of shampoo and conditioner. She finally looked what she was: a trick buster and whore. A prostitute. This was working out better than he had expected. He had her now where he wanted her, needed her, completely dependent on him and what he had to offer. He felt like a king in his castle. Everything Tiffany did from now on would be for him and him only.

A quick call to Social Services and the baby would be taken care of. Then he would have her at her lowest ebb, could pick up the pieces for her. A vicious circle was all that was needed. Once the kid was off the scene she would be devastated and the drugs would help the pain a little. He could kill two birds with one stone. What a clever boy he was.

He smiled again as he saw her burning the crack. Her nose seemed to grow longer with each draw she took. It was a strange optical illusion as she tried to take the drug deeper and deeper into her lungs.

Soon he could concentrate on the new girl he had picked up from Paddington station a few days ago, a little bleached blonde, fourteen top whack, with budding breasts and a mouth just built for blow jobs. She was on the ball as well, a succession of children's homes had seen to that. He was honeymooning her at the moment until he gained her trust. Then he would put the fear of Christ up her and rule her through terror and drugs. If only their mums could see their little girls after he had finished with them. Now that would be a laugh.

Life was sweet and Patrick enjoyed every second of it.

Tiffany slipped sideways on to the floor, her expression glazed. He heard Anastasia splashing about in the bath and felt a moment's anger. He would have to dry the baby now and he had an appointment at four o'clock. He pushed Tiffany on to her back with the toe of his Italian designer shoe. She stared up at him, her eyes like a newborn's, devoid of intelligence and milky, as if she had clingfilm over them.

She was hooked all right. Anyone with half a brain could work that one out. She would kill for it if she had to. Just like her mother before her.

As he wrapped Anastasia in a towel and stepped over Tiffany's prone body with the child in his arms, he felt the satisfaction of a job well done.

'Look at Mummy, sweetie, out of her fucking nut as usual.'

Anastasia grinned at him, unaccustomed to the gentleness in his voice.

'Da-da.'

He laughed delightedly, singing an old Curtis Mayfield track as he dried her. The little girl enjoyed the attention from her daddy and crowed with enjoyment at his words. She had learned at a very young age that when people were nice to you, you made the most of it. You never knew how long it would last.

Patrick was holding her up and looking into her face as he sang, his smile wide and happy.

'I'm your mummy, I'm your daddy.
I'm that lady in a hat.
I'm your doctor when in need.
Want some coke? Have some weed.
You know me, I'm your friend,
Your main boy to depend.
I'm your pusherman.'

As the rush wore off Tiffany watched him singing and dancing with his little daughter and her heart hurt so much she believed that it was finally broken.

Patrick grinned at Anastasia and said gently, 'Another few years and you will dance for your daddy, won't you?'

She just clapped and clapped, her face wreathed in smiles.

Lucy stared at her supervisor in obvious distress.

'Look, Luce, everyone knows the score here and I think you should take a few weeks off then decide whether you want to come back to work. Karen Black's husband and brother were seen here early this morning, asking for you, but you didn't hear that from me, OK? I sympathise, but I really have no intention of getting any more involved than I have to.'

He was embarrassed, and a part of Lucy felt sorry for him. The Blacks weren't the type of people anyone wanted on their case. But after the events of the last few days she wasn't emotionally strong enough to cope with this rejection on top of everything else.

'What are you saying? That you don't want me back? Fucking rich that is, coming from you. I assume your scam with the Blacks will continue even though Karen is locked up over trying to murder my mother?'

'That's unfair, Lucy, and you know it.'

'Do I?'

Her voice had all its usual belligerence.

'How do I know that? I came in today for one reason and one reason only. To ask for a few weeks' grace until I get back on me feet. But you more or less tell me to leave me job because you don't want to get involved with my problems. I bet a solicitor will be interested in what's happened here this morning. You'll be hearing from mine soon.'

She picked up her bag and the supervisor's voice stayed her.

'Do you realise the animosity this has caused? I am heart sorry for what happened, Luce, who wouldn't be? But this is the Blacks we're talking about, love, and the fucking Waltons they ain't. I am trying to help you here. They are lunatics and you know that. Look what they just did to your mum. Give it a couple of weeks, see how the land lies. I'll make sure you get paid in full, I promise.'

She knew that to argue with him was futile. He made sense but she was so low that she wanted to hit out at someone, anyone.

She took her bag and walked from the office. As she passed through the factory she saw the pitying looks and ignored them. All she wanted to do was put her head on someone's shoulder and cry.

But Mickey's mother had put paid to that, only letting Lucy have the sofa to sleep on and then leaving her bedroom door open so Mickey couldn't sneak down. Her father had not been in touch and she had no one else close. No real friends she could turn to. She had her mother, ill and difficult, and not another soul to call her own.

It finally occurred to her that her life was a wasted mess, but not that she was to blame for it. At least Karen Black had family to fall back on. People who cared. Lucy had no one.

Even Marie, the cause of everything bad that had happened, would have been welcome at this particular moment in time.

As she stood at the bus stop it took all Lucy's will-power not to break down and cry. She wasn't hurting for her mother, or her home, she wanted to cry for herself. For the terrible things that had happened to her. She would never understand that her own selfishness was the real cause of every single one of them.

Patrick smiled at the little girl beside him. Her roots needed doing, and her make-up was over-heavy, but she had a certain girlish charm that he liked. And more importantly, that he knew his customers would like.

Her name was Maisie, and she had huge blue eyes, a slim body with small pert breasts and skinny bandy legs. She was streetwise beyond her years and knew the score. As she was offered a joint she took it with a cool smile.

'What is it – grass?'

Patrick nodded.

'It's good grass.'

She lit the joint and expertly drew in the smoke, holding it for a few seconds before blowing it out. She sighed happily.

'So what's this going to cost me?'

Her voice was heavy with sarcasm.

Patrick didn't answer her. She looked into his face and grinned.

'Come on, Patrick. Let's put our cards on the table. You want to pimp me and I want to be pimped. It suits me. I just want to know what's in it for me? What do I get for my trouble, and what do you *want* for yours?'

He was impressed with her acumen. Most working girls never realised they were earning an actual living, they just lurched from one day to the next, spending indiscriminately. It was refreshing to meet one so young with a bit of nous.

'What do *you* want, Mandy?'

She'd expected his reply and answered him immediately.

'I want, Mr Connor, a fair whack of what I earn, a bit of grass now and again, and if possible another girl to do doubles with. Men like that more than most people realise. I don't do hard drugs. I don't need to. Don't want to. I like to keep me head about me when I'm working. I need a few quid up front to settle a flat, and I want good protection when working the street, from the other girls as well as the punters. That's about it in a nutshell. Oh, and I will not be treated violently. I do me work and don't complain even if they're eighty years old and stink of piss. This is all a means to an end for me, nothing more.

'I will take on anyone with the money, and that includes *you*. I don't do freebies for anyone, only Old Bill occasionally to get them off my back. I am discreet, reliable and clean. Always use a condom, always have. I will not work without one even if it's for a king's ransom. I don't drink because I like to keep me wits about me, and the same goes for crack or skag.'

She smiled to take the edge off her words.

'That about sums me up. And, by the way, the name is *Maisie*, OK?'

Patrick felt a sneaking admiration for the little girl sitting in his car. If only he had a few more like her he wouldn't need to work so hard for a living. But then he liked to coerce them as well. It appealed to his dominant personality. In fact, it was a prerequisite for his daily happiness. But this little one interested him; she was more than aware of her own worth and for a whore that was a novelty. Usually they had a self-hatred that was fascinating to see, especially after a few years on the game when they were ageing faster than their civilian counterparts.

'Aren't you going to answer me?'

Maisie's voice was bubbling with suppressed laughter. She was well aware of the impression she was creating on the man sitting beside her.

Patrick shrugged.

'You got a deal, providing you're as good at the job as you say.'

She sighed with pleasure and he saw that every now and then her right eye went skew-wiff. She had a lazy eye and instead of making her look bad it made her look appealingly child-like.

'Tell me more about the double act,' he suggested.

'Just another young blonde girl. I'll do all the work, but it can be lucrative. Especially with the ones who are just a touch off actual paedophilia. A couple of school uniforms is the only kit we need. Oh, and can I bring regulars to my flat when I get in? I like regulars, they're easy and they pay more. After a while you can finish them in minutes and they give you a bonus.'

Patrick was having a hard job keeping a straight face. He was in a good mood because he had broken Tiffany and everything was working out just as he wanted. He had left the bag of rocks at her flat and phoned Social Services playing the concerned father. They should swoop on her at any minute. He would miss the kid in some ways but she was better off without a crackhead mother so he could convince himself that he had done it for the best.

He debated whether to slap this little bitch in the face and put her through her paces right now, give her the fist and subdue her. But he liked her in a funny sort of way. She reminded him of himself at the same age, knowing instinctively what she wanted. He had been the same.

Instead of hitting her he smiled.

'I know just the girl for you to work with, Maisie. Her name is Tiffany and she's as amoral as you are.'

Maisie smiled back and held out her hand.

'Let's shake on it, I think we have a deal.'

As Patrick shook her hand he was beaming all over his handsome face.

'You have obviously done this before. What brought you to London?'

She shrugged like a woman a million years old who had seen it all.

'Let's just say my last pimp tried to move the goal posts, shall we, and leave it at that?'

As Patrick looked at her hard he realised that this girl was a complete one off, and for some reason she actually made him a bit nervous. She was *too* self-contained and cold.

Emotional people could be easily controlled; being unemotional himself he had soon realised its usefulness to him. He was seeing too much of himself in this girl and now it was bothering him. She was as calculating as he was and he knew that was only a good thing while she worked for him and not against him. He would have to watch her closely.

It was amazing in someone of only fourteen.

Linda Harrison was thirty-seven years old and felt that as a social worker she had seen it all. She'd arrived at Tiffany's flat with the police at a little after seven-thirty. She had tried to gain entry twice and been unsuccessful. The little girl's crying was clearly audible from outside and Linda could see the mother slumped in the lounge as she looked through the letter box.

PC Kelly broke the door open with a lock buster and they entered the flat together. Tiffany was completely out of it. Before he had left, Patrick had given her a large glass of Ribena laced with Librium and she could hardly move. Her mouth felt as if it was full of cotton wool and her head was heavy and sore.

The crack and the sedative had poleaxed her. As she saw the woman pick up Anastasia she knew she should try and stop her but could barely move. Her speech was slurred, and her eyes refused to focus. She just wanted to go back to sleep. The social worker looked strange, her teeth seemed to be too big for her mouth and face was blurred round the edges. It was the tiredness, Tiffany thought, the extreme tiredness. She caved in. She couldn't take any more. Her eyes were burning from trying to keep them open. She went back to sleep, the need to close her eyes overwhelming.

She dimly registered the policeman and something told her she was in trouble but she just didn't have the energy to think about it, let alone *do* anything about it.

'I'll phone an ambulance, shall I?'

PC Kelly's voice was flat, without emotion.

Linda Harrison picked up Anastasia and comforted her.

'I have to arrange temporary care for this poor little mite. Has the mother got a pulse?'

Kelly nodded.

'She's just out of her brains. How do you stand this, day in, day out?'

He sounded disgusted.

She didn't answer. Instead she got Anastasia a drink in a bottle and tried to calm the child down.

'Could be the first time this has happened, let's not write her off too quickly. Though according to the father of the child she's a crack addict and a prostitute. He's been worried for a while, apparently.'

She sighed.

'Tiffany's been in and out of care, and up until now she was supposed to be a good mum. Pressure, I suppose.'

They heard the ambulance in the distance.

When they'd taken Tiffany away, Linda packed a few bits and pieces for Anastasia and as she did so, registered the fact that the place was basically clean and the environment child friendly. Nice clothes, plenty of food in the fridge, and educational toys. This girl had tried to be a good parent whatever the policeman might think. She wondered what had gone wrong. Why she had just stopped coping.

Linda hoped the police left this as a case for Social Services and didn't summons the girl for child neglect and endangerment. Then she saw the bag of crack on the table and sighed. If the child had chewed on these the mother would have been locked up as soon as she came round in hospital. That reminded her – she needed to get the hospital to alert her as soon as Miss Carter was capable of communicating. She hoped she wouldn't have to take the kid permanently, but judging from the bag of crack she doubted the girl would be capable of looking after her child again. Crack addicts were like heroin addicts: totally dependent, physically as well as mentally, on the product of choice. It was heartbreaking to observe but it was far worse for the kids caught up in their parent's nightmare.

She looked into the small heart-shaped face of Anastasia and instinctively hugged her. She was a nice child, seemed well fed and cared for. It was all such a shame. Why did these girls feel the need to take drugs that were so potent and destructive? What was wrong with a bit of grass or a nice cold glass of white wine? Linda was a child of another generation and saw soft drugs as harmless. Couldn't understand the need for complete oblivion. She had never *needed* it.

She rubbed her eyes and finished packing the child's things. These cases always made her feel sad. She gave Anastasia a bit of chocolate and settled her down as best she could. She knew a nice foster family who were mixed race and hoped they were available to take in this pretty little girl for a while. This child needed some loving and Linda was determined to provide it. Even if it was only short-term.

On the mantelpiece was a photo of the child with her mother, a good-looking girl with lively eyes and a sweet smile. She looked very different from the unkempt ragbag Linda had seen slumped on the settee.

Anastasia pointed at the floor and said clearly, 'Mummy's pipe.'

The social worker closed her eyes and bit her lip. The child looked so pleased with herself. So very, very pleased. With those shocking words all Linda's kindly intentions flew out of the window. She was disgusted and shocked that the child was aware of what her mother was doing.

Linda's face grew grim. The sooner this poor child was out of this flat and away from her mother the better.

Carole Halter was in the club, her broken nose still evident and her make-up much heavier than usual.

'You can't work with that boatrace, I'm sorry, Carole. Fuck me, you'll scare off all the punters.'

Lizzie Banner was the head girl and well liked. She knew that Carole understood what she was saying. Though she felt sorry for her, there was no way she was working looking like a victim of a car crash.

'It's just simple economics, Carole. The other girls will get all the work anyway. No disrespect, but you only get the dregs these days.'

Her voice was kind but the barb hit home.

'I'm here because of economics, love. I need the bastard rent.'

Lizzie sighed.

'I can give you a sub and that's it.'

'How much?'

'Twenty quid.'

Carole was insulted and desperate. She shook her head and answered viciously, 'Shove it up your arse, Liz.'

Lizzie, hard and well able to take care of herself, grabbed hold of Carole's dress.

'Be careful I don't feel the urge to shove it right up yours, love. Now piss off and come back when you can fucking work.'

Carole saw the other girls laughing at her. Saw their unlined faces, their trendy clothes and make-up, and felt old. Old and ugly. Her days in this club were over and they all knew it. It was the Cross for her and the knowledge made her feel deeply depressed. All the time she was in a club she'd felt she had a bit of kudos. Felt a bit more upmarket than her pavement-walking counterparts. She hated getting in and out of cars. Hated putting herself up for violence on a daily basis. At least in the club they used a designated hotel and the porter would rap on the door when the time was up. The men were friendly because you had spent a while chatting to them and getting pissed with them.

Now it was King's Cross in all fucking weathers. Or Shepherd's Market in a cheap coat, having to compete with the little runaways and rent boys. She walked forlornly from the club and out into the bustle of Soho.

Clubbers were walking around, their smiling faces beacons to each other. The theatre crowd were making their way to warm restaurants to discuss the night's entertainment, and the homeless looked on with expectant faces, hoping for a few quid from the people walking past. She would miss it all, had loved the camaraderie of the club, the laughs they'd had at the men's expense. Had loved that feeling of belonging somewhere, of having somewhere to go where she could have a few drinks and a few laughs and get paid for it.

An over-boisterous young man shoved past her and knocked her into the road. She gave him the finger and walked through to Old Compton Street where she picked up an unlicensed cab to King's Cross. She had to earn tonight, had nothing, not even a pack of cigarettes. Her last few quid would go on this cab. Her mind was in turmoil now about how the hell she was going to cope. She'd spent every penny she had and her benefits were not due until next week. She was boracic lint and she was scared.

At the Cross she walked slowly towards the other women and

girls and saw them eyeing her suspiciously. It was dark and the wind was getting up. She had dressed for the warmth of the club and now she was starting to freeze. Her strappy shoes were no insulation from the cold pavement and suddenly she felt the urge to cry.

A large brunette with enormous breasts in a front-laced corset walked over to her.

'All right, love?'

Her voice was friendly and Carole responded in kind.

'Not really. Look at me boat.'

The other woman nodded sympathetically.

'You must be hard up. Want a fag?'

Carole took the proffered cigarette gratefully.

'What's it like tonight?'

The woman shrugged. 'Same as usual, a few bites, but it's early.' She drew heavily on her own cigarette. 'Come round the corner, it's better there. Gets rid of this wind and you can check for cars coming.'

A man kerb crawled past them and they both smiled into the window of the car but it drove on.

'Wanker!'

Carole laughed at the woman's exclamation. As they walked round the corner she saw a small crowd of other women and her heart sank. It occurred to her that she was being set up. A young girl with a long curly wig looked her over. For a few tense seconds Carole was paralysed with fear. They could rip her to pieces and she would be unable to defend herself.

'You look like you could do with a drink.'

The girl handed her a bottle of brandy and Carole took a deep swig from it gratefully.

'Thanks, love.'

They stood around stamping their feet and chatting. Every time a car came along they all smiled and walked out under the streetlight. When one got a punter they waved her off with ribald comments and eventually Carole relaxed.

'You got a pimp, love?'

This from the big woman who called herself Rosalie.

Carole shook her head.

'You got a choice of two here, one of Pat Connor's number twos or little Mo Reinhard. Go with Mo, he's fairer. He don't mind the older ones either. Connor only really likes the kids.'

'Where can I find him?'

'He'll find you, love, don't worry about that.'

Patrick Connor had put her back here on the street. Indirectly, she knew, but if she had not tried to help Marie and Tiffany she would be in a nice warm club now. Well, she would pay the three of them back. She didn't know how but she would.

Especially Connor.

A car pulled up and Carole had her first ride of the night.

As she climbed in she could smell after-shave and a magic tree. The man was small with a friendly face and badly cut hair. He drove to a piece of waste ground and shoved a tenner in her hand. As he undid his trousers he grabbed her hair and pulled her face into his lap.

It was all over in minutes and she realised too late that he had not put on a condom, the dirty bastard. When she had tried to raise her head he had pulled her hair so hard she nearly cried out. He came in her mouth and she gagged.

He was still laughing long after he had kicked her unceremoniously from his car. She spat on to the dirt, her body instinctively rejecting him, and then looked at the tenner in her hand. This was her life from now on and the sooner she accepted that the better off she would be. But it rankled.

She'd known her club days were nearly over anyway but chose to blame Patrick, Marie and Tiffany.

It made her feel so much better.

Chapter Thirteen

Karen Black was not impressed with Holloway. She hated the smell, the dimness and the close proximity of other women. She had already been warned that she had to shower regularly or she would get a kicking from her cellies or her cell mates. They were a pair of nutcases, one in for murder, the other for drug trafficking and conspiracy to murder. So she wasn't exactly top dog in her new environment.

As she walked through to her reception visit she was angry. Angry, hungry and tired. She had found it hard to sleep. The constant noise had driven her mad; the coughing, crying, laughter and shouting.

She saw her husband and tried to smile. He had to tell other people she was coping. He was her lifeline to the outside world and what was being said about her. She ambled over to the little table like a woman at one with her new surroundings.

'All right, Kal?' His voice was nervous and that placated her a bit.

She answered aggressively.

'What do you fucking think? What's the story then, on the street?'

She had the prison patois already and her husband was impressed. He was her second cousin on her father's side and they actually looked alike. The Blacks had a reputation for marrying in the family and her sister's two children were accredited to her own father as opposed to errant boyfriends.

Karen and Petey looked like brother and sister as they sat holding hands across the table.

'Everyone is talking about it, Kal. Fucking hell, you're a legend, mate! All I get all the time is, How's Karen? How's she holding up? Especially in the pub.'

She was practically preening. This would pat down her ruffled feathers and her husband knew it. He could not tell her the truth:

that people were cold towards them all. That the public consensus was she was well out of order. That she was as bad, if not worse, than Marie Carter, who in fairness had been out of her brains.

'How's me mum? Is she over the temper yet?'

'Well, she's upset obviously.'

In fact Rita Black had publicly washed her hands of her daughter. Unlike Karen she had an idea of how far you could and should go in the pursuit of revenge. Especially on a council estate filled with like-minded people. But Petey knew that now was not the time to mention any of this. Not unless he wanted to start looking for someone with a bollock donor card anyway.

'Love her heart. Tell her I'll drop her a line, OK?'

He nodded once more.

'Have you retaliated yet, Petey?'

He had been dreading this question. As he shook his head Karen frowned.

'What do you mean, no?'

She sounded upset now.

'Listen, Karen, we need time to see how the land lies before we all end up inside, don't we? If we do anything now then they'll suss it's us straight away.'

Karen didn't answer.

'Like I said, Kal, everyone is talking about you. I mean, you are like fucking Marilyn Monroe, an icon.'

She was placated once more. Felt a rush of adrenaline at the knowledge that she was top girl. That she was being talked about, that she was *someone*.

'Kevin Carter is on the missing list . . .'

She laughed at that.

'Sorted that cunt and all, ain't we? Fucking do that to me! Now people know what they get if they fuck with the Blacks.'

She was glad she had burned Louise Carter. It had helped her achieve her aim to be the baddest woman in her own little world, and it seemed she had achieved it with flying colours. Kevin Carter had run away. She wished she had done something like this before now.

Petey knew exactly what she was thinking and wondered what the hell was going on in his wife's head. They had even gone to Lucy Carter's workplace to try and make amends but he couldn't tell his wife that. They had received threatening letters and calls. The police were watching them all like hawks, and his wife was sitting in her own fucking fantasy world where she was the dog's gonads. Kevin Carter had disappeared all right, but he was also known to be looking all over the smoke for the men of the Black family. Petey had been told that by many people. Kevin Carter wasn't going to let his daughter's beating and his wife's injuries go unpunished. And who could blame him?

Yet Petey's wife thought she was Don Corleone and could do as she liked with no repercussions. He could smash her one himself for all the trouble she'd caused. But he knew he couldn't burst her bubble. Not yet. Karen had enough on her plate. Instead he smiled and got her another cup of tea and a king-size Kit-Kat.

Alan Jarvis was tired out, emotionally and physically. As he loaded another twenty keys of grass into the trunk he yawned loudly, making the two men with him start ribbing him.

'You are one lazy ponce, Alan.'

He ignored them. Used to their way of carrying on now, he didn't bother to retaliate. A key was 2.2lb. Loading in twenty at a time was over 40lb each lift and he was not used to manual work. Hated it in fact. But he wanted this load out of sight as soon as possible and that was why he was working fast and hard. The black bags were also awkward to lift and slippery from the sweat on his hands – sweat that had more to do with nervousness than physical exertion.

He hated these swaps, they made him nervous. It was still early evening. If anyone came to the yard they would suss the situation out in a few seconds. He had so much money now it frightened him, but in the process he had put himself in a situation he couldn't escape.

If he once voiced even a hint of negative thinking he felt the animosity from everyone concerned. They were all taking coke and all suffering from the Nick Leeson syndrome. All were in a drug-induced dream world where they felt and believed they were invincible.

Hence this daytime swap, in the open, in *his* yard where people dropped in and out all the time. Scrapyards were like that. Other mettlers would shoot in for a chat and a cup of tea or a beer. Talk about the prices they were getting or new contacts they had made. It was a sociable business, always had been. And they looked out for one another. Everyone scammed somehow, usually the taxman, but drugs were an anomaly these days. The sentences frightened people.

179

No one wanted to be associated with them if they had half a brain.

Not the people Alan knew anyway. He had the money to buy a shorter sentence if he had a capture, he was aware of that now, but he didn't want to do six years, six months or even six days.

He had to have a proper talk with Mikey Devlin. He was losing it. It had been bad enough doing the swaps at Thurrock services, but at least they'd had a chance of escape from there. In his own yard it was the capture of a lifetime for Old Bill. Especially where Alan was concerned.

As if his thoughts had conjured him up Mikey screeched into the yard in his Mercedes sports.

Davey and Jonas both stopped what they were doing. Alan felt the tension and wondered briefly what was going on. But these days Mikey Devlin made everyone nervous just by looking at them.

Mikey jumped out of the car, wrapping a bicycle chain around his fist. He looked demented with anger. Even his bald head looked angry. Alan felt his heart sink down to his boots. He racked his brains to think what he could have done to bring down Devlin's wrath on him.

But it was Jonas who was the recipient of the violence this time.

'Jonas, you slag!'

As Jonas tried to run, Mikey brought the chain down across his head with gusto, and pulled the boy to his knees. Then he began to lay into him. As Alan and Davey saw the blood and skin raining from him they moved away from the spray. They were powerless to stop it. The beating went on for over five minutes. Finally spent, Devlin threw the chain on to the boy's bleeding body and kicked him in the guts.

'Get that cunt out of my sight, Davey!'

He was breathing heavily, his blue eyes with the glazed look that was usual for Devlin these days. He was coked out of his brains and it showed. His heavy body heaved from his exertions and his head glistened with sweat. He looked the bully boy that he was.

Davey dragged the unconscious man towards his Lexus. He was shaking with fear. Mikey was going off more and more lately, for the most trivial reasons.

'What was all that about?'

Mikey didn't answer but walked into the Portakabin. Alan followed him warily. Mikey was cutting himself a line within seconds. As he snorted it he brought his head up and closed his eyes.

'He's grassed us up. That little cunt grassed us up.'

Alan felt his face drain of colour, so acute was the fear.

'Grassed us up?'

Devlin nodded. Then, seeing Alan's face, he started to laugh.

'Not to the filth, you prat. He's discussed us with the fucking coons in Brixton. Larry Marker told me this morning. He was approached by them to do a drop.'

Alan was non-plussed.

'What's wrong with that?'

Devlin looked at him as if he was a lunatic.

'What's wrong with that? Are you fucking stupid or something?'

Alan didn't answer, he wasn't sure what to say.

'He arranged a drop but never mentioned it to me, did he? So that is two fucking bastard things he's done, ain't it? One he gave them an in on what we are doing, and two the ponce was going to tuck me up.'

Alan didn't answer. Devlin had lost it big time and this fact alone terrified him. He finally took a deep breath and said, 'He *told* you about it, Mikey. You gave him a drink, remember? Last weekend, right here in this yard.'

Devlin's face was a picture as he tried to remember.

Then he shook his head like a mad dog and shouted, 'Did I fuck? What you trying to do, Jarvis, fucking wind me up or what?'

He was bellowing now.

'You taking the piss? You stuck up his arse or something? Is he your bum chum?'

Alan closed his eyes and hoped against hope that when he opened them the man in front of him would somehow have disappeared.

'For fuck's sake, Mikey, calm down before we have Old Bill on the doorstep.'

As he spoke Marie walked into the cabin.

'You can hear you two shouting down the road.'

'Who are you?'

Devlin's voice was calmer now.

'I'm Marie, Alan's secretary, and you are?'

Mikey stared at her intently for a few seconds before saying, '*You* have a secretary, Jarvis? Is this a piss take?'

Marie raised her eyebrows slightly.

'This is a business, a scrap business. I have to have someone to do me books and that so the taxman don't come sniffing round,' Alan told him.

The logic of the argument and Alan's deliberate way of talking penetrated the coke-induced haze. Mikey nodded and Marie could see him physically fighting to calm himself. Finally he forced a smile and walked from the office. She felt the tension seep from the room at his departure.

When she heard his car screech off she looked at Alan and said calmly, 'You bloody fool. What are you involved with now?'

Louise was in a haze of pain but she would not let it get the better of her. The strength she had always prided herself on served her well as she fought her way to health. The nurses and doctors were amazed by her. She hardly grimaced at the constant changes of dressings and only took morphine when the pain was overwhelming. But they didn't know that what kept her going was pure hatred.

Marshall's whole existence had been destroyed once more by Marie. Louise had only a few photos left of him now and she took that very personally.

The loss of the house and everything in it was as nothing to her. But her son's clothes were gone. His childish toys and paintings. Little stories he had written at school. All gone. And it was *Marie's* fault. Louise's husband had walked away from her, had taken *her* side as usual. Marie had always had her father in the palm of her hand and it would never change. Louise was better off without him. As she was better off without her daughter. The shame of Marie's prison sentence had been hard to bear but she had held her head up high and if anyone asked after her daughter would give them a look that should have floored them and kept silent. People had soon learned she had disowned her eldest child.

She tried to clench her fingers underneath the covers but the pain reminded her that she had to keep still. Stop moving around. She breathed deeply. Stilled the erratic beating of her heart. She might be a medical miracle, but that was nothing as far as she was concerned. She wanted out of here and into the world again.

Then she would pay them all back one hundredfold for everything that had happened. She had seen her bitch of a daughter off once and she would do it again.

Marie had tried to drag Marshall into her dirty life but her mother had stopped her. And she *would* stop her. Marshall had been as disgusted with Marie as her mother was. Having those bloody kids, humiliating the family over and over again. They were

182

respectable yet Marie had dragged them into the dirt as if it meant nothing. Every time Louise thought of how her daughter had taunted her, the pain was as fresh all these years later as it had been at the time.

That deep voice of hers that sounded like a whore's. 'Oh Mum, get a life. Who cares what the fucking neighbours think about me? I don't, so why should you?'

But Louise did care, she cared deeply what people thought about her. She had to run the gauntlet at the gates, at the shops, even at church. It was the pitying looks she had hated more than anything.

Other women with daughters, good girls who kept themselves to themselves and didn't give their bodies to any man with a pleasing smile and a few pills, looked at her with such sorrow she could have beaten them to the ground. She didn't want their sympathy. She was better than them, better than them all.

She went to Mass every morning of her life, took communion, she was *clean*. It was her daughter who was tainted, not *her*. It was Marie who had made them into a laughing stock. Marie who had dragged their name through the dirt. Had taken her family and destroyed it without a second's thought.

She stopped the tears from flowing, enjoying her own strength and mental stamina. Enjoying the hatred because it kept her going.

Once she was out of this bed she would stop that bitch once and for all. Of that she was determined.

'Wake up, love.'

The voice was penetrating and Tiffany struggled to open her eyes. Patrick was staring down at her, looking concerned.

'You all right, Tiff? I've been worried out of me mind.'

She blinked at him a few times before she croaked, 'Where am I?'

Patrick kissed her tenderly on the forehead before he answered.

'You're in hospital, Tiff. Don't you remember?'

She shook her head and the action made her wince. Her pretty face was grey and haggard, her eyes like a dead fish's. There was no life in her any more. The Librium he had dosed her with had left her with no memory of what had happened to her.

'You took an accidental overdose, Tiff, though they think you tried to top yourself. One of the neighbours heard the baby screaming and called the police. They've took Anastasia away, love. Social Services.'

As Tiffany took in what he was saying to her she pulled her lips back over her teeth. Before she could scream he had placed one hand over her mouth to quiet her.

'Shhh! Listen, Tiff, they'll do you for child neglect and endangering the baby. They're going to nick you, sweetheart. I told them I didn't know what they were talking about but they won't listen to me, will they? I said what a good mum you was and that. But someone has stuck the knife in, love. Probably one of the neighbours.'

Tiffany's world was tumbling around her ears and Patrick watched her with morbid fascination. She believed everything he said. That fact pleased him. On another level she disgusted him with her weakness. He hated weakness even though he played on it in everyone he came into contact with.

'What am I going to do, Pat? Poor Anastasia, she'll be so frightened without me.'

'Put this coat on and these shoes and we'll just walk out of here before Old Bill arrives. Then I'll get you a good brief, OK? I'll sort it out, I promise. She's my kid and all, you know.'

He sounded so sincere she believed him. She allowed him to help her sit up and drink a glass of water, then he put on her coat and shoes and they walked sedately from the busy ward and out of the hospital.

It had been so easy.

In Patrick's BMW she broke down crying and he petted her as he would have done a puppy or a kitten. She was absolutely in pieces and this knowledge made him feel powerful and in control. On the way to his flat he stopped and picked up wages from girls and lumps of cash from his dealers.

Business went on no matter what happened. Tiffany understood that so didn't wonder at a man who was still carrying on his nefarious enterprises while supposedly distraught over the loss of his little daughter.

He gave her a medicinal rock and she sagged against the leather upholstery of the car and felt her body relax and her mind empty.

'That's the way to go, Tiff. Put it all out of your mind for a while and chill, girl.'

She smiled tentatively and drew the smoke into her lungs once more. If ever she'd needed a lift it was now.

Patrick dumped her at his flat in Docklands and, after warning her not to burn the carpets or make a mess, left her to go about his daily business.

He had a living to earn as he frequently pointed out, and now

184

they had the court case to get the baby back he needed as much poke as he could get. Tiffany was grateful and it showed.

As he kissed her goodbye he said quietly, 'Have a bath, Tiff. You fucking stink, love.'

She nodded sadly and watched him walk away from her when she needed him more than ever.

She clutched the small bag of rocks Patrick had given her and sighed heavily. One hit to get her head together and then she would plan what she was going to do. Alone in the big apartment overlooking the Thames she felt lost. She wanted her little girl and Anastasia was gone, taken from her like everything had been all her life, starting with the loss of her mother and culminating in the loss of her child.

Tiffany was completely obliterated by crack within fifteen minutes of Patrick walking out on her.

Petey Black was locking the door on his D-reg Ford Sierra when he heard a familiar voice behind him.

He froze in fear and terror.

'All right, Pete? Burned anyone's house down today?'

Kevin Carter's voice was heavy with sarcasm.

Petey turned around, eyes scanning the street to see if he could do a runner.

'No escape, mate. I made sure of that.'

Kevin's voice was almost friendly.

'It was nothing to do with us, Kev. I swear on me mother's grave, mate. It was that mad bitch Karen. You know what she's like. I told her and all . . .'

'Shut the fuck up!'

Petey saw the shotgun. It registered instantly as Kevin took it out of a Sainsbury's carrier. He shook his head in disbelief.

'Leave it out, Kev. What the fuck you doing, man?'

Kevin laughed.

'What does it look like? I'm going to shoot you.'

Petey finally realised that this man was over the edge. Completely over the edge. His face crumpled and he started crying. Petey heard the loud click as Kevin cocked the gun and put his hands to his face instinctively.

Then a voice came from nearby.

'What's going on?'

It was an old voice, querulous, and Kevin swore under his breath, turned and walked away quickly. Petey collapsed on to the pavement. His legs felt as if they had completely turned to jelly.

He was still crying when his mother-in-law found him outside the house an hour later. She took him inside. She had his stuff packed and was ready to say her goodbyes. When she'd finally got the full story from her son-in-law Rita sat smoking in her favourite chair and cursed her own daughter over and over again. Bethany's daughter Tamara cried, convinced she was going to get hurt as well because it was her mother's death that had started off this chain of events.

'I hate Karen, Nana, I really hate her! I just want to be here quietly with you. I hated living with Mum and her men and the drugs. I hated it when men sat me on their laps and petted me and told me what a lovely little girl I was. I hated her for letting them *do* it. Marie Carter done me a fucking favour!'

Even her Nana couldn't answer that one.

Sally Potter knocked gently on Marie's door then opened it and walked inside. Marie was lying on her bed in a towelling dressing gown.

'How are you?' Sally asked.

She shrugged.

'OK, I suppose, considering.'

Sally sat on the bed and smiled, her round face over made-up as usual even though she was about to go to bed.

'I'm still working, you know. On the streets. Can't seem to keep away from it, can I?'

Marie felt sad for her but didn't show it.

'If they find out, you're straight back inside, you know that.'

'Maybe I want that deep down and just won't admit it. I felt I belonged in nick. I was there so long I had a good network of friends and companions. I feel lost out here. I think I went back on the game to feel I was in a familiar environment, with people who accept me for who and what I am.'

'Want a cup of tea?'

'You stay there, I'll get it.'

While Marie waited she wondered why Sally had picked tonight of all nights to open up to her. They knew each other's past form so she assumed it was because she had been a prostitute that Sally felt she could talk to her. People out of the game never understood the power it had over the women involved. For most it was a form of self-hatred. For others it was a substitute family. For the majority a means to an end.

Ten minutes later they were sitting side by side on the bed and talking as if they had known each other all their lives.

'Where are you working?'

Sally sipped her tea and swallowed deeply before she answered.

'I worked the Cross for a while but now I advertise meself in the local paper and visit people's houses. Sad bastards most of them with scruffy furniture and smelly bathrooms but the money is good.'

She sighed and then continued.

'I work for a woman over North London. She basically provides the mobile and the initial contacts. She puts in the adverts and we pay her a percentage as scrum money. So none of it can come back to me, see. I can only get caught if the police come to the actual house I'm working in. But I still do a stint with the girls on the street too because I enjoy the camaraderie. Trouble is, I have to be back here by ten-thirty!'

They both laughed.

The door opened and Amanda popped her head round.

'All right, girls?'

They nodded, feeling like school kids on a sleepover.

'I'm late passing you, Marie. From tomorrow you can have the ten-thirty curfew.'

She waited for Marie to thank her. It was a beat before she answered, 'Thanks.'

Amanda felt awkward. Smiling, she left the room, closing the door behind her.

'They act like they're doing us such a big fucking favour. Ten-fucking-thirty at our age!' Sally's voice was angrier than ever. 'Big fucking deal.'

Marie didn't answer her. Then she said seriously, 'Where the fuck will I go till ten-thirty at night?'

Sally laughed loudly.

'Come up the Cross with me!'

Marie grinned and shook her head.

'Been there, done that!'

'Nothing like flashing the old clout to give you a boost!'

'Old being the operative word where we are concerned!'

Sally screamed with laughter and Marie felt a spark of affection for this woman who was obviously desperate for human contact.

She wondered if that would ever happen to her. She hoped so. She was still dead inside. Wary of people. The only ones she wanted were her children and they were so far away from her mentally they might as well be on the moon.

'Be careful, Sally. Don't get yourself banged up again or you'll regret it, mate.'

'I suppose so, Marie. But it gets lonely out here, you know. Some of the girls you meet these days are so young! Honestly it's heartbreaking. Their stories . . . The world has changed all right since we were banged up, and not for the better from what I hear.'

'Life is what you make it, Sally. And there's another old saying I heard in nick: people only do to you what you let them. It's true, you know.'

Sally's full lips were quivering.

'I still think about him, you know. My old man. Bastard he was but I loved him. I was out selling me fanny and he was shagging anything with a pulse under the age of sixty. He was sex mad, him. All he talked about, thought about.'

She shook her head in reluctant admiration.

'He'd shag a table leg on a Monday if the time was right and we were skint.'

'Why did you do it then?'

Sally stared at the wall opposite as if she was picturing him in her mind.

'He got a real bird, didn't he? Fell in love. I could accept all the one-night stands and the slagging around but I couldn't handle him loving someone else. You know what I mean? I couldn't take that. It was the ultimate rejection. I had lost me kids over him. Lost me family. Me self-respect. Then he went and fell in love, didn't he? I couldn't live with that, Marie. I would see him dead before I saw him with someone else. I had told him that many times. He was like a disease, ate at me like a cancer. I killed him and nearly killed her. The worst of it all is, I'd do it again. Without a second's thought. I still love him. I expect I always will.'

Marie had a hand over her mouth. She wanted to cry for Sally and for the love that had destroyed everything in her life. Was still destroying her even after all these years.

'Oh, Sally. I'm so sorry.'

She shrugged.

'I miss him. That's the worst part of it all, I still miss him. His smell. His voice. The way he ate. The way he laughed. If I close me eyes I can see him smiling at me.'

The tears were flowing from her eyes and Marie put an arm around her shoulders and pulled Sally's head on to her breast to comfort her. Just then Amanda put her head around the door once more and with an exclamation left the room as fast as she had entered it.

Sally wiped a hand across her face and said loudly, 'That's all we need. Now she thinks we're a pair of carpet munchers!'

They both started laughing, high raucous laughter that reverberated all over the halfway house.

Tiffany walked around Patrick's flat. She felt ill with worry over her child and terrified of being arrested by the police. Guilt was eating at her. She was up for neglecting Anastasia, her worst fear had been realised, and she wasn't mentally strong enough to cope with it.

The phone rang, making her jump in the quietness. She heard reggae music and Patrick doing a rap on his answerphone. This annoyed her for some reason. Then a girl's voice came on the line, low and deep; she was obviously black.

'I am back, baby, and looking for you. Ring me.'

Tiffany sat on the white leather sofa and stared at the machine.

The voice was lovely, like softest velvet. But it was the confidence in it that struck her most. This girl, whoever she was, *knew* that he would ring her back. She wasn't a working girl, they didn't have this number. Tiffany had his child and even *she* didn't have this number. No, this girl was a real bird. A serious contender. The knowledge depressed her even more.

What had happened to her? Where was the girl who had sworn she would make something of her life? Who'd lain night after night in a children's home planning her future? She caught a glimpse of herself in the ornate mirror over the fireplace. She looked dreadful and this exacerbated the feelings welling up inside her. Self-disgust and shame were threatening to swamp her.

In a moment of stunning clarity she knew she had lost her child and that it would be an uphill struggle to get her back. She was a drug addict and a whore, like her mother before her.

Picking up the phone she dialled a number. Tears blurred her vision as she said into the receiver: 'Jason? Is that you, Jason?'

Verbena Melrose heard the girl's voice and the distress in it and said gently, 'Is that Tiffany?'

She listened to a torrent of words so confusing it was impossible to understand a thing. She passed the phone to her husband.

'I don't know what she's on about. She's crying.'

Oswald Melrose took the phone from his wife.

'Calm down, Tiffany, and tell me what's wrong. No, listen, Jason is in bed and I'm not getting him up at this time of night. He has school in the morning. Tell me what's wrong and I'll help you, child.'

Gradually he calmed her down with his quiet firm voice and his common-sense approach.

'Where are you?' He shook his head in despair. 'What do you mean, you don't know where you are? And who took the baby?'

Verbena's eyes opened wide.

'They've taken her baby – why?'

Her husband waved his hand at her to keep quiet. Eventually he put the phone down.

'What's happened?'

He sighed. A six foot five Trinidadian with soft brown eyes and the shoulders of a giant, he was a consultant haematologist at St Thomas's Hospital. Well respected for his work with blood disorders, he was a kind man who loved his wife and family with a passion.

'The bubble has burst, Verby, the girl is back to square one,' he said sadly. 'The baby has been taken and she is in a flat somewhere, she's not sure where, and she's on drugs or my name is Elton John.'

Verbena closed her lovely green eyes in distress.

'As you heard I told her to get a cab over here. Whether she will or not I can't say. The girl is in pieces. Patrick Connor! If I had him here, I'd . . .'

Oswald was lost for words.

His wife slid into his arms and cuddled him close, or at least as close as her five foot two inches would allow. He kissed the top of her blonde head.

'All we can do is wait and see if she arrives. But I don't hold out much hope. She's gone, I'm afraid. The drugs have got her now.'

Chapter Fourteen

Oswald and Verbena watched as Jason ate his breakfast. Neither of them knew how to tell him that his sister had been on the phone last night unable to say where she was or even who she was with. As he ate his bacon, eggs and plantain banana he was unaware of the tension between his parents.

Never a morning person Jason was quiet as he ate and drank his grape juice. He looked tired, but he had been studying hard the night before. Since starting sixth-form college he had really thrown himself into his academic studies and his parents were pleased to see him trying so hard. Never an A student, he had to try harder than others to keep on top. They were proud of him and it showed.

Verbena started to load the dishwasher. She saw the sun streaming through the window and felt a small lift in her spirits. Nothing bad could happen on a day like this, surely? Her white German kitchen looked clean and cared for; their whole home was bright, and she liked to think beautiful.

Jason completed their life and, as much as she liked Tiffany, Verbena was jealous of the closeness he shared with her. She knew it was silly, that he loved her as much as he would have loved his biological mother. Probably more, considering the home he had come from. But she still felt a chill whenever Tiffany became involved with them. Oswald, however, thought the world of the girl. But then, he was a nicer person than she was. Always would be, always had been.

Tiffany wandered in and out of their lives and Verbena found it unsettling. Felt that she let Jason down when she didn't get in touch for months and that it upset him. The girl was so unstable. But, like Oswald, Jason kept up his haphazard relationship with her whenever she felt she needed it. Verbena felt guilty for her own thoughts but that didn't change anything. She was *annoyed*.

She wished she was more like her husband. He was a good man, a decent man, and she loved him with a vengeance. Loved him so much it hurt her sometimes just to look at him. Since the first day she had seen him she had been in love with him and it had lasted twenty years. She adored him and he adored her. Now Tiffany was in trouble and she knew she would have to grit her teeth and help her because that was what Oswald would want from her. She would wait for Tiffany's next call and then see what she could do.

But the girl was part of her son's past and that was what hurt Verbena the most. She didn't want him to have a past. She wanted his past to consist of her and her husband. The years before he had come to them she wanted forgotten, only that wasn't going to happen and she would have to accept it. But why should he remember squalor, and drugs, and a mother who'd killed when he could remember laughter and brightness and parents who loved him to distraction? Holidays and Christmases full of laughter and joy instead of violence and drugs, hunger and distress?

Oswald would say he needed to remember because that was a part of his life too, whether she liked it or not. But Verbena didn't agree.

She wanted a picturebook upbringing for Jason but no matter how hard she tried to give him one, his past life would always mar that.

'All right, Mum?'

She had been in a world of her own. Now she turned to her son and hugged him. He was a handsome boy with a good physique and great bone structure, a kind nature and an electric smile.

'Sorry, Jason. I was miles away. I'll get my car keys.'

'That's OK. I'm walking in with Kelly and Tamsin from down the road.'

Oswald laughed.

'That's it, son, get the girls while you can. Only don't get caught like I did.'

He looked at his wife lovingly. This was a family joke.

When Jason had left, the house felt so empty to Verbena she longed for the days of his childhood when he would always be up to some mischief and their home constantly rang with childish laughter. Oswald guessed his wife's thoughts and pulled her roughly into his arms.

'Let him grow up, girl. He will be a man soon, you know.'

His voice still had a trace of the West Indian accent which had always turned her on.

'I wish we could have had children of our own as well, Ossie.'

He hugged her tight to his chest so she could smell his own particular smell: Paco Rabanne and fresh sweat. She loved the scent of him, always had. He kissed her gently on the lips. Even this early in the morning her make-up was perfect, he noticed.

'His sister is obviously in need of help. If she was our daughter we'd do what we could, right? Well, she's our son's blood and so we have to help if we can. She didn't have the advantages he's had, remember that.'

Verbena nodded.

'But she's so like her mother it worries me.'

Oswald just stopped his eyes from rolling upwards in annoyance. Her silly jealousy annoyed him at times. As much as he loved Verbena she could be such a snob. Consequently his voice was short as he answered her.

'Listen, Verby, that boy is half his mother and half his father, yet all ours. Stop this stupid talk and thinking. Let me get to my work without worrying about you too.'

He was sorry he'd spoken immediately. Verbena looked so hurt he kissed her again, hugging her close.

'OK. If she gets in touch I'll do what I can,' she promised.

'Ring me as soon as you hear anything, OK?'

He picked up his briefcase and left her then in her bright kitchen, her beautiful home that was feeling emptier and emptier by the day.

She made herself a cafetière of coffee and pulled the *Daily Mail* towards her to scan it. She took out one of her secret cigarettes and lit it, trying to concentrate on the news. But her ears were constantly alert for the phone which she knew was going to ring any moment and bring her family grief. Drag them into that girl's petty dramas and make Ossie feel he had to take on the cares of the world.

Kevin Carter turned off the radio as he pulled into Alan Jarvis's scrapyard. It was a beautiful day. He looked at his daughter's face as she walked towards him and remembered how lovely she had been as a child. Even as a grown woman with all the troubles she had endured Marie was still lovely.

Only now she tried to hide it. Her clothes, hair, everything was toned down so you had to take a second glance to make sure you were seeing a good-looking woman and that it wasn't just an illusion. He felt heart sore for her. None of her problems had really been her fault and he knew that, had always known that.

193

'Hello, Dad.'

Her voice was happy yet subdued. He guessed, rightly, that it was because of her mother. The fire would be another thing to lay at her door as far as Lou was concerned, but it was his fault it had happened; he was the one who'd gone after the Blacks, not poor Marie.

'Any chance of a cup of tea?'

He followed her to the Portakabin, made small talk until he had his cuppa then said seriously, 'Your mother is on the mend. No one can believe how strong she is, but then they never had to fucking live with her, did they?'

Marie was upset to hear the bitterness in his voice.

'She's been through a terrible ordeal, Dad . . .'

He held his hand up to silence her.

'I know, I know. But she'll make sure we never hear the end of it for the rest of our natural lives. Anyway, I've left her. I should have done it years ago.'

Marie's face showed the complete astonishment she was feeling.

'You what?'

He smiled sheepishly.

'I've left her. Didn't pack any bags, of course. No clothes left, were there? All I have is what I stand up in. But I left all the same.'

Marie was looking at him as if he was a maniac and it annoyed him.

'You can't just leave her now, Dad. Not while she's like she is . . .'

He ran his hands through his hair in agitation. Marie didn't feel she knew the man in front of her, so changed was he.

'What's the difference? I mean, I was going on the trot anyway. I couldn't cope with her well and supposedly happy so I definitely couldn't cope with her burned and miserable. No fucking way, Pedro. Her and Lucy can sort themselves out. Fuck them.'

Marie could not believe this was her father. Her quiet inoffensive father who had always taken her mother's side to keep the peace.

'She needs you, Dad.'

He sipped his tea then started to roll himself a cigarette.

'She don't need no one. Never did. All she wanted was kids, and even then she only wanted fucking Marshall. She should have had a house full of men and then she'd have been happy. You and Lucy were thorns in her side. I remember when you was only a few weeks old, she was crying one night and I comforted her, like, the way you do, and she looked at me and said seriously, "I don't like this baby, Kev. I really don't like it." I thought it was the baby blues, but it wasn't. She didn't want you from the second you were born and were a female. But Marshall! Oh, that was a different kettle of fish. All over him like a cheap fucking suit.'

He pointed the roll-up at her and she watched, fascinated, as the smoke curled around his yellowed fingers.

'She was a fucking weirdo from the off and I never saw it. We had to get married, did you know that? She got me lovely. Picked me like a ripe peach, she did, and I fell for it. Well, enough is enough. I've wasted too much of me life pretending I was happy and content and liked being dictated to by that fucking female Hitler, and I ain't putting up with it no more.'

It was as if a dam had burst and he was overflowing with hurt and pain. Marie listened to what she had always known at heart.

'Wouldn't let me visit *you*. Oh, no! Couldn't even mention your name without a fucking full-scale war erupting. And I went along with it. Wasn't man enough even to stand by me own daughter, the only person in the house I had ever really cared about. I admired you, do you know that? You told her where to get off when I never had the guts to. I never even got me end away, she put paid to all that. I just settled the bills and escorted her round the fucking shops and to weddings like a fucking badge of honour.'

'Oh, Dad . . .'

Marie felt his pain as if it was her own. She was crying and unknown to him taking all the blame on herself. She had caused all this and would pay for it for the rest of her life.

'Anyway, I'm here about Tiffany. I saw Cissy Wellbeck and she said that the Social Services had taken her baby and Tiff was on the missing list. I been round her flat. Old Bill had broken in and now the door's boarded up. I thought you should know.'

Marie sat down on her typing chair and sighed heavily.

'What is it with this family, Dad? We seem to be cursed. Since I got out there's been nothing but fucking trouble. I attract it.'

She was crying and Kevin wanted to comfort her but didn't know how. Because in some ways what she'd said was right.

Marie's return had set in motion a whole train of events. Though she was a victim too, she was also the catalyst for the major changes in all their lives.

Patrick had not come home and Tiffany was getting more and more wired. The rocks were long gone and she was relatively straight. Now she had to face the demons that were plaguing her. She was amazed to see a photo of Anastasia on the mantelpiece but guessed, rightly, it was for the benefit of the women he brought here as opposed to any real manifestation of fatherly love.

Her mother had been right, and that rankled. Her mind alternated between thoughts of her daughter and of drugs. In all honesty she didn't know which she wanted more.

She sat in the stainless steel kitchen and looked out over the river. It was bustling today, and she thought of all the people going about their lives without all the shit she had to deal with on a daily basis.

The phone rang constantly and she listened to the different voices and wondered who they were. Most sounded so normal, especially the women. It occurred to her that Patrick Connor had a *life*, a real life. That was something that had never occurred to her before.

She was sweating and knew she needed something soon.

She wandered into the bedroom and began opening drawers and cupboards, unsure what exactly she was looking for. She knew he would be too shrewd to keep drugs in the house. Then she opened a shoe box in the wardrobe and smiled widely.

It was full of money, twenties and fifties bundled up into neat thousand-pound wraps. She sat on the floor filled with fear and excitement. There was so much money, surely he wouldn't miss a little bit? All she could see as she looked in the box was rocks. Rocks, rocks and more rocks. She suddenly realised she was smiling, Anastasia gone from her mind as if she had never existed.

Taking two bundles of cash she stuffed them into her shirt and five minutes later was gone from the flat.

Tiffany flagged down a cab and made her way back into London. She was a woman on a mission and determined to fulfil her dreams as soon as possible.

She missed Patrick by forty-five minutes.

Marie was at Bethany's grave. She had locked up the Portakabin and made her way to East London Crematorium, needing proof of her own badness more than ever before. As she looked down at the dilapidated little headstone she felt the tears begin.

The sun was high and birds sang in the trees. Overhead an aeroplane buzzed and Marie wondered briefly where the passengers might be going. She had never been on a plane. The only time she had ever travelled was when they moved her from prison to prison, and then it wasn't like she saw any of the places she was confined to. Durham was apparently a fine city. She only saw the filthy old castle she was incarcerated in. She had never done most of the things normal people took for granted. She had been to Southend a couple of times as a teenager with friends, and once to Walton-on-the-Naze with her mum and dad when she was a kid. They had stayed in a caravan and she had enjoyed that. Her mum had seemed brighter on holiday, and they all seemed to put their natural antagonism on hold for two weeks.

Her whole life had been such a waste.

But, unlike Bethany and Caroline, at least she still had a life of sorts.

She laid the roses on the grave and then sat on the damp ground. She started to clean the plot, pulling up weeds and grass so it looked tidy. As she cleaned she talked to Bethany, trying to say sorry but unable to find the right words. She was assailed by memories instead.

She remembered them all going out, their hair styled in the trend of the day, bleaching it as they got older. Remembered Bethany's donkey-like laugh that made everyone grin when they first heard it. Saw dingy pubs and clubs where they had been the top girls. Fights they had been involved in and won, a few they had lost but that was because they had fought men.

How had they ever believed that they were living good lives? What had made them think that giving themselves to men for money or presents or even a few drinks had made them special?

She wiped her eyes with a tissue she had found in her pocket.

'Well, well, well.'

The voice broke into her reverie and she turned to see Janie Douglas, Caroline's sister, standing beside her.

'You're the last person I expected to see here today.'

Marie was mortified, and couldn't answer. Instead she started to stand up. Janie forced her back on to the grass by pressing down on her shoulder with a strong hand.

'Don't run off, Marie. I won't do anything, I just want to talk.'

'What about?'

Janie shrugged.

'I don't really know.'

She sat beside Marie and opened a large plastic bag. She took out a flask of tea and some sandwiches.

'Sad fucker, ain't I? I do this every year, come to the graves and clean them up, see how they're doing. You seem to have saved me a job. It's me day out when it's sunny. Caroline's over there.'

197

Marie didn't answer her, she just stared, waiting for the attack she was sure was going to come.

'Poor Bethany. Like Caroline and you as well she never did see the big picture. You all thought you were so clever with your drugs and your outrageous behaviour. And where did it ever get any of you, eh? Now your father is threatening people with guns and Karen, the silly fat whore, is locked up, and you think the whole world is against you.'

'What do you mean, my dad threatening people with guns?'

Janie looked at Marie and satisfied herself she really didn't know.

'Ain't you heard he went after Petey? Put the fear of Christ up the fat ponce and all, I can tell you. You look well, Marie, you look young. I expect that's from being banged up without any real problems to put lines on your boat, eh?'

Janie was overweight and looked years older than she actually was. She had the defeated look of a woman who had too many kids and not enough time. Her once lustrous auburn hair was shapeless and lank, needing a wash, her blue eyes were faded and her skin a spotty mess.

She saw Marie looking closely at her and smiled. Even her teeth looked grey, a couple chipped or missing.

'I married Stevie Baily.' It was almost said by way of apology for how she looked and they both knew it. 'Rotten ponce he is. I envy Beth and Caroline in a way. Always young and always remembered with affection.'

She poured them both a cup of tea and Marie took hers gratefully. They drank in silence for a while, listening to the sounds around them, the busy road, seeing the mourners at recent funerals milling around.

'Why did you do it, Marie?'

She shook her head. This felt surreal, sitting at Beth's graveside being asked questions about something that had happened so long ago but was still raw in her mind. Still felt as if it had happened only yesterday.

'I really don't know, Janie, and that is the gospel truth. I have gone over that day time and time again and I can't pinpoint anything that could have caused it. I was out of me box, I suppose, and it just happened. I think we must all have had a fight. It wouldn't have been the first time, would it? We were renowned for fighting, weren't we? All three of us were hard bitches. Remember Beth's T-shirt? "I can go from nought to bitch in two point five seconds!" '

They both smiled, remembering.

'She was a girl, all right.'

'Is that really true about me dad, not just Black talk? You know what they're like.'

'They are really feeling it. Public opinion is strong against them and Karen's mother has washed her hands of her. You're almost a martyr figure at the moment. I mean, at least you was out of your nut, like. Everyone knew you were an addict. You all made sure people knew that, didn't you? It was almost your badge of office. "We are bad girl druggies and we don't care who knows it".'

'We were so stupid and we really didn't see it.'

Janie shrugged and opened the sandwiches.

'You would all have been dead by now anyway if it hadn't happened. Heroin addicts don't make old bones, everyone knows that. Look at Gillian Wise. Found propped up against her radiator, dead as a fucking doornail, been there over two weeks. 'Course, the heating was still coming on and off. She was a maggot-ridden corpse when they finally found her. One of the neighbours had complained about the smell. Smacked out of her tiny mind as usual. That was ten years ago. It could have been any of you, couldn't it?'

Marie nodded sadly.

'I suppose so.'

They were quiet for a few seconds, thinking about everything, then Marie said: 'Gillian taught us how to highball. I remember it clearly. You get two mates. One injects you with speed and one injects you with heroin at the same time. As they meet in your body it blows you out of your head. Bethany loved it because it was dangerous.'

Janie shrugged. 'She would. Beth always had to go too fucking far. You all did. I'm only sorry it ended in such tragedy. I remember that day so well. I'd been up to see Caroline, score a bit of grass for Stevie, like. She was out of her box!'

She smiled at the memory.

'Funnily enough your brother Marshall was there. He nearly shat himself when he saw me. In case I told your mum, I suppose. He was waiting for you to come round, you'd passed out on the floor. Caroline was jacking up and that always made me feel sick so I shot off. That place was a shit hole. The smell! It was awful.'

They were both quiet again, remembering Marshall and how he'd died.

'I never knew he was there. Do you think he saw it all and

199

that's why he killed himself?' Marie asked.

Janie shrugged again.

'Could be. I never told anyone I saw him there. Everyone had enough on their plate. Anyway I wasn't getting involved with Old Bill so I kept shtoom. The way you do.'

Marie lit a cigarette with shaking hands.

'Poor Marshall, he so wanted to be one of the in crowd. If my mother had known she would have launched him into outer space.'

'Her little soldier, she called him. It would have destroyed her,' Janie agreed.

'She was destroyed anyway, only I did it to her and not him. When he killed himself she stopped living, apparently.'

Janie poured them both more tea.

'Depends what you call living, don't it? Cold woman, your mother. No one likes her though she has the sympathy vote at the moment, of course. Have you seen her?'

Marie shook her head.

'No. She hates me.'

'You're in good company then. She don't like anyone much, does she?'

Marie found herself smiling.

'I'm glad I saw you, Marie. Would you do me a favour?' Janie asked.

She nodded.

'Of course, anything.' She was desperate to make amends and it showed on her face.

'Live the rest of your life, live it for them two. Make something good come of it all, mate. It's happened, as the kids say these days, deal with it.'

Marie didn't answer her, too choked with emotion. She had come here to try and find comfort from her dead friends. Instead she had found it in the shape of Janie Douglas, a woman she had laughed at and ridiculed for being straight all those years ago.

Life was strange sometimes. Very strange.

Tiffany was freebasing and it felt good.

She had spent five hundred pounds in one go and had sought and achieved complete oblivion. She lay on the cold floor of a squat in Willesden and scanned the room for her friend Rosie.

But she was long gone. She had taken some of the money with her, Tiffany remembered that much, but what it had been for she couldn't for the life of her remember. She closed her eyes and let the good feelings roll.

Lionel Green was watching her as she lay on the filth-strewn floor.

'Who the fuck is she?'

Another man shook his head.

'Rosie brought her, she's loaded.'

Lionel raised his eyebrows. 'Loaded? How loaded?'

'She had a couple of grand when she came in. Rosie's took some of it and gone to score some skag, but that one's on the rock. Out of her box too by the looks of things.'

Lionel studied her. She could be pretty if she tried, but she looked like a street-living girl, dirty and unkempt. But unlike those girls her clothes were good quality and her nails still relatively clean. He noticed things like that, being a street liver himself. He prided himself on his acumen. It had kept him alive for ten years on the street. He had been eleven when he had run away from home. He had never gone back to the little terraced house in Essex and he never would.

He didn't miss Tilbury, but he missed his mother. He missed his brothers but didn't miss his stepfather with his great big boots and fast fists. He had a new life of sorts now and a new family.

He slid across the floor to Tiffany and she opened her eyes and smiled at him.

'My baby. I have to get my baby.'

'She's on more than rock, has Rosie jacked her up?'

The other boy shook his head, unconcerned.

'Might have, who knows? Do you want a quick blast?'

He offered Lionel the crack pipe.

'Nah, never been my bag. I like a drink.'

'Shame, 'cos she has loads of it and I intend to stick with her till it's all gone.'

'Has she got a baby?'

The other boy was getting annoyed.

'I don't fucking know. What are you, Old Bill? I couldn't give a fuck if she's got ten kids or gave birth to a litter of pups. All the time she's got a rock she can stay here, and that's it.'

Lionel was quiet. His years on the street had taught him that was best around druggies who were too unreliable to be rational. When he was sure he was unobserved he searched Tiffany till he found the last of her money and slipped it into his jacket pocket. The others

201

would only have done it anyway once they came round enough. He watched over her until she came back into the world and then, smiling, helped her sit up. It was evening now and she had lost nearly all the day.

'You OK?'

He gave her a can of lager and she drank from it deeply.

'Come upstairs and chill out, it's warmer.'

She followed him up the rickety staircase, fighting off the effect of the drugs. On a dirty mattress they sat and talked. Lionel knew the score and started off asking her easy questions: name, age, how she knew Rosie. Then he sat back and listened to her tale of woe.

'Why don't you go back to your flat?'

Tiffany shook her head.

'I can get done for neglect, see. They can nick me.'

She started to cry.

'I don't know what happened. I've never had that before on the crack, you know. Never passed out for all that time. Now my little girl is in care and I ain't sure what to do. I ain't been to work for ages either so I don't even know if I still have a job. It's all a fucking mess.'

Lionel had heard similar stories all his life but he was moved by this little blonde girl and her sad tale.

'What about the baby's father? Can't you go to him for help?'

Tiffany had not mentioned Patrick because his reputation always preceded him and the boy might have heard of him. But she was desperate for company, frightened of being on her own.

'He's no good.'

'Haven't you anyone at all to go and get help from?'

She remembered Jason and his family. They would help her.

'Me brother, he was adopted by this couple but I was allowed to keep in touch. We were close like, you know. They would help me but I'm so ashamed.'

She was also frightened they would want her to stop taking drugs and she liked the feeling drugs gave her. Liked being able to forget her life and everything that had happened to her. Wanted the feeling of well-being the crack gave her.

She couldn't cope with all her problems without the drug and had convinced herself that she had to keep on with this life until she was capable of coping with the old one. It sounded good to her, and even though at heart she knew all she was doing was giving herself permission to dump her child she was deluded enough to think that it would not be for long.

She just wanted drugs and the feeling they gave her. She was an addict and she knew it, but she didn't care.

She opened her jacket and looked for the money she had stolen from Patrick. As she started to panic Lionel gave her the notes he had taken.

'I had to take it or they'd have rolled you by now and disappeared. If you're going to squat with addicts you have to learn to live like them, mate. They'd nick your shoes to get the money for a fix, remember that.'

She stared into his face. He was good-looking in a rough and ready way: shaved head, skinhead-type clothes and a good solid body. He had a nice smile.

'Thank you.'

'Go back to your flat, Tiffany, or to your brother's. You'll have to when this lot goes anyway, so go sooner rather than later. I'll come with you, if you want. Sort it out about your baby before it's too late.'

She was wavering, he could see that, and it pleased him. Then Rosie, with her fat legs and loud voice, burst into the room and he knew she was lost to him.

'Look what Doctor Rosie has got!'

She held up a small plastic bag of heroin.

'Put a smile on all our faces, this will.'

As she prepared the drug Lionel went out and got a McDonald's for himself and Tiffany. He also got her a large shake. He would put a bit of food into her belly and wait his turn. He liked her and the fact she had her own flat and was capable of leading a normal life at times made her even more appealing.

Rosie would need to get back to her boyfriend at some point so he would do what he was good at: wait. Then, when the time was right, he would try again.

If nothing else he might get a bit of her dough, make his life a bit easier. She might even have a tap of it. Someone who could guarantee a few quid at a time. Two grand was serious money and should be treated with respect.

If she got that much once, who was to say she couldn't get it again? You had to look at things from all angles and try and get whatever you could from life.

He had learned that many, many years before.

Chapter Fifteen

Patrick was looking all over for Tiffany. She had left the wardrobe door open and consequently he now knew she had taken money. It wasn't the money itself that bothered him, but that it would give her access to other people which was just what he had been trying to avoid.

He had spent so much time and energy isolating her so that he could do what he always did with his women, make them totally dependent on him. The kid was gone and that should have been the finish of her. Now she would get out of her brains without him controlling what she took. She had a couple of grand, enough to get herself and the whole world high. Supposing she overdosed as well? All that time and effort for nothing.

He was angry. He had already lost a girl to an overdose today, and another one had had the gall to up and leave to get married. She had gone off with a fucking punter and left him with the rent on her flat and all her bills. He had the room rented again but it was the principle of the thing. She had bested him and that he would never forgive.

He didn't understand what was happening in the world any more. It was as if, for some reason, everyone was out to annoy him. Well, when he got his hands on Tiffany he was going to break open her fucking face for her. He was going soft in his old age, that's what was wrong with him, and the girls were taking advantage.

Now Tiffany, in whom he had a personal interest, was taking the piss. She was robbing him and he was going to take it out on her hide when he got his hands on her. And he *would* find her, he was determined on that.

Within twenty minutes he was at Maxie James's house. Maxie was in bed with his wife. Patrick gave her a ton and told her to get herself something to eat and drink and come back in a few hours. One look at his face and she did as he requested. Patrick was known as a mean fuck by everyone and she often wondered why Maxie kept up an association with him.

Maxie, who was also pissed off, was quite aware that now was not the time to say anything about it. Patrick had the manic look that meant he was after aggravation big time. In this mood he would argue with his own fingernails.

'What's the prob?'

Patrick was definitely not in the mood for his friend's street talk at this particular moment in time.

'What is it with you and the way you talk?' he bellowed. 'Why can't you talk fucking normal? "What's the prob?" What kind of fucking expression is that?'

Maxie stared at him and swallowed deeply. He was getting fed up with Patrick, a lot of people were. Who the hell did he think he was?

'Listen, Patrick, I don't know who the fuck has rattled your cage but you come here and get me out of my bed, where I was fucking the arse off me wife, and then give me a hard time. So I have to ask, what is *your* fucking problem?'

Patrick debated whether to kick his friend's head in or leave it for the moment because he had more pressing things on his mind. Maxie was a mate, probably the only real mate he had. He was more than aware of the fact that people were avoiding him these days. He was getting too big for everyone; no one knew how to handle him any more.

So he smiled – the smile that had got him whatever he wanted when he was a kid. It made him look innocent and trustworthy, and he turned it off and on when he needed to make people feel secure.

'Tiffany has gone and I have to find her.'

Maxie ran his fingers through his dreadlocks.

'What the fuck is the big deal with her, Pat? She's just a slag, why all this interest?'

He frowned.

'She *is* the mother of my child, remember.'

Maxie blew air out of his mouth noisily to denigrate Patrick's words.

'Lots of women have your kids and you still put them on the game. I thought you'd get the kid taken care of as usual and then have her in the palm of your hand.'

Patrick started laughing.

'Skin up, Maxie, I need to chill out. She's only fucking robbed me, ain't she? The bitch is stronger than I thought and she's rebelling. That's all it can be.'

His voice was almost jocular.

Maxie started to roll a joint.

'Let her go, Pat, she ain't a bad kid. You have enough girls, why do you want Tiffany so much?'

Patrick thought about what his friend had said. He thought seriously and hard.

'To be honest, Maxie, I don't know. I enjoy making women into what I want them to be. When I first met Tiff and realised who she was, I got a buzz, you know. I had fucked the mother and now I could have the daughter. It's a fantasy, ain't it? Lots of men get off on it. So I went for it and enjoyed it. She is my son's sister as well, don't forget. It just appealed to me. And she is a good-looking girl. Not a patch on her mother, though. Marie was a hard horse to tame, I can tell you.'

He took the joint and puffed on it deeply. It was good grass as he'd known it would be.

'I thought Tiffany would be a doddle but she is stronger than I thought. So much stronger that in a way I admire her spunk. But I *have* to break her now, I have to break her once and for all.'

Maxie looked at his friend in awe.

'You are one weird fuck, Pat, do you know that?'

They both started to laugh.

'Leave her be. She was happy enough with the kid, and a good mother and all. Just leave her alone, let her go.'

Patrick's eyes narrowed as he looked hard at his friend.

'What's the matter, Max, you want to go there then?'

'Of course not, you dick! Don't start all that. I just think she's a nice kid. Leave her be. You're too big for all that crap.'

'You just don't get it, do you, Max? I enjoy it. It gives me a buzz every time I break in a bitch and she starts to earn for me. The money is nothing to seeing them brought low – all women are basically fucking whores. Some do it for life with one geezer but that's still for money, ain't it? Housekeeping or whatever you want to call it, they still get kept, don't they, taken on holiday, whatever. Then they have kids and the poor bloke they snared is fucked for life. Well, not me, mate. I dump my kids like I dump my women. No one has any claim on me.'

Maxie drew deeply on the joint and finished it.

'This calls for a pipe, Pat. I can't believe I'm hearing all this. She's just one little bird, what's the big deal?'

Patrick put his head in his hands and sighed deeply.

'I have to trounce Tiff now, don't I? If I don't it will be all over the pavement before the week is out and we'll have more girls thinking they can do what the fuck they like. So I will rip her fucking heart out and laugh while I do it. She thinks she's on a roll. Well, she ain't. I want a crew out looking for her and I want her by the morning.'

Maxie was astounded and it showed.

'You *are* joking?'

Patrick shook his head.

'You want me to get the boys mobilised for an errant bird, is that what you're saying?'

Patrick nodded.

'Tell them if they don't find her I will personally beat all their fucking brains in, and that, Maxie, is a promise.'

'You sure you ain't in love, Pat?'

Patrick laughed loudly.

'I'm in love all right, Maxie, have been for years, but it's with meself! I even shout out me own name when I'm coming!'

Patrick was sure she would be traced so he relaxed. But he promised himself that when he finally got his hands on Tiffany he would teach her a lesson she would never forget. Taking his hard-earned money and trying to run away, who did the whore think she was?

When his fist came into contact with her smooth-skinned face she would finally realise who was the boss in this relationship. He was looking forward to it.

Marie had put everything on disk once more and tallied the overseas accounts. Though the scrap business was lucrative it did not take Einstein to realise that the money spent by Alan, and the money he earned, were two completely different sums. After seeing Mikey Devlin in the office she knew that some sort of skulduggery was afoot, and guessed it would be drugs or guns. Maybe both. They were the real money spinners, she had listened to enough women talking in nick to know that.

She was worried, not just for Alan who was a kind man and had given her the opportunity to be employed but also for herself. She could not risk getting involved even on a peripheral basis with drugs, or any other illegal enterprise, as she was on licence and would stay on it until she was dead. Her whole life could be jeopardised through his shady dealings and she could not take that chance.

There was already too much going on for her with her kids and her family. She needed to be able to think and it was getting harder by the day. Every second was filled with thoughts of how to sort everything out, and every second told her it was useless, that she could do nothing because she had to keep such a low profile. Patrick Connor was the problem, she knew. He had taken any chance of a decent life from her and from her daughter. History repeating itself. Now her mother was on her conscience too.

She was hurting and Marie couldn't even go and see how she was because Louise had no interest in her. Would just want her away, as far away as was humanly possible. She remembered her mother yelling at her once that she wished she would die so she would not have to listen to any more tales about her and what she had done. Now Marie could understand her point of view. Hearing about her own daughter's downfall had broken her, so Christ knows how Louise must have felt all those years ago. And the same man who had brought her low was now doing the same thing to her daughter, her little Tiffany, whom she wished with all her heart was just a regular young girl with a regular life.

She needed somehow to frighten off Patrick Connor, make him leave her child alone. But how? She knew she had to do it but wasn't sure how the fuck she could achieve her aim.

In her heart Marie acknowledged that she had been planning to do something drastic since the time she had been to her daughter's flat and seen the state of her. It was trying to work out *what* that had been the problem. She was willing to go away again, this time for ever if it gave her child the opportunity to make something better of herself. Without Pat, the girl would stand at least a chance in life. With him hanging round her neck, she was finished. Marie knew that better than anyone.

She heard a noise and turned to see Mikey Devlin in the doorway. He smiled at her, wired as usual, and Marie stared back at him for long seconds before she spoke.

'Can I help you?'

She had a good voice, deep and husky.

Mikey grabbed the crotch of his trousers lewdly and answered, 'Oh, yes darling, there is something you can do.'

Marie stared at him, the same dead-eyed look she had perfected in prison, and retreated into silence. Once again it was her salvation.

Mikey was uncomfortable.

She sat there on the typing chair staring him out, her face

completely expressionless and her eyes telling him she had no interest in him whatsoever, that he was nothing to her but a nuisance. For the first time in years he felt embarrassed.

Women usually wanted him. He knew it was chiefly because of who he was and what he did. He accepted that and used them as and when the fancy took him. They were a type, and they were a type he was used to. They wanted a bit of gear, a few quid, a good night out and the glory of spending a few nights on his arm. It was a good deal. He got laid and they got a bit of kudos.

Some were only kids, but grown-up enough to fill a short, low-cut dress. Others were grown women with a good mouth and the nous to bring him off and make him laugh. He was used to a different reaction altogether from the one he was getting from this good-looking, cold-hearted, murdering bitch before him.

He was high as a kite and now he felt malicious. He would bring her down, get a reaction.

'Murdered any of your mates lately?'

He was grinning at her, daring her to answer him.

She smirked back at him and it made her look very sexy.

'No. Have you?'

Her answer threw him as she knew it would. He floundered.

'Very fucking funny!'

She shrugged and carried on staring at him. He soon realised she would not speak unless spoken to. For the first time in years he was uncomfortable with a female and the knowledge amazed him. She was actually making him feel nervous!

'You done a lump, love, and I respect that . . .'

She interrupted him, saying scathingly, 'Fucking right I done a lump, and to be honest I did it well. I kept me head down and me trap shut. If you ever get a double life I hope you can cope as well. I dealt with the scum of the earth in there. I was A-cat and I done every maximum prison in the country and learned how to take care of myself. So I resent someone like you, who has never done a bit of bird in your life, talking to me like I am a cunt.'

It worked as she knew it would. He was a hard nut, but one who had never had to smell a real prison, let alone sleep in one. The nearest he'd got was a night in the cells for a D and D. She knew that in his world the fact she had done a lump would bring her the respect she wanted, and she was going to use that to her advantage because this man could be the saviour she was looking for. If she played him right she might just be able to use him to get her daughter a decent chance in life.

Mikey stared at her for long moments and she knew he was battling it out with himself whether to smack her one for her front or afford her the respect he would give a male lag.

'You got a big trap, lady,' he said finally.

She laughed.

'And you have a big ego. If your cock is half the size you'd be worth a fuck on the strength of that alone.'

Her words were so outspoken that he started to laugh. No one had challenged him like that in years. She was the first person to give him grief since he could remember.

She laughed with him, the tension in the cabin evaporating in seconds.

He saluted her.

'I apologise. You have the creds and I have to give you the respect due. Come and have a drink with me. Friendly, that's all. Just as friends.'

She picked up her bag and grinned.

'If you are very, very good you can buy me a sandwich too.'

He was still shaking his head at her front and smiling as they drove out of the yard. Alan drove in. When he saw them in Mikey's car together he felt as if someone had punched him in the solar plexus. He felt bereft because he thought the world of Marie and realised that his feelings for her were far more serious than he had first thought.

If she got caught up with Mikey Devlin then she was heading straight back to prison, and he only hoped she saw that before it was too late. He kicked the tyre of his car and hurt his foot. As he jumped around the yard he was swearing his head off.

The two men watching from the right-hand side of the yard wrote everything down in their notebooks.

Tiffany had heard that someone was looking for her. She also had a good idea who it was. Her newfound friend had scored for her again and they had cabbed it across London to a squat near Docklands. It was a dive, worse than the place they had left, but by all accounts it was safe.

She was freebasing once more and the oblivion she craved so much was a long time coming. She was becoming immune now and needed more and more to get the high she was seeking. A

211

dark-eyed girl with red hair and bad skin offered her a needle. Tiffany looked at it for a few seconds before nodding.

It was an urge she had, a craving to get off her face and out of the present. That seemed imperative to her at this moment. Patrick was bringing her down, worry about him ruining her high.

The girl injected her in the arm and Tiffany lay against the wall and waited for the first rush to come over her. When she slumped backwards the girl rifled her clothes, took her shoes and jacket and left the squat five hundred pounds richer and better dressed than she had been in weeks.

Tiffany was still out of it when Maxie found her.

As he looked down on her skinny body lying in the filth of the squat he felt sadness come over him. She had defecated, wet herself, and white milky vomit hung in strands from her mouth. Heroin always made people sick the first few times. To be a heroin addict took time and effort.

The two men with him looked at her in distaste.

'I ain't picking her up, Max.'

Eddie Loyal was adamant about that. Big and blond, he was dapper and well-dressed.

Maxie grinned.

'You are because Patrick wants her and whoever delivers her gets a grand for their trouble. Should cover the cleaning bills.'

Eddie shook his head in disgust.

'Always me, I always get the fucking shit jobs.'

Maxie was laughing; he could relax now she was found.

'Just pick her up, white boy.'

In the car on their way to Pat's office in Spitalfields Eddie was still moaning as he negotiated the traffic. Maxie lit another joint, and said loudly in the voice of W.C. Fields, 'I always wanted a white chauffeur!'

Even Eddie laughed at that and they cracked jokes until they got to the gym.

Tiffany, in the boot of the Mercedes, could hear the noise but had no idea where the fuck she was. She vomited again and the sour smell made her eyes water.

The fear had not set in yet. She was still too out of it to realise exactly what was happening to her.

Marie ended up having an early dinner with Mikey. He was enjoying her company, she was being charming and chatty, and it had occurred to him that this woman had done more time than anyone he knew. In his world the ability to do a long stretch and come out relatively normal was something to be proud of. He admitted to himself if not to her that he could not have handled it.

'You find a place inside yourself and you retreat into it. You have to free your mind and then you don't feel so confined. It was the smell I found hardest to cope with. The stench of other people: sweat, despair, hatred and anger. It's a smell you never, ever forget. And it's a smell you never want to go back to, believe me.'

He nodded, fascinated. Men didn't come and open their hearts about their stretch. Men kept quiet about it all or bragged about how they'd done their bird on their head. No trouble.

But this woman was telling him about things he could only imagine. She was putting into words his greatest fears. He watched her eat, she was graceful and precise in everything she did, and he suddenly felt protective of her.

'What were the screws like?'

She shrugged.

'I was A-cat, as you know, so I went to maximum security. Like Durham – well, Frankland. The Island. I was kept away from the men, of course.' Marie smiled. 'But I was treated pretty much the same as them, I expect. Cookham Wood towards the end. Plenty of women doing lumps there. Most women, though, had killed partners or kids, or were drug dealers. It was the same everywhere you went. That fucking smell felt like it was following you from place to place.'

He was nodding again, aware that they were getting a lot of strange looks in the pub restaurant from his cronies and friends alike. For him to be seen with a woman over the age of twenty-five was unusual, but actually to be having a conversation with one was unheard of. He found himself enjoying the experience.

'How did you feel when you got the sentence itself?'

Marie looked thoughtful before she answered. He was once more aware of what a good-looking woman she was. She could have been stunning, if she had wanted to stereotype herself. He was glad she didn't, it would have taken away from her natural dignity.

'I had a hard bench, you know. Really tough judge. But I was gutted even though I had resigned myself to it. You can't go round murdering your mates and expect to get away with it, can you?'

He laughed.

'I know a few people who have! Me included.'

She laughed with him.

213

'The worst of it all is, you come home to nothing. Everything and everyone you knew has changed. The areas, the clothes, even going on a bus is a shock because you have no concept of how much things cost nowadays. It feels so odd, you know. In prison you are static, the same thing day after day, and the newspapers don't prepare you for what you are coming out to because you haven't experienced it for yourself. I was used to an environment where physical strength brought survival. Now it's all about money and getting more of it. Thatcher's children, I think they call them these days.'

'So you came out to nothing? What about Connor, the black ponce – didn't he give you a drink?'

She shook her head then lied for her own ends.

'What, him!' She laughed. '*He* took me daughter, his son's sister, and put her on the game and on drugs like he did me. Now I'm biding my time until I can take him out. I've been away once and know what I'm letting meself in for, but it would be worth it to see him beg for mercy for what he has done to me and mine.'

She watched carefully for Mikey's reaction. He looked angry. Like most men the thought of whoring made him uncomfortable. Men who dealt in women were a one off in many respects. Other men looked down on them for it and they knew it. She was going to cultivate this man if possible and use him.

He covered her hand with his and Marie suppressed the shudder that ran through her body. If she had to she would sleep with him, she was adept at sleeping with men she didn't like, had done it for years. She was determined to get her daughter away from Connor, no matter *what* or *who* she had to do.

She might be putting herself up for more trouble from the filth but that was a chance she would have to take. This man could help her do what was necessary to get her daughter away from Patrick so any association with him would be worth it. He was interested in her, in the fact she was a double lifer. She would use that to her advantage.

'At the end of the day, Mikey, I love me kids.'

'Fucking hell, love, I ain't father of the year but even I love me kids. Especially me son, Mikey Junior. He is me life. I would kill for him.'

Marie gave him her most winning smile.

'Same here, Mikey. It's exactly the same for me.'

She sighed.

'I really have enjoyed meself today. It's hard for me, you see, I don't have anyone to talk to about me time away. No one else who understands, you know? Thanks for listening to me.'

He was practically preening himself now at her praise.

'Anytime, mate. Listen, I'll give you me mobile number, all right? We should get together more often, don't you think?'

He was leering at her and she smiled at him as if he was the most interesting and handsome man she had ever met in her life. It was as if the years had melted away and she was up for a trick once more. She was shocked at how easy it had been to slip back into the role of prostitute once more.

'That sounds good to me.'

He was calculating what she would be like in the snore after so long without it. He was also wondering if she'd had any lesbian encounters she could regale him with. Marie was interesting and fuckable, a winning combination as far as he was concerned. She would do wonders for his credibility, had the creds and the brains to make something of herself in this world. Everyone knew women were far more ruthless than men. Men got mad and women got even, there was a big difference.

On top of all that, though, he genuinely *liked* her and that fact amazed him more than anything. He had never liked a woman before in his entire life and that included his overbearing mother, God hurry up and rest her irritating old soul.

Patrick opened the boot of the car and understood immediately why Tiffany had been placed there. He stepped backwards at the stench.

'Oh, for fuck's sake!'

The car was behind the gym in relative seclusion. He stared down at her for long moments, his anger reaching volcanic proportions. Maxie and Eddie watched in trepidation as he dragged the girl out by her hair. He was livid. To see a woman in such a filthy state went against everything Patrick believed in.

'You fucking, filthy whore!'

He was spitting with anger. He dropped Tiffany on to the concrete like a bag of trash and started kicking her. Then he rained blows all over her head and torso, his whole body heaving with exertion. Suddenly, Eddie could watch no longer. He dragged Patrick away from the unconscious girl.

'That's enough, Pat. Enough! She has had enough! You want to kill her and go away for a piece of shit like her?'

Maxie watched in morbid fascination and made a mental note to give Eddie his own crew – he was one brave motherfucker. No one else he knew would interfere when Pat was like this, least of all himself.

Eddie was holding Pat down on the ground. He was frightened himself but could not watch the girl take any more punishment. Hitting women was not an option for him and deep down he had lost a lot of respect for Connor because he'd been so violent towards a defenceless girl.

'Enough, Patrick.'

He lay there, breathing heavily. Eventually Eddie let go of him. He got up heavily, his every movement exaggerated, and stared at the blond-haired man before him.

'Are you all the fucking ticket, Eddie?'

Eddie just stared back at him and didn't answer.

'That is my fucking bitch and my property. You do what I tell you because *you* are also my property.'

Eddie wiped one large hand heavy with gold rings across his face.

'I ain't no one's property, Pat. I mean that. I work for you because I *choose* to, but my work does not involve watching a little seven-stone bird get a kicking. Not off *you* or off *anyone*.'

Maxie watched the two men closely. He admired Eddie for his stand but also thought he was a fucking headcase.

'Get him away from me, Maxie,' Patrick growled. 'Get him away from me *now*.'

Maxie walked a few steps towards Eddie who whirled round to face him.

'Don't even think about it, Max. I will go but not until he leaves that girl alone. She has had enough, I tell you.'

His eyes were pleading with Maxie to back him up. Maxie made a decision that would affect the rest of his life.

'He's right, Pat. Leave go now. Look at the state of her, she's had enough.'

Patrick looked from one man to the other and weighed up his chances against them both. Spitting on the prostrate girl, he turned and walked away.

Maxie shook his head sadly.

'He won't let that go, Eddie, you realise that, don't you?'

He shrugged.

'I ain't in the business of beating up women or kids, Maxie, and I don't think you are either. Now help me get her into the car again, she needs a hospital and soon.'

They placed her gently in the boot this time. She was bleeding profusely and both men were aware of the dangers of HIV. After all was said and done she was a brass and they were the worst carriers of every disease because they were notorious for not doing anything to help themselves. The two men drove Tiffany to the hospital in silence.

Oswald arrived there three hours later after a call from the ward sister. When he saw the condition Tiffany was in he was shocked and sickened. She was not only badly beaten but also showing all the signs of drug addiction. A social worker informed him that she was signing an order for the girl to be sectioned into a mental hospital until they could decide what to do with her. She explained the situation with Anastasia and how Tiffany was being prosecuted for child neglect and endangerment.

Oswald listened with wide eyes and a heavy heart, said he would do all he could to help his son's sister and that he was willing to do whatever was necessary to get her back on track. The fact that she had given them his number spoke volumes as far as he was concerned.

When the woman had left he sat holding Tiffany's hand until she opened her eyes again.

'I knew you would come,' she said painfully. She was having trouble talking because of the bruising around her face. 'He'll kill me for this.'

'Who? Who will kill you?'

Oswald's voice was deep and rich and she closed her eyes against the kindness in it.

'Anastasia's father . . . Patrick Connor.'

'Excuse me? Did you say Patrick Connor?'

She nodded.

'I am so bad, Ossie, so very bad. Like me mother was.'

She was crying silently and his heart went out to her, she looked so small and defenceless.

'She came to warn me about him and I didn't listen to her.'

Oswald was finding this a night of revelations.

'Your mother came to see you?'

Tiffany nodded.

'I sent her away – sent her away and let her think I hated her. And

217

she was trying to help me! All those years I missed her so much, Ossie.'

She squeezed his hand gently.

'How did this happen to me? I only wanted to be loved. Just once in my life I wanted to be important to someone. Know there was someone somewhere in the world who was thinking about me, who cared about me. How did I get it so wrong?'

He smiled.

'Maybe you just wanted it too much, baby.'

She squeezed his hand again and he squeezed it back.

'It will be OK, sweetie, I promise you.'

As she drifted off to sleep he wondered how he was going to explain to Jason just how low his sister had sunk, and how he could make it better for them both. He decided it was time to talk to the mother and see what she had to say. If she had tried to warn Tiffany off Connor then she obviously cared what happened to her daughter. She'd been trying to help.

But his main problem was Verbena. She would not want Marie Carter near her son, he knew. No way. She was obsessed with the boy and at times he wondered if her attitude was healthy, consoling himself with the thought that at least he could temper her overpowering love with common sense and reality. He was a worried man but he stayed in the hospital all night. It was the least he could do for the battered girl lying so still in her narrow bed. He watched Tiffany as she slept, her face troubled and eyes flickering with images he could only imagine.

She was still a child in many respects, just a child. Yet she had already lived a thousand lifetimes and all because she had had a mother who was weak enough to succumb to drugs. Maybe it was genetic, who knew? Like mother, like daughter?

His real fear was the old adage, Like father, like son. Because where the hell did that leave his boy? His pride and joy, the thing that kept him working day and night and gave him the love he so desperately craved.

It was a long night for Oswald. As the sun came up he decided he had to see Marie Carter.

Chapter Sixteen

Marie and Alan were uneasy together for the first time and both felt it acutely. Since she had arrived for work the atmosphere had been heavy. She was wearing make-up, only a small amount but it proved to Alan that she was embarking on an affair with Mikey Devlin and consequently changing herself, making herself even more attractive.

It hurt him and made him feel angry. She was a good woman, and even if she didn't want him he didn't want her to take up with a piece of shit like Devlin. He would use and abuse her and Alan had thought she was better than that these days. Also she was on licence, would be for the rest of her life. What would happen if her association with Devlin was noticed by the police? If he dragged her into some of his nefarious dealings?

Marie had had the worst in life and now she was being given another chance. All of a sudden it seemed as if she couldn't wait to destroy herself once more. People could damage themselves in so many ways, drink, drugs, but also with the partners they chose. If she decided on Devlin she was a mug, no, worse than a mug. She was proving to him that blood will out – she was still the woman she had been all those years ago when she had killed her two friends.

That thought made him feel bad all over again. He was judging her and finding her lacking, and he had no right. She worked for him, that was all, her private life was her own. He had not done such a good job with his, he admitted to himself. He was involved with Devlin as well. And unlike her he knew how hard it was to get away from the man if he wanted you, for whatever reason. Devlin would enjoy having Marie on his arm, she was like a big present to him, and he would love her notoriety. Telling people who she was and what she had done would appeal to him. The big I am.

Alan was growing more and more annoyed.

Marie was such a good-looking woman. The sight of her long legs was driving him up the wall. She smelled of soap instead of heavy perfume, which was what he was used to from women these days. She was gorgeous, in fact. He could watch her for hours, just sit and watch her. Her hair falling across her face as she leant forward, her movements as she made a cup of coffee. It occurred to him that he was falling for her in a big way. Had already fallen, in fact, and that what he was experiencing was plain old-fashioned jealousy.

'Can I get you a drink?'

Her husky voice was quieter than usual and he suddenly realised he had been sitting there staring at her. He felt his face flush and looked down at the open paper on his desk. The phone rang and he grabbed it, glad of something to do.

'Hello?'

It was Mikey Devlin and just hearing the man's voice made Alan feel capable of murder.

'What can I do for you?'

Alan sounded jokey but was actually feeling depressed.

'It's not you I want, it's your rather luscious assistant.'

Alan had to stop himself from losing control completely.

'Hang on and I'll pass you over.'

He handed the phone to Marie and his eyes said everything he needed her to know. She took the phone and turned her back on him. The atmosphere between them was worse than ever after that.

Petey Black was terrified out of his life. Kevin Carter had been around looking for him again. He wished he could explain to the other man that he understood his anger. He would have been the same. How he wished his wife was a normal woman who cooked, cleaned and gossiped. But no, he had to lumber himself with Silvertown's answer to fucking Ma Baker – a big, fat, smelly nutcase.

He always said he could not remember for the life of him what the fuck had attracted them to one another. But he knew, deep down. It was that same nutter factor that had been the attraction once. Between them they had terrorised half their community and now it was coming back on them and they were finally finding out what it was like to be frightened to open your own front door or go out shopping.

Petey didn't like this feeling one bit. It was taking its toll on him. He was even losing weight from all the worry. While Loony Lil was safely ensconced in prison and largeing it up like there was no tomorrow, he was the one who had to sort out all the shit. He was so sorry for himself he was in fear of losing his grip once and for all. Kevin Carter was one hard fuck for all his respectable façade. That was mainly his old woman anyway. Miserable bitch she was, and now she'd been toasted and *he* was the one having to watch his back.

His mother-in-law had renounced her daughter and told Petey she wanted him out of the house soon. Then Kevin had been round looking for him. All he wanted was a bit of peace, that was all. Who would take him in now?

He glanced around the room. It was like a tip as usual. Cups everywhere, some with mould growing over them with wild abandon. Sweet wrappers on the floor. Even the wallpaper looked defeated as it was peeling in places and had a sheen of nicotine over it from all the years of smoking. The place stank. He looked at it as if for the first time. Saw the squalor he lived in and it depressed him even more.

On the TV was a makeover programme which he'd only watched because it had a fit bird fronting it. But as he looked at the lovely house she was in he realised that what he had mistaken for a life was in fact just an existence. All those years of cultivating a hard man rep were coming back to haunt him. He should have a little house by now, a few kids and a good woman with the dinner on the table and an interest in what he had done during the course of the day. He couldn't blame Kal over the kids, they had just never happened, but somehow he felt she was to blame for all the rest of it. He couldn't even use the pub any more in case someone grassed him to Carter.

That was another lesson he had learned. People were pleased this had happened to him. They would grass him given half the chance and that knowledge had been a real eye opener. The Blacks were thoroughly disliked and though on one level he had always known that, now it was proved it made him feel even more dejected. They were pariahs, and he knew it.

He rolled himself a cigarette. As he was lighting it two loud bangs erupted in the room and the windows blasted on to him. Shards of glass sliced into his body, embedding themselves in his face and head. One large sliver was hanging out of his hand and he watched in silent amazement as it dropped almost in slow motion to the floor. His eye hurt, and he guessed that he had glass in it. He couldn't blink.

What really amazed him was that there was no pain. He was still in shock.

He saw Kevin Carter through the blood dripping from his own face. He was standing in the front garden with his shotgun, smiling. It was only then that Petey realised he had actually been shot.

He could hear screaming coming from a far-off place. It was the last thing he heard before he lapsed into the blessed unconsciousness that preceded his death.

Verbena watched as brother and sister talked in low voices. She was sitting on the far side of the small sitting room allocated to patients and visitors. She didn't want to listen to them talk. She didn't even want to be here.

The whole place had the smell of death and decay as far as she was concerned. Scratched furniture and magazines that were years out of date littered the cramped space. High-backed leather chairs smelling of urine and God knew what else were the only available seating, and her child, her son, was sitting with his tart of a sister and it grieved her to see him there.

Tiffany had dragged him into her world once more, that twilight world of drug addicts and sleazy people she thought were so great. Verbena swallowed down her anger but each breath she took made her feel physically sick. This place was filled with the smell of despair, of people who had lost all hope.

An old man was trying to light a cigarette between fits of coughing and spluttering. He was obviously having trouble breathing and Verbena watched in fascination as he finally took a long hard pull on his man-made killing stick.

Standing up, she nodded to her son and hurried from the room. She couldn't stay any longer. She couldn't watch him with his sister. It was as if the past was rearing up before him and she was frightened it would steal him away.

Blood was thicker than water – how many times had she heard people say that over the years? Could it take the place of love and caring?

She would soon find out, but she wasn't sure she wanted the answer.

'I'm sorry I've caused all this trouble.'

Jason smiled gently. He was a good-looking boy but wasn't aware of the fact.

'Is it true what me dad told me about you and me real dad?'

Tiffany nodded sadly, a tear escaping from the corner of one eye.

Jason shook his head in wonderment. He had short locks, more to be fashionable than as an ethnic statement. He liked the fact he was different from most of the people he knew. They all came from liberal families with no racism in them. He realised just how lucky he had been there. Now, looking at his sister and knowing that the man who had destroyed their mother had gone on to destroy her, he wondered if he had any of his real father inside him. Ossie said you were the person you wanted to be. You made your own life and your own luck. Jason was desperate to believe that was true.

'You have to go away, Dad said. To get better.'

His sister tried to smile. She was desperate to get away from her life as it was now. She was in so much trouble with everyone, especially Patrick. He would kill her if he saw her again and she knew it. She wanted to lie low, just until she got her head together.

'Dad is going to ask for Anastasia to be given to us. I am your next-of-kin, aren't I? And she is my sister, the same as you are.'

Jason had said it out loud and still it made no sense to him.

'How was our mum?' He asked it softly, frightened that his adoptive mother would hear him even though she wasn't in the room. He didn't want to hurt her but he had to know.

Tiffany smiled.

'She looked all right. Different from how I remember her. Quieter. She's still really pretty. She wanted to help me but I wouldn't listen to her.'

He squeezed her hand, glad to hear something good about his mother. He barely remembered her, she was a hazy memory, a smell he couldn't quite recapture but which had stayed with him all his life.

He remembered crushing embraces when he had kicked his little legs to make her put him back down. Her love wasn't like Verbena's gentle love, which was all-powerful because she used her weakness to make you pity her. He had worked out a long time ago that in her weakness she was stronger than all of them put together. She made you do what she wanted because she made you feel bad if you didn't. Yet she loved him and he loved her, dearly.

'Dad is going to see her and said I could go with him.'

Tiffany heard the suppressed excitement in Jason's voice and envied him his confidence.

'Tell her I am sorry, would you?'

He nodded, his huge brown eyes full of sadness to see his sister brought so low.

'Was it me real dad who beat you up, Tiff?'

'I stole his money, he won't let that go.'

Her face looked like a parody of its real self, so beaten and bloated. He was amazed at how well she was coping with her injuries. But he wasn't allowing for the fact that she was used to bad treatment. Almost expected it off people. She needed the pain to remind her of what she had done.

'Try and fight for my little Anastasia. Insist on having her, please. I can't bear the thought of her with strangers even though I know she's better off with them than she would be with me. I let her down like Mum let us down and I can't forgive meself for that. Tell Ossie not to let her father anywhere near her. He'll use her to get back at me.'

'I promise, Tiff. You know Verbena, she's a good mum.'

Tiffany smiled, a distorted grimace as her mouth was still split and painful.

'Promise me?'

He kissed her gently on the forehead.

'I promise.'

She closed her eyes tightly. She was dying for something to give her a lift, having trouble keeping up this act about rehab. As soon as she was able to move she was out of here. Patrick would not find her, a sitting duck in some halfway house somewhere. She was gone. She just wanted to make sure her daughter was taken care of first.

She had to make sure *he* didn't get her. If Pat got the child he would use her as bait. Like her mother before her Tiffany was finally seeing him through her own clouded eyes instead of the rose-tinted glasses she usually wore.

All she really wanted now was something to get her out of the ball game, preferably a rather large rock that she could inhale at her leisure, and then lie back and stop thinking, period.

Mikey and Marie were in his house in Rettenden. It was a lovely old property with a pantiled roof and six acres of land. The house was Elizabethan in parts, beautifully restored, and obviously worth the National Debt. Despite herself Marie was impressed. Mikey had enjoyed seeing the expression on her face as he had driven her up the winding drive.

224

'Nice, ain't it?'

She nodded.

'It's beautiful, Mikey. A really fabulous-looking place.'

He was pleased at her reaction and it showed.

'Wait until you see inside. I bought it all off this geezer, furniture and everything. He was going bankrupt and glad of the dough, I can tell you.'

It had been a bargain and he'd enjoyed the fact he had got it at a fraction of its true value.

Inside was every bit as beautiful as outside. The entrance hall had been restored to its former glory and Marie stood there for a few minutes enjoying her surroundings. Mikey watched her and felt a glow of pride at her appreciation of his home.

She was overcome by the sheer age of the place. That people had lived here over hundreds of years amazed her.

'It is fucking fantastic, Mikey. Think of all the people who've lived here before you. It's just unbelievable, don't you think, that a building lasts so long? I used to think that when I was in Frankland, think of the thousands of people locked up in there over the years. People who had been hung there . . . died there. That their last sight was of such an ugly place. Yet to die here would be worse because think what you'd have to leave behind.'

He walked across the hall and hugged her, a real hug of appreciation. He was immediately embarrassed, but Marie hugged him back. For the first time they had really connected and they both felt it.

'Come and have a drink.'

He dragged her by the hand through to the large kitchen and made them both a drink. They sat at the scrubbed oak table and he pottered around getting cold meats and cheese from the fridge and fresh-baked bread from the pantry. Marie got out the ingredients and made a large salad. They chatted amiably as they worked side by side. She was surprised to find she was really enjoying herself. They drank wine, chilled and sweet from cut-glass goblets, and she felt she had stumbled into someone else's dream.

As they ate and drank the atmosphere changed. Mikey became more himself and it showed. He wasn't coked up either and that made all the difference as far as Marie was concerned. She realised that deep down he was a likeable man.

'The thing is, Marie, I only really feel comfortable in here. The rest of the house makes me uneasy.'

He was smiling as he said the words but she understood what he meant.

'I mean, when this house was still owned by the bloke I bought it off, I wouldn't have got past the front gate, would I? He wouldn't have wanted the likes of me in his home.' He stared off into space for a few seconds. 'Not until I had the poke to get him out of debt, which I did.'

Marie laid her hand over his and said gently, 'Well, it's your house now and if I was you I would forget all that and enjoy it.'

'It seems weird to me sometimes, being here. I came off a rough council estate and still feel more at home there than I do in this place. But I love owning it. I love the fact it's mine and no one else's. Unless the filth give me a capture, of course, then it will be me old woman's.'

He laughed loudly.

'Now *she* loves it here. She even tried to be all refined once we had it, and that was a fucking sight to see, I can tell you. She was pure Essex born and bred, from the roots of her bleached hair to her silicone tits. Kept referring to the place as "the estate". 'Course, she realised eventually that people thought she meant a council estate so she started calling it "the country house" so there would be no mistake.'

'Do you miss her?'

He shook his head.

'You don't miss people like Desrae, you just wonder how the fuck you married it. She was pregnant and it seemed like a good idea at the time. I was off me face on the day and had a fight with me brother. He told me what a prat I was for marrying her and he was right, but I didn't want to hear that, did I? I miss me kids, though, especially me boy, little Mikey. The girls are all right. The eldest is fourteen now and uses people just like her mother does. Looks twenty and thinks that clubbing and getting laid are what you do for a good night out. Desrae actually goes out with her, believe it or not. I have had to distribute a few slaps, I can tell you, because of them. My younger girl is heavy, a big girl, likes her school. She's away, private like. Me boy, he's like me, tough but with a bit of nous. His mother gets on his wick and I can appreciate that. He's embarrassed by her.'

Mikey gulped at his wine.

'How come I can talk to you, Marie, when I could never talk to anyone before? I think it's because unlike most women you actually listen to what's being said. You look interested as well and that helps.'

He was smiling at her. His big face still bore traces of his former good looks. When he was being himself she found she liked him. He wasn't as brash as he made out and she guessed that he got out of it on coke for the same reason she had. It was to give him confidence, bravado.

'You are a nice man, Mikey, why wouldn't I be interested in what you have to say?'

He looked sheepish and that fact amazed her and also endeared him to her even more.

'I shouldn't be drinking this wine. I have an addictive personality and I have to leave all drink and drugs alone,' she said.

'What quack told you that?'

'The prison quack.'

Mikey grinned and refilled her glass.

'Fuck him, what does he know, eh? You drink your wine and I promise to take care of you, OK?'

'Sounds good to me, Mikey.'

He held his hand gently to her cheek and said softly, 'What have you done to me, Marie Carter? When I'm with you I want to be a nice bloke.'

He looked so earnest, so sincere, that she felt a sudden urge to cry for him and the waste that had been his life. Like her he had chased the impossible, but unlike her he had found it and it had not made him any happier.

She kissed his hand, gently on the palm, and it was more erotic to him than if she had stripped off and laid across the table. It occurred to him suddenly that he was falling for this woman, and falling for her in a big way.

For all the bad things she had once been – and he had heard the stories about her, who hadn't? – she still had a dignity that he found irresistible. It was in her voice, in her face and in the way she carried herself.

She smiled, and as her eyes crinkled at the corners he was undone. For the first time in years he wanted a woman for all the right reasons and it felt good. He didn't care about her past. He was only interested in her as she was now and how she would be in the future. He wanted her in his bed and in his arms, and he wanted her there sooner rather than later.

★ ★ ★

227

Louise was still in tremendous pain but she was coping with it. Inside her was an overpowering drive to get out of this bed and get home – wherever that was now. At times she felt an urge to scream out at the injustice of it all. She was lying here day after day in pain, her body crying out for drugs to ease it, while her hated daughter was out there causing even more mayhem.

Marie was the worst nightmare of every mother living: a daughter who was nothing more than a whore. She had caused everything bad that had ever happened to them. From the loss of Marshall, Louise's heart, her son, the reason she got up in the morning, to her own near death by fire. Yet fire was supposed to be cleansing. Louise remembered reading that after plagues and epidemic illnesses everything was burned. If she was ever capable she would burn her daughter herself and watch as she writhed in agony, she vowed. Only then could she feel she had been avenged for all the trouble Marie had brought on them.

Her breathing was bad again and she fought to calm herself. She must concentrate on getting better.

The door opened and she was surprised to see her husband standing before her. Kevin looked dishevelled, his whole demeanour strange. He needed a wash, a shave and a change of clothes. He looked like a tramp. What must the nurses think, seeing him like that? She was so angry with him for showing her up, but that was him all over. Without her he was capable of nothing. Her spiteful thoughts were clearly reflected in her eyes and he knew exactly what was going through her mind.

'What do you want?'

Her voice still sounded muffled. She couldn't talk properly because of the scarring to her face.

He smiled at her and drawled out his words because he knew it would annoy her.

'You look terrible, Lou. Really fucking rough, girl.'

She shook her head in annoyance.

Kevin widened his eyes as if he was surprised he had offended her.

'Oh, have I upset you, Lou? Sorry. I was only doing what you normally do – plain speaking, remember? Please or offend, that was your motto. Especially when you were slaughtering someone's reputation. Or more often their kids' lives.'

Her eyes were black pools of hatred as she looked at him. She didn't need him to tell her what she looked like, she was well aware of it. She had insisted on seeing herself as soon as she was able, and she didn't care. It meant nothing what was on the outside, it was the inside that mattered and she was good inside. She was clean, which was more than her husband or daughter could claim.

'Get out of here.'

He laughed. 'You amaze me, Lou. Even like you are, you still think you're the dog's knob, don't you? Get out of here!'

He mimicked her voice and she closed her eyes against the onslaught she knew was to follow.

'Well, I come to give you glad tidings as they used to say in biblical days. I have avenged your burning up. I killed that fat cunt's husband today. Petey, who I feel drew an even shorter straw than I did, is no more. He has ceased to be, as they say on *Monty Python*. He has crawled up the curtain to meet his maker. He is an ex-arsonist.'

She was finally convinced that he had lost it. Once and for all he had gone over the edge.

'Kevin . . .'

He laughed again.

'Kevin! "Oh, Kevin, my husband". How often did I hear *that* when we were first married, eh? But not for long. Once Marshall was born I was redundant, weren't I? You had what you wanted, your glorious son. Well, he wasn't the boy you thought he was – he was a weak-kneed little fucker and I hated him almost as much as I hated you.'

'Stop it, Kevin. He's dead . . .'

He watched her distress and felt a small spark of pity for her.

'Oh, you noticed, did you? Would you have noticed if I had died, by any chance?' He slapped his forehead and bellowed, ''Course you would. When the wages didn't come in you would have wondered where I'd gone, wouldn't you, Lou? Only I didn't shoot meself, did I, like Marshall did? I shot someone else.'

He was laughing again.

Three nurses entered the room and looked at the man before them fearfully. One was very pretty with ginger hair and wide-spaced green eyes. Kevin smiled at her in a friendly way.

'Hello, girls, come to see the freak?'

Then he took the gun from the carrier bag and held it so it was pointed at his wife. Louise was terrified. She was dribbling with fear and unable to wipe her mouth. It was an Essex shotgun. Lazily he unscrewed the long barrel, then threw the piece to the corner of the room. It made a hollow sound as it hit the pale green wall. He held the gun underneath his chin.

'Husband *and* son topped themselves. How will you live *this* disgrace down, eh, Lou? Driving us *both* to suicide.'

Before he could pull the trigger, however, a burly porter grabbed him from behind. The report from the gun was heard all over the hospital, and the hole in the ceiling was there for months.

The police took Kevin away and charged him with murder. He was whistling and smiling all the way to the station.

Lucy listened to her mother's ranting afterwards and tried to stem the tears. She knew her father had murdered Petey and wondered what on earth had possessed him. They were now left at the mercy of the Black family and she was terrified of further revenge attacks. It seemed to her that as soon as Marie had been released all hell had broken out.

She grasped her mother's hand and the two of them stared at one another in shock.

'I bet she's laughing up her sleeve at us. She's evil, Mum. You were right, she's nothing but pure evil.'

Louise nodded her head in frustration.

'Mickey's mum is going to go mad when she hears this latest. He already hardly talks to me any more. I feel like Marie's done all this deliberately, and there was me starting to feel sorry for her!'

The two women sat together, bitterness overflowing from them both. For the first time in ages they were united and as usual it was over Marie who, no matter what she did or didn't do, was hated by them both for the same reason.

Marie watched Mikey sleep by moonlight. He slept like a baby, deeply and with small snuffling noises. She wondered what men would think if they knew how women watched them at their most vulnerable. Men asleep were like children. They thrashed about, farted, spread themselves across the bed claiming their space. Their faces relaxed and the real man was revealed, weak chin, saggy jowls . . . things that were not immediately obvious when they were strutting around being men. Thinning hair and pot bellies were hard to disguise asleep. Her eyes roamed all over him and she felt a strange affection for him. Sexually he'd been like a teenager, all over her, grabbing, wanting it all at once. His big hands were gentle in their way, but he was not the great lover he thought he was. That came from years of shagging women who just wanted something from him, who were with him because he was Mikey Devlin, who sucked his cock and groaned at all the right times because they knew it was what he wanted to hear.

Marie could spot women like that a mile away. Their only claim to fame was who they fucked, and they made sure people knew who that was. They held on to their man like a badge of honour. 'Look at me, people, I'm shagging a bank robber, murderer, burglar, whatever.' They didn't know what real love was, or real life come to that. Which was why Mikey was so drawn to her. She actually had more creds than him and that had been the attraction in the first place. Now he liked her because he had talked to her and she had listened to him, and she liked him back. This surprised her but it made this job so much easier. Mikey was her ticket to Patrick Connor; she was Patrick's nemesis, though he didn't know that yet.

But, she reasoned, the fact that she liked Mikey made it all much easier. She had shuddered and groaned for England and he had believed he had satisfied a woman who had not had sex for thirteen years. He was over the moon with his own performance and she hadn't had the heart to tell him that George Clooney himself couldn't have got a reaction from her. She had no sexual feelings left any more. She had used them up years ago and now sex was nothing to her. She had enjoyed the cuddle afterwards. Enjoyed feeling his heart beating against her chest. Even enjoyed his awkward compliments, such as the fact that she was apparently 'in beautiful condition'. She smiled at the thought of his awkward words.

He was used to babes with fake tans and fake personalities. Women who had no real intelligence except knowing how to garner money from him and maybe a holiday if they were lucky. Whose conversation was spattered with other hard men's names and gossip about their contemporaries. Who didn't read books or watch television unless it was a soap or a documentary on plastic surgery, the ultimate goal in their hollow lives. On one level Mikey was aware of all this and that was where his dissatisfaction stemmed from.

She kissed him gently and he snuggled into her. She pulled him into her arms and held him like a child and he responded like one, searching for a nipple and putting his hand in the crack of her behind. As he gently caressed her in his sleep she found herself beginning to become aroused. She moved against his hand and her movement woke him. She had her eyes closed and let the feeling wash over her. The fact that she was feeling anything was making her head reel. It had been so very long since the idea of sex had even entered her mind.

He pushed her on to her back and slipped his fingers inside her. He watched, fascinated, as she came in one long shuddering movement. She soaked him and she soaked the bed and when it was over he pulled her towards him and held her as she tried to control her breathing.

She felt free, really free for the first time in years. It was as if a dam had been emptied and taken away all her pent-up emotion with it. She was crying. Then he rested her back on the pillows and whispered softly in her ear, 'You can definitely sleep on the damp patch after that!'

They laughed together, holding one another close.

'I can't sleep on the damp patch anyway. I have to go, I'm late for my curfew as it is.'

Mikey felt deflated. He had forgotten about that.

'It's only eleven o'clock, Marie . . .'

'Let me ring and explain why I'm late and then I have to go, mate. Sorry.'

He stood up, annoyed she could tell. But it would just make him want her more.

'Tomorrow me and you eat fast and then get straight in the kip, right?'

She laughed at his boyish eagerness.

'We'll see, Mikey. We'll see.'

Chapter Seventeen

'**C**ome on, Verbie, it's only until the girl gets back on her feet.' Verbena stared at the man she loved above all else and wondered how he could have the gall to ask her to take on Tiffany's child.

Ossie felt angry deep inside. When his wife was like this he actively disliked her. She could be a snob, and though he joked about it to her, she knew that it annoyed him.

'I don't know, Ossie. She's trouble.'

Verbena knew she was annoying her husband and she didn't care.

'Who's to say Tiffany will even take the child back? She's too much like her mother for my liking.'

Ossie rolled his eyes to the ceiling and Verbena felt tears near the surface of her own.

'Look, Ossie, I'm the one who'll have to take care of the child, not you. You'll go off to work as usual and leave me here with her.'

'I'll stay home and help, Mum.'

Neither of them had realised that Jason was listening. Ossie turned and grinned at his son.

'She asked me to help and she is my sister. Whatever she's done she is my blood. Same with Anastasia. I feel I have to help if I can. Tiff would do it for me, I know she would.'

Verbena put her hand over her mouth as if she was going to be sick.

'And as for my mother, if Tiff is like her then so am I. We come from the same stock, remember.'

He walked from the room and Ossie shook his head sadly at his wife.

'We have to do this, Verbena, the boy needs to help his family.'

'I'm his family . . . *We* are his family.'

Ossie shook his head again, his handsome face troubled.

'Supposing we could have had kids of our own and had a

233

daughter who'd turned out like Tiffany – would you turn your back on her?'

Verbena lit a cigarette and drew on it deeply. 'We would never have had a child who turned out like that.'

Ossie laughed nastily.

'No? What about John and Mary Thompson then? Their son is a heroin addict who has been in rehab more times than I can count and has actually robbed them. But they don't give up on him and he was their birth child. No one can guarantee what a child will turn out like, Verbena. Remember that. That boy had everything a child could want, including an expensive private education, but he still turned out a thief, a liar and a drug addict.

'And what about the Rawlings – the mother is addicted to painkillers, has been for years. Laura Rawlings is an addict, for all her high talk and expensive education. Verbena, it *happens*. No one wants it to but at least Tiffany is trying to make things better.'

His wife just looked at him. Her eyes were pain-filled and her mouth was trembling ominously.

'I spoke to a solicitor. He said the boy has every right to ask for his sister's child. No one else is available. No one else *wants* the poor little mite.'

Jason had been standing outside the door and came inside once more, his face set as it had been when he was a little boy determined to get his own way.

'Please, Mum. Do this for me? She's a lovely little girl.'

His expression was implacable and Verbena knew if she didn't do what he wanted she would lose a part of him for ever. He was asking her for something so big she knew instinctively that if she let him down now it would seriously affect their relationship.

'I promised my sister I would try and help and I intend to keep that promise, whatever.'

Ossie was proud of his son, saw the man he would become and felt grateful that Jason was a part of his life.

Verbena tried to smile but it was more of a grimace.

'Looks like my mind has been made up for me, doesn't it?'

Jason hugged her close and his touch was worth everything to her. She would do whatever she had to do to make her son happy.

Ossie hugged them both, his big arms encompassing them, and Verbena prayed that she could take to the child. Because she was the one who would be with her all the time and both the men in the house had forgotten that fact.

Patrick sat outside Sadie Beasley's house with his music blaring. Her mother looked out from behind the net curtain and cursed under her breath.

Sadie was a pretty girl with long dark hair and deep brown eyes. She had olive skin, the legacy of an Italian grandmother, a high-breasted body with slim legs and a tiny waist. Her mother was frightened for her. She was only sixteen years old and already she was a handful.

Sadie came into the room.

'I'm going out.'

Mabel Beasley shook her head.

'No, you bleeding well ain't. Not with that black bastard any-way!'

Sadie laughed without a care in the world.

'Get a life, Mother, for crying out loud. What you going to do, stop me?'

She was ridiculing her mother and they both knew it.

'I mean it, girl . . .'

Sadie walked from the room and Mabel felt the frustration of a mother who had completely lost control of her child. Tears of rage and fear filled her eyes as she watched her lovely daughter get into the car of the local hard man and drug dealer, Patrick Connor. He would ruin her without a second's thought, without remorse, but Sadie was too stupid to see that.

If only her husband was still around, he would have stopped Sadie going out. But he was up north somewhere with his bird, a girl hardly ten years older than the daughter he had walked out on without a backward glance. The daughter he had once professed to love more than anything in the world.

Was it any wonder the girl was running the streets with Patrick Connor? He offered her everything that life had so far denied her and she was too young and starry-eyed even to suspect that some day soon she'd have to start paying him back.

Alan Jarvis saw Marie pull up in Mikey's Merc and felt his heart sink down to his boots. Mikey must have picked her up from the hostel and that smacked of some kind of ongoing arrangement between them. Mikey lived out in that big mausoleum in Essex so he'd have had to get up early to go and pick her up from the halfway house.

Seeing them together made Alan angry. What did Mikey Devlin have that he didn't? He had asked himself this question over and over in the last few days. He didn't care that Marie had the rep she had: prostitute, thief, drug addict, murderess. The list was endless, yet he would give anything to have her look at him just once as a potential lover. But it wasn't going to happen, and he could not for the life of him understand why he cared so much. He thought about her all the time and obviously Mikey did the same. Devlin had once remarked that he wouldn't get out of bed for less than ten kilos. Now he was getting out of bed to give a bird a lift to work.

That told Alan all he needed to know and he was gutted. Devlin was too heavy for him, far too heavy. Anyone else and he might have tried to interfere.

Marie must be off her head if she thought she could handle Mikey Devlin, the biggest nutter this side of the water. He was worried for her on top of everything else. Devlin exacted a price for everything he did to help someone and it was usually far higher than the person he'd dealt with had anticipated.

'Listen, Marie, I promise I will find out what I can. He'll be charged then held on remand. I can't see him getting bail, especially not at Magistrates' Court. The ponces are renowned for not having the guts to give it. We'll see how it goes at Crown. If push comes to shove we'll request judge in chambers, but don't get your hopes up, OK?'

She nodded. 'I can't believe Dad did that. Killing Petey of all people! He was just a prat. It was Karen who was behind the fire, not her husband.'

Mikey personally couldn't give a toss, but he knew better than to say that.

'Petey had it coming to him. I think your father done a good thing. I'd have done the same if someone crisped up any of my family. You can't let people get away with that! They'd start to think they could do what the fuck they liked. When you deal with a nutter, you have to be a bigger nutter. It's how the world works. Our world anyway.

'Now stop worrying. I'll call me brief and see what can be done. If he goes to the 'Ville I have a few faces in there who can give him an easy sit, OK?'

Marie nodded. Once more someone else's actions had turned her world upside down, but she knew what lay behind her father's rashness. All his trouble stemmed from her and it was getting her down.

Mikey put his fingers under her chin and kissed her gently on the mouth.

'Let me take care of you for a while, eh?'

He meant every word and Marie was grateful to him for his kindness. She needed a friend now. Mikey Devlin had turned out to be a much better man than she had anticipated and she was thankful to him.

'Thanks, Mikey.'

She got out of the car and braced herself for Alan's wrath. She knew how he felt about her and was sorry for him. It amazed her that she could attract both men even though they knew her past and her reputation. She concluded it was the fact she had no real interest in them that was the biggest draw. Because she *didn't* have any interest in them whatsoever. Men were trouble unless you could control them, as she intended to control Mikey and use him to help Tiffany.

Inside the Portakabin Alan had a fixed smile on his face. Marie tried to look businesslike and pleasant.

'I heard about your father. I'm sorry,' he said.

She placed her bag by her chair and turned on the computer.

Alan watched her warily.

'How was Mikey? Have a good time?'

Marie turned to face him, her blonde hair falling across her face as she was still leaning over the desk.

'Yes, thank you, Alan. Though the news about my father ruined the good time somewhat, as you can imagine.'

Her sarcasm hurt him but he still retaliated.

'Not too badly though, eh?'

He was leering at her and even though he knew that what he was doing was wrong he couldn't stop himself. Jealousy was a terrible affliction. Now he knew what had prompted his wife's acid comments all those times he had been on the missing list.

Marie's face was set and hard now. He felt the full force of her anger as she bellowed at him, 'My sex life is *my* business, Alan.'

He was so angry all his good intentions went out of the window.

'So you are having sex with him then?'

As soon as the words were out he regretted them. But it was too late to take them back now.

Marie looked almost manic as she shouted, 'Look, Alan, I work for you, remember? You are not me fucking father, who incidentally is banged up at the moment because like you he stuck his big conk in where it wasn't needed. If I want to see Mikey Devlin, I will, OK? And you can't stop me.'

They stared at one another for long seconds. Their relationship had shifted up a gear and they were both aware of that. She looked into his handsome face. He was weak and she knew that but he was also a kind man deep inside. She was sorry that she affected him so much as she was aware she was not worth it. All this jealousy was not worth his effort.

Marie was no good and knew that deep inside. It was her bad luck that she had this effect on people. Trouble followed her wherever she went. Always had, and it looked as though it always would.

It had been the same in prison. Women got crushes on her, screws as well as inmates. It was as if she attracted the weak and the lonely, and she didn't want them. Wanted no one in her life except her children and it was far too late for them, it seemed. All she wanted now was to help her babies. No more and no less. The rest of her life was mere existence. She really didn't need or want this man's love and he was too stupid to see that she would destroy him eventually. She never meant to do it, it just always seemed to happen. She picked up her bag.

'I'm going, Alan, before we both say things we'll really regret.'

He stood in the doorway, his face a picture of sadness.

'I am sorry, Marie. Please don't go.'

She looked at him. His face was crumpled with misery and she was so sorry for him she wanted to cry. She often wanted to cry lately.

'Please, Marie, listen to me. Who'll do my books, eh, if you walk out on me?'

She didn't answer him.

He was desperate. If she walked out now he knew she would never come back. He had to build some bridges, try and minimise the damage he had done. He had to have her near him whatever it cost.

'Come on, forget it. I was out of order. If you leave you won't be able to get a flat, will you? You'll have to get another job and everything. Let's just let bygones be bygones and pretend it never happened.'

She placed her bag down on the floor and he felt a rush of relief so acute he was actually shaking with it. Never in his life had he felt like this about anyone. It was as if she had put him under some kind of spell.

'I'm sorry, Marie. As if you haven't got enough on your plate at the moment.'

She sat down on the typing chair and put her face in her hands. She was crying so quietly he didn't realise what was happening for a moment. She was sobbing, her shoulders shaking with the effort of trying to stem the flow of tears.

He wanted to touch her, hold her to him, but he knew that if he did he wouldn't be able to stop himself from wanting her there and then. Instead he put the kettle on and let her cry. Eventually, after what seemed an age, he took her the tea and saw that she had brought her feelings under control.

'Why did my father do it, Al? It's as if he's gone mad and it's all my fault. Everything is my fault somehow. Me poor mother, me sister, me father, me kids . . . it's as if I'm cursed. Or I curse anyone who comes into contact with me.'

He placed a hand gently on her shoulder.

'You aren't cursed, Marie. You're the victim really, a victim of your own looks and personality. You attract people, and unfortunately they're sometimes the wrong people. But you have to keep trying to make it right, mate. It's all you can do, it's all any of us can do. Try and make everything turn out right.'

She stared into his eyes and the lure of her was so strong he wondered if he had been cursed too because he knew he would never look at another woman in the same way as he looked at her. She was in his blood, in his head, inside his very being, and he knew without a doubt that if he had to he would kill for her. That was how much she affected him.

'I'm tired, Alan, tired of it all. I'm a magnet for trouble, always have been. I'm sick and tired of always having to be sorry, apologising for living. Ruining people's lives without a second's thought. Look at my daughter – look how she turned out. Patrick Connor has taken her and turned her into a watered-down version of me. Maybe it's in the DNA, who the fuck knows?'

'Like I said, all you can do is try and make it turn out right.'

She laughed sadly.

'That's a tall order, Alan. Jesus Christ Himself would have His work cut out sorting this lot.'

'Drink your tea, mate. Things have a habit of sorting themselves out, you'll see.'

239

She tried to smile at him but it was so hard. She was fed up with putting on a brave face. Had been trying to do it for thirteen long years. It was getting harder and harder by the day.

'What do you mean, Patrick?'

He lit her another pipe and handed it to Sadie before he carried on talking again. As she inhaled the crack he suppressed a smile. It was so easy to make them do what he wanted. He was losing interest in her now. Before the week was out he would have her where he wanted her. But he smiled at her anyway, one of the winning smiles that made him look so handsome and affable.

He was undoing her top now and as he grabbed a breast he enjoyed the sight of his black hand against the whiteness of her skin. She was a lively fuck as well, really enjoyed it. But the crack would soon stop all that and then she would perform only for the drug and he could walk on to the next girl.

He liked the power he had over his girls. Some of them were so fucked up now that they hardly knew what day of the week it was yet they could still perform the sex act and that was all that bothered him and them. They knew they had to do it to get the drugs. Yet still they felt affection for him – he always found that strange. If he saw them and spoke nicely to them they still held a torch for him, would do anything he asked them, and it wasn't just from fear, though he used that if he had to. He made sure they kept in mind what he was capable of. If one of the women needed a hiding he made sure it was given in front of some of the other girls so they all learned he would take no nonsense from them.

As he slowly fucked this girl in his car, making sure she had the time of her life, he was actually thinking about Tiffany and how he could take her down properly. She was an accident waiting to happen and he was going to make sure that accident would be one no one would forget.

Sadie Beasley felt she was in ecstasy every time she made love with this man. He was everything she had ever wanted. He was handsome, sexy and hard. Everyone knew who he was, she loved being seen with him, telling her mates about him. He was also going to set her up in a little flat so she didn't have to listen to her mother's griping all the time. Now that would really be something. Her own drum, she would love that.

Her mother didn't have the sense to keep a man; her father had walked away from them without a backward glance. Well, it wouldn't happen to her. No way. She was going to make sure she kept this fucker on his toes. He was all over her like a rash and she intended to keep him that way.

She was buttoning up her clothes when someone got into the back of the car. She turned to see a young girl smiling at her.

'She'll be perfect, Patrick.'

Sadie looked from one to the other in amazement and saw that Patrick was grinning.

'You like her then, Maisie?'

The other girl laughed.

'Perfect.'

Sadie was nonplussed.

'What the fuck are you two talking about?'

'You are going to share a flat with Maisie, a friend of mine.' He introduced them with exaggerated courtesy. 'Maisie, Sadie. Sadie, Maisie.'

Sadie realised that there was something going on here that she was not party to. Maisie and Patrick clearly had their own agenda.

Suddenly she was frightened. The atmosphere was charged and she realised that all her big ideas about Patrick were deluded. He was in complete control here and she was a fool if she had ever believed otherwise.

'I want to go home.'

Patrick lit a joint and inhaled deeply on it before he spoke. He was looking into her eyes. She had nice eyes. Sexy-looking lazy eyes that gave away her youth. She thought because she looked so grown-up, she was grown up. She also disrespected her mother, and he found that disturbing. Black girls rarely did that, they respected their matriarchs. Wanted them to be proud of them even if they had to lie about their lives to garner that respect.

But then, girls like Sadie Beasley often had good reason to rebel against their mothers and the lives they led. He had worked that one out from the day he met Louise Carter. She had made her daughter Marie into what she was, and Louise knew it. Every time Marie did another outrageous thing her smugly condemning mother was just proved right. Marie had made her mother even more powerful with her actions, though she had never realised that. This girl's mother was doing the same thing. If they wanted to prove the mothers wrong they should get a good job and make something of their lives because that was definitely not what the mothers expected.

Instead the girls played right into their hands. And his. He marvelled at his own acumen and patted himself on the back because, unlike the mothers, he knew exactly how to control these girls.

'I want to go home now!'

He grinned.

'Listen to her! Demanding things.'

Sadie was really scared and knew that she had to get out of the car. All the things her mother had said to her about Patrick Connor came flooding back into her mind in a rush of fear.

'You will do what the fuck I tell you to do, right?'

She didn't answer him, just stared at him with those big eyes, so he slapped her across the face.

'I said, right?'

She nodded. He relaxed. He didn't want to mark her too much. Anyway she was a shitter. All mouth and no fucking push, like all her kind.

'Now Maisie is going to teach you all you need to know about being one of my girls, OK? From how to dress to how to put on a good show. You listen to her and you do what she tells you. I don't want to hear any stories about you because if I do I will go round your mother's and rip her fucking heart out. Do you understand what I am saying?'

She nodded, her whole face frozen from the terror inside her.

Patrick smiled gently and the action made him look handsome and kind again.

'You do what I tell you and you'll earn good wedge and get what you wanted: your independence and some street cred. If you go against me then I'll be cross, and you don't want to make me cross, do you?'

His voice was cajoling and friendly. He poked a finger gently into her chest.

'Smile, Sadie. You just got what you wanted, sweetie. Not many people get that, do they? Remember the old saying, love. Be careful what you ask for, you just might get it. Well, you got it, girl. Enjoy it.'

Sadie felt as though she had just woken up in her worst nightmare, and of course she was absolutely right.

DI Palmer listened to the doctor's diagnosis and sighed. He was a large man and he was sweating freely. The murder of Petey Black had been shocking if not entirely unexpected. Someone was going to kill him at some time or else he'd get a large lump of a sentence.

242

In a way Kevin Carter had done them all a favour. The manpower it took to keep going to the Blacks' house was phenomenal.

'In short Carter is unfit for anything at the moment. He is over the edge and needs proper psychiatric care. It will have to be arranged on remand. He cannot be released into the general population, the man is too disturbed.'

Palmer sighed again. He was itchy, the heat in the office was overpowering. He hoped to Christ they sorted it out soon; he was feeling a strong urge to put his head down on the desk and sleep. He had no real interest in what was going on here. The air was dry and he wanted to cough all the time. He sighed noisily and the doctor rolled his eyes.

'Look, I'm sorry if I'm boring you. I was asked for my professional opinion and I am giving it.' He stood up. 'If you would excuse me . . .'

Palmer stood up too.

'I'm sorry, Dr Jannet. I'm suffering here from the heating. It's broken and we can't turn the bloody thing off. Please, be seated and tell me what we need to do.'

The other man sat back down.

'Carter is suffering from a severe form of depression, that much is obvious. He needs medication and psychiatric help as soon as can be arranged. He is a danger to himself and to everyone around him.'

'Did he admit to the killing?'

Dr Jannet smiled.

'Now you know better than that, Palmer. When he's better you can interview him. Until then he needs care and medication.'

Palmer sighed again. He had never liked doctors and his opinion was not being changed by this supercilious prick sitting opposite.

'So we can't interview him then?'

Jannet shook his head.

'He needs a suitable environment, a secure hospital. I wouldn't recommend prison at this time unless we can't place him anywhere else.'

'So it's a no-no, then?'

Jannet nodded.

'A definite no-no. He really needs a secure place and some kind of help before he harms someone else.'

'Fair enough. But we know he killed Black, he admitted it in the police car. His exact words were: "I will do the whole family, they need culling like rats need culling".'

243

Palmer grinned.

'The worst of it is, he has a fucking point. The Blacks burned his wife but they're also responsible for a one-family crime wave. The dead man's wife is on remand for an arson attack on Carter's wife.'

'With respect, Palmer, that's your problem. He needs to be moved and soon, OK? I will see what I can arrange.'

The doctor left and Palmer took off his jacket. He stank of sweat thanks to his polyester shirt. He called in a subordinate.

'Give Carter whatever he wants food and drink wise. He's being moved to a secure hospital, no way we can interview him now. It's taken the doctors all this time to decide that. Still, he's a nice bloke, see he's taken care of, OK? But be careful, he's still a handful by all accounts.'

'OK, sir. His daughter rang and wants to know when she can see him.'

Palmer shrugged.

'Who the fuck knows when that will be? He's madder than the maddest madman at the moment, by all accounts. We'll pass him over and see what happens.'

Sadie looked around the flat and breathed a sigh of relief. It was lovely, with a TV and video and a decent hi-fi unit. It was decorated nicely, too, with pale walls and expensive furniture. She could easily envisage herself living in this luxury. There was a bathroom with mirrored walls and a large corner bath.

She was cheering up by the moment. She had expected a right dump but this was something different. This she could live with.

Patrick watched her closely. He had seen this reaction time and time again.

'Like it?'

His voice was friendly and she smiled brightly as she answered him.

'It's fantastic, Pat.'

'You got to work for it, girl, you know that, don't you?'

She nodded.

'I have hand-picked you to work with Maisie here and you will earn top wedge, right, but you have to be up for it. I mean, five hundred a week is a lot of money.'

'Five hundred a week?'

Her voice was excited. He knew she was already bragging to her friends in her mind. Imagining their expressions.

He nodded.

'And all the rocks you can inhale, girl. It will all be laid on.'

Maisie watched quietly as he groomed the girl for the bad news.

'What do I have to do?'

She knew, they could hear it in her voice, see it in her face.

'You do what you're told.'

Maisie prepared a pipe and offered it to the girl. She sat down and inhaled heavily, needing the drug so she could listen to what they were going to say. Patrick made her a Scotch and Coke and afterwards she drank it straight down. It was drugged, and when she was incapable Maisie started to undress her while Patrick set up the camera.

Maisie stripped the girl expertly and surveyed her like a professional.

'She's lovely, Pat. We'll do well with her. Get the make-up off her and she'll look a lot younger. I have just the punter in mind. Shall I ring him?'

He nodded, fascinated, as he watched the girl set up a complete stranger and patted himself on the back once more because Maisie was going to improve his business no end.

Twenty minutes later a large bald man arrived. He had ill-fitting false teeth and a heavy belly covered in stretch marks. He was a property developer with too much money and a confirmed deviant thrill-seeker. He had no idea he was being taped and as Patrick watched him at work with the two girls he wondered if he would care anyway.

He wondered how Sadie would feel when she saw the tape and he informed her he was going to take it to her mother's house. She would toe the line whatever then. He would play it by ear, but it should have been Tiffany at work for him tonight, not Sadie, and the thought rankled.

But she was going to be paid back in full. No one put one over on Patrick Connor, and if anyone should know that, it was Tiffany Carter.

Chapter Eighteen

M arie was at the yard. Alan and she had made a kind of truce and she was throwing herself into her work so she didn't have to think too hard about anything else. In the four days since the shooting, she had tried to come to terms with everything but was having no luck. She felt worse than ever. Every time she thought of her father locked away her heart felt as if it would burst in her chest. At least he wasn't in the 'Ville. He was getting medical help and that was the main thing, she told herself twenty thousand times a day. He was off his head, as Mikey so succinctly put it, and she knew it was because of her. She could imagine how her mother must have taunted him over the years, especially over Marie. If only Marshall had not topped himself her mother might not have been so hard to live with.

As she worked she felt the presence of another person behind her and turned to see who it was. Expecting a customer, or a friend of Al's, she was amazed to see a large black man in a suit smiling at her. Her first thought was that Al was going up in the world if this was his new type of clientele.

'Can I help you?'

The man smiled.

'Marie Carter?' It was a question.

'Are you the police?'

'No, I am not the police, Miss Carter. I am the adoptive father of your son Jason.'

He saw her face drain of blood and her worried expression as she gasped, 'Is he OK? Is everything all right?'

She was standing now and he saw a fine-looking woman with a good figure and a natural grace. He understood now where Jason got his good looks. He was like his mother, only darker-skinned.

'Calm down, he's fine. He wants to see you and I wanted to make sure you didn't mind.'

He watched the changing expressions on her face. The joy, the hope and the fear. He guessed that the fear was at the thought of actually meeting her child face to face after what she had done to him and his sister all those years ago. He understood that but was amazed to see that she had the same fine qualities about her that were evident in her son. They had an identical presence, a way about them that kept in your mind long after meeting them. He was bowled over by her and was shocked to realise the fact.

He understood finally what had got her into such trouble. Something about her would drive men crazy. Some women had it, most didn't. This woman had it in abundance. She was stunning yet she dressed conservatively and wore little make-up. But she made you feel that if you could only get inside her, she would give you the best sex you had ever had in your life.

These thoughts shocked him even as they aroused him. He had never felt like this before in his life. Her presence was almost electric and as she sat down again he stared mesmerised as she crossed her legs.

'He wants to see you because you're his mother. He needs to see you, Miss Carter, and I think you need to see him. Am I right?' Oswald said, trying to sound businesslike.

He was smiling again and she was so glad her son had been given to this kindly man. On just a few minutes' acquaintance she could feel his goodness.

She stared into his face, her blue eyes moist with emotion and her mouth trembling as she said, 'But he refused to see me. When I asked, they said he had been approached and had not wanted to resume any kind of contact.'

Ossie had no idea what she was talking about.

'Well, he wants to see you now anyway.'

He made his voice light and made sure he smiled at her. He was convinced that lots of men made sure they smiled at her, and he was no exception.

'He really wants to see me?'

Marie's voice was unsteady and his heart went out to her.

'Why would I come all this way if it wasn't to look out for that boy of mine, eh? He's determined to see you and is looking forward to it so much. I love him, I love him desperately, and I think Jason needs you, Miss Carter, needs you in his life. He is a good boy, a nice boy. You will be proud of him.'

She put her hands to her mouth in a gesture of shock and

surprise. Then she said honestly, 'I never thought this day would happen. I dreamt about it for so many years and it kept me sane. I prayed they were both OK, that they had people in their lives who cared for them, and at least half of my prayers have been answered. Thank you. Thank you for coming here.'

'Thank Social Services. They gave me your address. There is another reason I am here and that is Tiffany, but now is not the time or place to discuss it all. Shall I pick you up when you finish here and then we can all talk properly?'

'Is Tiffany OK?'

He heard the worry in her voice and smiled reassuringly.

'She's getting there. Now I must dash, I have to get back to work. I'm always cancelling appointments these days. Good job I have a private practice as well – otherwise I'd get the sack!'

Marie wondered what the hell he was talking about, but left it as she didn't want to rock the boat in any way.

'You will come back later? I can leave at five . . . earlier if need be.'

'Oh, don't worry. I'll be back.'

Then he was gone. She watched his car pull out of the scrapyard and wondered at a God Who could throw you a curve when you were at your lowest ebb. She was going to see her son, her youngest child. He wanted to see her, actually wanted to see her, and she felt as if her head would explode with the force of her emotions. After all these years she would hear Jason's voice again, breathe the same air; be in the same place as her beloved son.

She realised then how her mother must have felt about Marshall and a tiny glimmer of understanding for the woman who despised her crept into her heart. Marie would see her boy with her own eyes and all the years of wondering about him would be over.

She heard a commotion in the yard and went to the window, her mind still on her son. She watched as Mikey Devlin and his henchmen put a cache of guns into the boot of Alan's car. She saw Alan watching them from the sidelines and guessed he was not happy about the situation. She sighed. Alan was in over his head here and it was only a matter of time before he had a capture of some kind.

All her life she had been on the periphery of law breaking and it had never really bothered her before today. Now she had the chance of seeing her son and maybe starting some kind of relationship with him, all the skulduggery around her was suddenly menacing. If she was implicated she would be away for the duration, and thanks to a visit from one good man she finally felt she had something to live for. Now she was witnessing guns and possible trouble and didn't want any part of it.

Mikey spotted her and waved merrily. She waved back, but her heart was not in it and suddenly she wondered what she had been thinking of, trying to use him to save her daughter. She still had the mentality of a criminal and the knowledge depressed her. Was she fit to see her son again when she had ties to her old way of life? It was important that he respected her and saw the woman she was now, not the woman she had been.

She had prided herself on eradicating that part of her personality, and yet as soon as trouble had loomed she had slipped back into her old life and her old role as if she had never left it. Used her body for gain as if she had never had that long break between punters. Slipped back into it all so naturally. She sighed.

Marie felt ashamed of her own behaviour. Questioned her ability to cope with what was happening to her and her children. Once more she was beating herself with a big stick and no one could hit her harder or with more viciousness than she could herself. After all, she had had years of practice. Thirteen years in all.

She went to the doorway and stared out. It was a beautiful day and she had not noticed that before. The sun was high and the air was still. A breeze like a baby's breath stirred against her skin and she was assailed by the memory of her son's tiny hands after she had given birth to him in hospital. She saw the perfection of his long eyelashes as he had lain sleeping in her arms. Remembered the rush of love she had felt until the need for narcotics had taken over. Jason had been born addicted and she thanked God it had not affected him later in any way. She had so much to answer for and could never find enough words inside herself to say sorry. She had read once, while incarcerated, that the Japanese had over a hundred words for no. If she had a thousand words for sorry it would still be inadequate.

Mikey came over to her and smiled easily.

'Lovely day, ain't it? May is always a nice month. My birthday's in May.' He laughed as he said it and she smiled at him, wondering what he was after.

'Still on for tonight?'

'I can't, Mikey. I'm going to see my son.'

He was genuinely pleased for her.

'That's good, ain't it?'

She nodded. 'Very good. I feel really nervous, to be honest.'

He pushed a fist against her chest playfully.

'What for? He's a lucky boy. If you'd been my mother I never would have left home!'

The men with him laughed as he had said the last bit out loud and Marie smiled gently.

'Suppose he decides he doesn't like me? It's a lot to take on board, what I did all those years ago.'

Mikey was dismissive.

'So what? It happened. Let it go, Marie. Give yourself a break and enjoy tonight. Think of me on me tod in that bleeding great gaff, that should put a smile on your boat. Now give us a kiss, gorgeous, I have to go. Got to see a man about a dog.'

He grinned.

'That's true, actually. I have to see me brief about me ex-wife!'

Marie laughed at him and he was pleased he had cheered her up. He understood how she was feeling and he liked her a lot. Wanted to see her happy. If he wasn't careful she was in danger of turning him into a nice bloke!

He turned the music up loud and honked the horn as he drove from the yard and Marie waved, as she knew he expected it.

'Love's young dream, eh? You've got him by the short and curlies,' Alan commented. 'Make the most of it, Marie. It won't last long.'

'What do you mean?'

He smiled at her and shrugged.

'Nothing. Just that he never lasts long with anyone, that's all.'

'Well then, let's hope he gets fed up with bringing all his shit to this yard then, shall we?'

Alan didn't answer her. She knew he wouldn't which was why she had said it. She would have liked to tell him her news, though, but now wasn't the time or the place. She made them both coffee and as she sipped the hot sweet liquid envisioned seeing her child at last.

Inside she hugged herself for joy.

Tiffany looked and felt terrible. She had walked out of hospital in a stolen coat and was now on her way back to the squat. She felt so ill and afraid, not because of her injuries but because the need for the crack was overwhelming. The pain she could cope with, it was fear of meeting Patrick that really scared her.

Once out of sight of the hospital she opened the bag she had taken from the nurse's station. As luck would have it, there was a purse with fifty quid in it, an electric bill for forty-five quid, and a few credit cards. She hailed a cab and made her way first to Rosie, who wasn't in or wasn't answering the door, and then on to Carole Halter's. She owed Tiffany money and she was going to make sure she got it back. In full.

'You all right, love? You look rough,' the driver commented.

Tiffany smiled as best she could.

'Had a car crash.'

'Shouldn't you be in hospital?'

Tiffany grinned at the words.

'Shouldn't you be driving the fucking cab?'

Her voice was jocular but the man took the hint. He drove her in silence to the address she'd given and didn't get a tip. As she limped up the broken stairs of a block of flats he shook his head in sadness. So many young girls like her about these days.

Carole Halter was getting ready for a night on the street, and was more than surprised to see Tiffany on her doorstep.

'If you've come round here because I told your mother everything then you can fuck off. I ain't got the time or the energy for a row.'

Her strident voice was nervous and Tiffany guessed she had already seen Patrick.

'Look at me, for Christ's sake – do I look like I could even have a row? Just let me lie low here for a few hours and score for me, Cal. That's all I want.'

Carole pulled her in and slammed the front door shut. She sighed.

'You got some front, Tiff, coming round here. You're just like your mother. You attract trouble.'

Tiffany, used to this woman's complete two-facedness, didn't even bother to answer her.

'I have some cards here if you want them.'

Carole was immediately interested.

'What you got?'

'I stole a bag. There's a Visa, a MasterCard and a Switch.'

She passed them over and saw Carole smiling.

'Sixty-forty on whatever I get for them, eh?'

Tiffany nodded. She was tired. All she wanted was a rock and some peace.

'Whatever. Just score for me, would you?'

She handed over the fifty pounds.

Carole's haggard face was suddenly troubled.

'He made a right mess of you, didn't he?'

Tiffany shrugged.

'Have a bath, Tiff. You'll feel better if you have a soak.'

Tiffany walked through to the bathroom. It was filthy as usual.

'No, thanks. I don't want an infection!'

Carole laughed.

'There's an old tin of Vim somewhere. Scrub it with that. I never was tidy-minded as everyone knows.'

Tiffany went back into the chaos of the lounge and lay on the sofa. It stank as it always had. She remembered the same sofa from visits here with her mother when she was small. It stank then and it still did. The whole place was a disgrace. But she couldn't be a chooser today, she was a beggar and she knew that.

'Hurry up, Carole, will you? I'm getting fucking wired.'

Carole pulled a shabby coat over her revealing clothes and sighed.

'You sound like your mother. Drugs are a mug's game, Tiff. Have a fucking drink, that's my poison. At least you can sleep that fucker off and get on with what you got to do.'

Tiffany wasn't listening. If one more person said she was like her mother she would scream. She knew she was, didn't need to keep being reminded of that fact. Her daughter came into her mind and she pushed the thought away. She couldn't cope with the child and if her brother's parents took her then that was all to the good. He seemed to have done all right with them.

She was aching all over, but she told herself she had done the right thing. She wanted to give herself a few days, chill out and forget everything. Then she would be in the right frame of mind to sort out her life, she decided.

Deep down she knew she was fooling herself, though. That she had given up on herself and on her daughter. That the drugs now took precedence over everything else. But she was a good actress and could con herself into believing whatever she wanted to think. She had conned her brother and his family, and now she would con everyone else, but she would get to oblivion if it killed her.

An hour later she had made a makeshift pipe from an orange juice carton and had the lift she had craved so desperately. As she inhaled the substance she felt her brain react, felt the complete high, and as

253

she lay back against the grimy sofa let out a heavy sigh of relief. She closed her eyes and smiled.

Carole Halter watched her in fascination. Marie had jacked up on that same sofa and she had seen the same look of satisfaction come over her face as well. It was mad, the whole world was mad. She left the girl to her own devices and made her way to Chigwell and a man who would buy the cards and clone them.

All in all it had been a good day. She had earned a few quid and had a houseguest. She got lonely at times and Tiffany would be a bit of light relief for her. Especially as she had apparently unloaded the kid.

Carole missed her own daughters at times. As much as they got on her nerves they were company. Now LaToyah had got herself a further nine months for fighting in nick and so Carole wouldn't see her again for ages. She was determined to go and visit her at some point but it was hard getting it together. She was working all hours and then clubbing with her new found mates and asleep most of the day, so it was difficult to get things sorted at times. But now Tiff was here perhaps she could talk her into going with her.

She hurried herself along. She was determined to earn a few quid tonight. It was heavy going at the Cross because you had to take on so many punters to get any real money. The competition was fierce as well, especially with all the schoolies, the young runaways who made their way there.

Life was hard these days and it was going to get harder. She knew that better than anyone.

Maxie and Eddie were having a drink in the Dean Swift. They were meeting a man there who had a bit of information for them. They were off their usual manor and consequently uneasy. As they sipped their designer beers they looked around warily. But the place seemed friendly enough and they gradually relaxed.

Dino Carvalles came into the pub with his usual good-humoured smile and waved at them as he got himself a drink. Approaching their table he said genially, 'How's it going, guys?'

Maxie grinned. Dino was a big man and a funny one. He had a natural sense of comic timing that made his jokes all the more hilarious.

'OK. Yourself?'

Dino shrugged.

'Usual. Here, what do you say to a woman with two black eyes and a fat lip? "That will teach you to keep your trap shut!" '

They all laughed, along with three men from another table who had heard the joke. One of them shouted out, 'What do you call a coon in a suit? The accused.'

The men with him busted themselves with laughter but Maxie turned in his seat and looked at them menacingly.

'What did you fucking say?'

The joketeller was big with a shaved head and a tattoo round his neck that read 'Cut here'. Maxie had seen people like him all his life and he hated them. Hated their racism, the fact that they put themselves above him and his black brothers just because they were white.

Dino shouted, 'What has a white bloke with a big cock got that his mates ain't? A black forefather!'

The big man was not amused and he stood up menacingly.

'Outside, now.'

Eddie stood up with Maxie. He was upset at this treatment as well and was determined to show them that.

'In the car park now, you cunt!'

They all walked from the pub. As they hit the street Maxie saw five blokes in a white Cavalier. He realised before Eddie did that they had been set up. The men were tooled up and as they got out of the car Maxie felt his bowels turn to ice water. Dino was distancing himself from the action. As Maxie caught his eye he shrugged as if to say sorry.

Dino had set them up and it could only have been over one person. Eddie realised this was because of Tiffany Carter and cursed himself for getting involved in the first place.

He caught Maxie's eyes and knew that he was thinking exactly the same thing. They saw knives, wrenches and baseball bats. It was serious; this wasn't going to be just a hiding. They were dead.

The big white skinhead grinned.

'Patrick Connor says hello.'

The beating was fast and brutal. Eddie died on his way to hospital and Maxie never regained consciousness.

It hit the papers as a race crime, as Patrick had expected it to.

They never stood a chance.

Verbena was at home waiting for her husband to bring back the woman who had birthed Jason yet never been a mother to him. Her son – *her* son not this woman's – was already showered and changed into his best and waiting with bated breath for Marie's arrival.

The place was spotless. She had offered her cleaner double wages to come in and do the honours. It was now pristine. She would show this slut how they lived. What they had offered her child, the one she had abandoned without a second's thought. Just like her daughter had done.

Verbena was shaking and it was from anger pure and simple. Her whole body felt as if it was crying out for something. She knew, deep inside, that what she wanted was for her son to tell her he hated his natural mother and wasn't going to see her ever again.

She clung to that hope. Once he had seen Marie Carter in all her disgusting glory he would realise what he had in Verbena herself. Her fragrant cleanliness. Her love for him. Her devotion even. Wasn't she taking on his slut of a sister's child? Didn't that prove her love for him that she would do that?

Verbena did not really like girls, they were troublesome. She preferred boys. Boys needed their mothers for all the right reasons. Once he saw his birth mother Jason would understand her worries. Imagine introducing a woman like her to his friends! Youngsters from good, affluent homes. It was laughable.

But she couldn't laugh, not yet. Not until she had seen his reaction. Ossie said Marie had seemed very nice. But he would, her good old-fashioned liberal man who voted green and had no idea about the real world whatsoever.

'They're here!'

She heard the excitement in Jason's voice and sighed. Heard him running down the entrance hall to open the door. She lit a cigarette and carefully arranged her face into a neutral expression. She would wait and see what happened. When a big blowsy trollop came in she would smile at her and be nice. Jason was, after all, her son now not this woman's and Verbena would prove that to her. She looked at the photo albums on the table and felt a moment's triumph. She had the memories, not this woman, and would prove that to her with subtlety and cunning.

This was war and the other woman did not stand a chance.

Marie looked up at the large house and felt a moment's shyness. It was in a pleasant tree-lined street and all the drives had new cars parked in them. It was a good area and she saw a woman looking at them curiously as she went about her business. She looked pointedly at Marie's suit and suddenly she found it lacking, wished she had had time to buy a new dress before she met her son. First impressions were so important.

Then the front door was flung open and she gasped as she saw the boy coming towards her. It was Marshall, her brother, only with dark skin and hair. But the likeness was uncanny. It made her heart stop in her chest and her breath come in short shuddering gasps. This was her son, her child, her baby.

The tears came then, and as he stood before her, his smiling face so honest and sincere in its joy, the tears burst from Marie's eyes and she instinctively gathered him into her arms. As his went around her she felt as if God Himself had come down from heaven and performed a miracle. She felt happy, truly happy, for the first time in many long years.

She could smell him: a mixture of expensive soap and young man's sweat. He was shaking almost as much as she was.

Jason pulled himself free from her embrace and said shyly, 'Hello again, Mum.'

She hugged him as if afraid to let him go. She *was* frightened in case he disappeared from her sight.

'Hello, Jason.'

Her voice was a distant memory, but it stirred something inside him and he fell in love with his mother as boys do. He fell in love with her as the woman who had conceived him and borne him and without whom he would not exist. All his life he had needed something and now he knew what it was. He had needed to know where he came from, and he had come from this pretty woman standing before him. He would finally know what and who he was.

Marie looked down the hallway and saw a woman standing there, beautifully dressed and with an expression that made her look as if she had just had a knife stuck into her ribs.

Verbena walked back to the kitchen in a daze.

The woman was beautiful. Extremely so. The opposite from what she had expected. Marie had entranced her son and Verbena had a feeling she had also entranced Oswald. She had heard him telling Jason how nice his mother seemed and had assumed he was just trying to make the whole thing easier for the boy. Wrong. He was understating her attraction if anything.

She lit another cigarette and busied herself making coffee and tea. She was fuming inside and also feeling frightened. This woman could take her son from her, but that was never going to happen, not while Verbena had breath in her body. As she heard them come into the house she plastered a smile on to her face.

She was standing by the double sink when Marie walked into the kitchen, held out her hand and said gently, 'Hello. Thank you for letting me come to your beautiful home.'

As Verbena shook hands all she could think was, This woman is stunning. She is enigmatic, has natural grace, and my son and husband are hanging on her every word.

'Coffee, tea?'

It was all she could force from between her tight lips. She just wanted to take back her arm and fell this woman to the floor, so great was the jealousy inside her.

Carole Halter was in a pub having a quick drink between punters. The weather had turned again and it was cold, especially at night, so she was freezing in her flimsy clothing.

'Hello, Carole, all right?'

She turned to see Lally Turner, an old brass she had known for years.

'Fuck me, girl, you still going?'

Lally shook her head.

'Nah, I have a little bird scratching for me these days.'

Lally was a large woman, a renowned lesbian with a penchant for young girls whom she put on the game. She had worked the streets for years and was well known, a fountain of wisdom and also a hard nut to crack.

'You heard the news about Connor?'

Lally's voice was conspiratorial.

'No, what?' Carole was instantly all ears.

'He's put five grand on Tiffany Carter's head. Whoever delivers her gets the poke. He *must* be in love is all I can say.'

Carole's eyes nearly popped out of her head.

'Who told you that?'

'His new bird. Maisie, is it? She was asking round this afternoon.'

'I ain't heard nothing about it.'

Lally shrugged.

'Well, I spoke to her meself. Wouldn't mind getting a bit of action from *her*. Right up for it, as young as she is. He has a goldmine there, but knowing that black ponce he's already sussed that much out for himself.'

Karen finished her drink in double quick time and left the pub.

Her mind was reeling. Five thousand pounds, plus the chance to get back into Connor's good books!

She knew she was scum and she knew she was wrong but she'd make the call anyway. That was a lot of money and Carole needed it desperately.

She was humming as she walked to the nearest phone box. It crossed her mind that with five grand she could get herself a mobile.

Chapter Nineteen

Verbena watched as both her husband and son tried to get their ten pence worth in with this woman who had infiltrated her home. She studied Marie quietly, looking at everything from her hair to her shoes. Her clothes had seen better days but were still good quality.

'This is us in Barbados. My mum, I mean . . .'

Jason was unsure how to put things and Marie smiled gently and said, 'She is your mother, Jason, legally as well as emotionally. I don't mind you saying it.'

Verbena saw the look of relief on her son's face and could have screamed. Her boy was actually pandering to this murdering bitch! A tart who had been a drug addict and a whore, yet to look at her own husband and son you'd think the Queen herself had come to tea. She watched as they smiled happily at one another and wanted to shout at them all.

She didn't need this woman to give her son permission to call her *Mother* – she had been his mother for years. She stood up abruptly and went back to the kitchen; she could not stand to listen to any more.

She left them in the drawing room, laughing with the bitch as she was already calling Marie Carter in her head. The force of her own feelings scared her. She felt capable of murder herself. She took a few deep breaths and lit yet another cigarette. She could smell Marie, like a bitch on heat she was, drawing men to her. Taking the two most important people in Verbena's life and winning them over.

Her husband followed her and slipped his arms around her waist. Verbena pulled away from him and whispered spitefully, 'You want *that* around my son?'

Ossie looked at her sadly and answered her in the same vein.

'She is a nice woman, Verbena. Give her a break. She is trying to

261

change her life. She has done a degree; *is* a changed person. She is rehabilitated, darling. And your son is also *her* son and *my* son. Not exclusively yours. Not now, not ever.'

Verbena was hurting. She didn't want to hear what her husband was saying. She shook her head at him, as if looking at a complete fool.

'I knew this would happen. She waltzes in here with her flashy looks and her terrible clothes and invades my home – and you take her part. Well, I've seen the way you look at her. She knows how to get men on her side – it's what women like her are good at, isn't it? Prostitutes, whores, call them what you will.'

Ossie was shaking his head in bewilderment. He could not believe what his wife was saying. He had expected jealousy; she had always been jealous though she managed to keep it under control most of the time. But this was disproportionate.

'Have you gone mad, woman? And keep your damn voice down!'

Verbena's face was twisted with rage and hurt.

'There you go, defending her again. She looks like Christine Wallace, is that the attraction?'

Ossie sighed to have that thrown at him again. Christine had been a partner at his private practice. She had been clever, beautiful, and Verbena had hated her on sight.

'Christine and I were friends. She worked with me, that is all. I am sick of having to explain that over and over again. You know it's the truth.'

Verbena laughed nastily.

'Do I? How do I know anything any more? I saw the way you looked at that woman, and I know men. I know what you want from her – and she'll let you have it, I have no doubt about that. She likes black men, doesn't she?'

She turned from him and gripped the sink. She expected him to try and cajole her again but instead he walked quietly from the kitchen.

Verbena realised she had gone too far.

Marie smiled at Ossie as he came back into the lounge. He looked worried. She had already picked up the vibes from Verbena and was aware of the underlying tension here even though the boy wasn't.

Why did this always happen to her? Why did women hate her so much on sight without even trying to get to know her? She could have understood it if she was half-naked or if she flirted with their men, but she didn't. She *wouldn't*.

But Verbena was like her own mother. Her son was her all and no other woman was ever going to take him from her. Verbena had the same dead-eyed look as Louise and the same body language. Her smile never reached her eyes. She had a coldness to her face that seemed to reach out to Marie and lodge itself in her heart. She was more than aware that as far as Verbena was concerned, Marie Carter was not welcome in this house or their lives, particularly Jason's, and she never, ever would be.

It wasn't just because she was Jason's real mother; it went deeper than that and Marie knew it. This was a jealousy that was out of control. It would have been the same if she had been his girlfriend. Verbena was full of hatred for other women and if Marie wasn't careful it would be turned on her full force.

She would have to tread warily because she wanted this boy in her life more than she had ever wanted anything before. It was a dream come true. And through him she might even gain access to her daughter and grandchild. She could maybe have a bit of family around her, what she had dreamed of for so many years.

She'd just have to pretend she didn't notice anything and hope for the best. But it galled her that once more in her life she was at the mercy of an unhappy and vindictive woman. She forced a smile and made herself concentrate on her son. He at least was pleased to see her and that in itself was a miracle as far as Marie was concerned.

Alan was at Thurrock services once more. As he stood by smoking a cigarette, he kept his eye out for the Scania lorry that was going to deliver his cargo to Newcastle. This was a new venture, but with Tilbury docks having so much gear arriving on a daily basis it was good business. At least as far as Mikey was concerned.

Alan was not so sure. In fact he wondered what the hell he was doing here in the first place. He must have been mad.

The smell of diesel hung in the air, and the thunder of traffic on the M25 was loud and disturbing. He thought about Marie and hoped she was OK. He knew she was seeing her son. Mikey had let the cat out of the bag and Alan was hurt that she had not even mentioned it to him. But then again, why should she?

Things were still strained between them. It didn't matter what he told her, he knew he was never going to accept Marie and Mikey being together. It had given him the push he needed to expel

Devlin from his life. Alan wanted out and he was going to get out, no matter what. It might cost him, but it would be worth it.

His mobile rang and he answered it. The drop was all ready to go ahead and he glanced around him to make sure everyone was in place. He felt sick with apprehension but this was something he had to do. He had no say in it whatsoever.

Which didn't make it any easier.

Tiffany was still at Carole's and she was completely out of her head. The rocks were the only things she wanted. Needed. They had taken over every other feeling she had. Suppressing even her mothering instincts, which had been strong, they made her forget all the troubles in her life. The only bugbear was, the problems were still there when she came down, and then the depression caused by the crack made them seem much worse than they had been before. It was a vicious circle and she hated it. But she was in a no-win situation now and just had to go with whatever made her feel good at the time. This was her life and she had accepted it.

She understood why her mother had gone like she had. It had been because of Patrick Connor; he had worked his evil magic on her too. He was a destroyer of people, had been doing it for years. It had been in this very flat he had first taken Tiffany under his wing, bullshitting her about her mother and what a whore she had been. How he had tried to help her because she was the mother of his child, Tiffany's brother.

She had needed him then; just out of the council home and in the real world all alone, he had seemed like a rock to her. He had been so handsome, with money, a nice car, and well respected. Everywhere she went with him they were treated like royalty. She had been swept off her feet, had thought she was so clever. So on the ball. Then she had had the baby, and that was when he had changed towards her. The rest was a complete and utter travesty of love. He had taken her and given her drugs, talked her into whoring and made her into the person she had tried so hard not to be. Her poor mother . . . the woman he had said so many bad things about and convinced Tiffany was scum. But her mother had tried to help her and Tiffany had turned away, while simultaneously wanting to feel her arms around her and wanting to have her nearby.

She had just not realised it. Had not realised how lonely and frightened she was. The man who had made her so happy a little time before frightened her now. The man who had told her he loved her and wanted her more than anyone else in the world had deliberately set out to make her into the girl she was, a watered-down version of her mother. Or the mother he had told her about anyway. The one who had abandoned her kids, dumped them and lived for drugs. Well, Tiffany had done the same thing and yet she knew she wasn't really bad, just weak and unhappy. If her mother were here now she would beg her forgiveness. But it was all too late. Patrick Connor had knocked all the decency from her body and shame made her want to keep away from everyone, especially her own little daughter.

Like her mother she was ashamed of what she had become, and the more ashamed she became the more drugs she wanted to consume. They, at least, killed the pain. Tiffany hated herself inside and out, Patrick had seen to that. She had absolutely no self-respect any more.

He had done his job well, she would give him that much.

She heard the door and didn't even open her eyes. She assumed it was Carole back from work. She had drunk the last of Carole's whisky so was expecting a row but wasn't too worried. She should have dumped the cards by now and received the money for them, so they'd have a few quid to see them through the next few days. Then Tiffany would have to go on the street, but it would be far away from London. Far away from her daughter and brother. She was resigned to being alone now. Anastasia was better off without her.

She could smell herself, a sour smell like milk that had been left in the sun for a few days. But it was a comforting smell as well. It told her she was still alive. She watched the colours behind her eyes, bright vibrant colours that she loved to see. There was a whole world behind her eyelids that she had not enjoyed since she was three years old.

As she relaxed back on to the dirty cushions she felt a hand wrap itself around her neck and her eyes flew open to see Patrick's face close to her own.

'You smelly, dirty cunt! I have you at last.'

The fear was so acute she felt faint. She could smell his breath and was acutely aware that he could smell hers. He threw her back on to the cushion and she saw the look of disgust that crossed his face and closed her eyes against it.

'You are crunched, girl. I will make you sorry you ever decided to try and think for yourself. All I have done for you and this is how you repay me, is it? You made a complete cunt of me and you actually thought I would let you get away with it?'

He was poking a finger into her chest and it hurt, but she knew it was nothing to the hurt she was going to experience before too long.

'You are dead, Tiff, so you better start saying your prayers, mate.'

He slapped her heavily across her head and she felt her ear split. He wore a heavy keeper ring, and though the pain was sharp she was beyond feeling it. She was used to it. She didn't even cry, just looked up at him sullenly.

He saw the look and slapped her again, but he had a plan for her and was careful not to make her look any worse than she already did.

He cut himself a line on the dirty table and she watched enviously as he snorted it.

'Carole will wonder where I am.'

She was clutching at straws and knew it.

He grinned.

'It was Carole who told me where you were, Tiffany. She's five grand better off, the ugly bitch. She couldn't wait to sell you down the river, love. You ain't got no mates, you ain't got nothing.'

She kept quiet. She knew the last thing to do now was antagonise him.

'See what you cost me? See all the trouble you cause, and yet you still think you can treat me like shit, don't you?'

He was gone, she could see it from his eyes and decided to keep quiet and do what he wanted. Someone had once said that he was a psycho and they were right. Even without drugs he was unpredictable and vicious.

'I killed Maxie and Eddie today over you. Both good grafters. Maxie was the closest thing I had to a mate and now he's dead. All over you, Tiff. I hope you're happy now?'

She knew that he really believed she was the cause of what had happened. He was good at blaming other people for his own mistakes. According to him he never, ever did anything wrong. It was always someone else. Today it was her turn to take the blame.

She was finally convinced of the lunacy of the man before her and becoming more and more terrified by the second.

'You just don't realise the trouble you have caused me, do you? Well, it stops now. I am going to sort you out fucking once and for all.'

Tiffany was dragged from the sofa and even though her legs were like jelly she allowed him to frogmarch her from Carole's flat.

People were going about their daily business as he threw her in the car but she knew no one would interfere. It was that kind of neighbourhood.

You could be stabbed to death in this street and no one would have seen or heard anything because it made life safer to keep yourself to yourself.

Jason was more aware than any of them realised of what was happening with his adoptive mother. He also understood it all on one level. But his real mother, his birth mother, had affected him strongly. To feel her near him brought joy. She was beautiful and he could feel kindness exuding from every pore of her body. It was like his dad said: she had been a victim, like Tiffany was a victim now. She needed understanding and she needed him in her life, just like he needed her. He knew all this already, and he was going to talk to Verbena about it as soon as he could and reassure her that his birth mother would never take his adoptive mother's special place. He loved his adoptive mother and needed her as well.

As he listened to his real mother's voice, low and husky, he knew that this was someone who was good inside. It shone from Marie like a beacon. Whatever she had done, it had been many years before when she had been a different person. He had seen what drugs had done to his sister and understood that.

He felt he could look at her for hours, she was so still and tranquil. She made him feel calm and complete.

He heard Verbena calling him from the kitchen and excused himself. There were sandwiches and a cake ready to be brought into the lounge. He plastered a wide smile on his face as he walked to his adoptive mother's side.

'Thank you for doing this, Mum, it looks scrumptious. I know how hard it must be for you.'

Verbena looked at the boy she adored and forced a smile to her face.

'It's the least I can do for the poor woman. I just hope we're doing the right thing, that's all.'

'What do you mean?'

Verbena shrugged.

'Well, think about it. From prostitution to prison, drug addiction to a beautiful home like this. I'd be very careful for a while if I were you. She may only be out for what she can get. After all, that's what people like her do, isn't it?'

267

She saw the hurt on his face but couldn't stop herself now.

'Look, Jason, I don't want to upset you, son. But people like her, your so-called birth mother, they just use people. Especially men. Why do you think she's all over your father, eh?'

Jason was non-plussed, unsure where his mother was going with this.

'What do you mean? Dad likes her as much as I do. She's nice.'

Verbena could see the confusion on his face as he tried to convince himself that she meant no harm. Even though deep inside he knew better, knew what she meant to do and was trying to avoid a confrontation. She had always been protective of him and he had appreciated it over the years. He had never called it jealousy before, but he knew there had been an element of that to it. If he had said he liked another boy's mum, for instance, she had always been miffed. He had learned very young how to be a diplomat.

'Of course your dad likes her, Jason. She is making sure he likes her. I don't want to speak ill of the poor woman but I have to speak as I find. Don't forget what she was, is – a murderer and a prostitute.'

Jason stared into the face of the woman who had been everything to him for years and was surprised to find he didn't really like her. He loved her, but he had never liked her, and at this moment in time he was also feeling another repressed emotion which was anger. She often made him angry with her throwaway remarks. Like when his friend Thomas's mum had come round. She was fat and jolly, always laughing, and his mother had said she was OK, but just a bit too loud. 'A touch common' had been her exact words. It had angered him at the time.

'*That* was a long time ago. Why don't you leave her alone! I want to know her and I will know her, whatever you try and say.'

Verbena sensed the animosity coming off her child and felt sick at the thought of what he was saying. He would prefer that *thing* to her? The woman who had loved him, adored him, all his young life? It was as if a cancer had split open and all the poison was pouring out.

She was whispering feverishly as she grasped his shoulders, 'She may be your birth mother but that means nothing, *nothing*! I was the person who fed you and loved you. I don't really see why you need someone like her in your life. Her own family didn't even want her . . .'

'*Your* family didn't want you because of Dad, did they? Because he was black. So what's the difference really?'

Verbena was incensed at his defence of the woman she saw as her rival. A rival not only for her son's affection but also for her husband's.

'How dare you say that to me of all people? Without me, *boy*, you would have been in a home all your life like that sister of yours. I was warned, all right. Blood will out, people said. But I didn't listen, and my God, they were right. You've found your level with *her*, haven't you! For all the fine education I provided for you, it seems you still want the gutter I dragged you out of.'

Jason was stunned at her words and the vituperative way she said them. Her eyes filled with tears as he stared at her in utter disbelief.

Verbena was sorry as soon as the words left her mouth. As she went to take the boy in her arms he pushed her forcibly away. Then, turning, he ran from the kitchen and up the stairs to his bedroom. Ossie was out in the kitchen in seconds.

'What have you done now, Verbena?'

It was the accusation in his voice that was her undoing. She sat at the table, put her head on her arms and cried like a baby.

Tiffany was in Patrick's flat and he was getting weirder by the second. She had only ever seen him like this twice before and each time it had been over the murder of a close friend. She now realised he had probably caused those murders. He was capable of anything.

As she watched him stalking round the room she felt the familiar fear encompass her body. She was sweating profusely, and her heart was hammering against her chest. He was talking constantly.

'What is it with you fucking people? I give you everything you need and yet you still think you can mug me off. I spent poke on you and you will repay my investment or I will break your fucking neck.'

He stuck his face close to hers.

'Are you fucking listening to me?'

He was screaming the words in her face.

She nodded, her face crumbling with terror. She was aware that he was dangerously close to the edge and that if she antagonised him now he would really harm her.

'Look at the state of you! You fucking stink and you look what you are, lady, a fucking drughead. A slapper. An ugly whore. I am ashamed to admit I ever fucked you. You are a worthless piece of shit – what are you?'

She couldn't answer him, too scared to talk, knowing that the sound of her voice could be the trigger he needed.

'I said, what the fuck are you?'

'I am a worthless piece of shit, Pat.'

Her voice was low and trembling; she was having trouble talking properly. She knew that her fear pleased him and felt a great sense of relief.

He dragged her off the sofa by her hair and into the bathroom.

'You'd better be scrubbed in ten minutes, Tiff, because I have some work for you tonight, girl, and you'd better do it right or you'll wish you'd never drawn a fucking breath and died in that cunt's belly. I mean that, girl. Just give me an excuse to hurt you, Tiff, I dare you to just give me one excuse.'

She stood in the beautiful bathroom with its gold taps and its expensive tiled walls. It was over the top, pictures of nymphs and the Venus de Milo everywhere, and the glass ceiling made her feel she was being watched, which knowing Patrick Connor wasn't too off the wall. As she already knew to her cost he was capable of anything.

He had left the door open and as she stripped off she was aware that he could come in at any moment. She piled her clothes on to the floor in a heap and, turning on the shower, stepped into the cubicle. The water was hot and even though she felt so bad inside, it felt good on her poor bruised body. She saw herself reflected in the mirror; she'd always been skinny but now she looked emaciated.

She knew that he had groomed her well and that she was trapped with him now. It had all gone too far. Whatever he told her to do, she would do. She had no other option. In a way, being back with him made her feel a weird sense of safety. At least it was over now. Kiss or kill, she had faced him so whatever was going to happen would happen. At least she wasn't wondering if she would meet up with him any more.

She scrubbed herself. Turning to the door, she saw him watching her. He had a large crack pipe in his hand, and as she realised it was for her she smiled.

She stumbled from the shower, soaking wet and still covered in soap, and took it from him gratefully. Sucking on the pipe as if her life depended on it, she enjoyed the rush when it came, the euphoric rush that made everything better and her life that much more bearable.

Patrick was like a different man now. He was holding her to him gently, caressing her naked back and talking normally.

'Why do you wind me up, Tiff? You know what I'm like if I get annoyed, so why do you craze me up like you do?'

She was looking at him, trying desperately to focus on his eyes and also trying hard to make him like her again.

She was back in the cycle once more and he knew it.

As he looked at her he suppressed an urge to ram his fist into her face; she was battered enough as it was. He had a much more serious punishment in mind for her and that would help ease some of the pent-up anger inside him.

There was a hammering at the door of his flat then and it made him jump. People had to get past the doorman before they could reach his home. That was the whole idea of paying a fortune for this place. Access was difficult and it gave him the measure of protection he needed in his line of work. He had also given the doorman a hefty wedge to screen his visitors so that ponce was due a serious slap in the near future.

He walked quickly to the door and shouted, 'Who is it?'

'It's the police. Open up, please, Mr Connor.'

He glanced round the room and then pushed the crack pipe into the bin in the kitchen. He was panicking and Tiffany felt his nervousness. Then he shoved her back into the shower and she started washing her hair, as she knew he wanted her to.

Patrick needed her to keep out of the way of the police and she was going to do just that. She started to scrub herself once more. The crack had mellowed her out and she was once again only interested in the next high. A high she might get if she did exactly what Patrick wanted.

He opened the door wide and stared at the two men standing before him.

'What the fuck do you want?'

The larger man, a DI called Smethurst, smiled lazily at him.

'Calm down, Mr Connor. We only want to question you.'

The man had large teeth that were stunningly white and Patrick focused on these as he shouted, 'You got a fucking warrant?'

He knew they didn't or they would have shown it to him already and been in the apartment. Also there would have been a few more of them, and they would have expected him to put up some resistance.

The DI shook his head and Patrick started to shut the door in their faces.

271

'Not so fast, Patrick, we're here to give you some news. Did you know Maxie died today? We wondered if you'd seen him at all. We're trying to put together his last movements.'

The younger policeman grinned.

'We understood you might be able to help us.'

Patrick snorted.

'Well, you understood fucking wrong then, didn't you? And another thing – how did you get up here without me getting a buzz or a call from the doorman, eh? You pulled a flanker and now they think I'm a dodgy bastard. Well, my brief will have something to say about that, mate. I think you're racially harassing me, you cunts. I been with me bird all day, shagging the arse off her in my bed.'

He shouted over his shoulder, 'Oi, get out here.'

Tiffany had a towel round her head and another wrapped around her body. She walked out into the hallway.

'All right, seen enough, have you? Now fuck off.'

The DI was annoyed.

'You don't seem too bothered about Maxie.'

Patrick shook his head slowly.

'Oh, I am bothered, mate. But I am also bothered about the fact you come to my door without warning, making a cunt of me in the place I live, and have the nerve to question my whereabouts on the day my best mate died as if I had something to do with it.'

He shook his head again and turned to Tiffany.

'If that ain't fucking racial harassment, I don't know what is.'

She walked back into the lounge. She didn't want them to see her too closely because she was so bruised and marked.

Patrick's handsome face was twisted with rage. He was so angry that he could feel himself losing control once more.

The DI sensed this and decided to antagonise him.

'Would you please come to the station? Of your own volition, of course. We would appreciate a statement as to your whereabouts since last night.'

He slid one shiny shoe into the doorway. The two policemen watched as Patrick Connor battled with himself.

'You winding me up? You dare to fucking wind me up?'

He was shouting again though trying his hardest to keep a lid on his emotions. He had had a lot of cocaine and was getting paranoid. He knew he had to get them away from here before he went to his bedroom and came back to them armed with his newly bought machete.

He was capable of murder and he knew it. It wasn't the first time he'd felt like it and he knew it wouldn't be the last.

'Get your foot out me door or I'll use reasonable force to remove it for you.'

The DI was nervous and it showed. He was a big man; he had a tickle now and again, took a few quid to turn a blind eye, but Connor was a lunatic and needed putting away. It was imperative he was put away. Also, he was being paid a good wedge by another dealer to take Connor out of the ball game. And he would. It was getting personal now.

After a few seconds Smethurst removed his foot and Patrick shut the door in his face. He watched through the spy hole until they got into the lift, then he breathed easily once more.

They had come to his door, they had actually come to his home! He was on the big list now and knew he had to watch his back. But if he went down he would take a good few with him, police as well as civilians.

He went back to the lounge and saw Tiffany looking at him still wrapped in the towel. He had forgotten she was even there. He stared at her long and hard but she knew he couldn't see her. He was planning something and she knew that whoever was on the receiving end of his anger would regret it dearly.

He poured himself a large Chivas Regal and drank it down in one gulp. Then he dialled a number on his phone and shouted into the receiver, 'Paul? The filth just came to my home, motherfucker. My *home*!'

Chapter Twenty

Marie was sitting alone in the lounge. She knew something had happened between the other three but she wasn't sure what. She could take a good guess, though. Jason had just run upstairs and Ossie had followed him.

She glanced round the room. It was beautiful, decorated in creams and beiges. It must take a lot of upkeep. She had had no real possessions for so long that the thought of trying to make a home seemed alien to her. But then, she had not made a very good job of it when she had last had the opportunity. She thought of all the home classes she had attended in prison and smiled wryly.

'Your home is where you relax. Where you spend most of your leisure time.' She could still hear the lecturer's voice as she'd said it. Marie had nearly answered: 'And there is nothing like a wrap of the big H to relax you in your home, ma'am. That is why most of us are here.' But she hadn't.

That poor woman couldn't even imagine the so-called homes of the people she was preaching to. She had always seemed highly nervous of her class of degenerates. Now Marie was feeling that same nervousness herself.

She was more nervous than she had been on her arrival. She had known instinctively that Verbena was going to be a problem, just had not expected it to manifest itself so soon. In fact, she wondered if she should get a taxi or something and leave. Let them all talk about what was happening. It was obvious Verbena had a problem with her and Marie could understand that. She didn't want to take the boy from her, couldn't do that even if she wanted to. He had a lot of his life invested in the couple who had adopted him. She couldn't expect him to want her over all this – the lovely home and the holidays and the good education.

She only wished Verbena had given her the time to thank her properly for all she had done for Jason. And Marie *was* grateful. She

275

really appreciated it all. If only Verbena could see past her face and body she knew that they could get on with one another. Marie was capable of getting on with anyone. Her years inside had made sure of that.

Verbena walked into the room and the atmosphere was instantly charged. Marie stared at her for long moments. Verbena was a heavy woman, well-rounded. Her eyes were spectacular; their greeny-blue colour made them seem almost catlike. She obviously loved her son *and* husband, the only thing that differentiated her from Marie's mother. Louise had the same problem with wanting to own people, but unlike Verbena had had no time for her husband at all. This woman had the same air of simmering animosity; it came off her in invisible waves. Warning people to back off, leave her boys alone and if possible sever any contact with them.

Marie was heart sorry for the woman but she wanted her son in her life and she would have him. No matter what this woman thought.

'I hope you're happy.'

The words were spoken in a low voice, almost a whisper, and Marie knew that Verbena had thrown down the first gauntlet.

'Not at all. Why would I be?'

Verbena snorted in a most unladylike way.

'Oh, I don't know. You come waltzing into my home and try and inveigle yourself into my family. I never wanted you here and neither did my son. In fact, when the social worker asked about him seeing you, I told them he had said no. But it still happened, didn't it? My husband saw to that. You want the boy back and now you're determined to take him for me.'

Marie stood up. She was taller than Verbena and as she walked over to her saw the first flash of fear on the other woman's face.

Standing before her Marie said gently, 'I would never try and take him from you. Why would I? This is all he knows. You have done a fantastic job with him. Jason's your son now, not mine. You took care of him, something I had never been able to do. Not properly anyway. I understand how you feel. Believe me, I understand.'

Verbena refused to be won over.

'Don't you patronise me! I know what you're doing and you will never, ever get me kissing your backside like those two. I know what you are, and I know what you want, and I will do all I can to prevent you from taking my son and turning him into a piece of dirt like you and your daughter. Now get out of my home!'

276

Marie stifled an urge to slap this supercilious bitch across her fat face. Instead she smiled again, a cold smile.

'Do you know something? I wouldn't want to be you for all the money in the world. As bad as my life was, at least I can sleep at night now. I accepted myself a long time ago. I was a drug addict and a prostitute; I am also branded a murderer. But I would rather be me than you because people like you are leeches. You drive everyone away with your so-called goodness. You should meet my mother, darling, there's nothing between the pair of you. Self-righteous prig is the term that springs to mind. You will drive that boy away from you with your attitude as sure as you will make him hate you because of it. Whatever my faults, and they are legion, I have attempted to change my life. My advice to you would be to do the same before it's too late.'

She walked from the room and out of the house and as she shut the front door felt as if she could cheerfully commit another murder. Instead of feeling worried by her feelings, though, part of her welcomed them. Because at last, finally, she was feeling like a normal person again. She felt angry but she could control the emotion. Something that had frightened her for years was her fear of losing her temper again. She was over that, she was like everyone else. She got upset and she walked away.

It was a small victory, she knew, but at least it would stop her from thinking about what she had left behind in that house. Her son. Her future.

In prison a therapist had taught her to think about what she had achieved instead of what she had failed at. That had been good advice and she pondered it now.

As she walked down the tree-lined avenue she thought how astonishing it was, her son living in all this luxury, with everything money could buy. Yet even in this bastion of respectability there was still room for someone just like her mother. Money did not make you happy. The truth of it had never hit home before but she had just seen it clearly illustrated.

Verbena would never be happy because she couldn't let people go. If only people saw themselves as others saw them, how differently they would view the outside world.

But at least Marie had touched her child, he had accepted her, even seemed pleased to see her. That was one victory she had gained.

She wasn't crying and even that fact pleased her. She was stronger than she'd thought and that meant maybe, just maybe, she might cope with living on the outside. If only she could make things right with Tiffany as well as keep in contact with her son; little by little she could right some of the great wrongs she had committed in her life. And pay back some of the people who had wronged her.

She was going to best Patrick Connor and take her daughter from under his influence even if she had to kill again to obtain what she wanted.

Patrick felt the noose tightening around his neck and was powerless to do anything about it.

The fact that the police had come to his flat rattled him. It was their way of saying they had him in their sights. He wondered who the grass could be. Not Maxie anyway, he was dead meat. But Patrick was shrewd enough to know that he had made a good few enemies over the years and any one of them could be putting his face up for a capture.

The fear factor had always worked for him until now. So what he needed, he reasoned, was to make a big splash that would tell everyone in his world just what he was capable of when pushed.

The more he thought about that idea, the more attractive it became. He saw himself as an avenging warrior, someone to be reckoned with. He forgot that he was going against his own rule: never make important decisions while under the influence of cocaine. All sense of reality went out of the window then and the feeling of euphoric strength it caused made you feel invincible even when you weren't. It was why people took the damn drug in the first place.

But Patrick was rattled, seriously rattled. His eyes alighted once more on Tiffany. Was she the person who was grassing him? Helping to get his arse kicked by Old Bill? Could they be using her to get at him? He knew they had wanted him for a long time. That they had known about his nefarious dealings but had never been able to link him to anything except his legal businesses for years. He paid his accountant a good wedge to make sure that he was pristine on paper, but his reputation had as usual preceded him and they were sniffing round once more.

They had by-passed the security of his flat and come to his front door. That spoke of tenacity and determination. Told him they were serious about giving him a capture, and if that happened he would go away until he was an old man. He could see the fright on

Tiffany's face and that reassured him. She would not have the guts to grass him up. She was a shitter, like all her kind.

He would have to start putting the frighteners on people, it was all he could do. Scare them into telling him what he wanted to know. But first he had to sort out this girl before him.

He smiled at her tenderly.

'All right, Tiff?'

She smiled back at him, relieved that he was calmer now. That the main force of his anger was spent. All she wanted to do was keep him as sweet as she could and hopefully make him like her a bit again. It was important to her that he liked her again because then she could relax a little.

Mikey and Alan were at the house in Essex. As they sipped brandy Alan looked around at the great baronial hall and smiled.

'This is some drum, Mikey.'

Devlin grinned.

'I know. I paid the Nash for it. But it's like me mother always said – you get what you pay for, eh?'

Alan nodded.

'So it would seem.'

Mikey drank his brandy down and immediately refilled his glass.

'You don't like me seeing Marie, do you, Alan?'

The question startled him and he was caught on the hop.

'It's none of my business, Mikey.'

Devlin shrugged.

'I suppose not. But then she does work for you and I ain't fucking stupid. I can see the way you look at her. She affects me like that an' all, Al. There's something about her, ain't there? A sort of niceness only some people pick up on. Hard to believe she was a brass at times, she's so feminine and dignified. Know what I mean? Yet I don't care about her past. She's nice to be with, like. Calming is the word I'm looking for.'

Alan realised even if Mikey didn't that he was well and truly in love.

'She's a terrific woman, Mikey. Had a few bad breaks, but then haven't we all? I think she's coped well. I certainly couldn't do a lump like she did and come out of it still relatively normal. Most lags come out lunatics. Only a few are tough enough to survive it and those are the ones with strong minds and hearts.'

Mikey was nodding.

279

'That's what I think and all, Alan. She's a grafter, ain't she? Like me.'

Alan didn't want to answer but knew he had to. He nodded his head and said gently, 'Yep. She's a grafter all right.'

A car pulled up on the drive and Alan went to the french windows.

'They're here.'

Mikey went to the door and Alan sat and waited while the two guests were greeted. When they finally came into the room he stood up and stretched out his hand.

'Pleased to meet you.'

The first man smiled, showing a set of very white even teeth. He was a handsome Indian though small by any standards, no more than five foot one, and so thin he was almost emaciated. The other man was big, over six foot, with a paunch.

'Mohammed Ali and Perjit Amarera. Our Indian friends,' Mikey introduced them. 'And this is my associate, Alan Jarvis.'

They all sat down and studied each other warily. It was always like this on a first meet, everyone trying to suss the others out. Alan relaxed. He would have nothing to do. Devlin would work this room and work it well. He had seen him in action before. He listened as they discussed mutual friends and enemies alike. After a while, and a few brandies, the plan was discussed: how to bring in heroin from Sri Lanka and distribute it all over Europe.

Once the work talk started the atmosphere changed once more, became energised, and when Mikey left the room Alan knew he was going for a line and hoped that he didn't overdo it. The Asians were renowned for never touching the stuff they produced and had an aversion to working with people who did.

They knew how dangerous it could be in the wrong context. It was a recreational drug, not one to use while making serious decisions.

So Alan sat back and smiled at the two visitors and hoped their business would be concluded soon, then he could go home and try and get some much-needed sleep.

Carole Halter stood by the road and smiled at a passing driver. She was drunk, and she was also five grand better off so she didn't really need the work. But she knew she should keep at it so as not to arouse any suspicion. The girls would all know the trophy money had been paid and would soon put two and two together if she disappeared, then she would be in line for a good hiding. They might fight the fuck out of each other but they were loyal when a girl was sold or had a reward out on her head.

Unless they wanted the money, of course. Then they would have done what she had and pretended they'd had nothing to do with it, just as she was doing now.

But it was burning a hole in her bag.

She was going to get a cab soon and visit her daughters. Then Carole was going to blow the rest on a good time.

As she got into the car that had stopped for her she bashed her shin and swore under her breath. The punter was big, with iron-grey hair and a wrinkled face. She could smell the odour of sweat, old sweat, and decaying teeth. But she forced a smile anyway. After all, she was a professional.

'How much for a blow job?'

He had a Northern Irish accent and it sounded harsh in the confines of the car.

'Ten quid, money first, and I use a condom. Twenty-five quid without. Money first.'

He grunted and drove away.

She lay back against the upholstery and tried to stop her head spinning. She was really drunk and she knew it. Just as well with him. She would not have taken him on sober. He stank. He was still driving ten minutes later when it occurred to her that she had been in the car a long time.

'Where are you fucking going?'

She was belligerent with the drink and it manifested itself in her voice. He didn't answer her, just carried on driving. She looked out of the window and saw that they were in a derelict street.

'Stop the fucking car now!'

He carried on driving without answering her. Instead he turned on the radio. It played loud rock music. He was driving fast and she was getting frightened. She put a hand across the car and tried to undo his trousers. He pushed her hand away aggressively and she shrank back into her seat.

Carole was in trouble and she knew it.

She glanced around the car. In the back there was a baby seat and a few toys, a bottle half filled with orange juice and a hammer. It was the hammer that caught her eye. She tried to open the door of the car, but the man just grabbed her by her coat and smashed her head towards the dashboard. She hit it with a massive noise and knew she was in the company of a nutter.

281

He finally spoke.

'One more move and I'll batter your fucking brains out.'

He carried on driving then as if nothing had happened, the sounds of Meatloaf filling the car. 'Bat Out of Hell' had been a favourite of hers once, many years ago when she had been young and the world had seemed an exciting place. When her tits had still pointed upwards and she had no cellulite. When her body had been her fortune even if her face had never been that beautiful.

She had heard of people saying their lives had flashed before them but this was ridiculous. She was thinking back to a time when she had been happy, as if she knew she was going to die.

She was used to rough treatment from the men who paid her for oral sex, and occasionally for full sex. They were ashamed of themselves for the most part, that was why they were so aggressive. Now she tried to calm herself down and keep her wits about her but it was hard when she had drunk so much and, with five grand in her bag, had so much to lose. It would be just her luck to get murdered tonight of all nights, when she finally had a few quid at her disposal and was happy.

The car stopped in a disused warehouse. She looked at the man's face and saw he was smiling at her. He undid his trousers and said, 'Well, get on with it then.'

She looked at him properly. The light was on inside the car now and she saw that he was even uglier than she had first thought. His face was badly scarred, and he had broken teeth. 'A mouth full of dog ends' was how Marie would have described him years ago.

Carole lowered her head on to his erect penis, trying not to gag. She knew better than to try and put a condom on him. She had a feeling he was waiting for her to do something wrong. Do something to upset him.

He put his hands into her hair and forced her down on to him so she took it all up to the hilt. It was over in seconds and she tasted the saltiness of his semen. He held her head down on him so she was finally forced to swallow.

She heard him laughing.

He released her hair and she sprang away from him as if she had been scalded.

He gave her a hard look then said, 'Open your bag.'

She was clutching it to her chest now, her eyes straying to the hammer on the back seat.

'What for?'

282

He opened her coat and ripped open the flimsy top she was wearing so her breasts were free. Then he pinched one nipple as hard as he could. She squealed out loud and he laughed once more.

'Open the fucking bag or I'll burn them off.'

He had a silver Marlboro Man lighter on the dashboard. He flipped the top and put the flame close to her body. She opened the bag, her hands shaking with terror.

He looked inside and whistled.

'That's a lot of money for an ugly bastard like you. No one in their right mind would pay you, love. Where did you get it?'

Carole was mortified that her hard-earned blood money was now lost to her. She knew she was going to be robbed, raped, and possibly murdered. And it rankled all the more because finally she had got herself a little stake and now it meant nothing. Marie used to say, What goes around comes around. Carole was finally finding out how true that expression could be. But she wasn't going to give up the money without a fight. Her life was worthless, but money made it bearable for a while.

'It's me pimp's. Right hard bastard he is . . .'

The man interrupted her.

'Shut the fuck up, you stupid whore! Is that supposed to frighten me or something?'

He took the money from the bag and placed it on the dashboard of the car.

'Now strip off. I want to look at you.'

'Pardon?'

Her voice held amazement. He *really* was going to rape her. She looked around once more. She was in the middle of nowhere with a maniac. Like Tiffany Carter was stuck somewhere with a maniac called Patrick Connor.

'Hurry up, for fuck's sake. I have the urge to have a bit of fun with you again. So do what you're told and don't annoy me.'

His face was clearly visible in the light and she had a good look at him. It occurred to her then that he wasn't worried about her seeing him in all his smelly glory which meant only one thing: she wouldn't be around long to give a description.

She did as she was told. It was going to be one hell of a long night, but she had guessed that much already.

Verbena was mortified at what she had done. She could not believe that her son was crying in his bedroom and she was the cause of his distress. Her husband's face told her all she needed to know about his feelings. Her own anger had finally evaporated when she had tried to comfort Jason and he had pushed her forcibly away. The look of disgust on his face had been almost as strong as a physical blow in its intensity. He had never looked at her like that, ever. It was strange to see him without a smile on his handsome face.

She remembered the night they had brought him home, a dear little boy, undernourished and so painfully eager to do what was wanted of him. His reaction to the toys they had supplied him with. The expression on his face at the sight of his bedroom, with its gaily painted cupboards and own little bathroom. He had been just three years old but with a world of experience behind him already.

His voice as he had thanked her for everything . . . He had had good manners, she had been amazed by that at the time. He rarely mentioned his mother after the first week and Verbena had hoped that was how it would always be. Marie Carter's life sentence had made it seem possible and she had been pleased by the verdict, though she had never spoken her thoughts out loud. To Ossie she'd expressed sadness at the other woman's plight, but deep inside she had been euphoric. The little boy would cement them together and give her something to do with her days, she'd believed. He had been perfect for her. No nappies to contend with, added to the fact he was always trying to please them, made him perfect in her eyes. Ossie adored him as much as she did. He did all the boyish things, playing football with Jason, wrestling with him. She had provided the child with gentler amusements, drawing, painting and Play-dough. It had been idyllic, just the three of them, Marie Carter firmly in the background. Locked away from her son and unable to mar their happiness in any way.

Until now, of course.

Her own jealousy had astounded Verbena. She had been unable to control it, seeing the woman she was supposed to pity looking so good. Seeing her own husband turn his face from hers towards Marie's had made her so incensed she had wanted to lash out, hurt the other woman in some way.

Exactly like Christine Wallace, with her power suits and her red lips. Ossie might not have been having an affair but Verbena was not going to risk anything developing. She had chased that rival off and she would do the same with Marie Carter, who wanted not only her husband but her son as well.

She was finding it difficult to breathe again. Could feel the swell of her anger surging through her body and tried desperately to quash it.

She had done enough for one night.

More than enough.

She had to mend a few fences here before she could concentrate on that bitch. She would be humble to her two men if necessary, make them sorry for her by the time she was finished, and if nothing else had come out of tonight she had at least made sure Marie Carter knew she was not welcome in this house.

And never would be.

The dismay she'd felt as she had watched her son try and endear himself to a woman who had the social graces of a psychiatric patient on day release was palpable. Inside she had felt the rage building up until finally she could not help but unleash it.

Yet, she was the bad person. She was the one who was in the wrong. She was the scapegoat for everyone. That is what hurt. But she was shrewd and she knew exactly how to get herself out of the mess she was now in.

She would just make a point of apologising and looking forlorn and sorry for herself and for what she had done. She knew how to play that bitch back at her own game. A double murderer, sitting looking like butter wouldn't melt in her mouth. It was laughable the way her husband and son could be so gullible. But then men were gullible where a pretty face or big breasts were concerned. Marie Carter had proved that tonight with her very presence.

She felt someone behind her and turned to see her husband in the doorway. Verbena looked devastated, her face ravaged by tears, eyes swollen as if she had an allergy of some sort.

'I am so sorry, Ossie.' Even her voice sounded broken, as if she was running out of energy. He stared at her for long moments, the anger he felt still evident from the stony glint in his eye.

It occurred to her that this was going to take a little longer than she had anticipated. She began to cry again, heart-wrenching little sobs that were usually guaranteed to sway her husband even when he was as angry as he was now.

But not tonight. Ossie had had enough of her and it was clear from his voice as he said coldly, 'It won't work, Verbena, not this time. All the tears in the world wouldn't be enough this time.'

'I am so sorry, Ossie. Please believe me when I tell you that.' She was crying harder now as she sobbed out, 'How is my boy? How is my baby?'

285

Ossie didn't answer her for a while. He seemed to be trying to control his temper and this fact alone frightened Verbena. Oswald was a good man, a very good man. He had been her rock all her married life. Her biggest fear was of losing him. She would rather he was dead than with another woman, that was how strong her feelings for this man were.

'Your baby, as you put it, is upset and embarrassed. Embarrassed that you could have humiliated him, yourself and me so badly in front of his birth mother. And it doesn't matter what you say or do, she is still the woman who bore him. Not you. We were lucky enough to be given the opportunity to take that boy into our home and our lives. Our opportunity came through another poor woman's misfortune, and if you can't be grateful to her for that much then you are even more selfish and egotistical than I thought.'

His words were meant to hurt her and he felt a moment of petty euphoria as he saw just how badly he had wounded her. Her face was white now, pinched and closed. This was the real Verbena, not the cringing little mouse she was trying so hard to portray. He had sussed her out a long time ago but had indulged her because he loved her. So far her insecurities had made him protective of her. Now he realised that all he had done was feed her fantasies. She wanted to keep him pinned by her side and would do the same with the boy if he didn't do something now.

'You'd better leave him for the time being, Verbena. He doesn't want to see you or talk to you.'

She bristled with rage and denial, walking briskly towards the door to go in search of Jason, but Ossie blocked the doorway with his big frame.

'Out of my way! I want to see my son!'

Her natural belligerence was back now. She would not be told how to behave with her own child. Who did this man think he was?

Oswald shook his head slowly.

'You heard me, woman. I said, leave him alone! He needs to be by himself for a while. Haven't you done enough tonight already?'

Verbena confronted her husband and completely lost control. Her face was almost unrecognisable from the force of her emotions, the jealousy and rage twisting her outside and in.

'Oh, I see. You and him against me, as per usual. Is that it?' She laughed nastily, her head thrown back dramatically. 'She was even better than I thought then. She has you eating out of her hand already. Taking her to lunch, are you? Like that Wallace woman. Will Jason be going as well or will it just be the two of you? Nice and cosy, like.'

Ossie was amazed at the way she twisted everything to make herself appear the victim.

'You are mad, woman, bloody mad.'

She smiled at him.

'Of course I am. It's always me, isn't it? I'm the one who is wrong. Who imagines everything. Who makes life so difficult for you. Well, it won't work this time, Ossie. I will take that boy and leave if necessary.'

He said gently, 'That boy, Verbena, wouldn't cross the road to speak to you if you were being mugged. You have gone too far and the sooner you realise that the better. So keep away from him tonight, he doesn't want to see you.'

'I'm his mother . . .'

He had had enough of those words. She repeated them constantly, like a mantra.

'Who are you trying to convince? Him or me? Or is it yourself, because you're his mother only if he lets you be. Even real parents find that out, lady. If you want to walk out, go, Verbena. Just go. But the boy stays here with me.'

Her hand was out and she had slapped his face before she'd even realised what she was doing. That was when they realised Jason had heard the whole exchange. He was in the hallway listening to everything they had said. Verbena nearly fainted when she heard his voice.

'Don't you dare hit my dad like that! I hope you *do* leave. I hope you go away and leave us alone!'

'Jason . . . please. Listen to me.'

He shook his head sadly.

'Leave me alone, Mum. You had no right to do what you did to me, my dad or my real mum. She was trying her hardest to be accepted by us all. And I liked her, I liked her a lot. If nothing else she has good manners. You've always set such store by that yet it seems it's something you lack yourself if tonight's anything to go by. In future I'll meet her away from the house where you can't interfere. But I will see her, and my sister, and my niece. Whatever you might think or say about it.'

He walked back up the stairs and Ossie thought that the boy had handled himself admirably. Verbena had needed to be put firmly in her place by her child, and it seemed the boy had done it without even raising his voice.

He felt a moment's pity for the crushed woman before him, but he stifled it. She had needed a wake-up call and now she'd had one. It was up to her from now on.

Chapter Twenty-One

'How do you think it went, Marie?'

She didn't answer.

'Come on. You must have some thoughts about it?'

'I think he liked me – Jason. He seemed pleased that I was there. I only wish I could say the same for Verbena.'

Marie gave her usual little shrug.

'She was like a maniac. Honestly, she reminded me of a woman I was banged up with – all that suppressed anger. You could feel it off her, you know.'

Amanda smiled.

'I understand from Mr Melrose that you handled the situation very well. His wife, I hear, can be unstable.'

Marie sighed, her eyes sad, and Amanda Stirling once again marvelled at a woman who really didn't understand the effect she had on other people. Marie Carter was a woman either loved or hated by her contemporaries. It seemed Verbena Melrose had chosen to hate her.

Amanda also knew that if Mr Melrose had not rung and explained what had happened then she would never have heard about it. He had obviously been concerned how Marie would cope after her visit, and that was a good sign. The boy had taken to her, by all accounts, and that again was good.

'Tiffany is still on the missing list, as you know.'

Marie didn't answer her.

'Her daughter was supposed to go to the Melroses. I can't see that happening now, can you?'

Marie shook her head.

'Another thing to blame me for. Tiffany will blame me for it all.'

'At the moment I understand Anastasia is with foster parents in Bow. I can ask for a visiting order for you, if you like? After all, you are the grandparent. You could see her – I can't see any reason why they wouldn't allow it.'

'The fact I'm a double lifer will go against me . . .'

Amanda held up her hand for silence.

'Excuse me, but even paedophiles have access to their children. Tiffany is off the scene, and you are now a fully functioning member of society. You have to remember that, Marie. You have paid for your crimes and now have a clean slate. What you do with your future is completely up to you. I can officially recommend allowing you visiting rights to the child as her relation. You are seeing your son, why not your grand-daughter? Jason has requested to see her as well, and while family members are involved with her it stops any moves to put her up for adoption. It will give Tiffany more time to sort herself out, too. I understand she was a good parent until she hit the crack.'

'What's happening about her flat?'

'Well, it's council, and as long as the rent gets paid they will keep it open for her because the Social Services will request that much, what with the child and everything.'

'I'll take over the rent if needs be.'

'I thought you would say that. It would make life much easier if they could find her.'

Marie didn't answer, just looked at her with those big eyes and Amanda knew she had more idea of what was going on than any of them but she would never say.

'She might turn up, Amanda. Stranger things have happened.'

Her face was closed once more and Amanda decided to let things lie. For all the talks they had had over the last months she felt she knew no more about Marie Carter than she had on the first day they had met. One thing she did know, though, Marie was gradually coming out of her shell. She had lost her nervousness of seeing people. She greeted her fellow residents and had brief conversations with them. That was a big step.

Amanda knew how hard it was for people who'd been shut away from society for long periods of time to adjust to everyday things – let alone a divided family, a whole new set of rules, and in Marie's case coming to terms with why she had been incarcerated in the first place.

She also had to deal with the knock-on effects of what she had done. The burning of her family home had been traumatic, exacerbated by the fact that her mother had long ago disowned her anyway and Marie now felt it was her fault Louise had been so badly injured. Guilt was a strange thing. She was guilty of a double murder and also of being far too hard on herself.

What she had done all those years ago had been terrible but she had been a girl then, a very different person from the woman she was today. She would accept that eventually. It would be hard but one day she would find herself laughing out loud and realise that she had not thought about what she had done for a few days. It was all part of the healing process.

Marie had been as much a victim in her own way as the two girls who had died.

Amanda had gathered from the social worker that the daughter was going down the same path. What Marie had to be careful of was getting too involved in Tiffany's affairs. Anastasia's father was the same man who had fathered Jason. Nothing like keeping it in the family, as the social worker had put it. People's lives could be so complicated.

Amanda had seen it time and time again over the years. Women like Marie had lived complicated lives since childhood. Mothers might have three or four children, all by different men. The product of those brief relationships lived with the knowledge that they were no one really. They had no roots. The women had given birth to them then abandoned all responsibility for the by-products of their brief flings, leaving the children to the mercy of children's homes or eventually secure accommodation.

It was so heartbreaking to see them come here, over and over again, knowing that it was only a matter of time before they were banged up once more. They were institutionalised at an early age, and deep down they only felt safe when locked up.

After Marie had left she felt the usual feelings of helplessness. There was so much that needed putting right in this woman's life, and so little Amanda could do for her. And she would like to help Marie Carter, sure that deep inside she was a good person.

If only she would give herself a break.

Patrick was still convinced that he had to do something spectacular to get himself back on form. Since Maxie's death he felt that people were suspicious of him, and the police coming to his home had shaken him badly. Every time he thought of them at his front door he felt almost faint with anger. Someone had to pay for that. People had to be made aware that he was not a man to fuck with. He needed a fix, and his fix was fear. Pure unadulterated fear.

He needed people to be scared of him, to respect and revere him. That was the key to getting away with murder.

Even that cunt Tiffany thought she could mug him off! He had had to chase her all over the fucking smoke, the stupid cunt. Even she thought he was a fucking pussy eater with nothing better to do with his time. Maybe she thought that now that murdering whore of a mother of hers was on the street again she could walk all over him. Fucking Jonah! That Marie had always been a Jonah. Since she hit the pavement he had started getting aggravation. She was like all her kind, nothing but trouble.

All women were trouble. They were either fucking whores or they were religious nutcases. Never a happy medium with them. All fucking pot pourri or living in shit holes like fucking trollops the lot of them. Get them on their backs and you could make them do anything. And anything would get them on their backs. Drink, drugs, a fucking meal at a Bernie Inn for most of them. All women were nothing but fuck busters, worth a shag and that was it. He knew how to make money from them, and it was what they were put on earth for – to be used by men. All the laws in the land would not make a woman his equal. They could say it over and over again, it would not make it true. Women were only equal to animals, natural scavengers living off the carcass of their mate. That was the reality of the situation and anyone who thought different was a fucking moron. Women went to the strongest man who'd have them for protection, money and sex. Well, Patrick gave them all that and didn't even have to put up with their miserable fucking faces at the breakfast table.

Now he was going to do the big one. He was going to take out a face, a London face. A man who instilled fear into Brixton and its boundaries, and made the rest of the South East think twice before they offended him. A bona fide nutcase, and also a nice bloke in many respects. He had taught Patrick a thing or two, that much had to be said for him. Credit given where it was due. He was a good Gangsta man, a Rasta killing machine and a man who commanded respect. And Patrick would garner that respect for himself before much longer. *He* would deal with the Yardies in future. *He* would bring in the drugs, and take over all the women.

For all his respectable front there was nothing like a good expanse of complete bastardy to get the juices flowing. Make you feel like a man. Bring your brain into action and your body into line. There was nothing like causing a bit of mayhem to give a bloke a buzz. No drug could match it. If he could bottle that feeling of ecstatic pleasure it gave him he would be a fucking billionaire. It was addictive, it was the best feeling in the world. Better than sex. Or better than the kind of sex his girls provided anyway.

He was looking forward to it. But first he had to sort out Tiffany.

Carole lay in her filthy bed and breathed in the fumes of alcohol and vomit. She knew on some level that she should see a doctor, but she was too scared. Her whole body ached. The alcohol made her sleep for a while but it was wearing off, and she knew she should try and wake herself up. At least take a soak in a hot bath. She could feel the vomit in her hair as she moved, it was stiff and it stank.

She tried, unsuccessfully, to get up. It was too much trouble and she slumped back on to the pillows again.

She thought about the money again and felt the futile tears. He had taken her money and given her the most terrifying time of her life. She had really thought he was going to kill her. He had been at her for hours and she had wondered all that time how he would finish her off. But in the end he had dropped her at the end of her street as if they had been on a date, and she had been terrified to leave the place since.

He had her address and he had her money.

She hated him.

What goes around comes around. Marie had always said that and she was right. It was the fact Carole had done what she had to Tiffany that made this even worse. Tiffany had been grassed for that money and now it was gone. No good had come of it whatsoever.

Carole tried to get up again and this time she managed to get herself to the edge of the bed. Her thighs were heavily bruised and already scabbed. He had scratched her, pinched her. She hoped she had a disease of some description, at least a dose of hepatitis so the bastard had a memento of her.

But then, what the fuck was he carrying?

Last night had been a wake-up call. Carole had lost a lot more than the money. She feared she had lost her bottle and in her job, especially at this end of the market, that meant she had lost her earning capacity.

She stood up, wincing at the pain all through her body. She caught a glimpse of herself in the stained mirror on the old dressing table. Everything here looked scuffed and dirty, like her. She was aware for some reason of the real state of her home, though it had never really been that, not by other people's standards. It had just been somewhere to go when her night's work had finished. Even her daughters had never wanted to be there for any length of time, and who could blame them?

Carole didn't want to be here either and now she had no choice. The place looked even more depressing than usual. All those years ago, she had meant to do something with her new flat. She had watched TV and thought, I would like a place like that, furniture like that, whatever. But she had known deep inside that she would do nothing about it. Even little Tiffany had tried to get a place together for Anastasia. Her flat had looked lovely, brightly painted and warm. She was just like her mother in that way. When Marie had got her first place it had looked nice. Until she got on the skag, then it had all been turned upside down. Patrick Connor smashing the place up regularly had not helped matters. She had given up, like many women before her. It was pointless trying to get a place around you when you had a man who was out to destroy you and anything you possessed.

Carole walked unsteadily to the dressing table and gripped the top of it. Her fingers felt sore where the man had bent them backward at one point in the evening. He had also burned her with a cigarette. Remembering made her feel faint with fright once more and she sank down on her knees. Her reflection told her all she needed to know and she started to sob: with guilt, remorse, and the realisation she had finally reached rock bottom. It had been a long time coming, but it had arrived.

She closed her eyes tightly and saw Tiffany with Anastasia on her lap. The little tableau made the tears fall thicker and faster. Marie would kill her if she found out what she had done. What she had caused to happen.

She had given that girl up like a sacrifice to the man who had destroyed everyone he had ever come into contact with, male or female. Marie's voice was in her head once more: What goes around comes around. How true those words were.

The psychiatrist listened to Kevin rambling on. He had said the same thing over and over. That his wife was evil, that she had caused everything bad that had happened and now she was getting a taste of her own medicine.

It was like a mantra. One thing Dr Bewly knew for sure was this man was not fit to stand; he was not fit to mix with society either. Kevin Carter was suffering from a personality disorder, he was paranoid and he was also in a deep depression. Every now and then he seemed lucid but the things he said were unbelievable.

Bewly reviewed his notes and decided that what this man needed was a course of intensive psychiatric therapy and drugs, then they could decide his fate.

He was meeting the police later in the week and they would review his findings. He felt sure that once they observed the man for themselves they would agree with him. Kevin Carter had lost all contact with reality.

He listened once more to his patient's raving.

It seemed the wife had driven him mad over the years. A very difficult woman by all accounts. She would have been called a nag years ago, though that was politically incorrect, he knew.

He watched as Kevin leaned over the table and said conspiratorially: 'You don't know what she's like, doctor. She made us all do what she wanted. Everything was for Marshall. None of us mattered, but he was as bad as she was. She made that boy as bad as her. Looking down on everyone, thinking he was better than he was. But it was Lou – she made him like it. She gave him an inflated opinion of himself from a child.'

Kevin stopped and concentrated on rolling himself a cigarette. His hands were shaking from the medication and suppressed anger. He carried on whispering to himself, oblivious now to the man sitting opposite him. He looked demented. He was demented.

And he was also telling the truth most of the time but it sounded so incongruous that no one could be expected to believe him. Least of all a doctor who had no real idea what had happened all those years ago. For the simple reason the truth had never been spoken aloud.

Patrick was in a Wimpy drive-through when he got the call he was waiting for. He wheel-spun out of the queue, ignoring the many shouts and rude gestures from the other patrons.

He was sweating with excitement, driving erratically through London, weaving in and out of traffic and listening to Jungle music. The beat stirred his blood and he luxuriated in the knowledge of what was going to happen soon. Violence was a funny thing; he had courted it all his life and as long as it was not directed at him he enjoyed it. He felt good about himself when he was in control of it.

Now he was about to cause an act of violence that would reverberate throughout London. The buzz was astronomical, the feeling giving him a natural high, and that was what he craved these days.

He knew that everyone was mugging him off, from his girls to his so-called mates. Well, after today they would all have to have a rethink. He was going after the big one and he was going to get it.

He had settled a few old debts in the last twenty-four hours. Today marked a new era in his life. He was soon going to be in charge of every major scam in the smoke, and couldn't wait to get started.

Mahogany Statter was tall and she was pretty, very pretty, with relaxed hair and large brown eyes. Her slim frame was perfect for displaying the latest fashions; she turned heads wherever she went.

As she walked into the block of flats on the corner of her road she heard a groan, low and barely audible. She stepped into the lobby and looked around. Nothing. She was about to walk to the lift, thinking that she had imagined it, when she heard it again.

It was coming from the bin cupboard. She was scared now, but she walked over and opened the door slowly, frightened of what she might see.

Her screams brought all the people out of the flats.

Marie was in a restaurant with Mikey. They were having a late lunch, and she was telling him all about Jason and his adoptive mother.

Mikey was listening with half an ear. He had a lot on his mind, but the sound of her voice was soothing. He loved listening to her whatever she was saying. It had occurred to him that he was in love. Or at least as near to it as he had ever been. When he had first met his wife he had been in lust. It was how he always was with women. He never could resist a good pair of tits or a nice tight arse. Or, come to think of it, a pair of long legs or a naked thigh.

It was just the way he was, and he had money and a good reputation so all these things were available to him as and when he wanted them. Now he had Marie, and liked her for more than her looks which, he admitted, were nevertheless good for her age. Considering what had happened to her, he thought she looked phenomenal. But what he really liked about Marie Carter was her quietness. She had a quiet voice and a quiet nature. He could relax when he was with her, secure in the knowledge that she wanted nothing from him except his company.

All the shit that had happened to her, and she never felt sorry for herself. He admired her for that. So many people blamed others for what had befallen them. He had even knocked the coke on the head because he didn't need to be on it when he was with her.

His phone rang. He saw it was Alan's number. They were waiting for another shipment so he took the call even though he was with Marie. He was not expecting to hear the words Alan said to him. Mikey replaced the phone on the table and immediately called for the bill.

Marie watched him warily. There was obviously serious trouble of some kind and as they walked from the restaurant she hoped that everything was OK.

Malcolm Derby was with his baby daughter Alisha. She was a very pretty little girl with his dark eyes and her mother's crinkly hair. He adored her and she adored him. He was a good father to all his children, acknowledged his responsibilities, paid for them all to go to private schools and gave them the best of everything.

Alisha loved to chew on his dreads and he smiled at her as she did her teething on her father's hair.

Her mother took the little girl and put a coat on her. She was going shopping and Malcolm pushed a wad of money into her hand, as she knew he would. He was a good provider and she loved him dearly. She turned a blind eye to his business and an even blinder eye to his other women, especially his wife. It worked for her and it worked for him.

He kissed his little daughter on the cheek and she crowed with excitement. Malcolm buckled her into her buggy and waved her off from the spacious lounge.

'Listen out for Georgie upstairs.'

He nodded and turned on the monitor so he could listen out for his two-year-old son. He settled back into his chair and picked up a twist. As he lit the grass he inhaled deeply. Three of his henchmen were in the room with him and he ignored them as usual.

'She is gonna break a few hearts that one, Malcolm.'

The man's voice was kindly and Malcolm smiled at the compliment.

'She me baby, Alisha. She's in my heart. That Georgie is a boy too. He is a big man. He will be a good boy, I think. He is clever, you know. Loves his picture books.'

He often talked this way about his children and his men admired him for it. They all loved their children, too, but Malcolm had a special bond with all his kids and made sure they were all well taken care of.

Malcolm looked at his best boy, a young man with well-developed muscles and a quick mind. His name was Stanley, and he had gradually risen in Malcolm's business from collector to personal minder. Stanley thought the world of Malcolm, admired and respected him. He was also grateful because Malcolm had paid off the CPS and got him off a robbery charge. He knew he would lay down his life for the man before him – and that was going to be proved sooner than any of them realised.

This room was large and well-decorated with white walls and expensive furniture. Malcolm loved it as he loved his whole house. It was the epitome of all he had worked for. He had arrived from Jamaica with nothing, and now he was coining it in. He was proud of what he had achieved. He was a hard man but, it was generally agreed, as bad as he could be, he was also fair. He never used mindless violence, there was always a good reason for his outbursts.

At least that was the general consensus and he agreed with it. He knew he dealt in fear and in his line of work that was mandatory. It was par for the course. If someone upset you then they had to be taught a public lesson so no one else made that same mistake. It was how you kept on top, how you sorted out your business. It also kept any usurpers at bay, made people wary of taking you on, and with his many illegal businesses that was also mandatory.

He had to use the fear factor, and he made sure people saw him enjoying what he did. They were always more frightened of someone they thought would get a kick out of hurting them. Although, if he was honest, he did enjoy it; he especially enjoyed the status it won him.

But at home, in this house, he was a different man from the one on the street. He was calmer. He was happier. He could be normal. Forget what he did outside the walls of his home and enjoy his ill-gotten gains.

The house had two entrances. The front was on to the street and the back on to a very large garden with swings and a slide. He was toying with the idea of putting in a swimming pool for the kids. There was plenty of room if he decided he wanted to. But he was also thinking of moving the families out to Hampstead. That thought made him smile because Hampstead was named after hemp, and hemp had been his first big money spinner. It was where they'd originally processed hemp for ropes. He didn't sell hemp itself, he admitted that, he sold the leaves and the buds, but it still seemed ironic that he should move there. At least it did to him anyway, the boy from a shantytown near Kingston moving to an affluent suburb of London. But now he was a rave king he had a lot of legal money to play with. The filth could not touch him and they knew it.

As he put on a Bob Marley CD he could hear Georgie chatting away in his sleep. Malcolm got up and walked towards the kitchen to get some cranberry juice for when the little boy woke properly. He always wanted a nice cold drink when he woke and Malcolm made sure he had one to hand.

He said to Stanley, 'Go up and get the boy for me.'

Stanley immediately leapt from his chair and made his way out to the hallway. As Malcolm opened the kitchen door he stepped back in surprise.

'All right, Malc?'

Patrick brought the machete down on the man's big dreadlocked head. He split the skull with the first stroke, then attacked again in a frenzy. Malcolm was half-dead on the floor, his life's blood slipping away, as his two other men stepped out to see what the commotion was.

Patrick's two sidekicks attacked them and the noise was loud and brutal. Upstairs Stanley was holding the boy in his arms. He could hear the commotion and bundled the child into the wardrobe as quick as he could and put a chair against the door. Then he ran to Malcolm's bedroom and grabbed a gun from the hiding place in the window recess.

They caught him at the door. The machete hit him full in the face and the gun went off but injured no one.

The whole house was a blood bath. Patrick was naked. He had stripped off in the garden as had his two accomplices. They could hear Georgie crying and the mortally wounded Malcolm could hear him calling for his daddy.

'Your daddy is dead, boy!'

Patrick was laughing as they walked back down the stairs. In the large secluded garden he and his men hosed each other down and then got dressed again. Malcolm was still alive and watched them leave.

Patrick waved to him merrily. He liked the fact that Malcolm could not survive those injuries, no one could, and half admired him for hanging on as long as he had. But he also enjoyed Malcolm knowing who had beaten him, who had taken what he owned. It appealed to Patrick.

Malcolm was worried for his son, all alone upstairs, wondering if they had killed him as well. It was a terrifying and lonely death. He had crawled to the bottom of the stairs before he died. His last thought was to get to his child.

Mikey had driven Marie to the Old London without a word. She had sat beside him, knowing that whatever the call had been about it concerned her. Which meant it was about one of her children. Consequently she was too scared to ask him and he was obviously too scared to tell her.

When they'd finally parked he turned to her and said, 'Tiffany was found this morning. She's bad, Marie. The hostel phoned your work. She's asking for you.'

He saw Marie's face go even paler than usual.

Ten minutes later they were in the ICU and she was looking down at her daughter's battered face. Tiffany was beaten so badly she was barely recognisable. At the sound of her mother's voice she tried to open her eyes.

'Mum?'

Her voice was stronger than either of them had thought possible.

'I'm here, Tiff. Just relax. Try and rest, love.'

Tiffany shook her head weakly.

'No. Listen, Mum, I'm bad. You have to promise me that if anything happens, you will take my baby. Take my Anastasia, please?'

Marie took her hand gently and Tiffany squeezed it tight.

'I'm sorry, Mum. I should have listened to you. Pat gave me to his mates, Mum. Last night. They taped it – he has the tape. He was laughing, Mum. He's mad. Said he was going to take my baby, too, and that he was going to get you and Jason.'

She was crying and as Mikey looked down at that broken body he felt rage stir inside him.

'Is she talking about Patrick Connor?'

Marie could hear the disbelief in his voice. She nodded.

'He's done this to her before. I told you he put her on drugs and took every bit of her self-respect. Like he did me.'

'Fucking hell!' Mikey was in absolute shock. 'I'll fucking kill him meself.'

Tiffany opened her eyes again.

'I am sorry, Mum, for all the trouble I've caused.'

Marie kissed her daughter's forehead gently.

'Don't worry, sweetie, Mummy will sort it out, OK? I promise you, everything will be OK.'

She was shaking with anger and knew that if she had Patrick in front of her now she would tear him apart with her bare hands. If she had been there over the years this would never have happened. This was her fault and no one else's. She had let down both her kids, but whereas Jason has fallen on his feet in many respects, this poor little girl had not. She had been left to the care of councils and foster homes, finally abandoned to fend for herself when she wasn't equipped to take care of a kitten, let alone herself and a child.

She had been easy prey for Patrick Connor and Marie knew only too well he would have got a buzz out of Tiffany's being her daughter and his son's sister.

Well, he had better watch his back because he had to deal with her now. Fuck Mikey and all the rest of them. She wanted him herself and she would enjoy taking that bastard down.

Chapter Twenty-Two

M ary Watson stared into her son's face.
'I am telling you now, boy, you get rid of that Lucy and you get rid of her soon. How I have stood the shame and degradation of the neighbours knowing she's living here, I don't know!'

Mickey Watson was caught between a rock and a hard place. As much as he loved Lucy, his mother was such a strong personality he was terrified of upsetting her. Since he was a boy she had dictated his every act: what he wore, what he did, who he played with and where he worked. It was hard to break the habit of a lifetime.

Also he was afraid that Lucy was like his mother. She was very domineering at times, even though she wasn't brave enough to front up Mary Watson. Since her dad had shot one of the Blacks Mickey's mother had been almost demented from the gossip that had been going around. People were glad to see her get some of what she doled out so often. She was now the subject of the gossip by her association with Lucy and that was not what she wanted at all. Mary was the gossip queen of East London and had prided herself on the fact that she was whiter than white, which gave her the right to slaughter everyone else as and when it pleased her. To be on the receiving end of the wagging tongues was hard for her and on one level Mickey understood how much it was upsetting her. For all her faults, and they were legion, she was as straight as a die, he had to give her that much at least.

He glanced at the black bin bags in the hallway. She had packed all Lucy's stuff and was now telling him she wanted his fiancée out. But where was Lucy supposed to go? She spent most of her time up the hospital with her mum, though she was back at work part-time now. He was bewildered by it all, if truth be told, and wasn't really sure what the fuck he wanted from either his mother or his fiancée.

If he was honest with himself, Lucy was getting on his nerves.

She was like his mum in many respects, bossy and short-tempered. Even in bed she was in charge and there was definitely nothing out of the ordinary there. The same routine each and every time, it was boring him.

He watched as his mother opened her mouth again. But he was long past listening to her. He knew the gist of what she was saying, that was more than enough for him. She was like a cracked record, going on and on and on about the same bastard thing, morning, noon and night.

He pictured himself taking back his arm and clumping her one right across the face. It made him smile and she shouted at him nastily, 'Like fucking Dilly Daydream you are! With your stupid smile and your stupid gormless bloody face. Why don't you act like a man? Why am I plagued with men who are fucking useless? Like your bleeding father you are, a gutless ponce . . .'

Her voice went on and on once more.

Mickey listened once more with half an ear and wished his mother would just dry up and blow away.

'I am warning you now, boy. You tell your lady love that she is out and you tell her today. I have had enough of the lot of you.'

'But where will she go, Mum?'

Mary rolled her eyes to the ceiling in an exaggerated manner.

'What do I care? Just give her the bad news. I want her out and that's the end of it. If you had half a brain you'd have given her the elbow long ago.'

His mother had spoken. That was that.

Mickey felt almost relieved if he was honest.

Patrick was euphoric. He had never felt so good in all his life.

Blood being what it was, he was still finding dark brown stains all over his body. He knew he needed to get showered and changed so was making his way to the gym in Spitalfields. Afterwards he'd have a large brandy and a joint to calm himself down.

He felt absolutely fantastic. Like he had been reborn. So good was the feeling that he didn't even see the colour change at the traffic lights ahead. He heard an insistent honking coming from behind him and glanced into his mirror.

It was three blokes in a white Transit. He smiled to himself before he stuck up two fingers in a blatant act of aggression. He was daring them to do something about it, and hoped they decided they were going to. He was running on adrenaline and it felt good.

The lights were on red again. They all had to wait once more for them to change.

He saw a large man get out of the driver's side of the Transit. He was heavy, more fat than muscle, a forty-five-year-old skinhead. Patrick could see the blue and red of his tattoos even from this distance. He watched as the man ambled towards him, his heavy body encased in a white sleeveless T-shirt and baggy jeans covered in paint splatters.

Patrick could just see this man in his local pub, a pint in one grubby hand and his big flabby mouth going. He obviously thought he was hard. He had to think that or he would not have bothered to get out of the Transit in the first place. Thought he was a diamond geezer, a bit of a face. Well, he and his mates were about to get the shock of their stupid pointless little lives. Patrick was up for it. More than up for it.

More to the point, he *wanted* it. Wanted the man to force his hand. Wanted to take this bastard down, quickly and efficiently and violently. He was grinning with the knowledge that he had the upper hand. He had a machete, he had a hammer, and he had something none of these blokes would ever have: the fucking bottle actually to kill someone. These were ice creams, local bullyboys. Well, they could fuck off. He was ready, he was willing and he was more than able. As the man walked towards him he was practically giggling.

Patrick opened the car door just as the other man got to the driver's side window. The man looked into a pair of piercing blue eyes in a black face and that in itself threw him. He opened his mouth to speak, displaying yellowing teeth and a thickly coated white tongue.

But Patrick got in first.

He opened his coat and let the man see his blood-stained machete, then he said in a low voice, 'Do you really want some of this, mate? Do you want your old woman to know you were beheaded at a set of fucking traffic lights because you were an impatient cunt?'

The man, a decorator from Canning Town called Stevie Bowler, looked once more into those piercing blue eyes and saw a man who was ready to kill over nothing. It speedily occurred to him that his own natural aggression was more than matched by this black man in the BMW. He weighed up the pros and cons of taking the man on and decided against it. This was a man on the edge and it showed.

305

From his belligerent stance to his practically daring Stevie to damage him, this man wanted a tear up far more than he did. Stevie was just being a hard man in front of his mates. This bloke *was* a hard man, that was the difference. He had no one else with him yet he was willing to break open heads for what was, in fact, nothing at all.

A fucking machete! He couldn't believe it. And this bloke was ready to use it, *wanted* to use it. He was more than up for it. You could see it in his eyes. This should have been a war of words, a few fucks flying about and maybe a slight fracas. But this bloke was ready to kill over something that was childish and stupid and Stevie wanted none of it.

It occurred to him that he was as bad, getting out of the Transit in the first place. What the fuck was he trying to prove? He had a nice little wife and nice kids and this bloke was willing to extinguish his life without a second's thought over something so trivial it should never have mattered to either of them.

Stevie's eyes were glued to the machete. It had recently been used, he could see that much for himself. He stepped back slowly. Turning, he made his way back to the Transit van. It was the brownish stains on the machete that had been the deciding factor. It was very obviously blood, and more than likely human blood. Well, it was not going to be his blood, he was determined on that.

He got into his Transit and they drove away after a few moments. He had never felt so relieved in his life. His friends, asking what the fuck had occurred and getting no information whatsoever, wondered what was going on. But Stevie's face stopped them from enquiring. They guessed it was a heavy situation and it quietened them all.

As they turned towards the Becton flyover a radio news announcement stated that four men had died in a bloodbath, all killed with machetes. Police were looking for two black men and a white man with bleached blond hair.

Stevie pulled over and jumped from the white Transit. He brought up his lunch – three pints of beer and a cheese roll he had eaten not an hour before. His friends were still unaware of what he had seen and exactly what had happened, and he was not about to tell them.

All he knew was that he had had a very lucky escape, and the knowledge left him almost faint with relief. He suddenly realised what mindless violence really meant, and that he had nearly become the latest statistic because of his own foolishness and arrogance.

It was a sobering afternoon.

Tiffany was dying and she knew it. Her kidneys were packing up and her liver was so badly damaged it was not functioning. Her face and body were bloated and they had put her on life support. Marie held her daughter's hand and wondered at a God Who allowed something like this to happen. Hadn't her daughter had enough thrown at her in her short life without this? Dying like an animal, used and abused and finally thrown away like rubbish. The fact that Patrick had put her daughter in a rubbish bin had been the hardest fact of all to take. Her lovely child degraded even further as she lay dying amongst the filth. How had God allowed that to happen to this beautiful girl? Where was He when she was being beaten and raped? How did God distinguish between those He would give to and those He would take from? Marie hated Him at this moment in time because she needed Him and knew He was not going to help her. No one would help her or her child.

But still she prayed, prayed as she had never prayed in her life. Even when she had been awaiting the verdict from the jury she had not prayed as she was praying now. She looked at her child, the daughter she had abandoned without realising just how much she had loved her. Drugs had been everything to her then as they had become to the dying girl before her. Two wasted lives.

What was the attraction really? What made someone put a chemical before everything and everyone? The belief that getting so out of it you couldn't repeat your own name made problems disappear was outdated and, worse than that, it was a cop out. Her daughter had left real life behind just as Marie had. Tiffany had opted for the pretend world of drugs, dingy night clubs and the scum of the earth. Just like Marie. Why had she allowed history to repeat itself, why hadn't she tried to get out sooner? Fought the courts for contact with her children? She had thought she was doing the best for them by getting out of their lives, when all she was really doing was giving her daughter to a man who preyed expressly on young girls without family or anyone who cared. Patrick had taken her child as he had taken her, and this was the result: Tiffany dead at nineteen, her body and mind ravaged by crack and a series of beatings that would have killed most people already. Even the doctors were amazed she had hung on so long.

She could not have a transplant because her body would not take the anaesthetic. Also, being a crack addict, she would not be considered a worthy donee.

Her daughter's beautiful hair had been ripped from her head, and her face was a black mass of bruises. Her whole body was broken, another victim of Patrick Connor's evil. She had a perfect boot print across her face. But the police would not be able to pin it on him, he was far too clever for that. He wasn't going away for the likes of Tiffany. She was old news by now as far as he was concerned, Marie knew that.

Patrick took people and he used them. When they were no good to him any more, he destroyed them without a second's thought.

Tiffany had slipped into a coma. As she held her daughter's hand Marie wished her to a better place. Wanted her somewhere where no one could ever hurt her again. She pictured green fields and bright sunshine for her child. She hoped to God that was what she got wherever she was going. Marie prayed it would be somewhere warm and beautiful, somewhere Tiffany could laugh and relax and be a normal young girl. 'Please let her find peace and happiness,' she prayed. God Himself knew there had been little enough of it in her life up to now.

Marie wished she could go with her, be there with her to keep her company, keep her safe. But she had promised her daughter she would try and take on Anastasia, and that was a promise she was determined to keep. She was a different person now from the girl she had been when she had murdered Bethany and Caroline. She was clean, was decent. Even taking on Mikey had ultimately been for her daughter. She had gained a valuable friend there when in fact all she had wanted was a nutter to take on Patrick for her. Mikey had been with her through all this heartbreak. Another man would have run a mile.

Now she was going to fight for her grand-daughter, would not let her get lost in the system which seemed to breed girls like poor Tiffany, fodder for pimps and drug dealers. She would fight for the child and maybe she would redeem herself through Anastasia. Make up for all her past mistakes with her daughter's child. It was the least she could do.

But first she had a date with Patrick Connor. In fact she was quite looking forward to it. She wanted to see his face when she told him what she thought of him. As she made him suffer as he had made her child suffer. Wanted him to know it was Marie Carter who was going to take him out of the ball game. Violence solved nothing, she knew. But this time it would make her feel a whole lot better.

First, though, she had to watch over her child as she took her last breath. Watch her son's heart break as he lost his sister, knowing that it was his own father who had brought Tiffany to this.

It was a tragic, terrible mess and she was responsible for the lot of it. But this time she was after revenge and she was determined she was going to get it. Patrick Connor did not know what was going to hit him. Neither did her so-called friend Carole Halter who had given Marie's child up to him for five lousy grand. But then money was her God. Marie had been the same once herself.

Now it was payback time for them all.

Mikey was at home, pacing the room like a parody of a man waiting for his child to be born. The men with him could feel his anger. It was in his eyes, in his body language.

'What have you found out?'

Old Billy spoke. He was an old friend of Mikey's and always had first talk because of that fact. The others knew their long friendship gave Billy first call on everything. He was the only person ever to have openly disagreed with Mikey and still lived to tell the tale. Consequently, he was well-respected and liked. A powerful man, with a bull neck and sparse hair, he was also easygoing and funny.

'Connor done Rasta Malcolm today. It was definitely him from the word on the street. Cut him up with a machete. Ironic, really, since that was always Malcolm's weapon of choice, as we all know. Done him in his house with his little boy upstairs. Also done three of his blokes. Surprise attack, I'd say. Well-executed and neatly done. Filth are all over the place but Connor will walk away as usual. Obviously he wants Malcolm's pitches, businesses and henchmen. He will get them and all if we ain't careful.'

Mikey looked disgusted.

'He done him with his little kid in the house?'

The men could hear the absolute horror in Mikey's voice.

'That is what we are dealing with now, boys. It's pure fucking laziness. Get to people through their kids. The piece of shit cunt! Give me back the old days when we just spanked the perpetrator of our troubles and left the families out of it.'

Mikey shook his head in disbelief.

'Well, I want him done and that is that. Get his movements and then we swoop.'

Billy looked puzzled and said, 'What for, Mikey? That's not our turf, it's nothing to do with us. Why stick our neck out over the coons? They want to fight one another – what is it to us?'

Mikey was expecting this question and knew only Billy would have the front to ask it.

'One, I liked Rasta Malcolm, I was dealing with him years ago when he first come over from the Big J. He was a sound geezer and he knew his place. He kept out of other people's business and he'd lend a helping hand if one was needed. One hard fuck, I tell you, but he never tried to take what was someone else's. He kept to his own turf and I respected him for that. Two, I have a private score to settle with that ponce Connor. He is a cancer and I want him dead. Three, he picked on a kid, has a penchant for picking on kids, and four, he is a pimp and I fucking hate pimps. They are carrion and they are scum.'

Old Billy was quiet for a few moments before he said, 'I agree with all you say, Mikey, but we could cause a fucking war by topping Connor. Are you prepared for that to happen? He'll be busy making peace with all the other people involved. Drugs cause havoc, you know that.'

Mikey nodded.

'We'll take him out with his henchmen if need be. I want all Rasta Malcolm's men on my payroll by the end of the week. That'll stop them from going over to Connor. I think I'll take a cut from South London. It'll be lucrative and I know most of the main faces personally, black and white. We need to work together anyway with the fucking Bosnians running amok. But I digress – I want Connor dead as a fucking dodo at the earliest opportunity, OK? No more discussion, I have spoken.'

The men were silent, all contemplating what the knock-on effect of their boss's orders would be. Connor was a ponce in every way. He even lived off his birds' earnings. But he was also a nutter, and nutters were not to be taken lightly. Chances were Patrick Connor, that blue-eyed bastard, was about to start another war. They all knew they had to take him down at the first opportunity before he had time to regroup and come back at them. They also knew they were in this spot because the boss had taken up with an ex-jailbird and murderess who had got so far under his skin he was willing to cause the Third World War to make her happy.

Whoever would have thought that Mikey Devlin, all-round bastard and known lunatic, would fall for a bird like her and this would be the upshot? She was an ex-brass and an ex-druggie. Love was a strange fucking thing as far as his men were concerned. Most of them wouldn't have touched her with a barge pole, but then Mikey had always been different.

310

Still, they would do what they were told. It was the way things worked in their world and they would not question it in any way, shape or form.

Not to Mikey's face, anyway.

Lou was bad and she knew it. The pain was not getting any easier but they were lowering her dose of painkillers. She moved painfully to make herself more comfortable. She sat in a high green-covered chair where she could see out of the window over the car park.

She was not admiring the view.

Lucy sat with her, her face white and haggard, wondering where the hell she was going to go. She had been given twenty-four hours to leave her so-called fiancé's house. She could not believe it had come to this. She stared at her mother's burned body. The scars were red and livid. Lou had refused plastic surgery except on her hands. She wanted to be able to use them so had agreed to go through all the pain of the skin grafts.

The events of the last few months were still unbelievable to Lucy. She could not understand how it had all happened but she knew who was to blame all right: Marie. It was as if she'd deliberately set out to ruin everything for everyone.

Lucy gave her mother a drink. She was sipping the orange juice through a straw when Lucy tentatively made a suggestion.

'The insurance company have to put us up, don't they, while the work is being done on the house? I'm going to see about going to a hotel or something. Maybe renting a little flat . . .'

Lou's eyes narrowed and she pulled her head back sharply and said, 'I thought you was staying with Mickey.'

Lucy shook her head.

'They aimed me out. I have till tomorrow to find somewhere else. In fairness, Mum, it ain't him, it's her.'

Lou nodded. Her terrible face and head were like a grotesque parody of her former self. She had always kept herself nice, clean and tidy. Had prided herself on her trim figure and her unlined face. Lucy still had trouble looking at her mother for any length of time.

'That woman, she's a scourge. And Mickey's nothing but a fucking mummy's boy. She rules him. Some women are like that, Luce. They interfere in their kids' lives when they should keep their bloody noses out of it.'

Lucy didn't answer her. She didn't know what to say. That her mother could not see herself in her own words spoke volumes.

311

'Old bitch she is. Bitterness is a terrible thing, you know. It's like a cancer and should be cut out. He'll rue the day he let you go. I take it the engagement's off?'

Lucy shrugged.

'Well, no. Not as such. He ain't said it outright . . .'

Louise rolled her eyes heavenwards.

'You don't mean to tell me you are still going to go out with him when he has in effect put you out on the street?'

Lucy was defensive, her strained face on the verge of crumpling. Because she wanted to cry her eyes out. She wanted her mother to take her in her arms and tell her it would all be OK. She knew that wasn't going to happen though. Even if her mother had been fit and well it would still have been the same scenario.

'It's not him, it's his mother . . .'

'Same difference, Luce. He's a mummy's boy, and the sooner you realise that the better. You'll always come second to her.'

Lucy listened to her mother but on another level she was laughing. In her head she could hear loud uninhibited laughter.

'I mean, I was close to my Marshall, God rest him, but he was not a mummy's boy. But Mickey is. A classic mummy's boy at that. You're better off out of it. Keep a bit of dignity, tell him to get stuffed, give him his ring back. No one will blame you, they all know what his mother's like. Some women have a lot to answer for where their kids are concerned. Look at me with Marie. I tried everything to keep her on the straight and narrow but I was wasting me time. From birth she was trouble, never let me get a night's kip. Your father was no better. Always taking her side. And look where it's got him . . .'

Lucy listened to her mother's tirade about Marie, her father, Marshall, and anyone else she felt had done her down. She was sick to death of hearing it all. She knew, deep inside, that her mother was the instigator of many of the troubles that had befallen her. She was like Mickey's mum, a vindictive old bitch. Even as she was now, scarred and in pain, she still had the energy to give out yards about everyone else.

Lucy remembered how Marie, as a girl, would stand behind Lou, mouthing her mother's words off pat. They had all heard the same thing over and over and all knew exactly what she was going to say next. Lucy and Marshall had laughed like drains and her mother had beaten Marie black and blue. It was one of the few times the three children had been in agreement about something.

But then, Marshall had loved Marie, though her mother was not aware of that, and Marie had loved him. Lucy had always felt left out. Marie would call her Bertie Smalls, meaning she was a grass, because she always told on her brother and sister. Not that it had ever done her much good. Her mother would not have a word said against her son, though she was never surprised at what Marie was up to.

Lucy sighed heavily.

'Oh, am I boring you?'

Louise's voice was nasty, and Lucy knew another tirade was about to start.

'Look, Mum, can't you just let it go for a few minutes, eh? Do we have to go over the same thing again and again? You're driving me mad. Marie is at this moment at the hospital with her daughter. Tiffany is dying, Mum.'

As soon as the words were out she regretted them.

'What are you talking about? How do you know anyway?'

'I saw Cissy today. She was asking after you, and as you know her daughter lives in the same block of flats as Tiffany. She heard it through Marlene Morrison who works at the Old London. Tiffany's been really badly beaten, she's dying.'

Lucy's voice was sad. Her niece had not been part of her life but she was only a young girl and it was a horrible thing to happen. She saw the smile that spread over her mother's face and felt sick with disgust.

'Hah! God pays back debts without money. How often have I said that, eh? She'll know what it's like now to lose a child, like I lost my baby, my boy. That was all *her* fault, he topped himself over her. What she made him do . . .'

Lucy frowned.

'What on earth are you on about? Marie never made him do anything.'

Louise shook her head.

'I know what I know. But God has been good to me today. I needed something to cheer me up and you provided it with that news. So that whore will know what it's like to suffer at last!'

She gave a ghastly smile.

'What about poor Tiffany, Mum? Your grand-daughter? She's suffering as well. Surely even you couldn't wish that on the girl. What about her baby?'

'What about her? Probably end up like her mother, who was like

313

her own. What's bred in the bone comes out in the blood.'

'So who did Marie take after then, Mum? You?' The words were out before Lucy could stop them.

Louise looked at her daughter in such shock Lucy wondered how she had ever dared say the words out loud.

But she had.

'You little bitch! Don't take it out on me because your bloke has put you out on the street. Don't make me your scapegoat because you can't get your life together. Like your bloody father, you. Couldn't get a blasted cold without me to help you. I'll be lumbered with you all me days because you couldn't get a man if he fell out of a tree and hit you on the bloody head. Joke, ain't it? One daughter man bloody mad, the other couldn't get one if she advertised naked in the paper. You are a loser, Lucy, always were and always will be. Even that prick Mickey was too good for you, and you couldn't even hang on to that useless bloody twit!'

Lucy picked up her handbag.

'I am not listening to this. In future you can sort your fucking self out, you vindictive old witch! I might not have a man, Mum, but I'd rather be alone than be with someone who didn't love me or care about me like you were. Dad hated you and so did me and Marie. Even Marshall laughed at you behind your back. You were a fucking joke to him and to us girls as well. Even me father laughed at you.'

She could hear herself talking and on some level knew she was going too far, that her mother had enough to contend with, but she couldn't stop herself. It was as if a dam had burst inside her.

'The neighbours would say to us, "How's your mum? At Mass as usual?" But we knew they were taking the piss. You put yourself up as a paragon of virtue when you were just a fucking joke to everyone. I remember my Confirmation. You caused murders that day and even I could see the priest was fed up with you as well.

'Listen to yourself, you're so bitter and twisted you can't see what you've become. You were never a mother to any of us, not even Marshall. You suffocated him and you neglected us. Face facts, for Christ's sakes.'

Louise sat back in her chair and smiled smugly. A patient expression had come over her face. She really knew how to annoy someone; she was the master of nasty.

'So I'm bitter and twisted, am I? Well, at least I had a family and a husband, something you will never have. Dried up and old I might be, but I *am* old. You're like an old woman already. Look at yourself, over thirty years old and neither chick nor child to call your own. I pity you, Luce, and I pity the man you finally settle with. Because no man would have you unless they were at rock bottom. Scraping the bottom of the fucking barrel.

'My Marshall was my life. He was all I wanted and all I needed. You and Marie were nothing to me. If you had died I wouldn't have shed a tear over either of you. But you both lived and my boy died. Well, I'm glad she is losing her daughter and I'm glad that Mickey has seen through you once and for all. May you both die lonely, manless and friendless. That's me prayer to God every day from now on.'

Lucy was devastated at her mother's heartfelt words.

'We will die like you then, won't we? Only I don't see anyone coming to visit you except me. Even the priest tries to give you a wide berth. I won't be back, Mum, not after what you said today. And do you know something? I'm glad I won't have to look at you ever again. You were always ugly on the inside, now God has seen fit to make you ugly on the outside too. I hope you live for years and years, and I know you will die the lonely death you predicted for Marie and me. Dad was seeing a woman, you know, a nice woman and all. Even he had someone in his life and she'll stand by him as well. Like I will and Marie will. I hope you stew in your own hatred and it eats away at you like a cancer. It's what you deserve.'

As she walked from the room she felt her mother's dislike of her like a physical thing. She had always known that Louise was not as fond of her daughters as most mothers would be. She had accepted that. But to know that her own mother despised her hurt more than anything. Her father was locked away, her sister was estranged from her, and her boyfriend had given her an ultimatum. Even her own mother had no time for her. Did not even like her by the sound of it, and never had. Lucy had never felt so low in all her life.

She could hear her mother screaming out to her for the name of her father's mistress. But she ignored her. She would find out soon enough. It was common knowledge. It spoke volumes that no one had grassed him up before now, because so many people knew about it. But her father was well liked, always had been. People had felt sorry for him, chained to her mother and her so-called goodness.

Lucy cried.

315

Louise sat back in the chair. She was exhausted by all the emotions running through her body. That her own daughter could talk to her like that! She was another Marie and Louise had never seen it until now. But that last shot about Kevin having a woman had hit home. She had half guessed at it, he had seemed happy at times, and now she knew why.

The filthy bastard of hell! She hoped they put him away for life. He had betrayed her and now he was locked up. God knew what He was doing all right.

He moved in mysterious ways and He was working His miracle for her now, as she sat here in this chair. He was taking Marie's daughter from her and he had taken Lucy's man from her. He had also seen fit to put the adulterer in prison. He *was* a vengeful God and the sooner they realised that the better off they would all be.

Louise stared around the room that was like a prison to her and smiled. Marie would cry bitter tears and she was glad of that fact. She rejoiced to think her daughter was getting a taste of her own medicine at last.

The room was very quiet as Louise said a decade of the Rosary as she always did when she was upset. The Sorrowful Mysteries always made her feel better. But for some unknown reason, they didn't comfort her this time. She didn't feel that Marshall was close as she usually did.

In fact, she felt lonelier than she had ever felt in her life.

Marie was holding Tiffany's hand as the girl drew her last breath. It was all over in seconds, and she was at peace. Marie knew she was at peace, she could see it in her daughter's face.

Jason put his arms around her waist and she held him as he cried, his body racked with sobs. She held him tightly to her, enjoying the smell of his hair even as she mourned for her daughter. She had lost her child and gained a grand-daughter. It was unbelievable, and she felt responsible for it all. Would always blame herself for what had happened to her daughter.

Her own guilt would make her hurt Patrick Connor. Guilt and revenge were both powerful emotions. Together they were stronger than anything.

She held her son and she cried. For her daughter, her grand-daughter and also for Jason. Finally she cried for herself, at the wasted life she had lived and the knowledge that she was the cause of all the problems her children had encountered. But she could right some of the wrongs she had done and she was going to start with her son's father, Patrick Connor.

She was looking forward to it.

Book Two

'Those who cannot remember the past are condemned to repeat it.'

George Santayana (1863-1952)

'I am condemned to be free.'

Jean-Paul Sartre (1905-1980)

'My son, may you be happier than your father.'

Sophocles (496-406 BC)

Chapter Twenty-Three

Patrick was in his office at Spitalfields. He watched through the window as members parked their cars before going into the gym. Everything he touched was turning to gold. It was as if he was being watched over by an angel. His legal businesses were raking in money, but it didn't give him the buzz he got from his scams. Every time he fucked with a young girl's head, or pulled in a few quid on a drug deal, he felt a euphoria that was becoming addictive.

He lit another joint and blew out the smoke lazily. As he finished it two men walked into his office. He knew immediately that they were police. He smiled and finished blowing out the smoke lazily.

'What can I do for you gentlemen?'

He was Mr Nice Guy today and knew it would throw them.

'Mr Connor?'

He nodded.

'I am Detective Inspector Ragfield and this is my associate, DC Spicer. We need to talk to you about an event that took place yesterday in South London.'

Patrick looked suitably bewildered.

He was in businessman mode today. He knew these two police-men had nothing on him or they would have pulled him in for questioning proper. He was dressed in a crisp white shirt and Italian designer jeans, knowing he looked every inch the young City entrepreneur. He smiled once more, showing his pearly white teeth. He was a very good-looking man and he knew it. He could also be charming when he wanted. It was a prerequisite of being a pimp. Charm got you further than anything with working girls. Until you had them by the throat, of course.

'So, how can I help you?'

It was a question apparently asked by an innocent man with no idea what was going on. Ragfield was impressed despite himself. This was a consummate actor. He knew that Connor was suspected of enough skulduggery to keep the whole of the Met in forms until the next millennium. It was proving it that was the difficult part.

As he looked at him now it was hard to believe that this man was responsible for murder, arson, rape and drug dealing, and that was only the tip of the iceberg. It was rumoured he had high-up friends; in the Met and in the CPS. He must have someone because they were finding it increasingly hard to pin anything on him. Ragfield had been warned to go easy on Connor by his own supervisor and that in itself told him all he needed to know. This was one slippery bastard, and the worst thing of all was Patrick Connor knew exactly what he was thinking and found it all highly amusing. Well, the DI would enjoy taking him down once and for all. In fact, he was determined to do it. So he smiled back at Patrick, an easy smile very like his own.

'We had an incident yesterday in South London. A Mr Malcolm Derby and three of his associates were murdered.'

Patrick butted in, 'And what has that to do with me?'

He sounded shocked and affronted. As if it was ludicrous for anyone to think he could have had anything to do with a murder.

'We were given your name by an associate of Mr Derby . . .'

Patrick was swiftly on his feet, a deep frown on his forehead and his stance belligerent.

'Do you have anything to substantiate your claim that my name has been put forward in connection with this terrible occurrence?'

Spicer was trying to suppress a smile and Patrick noticed.

'Do you find this amusing, is that what you're trying to tell me? I think I had better see what my solicitor has to say about it. Have you a warrant for my arrest? Have you anything to tie me into this investigation in any way?'

Spicer said clearly and loudly, 'Have you been smoking grass in here, Mr Connor?'

Ragfield closed his eyes in distress at the crassness of his colleague.

Patrick also seemed to lighten up as he said, 'Is this fucker for real, man?' He was all West Indian now. 'I can't get nicked for a joint, you damn fool boy. I get a caution if that.'

He shook his head in amazement at the complete stupidity of the men before him.

'No warrant, no talking. So either show the paper, man, or take a fucking walk. Who you think you dealing with, eh, a beastie boy? A fool? I'll blow you so far out of the water, man, you will need a fucking rocket ship to get you home. Now get out and stop wasting my time.'

Ragfield smiled again, in control once more.

'We'll be back, Mr Connor.'

Patrick laughed aloud.

'When you come back, boy, make sure you got something to talk about, OK? Don't be wasting my time. It makes me angry, you know. I am a busy man, and a rich and busy nigger is not a man to cross. Because this is what it's all about, ain't it, eh? I am a rich boy, and I am black, and I don't fit the mould. You better take care, man, because I have good representation in the City and they love cases of racism by the police. I'll whip your arse and smile while I do it. You understand where I am coming from?'

He was baiting them and they knew it.

'You will not make an example of me, you hear? Oh, a girl was found in a rubbish bin recently, are you going to charge me with that one as well?'

Ragfield could not believe what he was hearing.

'She was the mother of your child, wasn't she, Mr Connor?'

Pat grinned again.

'Lots of bitches have my kids. If one of them gets hurt, are you automatically going to blame me? She was a whore and a lap dancer, a heroin addict, a *fucking loser*. She would fuck anyone for a fix, even you. Anyone could have done that to her. So remember that when you're looking for a likely culprit, OK?'

Patrick pressed a button on his desk and two muscle-bound men came in. Both were white-skinned and blond.

'Escort these gentlemen from the premises, please.'

He was smiling once more as they left the room. He felt invincible because he knew they had nothing on him.

But they were at his door once more, and that was two visits too many as far as he was concerned. He would have to spread a few more grand around to stop any repetition of this foolishness. He had it all sewn up, he was the king and he knew it. Now he just had to convince the filth and he was home and dry.

He rolled himself another joint and smoked it slowly, savouring the taste and the buzz. It calmed him and he needed calming now more than ever. He was ready to explode again. Anger always did that to him.

He stood up and looked out of the window once more, master of all he surveyed. Gradually he calmed himself, but it was difficult, really difficult. Because he had the taste for blood again and it was making him excited.

He thought about Tiffany and wondered if she was dead yet. He hoped so, he wanted her obliterated from the world. It occurred to him that he would have to remove the witnesses as soon as possible. Grassing was a lucrative business these days, so it was just as well to watch your back.

He felt pleased with his own forethought. All in all he was doing well. Very well. That was what happened when you worked hard for a living.

Marie lifted the letterbox and felt for a string. She found it and pulled the key towards her. Old habits died hard.

She opened the front door carefully, so as not to make too much noise, and walked into the damp dinginess of the flat. She wanted her visit to have the element of surprise. She stood still and listened. All she could hear was the muted sound of the TV. The familiar smells of old food and broken-down furniture pervaded her nostrils. How did people live like this? How had she lived like it all those years ago? Every time the smell invaded her nostrils it reminded her of a life that was wasted and useless, even though it had seemed so exciting at the time.

Carole Halter was still lying on the sofa. She was in agony. All night she had tried to sleep but not even whisky had brought her any relief from the aches and pains that racked her whole body.

As she watched Richard and Judy she lit another cigarette. She liked Richard, would give him one as she'd often said to anyone who would listen to her. Though it was the furthest thing from her mind at the moment.

She was frightened she'd lost her will to work, the nerve to go out on the street and consort with strangers for money. If she couldn't get that back she was finished.

Then she heard a noise; it sounded like the front door. She felt the sweat break out on her forehead. It might be the madman coming back to finish her off. When the door opened and she saw it was Marie, for a split second she felt relief. Until she remembered what she had done, and acknowledged the fact that Marie had walked into the flat unannounced. Carole prided herself on the fact she could smell a rat before it was stinking and realised she was in deep shit. Marie was after her for what she had done to little Tiff, and who could blame her?

'All right, Marie?'

It was a form of address and a question all at once.

Carole was so scared she was having trouble breathing. She knew what Marie was capable of and in her heart of hearts she knew that she deserved whatever was coming her way. The law of the street dictated that Marie should take an eye for an eye. Carole Halter was expecting the worst.

Marie stared at her. Her eyes were cold and her face so still she looked as if she was carved from stone. Karen was reminded once more of how beautiful Marie actually was. Tiffany had the look of her mother but had never had her presence. Marie had always had a way about her; men either adored her or wanted to fight her. But one thing they all had in common was they wanted to fuck her. It had made Carole jealous as a girl, and it still made her jealous as an adult.

Now, looking at Marie standing in her home, she realised just what she had done to the woman she had been friends with for so many years. One thing she was sure of: she was going to be the recipient of some serious physical retribution.

Marie stood and stared at her. She took in Carole's battered face and body, knew she had got a rogue punter and inside herself was pleased that her old friend had at least experienced something of what her daughter had gone through over five lousy grand.

'Where's the money, Carole?'

Her voice was low and clipped. It felt like a slap it was so cold.

'What money?' Carole was silly enough to try and front it out. Her voice was high and nervous. A tic was working just by her left eye and she could feel it even as she tried to control it.

Marie shook her head in utter disbelief. Then, moving quickly, she had Carole by the throat.

'The fucking money Connor paid you! Five grand, if I remember rightly. Now don't fuck me about, Carole, I really am not in the mood. I watched my Tiff die over you, you piece of fucking shit. So, I am begging you, don't wind me up any more than I already am.'

Carole knew she was in deep trouble. Could see that Marie was on the edge. Tiffany was dead . . . the words penetrated her brain. In a split second she realised exactly what she had done.

She saw Tiffany as a little girl; saw her grown-up. Saw her taking care of Anastasia, the pride in her face as she'd looked at her baby. Remembered introducing her to Patrick Connor. Went red with shame as she remembered telling Tiffany what a bad mother Marie had been to her and her brother. Patrick had given her money then.

The worse she had made Marie out to be, the bigger the sum.

Shame washed over her like a hot flush and she could not look at Marie, aware finally of what she had done and the trouble she had caused. Marie threw her back against the sofa and pain raged through her body like a fire. Carole was in mortal agony and it didn't matter any more. For the first time in her life she was thinking about someone else and it felt strange. Even her own children had come second to her and her lifestyle.

'I'm so sorry, Marie. So very, very sorry. I don't know what made me do it, I swear. I must have been mad or something.'

It was useless, she knew, but she had to say the words because for once she actually meant them.

'You did it for five grand. Money is the reason why my child is dead. Money, Carole. Something you and I worshipped many years ago. Me for skag, and you for drink and speed. I can remember me and you going to see Doctor Grass in Hampstead for slimming pills. Neither of us was over eight stone them days. Then scoring grass at the Roundhouse. It was all drugs and drink then, and now you've sold my baby like you'd have sold your own fucking mother for a drink in those days. Eventually we would do anything for a few quid. I killed over drugs the first time, and I'm going to kill over them a second time, aren't I?'

The words penetrated Carole's brain and she started to cry. As bad as her life was she did not want to die. After her recent brush with death she finally understood what life was all about. Money meant nothing if you had no friends or bad health. It was a bonus in life, nothing more and nothing less.

Easy money had always been her lure as it had once been Marie's. But even though she had been locked away for years she had come out a better person.

'You were supposed to be my mate. I would have looked out for your daughters, you know I would have. I looked out for us all until I cracked up. Even Caroline and Bethany would come to me if they had a problem. How many times did I share what I had with you, eh, food, drugs, whatever I had? Whereas you would buy twenty fags and leave fifteen indoors and come and smoke everyone else's. You were a ponce then, and you are still a ponce now. But you killed my Tiffany as sure as if you'd given her the kicking yourself. She died hard that girl, without anyone giving her a kindness in her young life. She could trust no one, not even me, thanks to you and Patrick. You turned her away from me and you know you did. I would have got her away from him but you two poisoned her mind against me.'

Carole was crying, her face already blotched and swollen. She looked terrified.

'Are you going to kill me, Marie?'

The words were low, spoken in terror but with a certain bravado because at least she had the front to ask the question out loud.

Marie started laughing.

'I'm not killing you, Carole. You're not worth doing the time for. I'm after Mr Connor, the big man, love. What I want from you is all you know about him. No more and no less. You tell me about his prostitution ring and I'll leave you in peace, OK? But I want the truth or else I will really harm you and I take oath on that one. I want to know where his girls hang out and what they expect from him these days. I want to give him a surprise, see.'

Carole saw the blackness in Marie's eyes. If was as if her pupils covered her eyeballs. She looked drugged up, but it was adrenaline and hatred that had given her that look, two of the most powerful chemicals ever so far as Carole was concerned.

'What you going to do, Marie?'

'Why? You thinking of ringing him up and earning another few quid, you two-faced ponce?'

Carole shook her head furiously.

'Never, Marie. I wouldn't.'

Marie looked at her old friend, and in one part of her didn't really blame Carole who knew no better. Her whole life had been spent tucking people up, looking out for number one. It was the law of the pavement, the law of the street. She was too long in the tooth to change now; the course of her life was set.

'What happened to your boat?'

Carole shrugged painfully.

'I had a rogue punter. Right fucking nutter. He skanked me dough and all. Five grand, up the fucking Swannee.'

Once more, even in the face of Marie's distress, it was all about *her*.

'One of them will kill you one day, Carole.'

It was said caringly and Marie wondered how she could still be bothered about this woman who was a piece of dirt by most people's standards.

Carole shrugged.

'Who gives a fuck? Not me. But I wanted that dough. I really had plans for that money, you know?'

Marie sat on the edge of a chair and, taking back her hand, slapped Carole a resounding blow across her face.

'It means nothing to you, does it, my Tiffany dying all because *you* wanted a few quid?'

Carole realised then what she had said and could have kicked herself. Why could she never remember what she'd said to people even a few minutes before? She really must start listening, and concentrating on what was going on.

'Patrick threatened me, he was gonna really hurt me. You know what he's like . . . Look what he did to Tiff.'

The old Carole was back, the lying scheming Carole. The woman who looked for the scam in everything and everyone she came into contact with.

Marie was amazed at how easily her old friend fell into the role of poor weak woman.

'If the truth be told I bet you got a hiding because you tried to scam the punter. It wouldn't be the first time, would it?'

Carole was shaking her head once more.

'No, I swear on me grand-daughter's head.'

Marie held up her hands for quiet as if she was in a classroom full of little children.

'I don't want to hear it. I think you got what you deserved, Carole, no more and no less. Now talk to me about Connor and let me get on me way.'

Carole lit a cigarette with shaking hands and began to talk. She knew she had to tell Marie what she wanted to hear if she was going to get her out of her home. Suddenly it was important to get her out of the way. Carole would just dig herself in deeper and deeper otherwise, she couldn't help it.

She was loose-lipped, always had been and always would be. And this time she had gone too far, even she could see that much. But deep inside, as sorry as she was for what had happened to Tiffany, the loss of the five grand was hurting her more. She convinced herself that anyone would have done the same, even Marie.

Old habits really did die hard. She had been deluding herself all her life. It was impossible to change now.

Alan had a meeting that ran on much longer than he'd expected. When he got back to work he was not surprised that Marie was not there. He stared around the yard for a while. Soon he would be gone from here for good. It was the only way out. The meeting

328

today had put the final nail in the coffin as far as this place was concerned.

It was strange but it was the death of Marie's daughter that had made him take the final drastic step. That was one tragedy too many as far as he was concerned.

He could smell Marie's perfume in the office space. It was light and fragrant and like her it was subdued. He missed her around the place. But every time he thought of her with Mikey Devlin he felt sick to his stomach. They were hardly what he would have called a natural couple.

Mikey was a diamond geezer. He should have his usual armful, a young bird who was grateful to be seen with him. Not his Marie. She, whatever she had done, was intelligent and kind. She deserved better than Mikey whatever she might think. She had overcome so much and come out the end of it all a better person. Mikey would only drag her back down into the gutter with him because Mikey was going away and he was going away for a long time, whatever he thought.

None of this could go on much longer. Alan was amazed they had carried on as long as they had without a capture, though that was on the cards, he knew for a fact.

The phone rang and he answered it quickly. It wasn't Marie and the realisation made him feel sad. She was under his skin and he didn't know what the hell he was going to do about it. He thought about her all the time and dreamt of her in his home and in his bed. He had it bad, he knew he did. Love was a strange thing. It made you brave and it made you sneaky. As Mikey was going to find out very soon.

Verbena and Ossie had a truce for the moment but she wondered how long it was going to last.

Jason was devastated over his sister's death, and she understood that; she just couldn't see, as her son and husband apparently could, what the big deal really was. Sure, it was sad the girl was dead but the life she'd lived had made that inevitable. It was going to happen sooner or later, and if they'd chosen not to see that then more fool them. It was not like she'd been a regular girl, a *respectable* girl.

But Verbena was too shrewd to say any of this out loud, though privately she had made her feelings clear to Oswald.

She had also vented her feelings loud and clear on Jason's

so-called birth mother. She was damned if she was going to act like Marie's best friend when in fact she should not be allowed anywhere near her son. If she were a neighbour they would be warning him to keep away, not encouraging him to see her and forgive her for the terrible things she'd done.

It was all completely laughable, but because Marie was a sexy piece Ossie had decided she was OK. Was to be welcomed. Well, that was not going to happen, not in Verbena's home, she was determined on that much.

Marie Carter was not coming in here like a longlost sister, no way. Her with her big tits and her brash clothes, her smarmy smile and hangdog expression. 'Look at poor me, I killed two people so feel sorry for me!' It was as if the men in Verbena's life had gone mad.

All Marie had done was give birth to those children. She'd never nurtured them, or loved them, or comforted them. Look at Tiffany, dead at nineteen. Beaten to death, mind, and raped, and the police had no interest at all. Because like Verbena they knew that it was par for the course with tarts like her. If she was honest Verbena was pleased the girl was gone. It was one less bloody relative to have to deal with. One less nuisance to have to listen to and smile at and pretend to welcome.

Shame the bloody mother had not gone with her. At least a small child could be moulded into something else. Look how well she had done with Jason. He should be down on his bended knees thanking her for the new life he'd had, not giving out to her over his mother. Her friend had said years ago that children were a thankless task and Verbena had disagreed. Now she understood only too well.

Well, she would bide her time and when this was over she was going to give them both the shock of their lives.

To think that her husband, the man she had adored all these years, could have his head turned by Marie Carter! It was unbelievable.

She finished making the sandwiches and put the soup on to heat. She had made her special vegetable soup, both her men loved it. She was making all their favourite food because she wanted them to realise what they could be giving up. When she gave them her ultimatum she wanted them to be fully aware of exactly how much she did for them.

She still could not believe that in a few short weeks her life had been virtually destroyed because of that woman. But one thing it had proved to her: Ossie was as weak as the next man before a pretty face and a comely figure. It didn't matter that this one had been a drug addict and a double murderess, she was pleasing to the eye and for that he would forgive her anything.

It broke Verbena's heart to know that the man to whom she had given herself, had fallen out with her family for, was not worth it. But he was hers and she loved him, and she was damned if she was going to let that other woman have him without a fight.

As her husband and son came into the bright airy kitchen she plastered a smile on her face and turned to them.

'I'm not really hungry, Mum.'

Her son's face was ravaged by tears so she walked over and hugged him to her. It was a tight hug and he tried to pull away but she held him in a vice-like grip so he just relaxed against her as he always did.

Watching them, Oswald sighed. Verbena was too overpowering. Why had he allowed her to become like that over the years? Why had he indulged her?

If only she'd believe she had never had any reason to be jealous, but she had always been like this, from the day they had met.

He forced himself to smile and eat the soup and sandwiches when in reality all he wanted to do was take his boy and go out somewhere. Get him some fresh air and talk through his sister's death with him. Instead he had to sit it out with Verby for a while at least. He knew all the signs and how to deal with them. But he was getting bored with the constant drama. She controlled them both with her assumed helplessness when in reality she was the least helpless of the three of them.

Maisie answered the door with a smile. She looked quizzically at Marie before saying gaily, 'Can I help you?'

Marie pushed her into the flat none too gently and answered her sharply.

'I hope so, love. Maisie, isn't it?'

Maisie looked like a child but though Marie was shocked at her youth she made sure it did not show. Patrick had always liked kids, it was in his nature.

Maisie was nothing if not streetwise. She felt the animosity coming from the woman before her and decided to listen first before she tried to fight her way out of anything. She wondered if this was one of Patrick's real women, a proper girlfriend who had found out about her.

331

She walked into the lounge and Marie followed her. They surveyed each other warily. Finally Marie smiled.

'Relax, love. I'm not here for a tear up. I'm Tiffany's mother.'

The words had the desired effect. She saw the girl swallow noisily and sit down. She was wearing a tiny leather skirt and her narrow little face was thickly covered in make-up. This somehow made her look much younger and Maisie obviously knew that. It was all part of the act.

Her tiny breasts were held in place by a white crop top. On her feet were impossibly high black leather stilettos. Her hair was backcombed to within an inch of its life. She was obviously expecting a punter and this depressed Marie even more. It was like looking at her own daughter, like looking at herself. Fools . . . they were all such fools.

'I heard about her, I really am sorry.'

Marie laughed.

'I'm sure you are! Now, I understand you and Pat are close. So who did he give her to? I need to know exactly who he gave her to. And before you answer, remember, if you hold out on me I'll kill you, sweetie, without a second's thought. You must have heard about me from people? I'm a known face with the girls old and new. A legend, you could say. And I am more than capable of killing again. So think on that before you answer me. This is personal, love.'

Maisie was hard, she knew she was hard. She'd had to be to get as far as she had. But she instinctively knew that this woman was capable of all she said and that she would extinguish her without a second thought.

'Can I get you a drink only I think we need to talk properly, don't you?'

As they sipped coffee together Maisie put her case.

'I don't take drugs and I don't drink, right? I am here purely for the dough. I am young and I am streetwise. I saw my own mother used and abused by men, and though I sleep with them for money it is purely a means to an end. Patrick Connor means fuck all to me and if you want to turn off his lights then I will do nothing to stop you. What he did to Tiffany was wrong, and I am as guilty as he is in some ways. I get girls on the game, they trust me and I connect with them. But Patrick is too far off the wall even for me. I was going to tuck him up when the time was right anyway. But I digress, as they say. I'll tell you all you need to know on one condition.'

Marie was shocked at the way the girl was talking but hid her feelings and answered her.

'What's that?'

'I take what he's got, and you leave me alone.'

Marie was silent for a few moments.

'Fair enough. I give you my word,' she said finally.

Maisie smiled and her whole face changed. This was a real smile, not a professional one. Marie found herself smiling back.

'There are three men he uses who are into the gang thing. I don't know them but I have seen the videos. Tiffany's is over there.'

She pointed to the wall unit and Marie felt her breath catch as she realised she would have to watch it. Needed to watch it to get her anger up for what she intended to do next.

'He was watching it all night. Tell the pathologist to look for GHB in her system – they dosed her up on it at the finish because she was screaming so much. He knew she would die, he told me that. He wanted her to know she was in the rubbish bin. He also wanted her found quickly so he could hear about her death. He is one weird fuck, but I expect you already know that.

'He used her death to keep all the other girls in line, me included. He also intends to blackmail the men, though they don't know that as yet. One is a high court judge, the other is in the CPS. So as you can imagine they're worth more than money to Patrick Connor. They keep him on the street. He's sure he'll never get burned. So there you are, a potted history of Tiffany's death. He used her to get to them and used them to get to her. One of the girls in the other videos is only about thirteen. Even I balk at what they've been doing to her. Fred West eat your heart out, eh?'

'Do all the girls die?'

Maisie shook her head.

'Wished they had, most of them. But no, only your Tiffany and one other girl. A runaway from Bradford.'

Marie digested this information.

'More coffee?' Maisie offered.

She nodded.

'Aren't you expecting a punter?'

Maisie shrugged.

'He can wait. If I don't answer the door he can't come in, can he?'

She went out to the kitchen.

'Can I slip in a drop of hard for you? Brandy? Scotch?'

333

Marie followed her out and watched her every movement. She didn't trust the girl that much. Not yet anyway.

Maisie read her mind and grinned.

'I tell you something, mate, I wish you'd been my mum.'

Marie shook her head.

'No, you don't. Believe me, that's the last thing you would have wanted.'

'At least you're trying to make amends now. My mum doesn't give a flying fuck about me or me sisters.'

'Will you watch the video with me, Maisie?'

She smiled sadly.

''Course I will. But I warn you, it's not pleasant viewing.'

Marie held back the tears with difficulty.

'I didn't think it would be.'

Maisie put a slim arm around her shoulders and hugged her gently.

'I ain't never having kids, I know that much.'

Marie answered her seriously, 'Much longer in this game and the choice will be made for you, darling. Remember that. You'll end up like me or my daughter. Bear that in mind.'

Maisie didn't answer her but it was a sobering thought.

Chapter Twenty-Four

M ikey was at Patrick's flat. It had taken a five hundred bar and a good few shouted fucks to get past the security guy. He was obviously scared out of his life of Patrick Connor and Mikey was reluctantly impressed by his adversary's ability to keep his security tight. He had always admired tight security and loyalty, even if that loyalty was born of fear. If you kept your own house in order you had nothing to worry about. You could relax and let life pass you by without the constant fear of either a capture or a takeover.

At least, that was how it should work out anyway. But the security guy had soon been had over with threats and a few quid. Still, in fairness, he was a straight guy, not a worker as such, so Mikey still felt the man had acquitted himself well. He knew his goons looked what they were and the bloke must have realised at some point they were serious trouble.

He looked around the luxurious Docklands flat with interest. It was the usual naff place. Fitted kitchen with barely enough space to swing the proverbial cat but good solid units. A coffee maker that was never used, all stainless steel and designer nameplates. A lone jar of Nescafe told its own story. He was disappointed in a way. The place was so predictable. Like something from a BBC2 drama production.

He headed into the bedroom. It was all mirrored wardrobes and Schreiber units once again. As he searched the place, putting any money he found on the bed, he came across a video hoard and smiled to himself as he looked through the titles. One was marked in black felt pen: Judge.

He already had a good idea what they were for. He slipped one into the machine in the bedroom and sat on the edge of the bed to watch it. He lit a cigarette and drew the smoke into his lungs noisily. He could hear his blokes tearing the rest of the flat apart. He knew they would do a good job, and pushing a pair of Calvin

Kleins away from him with his foot Mikey settled down. It was a comfortable bed, he would give the ponce that much. He would bet it had seen some action as well.

The film came on.

He'd expected the usual bit of old bluey, namely some old geezer giving a young bird one. He had already sussed the tapes were for blackmail of some kind. But what he saw shocked Mikey to the core.

This was not the usual old crap he had expected. Instead there was a young black girl, still in her teens and terrified. This was not acting, this was for real. The man, middle-aged with grey hair and a large gut, was unaware he was being filmed. That much was obvious because he kept going out of focus. He was definitely unaware of what was going on, and judging by what he was doing to the poor little mare, he would not have wanted any of it filmed.

No one in their right mind would want anyone to see that, not unless they were after a twenty-year stretch in a nonce home anyway. This must have been what had happened to Marie's daughter. She was a slapper by all accounts, but even slappers were entitled to have a say in what happened to them.

He thought of his own daughters, their trusting faces as he had picked them up as little kids. Their innocent smiles when he'd said something amusing. Rage built inside him. He could not believe that anyone could peddle this shit with a clear conscience. The world had gone mad as far as he was concerned.

He ground the cigarette out on to the cream-coloured carpet and immediately lit another. He was mesmerised by the figures on the screen, unable to believe that anyone could get their rocks off by causing so much pain and suffering. The girl was bleeding profusely now, her face a mask of terror as she tried unsuccessfully to escape her attacker. She was losing consciousness rapidly and the man was still at her. He watched in morbid fascination as the figures on the screen went through their grisly ritual.

Of all the things Mikey had ever seen or heard of, of all the things he had done and been accused of doing, nothing had prepared him for the feelings this film engendered in him. It was fucking unbelievable what some people wanted to do, and the fact that someone like Connor made their sick fantasies possible just made Mikey want the man dead more than ever. It was a righteous crusade as far as he was concerned. Even if the filth knocked on his door, one peep at this lot and Mikey would be the recipient of a rather large round of drinks, surely, rather than a capture of any kind. No man could look at this obscenity and not be moved. Unless they were weirdoes like the geek he was watching.

The plight of the girl on the screen made him feel so helpless and disgusted that he knew when he got his hands on Patrick Connor the man was going to die. Painfully and begging for mercy, he was going to die.

'Jesus fucking Christ, Mikey!'

He turned to see Old Billy watching the screen in amazement.

'What the fuck is all that about?'

'That, mate, is Connor's idea of a lucrative business.'

'That old geezer is Judge Martin. The hanging judge of the Bailey. Old ponce! Been up before him meself. Cunt he is, put away Jimmy Lauder and Morrie Burns. And all the time he was a fucking pervert, the dirty old cunt!'

The other men were watching now, brought in by the sound of Billy's voice. They all stared at the screen as the girl breathed her last and the judge still kept at her.

Twenty minutes later they were on their way. They had over twenty videos and nigh on sixteen grand in a black bin bag.

They all fell quiet as Mikey made sure his cattle prod was in perfect working order.

Marie was waiting for Patrick outside the gym. It was early evening and she was looking out for him as she sipped coffee in the café opposite. As she watched the people walking by she marvelled at how easy some people's lives were. Though they didn't realise that, of course. Everyone's troubles were their own. How many times had she heard that old chestnut over the years?

She saw pretty girls with their boyfriends, saw the innocence of their love and was sorry that her daughter had never experienced any of this. Neither had she, come to that. Her whole life had been nothing but a waste.

But she was going to take retribution for her daughter's death, she was determined on that. No one else's child would have to endure what her daughter had because of Patrick Connor.

Marie only wished she could remember what had happened the last time she had killed. It would help her now to know what had triggered the outburst.

The day was still vague and clouded in her memory. She

remembered going to score early in the morning. It had been a lovely morning, bright and sunny. She had been wired, out of it as usual. Her nerves shot. She remembered sweating, the feeling of nausea that assailed her as she poured milk over the kids' cornflakes.

No matter how out of it she was, she had always made sure the kids had the basics. At the time she had thought that made her a good mother. Oh, if only she had known what trouble her lifestyle was going to cause she would have changed it, she'd sworn that to herself every day of her sentence. Not for her, but for her two babies. That day she had finally scored and been happy again. Until it wore off, which was when Bethany and Caroline had turned up, telling her to come to Kensington with them to a squat that was used by addicts and was always worth a visit for a good fix. They were all going to Mayfair anyway, to work Shepherd's Market, so it was on their way.

The Market had always been a lucrative earner, and again they could score easily there as well. A Rasta would come round every hour with rubbers and heroin. The prostitute's friend, they had called him. He was a nice bloke in his own way, earning a living like them. It was amazing where people saw business opportunities.

If only she could remember what had happened next. She remembered getting drunk, remembered the smell of Thunderbird wine and grass. Then arguing with her mother, she remembered that as well. She had gone round there to try and borrow some money off Marshall. It showed how wired she must have been to have gone to her mother's house. She never went round there unless she had to. Unless she was desperate. It was not as if her mother wanted to see her grandchildren, she hated them both. Especially Jason, God love him. Because he was black, and because his father was Patrick Connor.

Well, Marie finally agreed with her mother on something. Patrick was all her mother had said he was, and more.

The killing itself was as usual a blank.

Tiffany had been really chatty that day and had made her mother laugh. She remembered that clearly, could see her daughter in her mind's eye, in her little blue dress and her little white jellies, her hair half brushed as usual and her face smeared with Smarties. Tiffany had been such a nice little kid and she had never appreciated that fact until it had been too late. After a year on remand, clean and sober, she had said goodbye to them both. She still remembered the smell of Tiffany's hair: Pears shampoo and bubble gum. Remembered Jason being frightened of her, unable to place who she was, and Tiffany's little piping voice asking her when she was coming to take her home.

That had been the hardest day of Marie's life. She had looked at her two kids and seen them as if for the first time. Tiffany had been beautiful, all hair and eyes, her long blonde curls silky to the touch. Jason had looked handsome, with a big red dummy sticking out of his face. His eyes had burned into hers as he tried to place her. But he had hugged her in the end because Tiffany had hugged her tightly. She'd thought at the time that Tiff knew she would not see her again for years. She had always been a shrewd kid. She had needed to be. She'd had to grow up fast because Marie had been such a useless mother.

If only she had known then what she knew now, how different it would all have been. Yes, hindsight was a marvellous thing. But she had been warned, over and over, and had ignored the advice she had been given. Her life then had been lived purely for fun; one big blurred adventure.

She felt tears start once more but swallowed them down. This was no time for crying. There would be plenty of time to cry when this was all over and she had to bury her girl, her child, who had rejected her over Patrick Connor, the man who was to take her life. Had already taken her life in many ways. The moment he had given her crack he had in effect given her a death sentence.

Tiffany would have been too young and naïve to understand that if a man was willing to let others use you it meant he had nothing but contempt for you as a person, a human being.

But he'd had Tiffany so she didn't know what was right and what was wrong. From what Carole Halter had said she had been a good mother until he had decided to put her on the game. Decided to use her. Marie knew better than anyone did how charming he could be, and then how vicious he could become.

Carole had made her so angry with the stories she had told her. Marie hoped she had finally learned *her* lesson once and for all. She had left her with something to think about for a while.

She smiled at the memory.

She was sorting out every person who had hurt her daughter and it felt good. She had felt so useless for so long, but now she was finally doing something for her child. Even if it was too late.

If nothing else, it would make her feel better.

She wanted the names of the men in the video, then to see them with her own eyes. If they had children she would make sure they got a copy. Let them see what their fathers were capable of.

Thinking of children reminded her of Anastasia. She was happy enough in foster care, by all accounts. Liked the people. Probably enjoyed the normality of her life for once. Regular feeding and plenty of hugs worked wonders with little children, or big ones for that matter. Big grown-up children like herself.

Marie wanted to hold her grand-daughter, take her into her arms and love her like her mother had tried to do. Wanted to make amends for all the mistakes she had made with Tiffany and Jason. And she would. Whatever happened she would let that child know what a good person her mother had been underneath. Marie ached to hold the child, her own flesh and blood, her only link with her daughter now. She had promised Tiffany she would look after her and hoped that would be possible. That she didn't get caught for what she was going to do to Patrick Connor. But whatever the turn out, she had to take that man off the street once and for all.

Maisie knew the names of judges and other people she said could help them. She had even given Marie a mobile, the first phone she had ever owned. If Patrick turned up there Maisie was going to ring her. She wanted what Pat had and, as far as Marie was concerned, was welcome to it. All she wanted was to know he was dead and buried then she could relax. Could breathe easier. Could try and get on with her life – what was left of it anyway. She knew she would never know another happy day. All that was gone from her with Tiffany's death.

Marie trained her eyes on the gym and watched the world go by. She was on a mission now and would not rest until it was over.

She was looking forward to seeing Patrick's face when she confronted him. He had always been wary of her because she was so strong. Unlike most women she knew how to fight. She had always been able to fight and had given him a few right handers over the years.

Now he was going to find out exactly what she was capable of. Years ago he used to brag to her about how the element of surprise was always a good frightener. Hit people when they least expected it, that had been his motto. Well, she'd see how he got on when suddenly confronted by her and her wrath.

Unlike everyone else he dealt with, this was personal, this was payback, and this was going to be vicious. Marie wanted him to see her face before she struck. Wanted him to know exactly who was taking him out.

Patrick had left the gym by the back door, and as he roared off in his BMW congratulated himself on his cleverness. He had taken out Malcolm Derby, wiped away Leroy and Maxie. Now the whole of the smoke was his for the taking. He wasn't even worried about Old Bill because he had enough well-connected people on his payroll to feel that he was untouchable.

He turned up the CD player. It was Sade, and he remembered how much Tiffany had liked her songs. Well, perhaps they would play them for her at her funeral. He laughed to himself at the thought.

He remembered his daughter fleetingly then pushed her from his mind. He had a meet later in the evening and now he was going to dinner at his sister's. He had to talk her round and get her to do him a favour. Busby would do anything for him, he knew. She had always done whatever he asked of her.

He was unaware of the car following him because he was so wrapped up in himself and what he was going to do. He made plans as he drove and sang along to his music like a man without a care in the world.

As he passed the Beehive on his way to his sister's he saw three young girls sitting at the bus stop. He watched as they surveyed him hungrily. The clothes, the car and his blue eyes always made sure he attracted attention. He smiled at them. If he had the time he would stop and chat. Pretend he was lost and ask them for directions, all the time sussing them out. Seeing if any of them were live ones, ready to go out into the big bad world. It was amazing really. People told their kids to keep away from bad men, not the smiling one with the big bag of sweets and some nice puff in his prestigious car. Well, he was still a bad man in every sense of the word, the baddest man who'd ever walked the streets of London.

One of the girls was mixed race, about thirteen years old and already well-developed. Judging by her clothes, a small tight top and leggings, she was rapidly discovering the power of her body. She was just up Patrick's street. A bit of flattery and she would be his for the taking. He filed her away for future reference. He was always around and about, he would see her again, he would make sure of that.

341

As he pulled up at his sister's he was in a good mood, buzzing with it in fact. In the car he spooned some coke up his nose and snorted it in noisily. He needed a lift. He had had a long night and a long day.

Busy, busy, busy, that was him.

As he locked his car he was grinning and prepping himself for what he would say to his sister. She was another silly bitch with her African awareness and her ethnic clothes. But she was cool, she adored him. And why wouldn't she? Every woman he met loved Patrick Connor. He checked himself over in his wing mirror. As far as he was concerned, he was fucking gorgeous.

Marie arrived at Verbena and Ossie's at just after nine-thirty. She knew that Pat had left the gym unseen by her and also knew that she could wait for him. She had all the time in the world. She wasn't expecting a warm welcome here but she was past caring.

She'd felt an urge to see her son and didn't care what trouble it caused. Verbena's feelings were not high on her list of priorities at the moment. She was a woman who needed to get out into the world and find out what real problems were.

Ossie answered the door. His handsome face seemed pleased to see her, but he had the hangdog look of a man who knew he was in for trouble. Verbena was not going to be over the moon at Marie's visit, especially as it was unannounced. But the boy needed to see his real mother, whether she liked it or not.

Ossie welcomed Marie with a smile and a hug. She felt the strength of him as he put his arms around her and longed to bury her face in his shoulder, just for the comfort it would bring.

She knew that part of her was only here to delay what she was going to do. She was shocked inside that she was now contemplating murder in such a calculated way. All the years she had served Her Majesty, she had told herself over and over that violence solved nothing, it was a mug's game, and she had been determined to be a better person. Now that was all turned upside down because she had to take revenge on Patrick Connor. But first she would see her son.

She walked into the beautiful home where he had been brought up and relaxed. She would see her boy, her child. He would stop the ache in her breast, stop the madness in her blood.

Jason ran to her and hugged her tightly.

Marie put her arms around him and felt at peace with herself for the first time since her daughter had died. As she pushed her face into his springy hair she was reminded of him as a baby. All her memories of her children were like that. She had missed out on so much of their lives.

Even their first steps were a blur to her. She still beat herself up over her neglect of the two most important people in her life, but they had not been important to her then, not really. Heroin had been her passion, her love. It was a destructive love. To want something above your children, whether it be a drug or a man, was wrong. How many women had she met over the years in prison who had put a man over their children? Hundreds probably. Why did it take so long for them to realise that you would not be young for ever? That sex was peripheral and drugs only an escape? Your children were to be enjoyed and loved because they endured, and loved you no matter what. Look at her son now, hugging her even though she had been away for most of his life. She wasn't sure she could have been so forgiving in his shoes. But then, she knew so much more about her life than he did.

Which was probably just as well.

'I was wishing you here, Mum.'

His words were like a balm to her. He had called her Mum. If she died now she knew she would be happy. It was so long since anyone had called her that and she'd never thought she would hear it again. Had expected him to call her Marie or even Ria. The POs had called her Ria in Cookham Wood.

She was assailed by grief once more and cried into her son's hair. He cried with her. Together they felt their combined grief and it made it easier to bear.

'I am so sorry, Jason, so sorry for leaving you.'

He half smiled, his handsome face so like Marshall's it was eerie.

'You're here now, Mum, that's all that matters.'

She kissed him again but in her head she was screaming out: For how long? If she did what she planned she would soon be gone from him again.

Verbena watched them from the hallway that had been painted a pale lemon yellow because that was the colour of the moment. She still found it hard to believe that her son could find anything even remotely likeable about Marie Carter.

Marie locked eyes with her and the animosity between them was almost tangible.

'I don't recall you ringing?'

Verbena's voice was superior and very clipped.

Marie didn't answer her.

'I said . . .'

Marie forced a smile.

'I heard you the first time. Your husband gave me free rein, told me to pop in whenever I wanted to, remember? I wanted to see my son. I needed to see my son.'

She had said the word out loud. *Son*. A word that so many women took for granted.

Jason hugged her closer.

'I'm so glad you're here. Tiffany missed you as much as I did, she just didn't know how to put it into words.'

He was trying to make her feel better. She realised that he was a kind boy. Patrick had not passed on any of his malice and evil. Jason was a good kid.

'Go to your room, Jason.'

'NO!'

The word was loud and it was final.

Marie found it in her heart to be sorry for Verbena. She was one sad fuck, as they would say in prison.

'Look, Verbena, why don't you just go and make some coffee or something?'

Ossie half pulled and half pushed his wife into the kitchen as he spoke. Shutting the door on his son and Marie, he whispered harshly, 'What is it with you, woman? Can't you see that she is what Jason needs at the moment? She is his only link with his sister. His only link with the past.'

Verbena snorted.

'What past? You and I were both told the true circumstances of his early life. Mother a drug addict, both kids neglected, she killed two of her so-called friends. What kind of bloody link is that, for Christ's sakes? Remember what he was like when they brought him here? A bundle of nerves, crying all the time, not eating! Remember all that, do you?'

Ossie shook his head slowly at his wife's angry words.

'I remember all that, Verby. I also remember that he missed his mother. Cried for her and called out her name. That is what I remember. I also remember us discussing the bond that could make a child love someone who had in effect abandoned them. And he did love her. He still *loves* her. There are many types of love, Verbena, and if you are not careful you will destroy what love that boy has for you because you are making his life so difficult! He has lost his only sister – doesn't that make you in the least bit sad, woman? Can't you find it in your heart to let Marie have a little piece of his life?'

She shook her head furiously.

'It's either her or me, and that goes for you as well, Ossie. I haven't invested all these years in Jason for her to come waltzing into my home and take him away from me. I love him more than she ever could. *I* sat up with him through chicken pox and measles. *I* took him to school and fed him and read to him and made sure he was secure. Not her! *I* made sure he was dressed well, spoke properly. *I* played with him, and taught him to read and write. I don't have room for her in my life and neither does he.'

'But that is where you are wrong, Verbena – he does have room for her. And if you want my advice you'd better make room for her too. Because I intend to do that. I don't think Marie is as black as she is painted.'

He put the kettle on and she could see by the stiffness of his back that he was really angry. Part of her wanted to go to him and caress him and tell him he was right. But she didn't. Pride had always been her biggest failing. That wasn't going to change overnight. Not even for her precious child.

Busby was overjoyed to see her little brother. Her large frame was wobbling with mirth as usual as she showed him into her lounge and sat him down. She made him a white rum and Coke expertly and placed it on a coaster on the table beside him. He could smell rice and peas and his mouth watered in anticipation.

'Let me check on the food.'

Alone he sipped at his drink and surveyed the room. A large picture of the Last Supper adorned the main wall over the fireplace. Jesus and all His disciples were black. It had to be a truer depiction of the night than the white version. A blue-eyed blond man walking round North Africa two thousand years before? He was with Busby on that if not much else.

Patrick saw religion as a big scam, did not believe in any power higher than his own. If God was so good, what the fuck was He doing all day while people starved and died of illnesses like cancer and TB? Patrick believed that people who needed a God were fools, could not bring themselves to take on board that this was it. Once you were dead that was the end of you. Fuck eternal life, live this one as best you could, that was Patrick's motto.

He had finished his drink and poured himself another. He could hear Busby pottering around in her kitchen. It reminded him of when they had been kids. His mother had been white, a fact that shamed him though he would never admit it. Unlike his sister, whose father and mother had both been black, he had always felt left out because his mother had been a low-class white woman whereas his father had been a respected religious man. Not that religious though, obviously, or he would not have been taken in by the white whore he had met at one of his domino nights.

Patrick had hated her, her drink-fuelled rages, even her smell of cigarettes and cheap perfume. But his father had been besotted with her.

When she had finally gone on the trot Patrick had been over the moon, though he had loved his grandfather, the man she had named him after. He didn't have his father's surname. In those days if you were illegitimate you took your mother's. But old Pat Connor had loved him. He had been a hard-drinking, hard-fighting Irishman who had loved his grandson, loved his blue eyes and his sturdy body. He had also adored his daughter, and had faced out the people who'd thought mixed-race relationships were wrong.

When his mother had left, Patrick had been brought here by his father and raised by Busby, the elder sister who had adored him from the moment she had set eyes on him. Twenty years older than he was, she had seen him as the child she had never had.

He had visited his grandfather until his death from cancer when Patrick was fifteen years old. He still thought about the old man as he'd fought the disease, his big frame ravaged, leonine head of red hair on a screaming skull.

Patrick always told people his mother was dead. She was to him anyway. It was better that way.

He looked at the photos round the room. Nearly all were of him at various stages of his life. In his school uniform, or on his motorbike after passing his test. He stared at that smiling boy and marvelled that no one had ever sussed out what had been going on inside his head.

Busby came back into the room. She smelled of food and comfort. He smiled at her. She was the only person he actually cared about.

'I had a letter from Lilian today. Do you want to see it?' She was already holding it out to him.

He shook his head and Busby sighed as she saw the look that came over his face.

'I heard about Tiffany, you know. One of the ladies at the church told me. I'd rather have heard it from you, brother.'

He closed his eyes slowly and looked suitably upset.

'I didn't want you worrying. I told you what was happening to her, didn't I? I tried to stop it all but she was bad. Like her mother, she was bad.'

'I know you were only trying to help. But Marie was her mother and it always seemed wrong to me . . .'

Busby's voice trailed off.

They had been over this so many times and on each occasion he just went quiet. He had been the same as a child. But she was determined to get a reaction of some sort this time. 'What about the baby, little Anastasia? Who is taking care of her? Has Marie seen her at all?'

Then she said the words he had been expecting. Only now he had changed his mind. If Busby took the kid he would be lumbered.

'She could come here, you know.'

He shook his head.

'No. Now, Busby, you listen to me. You can't take on a little girl like her. She's better off in the hands of the professionals.'

'You said the same thing about Tiffany and look how she ended up.'

He closed his eyes to show her she was annoying him.

'Don't get vexed with me, Patrick. I am trying to save that child from the same fate as her mother. We are her blood, this is where she should be.'

'Are we going to eat, Busby, only I have an appointment in about an hour and I'm starving.'

'You always starving, Pat. Don't you eat in your big flat? Don't you even go to a restaurant to get some food? And why do you always change the subject when I talk about the family? Poor Lilian . . .'

'Lilian is a fucking whore, and you and I both know it.'

'Lilian is your mother and she was just a young girl when she had you. How long you going to keep all this up? You must learn forgiveness, boy. She wants to see the child as much as I do.'

Patrick stood up angrily.

'*What* is it with you fucking people?'

Busby prised her large bulk from the chair and bellowed, 'Don't you bring your gutter talk into my home, young man. You have to face up to things at some point in your life. You are nearly forty years old, boy. Grow up and take on your responsibilities. Your mother is a car ride away, and she is heartbroken over you. Daddy was not the man you thought, may God rest his soul. She was just a young girl and he took advantage of her. In those days having any kind of baby without a husband was frowned upon, let alone a black baby with blue eyes! Have some compassion for the woman who bore you. Who loved you.'

He knew he was on the point of exploding so used the ruse he had always used when dealing with his sister.

'You are my mother, Busby. The only mother I have ever wanted or needed. We have been over this time and time again. Lilian is nothing to me. I don't want to see her or talk to her. She is dead to me and has been for many years. You are all I ever needed in my life. So can we please drop the subject before we both say something we'll regret?'

Busby never could resist him, though deep inside she knew he was bad. She had heard the stories about him.

At school it had been the same, one story from the teachers and one from Patrick. She had always believed him because she had wanted to. But as time was marching on it was getting harder and harder to listen to him and what amounted to his delusions about her and himself.

She needed to think hard about what she was going to do this time. Tiffany was dead and there was a child in the world with no one to care for her. As a good Christian woman Busby could not allow that to happen. As a woman who should have been surrounded by babies it was also a need she wanted fulfilled.

She had to think her way carefully through her next step and try and get him to do what she wanted. Reclaim the baby, settle the yearning inside her, and give her something to live the next twenty years for.

Chapter Twenty-Five

Mikey went into Patrick's drinking club mob-handed. As he walked up to the bar he surveyed the place with one quick look. He noted two men in the corner who were obviously tooled up, but wasn't too bothered about them. He knew them both and one even nodded an acknowledgement. He also noticed a couple of young men with dreams of the big time. He pulled the barman to one side and with a mixture of menace and joviality found out Patrick Connor's mobile number and his local haunts. Then he watched as his henchmen wrecked the place.

No one said a word, the club just quietly cleared, one man even taking his drink with him, a large smirk on his face.

Patrick Connor was evidently not a well-liked man.

The place was damaged beyond repair and Mikey knew that Connor would hear about it within minutes.

Which was exactly what he wanted.

Now all he had to do was wait for Connor to come to him. It was a game he was playing and he found he was actually enjoying himself. He would start hassling Connor on the phone when he had had a drink, and was going to get other people to ring him as well. If that didn't bring him out of the woodwork, nothing would.

Mikey walked behind the bar and poured himself a large Scotch. All he could think about was how Marie must be feeling, knowing what had happened to her girl. He had not been able to contact her and guessed she was with her son. She would need her boy around her now after all that had happened, he understood that.

He wanted to see her face when he told her what he had done. He knew she would be grateful, understand why he had done it. They were like-minded and he knew she understood him. That had never happened with any other woman before. Until Marie he had used women and knew that now, could see why all his relationships had all foundered. No respect, no real love. Lust was a completely different thing. You could lust after anyone but once the bonking was over, what was left? Nothing. Just a few warm memories and not much else. He always seemed to be out of pocket afterwards, too, but that, as he told himself, was another story.

He finished his drink and then kicked open the locked door to the office and looked through everything he could find. It was always worth a nose when you were trouncing someone, you never knew what you might find.

There were more videos and more money, a hell of a lot more money. Not that he needed it, but it would wind up Connor no end if he thought he had been robbed. As Mikey looked through the videos and counted the money he was smiling. All in all it seemed this was his lucky night.

They bundled the barman into the boot of the car to make sure they had someone who knew Connor's usual haunts and who had the means of contacting other members of his workforce if necessary.

The boy was terrified and it showed. Before shutting the boot on him Mikey said warningly, 'I hope you aren't a hero, son. I am in the mood to hurt someone badly – don't let it be you.'

Then he was in total blackness and had wet himself with fright before they had even turned the corner of the street.

Lucy was round at Susan Tranter's place. She wanted to know what was happening with her father. It felt strange to be knocking on this door but for now she could not face going back to Mickey's house, could not face seeing his mother and her rat-like eyes. So she thought she would come and visit her father's mistress as a means of delaying her return to a place where she was not welcome.

Anyway, Susan was nice by all accounts. Lucy knew her by sight and had nodded to her before, but it still felt odd knowing that this was the woman her father had been with sexually. She had also heard that Susan's house was filthy though she was clean enough in herself.

One thing she knew for definite, Susan Tranter had stood by her dad through everything and as far as Lucy was concerned, that counted for something.

The woman answered the door. Her face betrayed none of the surprise she was feeling.

'Yes? Can I help you?'

'Hello. I'm Kevin Carter's daughter Lucy.'

Susan stared at her blankly and she hurried on, 'I wondered if you had seen him? Could tell me how he was?'

'Well, there's visiting for family and friends. Any time you want to go, you can. He's not banged up as such, he's in a psychiatric hospital. Rampton, actually, as I'm sure you already know.'

The sarcasm was not lost on Lucy and before she could stop herself she was crying. It was the last straw. Everyone had a downer on her and she was feeling incredibly lonely and sorry for herself.

Susan had a kind nature. Seeing the younger woman on her doorstep looking so distressed, she relented and brought her into the house. Twenty minutes later, the recipient of a cup of tea, Lucy poured out the whole story of her mother and her own broken engagement.

Susan listened sadly. Kevin had spoken of Lucy many times, had felt sorry for her, saying that she was her own worst enemy. And as she listened to her now, Susan was inclined to agree with him.

Lucy was eaten up with bitterness like her mother before her. It was a shame because when she smiled she looked lovely. She just needed to make herself a happier person and then she would attract people to her. As it was she drove them away.

'I want me dad. I miss him so much.'

The loneliness in her voice made Susan sorry for her but she was also sensible enough to see that she was Lucy's last resort. She had no one else to turn to so she wanted her daddy and Daddy's bird if necessary.

But as Susan tried to explain, Kevin wasn't right in the head. He had had a complete breakdown and she wondered at a daughter who could not even be bothered to go and visit him. She told Lucy the doctors believed it was because Kevin had kept so much bottled up inside him for so many years. His daughter's imprisonment and his son's suicide had been hard on him, but he had had to suppress his natural feelings of grief because of his wife and the way her own mental condition had deteriorated after these events.

It was all a sorry tale and now she had his daughter and her problems on her doorstep. In one way Susan was glad because she missed Kevin very much. Lucy was better than nothing, at least she was a part of him. If Susan could help her, maybe she could help him. Kevin needed to see his children, the doctors were all agreed on that. Maybe she could talk Lucy and Marie into going to visit him and the psychiatrists; it might keep him from being locked up once and for all. She would do anything for Kevin, she loved him with every ounce of her being.

So she listened to the younger woman with half an ear. Until Lucy spoke of her and Kevin.

'I beg your pardon?'

'I said, I don't blame my father for turning to you. My mother was never the easiest woman to be around. How long has it been going on? You and him, I mean.'

Susan shrugged nonchalantly.

'Years. I loved him for years and he loved me. But he would never have hurt your mother though she was a trial to him, as we both know. I feel sorry for Lou really. People like her, eaten up by bitterness, never find happiness. Even her own grandchildren were tossed aside. Your father found that very difficult, you know. As he found not seeing or hearing from Marie difficult. If it had been left to him, I think he would have taken the kids on and tried to make the best of it. But your mother was determined that they would never be a part of the family. I assume you've heard about Tiffany's death? Marie must be in bits, the poor woman. Her whole life has been a struggle.'

'She chose to kill her mates, no one made her do it.'

The old animosity was back again.

'Drugs made her do it, Lucy. Drugs are a terrible affliction, especially for the person caught up with them. It's hard enough for the family who have to cope with knowing their child is an addict, but for the person themselves it must be doubly hard.'

Lucy didn't answer.

'So where are you going to stay?'

She looked around her at the untidy room and shuddered. She did not want to stay here but it might be necessary for a few days until she sorted herself out. She certainly didn't want to go back to Mickey's house and have to deal with his bloody witch of a mother.

'I don't know, to be honest. I was going to go to a hotel . . .'

Susan had seen the way Lucy looked at her home and had obviously found it lacking so she didn't offer her a bed. She had been going to but now she felt that Lucy deserved all she got if she would only realise that fact. She could look down her nose at Susan all she liked. No one was forcing her to sit in this mess, were they?

She glanced around her and felt like smiling for the first time in weeks. It was a mess, she'd be the first to admit that. But it was a comforting, clean mess. Papers and books everywhere. Plants growing wherever they were put and just left to overrun windowsills and shelves. She liked her home. Liked the sense of tranquillity it gave her.

'Your father loved it here. Said after your mother's regimented cleanliness it was refreshing. I think he liked the fact he could put his feet up on the furniture and there wouldn't be a fight. Could put his plate on the floor if he wanted to and just chill out, as the youngsters say nowadays.'

She didn't know why she had said that but she wanted this girl to know her father had had happy times in this shithole. Because she knew that 'shithole' was the word that Lucy and her mother would use to describe her home. And maybe it was, but not to her and certainly not to Kevin. It had become his refuge and they both knew that.

'I can understand that, actually. My mother could be overpowering at times. I am looking forward to seeing him. Do you think he will want to see me?' Lucy asked hesitantly.

Susan grinned.

'He'll be over the moon to see you, Lucy.'

She shrugged.

'I don't know why. Marie was always his favourite.'

The bitterness was back once more.

'Oh, really? He talked mainly about you to me. I got the impression he saw you as the stronger person, far more able to cope with the world than Marie.'

It was lies and they both knew it but Lucy appreciated the fact that this woman would do that for her. It was so long since she had been shown even a small kindness that she was near to tears.

The messy house was forgotten now as she finally saw what had attracted her father to the rather blowsy lady sitting opposite her. Susan was kind and she was nice and she had a quiet way with her that was very relaxing.

Seeing Lucy with her guard down, Susan saw a woman in her prime who needed a friend. Someone who would not judge as her mother had done, but would just like her for herself.

'You could stay here for a few days until you get on your feet, I suppose. But as you can see, I'm very untidy.'

She saw the relief on Lucy's face and any qualms she had felt about her offer disappeared. She had always been a sucker for lame dogs. She only hoped that this one wasn't going to bite her at some point in the future.

But she was doing this for Kevin anyway. At least he would see one of his remaining children. She only hoped she could get Marie to visit him as well, though she had her own priorities at the moment and Susan understood that. To bury a child must be the most traumatic thing a person could do.

'If it's not too much trouble?' Lucy said timidly.

Susan smiled without answering. Deep inside she was wondering if she had gone stark staring mad.

Jason and Marie were in the TV room at the back of the house. Like everywhere else it was spotlessly clean, though the furniture was shabbier here than in the rest of the place. Marie guessed that this was the room they used when they were not entertaining. It was more relaxing here than in the other rooms because it was not like a magazine picture. As they sat together and talked, Marie felt herself unwinding.

'She doesn't mean it. My mum . . . I mean, Verbena. It's just that she's had me to herself for so long she finds it hard to share me now, that's all it is.'

Marie grinned at her boy. Soon he would be a man, and from what she had seen he was going to be a good man. A decent man. He was certainly going to be a handsome man.

'I am sorry if I've caused a rumpus but I felt the urge to see you. I missed you so very much when I was away from you.'

He looked into her face.

'Why did you do it, Mum? Why did you kill your two friends?'

She shook her head sadly.

'I wish I knew the answer to that, Jason, I really do. But I don't remember it, any of it. I woke up covered in blood and that was when I realised what had happened. My handprints were on the weapons used and I was charged with murder. Two counts. My brief tried for manslaughter due to diminished responsibility but it was rejected. I was deemed fit and able mentally, and they assumed I had known what I was doing and why I was doing it, I just wasn't telling them. But I have never been able to remember any of it.'

'Truly?'

She nodded.

'Truly. But you have to understand, Jason, I was a different person in those days. I was an addict and they're not like everyone else. Their whole life revolves around getting drugs or drink, whatever their preference is. I would take anything I could lay my hands on. It's like an illness only people don't understand that. People who can control their lives do not become addicts. I could never control mine. I did far too much too soon and it took its toll on me. I was fifteen when Tiffany was born and just seventeen when I had you, and I was just far too young for all that responsibility. So I started to get out of it, take drugs. Tried to stop the pain and the hurt that my life had brought me.'

She saw the searching way he looked into her eyes and felt a desire to lie to him, but she knew she couldn't. He had to know the truth and he had to accept her for what she had done and who she was now, otherwise they would both be living a lie.

'It's hard to believe you did something like that.'

She clasped his hand tightly.

'I know, I feel like that myself. I have had to learn to live with the knowledge that I went out of control and took the lives of two people I liked and cared about.'

He nodded like a seventeen-year-old ancient.

'I'm not going to take drugs ever.'

It was said fervently and with complete candour.

'Some of my friends have taken Es and smoked grass, but I won't. If Mum knew who the boys were she would freak out because they're all what she classes as good lads from good homes. But the world is different these days, drugs are practically socially acceptable. In Amsterdam the government check out the drugs to make sure they're good quality. My friend James said his dad reckons that will happen here eventually.'

'I hope not. Drugs can never be a good thing, can they? Not if they destroy lives. They destroyed my life and yours.'

He nodded solemnly.

'And Tiff's. Are you going to get Anastasia? Only I hate to think of her being adopted. She's all that's left of Tiffany, isn't she?'

'I am going to try. I just have a few things to sort out first.'

'What things?'

'Oh, just a few things that need doing. Nothing for you to worry about.'

As she said the words her decision to be honest with her son went out of the window. She would be as honest as she could about everything else, but she could never admit to him that she was contemplating killing his father.

Though she didn't remember killing the first time, she was determined to remember every second of it this time. This was retribution, not murder – there was a difference as far as she was concerned.

Her phone rang and she was glad of the intrusion. As she answered it and heard Maisie's voice she felt her heart begin to beat faster.

Patrick was driving around the streets erratically. Since the call telling him about the raid on the club he had been possessed by a rage so acute he could feel it eating into his very soul. When he found out who was responsible he was going to bite their heads off personally and after ripping out their hearts he was going to get seriously nasty. As he drove he thought up more and more elaborate ways to inflict pain on his enemies.

He just could not believe it! He had taken out the most dangerous and notorious Gangsta in the country and now someone had the gall to try and fuck him over. He was absolutely livid. He was meeting with his boys and they had better come up with some answers or he would want to know why.

This was typical of the British mentality. He did all the collar, the hard work, and now some little firm thought they could capitalise on it. Well, it was not happening. No fucking way. If it was the Yardies he would have heard by now, he kept a couple of boys in their camp to be on the safe side, and anyway they would just have taken him out. This smacked too much of retribution; this was revenge, and he was racking his brains trying to think of someone who'd worked for Malcolm Derby and would actually have the gall to front him up. He could think of no one at all. He also had to allow for the fact that someone in his pay was giving out to all and sundry about his business. That was another thing he had to think about.

As he pulled up at Maisie's flat he saw the gleaming BMWs of his workforce and sighed. Why didn't they all just leave out a dirty great fucking sign saying: 'Meeting going on, knock on the fucking nearest door'.

He was surrounded by a bunch of fucking morons, but then again, what was new? He didn't want anyone too intelligent working for him because they eventually wanted what you had. It was the unwritten law. But this lot were just above the level of a class of five year olds and he had to have a good sort out in the near future.

As he walked past the line of cars he scratched his keys down the side of each one. He couldn't even get parked at his own meeting! What a fucking performance this was turning out to be.

He stomped towards the building and was amazed to see Marie Carter standing in front of him. She had walked out of a doorway right into his path.

'All right, Pat? Long time no see.'

Patrick looked at Marie in abject horror. She was the last person he had expected to see tonight.

'Well, well, well. Marie Carter. What the fuck do you want?'

'You took my baby . . .'

Patrick laughed. 'Oh. That's what brought you here, is it? Little Tiff.'

She stared at him warily and he started talking to her again.

'She was a whore, like you are.'

As he spewed out his venom to the woman he had destroyed, he saw the iron bar coming towards his face but as he tried to sidestep it, he stumbled.

Marie hit him, over and over again. And with each blow she felt the anger and the hatred leaving her body. Eventually she stopped. Breathing heavily from her exertions, she smiled down at his crumpled form.

'That was for my Tiff.'

Then she walked away from him without a backward glance.

It occurred to her that she had killed again and probably jeopardised her relationship with her son and granddaughter. But someone had to take Patrick Connor out once and for all.

It seemed fitting that it had been her.

Kevin Carter was screaming out obscenities at everyone and anyone. Heavy sedation had been prescribed and he was now being held down once more and injected with Librium.

'By rights he should be out cold!'

The night sister was always amazed at what the human body could take when it was under pressure. A tall thin Nigerian woman, she had worked on agency at the hospital for over four years and was more than aware of the state of mind of each of her patients.

'Keep hold of him until the drug takes effect.'

The two male nurses and a female orderly held him tightly. They did not need to be told to keep hold of him; one man was already sporting the beginnings of a black eye from their last encounter.

'What set him off?'

The nurse shrugged.

'Who knows? He was talking away to old Sally about his kids, she was smiling and nodding like she always does – God knows she doesn't know what's going on from one day to the next – when he suddenly started going berserk.'

357

The female orderly said quietly, 'Whoever this Lou is, I hope he don't get hold of her. He hates her.'

Kevin was still talking, quietly now but they were wary of letting him go.

'She knows I know all about her and what she can do. I should have told but it's too late now. My girls are destroyed . . . Both of them destroyed. She should have been burned up a long time ago, the fucking old bitch! What she done to those two girls was wrong, so wrong. My daughters were both ruined by her . . .'

'Shhh now, calm yourself, Mr Carter. You are in hospital, remember?'

He was nodding. His eyes were closing but still he fought to keep himself conscious. They held him till his body relaxed and his pulse was back to normal. Then they let go of him.

'Off his trolley!'

The Nigerian nurse nodded sadly.

'Poor man.'

'He *is* a murderer, don't forget.'

The female orderly was in her element. She kept her neighbours regaled with stories about the patients on her ward. At the moment Kevin Carter was a favourite topic of conversation.

'How can we forget when you keep reminding us?'

Kevin was still mumbling in his sleep. He was quieter for the rest of the night, but his explosive outbursts were getting more violent and frequent as the days wore on. The doctors would have to up his medication before someone got seriously hurt.

As she wrote up her report the nurse wondered what the fate of this man would be. Prison would not be the answer, he was completely over the edge. Sighing, she stretched and wished the night would end so she could get herself some well-deserved sleep.

Mickey was upset and it showed. With his mother at Bingo he was now acting the man of the house. The fact that he had told Lucy she had to find somewhere else to live was forgotten in the surprise of her turning up in a taxi to collect her stuff. She looked different somehow. More in control, more relaxed. For some reason her doing what he had asked had wrong-footed him. Especially as she had done it so quickly. It occurred to him that she might actually have wanted to leave. There was also the fact he was going to miss her and that was the worst thing of all. He had been all ready to front up his mother for her as well!

As she dragged the bags out to the waiting taxi he didn't attempt to help her. But she didn't ask him to either so he let her get on with it. As she walked back into the house she said, 'You could have folded the clothes up for me, Mick. Most of the stuff is new and hasn't even been worn yet.'

She said it without any animosity whatsoever but the words set him off.

'You should have packed yourself then.'

Lucy laughed and that annoyed him even more.

'I could hardly have packed if I didn't know I was leaving, could I? Anyway, who's rattled your bleeding cage? I'm doing what you wanted so why you have the hump I don't know. Perhaps you're going through the change. You're like an old woman, perhaps you're turning into one.'

She laughed once more at her own joke until she saw the look on his face. Then she surprised them both by saying gently, 'Come on, Mick, play the white man. How can you be cross with me when I'm only doing what you wanted? Or, more precisely, what your mother wanted?'

'Where are you staying?'

'With a friend.'

He didn't know what to say to that. He wasn't aware she had any friends. Not close friends anyway. They both had lots of acquaintances but neither had an actual bosom pal. With mothers like theirs friends were never encouraged, there was always something wrong with them, and so eventually they stopped bringing people home.

'Who are you staying with then?'

She shrugged.

'No one you know.'

He was suspicious now and thought it might be another bloke.

'Male or female?'

'Who the fuck are you, the friend police? Giving me the third degree like you own me or something.'

He was taken aback and it showed.

'I thought we were supposed to be engaged, Lucy? In case that fact has slipped your mind.'

He was self-righteous now, on his dignity, and she wanted to laugh at him again.

'Hark at you, you pompous little twat! I was under the impression we were engaged as well until I got me fucking marching orders from you and the East End's answer to Bonnie Parker. But I think we both know it's time for a rethink, don't we? I ain't marrying your fucking mother, mate, I have enough trouble with the one I've already got. So you think on that when she gets in from Bingo and wants you to make her a cup of tea while she regales you with stories of how she "only wanted one number" all fucking night. What woman in her right mind would want to take *that* on?'

She walked out of the door and he grabbed her arm, pulling her round to face him.

'I want to know where you're staying!'

'And I want world peace, to win the Lottery and a shag off Denzel Washington, so like me you'll know what it's like to want, won't you?'

As she walked down the path the cab driver smiled at her. He was about thirty-five, dark-skinned with thick black hair. That smile tipped Mickey over the edge.

'Who's he fucking smiling at?'

As he spoke his mother turned into the street with one of her cronies, Gladys Lancaster. She was like his mother, old before her time, dried up and vicious. Lucy thought it all highly amusing. Inside she was pleased to see Mickey was jealous. It proved to her that there was a man in there somewhere.

Only a small man, she admitted, but a man nonetheless.

For the first time in ages she was in control and it felt good. He was looking at her like he used to before they got bogged down with the wedding preparations and their mothers. Before he let her boss him about and she had lost all respect for him.

'Oh Mickey, don't be silly.'

As she spoke his mother came up to them with her friend.

'Good riddance to bad rubbish, that's what I say.'

She'd had a couple of brandy and ports, plus four barley wines in the Bingo hall, and was ready for a fight. She was determined to see Lucy off and determined to do it now. In fact, if it was left to her then her boy would live with her for the rest of her days.

'Mum!'

Her son's voice was high.

'Don't you "Mum" me! You're better off without her and the tribe she comes from. You can do better than the Carters.'

Lucy opened the taxi door without even answering. The driver was finding it all highly amusing and his laughter was making Lucy want to laugh too.

'Drive.'

Her voice was full of suppressed laughter as the taxi pulled away quickly from the house, leaving Mickey, his mother and her friend speechless.

'She's gone then?'

He heard the satisfaction in his mother's voice and answered her in a shout that could be heard three streets away.

'It fucking looks like it, don't it? Happy now, are you? You fucking miserable old bag!'

Her face was ashen as she watched her son stalk off down the street in his slippers.

Her hand was still pressed over her mouth in shock as Gladys said happily, 'What a bleeding night this turned out to be.'

Mary Watson had won three hundred pounds with a full house, hence the over-indulgence in drink. But it meant nothing now as she realised she had finally gone too far. Like his father before him Mickey had his limit and she had pushed him over it this night. She had won a few battles but she had a feeling Lucy Carter would win the war.

Marie had lain in the bath at the hostel for over half an hour and now she was lying on the bed in her room, staring at the ceiling. She could not believe what she had done, what she was still capable of doing.

All those years of controlling herself were for nothing. The degree, the hours of dedicated learning, trying to be a better person, were all for nothing. She was still a killer and this time she didn't have the excuse of drugs.

She had always had a temper, had always been capable of taking care of herself. At school she had been the best fighter in her year and had been proud of that fact. No one had dared to mess with Marie Carter, and when she had gone right off the rails, her reputation as a hard nut had made it all the easier because no one had the guts to tell her to her face what an arsehole she was.

When she had had her Tiffany at fifteen she had looked everyone in the eye with a steely glare and no one had ever had the front to say anything to her face. It had become a habit in the end. The worse she was, the more aggressive she got with people. That way they didn't say anything to her she didn't want to hear. No one ever had the guts to tell her where she was going wrong because they were too frightened to. Then the drugs had taken over and it had

361

seemed at the time like a natural progression. She was bad, wasn't she? She was off the rails and didn't care about any of it.

Only she did. Deep inside she cared but she was too far gone to admit it to herself, let alone anyone else. So the cycle had started all over again until finally she had gone too far. She had killed two young women whom she had liked and had thought she cared about.

For all these years she had told herself that it was out of character for her to do something like that, when in fact it wasn't. Tonight had proved to her that she was more than capable of harming someone even stone cold sober.

She didn't feel that she had done a good thing; now in fact she knew she had done a bad thing. Even worse than the first two murders because at least then she'd had the excuse of drugs.

But tonight would never leave her and she knew it. She would remember everything in vivid detail all her days. She didn't feel she had righted any wrongs. If anything she felt that all she had done was come down to Patrick Connor's level.

She should have let the police take care of him. Why had she been so adamant that she wanted to do it herself?

But she knew why: because she couldn't be sure they would have put him away. He was slippery, always had been, and she knew better than anyone that you could buy justice in this country. She had spoken to enough people while in prison who had done just that.

But it still didn't justify what she had done. She didn't feel that she had avenged Tiffany, she felt that she had used her daughter's death as an excuse to do something she had wanted to do for years.

And she *had* wanted to. Patrick should have been locked up, not her. He had made her into the person she had become. He had fed her heroin until she would do anything for it, even kill by the looks of it.

She closed her eyes as she saw him again, covered in blood and trying to crawl away from her. If only he hadn't laughed at her . . . it was his laughing that had sent her over the edge. Because when she had confronted him she wasn't sure she had the nerve to kill him.

She wiped the tears from her eyes with the back of her hand and waited for the police to come and take her away once more. Her lips moved in a silent prayer, but it wasn't to God she was praying but to her dead daughter. She was apologising for what she had done and for the fact that now she had fulfilled her task she had in effect lost her son and grand-daughter as well.

Every time she closed her eyes she saw Patrick laughing at her again, with that arrogant way he had, and the anger boiled up inside all over again.

Her mother had been right all along.

She really was bad. Inside and out, she was bad.

Chapter Twenty-Six

Alan watched the sun come up from the Portakabin window. He had not slept all night, was far too wired. Sleep could not have claimed him even if he had taken fifty downers. He had drunk a litre of Scotch and that had not made any difference. He wasn't even drunk.

Today was the day he had longed for and dreaded in equal measure. But whatever else it brought, it was the end of it all and for that he would be forever thankful.

He sipped at his coffee and savoured the last of the Scotch. He still needed something to take the sting out of the morning. He glanced at his Rolex and sighed. He had another hour before it all went off.

His mind wandered to Marie and her predicament. He hoped she would still be a friend after this was all over. But he doubted it. He doubted it very much. Out of the corner of his eye he saw a man with a gun and felt fear once more. Mikey would be mad at him for this double-cross, but what choice did he really have? He had to get out of this mess and he was going to get out of it with the least trouble to himself. That was what he had decided and that was what he was going to do.

His kids needed him and he needed them. Wanted to be around for them, not banged up. When this was all over he was going straight. He was never going to do one thing wrong again in his life, it had brought him nothing but trouble. He was also going to give up on the horses and the dogs. It was his gambling debts, plus the extravagant lifestyle of his ex-wife, that had brought him to this impasse in the first place.

He had been lonely when Beverley had gone. He would not admit that to anyone else, but he had been so desperately lonely. Missed his girls in the morning jumping all over him. Missed the smell of tea and toast and the girlish banter of his daughters as they got ready for school. Even missed his ex-wife's inane chatter, though at the time he could have murdered her, especially when he had one of his marathon hangovers. She had always known when he had been at it with another woman and her eyes would betray her hurt. Why had he done it? What had been so wrong with his life really?

They'd had the big house, the nice cars, and his and hers Rolexes. All the things that people like them aspired to. Yet it was then that the rot set in.

With money in your pocket other women were willing to climb into your lap without a second's thought. A nice meal, a few quid, and Bob was your proverbial uncle. You had some sort getting her tits out without an argument about the kids or wanting to know who you were with or what you were doing. It was mindless sex, something that was no longer possible at home once you had a houseful of children.

But the closeness was not there, the lying together afterwards and talking about mutual acquaintances or family. That was gone, to be replaced by chatter about fuck all because you didn't actually have anything in common. Not really. It was just a bartering system. The girl had to have a reasonable boatrace and big tits, and you had to have the means to give them a night out up West and cab fare home.

What was it his old dad used to say? Fair exchange is no robbery. That was it, but Alan never got a fair exchange. Most of the women he wouldn't want to see in daylight, and he certainly wouldn't want to be seen with them unless he was drunk, drugged or both.

He had seen one girl three times. She had seemed OK at the time, nice little bird with a baby. She had been a laugh, a crack. Nothing serious until she had turned up on his doorstep one morning and caused the Third World War and now here he was, a grown man, pretending he liked his divorced status and hated his ex-wife. A man who was lusting after a convicted killer and just about to tuck up one of the most dangerous villains in the South East, who was incidentally also lusting after the same convicted killer. Except he *was* trumping her and by the look on her face she was enjoying it immensely.

Alan Jarvis had certainly come up in the world, no doubt about that. All he needed now was to fall out with fucking Saddam Hussein and he could get to keep the fucking match ball. He glanced at his watch again. The minutes were ticking by so slowly he feared he might have a heart attack with the strain.

The phone rang and he grabbed it with a mixture of relief and trepidation.

'Hello? Is that you, Alan?'

It was an Irishman called Tommy the Pig, on account of the fact he was a pig farmer in Devon. It was a few seconds before Alan placed him because he was so nervous.

'All right, Tommy. What can I do you for?'

He was trying to act as normal as possible.

'I have some scrap coming in the end of next month. From Yugoslavia. A good few quid for the man who can get rid of it.'

'How much?'

'A lot, Alan. It's tanks.'

He rolled his eyes to the ceiling.

'No, thanks, Tommy. I am out of that business from today.'

He replaced the receiver gently and felt an urge to cry. How had all this happened to him? Where was that young man who'd been going to set the world on fire?

You got the life you deserved. How many times had his father said that to him? And why had the old fucker always been right?

He drank the last of his coffee and continued his vigil at the window. His life was going to change drastically after today. He only hoped it was all worth it. He saw that the men outside were getting impatient and hoped it all went off without too much hassle.

But the way things were going for him lately, that was too much to hope for.

The knock she had been expecting finally came on Marie's bedroom door at six o'clock in the morning. She was ready for it; she was up, dressed and ready to go. Taking a deep breath, she opened the door.

'Phone for you, Marie.'

She stared at Amanda for long seconds before forcing a smile.

'Who is it?'

Amanda smiled, her eyes still full of sleep.

'Some woman. She didn't give her name.'

Marie didn't answer her, just walked down to the hallway and picked up the communal phone.

It was Maisie.

'How are you, Marie?'

'OK.' She was so aware of Amanda hovering in the background

her words sounded stilted and false even to herself.

'Has this line got a hook on it?'

'I don't know.'

Amanda was miming drinking a cup of tea and Marie was nodding now furiously, indicating that she was dying for one.

'Well, I'm ringing about last night. You know, when we went to the Bluehouse Club together? You had a disagreement with Candice, the little black girl from behind the bar? Well, her sister is here and said to tell you Candice was sorry, she was out of order. Are you OK about that? Only Lizzy Waite who owns the club was upset about it. The last thing she needs is the bar staff giving the customers grief, ain't it?'

Marie nodded, forgetting that Maisie couldn't see her. But she was so nervous she would be hard pushed to write her own name.

'OK, Marie?' Maisie's voice was more insistent now.

'Yeah, thanks. Tell her to forget about it and lay off the vodka.'

Maisie laughed, as she knew she was required to if there was a hook on the phone.

'Did you charge the mobile like I showed you?'

'Yes, 'course I did.'

'Good. Well, turn the bloody thing back on! I'll ring you later then. 'Bye.'

The phone went dead and Marie had to hold on to the grubby wall to keep herself upright. Amanda called her into the rec room for her tea and she walked as normally as she could get to it. But it felt like she was walking underwater. The lying and scheming had already started, but how could she hope to get away with what she had done?

And, more to the point, why was Maisie doing this for her?

She sipped the tea gratefully, its hot sweetness reviving her flagging spirits. An old con she was once locked up with used to do the tea round for the other prisoners. She had been a gofer, which in prison terms meant 'go for this' or 'go for that', but she had loved it. Said it gave her something to do with her days. 'The cup that cheers' she had called it. She had died in her cell one night and the whole prison seemed to go into mourning for a nice old lady who had once made a terrible mistake. Was that how people would think of Marie one day?

'She sounded OK.'

Marie smiled. She wasn't going to tell Amanda anything. She was a lovely woman but she was also part of the prison service, even if she didn't see herself in quite that light. At the moment she was the enemy.

Marie was amazed at how quickly her prison ways had come back to her. A natural distrust of anyone was a must in that environment, especially anyone in the pay of the Home Office. She sighed inwardly. She wasn't sure she could live like that again for years on end. At least before she'd had the knowledge that whatever she had done it was while under the influence of drugs, so even though that didn't make it right, at least it wasn't premeditated. Now it was a different kettle of fish altogether. Though thanks to Maisie she had an alibi at least.

So she *was* going to try and walk away from this; she had made that decision, or she wouldn't be thinking like she was. She wondered how the alibi had been concocted and whether the women referred to would be willing to commit perjury when the time came. Because that time would come, she was sure of it. Once Patrick's body was found the police would come knocking on her door.

As Amanda chattered on Marie was still contemplating her own predicament, and wondering if it all came on top how she would cope with life inside once more. As a three-times killer she could not expect to get out for a very long time. And rightly so.

As her mind raced from one thought to the next Amanda stared at her curiously. There was something going on here, she knew that much. All her years in this place had given her a shit detector and it was working overtime at the moment. She hoped there wasn't going to be any more trouble for Marie; the poor woman had had quite enough to contend with in life already.

Mikey and his cronies pulled into the scrapyard at twenty-past seven. They were late and they were all quiet. Last night's events had subdued them all. As Mikey listened to the morning news they all made a point of looking out of the car windows as if they found the scenery fascinating.

Suddenly he spoke.

'He was a cunt and cunts need to be sorted out. Trying to fucking lie to me! To me of all fucking people!'

Old Billy nodded his head in agreement.

But he didn't speak. He was still seeing that bloodied body as it jerked into the air from the cattle prod. Could still hear the screams of the man as his eyes popped out of their rightful place in his skull. He closed his eyes to assuage the sickness rising up inside him. Mikey had gone over the top, there was no doubt about it. Even the hardened criminals who worked for him had been disgusted and frightened by the ferocity of the attack. Considering the man had been half dead already from the beating he had been given it had seemed unnecessarily cruel to make him suffer as long as he had.

And all that blood . . . It had taken place in one of their garages. They would have to go there often and the blood stains would be a permanent reminder of what had occurred. They would also be evidence if the filth ever poked their noses in.

Billy understood Mikey and the way his mind worked. His anger had had to be unleashed at some point, and better it was unleashed on a piece of shit than on someone far less deserving. But they were supposed to be the new breed of criminal who used the minimum of violence, and then only in a work-related capacity. It was one thing killing a man because he had crossed the line inside your manor; quite another killing someone painfully and with relish over something that in fact had no direct connection to you, no matter how sickened it might make you feel.

What Mikey had done last night would result in a capture, Old Billy was convinced. The victim should by rights have been taken well away from the smoke and disposed of quietly and with the minimum of fuss. Perhaps he was getting too old for all this. That thought had occurred to him more than once of late.

As they all got out of the car they saw Alan watching them from the window. Mikey was still covered in blood and gore and looked eerie in the bright morning light. His men could not understand why he had not showered and changed. He was fucking crazy to drive about looking like he did. It was as if he had gone mad or something.

But then, he had sniffed a huge amount of coke the night before. They wondered if he had needed it to make him do what he felt needed to be done. But it was still fucking mad. Like a nightmare.

One of the younger men had thrown up and that had made Mikey laugh even more, though how anyone could have laughed at what was going on was beyond any of the rest of them.

It seemed that Mikey's good boy mode was a thing of the past and he was back to being the violent psycho that had made him the rich man he was. If that murderer bird had done anything, she had at least calmed him down. Without her around it seemed he'd reverted back to his old self. But who in their right mind would go to pick up three million pounds' worth of cocaine with the blood of their latest murder victim still on their hands?

Old Billy shook his head sadly as he contemplated what the upshot of all this was going to be.

'All right, Billy?'

''Course I am, Mikey. Are you?'

He laughed good-naturedly.

'Better than I've ever been.'

As he said the words the whole place seemed to go mad. There were men coming out of every nook and cranny and they were armed and they were also Lily Law. As they all reached for their weapons Mikey's men knew they were already defeated. Two police cars and a meat wagon now blocked the only exit and trained marksmen covered their every move.

'Bollocks!'

Old Billy's voice was annoyed, but he dropped his weapon and put his hands behind his head. The younger men followed suit. It was a capture and a half and they all knew that Alan had been behind it. As they were bundled towards a meat wagon Mikey looked at his men and said calmly, 'It's a fair cop, guv'nor.' And started to laugh like a drain.

No one answered him; there really was nothing to say.

Then Mikey pulled a small gun from the waistband of his trousers and spun quickly round to shoot at the first person he could get his sights on.

He was shot down in a second. A high-velocity rifle bullet hit him square in the chest. And as the birds sang and the flies buzzed around he lay on the dirty ground and felt his life's blood drain from his body.

He was smiling still.

Old Billy knelt beside him and took his hand. Whatever he was, he had always looked out for his old mate and Billy had been grateful for that over the years. He had tears in his eyes as he saw his friend die.

Then there was pandemonium once more. They were all rounded up and searched properly, roughly treated by the masked men. All the time Old Billy gave out to them, his voice getting on everyone's nerves as he insinuated that none of them had any fathers and that their mothers were women of dubious sexual character.

Finally they were herded once more towards the meat wagon. This time they were all subdued. Inside it was sweltering hot from being parked in the sun so long. As they stepped inside they knew they were all going away for long sentences, at least twenty years apiece.

They were gutted.

That a capture was always on the cards they were always aware of on some level. When it did finally happen it was still a big shock, though. Even living with the possibility every day of their lives they still didn't quite believe it would happen to them. It was like car crashes and your house burning down – it happened to other people, not you.

But it had to happen to someone and they realised it was their turn as they were cuffed and read their rights.

One of the younger men, Willie Forrester, had just got married and his wife was pregnant with their first child. He was only two years out after completing an eight-year sentence for armed robbery. Even in their own misery they all felt sorry for him. His new wife was a foxy piece and had a wandering eye as well. His marriage would be over by Christmas and he would have to face the next ten years on his tod.

When they finally pulled away, Old Billy saw Alan sitting in the doorway of the Portakabin with his head in his hands and shouted out, 'You are fucking dead, you filthy grassing bastard!'

Alan couldn't hear him but it made the old man feel better anyway. If it was the last thing he did on this earth he would pay Jarvis back for this act of utter cuntishness. That would be his mantra as he sat and rotted in jail.

'He is dead. On my daughters' heads that ponce will breathe his last before I ever sleep easy again.'

Even the policeman in the meat wagon was amazed by the sheer hatred in the old man's voice. The men listening were all glad not to be Alan Jarvis. This day's work would bring down the wrath of every villain in the country on his head. He was a marked man and from now on would have to live with that. And with himself, of course, there was that to be considered as well.

All Alan could do was stare at the body of Mikey Devlin and know that he was responsible for what had happened. But would Mikey have wanted to do the time he was guaranteed if they had brought him to trial? He thought that maybe Mikey had done what he did so he *would* be shot because he couldn't face the long years inside.

Already Alan regretted his decision to grass. At the time it had seemed like the answer – now he wasn't so sure. He had just wanted out, that was all. And Mikey would never have allowed him to walk away. Until he was finished with you, you danced to whatever tune he requested.

DI Stanton came over to him.

'Bad business this, Alan. The main protagonist dead – doesn't leave us with much, does it?'

He shrugged.

'Who gives a fuck, really?'

And he went back to smoking his cigarette and watching the police ponce around his yard, going over and over in his mind exactly what he had let himself in for. He finally decided he must have been stark staring mad. He had grassed everyone up and now would have to look over his shoulder for the rest of his natural life.

Maisie was amazed by Patrick's so-called workforce. Without him they obviously could not arrange a prayer meeting in a convent. She listened to them talking, all bragging about what they would do when they found Pat, and how the person who had kidnapped him was going to suffer. Only no one seemed to have the least inclination to go out and look for their boss. It was true, she thought as she looked at the assembled men. If you paid peanuts you got monkeys.

'His car is outside so what does that tell us?'

Her loud voice commanded everyone's attention.

Chrissie Jordan, a young mixed-race lad with a handsome face and a natty way of dressing, answered her.

'That he must have been here at some point?'

'Exactly. So someone took him off the street – I think it's safe to assume that much, don't you?'

They all nodded as they listened to her. They knew Pat rated her and would give her a level of respect because of that. Especially if he was still alive somewhere, though secretly they all doubted that. Like a rudderless ship they needed guidance and she seemed to be the only one offering any at the moment.

'Then we should also assume that he's dead.'

No one answered and Maisie carried on talking.

'And whoever killed him is now in possession of whatever he had, aren't they? Which includes us lot as well.'

'She's right.' Chrissie's voice was subdued.

'So what do we do?' This from Winston Halliday, a quarter-caste from Whitechapel.

They all automatically looked at Maisie and she noted this with satisfaction.

'We wait, of course. Leave everything to me and I'll see what occurs. I have to do a drop later, still have to pick up the money from the girls. I'll need a couple of you to come with me in case we're going to be had over. Business must be seen to carry on as usual, agreed?'

They all nodded meekly and as she looked around the room at these so-called hard men of Patrick's she felt the urge to laugh. Men were so easy to manipulate. But only if you knew the magic buttons to press. Maisie had the edge here because *she* actually *knew* what had happened to him.

She also knew that he was dead.

As she made them all more coffee and tea she contemplated how much easier her life was going to be from now on, and sighed happily, secure in the knowledge that unlike most people she had got what she wanted and it felt good.

In a couple of weeks when the furore died down she would just take over and no one would question her doing so because by then they'd be used to her giving the orders. She would gradually assume control of paying them each week and they would start to work for her without even really thinking about it. They would soon forget all about Patrick Connor. Already he was old news.

Maisie was a clever little bunny when the fancy took her.

Ossie had woken up on the sofa in the study, as Verbena insisted on calling the small room at the back of the house. His neck was sore and he was not in the best of moods when he walked out to the kitchen.

Verbena was still sitting where he had left her the night before, at the kitchen table nursing a cup of tea. She wore the ravaged expression of a hunted animal and it annoyed him more than ever. He was damned if he was going to be the one to make things up this time. It had become a pattern early on in their relationship that he was the peacemaker. He was always the one who bought her flowers or perfume and made the first move to get their relationship back to the happy state it was in before they had rowed.

But not this time. He was determined to make her take responsibility for her own actions and petty jealousy.

How could she be jealous of Marie Carter? The woman had led a terrible life even though she looked good on it, and he was the first

374

to admit she looked a bit *too good* for the likes of Verbena. But that had nothing to do with the basic fact that she was Jason's natural mother and he wanted her to be in his life.

The worst part of it was that Ossie knew if a fat ugly woman with no dress sense and a grateful demeanour had turned up at the door, Verbena would have been over the moon. Even taken her under her wing, because she loved to be in control of everyone. But Marie Carter, although grateful, had no need of the help his wife would have loved to bestow. In fact, *she* could probably help Verbena. At least Marie Carter lived in the real world and not the one of tree-lined avenues and dinner parties that his wife inhabited.

Ossie was angry with himself for his thoughts as he felt they were mean. But Verbena had pushed it too far this time and he had had enough. As he put the kettle on she spoke, her tone aggrieved and her voice soft as if she was still on the verge of tears.

'There's fresh coffee in the percolator.'

'Instant will do for me. You know I prefer Nescafe.'

She did know and it annoyed her. Even when they went to dinner at people's houses he requested it, and every time he did so he angered her that little bit more. He didn't even drink decaf like everyone else. He enjoyed saying he needed the jolt of the caffeine to wake him up. And him a doctor!

As he spooned two heaped teaspoons of coffee into his cup she stopped herself from saying another word about it. For the first time ever she was worried, really worried, because he had slept in the study and he had never done that before. She had expected him to come out to the kitchen and cajole her into going to bed as he normally would. Instead she had heard him go into the study and that had been that. She had even had a shower and put on perfume in case he wanted to make love to her to seal their making up. That was what usually happened. In fact, if she was honest, that was usually the best bit.

But since Marie Carter had come on the scene he had changed. Her son had changed too and she felt strangely alienated by it all. They wanted her to capitulate and at least pretend she liked that woman but she couldn't do it. She just couldn't.

She watched as he poured water on to the coffee granules. As she looked at him in profile she was reminded of what a handsome man he was. Many women gave him a second look, she had always been aware of that. Even some of her friends gave him the glad eye now and again. As he was now, in his boxers, barefoot, he reminded her of an African prince. She could see him in her fantasies coming to save her and then taking her roughly on a dirt floor somewhere.

She blushed as she thought of it but it had always turned her on. He was everything to her, he and her son. If they would only realise that fact, and maybe appreciate her for it, how much happier they would all be.

He padded past her without another word and she heard the door to the study close. A few moments later the TV came on and she felt lonelier than she had ever felt in her life. He was watching the news, completely uncaring about the fact that he had broken her heart.

But she would *not* give in, she was determined on that much. She decided that if he liked sleeping in the study so much then that was where he could stay. See if she cared.

Jason came into the room, still looking sleepy. He kissed her automatically and she hugged him to her.

'Are you OK, sweetie?' Her voice was tender as she spoke to him. He nodded.

'I just feel a bit funny, Mum. I woke up and felt as if Tiffany was near me. I really felt that she was close by. It was eerie.' He paused and she could see him frown as he tried to find the words to explain what had happened. 'I sort of felt like she was trying to tell me that everything was going to be all right now.'

They both turned to the doorway as Ossie appeared there and said gently, 'She loved you, Jason. She was trying to let you know that.'

'Do you think so, Dad?'

His voice was hopeful. He was desperate to believe what he was being told.

'I *know* so. So be glad you had the chance to say goodbye properly. Come and have some breakfast, son. Shall I do us all some ham and eggs?'

He was trying to bring normality into a house that had been anything but normal for days. And twenty minutes later, as he watched his son eat enough for a platoon of soldiers, Oswald was grateful to whatever God there was for bringing this child into his life.

Chapter Twenty-Seven

'I know you're in there, Marie.'

Sally Potter's voice was a harsh whisper.

Marie opened the door slowly and Sally walked into the room before she could be refused admission.

'Look, Sal, I'm really tired . . .'

'I'm not surprised! I heard you pacing the floor half the night. What the fuck is up, Marie?'

The two women stared at each other for long moments; it was Marie who looked away first.

'What have you done, love?'

Sally's voice was gentle but elicited no response from her friend.

'You look dreadful and you look guilty. You look like I did after I wasted my old man. Now your business is your business, I accept that. But you don't need any more trouble in your life. None of us does. So tell me what's wrong.'

Sally's earnest plea broke through Marie's reserve and she said in a frightened voice, 'I did it again, Sal.'

'What are you talking about, Marie? You did what again?'

'I killed someone.'

Now she had said it out loud she felt easier inside. It was as if by saying it she had made it true.

Sally's face paled.

'What the hell you talking about, girl? Who the fuck you supposed to have killed?' The prison jargon was back without a second's thought.

'Patrick Connor.'

'What – the black pimp?'

Sally's voice held admiration now.

'That is one bad bastard.'

'Was. He *was* a bad bastard and that's why I did it. He was my son's father – I think I told you about that? Well, he duffed my

377

daughter, put her on crack and then he killed her. Had her killed in the worst way possible. I *had* to do it.'

'I heard about your girl. I didn't come in because I know that, like me, you need to deal with your grief in private. One of the legacies of a life spent in prison. It was only last night I started to worry about you because you were pacing the room.'

They were quiet for a few moments and then Sally left. She returned a few minutes later with a half-bottle of brandy. She poured out two glasses and, giving one to Marie, watched her as she downed it in one gulp.

'That's it, girl, it will help settle your nerves.'

They both sat on the bed.

'How did you do it?'

Marie sighed and said gently, 'I beat him to death. It seems that's what I do best.'

She held out her glass and it was refilled instantly.

'I took an iron bar, which is obviously my weapon of choice, and confronted him over my girl.'

She gulped at the drink before she carried on talking.

'He laughed at me. That rotten bastard just laughed at me as if it was the funniest thing he had heard in years. He said, "So what you going to do, Marie, kill me? You ain't no fucking killer, girl, you're just a stupid whore." And he kept laughing so I hit him.'

She finished the drink quickly and held out the glass once more to be refilled before she continued.

'And I hit him and I hit him and I hit him. And then he was on the pavement trying to crawl away from me and so I hit him again. And then I knew he was dead. So I ran.'

'What did you do with the wrench, Marie?'

'I slipped it down a drain hole then I went into the toilet at a train station and washed the blood off my hands. My shirt was spattered as well, so I slipped that off and threw it away and just wore my dark jacket pulled tight round me.'

Sally was nodding as if in agreement.

'Good, so there's nothing to tie you to it. Where did you get the wrench?'

'From a builders' supply merchants round the corner. I went in there and sorted through the tools until I found something smallish but heavy. He is one strong fuck as I have always known, but then so am I. He used to joke about my right hook years ago. Anyway, I binned it, just walked out nonchalantly. I didn't want to be seen buying it, you know.'

'Are you sure he killed your girl?'

Marie laughed nastily.

'I have the fuckers doing it on video. That's what sent me over the edge. He gave her to three nonces. He not only got shot of her, he made a few quid on the deal – now why am I not surprised about that? One was a judge and one was in the CPS. The other bloke is a barrister or something. Just pieces of shit who took my baby and literally beat and fucked her to death. What kind of way is that to go, screaming, and terrified out of your mind? Who the fuck do these people think they are – and what makes them tick? What made them want to *do* something like that to someone else? A lovely young girl with her whole life ahead of her.'

Marie was sobbing now, the crying of a woman completely over the edge. One of the other women knocked on the door, alerted by the high-pitched noise coming from the room. As she popped her head around it Sally said softly, 'Her daughter died, she's upset. Got any hard?'

The woman came back a few moments later with a bottle of Scotch.

'Take this. I hope she feels better soon.'

She looked at Marie with compassion. They had all heard about it. She left the room and Sally cradled Marie in her arms until her crying subsided. Then she held up the bottle of Scotch and said craftily, 'If they knew how much contraband was in the place they'd freak out. Feeling better?'

Marie nodded.

'A bit.'

'Listen, Marie, what you done was right. You done a good thing and you should be proud of yourself. Now have another drink and try and get a few hours' sleep. You'll feel better if you do.'

'Will you stay with me?'

Sally nodded.

''Course I will, for as long as you need me.'

Alan listened to the policemen talking and wondered what the hell was going to happen to him now. If they put him on remand it had to be in segregation or he'd be dead in hours. Because Mikey was dead, he wasn't that important to them any more. He knew it, and more to the point they did.

'Why would Mikey Devlin have killed Patrick Connor?'

That name frightened Alan Jarvis so much he was rendered speechless. Connor could bring Marie into the equation. She had had a child by Connor and now she was seeing Mikey. The implications were legion, especially as she was out on licence and should not be near anyone with form.

'Did Mikey kill him then?'

The policeman frowned.

'I'm asking the questions here, remember.'

Alan shrugged.

'I know nothing about that. If I did I'd have said so. I opened me trap about everything else, didn't I? I'd hazard a guess that if he did kill him – and that's a big if, mind you – it would be over the old Persian rugs. They were both at it after all, and Mikey, like I said, wanted to become even bigger. Supply the whole of the fucking country. Saw himself as a bit of an Escobar, if you know what I mean.'

The plainclothes policeman rolled his eyes to the ceiling in mock boredom before he answered sarcastically.

'What – he wanted to score an own goal in the World Cup and get shot? Well, one out of two ain't bad. At least he realised one of his dreams. I can't see Mikey in the England squad. A bit old like, don't you think? Though the way they've been playing he could still get a shot at it, I suppose.'

Alan shook his head in disgust.

'Very fucking funny, I don't think. He saw himself like the Colombian drug dealer of the same name. You know, the Mr Big of the smoke. Don't forget that cunt Escobar ended up running his country. He even owned the jail they banged him up in.'

'Well, bully for fucking Escobar. But none of this answers my fucking question, does it?'

'Well, that could be because I don't know the fucking answer. I can only hazard a fucking guess.'

The policeman, DI Teddington, was not a happy man at the best of times. Even his colleagues didn't like him.

'I'll hazard my fist in your fucking face in a minute!'

Alan had finally had enough.

'You dare and I'll beat your fucking brains out, you ponce! Now bring me a real filth with some real fucking power in this place and I might have something to talk about, mightn't I?'

Teddington was incensed. He was small fry by police standards and it bothered him. He acted the hard man all the time, but with his balding red head and extremely white skin, he was constantly the butt of jokes. He was always looking for the worst in people and invariably found it.

'You cunt! You fucking lairy cunt!'

As he started beating Alan three PCs came running into the room and pulled him off. As they dragged him out of the door he was still screaming obscenities.

'Piss off, you prat, I ain't scared of you! I ain't scared of no one! You fucking white-skinned ghost, come back and fight like a man. You hear me? I ain't fucking scared of you!' Alan called after him.

But he was scared, and he knew it. More to the point, Teddington knew it. But it made Alan feel better to say it.

Alone he put his head into his hands and tried to stem the tears that were threatening to fall from his eyes. He was frightened that if he started crying he would never stop.

Marie was in a cab on her way to Spitalfields after a call from Maisie. As she had walked out of the hostel she had half expected to be arrested. Instead she'd left without anyone taking any real notice. But she felt inside that it was only a matter of time before the police sought her out.

She was going to plead guilty and get it all over with. That was the easiest way. As Sally had said, showing the police the video would be her best defence. No mother could be expected to see that and not react. But she knew that the men in the film would not be easily incriminated. No, they'd have their arses well covered. The video would disappear or something else would happen to discredit her story.

It was how their world worked.

Her only other option was to contact them personally and try and get a deal from them. But if she did that she would be letting them get away with it. Strangely she didn't feel the urge to kill them any more, she had had her fill of killing since Patrick. She still couldn't believe she had really done what she had.

But in one part of her, no matter how bad she felt now and would feel for the rest of her days, she was glad he was no more. She wouldn't go so far as to say she was pleased she had done it, but she was pleased that he could never hurt her or her loved ones again.

Inside the restaurant she saw a beaming Maisie, who out of her working clothes and make-up looked just like any other young girl. As Marie sat down she poured her a large glass of ice cold Chardonnay.

'Let's have a toast, shall we?'

Marie didn't answer her.

'Well, come on, love, get that down your neck. Cheers! I can see you've already had a few, already been celebrating.'

'I am not celebrating, Maisie. I can't, not yet.'

She shrugged.

'Fair enough. But Christ, Marie, you gave him a braying and a half, didn't you? I was watching you. I saw it all.'

Marie was quiet, wondering where this was leading. Was Maisie going to try and use the knowledge against her in some way?

'When you hit him, he didn't know his arse from his elbow. It was perfect! And the way his head opened up with the first whack . . . Girl, I never, *ever* want to fall out with you. It was like something from a fucking film! Then you just laid into him. I couldn't believe he was still alive when the others turned up. It was so fucking freaky! And then I had to go back inside the flat and act like I knew fuck all when inside I wanted to roar with fucking laughter!'

Marie said loudly, 'What the fuck are you going on about? What others? Who else turned up?'

It was then that Maisie realised Marie had absolutely no idea what had happened after she'd left.

Jason was sitting with his father watching the news when they were both startled to see Patrick Connor's picture appear on the screen and hear a brief resumé of his life of crime. The story went on to say he had been tortured to death by a well-known drug baron, Mikey Devlin, a man who had himself been shot by police marksmen at a scrapyard in East London after a surveillance operation that had lasted for months.

Jason was in shock but as Ossie tried to turn off the news he held out his arm to stop him.

'Leave it, Dad, I want to hear it all.'

Ossie listened with his boy as his natural father's murder was talked about calmly and dispassionately by the nice Welshman who read the news on BBC1.

'Haven't you seen the news today, Marie? Some bloke called Devlin was shot at a scrapyard in East London. Well, by all accounts it was him who lifted Patrick after you'd brained him. I didn't know the blokes who turned up, assumed they were just another set of enemies. Christ himself knew Patrick had more than enough. But his body was found in one of this Devlin bloke's lock ups. They had tortured him, used everything on him . . . cattle prods, a welding iron, you name it. Fuck, I wish I'd seen it!'

Marie stared around the crowded restaurant and watched all the people laughing and joking and drinking. In the corner was a middle-aged couple. They were gazing into each other's eyes oblivious to everyone around them. They looked to be in love. Would she have fallen in love with Mikey eventually? She had wanted to use him, to make him hurt Patrick for her, and he had done that without her prompting. He had done it because he cared about her. She didn't deserve such caring.

The relief of knowing she had not actually killed Patrick was overshadowed by the knowledge that Mikey Devlin had done the job *for* her. Because he cared.

She gulped at the wine and tried to work out what the hell she was supposed to do next. She still had the video in her possession. Could she use it in some way to bring the three men to justice?

Something had to be done. This could not be the end of it – too many people had been hurt. She had to make sense of it all or it would send her as mad as her father.

Thinking of her father reminded her of what had happened to him and her mother. Whatever Louise was, she did not deserve to be burnt alive for it and yet that was exactly what had happened to her, and it was all Marie's fault. Her father had avenged that and had been locked away. Her own daughter had been determined to show her that she didn't need her, and now she was dead. Her grand-daughter was in care. Her son was the only bright spark in her life. Yet she was causing him problems by her association with him.

She had inadvertently caused chaos in so many lives by her release from prison. If only she had never been paroled, so much hurt and trouble could have been avoided.

Her mother was right after all. She was nothing but a Jonah.

Alan was getting tired and irritable. He had been left half the day in a cell without even a cup of tea or a cigarette. He was gasping for both and when the door was finally opened was ready to tell whoever it was exactly what he thought of them.

It was Teddington, as he knew it would be. He could see by the policeman's stance that he was after another row. It was why he was in the cell and had not had Alan brought to an interview room.

'What do you want, cunt! Another history lesson on the Colombians or a smack in the fucking teeth?'

Teddington had three other men with him and grinned at them as he said, 'See what I fucking mean? He has to be on a fucking death wish.'

Alan held up his fists like an old-time prizefighter.

'Come on then, one at a time. Or are you too scared to take me on? Come on then, I fucking dare you. You come in here like four mad fairies and think you can intimidate me. Well, fuck you!'

Teddington was half impressed with this man though he wouldn't let him know that.

'Come on then, you load of fucking filth poofters. Show me what you can do, or are you all after my arse?'

Alan started to laugh again.

'That's it, ain't it? You're all shirt lifters!'

That was when the kicking started.

Alan had made the mistake of forgetting he was actually no good to them now that Mikey was dead. Instead of trying to make things easier for himself, he had only succeeded in making everything worse. Fifteen minutes later he was bruised, bleeding, and back on the street. The sound of Teddington's laughter was ringing in his ears as he came to the sickening realisation that out here his life was in mortal danger because he was a known grass.

Everyone he knew would be scared to help him. He was finished. He was the reason Mikey had been shot and his boys banged up. Alan Jarvis had gone from respected businessman and scrap metal tycoon to drug dealer, importer, and finally grass.

What a glittering career he had carved out for himself.

Now he was completely on his own. He would never see his girls again because he could be traced through them. His name would be spoken with hatred and everyone would wonder if he had opened his trap about them as well. He had no one to turn to and no one to rely on.

The sooner he disappeared the better.

Anastasia was laughing, her little face red from the exertion. As Lorraine and Peter Porter watched her they both felt extremely happy. She was everything they had ever dreamed of in a child: bright, pretty and with a lovely nature. She had settled in well and already hugged them as if they were her real parents. That in itself felt like a privilege.

Since the sad news of her mother's death they hoped they might be considered for adoption. After all, they were mixed race like her. Lorraine's father was from Bangladesh though Peter was pure Yorkshire. They had met at university and had fallen in love in seconds, but since Peter had found out he was sterile their cosy little world had been destroyed. Until they had started fostering, that is.

Although they'd loved all the kids they had looked after, this little one was special. As she grinned at them now they both felt a lifting of their heart like a physical sensation.

'Annie's!'

She spoke the name they had given her with pride as she grabbed her dolly from the table. They had thought 'Anastasia' a bit of a mouthful and so they had shortened it accordingly. Annie had liked it. She found it easier to say than her other name and so she used it at every opportunity. After a few short weeks she felt like their very own child and they were terrified of the day she might be taken from them.

Anastasia had never been so happy, and if every now and then she briefly remembered and asked for her mummy it soon passed, especially when she was hugged close by Lorraine.

She was getting used to the regular food, and a house where no one shouted. Of getting up at the same time each day without having to lie in bed for ages waiting for her mummy. She was used to getting plenty of attention now and plenty of treats: swimming, the cinema and regular play school.

It was an idyllic life for the little girl with the curly hair and the effervescent personality. She had a look of her mother about her, but a darker, more honed version. Her character was actually more like her grandmother's, had the same self-contained quality. Now her personality was developing properly she was also getting strong-minded. Her foster parents put this down to her feeling more secure. They were right, she was blossoming under their tutelage and it showed. Even the social worker was impressed with the way she had come on since they had placed her.

When the news came on the TV and her father's photo was displayed, Annie opened her arms wide and said loudly: 'Daddy gone!'

Both Lorraine and Peter noticed that she seemed happy as she said it and they laughed together, not understanding what the joke was.

Then, her face serious now, she said, 'Mummy gone.'

And Lorraine hugged her and said gently, 'Yes, Mummy's gone, darling, but Mummy Lol is still here.'

'Big hug!'

Annie's voice was loud and Lorraine hugged her hard.

'Yes, my little darling. Big hug.'

'All right, Dad?'

Lucy was shocked at her father's appearance but tried her hardest not to show it.

He smiled at her, his face lighting up with recognition.

'Hello, love.'

Kevin was unshaven and it made him look like a tramp. He had lost weight and his body movements were jerky. Though she had been warned what to expect, actually seeing him with her own eyes was still a big shock. He had always been such a dapper man. Smart and well-groomed. In control of himself.

'Hello, Sue. I didn't know you two knew each other!'

He was delighted by his daughter's visit and it made them both feel good to see him so happy.

'Me two best girls! I've been wanting to see you. I have something to tell you, see. I should have told you before but I couldn't. Kept it locked away in here for years.' He tapped his head with a nicotine-stained finger. 'And I have to tell you now otherwise I won't be allowed to go home. Will I, Sue?'

He looked at her as he said her name and she smiled her agreement. He spoke in riddles a lot of the time these days.

'Do you want a cup of tea? They'll make you a cup if you want one, they're very good like that here. It's because we're all as mad as hatters!'

He laughed again and Lucy wanted to cry for the man she'd loved as a father and who seemed to her now more like an overgrown child.

He was gone, completely tipped over the edge. Like Marie, he had killed. Unlike her, it had sent him off his head. Although Sue had told her what to expect Lucy still could not equate this scarecrow of a man with the strong father she had lived with for so many years.

But then, he wasn't that strong. Not really. He had been ruled by her mother as they all had.

'Have you seen your mother?'

Kevin shook his head at his own question and carried on talking without waiting for an answer.

'Of course you haven't! No time for her girls her, only had time for Marshall. God rest his soul, she drove him fucking mad with her stupid ways and her pseudo-middle-class shit. He wasn't all bad, God love him. She made him like it. Made him weak because she always took care of him, didn't she? At the expense of the rest of us.'

No one answered him. They just listened, both guessing that he needed to get it all off his chest.

'She protected him and I protected her. Why did I do it, eh? And who protected you, Marie?'

Susan saw Lucy's eyes widen as she realised what her father had said and her heart went out to her. She held on to Lucy's arm as she made to leave.

'Stay. This is the most he has spoken since he arrived. Let him say his piece.'

Lucy stayed in the chair but the hurt lay heavy on her heart. It was always Marie for him, and her mother had had her Marshall, so where the fuck had that left *her* all these years?

'Them poor kids dumped. I wanted them, I did! I told her we should have them, but then Marshall killed himself and she had the breakdown and that was when I knew I had to keep me trap shut. I let you go away because I was terrified that if the truth came out it would destroy Lou. Now I wish it *had* destroyed her.'

Kevin started to cry.

'I'm sorry, Marie, please forgive me. She used it against me in the end, see. Because I let you go away, she knew she had me. I did it for her, for her son, and so people wouldn't know what had happened . . .'

'What are you talking about, Dad?'

Lucy's voice was small. She wasn't sure she actually wanted to hear what he was going to say.

'All those years it ate away at me like a cancer. She knew . . . your mother knew, deep inside. But because I couldn't tell her she used it against me, do you understand that?'

Lucy shook her head.

'Explain what happened, Dad. Please.'

'I heard her at him – Marshall. She knew he'd been at the squat that day. She knew he'd been to see you, Marie, and had searched his room. He was a dealer and she had known that for some time.

387

She blamed Patrick Connor, of course, but it wasn't just him. It was always in Marshall's nature to go after easy money. But Marshall, you see, was in *deeper* with Connor than she'd realised. When he told her it was Connor who had beaten those girls to death, had actually seen him do it, Lou went berserk. He told her he'd kept quiet because he was terrified of her finding out what he was really doing. That's how deeply she affected him. And *she* decided she would rather Marie went away and those two children were left motherless than have people know that her wonderful Marshall had gone off the rails. She was terrified of the neighbours finding out what he really was.

'He was her golden boy, see, the one she held up as a beacon of goodness to everyone. The truth getting out would have killed her. As it was, it destroyed their relationship. He still hadn't told the whole truth, see? That's why he shot himself. I think he knew he was cornered by her. She had said she would kill herself if he went to the police and that would always be on his conscience. By this time Marie had been charged, and even she thought she had done it. Everyone thought she had. It had gone too far.'

He lit an Embassy cigarette with shaking hands and puffed on it deeply.

'But you didn't know the extent of his dealings with Connor, he made sure of that. He knew you'd cause trouble over it. Always looked out for her brother and sister, did Marie.'

He looked into Lucy's face.

'Didn't you, darling? Tell her what I'm saying is true.'

Lucy looked at Susan and nodded her head.

'See, she knows the truth of it. Over the years after his death Lou convinced herself that Marshall just lied to help his sister out of trouble. Do you see what I'm saying, mate? Yet another good thing he had done in her eyes. She had it all worked out to her own satisfaction.'

He was shaking his head once more and the sadness in his eyes and voice was so terrible that Lucy closed her eyes.

'Even I believed it. Until I found his note after he topped himself. I still had it. I hid it in a safe place. I don't know why I kept it but it's all burnt up now, I suppose.'

He laughed. 'Like Lou, burnt to a fucking crisp!

'In the letter he said that he got to the squat with Patrick, and Marie was out of it on the floor. Stoned out of her skull as usual. It was then that the argument started and Patrick lost it. Marshall said in the letter that he picked up a baseball bat to stop Bethany attacking Patrick. Marshall killed her with the first blow. Caroline lost it then, and that's when Patrick Connor and he both went berserk. Marshall was on mescaline, see. He was as out of it as his sister. He'd been using for a while. He said in the letter that afterwards they wiped the weapons and then placed them in Marie's hands to put her prints all over them. She was covered in blood anyway; it was all over the ceiling, everywhere. Marshall was terrified by what he had done, and what his mother would do if it ever came out, and that's when he decided to shoot himself.'

Kevin started to cry again.

'And I never done anything about it! I let my daughter rot because my wife was so devastated by her loss, I dare not give her any more grief over her son. So what does that make me, eh? But I hated her for what I'd done; I hated her from that day on. And she knew I did. She fucking well knew!'

He was sobbing and Susan and Lucy stared at him with their mouths open and their eyes wide.

Lucy broke the spell.

'Oh, Dad.'

He put his arms around her and said loudly, 'I am so sorry, Marie. I was caught up in her fucking madness, you see. I am so fucking sorry for what I did to you. Forgive me, Marie. Please, forgive me.'

Chapter Twenty-Eight

M arie felt as if she had had the weight of the world taken off her shoulders. Even though she was more than aware that she had seriously hurt Patrick, that meant nothing compared to what she had *thought* she had done. The knowledge that Mikey had done the real killing for her made her feel strangely humble. He was bad, and she had known it, but he had tried to help her and she was grateful for that.

He had been a villain, but then he had never pretended to be anything else. He had given her peace by his actions and she would always remember that.

She looked around the room that had become her home and felt strangely nostalgic for it. She knew that was because she had been convinced she was going back to prison so even this little place felt like a haven. But she knew she had to leave now and go out into the world proper. It would be a big step for her but she would do it, for her son and for her grand-daughter and ultimately for herself.

She would immerse herself in her remaining family and try and make amends for the years she had lost.

Time passed, slowly but surely time passed, and with each passing year of her life imprisoned as a murderer she had felt stronger and more able to cope with what she had done. She remembered lying in her cell, knowing the door was bolted on her and the light was turned off. Durham had been so cold. Even in the summer it had been chilly. Cookham Wood had seemed like a five-star hotel after that place. But no matter where she was she would think of her children, try and imagine them at the age they would be. Scramble for memories of them: their smells, skin textures, any little fact to hold on to. To cherish as a reminder of her time with them, wasted in her stupidity.

Unlike the other women she had no photos to keep them fresh in her mind. No pictures were sent in, no childish letters to look forward to. She had had nothing. Not from her kids or anyone else for that matter. Even her father had abandoned her. She had done her time alone, both physically and mentally. Now it was time to try and make a different life for herself. She had been given another chance and must not waste it this time.

The hardest part was going to be burying her daughter but she knew she had to do it and do it with dignity. People would come not so much to mourn as to catch a glimpse of the famous murderess. She knew that. Faces from the past would seek her out under the pretext of paying their respects to her dead daughter.

But it was her son she would be strong for. For Jason.

She had an interview with a social worker on the coming Monday. Amanda had arranged it for her and Marie was going to find out about access to her grand-daughter. Amanda seemed to think she was entitled to see Anastasia.

Marie wasn't so sure. She wasn't the normal grey-haired granny they were used to dealing with. But she was going to try; she had to do that much for Tiffany, and for Jason who wanted to have contact with his sister's child.

As Sally said, she had to stop dwelling on the past, especially the recent past. She had to mourn a child and a lover. She would do that as best she could, hopefully with dignity and forbearance. After all, she had mourned her children for many years; they had been all but dead to her for so long.

But every time she thought of what she had wanted to do to Patrick, had tried to do to him, she felt her resolve start to waver. She was still capable of inflicting mortal damage on people who hurt her and had to make sure she kept herself away from any potentially explosive situations. Unlike other people she had to take a back seat because she could not trust herself when hurt or upset. The knowledge still made her feel like a freak of some kind.

She glanced at the mobile phone on the night table and noted that it was still turned off. She decided she didn't want to hear from Maisie again. She would throw the bloody thing away. She didn't like them anyway. They were intrusive and made you accessible twenty-four hours a day. Didn't people feel they wanted any peace any more, on call twenty-four seven? She found it almost Orwellian. No one seemed to have any privacy. CCTV cameras everywhere you went and even TV programmes dedicated to watching complete strangers make arses of themselves. It was a different world from the one she had left all those years before. Although they had had TV and computers in prison their viewing had been controlled and so it had not really made any impact. Now even little children were computer literate. Knew about soap operas and adult problems. It was amazing how much everything had changed.

Even this Archer scandal, which had inadvertently knocked Mikey off the front pages, was all a scam. He wouldn't do any real time, not like she had done and countless others were still doing. She had come out to a pretend world, filled with pretend people. She had to learn to survive in it if she was going to have any real chance in life. And she was determined to have a life of sorts. Even if it was always to be tinged with sadness and regret, she was going to live her life to the best of her ability, not just for her but for Tiffany as well as Caroline and Bethany. Otherwise it had been a waste of time. All the hurt and the pain would have been for nothing.

She glanced at the little travelling clock that had ticked away beside her all through her years in prison and saw it was time to go to Jason's house to discuss the funeral arrangements.

She glanced at herself in the mirror and saw a woman in a shabby suit. She had good skin and a trim figure and the saddest eyes in the world. But she was alive, she had a son and a grand-daughter, and at last she was looking to the future. Tentatively maybe, but at least she now felt she had something to look forward to.

So many people couldn't even say that, could they?

Count your blessings was going to be her new philosophy. She was also keeping her old prison mantra, which was tried and tested: It's not what happens to you but how you deal with it.

She had forgotten that one – and look where it nearly got her.

She closed the door of her room gently and made her way to her son's house. Inside, her heart was singing at the thought of being in his company once more. If she hadn't had Jason she didn't know what she would have done.

Alan was in his flat packing a case. He was clumsy, the large amount of Scotch he had drunk affecting his co-ordination. He had been drinking for twenty-four hours solid and it was taking its toll. He was trying to shut the case when the door went.

He opened it with a flourish and saw Steve Camble standing there.

'All right, Alan?'

He nodded.

'Can I come in?'

The man's voice was friendly enough and Alan stepped back to let him into the flat.

'What you going to do, Steve?'

The other man shrugged.

'It's nothing personal, Al, you know that. But you done a wrong 'un. You know it can't be left like that.'

Alan walked unsteadily into the lounge.

'Was it Teddington?'

Steve nodded.

'He's as slippery as a fucking greased eel. He'd sell his granny for a fiver and he got considerably more for you, I should imagine.'

Alan laughed.

'I should fucking hope so!'

Steve was depressed. He liked Alan, always had. But he had a job to do and that was that.

'Kneel down, Al.'

Alan looked into the man's face. He had drunk with him on numerous occasions. Gone to barbecues at his house with his family, and now Steve was going to kill him. Friendship was worth nothing in their world once you transgressed the rules. He was a grass and he was finished.

'There's twenty grand in the bedroom . . .'

Camble held up his hand for silence.

'Don't, Alan. You can't buy your way out of this.'

'I don't want to, Steve. You're doing me a favour really. The insurance will pay out for the wife and kids, and they won't get hassled by people looking for me. I meant, take it and give it to my old woman.'

''Course I will, Al. Like I say, this is nothing personal.'

Alan knelt down. He knew Camble would do as he asked, he was a straight-up geezer. As he waited for the inevitable he concentrated on a photo of his three little girls and the knowledge he would never see them again was hard.

But he knew this was for the best, especially for his children. Gone he was old news and they would not try and get to him through his kids.

But he was sorry he had wasted so much of his life on chasing the dollar, on betting on the horses and drinking and drugging in scummy clubs with scummy people. He could have been a million-aire now, twice over, legally. And he could have taken his kids away on holiday and done the things regular people do.

Instead he was going to die on a sunny day when he was still fit and well. There were people dying all over the world through illness, starvation, whatever. He was dying through his own greed and stupidity. It was laughable really, except he didn't think he had a laugh left in him.

The gunshot was loud and unexpected. He dropped forward on to the carpet with a surprised expression on his face.

Steve Camble picked up the money and placed it in a Tesco carrier bag. Then he left the flat and went to his car. He was whistling as he drove away. Alan Jarvis was already history.

Karen Black was in her cell. She was crying, really crying, and one of her cell mates snapped, 'Put a fucking sock in it, will you? You're getting on my tits!'

Karen sniffed loudly, trying to stem the flow, but it was impossible. She glanced down at the letter again and the tears started once more. She could not believe what she was reading.

Her mother had in effect cut her off from the family. Wanted nothing more to do with her. Said they all felt the same. They would not visit her or write to her, and she was requesting that Karen stopped writing to them. They had no interest in her any more.

She screwed the letter up into a ball.

Her solicitor had said she should get her head around a long sentence. The prosecution was refusing to let her plead to a lesser charge. She was up for attempted murder, and the state her victim was in would be seen in the courtroom because Louise Carter was going to give evidence. No jury in the land would find her anything but guilty.

Her argument that she'd thought there was no one in the house when she torched it would go nowhere. As her brief had pointed out, why had she blocked off the exits if she'd thought the place was empty? She had to have known there was someone in there whatever she said. She was better holding up her hand and taking it on the chin.

But Karen was frightened. She didn't want to be in prison for years without anything on the outside to keep her going, and yet that was what was going to happen. It was ironic really, because she knew it was exactly what had happened to Marie Carter. Karen would have to walk in her shoes now and she wasn't sure she had the guts to see it through.

395

She was crying again, her face awash with tears.

Juliana, her cell mate, jumped off her bunk and punched Karen in the head with all the force she could muster. The blow was heavy and loud.

'Shut the fuck up!'

Juliana was screaming now, fed up with the noise. She had just been informed that her two children were going into long-term foster care because their father had disappeared off the face of the earth, and she really wasn't in the mood for this miserable bitch at the moment.

Karen knew that this environment was all she could hope for in the years ahead. She had thought *she* was violent until she had come in here. Her head was smarting from the blow and she felt an urge to scream at the sheer terror building up inside her.

She couldn't do the time. She knew already she couldn't do jail time. But all her options had been taken away from her. She had no say in what happened to her any more.

Like Marie Carter before her she was doomed to serve a sentence without anyone giving her even the time of day or any letters from home to cheer her up. Her Petey was dead, and in effect, so was she. It was like being one of the living dead. Going through the motions of breathing, of living, but for what reason?

She started to cry again and Juliana rolled her eyes to the ceiling and shouted, 'Grow up, woman! You were big enough and ugly enough to get yourself in here. So be a woman and take it on the chin, for fuck's sakes. And stop that whining, I'm trying to think!'

Karen just buried her face in the pillow and cried her heart out. Self-pity is a destructive force as she would find out over the next few years.

Louise Carter was alone in her hospital room. She was in bed because she felt tired even though it was only early afternoon.

A sympathetic nurse had told her it was the pain. Louise had felt like laughing when the girl said that to her. Telling *her* about pain! These people didn't know the meaning of the word!

She had experienced pain all her life, and extreme pain from the moment she had seen her dead son. His face gone, his lovely handsome face destroyed by the gunshot. And all because of *her*. Marie.

She closed her eyes to try and shut out the mental picture of Marshall without his face and her husband looking at her with that accusing stare he could summon up when it suited him.

She knew the neighbours had laughed at her behind her back because she'd bragged about her son's achievements. But it was just jealousy, nothing more and nothing less. He was cut out for better than hanging around the streets like their children. Marshall was going to be someone, and as honours were heaped on him she would bask in the reflected glory. That had always been her dream.

The pain was burning in her hands once more, but still she flexed them. She was terrified of losing her hand movement. It was her biggest fear.

She didn't care about the facial scarring, she would wear those marks with pride and had refused any offer of skin grafts. At her age she didn't care what she looked like. But she wanted her hands mobile so she could arrange the flowers on her son's grave. She had made the priest promise that he would take care of it until she was better, and being a priest he had to do what he said because he was a man of God. She hadn't bothered to ask her lazy bitch of a daughter.

Lucy had no interest in anything other than getting a man. All man mad, the lot of them. Like Marie she was, deep inside. A right pair of them she had given birth to. Louise closed her eyes once more as the pain shot up her arms. But still she carried on flexing her fingers.

She heard the door open and kept her eyes closed. The nurse might think she was asleep and go away and leave her alone. She was sick of the lot of it: saline drips, painkillers, ice baths, the whole kit and caboodle. She wanted to go home. Except she didn't have one any more.

The presence was still in the room and Louise opened one eye.

'Oh. It's you.'

Her voice was bored-sounding.

Lucy stood at the end of the bed and did not say a word. The two women eyed one another.

'Well?' The single word was spoken with disdain and it set Lucy off.

'I've been to see Dad.'

Louise's flexing was getting faster, a sure sign she was agitated.

'He's in Rampton. The mental hospital.'

'So I heard. What do you want, Lucy?'

'I just wanted to see you. Dad's been talking about you a lot.'

There was something about Lucy's voice that was wrong. The usual whine was gone from it.

'Really? How thrilling. We've been married long enough, I should imagine he *would* talk about me. Fuck all else going on in his life, boring bugger that he is.'

Lucy grinned.

'He can't stop talking about you and Marshall.'

She was looking straight into her mother's eyes now and they connected like they had never connected before. Lucy saw her mother afraid for the first time ever. It was almost tangible it was so acute. She breathed in, convinced she would be able to smell it. But all she could smell was the stench of sickness, aqueous cream and the odour peculiar to all hospitals – disinfectant and urine.

She wondered at the fact that she could feel no pity for this broken woman in the bed, but Louise's hatefulness had stopped anyone pitying her. In fact, she seemed even stronger since the accident. *Was* stronger in some respects because she bore battle scars to prove her righteousness. She was quite convinced she'd acted for the best. How she could have allowed Marie to go away for all that time without saying a word was the most amazing thing Lucy had ever heard. But it was all for Marshall as usual, her son, the light of her life. He had to be protected no matter what.

'I'm living somewhere else now.'

Louise was glad of the change of subject and it showed.

'Really, where?'

Lucy's voice was matter-of-fact as she explained, 'I'm living with Dad's girlfriend Susan. She's a really nice woman, Mum. You wouldn't like her, though. Not really *your* cup of tea. But then, that's probably why Dad and me like her so much. And Marie. Marie *really* likes her. Even more than I do, I think. She's the opposite of you, Mum, a really nice woman.'

Louise Carter felt as if she had been slapped in the face.

'How could you do this to me, Luce? Knowing the state I'm in thanks to that bitch Marie, how could you come here and do this to me? Your own mother. Have you no decency, no compassion?'

Lucy shook her head and said in a bored voice, calculated to inflict on her mother the maximum hurt, 'Nah. None whatsoever. But then, I had a good teacher, didn't I? You, Mum.'

'Get out!'

Lucy laughed at her mother's display of anger.

'But I have a visitor for you, Mum. You don't get many, being so unpopular, like. What with the neighbours avoiding you like the plague and that.'

She chuckled at her own wit.

'I *said*, get out, Lucy, and don't come back!'

The old Lou was back with a vengeance now and she was furious.

Lucy called over her shoulder, 'Come on in, Marie.'

She grinned at her mother and said lightly, 'A family reunion, Mum. Isn't that lovely?'

Lou's eyes stared in horror as she saw her eldest daughter walk into the hospital room. To see the two girls together was shock enough. But Marie had the same calm look about her she had had as a small child. That accepting demeanour that had driven her mother mad whenever she had picked on her and got no reaction. It was strange because she had pushed the girl for a reaction for years and when she had finally got it, it had exploded in her face.

'Hello, Mum.'

Marie's voice was quiet and pleasant, something her mother had forgotten. Seeing her standing there she was reminded of how she had always been a help with Lucy as a little girl. She had always loved her brother and sister. Marshall had adored Marie, preferring her company to his mother's because Marie had always been able to make him laugh. She had been a comical person in her own dry way.

'Why did you let it happen to me, Mum? I lost everything. Me kids, the best years of me life, gone.'

Louise shook her head as if unable to believe what she was hearing.

'I did it for my son, of course. Because I was not going to have that boy's memory sullied over a pair of bloody whores. He was not going to be pulled down into the gutter with you. You tried to make him like you. *You* brought Patrick Connor into our lives, you with your men and your drugs and your filthiness. You broke my heart and you killed your brother. You *deserved* to go away in exchange for the life of my boy. Now your own child is dead you might understand what I went through over my Marshall.'

Marie didn't answer her for long moments. Then she said quietly, 'I hope you live for years, Mum, in pain and alone. Me dad has a good woman now. He will find a measure of peace and I wish that for him. I hold nothing against him because, like everyone, he was terrified of you. You deliberately left me to rot. Left my children, your own flesh and blood, in care. Well, I'm the strong one now. I'm the one who is on top because I feel nothing for you any more.

'I had beaten myself up for years over what I thought I had done to Caroline and Bethany, and to Marshall, and to you – yeah, even

399

to you who despised me from the day I came out of you. All those years I was convinced I had killed my two friends when I had done *nothing*. Now I might have lost my poor Tiffany, but I still have my son and he's a good kind boy. He passed all his exams and is on his way to university. I also have my grand-daughter, my Tiff's little one, so all in all I have more than you ever had or ever will have. Because they are in my life through choice, not through emotional blackmail or fear like we were in yours.'

Lucy listened with a mixture of fear of her mother's possible reaction and complete and utter shock at the calm way Marie was recounting all that had happened to her. If it had been her, she would have been screaming the place down.

'Come on, Luce, let's go and have some lunch. This place gives me the creeps.'

Louise watched as her two daughters left the room. At the door Marie turned and said, 'I understand Dad wants this all to become common knowledge, so I thought I'd better warn you.'

Then they were gone without a backward glance.

Lucy was finding it hard to accept she was sitting in this beautiful house with her nephew and sister and actually enjoying herself. She watched as Jason smiled at his mother and felt a lump form in her throat. She had told him what had really happened all those years ago, and he, like his mother, seemed happier for the news. Even that Verbena bird she had been warned about seemed friendly.

Lucy still wondered at her sister, though. How could she accept what had happened to her without any show of bitterness or anger? Lucy supposed it was the years of prison. It took a certain type of person to be able to put up with that amount of time away from everything and everyone they knew without cracking up.

It seemed all Marie was interested in now was building a solid relationship with her son and grand-daughter, and who could blame her for that? Unlike most people she actually had her priorities right.

Lucy was pleased with the relationship that was blossoming between her sister and herself too. All her bitterness was gone now because every time she thought of what had happened to Marie her heart felt as if it would break.

All those years poor Marie had believed she was the cause of two deaths when all she was really guilty of was stupidity. Of being an addict. She had even said that maybe it was a good thing it had happened because she would probably have been dead now, the way she had been carrying on. It was the bigness of her, the forgiveness in her heart, that made Lucy feel sad for her. She knew she would never have been so good about it if it had been her.

One thing was sure, their mother was no longer a part of their lives and that in itself was helping Lucy to build a new relationship with her sister.

Verbena felt her husband's hand in hers and sighed with relief. It had been a frightening few days when he had given her the ultimatum: either sort herself out or they would part. Now as she watched her son and his natural mother she made herself smile and function normally, and if it got too much for her she just went out to the garden or up to her bedroom.

She was not going to lose her man over Marie Carter. Since they had found out what had really happened even she had felt compassion for the woman. To be locked up for all that time, during the best years of her life, when she was innocent all along must have been terrible.

It was a tragedy, but one that had given them Jason. So she couldn't be too sorry about it no matter how hard she tried.

She squeezed her husband's hand tightly, aware of just how lucky she had been in life compared to so many other people.

Marie Carter being one of them.

Susan and Kevin sat holding hands in the garden. Since he had spoken about what had happened he was getting better in leaps and bounds. He would not be tried for murder, but for manslaughter through diminished responsibility. The entire sorry tale would come out at the trial, and what a can of worms that would open.

Still, from Marie's point of view it could only be a good thing. Her solicitor seemed to think that they had a good case for wrongful imprisonment as the police had failed to make a proper forensic examination and made mistakes in the arrest procedure. Added to which, Marie's drug levels were never given in evidence in court, only the basic facts that she was an addict. It seemed she was assumed to be the perpetrator because of her reputation, and that was not enough, not nearly enough, to put someone away for so long.

They had wanted a conviction as quickly as possible and that was what had happened. Marie, believing she had committed the murders, never tried to defend herself.

But whatever miscarriage of justice had happened, Marie was just pleased the years of remorse and shame were over now the truth was known. That seemed to be enough for her.

As if she had been conjured up, Marie came into the garden with Lucy and a young man. A handsome young man.

They came quickly across the grass to Susan and Kevin. She saw Kevin's eyes light up as he recognised his daughters, then his face froze as he saw the boy.

'Marshall?'

Marie smiled as they all sat down.

'I know, Dad. Uncanny, ain't it? Jason, this is your grandad.'

Her voice was matter-of-fact and helped ease the situation.

'Hello, sir.'

Jason held out his hand and Kevin grasped it and held it to his cheek. Tears were standing in his eyes as he said, 'Don't worry. I'm crying from happiness. I never thought I would see the day when I finally had all me family around me.'

He looked at his daughters and grandson as if frightened they would disappear if he took his eyes off them for one moment.

Marie sat and felt the peace she had craved for years wash over her as they all chatted together like a normal family.

She only wished her Tiffany could have experienced this day with them. Had lived to find out that her mother was not the monster they had all thought.

But one thing she had learned in prison was that regrets were a waste of time. She was living for the future now and putting the past firmly behind her.

Epilogue

The man tending his wife's grave saw the woman with the little girl and smiled. They came every week to the cemetery and she always said hello to him and he was always happier after they had spoken.

She was a very attractive woman, with a wistful smile and a lovely nature, it was plain to see.

She knelt down to place flowers on her daughter's grave and he smiled to himself as the little girl's voice drifted over to him.

'Hello, Mummy. I done writing at school, and drawing.'

He liked the way this woman encouraged the child to talk to her mother. Tell her about all the little events in her life. She seemed an extraordinarily kind person.

Marie watched Annie, as she was now called, dancing for her mummy. Since going to ballet she had decided she was the next Margot Fonteyn. Marie suppressed a smile as Annie danced on the grass. She was all legs, was going to be very tall, that much was evident. Lorraine and Peter gave her such a good life and the fact they allowed Marie to be a part of it too made her feel happier each and every time she hugged her grand-daughter to her.

'Look at me, Nanny, I'm dancing!'

'I can see you, sweetie.'

'Can Mummy see me? Mummy Tiffany?'

Marie nodded.

'I told you, Mummy is in heaven. She is in every flower you see and every butterfly and in the clouds and in the trees.'

'She's taking care of me, isn't she?'

Marie nodded.

'She's with you all the time, sweetie. All the time.'

They sat together on the prickly grass. Marie unpacked the little picnic she always brought. As she laid a cloth on the ground she was greeted by different people as they made their way to their own loved ones' graves. She was a fixture here and it gave her a measure of peace to come here and be with her daughter as she had never been with her in her child's life.

'I love chocolate cake.'

'I know, Annie, that's why I brought it.'

The little girl kissed her on the lips, a big fat smacking kiss that made Marie laugh.

'Is that a chocolate cake kiss?'

Annie nodded and bit into the sweet confection with relish. 'Oh!' She put her hand to her mouth, her eyes wide. 'I forgot to tell Mummy where we're going later.'

She looked at the photo of Tiffany on the gravestone and said happily, 'We're going to the cinema and then to Burger King with Grandad Kevin, Sue and Auntie Lucy!'

'Hello.'

Marie looked up to see the tall black man who tended his wife's grave every Sunday. Over the last two years they had got on to first-name terms.

'Hello, Easton.' She smiled. 'Beautiful day, isn't it?'

He nodded.

'It certainly is.'

He looked at Annie and said kindly, 'I heard you say you were going to Burger King, you lucky girl.'

She grinned.

'That's right. With my Nana.'

'Would you like a cold drink, Easton?'

It had become a regular thing, his dropping by to talk to them both.

'I would, Marie, if you don't mind.'

He seated himself on the grass beside her.

'How's work?'

She shrugged.

'The usual. I enjoy it, though. Teaching is rewarding. A bit like your job, I should imagine.'

He nodded his agreement.

'*Only* if I win my case. If I don't then it's not too good.'

She didn't answer. He was a barrister and she knew he knew all about her. It seemed everyone did these days. Her father's trial had been big news in its day, as had hers. Both had been acquitted, although for different reasons. Then Easton surprised her with a question.

'What are you doing after Burger King?'

She shrugged.

'Going back to my flat. Catching up on some housework. The usual Sunday routine. Annie's parents pick her up around seven on a Sunday.'

He took a deep breath and said lightly, 'How about a drink later, or a meal?'

Marie was nonplussed for a few moments and then she looked into his kind brown eyes and said gently, 'A drink would be lovely, Easton, thank you.'

He was really smiling now.

'The pleasure, Marie, is all mine.'

Out of the corner of her eye she could see her mother struggling to get to her brother's grave but Marie ignored her though they were very much aware of one another. Marie had already laid her own flowers there when she had first arrived. She knew her mother watched Annie, and especially Jason, when they came here. She must have noticed his uncanny resemblance to Marshall.

'Can I give you a lift to the cinema?'

'That would be lovely, thank you.'

A little later they strolled out of the cemetery together, Marie holding Annie's hand and the little girl chattering away twenty to the dozen as usual. Her mother was only five yards away at one point but Marie still ignored her.

Instead she said loudly to Annie, 'Wave goodbye to Mummy, darling.'

Annie turned and waved in the direction of Tiffany's grave.

The sun was high and the breeze was cool and her Annie was a beautiful and graceful child. Marie knelt down and held out her arms. The child hugged her tightly. Over the little girl's shoulder Marie looked directly into her mother's eyes.

She was telling Louise that there was a little girl with the whole world waiting for her. Unlike her mother and grandmother had done, she had people who loved her and cared for her and were going to make sure she had every chance available.

'I love you, Nana!'

Marie hugged her even tighter.

'And I love you, tiger!'

She picked up the little girl and carried her, laughing, to Easton's car. Marie's life was all laughter these days and she wouldn't change any of it for the world.

SUB-REGIONAL PLANNING STUDIES: AN EVALUATION

BY

T. M. COWLING
B.A., Dip.T.P.

AND

G. C. STEELEY
B.A., F.R.T.P.I.

PERGAMON PRESS
OXFORD · NEW YORK · TORONTO
SYDNEY · BRAUNSCHWEIG

Pergamon Press Ltd., Headington Hill Hall, Oxford

Pergamon Press Inc., Maxwell House, Fairview Park, Elmsford, New York 10523

Pergamon of Canada Ltd., 207 Queen's Quay West, Toronto 1

Pergamon Press (Aust.) Pty. Ltd., 19a Boundary Street, Rushcutters Bay, N.S.W. 2011, Australia

Vieweg & Sohn GmbH, Burgplatz 1, Braunschweig

First edition 1973

Library of Congress Cataloging in Publication Data

Cowling, T   M

   Sub-regional planning studies: an evaluation.

   (Urban and regional studies, v. 6)
   1. Regional planning—Great Britain. 2. Regional planning—Case studies. I. Steeley, G. C., joint author.   II.   Title.   III.   Series.
HT395.G7C68   309.2′5′0942   73–4476
ISBN 0–08–017019–6

Urban and Regional Planning Series
Volume 6

Printed in Great Britain by
Western Printing Services Ltd., Bristol

SUB-REGIONAL PLANNING STUDIES: AN EVALUATION

Contents

v

Preface

IN THE early months of 1970 a technical unit was being set up in the centre of the East Midlands Region of England by a Conference of its Local Planning Authorities. Among the tasks of the Unit, of which we were then both members, was the requirement to advise the constituent authorities of the Conference on the technical co-ordination of their Sub-regional planning activities and to integrate their Sub-regional strategies with the Regional Plan, whose preparation was a required task of the Technical Unit.

This co-ordination was especially appropriate because the Region was the scene of Sub-regional planning processes that covered almost its entire extent, the first initiated in 1969 and the last to be completed in 1973. They vary widely in complexity, field of interest, technical methods and policy functions, and exhibit a high degree of competence and achievement. They also, of course, reveal weaknesses, some incompatibility and differing relevance for Regional Planning.

The Technical Unit therefore instituted a review for internal office use of these Sub-regional activities, and of those bordering the Region, to act as a basis (a) for disseminating advice on techniques and overall methodology, (b) to assist the constituent authorities in evaluating their findings, and (c) to examine their contribution to the Regional Planning activity of the Technical Unit. This work was the context within which Malcolm Cowling privately prepared a dissertation for the Department of Town and Country Planning of the Trent Polytechnic.

Late in 1970 it was suggested that the review, together with Cowling's work, could be useful to other people. The Regional Development Conference, through its Chairman, Alderman Wilson, and its Secretary, A. R. Davis, and the Planning Officers of the Region, whose Chairman at that time was M. Gregory, were therefore consulted and gave their consent.

We have therefore prepared this text on evaluating Sub-regional plans, endeavouring to keep it simple and eschew technical virtuosity—to which we lay no claim in any event. The views expressed here are our own and not necessarily those of anyone concerned with Planning and Government in the East Midlands.

T. M. C.

G. C. S.

Acknowledgements

WE WOULD like to pay tribute to the members of the Notts./Derby. Sub-regional Planning Unit with whom we spent two eventful years, and to Andrew Thorburn, without whose leadership our interest in this field could not have developed. We are especially indebted to Joan Ellis for preparing the successive versions of this text and to members of the East Midlands Regional Technical Unit, the Notts./Derby. Monitoring and Advisory Unit and the Trent Polytechnic, Nottingham, for their forebearance and advice.

We acknowledge with thanks the permission of Faber & Faber Ltd. to reprint the quotation on p. 104 from *Urban and Regional Planning—a Systems Approach*.

KEY TO ABBREVIATIONS OF SUB-REGIONAL
STUDY TITLES USED IN THE TEXT

Ashford   *Ashford Study: Consultants Proposals for Designation*, H.M.S.O., 1967.

Central Borders   *The Central Borders: a Plan for Expansion*, H.M.S.O., 1968.

Central Lancs.   *Central Lancashire Study for a City; Consultants' New Town Designation Proposals*, H.M.S.O., 1967.

Coventry/Solihull/ War.   *Coventry, Solihull, Warwickshire Sub-regional Study*, 1971.

Dee Crossing   *Dee Crossing Study Phase 1: a Report to the Technical Working Party*, H.M.S.O., 1967.

Deeside   *Deeside—a Planning Study by Shankland, Cox & Associates*, 1971.

Doncaster   *Doncaster: An Area Study*, H.M.S.O., 1969.

Donegal   Donegal County: Planning for Amenity and Tourism, *Speamen Development Plan Manual*, 1966.

Eastern Lowlands   *The Eastern Lowlands Sub-regional Study*, Kesteven County Planning Offices, Sleaford, 1971 (2 sections published to date).

Grangemouth/Falkirk   *Grangemouth–Falkirk Regional Survey and Plan*, H.M.S.O., 1968.

Halifax/Calder Valley   *Halifax and Calder Valley: an Area Study*, H.M.S.O., 1968.

Humberside   *Humberside: a Feasibility Study*, H.M.S.O., 1969.

Impact on N.E. Lancashire   *Central Lancashire New Town Proposals—Impact on Northeast Lancashire, Consultants' Appraisal*, H.M.S.O., 1968.

Ipswich   *Expansion of Ipswich Designation Proposals: Consultants' Study of the Town and its Sub-region*, H.M.S.O., 1966.

Leicester/Leics.   *Leicester and Leicestershire Sub-regional Planning Study*, Leicester City Council and Leicestershire County Council, 1969.

Lothians   *The Lothians Regional Survey and Plan*, H.M.S.O., 1966.

Ljubljana   *A Demonstration Study of the Ljubljana Region*, Urbanisicni Institut S.R.S. Titova/II, Ljubljana, Yugoslavia, 1970.

Milton Keynes Interim Report   *Milton Keynes Plan: Interim Report to the Milton Keynes Development Corporation*, Llewelyn-Davies, Weeks, Forester-Walker & Bor, 1968.

North Glos.   *North Gloucestershire Sub-regional Study*, Gloucester City Council, Gloucestershire County Council and Cheltenham Borough Council, 1970.

xi

Northampton/ Bedford/N. Bucks	*Northampton, Bedford and North Bucks Study: an Assessment of Interrelated Growth*, H.M.S.O., 1965.
Notts./Derby.	*Nottinghamshire and Derbyshire Sub-regional Study*, Derby County Borough Council, Derbyshire County Council, Nottingham City Council and Nottinghamshire County Council, 1970.
Peterborough Impact	*Peterborough Sub-regional Study*, Huntingdon and Peterborough County Council, 1970.
Severnside	*Severnside—A Feasibility Study*, H.M.S.O., 1971.
South-east 1964	*The South-east Study, 1961–81*, H.M.S.O., 1964.
South-east 1967	*A Strategy for the South-east: a First Report by the South-east Economic Planning Council*, H.M.S.O., 1967.
South-east 1970	*Strategic Plan for the South-east*, H.M.S.O., 1970.
South Hants 1966	*South Hampshire Study: a Report on the Feasibility of Major Urban Growth*, H.M.S.O., 1966.
South Hants 1972	*Four Possibilities for the Future*, South Hampshire Plan Technical Unit, Working Paper No. 14, 1970.
Tayside	*Tayside: Potential for Development*, H.M.S.O., 1970.
Teeside	*Teeside Survey and Plan: Final Report of the Steering Committee*, H.M.S.O., 1969.
West Cornwall	*West Cornwall Study*, Cornwall County Council, 1970.
Yorkshire and Humberside Review	*A Review of Yorkshire and Humberside*, H.M.S.O., 1966.
Yorkshire and Humberside Strategy	*Yorkshire and Humberside Regional Strategy*, H.M.S.O., 1970.

Other Abbreviations

The following are used when giving references:

A.I.P.	American Institute of Planners.
C.E.S.	Centre for Environmental Studies.
H.M.S.O.	Her Majesty's Stationery Office.
O.A.P.	Official Architecture and Planning.
P.T.R.C.	Planning & Transport Research & Computation Co. Ltd.
R.T.P.I.	Royal Town Planning Institute.

CHAPTER 1

Sub-regional Planning in Britain

INTRODUCTION

Interest in Sub-regional planning has quickened in the last few years and the number of studies produced by co-operating Authorities has been increasing. One remarkable feature, however, has been the wide variety of studies produced, associated with very different manpower, financial and technical resources as well as variations in the physical, economic and political problems to be solved. At the same time technical knowledge has been increasing so rapidly that studies produced only five years ago now seem technically outdated.

These developments have taken place so quickly that it seems to the writers that we have not had time to take stock: to ask what makes Sub-regional planning necessary, what are studies intended to achieve, why do they differ so considerably even when produced in very similar circumstances, what technical processes are necessary, which aspects have been over-emphasised (if any) and which have been neglected, and where critical weaknesses exist? If this can be successfully accomplished the thought and discussion may be beneficial not only to Sub-regional planning, but to planning generally. This book is intended as an opening contribution to such a debate.

It seems to us that clients and practitioners in the field of Sub-regional planning might find it difficult to make use of our discussion unless our findings and conclusions are organised in such a way that they have direct relevance to their decision-making activity. For clients a critical question is the significance and trustworthiness of the Plan, for practitioners the validity and relevance of their work. We have decided, therefore, firstly, to write a "non-academic" text which nevertheless uses a level of language currently found in the more general writings in the planning field. Secondly, we address ourselves to the specifically interested, but not necessarily specialist or widely experienced, groups of clients and practitioners. Thirdly, we present our argument in the form of guidelines for the evaluation of the Plan by its clients and interest groups, guidelines that can also be used as a checklist for the practitioner in planning and managing his task.

This first chapter is concerned with the origins, general characteristics and future of Sub-regional planning. It is followed by seven chapters on the technical process. A final one brings together all of the various ideas and criteria which have been identified, and suggests how they might be combined in a procedure designed to enable client and interest groups to make their own assessment of the completed Sub-regional Study.

The general approach is to consider the function of each stage in the process in relation to the purpose of the Study as a whole and try to suggest how these various tasks might best be accomplished at the present level of technology and thinking. The emphasis is therefore on trying to identify the most promising and recent ideas and techniques rather than on a detailed examination of studies which may already be out of date. Many examples are, however, quoted to illustrate particular strengths and weaknesses in studies which have been produced in the last decade.

It is intended that our method should be capable of being applied to the published document only. Evaluating a study in this way, without access to background material or knowledge of the political and other constraints under which the team operated, is very difficult. It is nevertheless what may be expected of planners who work in this and related fields when they are asked to comment on a study produced outside their own immediate area. We have therefore tried, in each chapter, to suggest tests which will indicate if, and how successfully, the various operations have been carried out, even where these have not been described in a published volume. Of course, evaluation is likely to be much more thorough and satisfactory if access can be gained to unpublished material and if the work can be discussed with members of the Study team.

THE VARIETY IN SUB-REGIONAL PLANNING

Perhaps the first thing which strikes one about Sub-regional planning is the wide variety of plans and policies which have been classified under this single heading. Exploring this variety is our chosen method of describing the present state of Sub-regional planning. As an opening statement, we think Colin Cooper[1] gets to the heart of the matter writing on the "regions" of Wales (which would be classed as Sub-regions by many of us perhaps). He explains the variety in terms of the absence of legal constraints and suggests that a (Sub) Region may be any area over which a common policy framework is needed:

> The interesting thing about (sub) regional planning is that plans are still what we choose to make them. They do not have to conform to any statutory definition or regulations. This is in contrast to other levels of planning, notably the old development plans and the new structure plans, where the form and content are specified in some detail, even down to the colouring of maps. . . . I conclude, . . . that a planning (sub) region is determined primarily by the need for a policy framework which is markedly different from—or independent of— that of its neighbours. Whether the area is entirely rural or urban in character, or a combination of both, is irrelevant.

CO-OPERATION BETWEEN AUTHORITIES

Sub-regional plans are what we choose to make them, but that choice is often "political". The complexity of politics and administration is difficult to codify, but some of the more simple influences on Sub-regional planning have been widely recognised. It often happens, for example, that local planning authorities in adjacent areas have a long history of non-cooperation and even mutual antagonism. There may be a variety of reasons for this: fear on the part of semi-rural counties of the land needs of expanding towns or the sheer political weight of densely populated urban areas, different political opinions, competition for rateable value and so on. In the last few years, however, there has been a greater awareness of a need for co-operation between neighbouring authorities and one means of achieving this has been to encourage them to join together in joint sponsorship of a Sub-regional study of their areas. This point is made in the Coventry/Solihull/War. Study. J. Brian McLoughlin[2] also makes it in relation to Leicester/Leics.:

> The relationships between Leicester County Borough and the County of Leicestershire provide in recent years a good example of the difficulties which prevail in such situations. City housing developments in the county area, public transport arrangements, the public services and major highway plans are just a few of the specific issues which have given point to underlying city/county rivalries. Rivalry has on occasion come near to hostility on an issue like boundary amendment discussed before the (1960 Act) Local Government Commission. The disputes centred around submitted evidence concerned with levels of service, administrative efficiency, rate burdens and such-like matters. Nevertheless there was the suspicion in many people's minds that the real (but

unspoken) issues at stake were ward boundaries, votes and the local political machines. It is therefore commendable that these two large authorities should have responded so quickly to Mr. Richard Crossman's initiative, when, as Minister of Housing and Local Government, he invited several city/county "pairs" to join forces in the setting up of sub-regional planning studies.

CONTROLLING SYSTEMS

Although these sorts of considerations have undoubtedly encouraged the setting up of Sub-regional studies, they are not sufficient in themselves and we are bound to ask why the need for co-operation should have become so much more pressing than it has been in the past. The answer to this lies mainly in changes in the behaviour of the public—as car ownership has increased and more and more people have chosen to live away from the districts in which they work, shop and seek entertainment. With more movement across administrative boundaries there has been an increasing possibility that unco-ordinated policies in transport planning by neighbouring authorities might be mutually defeating. This has been emphasised by the introduction into planning of "systems theory" and the development of mathematical techniques to simulate behaviour such as travel to work and shop.

In a passage, which we seem to recall is from the works of Stafford Beer, the Law of Requisite Variety is discussed in relation to cars travelling along a section of road. In the first instance there is a great deal of variety in the system (think of the movement of pedestrians on a busy footpath) and very little control over the movement of vehicles. The introduction of a white line down the middle of the road and the adoption of a "keep left (right) rule" reduces the variety in the system and increases the degree of control. Dividing the road into three or four lanes further increases the control instruments, reduces variety in the movement of vehicles and results in a higher degree of control over the system. So do the introduction of road signs and traffic lights. As the number of control instruments is increased and variety is reduced, so there is greater control over the system.

A behavioural system such as the pattern of travel to work in and around a freestanding city might well extend across the boundaries of two or more local planning areas. If this is so the degree of control which can be exerted over the system is limited by the extent to which each of the authorities concerned is willing to co-operate in applying the same sorts of controls, at the same time and towards the same ends. If they are not willing to co-operate in this way, the degree of control may well be negligible and the plans of each authority may fail in an important respect. Sub-regional plans are therefore necessary as instruments to assist authorities to achieve the benefits of control that the Law of Requisite Variety shows to be possible.

The control of behaviour is not, of course, the exclusive concern of Sub-regional planners: as Beer[3] has pointed out the Universe may be perceived as being made up of sets of systems each contained within one somewhat bigger, like a hollow set of building blocks. Many systems with planning implications lie wholly within local government boundaries and the related problems can be solved at Structure or Local plan level. Many are not appropriately tackled by physical planning measures at all, but nevertheless remain within the competence of the Authority and the Community it serves. But there are systems (both spatial and aspatial) of major importance in planning, over which the maximum possible degree of control can only be achieved by means of Sub-regional co-ordination of policies.* (We are assuming that the communities consider such self-control desirable.) This is recognised in the Development Plans Manual,[4] which lists some of the activities of Sub-regional concern:

> The preparation of structure plans will involve studies of, for example, the spheres of influence of such activities as employment, shopping, education and recreation which seldom, if ever, draw their population exclusively from the area of one authority. The limits of these spheres of influence are not static (increasing car ownership, for example, makes it possible for more people to travel greater distances to work or to shop), they seldom coincide with each other or with local authority boundaries. Furthermore, there are considerable overlaps between the areas of attraction of different major centres, and there is often an hierarchical relationship between centres of different size. . . .
>
> . . . This complex and constantly shifting pattern, which is the basis of the structure, has to be examined and planned comprehensively. It bears little or no relationship to administrative areas and, therefore, structure plans prepared for individual counties and county boroughs will need to be set in the context of decisions taken jointly by neighbouring authorities, working together in conurbation or sub-regional groupings.

BOUNDARY DEFINITION

On the problem of boundary definition, as Colin Cooper's reference to a "policy framework" infers, Sub-regional boundaries are not completely flexible. They are usually defined with reference to the boundaries of those

---

* There are also, of course, systems requiring regional and national co-ordination.

authorities who are to participate. A first step, however, must be to recognise the extent of the system (or complex of systems) which is of primary concern and ensure that the whole of it is included in the Study area. This may be fairly obvious in the case of a Land Use/Transportation Survey since the relevant behaviour can be easily discerned and measured. It will be less clear in many other cases, e.g. where an area is suffering from general economic or social malaise. Information available which will help in identifying areas which contain particular systems can be grouped under the following heads:

> Geographical—physical features, buildings and infrastructure, communication channels etc.
> Homogeneity in statistical terms—activity rates, employment by industry, population age structure, etc.
> Behaviour—e.g. travel patterns.

THE ADVISORY ROLE OF SUB-REGIONAL PLANNING

Sub-regional studies are not "plans" in the sense of being the declared intentions of agencies possessing at least some of the statutory powers necessary to implement them. They are usually produced by agencies having no statutory powers at all, and perform advisory rather than executive functions. For this reason we prefer to think of "studies" rather than "plans" in a Sub-regional context. There seems to be no consensus of opinion in the profession on this point, however, so that we have been unable to maintain a strict observation of the rule throughout our text.

The fact that Sub-regional studies are advisory has been a source of weakness in the past and we have had situations in Sub-regional planning where the commissioners of the plan have been seen to be uncommitted. The idea of co-ordinated policies to control systems and the need to monitor (to which we shall refer later) is leading us to foresee a situation where Sub-regional work will come to have much more involvement on the part of the commissioning agencies and others working together over time. Sub-regional work may change from a consulting role to a joint behaviour role, since trade-off decisions* between agencies often need heavy involvement over a long period.

* Trade-off decisions are aimed at the establishment or maintenance of productive compromise.

In a sense, all plans are advisory until they are converted into legally binding contracts, and the important point here is that Sub-regional plans come early in a series of stages during which the degree of commitment is progressively increased. Working backwards through these stages, commitment is greatest when legally binding contracts are signed to implement a plan. Before this stage, plans are approved and become legally endorsed propositions which may or may not become contracts. Before this, propositions are embodied in plans which are prepared by the agency with powers to legally endorse them (submitted as provisional Structure or Local plans). Before this, the Sub-regional proposals are submitted to the agencies with statutory powers for possible inclusion in Structure and Local plans. An even earlier stage might involve the preparation of Regional plans to be submitted in the first instance to an agency which itself has no statutory powers but performs an advisory function to local government on the one hand and central government on the other. The advisory nature of a Sub-regional plan is therefore inevitable, and if the above argument is valid, properly so.

STRATEGIC PLANNING

The *Oxford Dictionary* defines strategy as "management of an army or armies in a campaign, art of so moving or disposing troops or ships or aircraft as to impose upon the enemy the place and time and conditions for fighting preferred by oneself". This overall management is distinct from tactics which are concerned with localised movement of troops actually in contact with the enemy.

Sub-regional teams are concerned with "strategic" planning, which is usually, though not necessarily, planning for the longer term. Whatever the time scale, strategic planning is concerned with the critical issues where control will enable the community/client goals to be achieved. The "critical" issues have often been identified as the activities whose control by an authority enables that authority to control other activities.

Because the "systems" in a society are to varying degrees related to its power structure an hierarchical model of National–Regional–Sub-regional–Local planning is often used, and the strategic planning is identified with planning by the upper levels of the hierarchy. In a rapidly changing society this does not have to be so, nor where many of the real world systems have not been recognised or used as a field of political action ("the market forces"). Consequently, Sub-regional planning as strategic planning cannot be confined to such a place in the hierarchy. It is, however, widely believed that Sub-regional planners give advice for decision-taking at the apex of the local government planning decisions pyramid: level A, not levels B, C, D. The plan so preferred will no doubt be evaluated taking into account the implications for lower levels of decisions and feedback from these levels, but the advice itself is to assert decisions at level A. It is this rather than the time scale involved which is said to make Sub-regional planning "strategic". In our view it is capacity to control with economy of effort that can make Sub-regional planning "strategic".

UNCERTAINTY

Another important characteristic of Sub-regional plans is that they assist local, regional and national government agencies by exploring problems at a level of planning where there is a high degree of uncertainty. This gives both the nature of the process and the resulting plan or strategy itself a unique quality. Thus Geoffrey Steeley[5] notes:

> A sub-regional plan is not a very large "local" plan—nor even an extensive county and city "structure" plan. On occasion it can be coincident with "operational" plans, e.g. for transportation. All these have as a characteristic a degree of firmness that permits and governs the execution of the projects involved. Criteria can be specified in considerable detail, performance standards can be defined and be found to be acceptable, institutional and agency procedures are available. But at the Sub-regional scale the principle of uncertainty holds such sway that firmness becomes illusory, criteria become platitudes and visions, performance standards fail to be demonstrable, and institutions and agencies have yet to be evolved or even conjured up.
> Planning over a large area, with many (and often only partially included) urban systems and few control totals, becomes an exploratory process, not a design nor yet an executive or management one.
> This degree of uncertainty does not necessarily progressively increase as one moves towards regional or national levels of planning. These are encompassing a sufficiently large proportion of the sub-systems, approaching sufficiently close to the control totals, and operated by agencies with many of the relevant powers and sources of judgement. . . .
> . . . The contribution that can be required of sub-regional planning is that the uncertainty is explored and that advice for local, structure and operational planning be propounded that assists their planners and managers to define the error levels to which they must work, to include sufficient flexibility in their

proposals, to exploit the advantages of joint action, to avoid harmful competition, to assess the impact of the unexpected, to respond to anticipated changes, to maintain and achieve performance standards . . . and so on. . . .

CORPORATE PLANNING

Our discussion of Sub-regional planning so far has been in spatial terms: of co-ordinating the actions of planning agencies operating across local government boundaries. Recently, however, there has been a growing interest in corporate planning, which implies a different kind of co-ordination and involves a variety of agencies not directly concerned with physical development. Thus with many social problems, agencies operating within the local government boundary may exert control over a sufficiently large area to make a reasonable degree of control possible. But these powers may be so dispersed between a variety of different bodies that they can only be effective with co-ordinated effort.

Such corporate planning problems may or may not involve cross-boundary co-ordination in spatial terms, but Sub-regional planners do have something to offer. Their range of vision has, in the past, been much less closely defined than that of the statutory planning authorities so that a number of teams have found it necessary, and have felt free, to move well into areas of social and economic planning. They have offered advice to non-planners both to secure the objectives of the Sub-regional plan itself and to provide advice on the spatial implications/requirements of the interests of the non-planners. There is thus experience of deriving advice for both kinds of co-ordinated action. A start has also been made on thinking of ways in which agencies might be induced to act together and of monitoring these actions and their results. The concept of "systems" that we have earlier noted as contributing to the popularity of Sub-regional planning is relevant here. Spatial components of the systems are often referred to by planners as though they were the whole of the systems under examination. We believe it to be much more the case that study of the "aspatial" characteristics of the systems is essential if the range of objectives and controls a planner promotes are to be soundly based. The implications are that (a) planners will become more involved in the management and government of communities and localities than has been customary or acceptable in the recent past; and (b) that the limited controls of all government activity over the observable systems will be recognised, so that planning for uncertainty will grow in importance. In both these fields Sub-regional planning has valuable experience to offer.

At this point it is perhaps appropriate to mention a quasi-philosophical argument which has recently been put forward that all planning activity is irrelevant. This view is most ably expressed in the writings of Etzioni [6, 7] and Lindblom. [8] The latter describes government decision-making in practice in terms of "Partisan Mutual Adjustment" and the results of such activity as "Disjointed Incrementalism". These have been put forward as the characteristics of decision-making that make all planning, let alone Sub-regional planning, an irrelevant process.

There are in any society various groups and individuals who are able to exert an influence on the decisions of government. Each of these has its own particular goals and objectives, some of which are in accord with those of other groups, some in conflict. Partisan Mutual Adjustment is what takes place when all of these various influences come together and some compromise agreement is thrashed out between them as to the action to be taken. Government action over the years is the result of a series of Partisan Mutual Adjustments, a process which can be described as Disjointed Incrementalism. Partisan Mutual Adjustment reflects the balance of power between various interest groups at the time of the relevant decision. The power of each group depends on a variety of factors such as size of membership, status of members, strength of feeling about particular issues and so on. Clearly the power of any group will vary from time to time and its objectives will also change. Under these circumstances it is impossible to predict with any confidence the nature of future compromises and hence future government decisions. Planning therefore becomes irrelevant.

Two propositions might be derived from this argument:
(a) that planning is ineffective because, whatever is proposed, Partisan Mutual Adjustment in terms of a balance between the interests of various groups will take place so that the plan will be irrelevant; and
(b) that planning is undesirable. This is based on an analogy with perfect competition in economics. A natural balance occurs which is seen as the most satisfactory solution because it enables the wishes of all the various groups in society to be traded off one against another.

We have insufficient space to discuss these propositions fully here. We suggest, however, that the first is impossible to prove because no two situations are ever exactly alike and one cannot therefore compare a "plan" with a "no plan" situation directly. Our own feeling is that plans *are* a factor in influencing the outcome of the Partisan Mutual Adjustment process, because of their role of providing information about possible (optimal) solutions to conflicts. We do, however, concede that they may be less effective than is usually supposed. So far as the second proposition is concerned, our government has taken the decision that land use and (more recently) corporate plans should be prepared and until the millennium is reached, when all groups have perfect access to power and where the political structure accurately reflects the operative systems of society, we would support that decision. The role of planners in seeking to articulate the interests of *all* groups we believe to have significance for democratic government.

LINKING LOCAL AND REGIONAL/NATIONAL PLANNING

Another role of Sub-regional plans that helps to account for their variety is that of linking local with regional and national plans. Richard Crossman, when Minister of Housing and Local Government, took the initiative in encouraging selected counties and boroughs to co-operate in Sub-regional studies of their areas. Leicester/Leics. was one of the first. At this time the Government were particularly concerned to set local planning in a regional and national context and this is reflected in the approach adopted by McLoughlin's team as we shall see later. It is still an important part of the Department of the Environment model terms of reference and formed part of the instructions to Coventry/Solihull/War. This concern for linking is also reflected in the Development Plans Manual which specifically requires Sub-regional co-ordination.

In some cases the work of Economic Planning Boards and Councils has been an important factor in leading to the setting up of Sub-regional studies. The North-east Regional Review,[9] for example, pointed to Teesside as a suitable growth area with sufficient potential for development to attract industry from the South and migrants from less well-placed areas of the North-east. Thus the Teesside Study is very concerned to exploit the advantages of its location for industrial development and this certainly influences the form of the final strategy.

INVESTMENT PROJECTS OF NATIONAL IMPORTANCE

So far, we have been concerned essentially with joint studies undertaken or sponsored by two or more local planning authorities to improve the effectiveness of their statutory planning activities. There is, however, another major group of Sub-regional studies with quite different origins and purposes. These are to advise planning decisions on a national scale rather than local, and are usually concerned with massive capital investment such as the establishment of New Towns or major road or air transport developments. At the Sub-regional scale, work is needed on such questions as the feasibility of sites, in general areas selected at national or regional level, and the likely impact of such proposals on the existing environment. In the last decade, Sub-regional studies concerned with the reception of large-scale inward migration have been initiated in two ways. On the one hand, there has been concern to relieve the present overcrowding of major cities and, in the South-east particularly, this has encouraged regional and national planners to look for sites for more New Towns. Thus there have been several Sub-regional studies, e.g. Northampton, Bedford and North Bucks., Ipswich, Ashford and South Hants. On the other hand, national planners have also been concerned with longer-term population growth and the possible need for much more radical changes in the distribution of national population. This has generated studies of Humberside, Severnside and Tayside.

These studies are largely concerned with urban systems which have yet to be created or which will be created out of much smaller, and perhaps quite different, existing systems. They have been very concerned with urban form, particularly from the point of view of accessibility, and make recommendations as to whether the large-scale investment involved is likely to prove worth while. They vary considerably in speed of implementation. Some, like Northampton, Bedford and North Bucks., are translated very quickly into firm proposals for a new town (Milton Keynes). Others, like Tayside, have a much more speculative air and may remain only an idea for a long period of time. Others still, like Ipswich, may not be proceeded with.

Clearly proposals for a new town raise many questions other than cost and the shape of the new settlement to be created. These may all be tackled in one study, but in some cases they call for separate investigation. Examples include the Impact studies of Preston–Chorley on N.E. Lancashire, Peterborough or the Huntingdon and Peterborough County, and the cost-benefit study on the Ipswich expansion proposals.

REGIONAL AND SUB-REGIONAL PLANNING

There is a great deal of confusion over the difference between Regional and Sub-regional planning and, indeed, the terms are sometimes used incorrectly in circumstances where we would have thought the position reasonably clear. There are, however, many similarities between them: neither Regional nor Sub-regional bodies have statutory powers or statutory limits to their interests in terms of policy areas; both operate in similar policy areas and so on. In addition, definitions are difficult to maintain over the country; for example what is "Regional" in a megalopolitan area may seem "Sub-regional" in another part of the country. Further, the majority of studies contain advice for more than one level of planning and it sometimes happens that a team is concerned to influence not its sponsors but some other body operating at another level entirely. It is not therefore possible to define the limits of our work with scientific accuracy. We have accordingly elected to compare Sub-regional and Regional planning at some length, quoting examples liberally, in the hope that this will convey a general impression of the more important similarities and differences between the two levels.

The principal difference between Regional and Sub-regional planning lies in the way in which the areas covered are defined. As we have seen, Sub-regions are usually defined so as to cover the whole of at least one major system which is critical in planning terms to the local authorities in the area. This system may already exist, or it may be one which is to be created. In contrast, Regions usually have meaning in administrative terms rather than physical form and behaviour. In fact there are several examples of regional boundaries which cut off major towns and cities from their hinterlands. They are nevertheless an important fact of political life and are of major significance in terms of central government administration. Thus the East Midlands Regional Technical Unit[10] notes:

> We have investigated the physical, economic and social characteristics with which planners are concerned, but there remain the administrative and organisational activities which are also fundamental to the purpose and practice of planning.

It is in these aspects that the Region as a whole displays significance—the Region is of course an administrative and organisational unit of central government, in addition to the grouping of local government bodies which constitute the area. These simple facts, which have on occasions been the basis of criticism of the Region as a coherent entity in the light of the evidence suggesting the inadequacy of any other activity as an embracing system, are of critical significance if advice is to be given for the Region.

The essential nature of the East Midlands, therefore, is composed of an overall administrative/organisational system (in which many Central Government decisions are made), within which physical, economic, social and cultural activities display a complex pattern of sub-systems related to parts of the Region (and of neighbouring regions).

Planning work undertaken by Regional bodies may be grouped into the following categories:

(i) Giving advice on the impact of national government decisions on the Region and its parts. These may be concerned with capital spending but they are also likely to include taxation, distribution of industry and so on. Also under this heading would be activities of nationalised industries and similar bodies operating on a national and regional scale.

(ii) Bringing together Central Government interests and Structure planning by publishing Regional Strategies and Plans, commenting to Structure planners on the local implications of central policies and attitudes and (probably) evaluating structure plans in the light of regional and national criteria.

(iii) Co-ordinating Structure planning activity in those conurbations which are so large that their problems must be considered on a regional scale.

(iv) Giving a technical service to Structure and Local planners by making forecasts and analysing data which are best handled at a national and regional scale.

An important point to be made here is that Regional planning often involves making a choice between areas which vary tremendously in terms of culture, population density, industry and topography, in allocating benefits, establishing priorities and so on. Clearly these decisions must have a much higher degree of political judgement, and technical arguments are likely to be less conclusive, than at Sub-regional level.

The foregoing text has shown that there is a great deal of variety in both Regional and Sub-regional planning work. One document may perform several different functions and advise different agencies. For this reason, no classification of studies at either level can be entirely satisfactory. Nevertheless it is possible, we feel, to arrange the studies produced to date in a simple grouping which brings out their more important similarities and differences. This is set out, with examples, in Table 1.1. The distinction between Regional and Sub-regional studies is retained and there is a further division between those which are concerned with the allocation of resources and others which co-ordinate the planning activities of a number of agencies.

TABLE 1.1. CLASSIFICATION OF REGIONAL AND SUB-REGIONAL
PLANNING STUDIES

		Areas	
		Regions	Sub-regions
Functions	Allocation of resources	Yorkshire and Humberside Review East Midlands Study	Northampton, Bedford and North Bucks. Ashford Humberside Severnside
	Co-ordination of planning activity	Strategic Plan for the South-east Yorkshire and Humberside Regional Strategy	Leicester/Leics. Teesside Impact on N.E. Lancs

A major part of the work of the Economic Planning Boards and Councils in the sixties was geared to advising central government on the needs of the Regions and the effects on them of government policies. One of their functions was the allocation of national resources and ensuring that the share which accrued to their area was related to its needs. The first wave of studies produced in the middle sixties were intended as a basis for this activity. In this respect these have something in common with Sub-regional studies such as Humberside and Severnside, which are also concerned with the allocation of resources on a national scale. Both are usually concerned with advising central government and they may also wish to influence public utility suppliers and others who have a major impact on the Regions.

At the Regional scale, both the Economic Planning Councils and Standing Conferences of Local Planning Authorities have been concerned with co-ordinating Local Planning activity by producing a Regional framework into which Local plans may be fitted. These are concerned with both vertical co-ordination between National:Regional:County levels and horizontal between county authorities. At Sub-regional level the co-ordination group clearly includes those which arise from the need to plan for and influence cross-boundary movement. It also includes impact studies which are intended to enable authorities to respond to major exogenous changes.

DISTINGUISHING LEVELS OF PLANNING IN PRACTICE

To illustrate the difference between levels of planning in practice, we discuss the South-west Region, where several interesting examples are to be found in a relatively uncomplicated area. The discussion is in terms of the pre-Local Government Reform situation.

Cornwall is a predominantly rural county with a number of towns of 10,000 to 20,000 population, most of which are either surrounded by land in agricultural use or are on the coast. Some of the towns are, however, sufficiently close together to have interaction between them. In either case they represent County planning problems because they lie wholly within Cornwall.

The Plymouth area on the other hand is one where Sub-regional co-ordination could make a contribution in the planning of urban land use dispositions and communication channels, since the urban system extends beyond the city boundaries into both Devon and Cornwall. A more extensive Sub-regional system is retailing activity, since Plymouth is a centre for more expensive consumer durables for the whole of Cornwall. Similarly there is a behavioural system formed by tourists in the area who find Plymouth a useful centre for Dartmoor and the coasts of both Cornwall and Devon (it is possible to travel from St. Ives to Plymouth in a morning and from St. Ives to Exeter in a day by road). It would thus be perfectly reasonable to plan tourism in the area at a Sub-regional level.

It will be noted that the distinction being made here between County and Sub-regional planning does not depend on the geographical extent of the systems involved, on the number of such systems or on the complexity of their interaction. Thus a major urban system could represent a "county" planning problem so long as it lay wholly within the boundaries of one authority. Similarly a major urban system comprising a chain of sub-systems all interacting in a highly complex way could be appropriate to County planning. On the other hand, a single, comparatively simple urban system could call for Sub-regional co-ordination if administrative boundaries had been drawn in such a way as to prevent a single authority from exercising its Structure planning powers over the whole of its extent.

An interesting example which shows the way in which Regional planning and Structure planning may overlap is the West Cornwall Study. This arises from the South-west Economic Planning Council document, "A Region with a Future—a Draft Strategy for the South-west", which expresses the view that West Cornwall has an insufficient basis for growth and for this reason applauds proposals (not now being proceeded with) for the reception of London overspill into the area and suggests that growth should be concentrated in the Truro–Camborne–Falmouth triangle. While accepting the need for special action to stimulate growth in West Cornwall, the County Council were not happy about either of these ideas: they felt that sufficient potential existed in the area, together with Development Area concessions, to contain the economic problems of the area at an acceptable level.

The West Cornwall Study is the County Planning Department's assessment of the economic potential of the area and the intention of the Study is to enable a decision to be taken on the issue of planned migration. It thus contains advice for decisions at both levels: Regional as to whether inward migration is desirable and Structure/Local on what should happen if migration does not occur. The Study is not, on the face of it a Sub-regional one, for the responsible authority wholly contained the area and, in so far as existing powers are adequate, is able to control its performance. However, had the study been commissioned as a co-operative venture by the much smaller local authorities then it could well have been Sub-regional, for without their joint activity each would have lacked so much spatial extent of its powers as to be unable to control the area, and moreover, lacking the powers of the County Council would have found it essential to enter into a co-operative relationship with it. Sub-regional planning of this sort is a special case of General Community Management in which spatial systems are controlled through political co-operation on the basis of planning advice.

CHANGES IN PLANNING AND GOVERNMENT

Having established some understanding of Sub-regional planning functions and the way these relate to and are differentiated from other levels of planning, we may now go on to consider changes which are likely to affect its future. These are (i) changes in the form and content of plans arising from the recommendations of the Planning Advisory Group, and (ii) changes in government boundaries and powers.

(i) One of the most striking features of the new planning procedures is that Structure Plans are much more similar in character (technical and procedural) to recent Sub-regional plans than they are to the old County Development plans.

This is primarily because in future County level planning is to be much more explicitly strategic planning than it has traditionally been. The old County Development plan, for example, was a map with supporting documents; the new Structure plan is a text with explanatory diagrams which do not have an Ordnance Survey base. It is also clear from the notes on publicity and the elimination of the right of all objectors automatically to be heard at public inquiries into overall strategies, that at this level comment will only really be sought from those organisations and individuals who are willing and (hopefully) able to think in very broad terms. Haggling over individual pieces of land is to be discouraged at this stage. Similarly, only Structure plans are to be submitted automatically to the Secretary of State for approval. Local government agencies will generally be allowed to authorise their own non-strategic plan documents.

The technical work to be carried out for Structure plans will also follow the pattern which has become familiar at Sub-regional level and great benefit should be derived from the technical advances which have been made in the last few years. In particular County planners will be expected to go much further in generating and evaluating alternatives than in the past. There will also be greater emphasis on transport proposals and their integration with land-use planning, which has always been a feature of Sub-regional work.

Greater integration of the policies of different local government departments is hoped for and Structure plans will cover economic and social as well as purely physical planning policies. They will also show proposed allocations of resources between the various activities, but this will cover a shorter period than land-use strategies, for obvious reasons. The intentions of other bodies such as Public Utility operators and Hospital boards will also be indicated. These corporate planning characteristics have also been seen in the more recent Sub-regional plans.

The need for Sub-regional co-ordination is formally recognised in the *Manual*[4] and evidence will be expected of consultations between authorities in adjacent areas, where necessary. In some cases it is anticipated that the preparation of group Structure plans will be necessary. Regional considerations are to be taken into account through liaison with the Economic Planning Councils and Boards.

(ii) With the redrawing of local government boundaries and in particular the merging of many county boroughs with the County areas which surround them, many Sub-regional planning problems will disappear. The problems investigated by the Leicester/Leics. and N. Glos. Studies, for example, could now be dealt with at Structure planning level, and Humberside is to have a County authority. Even so, many problems will remain after these amalgamations have taken place: in Derbyshire the County and County Borough will be amalgamated but the problem of the Erewash Valley towns along the Notts./Derby. border will remain.

Boundaries in some areas of major importance have, however, been drawn in such a way that Structure planning will be virtually impossible without Sub-regional/Regional co-ordination. The most remarkable examples of this are in the West Midlands and North-west, but Derek Senior[11] lists several others: Brighton, Burton on Trent, Luton, Milton Keynes, Peterborough, Plymouth, Stoke and Teesside.

So far as functions are concerned, County Boroughs are to lose their Structure planning responsibilities which will be taken over by the Counties. District authorities will, however, take over Development Control as of right, excepting those decisions which are of strategic importance and Districts will also have the right to produce their own Local plans.

The loss of implementation powers and the lack of development powers is bound to weaken the Structure planner's hand and it seems likely that existing problems of lack of understanding between Development plan and Development control practitioners will be exacerbated. On the other hand, the control of borrowing of capital by Central Government, and powers held by counties, will presumably be operated in accordance with Structure plans. Local elections held once every four years for counties as against three years out of four for districts will also strengthen the hand of counties, as will the rule that an individual cannot be a member at both levels.

Since counties are likely to lose a lot of planning work, their strength in terms of numbers of staff could well go down and this will affect the attitude of counties towards the setting up of separate ad-hoc teams to perform Sub-regional functions. It may however promote joint working between County and County District Planning authorities in order to achieve effective managerial control through joint availability of powers. This is referred to in the chapter dealing with Monitoring.

At the Regional level, the question of functions may be settled after the publication of the Kilbranden Report which is not available at the time of writing, but a strengthening of the regional Civil Service and some decentralisation of decision-making is already taking place with the creation of new posts combining the functions of Regional Directors of the Department of the Environment and chairmen of the Regional Economic Planning Boards. Some of the metropolitan area boundaries have been drawn in such a way that strategic planning will have to take place at the regional level. It is also the avowed intention of the Government that regional planning strategies should be completed for all regions.

These changes which we have been discussing have implications for the future of Sub-regional work of the co-ordinating kind. Allocation studies seem likely to be less affected. Clearly it is impossible to make firm predictions as to the future of co-ordinating work at Sub-regional level, so many imponderables are present. Nevertheless, it is interesting to speculate on a few possibilities.

Work of a co-ordinating kind will certainly continue to be necessary: even if proposed local government boundaries were all to be drawn in terms of urban activity and behaviour (which they are not), the two would not correspond for very long because systems change. Since it is easier to set up co-ordinating machinery than to continually revise boundaries, Sub-regional work is likely to survive. It is quite possible, however, that fewer teams recruited from outside will be involved in future, since other bodies who are capable of undertaking the work may have greater claims. In most areas joint Structure plans will probably not be seen as necessary, and more limited contacts between separate planning teams will have to suffice.

Where joint teams are set up, seconded staff may well be used to a much greater extent than in the past. This will involve a loss in some ways, a gain in others. The team will no longer take so fresh a look at the area and long-standing prejudices and misconceptions will have a greater chance of being carried forward. It might be too that fewer technical innovations will occur. On the other hand, whatever proposals are put forward, joint working will probably involve greater commitment on the part of the statutory authorities than recommendations of a team from "outside".

Regional planning agencies could well become more involved in essentially physical planning studies to control the growth of major conurbations and again there could be advantages in terms of commitment on the part of both local and central government if joint teams are involved.

CHAPTER 2

Information Services

WE SHALL be describing later how the Sub-regional planning teams have carried out their tasks, variously following the revered formula of "survey–analysis–plan". Some have given more weight to one phase than another, and some have developed significant variations on the theme—of which more later. The distinction between each of the three classic phases has, moreover, become blurred as the richness and elaboration of the process has grown. For our present purposes we have chosen to present our discussion in as simple an order as possible and not to reflect this growing complexity in the sequence of our chapters. Consequently the next three chapters are concerned with the collection and analysis of information about the area and forecasting its future on the basis of no change in existing policies. These activities reappear from time to time in later chapters under the guise of "plan" just as the activities of "plan" are prefigured here.

The design of the information services is an important area of inquiry for the client when evaluating a study, not only is this because of the need to assess the effectiveness and efficiency of the system, but also because its design was prepared at the crucial early stages of the whole process. Its character can illuminate the early thinking of the team and reveal assumptions, both good and bad, that have influenced the whole course of the study. It is not infrequent to hear of professional planners bemoaning the effort involved at later stages trying to rectify the effects of early mistakes in the design of their information services.

INITIATING DATA COLLECTION

When the team first assembles, probably knowing very little about the area which is to be their concern, a preliminary consideration will be the collection of information, not merely impressions about the area but large quantities of statistical data. A start must be made on this as early as possible because it is very time-consuming and having information available at the right time will be critical in meeting deadlines. Since it will occupy a large proportion of available resources of manpower (and cash) it is also important in the planning of the team's work. In other words major decisions regarding the allocation of manpower and resources to specific tasks and guiding the team into particular lines of investigation must be taken at a very early stage in the process. It is therefore worth considering briefly how these decisions are taken. Of course the team's knowledge of the Sub-region is increasing rapidly at this stage, but as a starting-point they draw on two sources: their own skill and experience or "culture" as planners and the terms of reference drawn up by the Study sponsors.

Sir Geoffrey Vickers[12] explains that culture embodies experience of "facts" and of norms by which facts may be valued. It enables us to recognise problems, devise solutions and decide upon action. It operates in the following manner:

> The culture in which we grow up is intensely normative in all three dimensions. The simplest discrimination—"This is a that" (whether "that" be a cow, a contract or a sin)—is no mere finding of fact but a judgement which carves something out of the field for attention and assimilates it to a category which has been generated by previous acts of the same kind. The simplest valuation— "This should be thus"—is equally a judgement arrived at by comparing some object or event or course of events (real or imagined) with some standard which has come to be accepted as the appropriate norm. The simplest decision on actions—"In these circumstances this should be done"—is the selection of a response from a repertory by rules which determine what is suitable to what occasion. The categories by which we discriminate, the standards by which we value, the repertory of responses from which we select, and our rules for selection are all mental artifacts, evolved, learned and taught by the cultural process and more or less peculiar to the culture which produces them. This process is a circular process, in which all these settings of the appreciative system are constantly being modified by its own exercise.

The planner participates in a general culture as a member of the community but he also has a particular sub-culture as a planner, which derives from his professional training and experience. It is this sub-culture he is hired to exploit on behalf of the political decision-takers. The freedom allowed by sponsors varies from area to area, but however close their supervision, the sheer complexity of the work at the Sub-regional scale means that the planner will himself make many of the important value judgements. It is impossible to consult the whole community on many value judgements and it is often considered impracticable to consult even élected representatives on the grounds that, if this were done, the task would never be completed, or data would have decayed to the point of uselessness before publication of the plan.

This brings us to a major philosophical problem as to how far a planner is justified, in his position as professional advisor, in taking the initiative on major issues where no clear line has been adopted by community leaders. We cannot deal adequately with this subject in the space available here, and merely note that finding the right balance is largely a question of professional integrity and experience.* In evaluating Sub-regional work we would, however, expect to be satisfied that a genuine attempt had been made to take community feeling into account on all issues of major importance, and that such issues had been brought out and discussed openly in the text.

The second starting-point for Sub-regional work is the Terms of Reference. These set out the task to be undertaken and may indicate the problems of the area, as they are perceived by the sponsors. From these Terms of Reference and their preliminary ideas about the area, the team will set out provisional goals and objectives. These are likely to be continually revised up to the point at which plan generation begins—which is why we have deferred a full discussion until Chapter 5—but a provisional list at this early stage is useful to help the team plan their work, and to indicate to the sponsors the direction they intend to take.

QUALITATIVE AND QUANTITATIVE DATA

The first information which the team collects is qualitative data in the form of general impressions about the area. Qualitative data plays a major role in the Sub-regional process and covers a wide range, from impressions about the climate of opinion in the area to judgements about the quality of landscape and environment. Problems associated with this kind of data, however, are best discussed in the context of the particular stages of the

---

* The ability and personality of the team leader is of crucial importance. We believe there is scope for a social/political study of the team leaders who have worked in Britain in order that sponsors may be more informed in selecting team leaders for future studies.

planning process at which they become of major concern and are therefore deferred until later chapters. In this chapter we are concerned primarily with the collection and processing of large amounts of quantitative information, some of which may be collected through special surveys, but with a large proportion being supplied by outside agencies.

The amount of quantitative information which is used by Sub-regional teams is enormous. Before the general spread of computing facilities, the problem of data handling for analysis and forecasting purposes usually had to be avoided by making do with simple tabulations and a refusal to go into detail. Similarly in devising and assessing plans, the methods used had to be simple and demand only a minimal amount of data manipulation. Now that facilities are available for processing large amounts of statistical information, however, these old methods are no longer acceptable. Moreover, in addition to the more familiar analytical work, many teams prefer to have the benefit of advice from at least a transportation model and often from shopping and Lowry-type models and potential surfaces as well. This naturally generates demand for data at a much higher level of disaggregation, both by subject and by area, than is usually called for by manual techniques. Thus, for example, although Notts./Derby. kept their data collection down as far as possible, they nevertheless felt obliged to store over 100,000 items of information on employment alone, roughly 60% of which were used primarily for economic analysis and 40% for simulation purposes. Information requirements on this scale are normally taken to justify electronic data processing.

SUB-REGIONAL DATA BANKS

Data Banks now being developed at the County level often involve holding data at one central point (the computer files), from which it is readily available to all departments and agencies of the Authority. This brings obvious benefits through eliminating duplicate records, greater accessibility and more intensive use of the data. In the context of this chapter, however, we use the term Sub-regional Data Bank in a more restricted sense. This is simply computing facilities for storing and processing large quantities of the various statistics required by the Sub-regional team. These statistics will not normally be made accessible to other agencies and professions during the course of the Study, although they may become so afterwards. Such an arrangement is, however, a bank in the sense of giving interest: greater understanding is achieved through the association of data on a variety of topics than if they were held separately in paper files. At the present time, most Sub-regional teams find it desirable to initiate such special data banks although, in the future, the existence of data banks at County level may make this unnecessary.

The most important advantages a data bank has to offer a Sub-regional team are time saved in data manipulation and the completion of certain tasks with a degree of accuracy which would be practically impossible by manual methods. Another organisational factor is that, with the growing use of computers in local government, it is often easier to secure computer time and cash for these purposes than it is to get permission to increase the manpower of the team. Any savings in money as a result of using a computer are not likely to be substantial: the Notts./Derby. team estimated the balance of cost between computer and manual methods to be about equal, especially if one ignored overheads incurred in a rather longer period of study.

The money cost of establishing a data bank is in fact heavy, particularly if point referenced data is prepared and stored. As a rough indication of the scale of investment involved, given an available computer with sufficient capacity, the Newcastle Point Referenced Data System may be quoted as reasonably representative of a city of its size (222,000 population). This was established over an 18-month period at an estimated total cost of £22,000 and required two planners, three technicians, one systems analyst, one programmer and a clerk. Each person was involved for at least 12 of the 18 months taken for the project, and eight temporary workers were also recruited for a 6-week period.[13]

CRITERIA FOR ESTABLISHING A DATA BANK

In view of the time constraint, and cost involved, it is essential to plan the data system carefully from the start and we would put forward the following criteria:

1. A Sub-regional data bank should be an output-oriented device, not an input one. Experience has shown that it is easy to fall into the trap of collecting large quantities of only marginally useful data and this may be to neglect the primary task of deriving useful planning advice. Considerations

such as the number of purposes for which items of data can be used, the availability of proxies and statistical techniques for reducing data requirements are relevant here.

2. The data should be of sufficient quality to give confidence in the results. It may not need to be compatible with data held by other agencies, but it should be acceptable to them in demonstrating the team's conclusions. Accuracy of the data in relation to the crudity of assumptions built into simulation techniques and the sensitivity of conclusions to possible errors in the data will be important.

3. Account should be taken of data needed at each stage of the process, including monitoring. The possibility, if it exists, that the Study data bank may be required on a permanent basis for monitoring purposes is important since an on-going project may well justify larger initial investment than a "once and for all" job.

THE KIND OF DATA COLLECTED

At this stage it would have been useful to have conducted a survey of recent Sub-regional studies so as to be in a position to discuss actual Sub-regional data systems in depth, but this has not been possible. Instead, use may be made of a recent study by Erlet A. Cater.[14] This describes information collected for planning at County, Borough and Regional as well as Sub-regional level, but Mrs. Cater gives the results of her survey work in sufficient detail for some conclusions to be drawn relevant to our task.

Visits were made to nine of the "first wave" of authorities who had been asked to produce new-style Structure plans, thirteen other planning authorities "known to be active in their attempts to develop the uses of a computer for their planning procedure" and three Sub-regional/Regional studies. In addition to these three teams, however, another three studies were covered in discussion with sponsoring planning authorities, so that information is given for:

> Coventry/Solihull/War.,
> Notts./Derby.,
> West Midland (Regional),
> South Hants,
> Leicester/Leics. and
> Teesplan.

Mrs. Cater uses a Chapin-type[15] systems-based classification, distinguishing:

Within place data   Activities
                     Adapted spaces
Between place data   Activities
                     Adapted spaces (channels)

She deals with twenty categories of data under these headings and discusses their collection by different planning bodies, who are mentioned by name. A count of the number of times the six Sub-regional/Regional bodies are mentioned under each of the headings has been made, to see what is suggested about the general pattern of data collection by these teams.

The results of this exercise are set out in Table 2.1. There is, of course, no guarantee that all bodies using a given category of data at the time of survey are mentioned in Mrs. Cater's text. Indeed this is not the case, and there is naturally a tendency for those using the latest or most novel methods to be mentioned more frequently than those using methods which are more generally applied and widely known. The table must therefore be treated as giving only crude indications of the frequency with which data is used. The general pattern does, however, conform with our experience over a number of years in Sub-regional/Regional planning, conversations with others working in the field and general reading on the subject. The inferences we draw are as follows:

(i) Between-place data is more common at Sub-regional than County level and this reflects a greater emphasis on modelling in general and use of transport models in particular.

(ii) Within-place data—activities are mentioned relatively more often for Sub-regional studies, while for other bodies adapted spaces (buildings) have more emphasis.

(iii) Of the various within-place activities, only two assume major importance at Sub-regional scale: residential and industrial, with industrial activity seeming particularly important. So far as residential activity is concerned, however, the results are probably biased because census data are normally purchased on magnetic tape or sheets and processed in familiar routines which do not call for attention in Mrs. Cater's work. For example, Notts./Derby. are not mentioned here, although they processed 1961 data for all wards and parishes and 1966 data for every Enumeration District

TABLE 2.1. ANALYSIS OF NUMBERS OF COMMENTS ON USE OF DATA
BY SUB-REGIONAL/REGIONAL AND COUNTY/COUNTY BOROUGH PLANNERS
IN *Information Needs of Planners* by ERLET A. CATER

Data	Sub-regional			Regional studies			Total	Counties, Boroughs, Cities
	Coventry/ Solihull/ War.	West Midlands	Notts./ Derby.	South Hants	Leicester and Leics.	Teesplan		
1. Residential activity	1	2	—	1	1	2	7	23
2. Industrial activity	4	1	1	1	1	6	14	28
3. Service activity	—	—	—	—	—	—	—	10
4. Education activity	—	—	—	—	—	—	—	11
5. Recreation activity	—	—	—	—	—	—	—	15
6. Other activities	—	—	—	—	—	—	—	7
7. Housing	1	1	—	1	1	3	7	30
8. Factories	1	1	—	1	—	2	5	23
9. Offices	1	—	—	—	—	—	1	13
10. Shops	—	—	—	—	—	2	2	8
11. Education buildings	—	—	—	—	—	1	1	9
12. Recreation land	—	2	—	—	—	—	2	10
13. Land in all uses	3	1	3	2	—	3	12	60
14. Journey to work	—	—	1	1	—	4	6	12
15. Journey to shop	—	—	—	1	—	—	1	1
16. Journey on employers businesss	—	—	—	—	—	1	1	2
17. Journey for recreation, entertainment	—	—	—	—	—	—	—	1
18. Journey for all purposes	1	1	—	—	—	3	5	10
19. Service infrastructure	1	—	1	1	—	—	3	7
20. Movement networks	—	—	1	—	1	4	6	21
Within place:								
1–6. activities	5	3	1	2	2	8	21	94
7–13. adapted spaces	6	5	3	4	1	11	30	153
	11	8	4	6	3	19	51	247
Between place:								
14–18. activities	1	1	1	2	—	8	13	26
19–20. channel spaces	1	—	2	1	1	4	9	28
	2	1	3	3	1	12	22	54

(ED)* in the area. There is however no reason to think that this biases the results as between Sub-regional and other levels of planning.

(iv) Land use, which is of paramount importance to other planning bodies, appears less dominant at Sub-regional level.

(v) Some Sub-regional studies seem to emphasise data collection much more than others. There is no clear indication why this is so and no obvious relationship can be seen between size of Sub-region and amount of data collected. Other factors such as size of budget and personalities involved are presumably more important. There is, however, some reason to believe that the nature of the area has some effect on data collection.

DATA SOURCES

For information on data sources we may again refer to Mrs. Cater's paper. Although her comments refer to use of statistics by planning bodies at various levels, by confining this examination to data which are of particular interest to Sub-regional studies we may draw some useful conclusions.

(i) *Industrial activity.* The most important source of information on industrial activity concerns employment. Employment Record II's† are the main employment statistics and are used by nearly 90% of all bodies visited by Mrs. Cater. Employment information from the Census is also widely used and many agencies collect data through their own special surveys. Unemployment and job vacancy statistics are also frequently held. On the other hand, data collected under the provisions of the Shops, Offices and Railway Premises Act and by the Factory Inspectorate are used by only a third and less than a fifth of bodies visited respectively. From these data sources, numbers employed and the industry breakdown are used by every-one visited and just over half have developed their own industry classifications in addition to the SIC. Full-time/part-time and self-employed data

---

* These are the smallest areas for which 1966 Census of Population data is available.

† Employment Record II's (ER II's) give numbers of employees (males and females separately), for 180 separate industrial categories or Minimum List Headings (MLH's) of the Standard Industrial Classification (SIC). These MLH's are also grouped into twenty-seven "Orders". ER II's relate to Employment Exchange areas which are defined with reference to journey to work patterns,

are used by a third, unemployment/vacancy statistics by three-quarters, and output and trip generation data by just over half.

(ii) *Land in all uses.* Most of these data are collected by special survey. Very broad categories tend to be used at Regional/Sub-regional levels, e.g. the Coventry/Solihull/War. team use ten categories and South Hants cover only shops, offices and factories, transport establishments and "other establishments". On the other hand, Teesplan data are very detailed indeed and they go "down virtually to MLH level for industrial use".

(iii) *Residential activity.* Principal sources are of course the Census of Population and the Registrar-General,* but over half of those bodies visited also make use of Medical Officer of Health† and special survey data. The electoral register is relatively unimportant, with only about a fifth using it. Items of interest to everyone are population and its age/sex characteristics. Other items, in descending order of importance, are car ownership, socio-economic groups, migration, consumer expenditure, occupations, household composition, marital status and trip generation. Fewer than half of those visited use birthplace data. This is also true of incomes, although here the explanation probably lies in non-availability rather than lack of interest.

(iv) *Housing.* Principal sources used are Census of Population (by everyone), land use and other special surveys, local authority housing records and the then Ministry of Housing and Local Government (MoHLG) quarterly returns. Less than half use rating records,‡ MoHLG local housing statistics, building surveyors, inspectors or architects' records, planning applications and Medical Officer of Health data. Variables of interest are mainly age, condition, amenities, size and site condition. Less than half use characteristics of tenure, rateable value, price and type.

(v) *Journey to work and movement networks.* Use of these data depends very much on the nature and extent of the team's involvement in mathematical modelling. The main published source is Census Workplace and

* The Registrar-General (RG) produces annual population estimates for Local Authority areas by adding recent births and subtracting deaths from Census figures.
† House Condition Surveys conducted by Public Health Inspectors; Slumclearance and House Improvement Statistics; Social and Demographic characteristics of people involved in Redevelopment and Overspill.
‡ Records maintained by Local Authorities for the collection of rates (local property based taxes).

Transport tables and Mrs. Cater notes that several of the authorities visited made special purchases of journey to work data between very small areas (parishes). Special surveys are the other main source but private industry sometimes has information.

AREAL UNITS

Many of the systems of interest to Sub-regional planners are spatial, consequently information must be stored so that any given item for different areas, or several items for a given area, can be easily combined and processed. Map presentation is, of course, often called for. It is important therefore that data be described with reference to location. Some believe it necessary to use code numbers that refer to the precise place (geocoding), others are content with the general area concerned (zoning). Cripps[16] recommends geocoding as having "the merits of performance universality, impartiality, uniformity . . .". Unlike Enumeration Districts, local government boundaries, and Employment Exchange areas, the National Grid does not change over time and Britain is fortunate in having a single grid system. Grid squares are "neutral" in that they are not defined with reference to land-use or population characteristics, and they are easily manipulated by computer.

Few planners would dispute that a data system based on co-ordinate grid references is to be desired and such systems have been made more feasible by the availability of co-ordinate referenced Census data for the first time for 1971. However, study teams recruited for a specific task over a limited period may find that to achieve a completely grid-based data system would leave insufficient time and/or manpower for other important stages of the planning process. Thus the Notts./Derby. study only gave grid references to employers' establishments and model zones were based on groupings of 1966 Census EDs. This gave quite enough flexibility for transport, shopping and activity allocation model purposes.

COMPUTER MODELS

We will be discussing the role of computer models in later chapters, but it is relevant here that their use seems to be changing in two ways. First, as more experience is gained in using an established model it may be possible to dispense with some of the more marginal parameters without significant loss of value in the output. Thus it is being argued that we need much simpler and less demanding models which can be run many times in evaluation and at frequent intervals in monitoring, rather than elaborate ones which are so demanding that they are rarely used. Second, as we shall see in Chapter 4, new models are being developed, notably to simulate change over time, and these must necessarily be more complex than the ones currently in general use.

Both of these changes have implications for data collection. The first will tend to reduce demand for some kind of data. In so far as cruder models are cheaper to set up and run, they will also be more widely used which will stimulate a demand for data banks in more authorities. The second will, of course, stimulate a demand for more information and particularly time series data.

GEOGRAPHICAL AREA

In defining the geographical area for which data are to be collected the Sub-regional planner must, of course, trade-off what he would wish to achieve in an ideal situation against his constraints of time, manpower and other resources. Perloff,[17] writing of "regional planning" (which is ". . . at a scale greater than a single community and less than a nation . . ."), goes so far as to assert that the whole nation should be covered in some detail:

> The information-analysis phase of regional planning can, and normally should, cover the total area of the nation (or of the multination region). This is particularly important in order to understand the evolving role of each activity, industrial sector, and area within the larger national scheme. Activity, sector and region are simply various categories in which to record the totality, each being a convenient way of describing the sub-systems involved. The inter-relationships of all these among themselves are important, as are the relations of each to the total.

We would not dispute this, and the need to see Sub-regional problems in a National and Regional perspective will be argued in later chapters. Obviously, however, the amount of detail which can be accumulated for other areas must be limited by manpower and other resources. Usually the best that can be done is to restrict detailed data collection as far as possible to the Sub-region and its immediately adjacent areas, but to recognise that for certain key topics a much broader view must be taken. The identification of what constitutes the broader view has often, in the past, been left to the "planner's culture". More recently, experience of using systems concepts in analysis has led to greater rigour in defining the spatial sub-systems of these key topics so that these areas, and a relevant level of disaggregation within them, have been used as a basis for data collection and analysis. Major advances in analysis and plan making are possible when such an approach is adopted.[18]

A great deal of duplicated effort might be saved by the exchange of data between Regions/Sub-regions for such purposes as input to transportation models, and this applies particularly to forecasts. Such an exchange might be encouraged, and perhaps organised, by central government. It presupposes the existence of a common approach to the problems of forecasting and here again central government might help by providing a set of economic forecasts at national level which planners could use as a background to their work. These might be along the lines of the 1964–70 National Plan forecasts, but covering the next two decades for broad categories of industry and perhaps making general comments about the period to the end of the century.*

CONFIDENTIALITY

We have looked at the problem of data collection primarily in terms of demand—the Sub-regional planner's need for information and what he chooses to collect. Finally we consider briefly one aspect of supply. At this point we are not concerned with important topics on which no information is collected—these will be mentioned in later chapters when we discuss the particular stages and operations at which such data is needed. Our concern here is with restrictions placed on the availability of data which have in fact been collected.

A considerable amount of data which does exist and is relevant for the Sub-regional planner is not available to him because of the problem called "confidentiality". This information usually refers to individuals and to firms. It is collected, usually by central government, under Acts of Parlia-

* The validity of the forecasts for medium- and long-term economic planning is not here being proposed. We are convinced, however, that such forecasting exercises are valuable for the planner in developing his speculative intelligence about the area of his study and the levels of uncertainty to which his plan must relate.

ment that guarantee the secrecy of the information and limit its availability to the government departments authorised to collect it. Its use could also be limited, by law, to the specific purpose for which it was collected. In Britain statistics on income, migration movements, the financial affairs of companies, employment statistics of firms, business turnover, input/output data and retail turnover are all restricted in various ways by confidentiality rules.

There is in addition the problem of national security and in areas of the country where many defence establishments are located this has, on occasions, prevented material that is normally available from being disseminated.

Much of the data that is subject to these statutory limitations can be made available by grouping information about individuals and firms into sufficiently large batches so that personal and business security is safeguarded. It is on this basis, for example, that census statistics are made available. But the Sub-regional planner has found it necessary to deal with very large numbers of very small groups because of the techniques he has to use, particularly because of his need to reassemble figures into many different zoning patterns (which requires that very detailed information be available as a prime source). Considerable assistance has been provided to him in this respect by the Government departments, but many believe that this assistance has not gone far enough. Progress is being made in some directions. The 1971 Census will be made available, subject to confidentiality rules, on a co-ordinate reference basis with a pattern of zones very much smaller than has hitherto been the case. On the other hand, the collection of employment statistics under the Statistics of Trade Act has recently imposed greater restrictions on the supply of this information.

The Sub-regional planner needs to take special care to ensure that his use of data does not infringe these confidentiality requirements. This can imply that material and types of analysis that he has been able to use may not be divulged to his clients and that he may not even reveal that he has sought and used certain methods of analysis. In evaluating the statistical viability of proposals contained in a Sub-regional plan the client would need to bear this in mind. For our purposes we would wish to investigate the extent to which the Sub-regional planner had negotiated access to essential information and used it efficiently and with discretion. The design of his data bank and a description of his operating routines is thus a very important field for inquiry.

CONCLUSIONS

Data collection goes on all through the Sub-regional planning process and may continue after the plan has been published for follow-up studies and monitoring. The significance of considering data at this stage is that the team must allocate manpower and plan the setting up of files and writing of programs very early if the data are to be available for analysis and forecasting, while the size of the resources involved mean that such decisions, once taken, are not easily reversed.

We have noted that the computer may not be cheaper than manual methods, but it has given the planner greater power than he has ever had before in analysis and, more recently, in exploring various plan alternatives. This in turn has led to demands for more data and finer levels of disaggregation for input to computer models. As these continue to develop demand for data is likely to continue to increase. Some of this demand will, no doubt, be satisfied by information from the Census which can be purchased on magnetic tape at a very disaggregated level. Other information will be collected from less accessible sources and perhaps special surveys. To the extent that this is necessary it will call for a high degree of efficiency in anticipating data needs correctly and being ruthless in eliminating items which are only marginally useful. The criterion for evaluation by the clients will therefore be the degree to which the stages of the planning process are aided and not constrained by the information services designed by the team.

CHAPTER 3

Analysis by Topics

THIS chapter and the next are concerned with preparing the ground for the generation of alternative sets of development policies or "strategies", that is, with the stages commonly known as "analysis" and "forecasting". The purpose of these operations is as follows:

Firstly, the team set out to understand the area as it exists and as it is evolving through time, in order to learn something of its problems and the kind of planning intervention which is needed. This will be particularly important where a study has been commissioned to foster co-operation between planning authorities in adjacent areas, because here there will be emphasis on a fresh and independent view of the area.

Secondly, topic studies of the kind described in this chapter are important in giving the dimensions of the strategy in terms of population, jobs, houses to be constructed and so on, and providing input data to the processes which will follow.

Thirdly, the analysis/forecasting stage must give the team indications as to how much room to manoeuvre exists for devising alternatives. This will be limited by physical obstacles to development, commitments which the sponsoring authorities have already accepted for the future, political constraints in terms of what is acceptable, and so on.

There is a great deal to discuss in all this, particularly so because for many years plans were based on survey and analysis alone, so that a lot of experience has been gained and some highly developed examples are available for discussion. Therefore what is essentially one stage in the plan-making process has been divided between two chapters. This one deals with the more familiar topic headings. The following one discusses attempts to simulate urban systems as a whole, develop overall indices of "potential" and forecast changes in society on a global scale.

In Chapter 2 it was seen that Sub-regional studies collect information about activities and behaviour and also, though to a lesser extent than Counties and Boroughs, about buildings, roads and land uses. The balance of the present chapter reflects this emphasis. The topics selected for discussion are population, industry and employment, mobility, housing, investment and resources, physical constraints and commitments. We emphasise that it is not our purpose to describe techniques, other texts[19] do this—but rather to illustrate the general approaches adopted for topic studies by various Sub-regional teams.

SELECTING A METHODOLOGY

In topic analysis, as with the plan-making process as a whole, it is necessary to select those techniques and data sources which are most appropriate to the problem in hand. Many teams produce technical notes in which the procedure to be adopted under each item is set out and discussed in some detail, both as a necessary mental discipline for the team itself and for the benefit of the sponsors of the Study. Some of the considerations which may be taken into account here are as follows:

The most important factor is the purpose of the Study, because the importance attached to each topic will vary according to the nature of the problem. A New Town study, for example, will be concerned with such questions as identifying a suitable site, the appropriate form of development, the impact of mass immigration on existing communities, resources needed and the way development should be phased over time. A co-ordination study, bringing together planning authorities in an established area, will be much more concerned with analysis of population and employment trends, quality of the existing housing stock, reconciling conflicts in existing policies and making proposals which will bring unity of purpose. A study in an area where pressure for economic growth is lacking will concentrate on ways of introducing new growth potential and exploiting whatever potential exists at present. Another in a prosperous area may simply ascertain from the Department of Trade and Industry how far it will be allowed to go in steering mobile industry within the area. A study which is simply concerned to assess the impact of major items of investment or to consider development in relation to investment thresholds may require only global population forecasts, but one which argues for social and welfare policies will need population figures detailed by age/sex groups and social class. Similarly, long-term proposals are likely to be much broader in outline than short-term policies on which detailed decisions are to be taken immediately.

The analysis/forecasting stage is important in supplying data for use in generating and evaluating alternative strategies. Thus the techniques which the team intends to use for generation/evaluation will be important: a cost–benefit analysis requires very disaggregated forecasts for example, and some traffic models are more demanding than others in terms of data input. The availability of forecasting techniques is also relevant. For example, nowadays it is often simpler to use a computerised cohort survival forecasting programme for population projections than to make crude manual extrapolations.

Demonstrating the strategy also leads to some problems in that some agencies need data in a different form for their internal evaluation of the Study recommendations than the team require for their own purposes. In Teesside, for instance, the team asked the Registrar-General to use his own forecasting model for the area, which had the satisfactory result that the estimates were not questioned by central government, but later the forecasts proved to be insufficiently detailed for implementation purposes.

Implementation agencies usually need more detailed figures than are necessary to define and demonstrate the strategy and the team must decide whether, and if so how far, to accommodate their needs. Some, indeed, may insist on forecasts disaggregated beyond the point where the team feel they have statistical validity, and they may be prepared to make their own guesses if the team refuse to co-operate. This kind of situation could arise, for example, if the financial implications of a strategy were being tested by accountants and valuers or if further transport modelling were needed to test the strategy in a critical part of the area. One point here is that assumptions made by the team are more likely to be realistic than those made by someone with less knowledge of the overall situation. Another is that it is not always possible to ensure estimates made for one purpose will not be used for another, so that the consequences may be unpredictable. Each situation must be judged on its merits, but the extent to which the policies so devised are likely to be harmful if the assumptions on which they are based prove inaccurate will clearly be a major consideration.

The team's primary aim in designing a project is to identify the role of the topic in terms of the total process and to ensure that the techniques and methodology are appropriate to that role. Once this has been achieved a trade-off can be made between other considerations such as what they would like for their own purposes given no constraints on time or man-power, what is desirable for demonstration purposes and the needs of implementation agencies. It is, of course, important that a topic study is no better than it needs to be!

TIME HORIZONS

The period of time to be covered may or may not be laid down in the Terms of Reference, but in either case it will be related to the purpose of the Study. For example, if the intention is to compare labour supply and demand in order to assess the likely extent of future unemployment and social hardship, there is likely to be a high degree of uncertainty. Thus studies produced by Economic Boards and Councils tend to produce employment forecasts for only 5 years or so ahead. In contrast, Co-ordination studies and New Town studies are concerned with fixed investment which has a long gestation period and a life of several decades thereafter, so that the recommendations they make involve commitment over long periods of time. In these cases it is desirable to take into account whatever information is available about the longer term future in coming to a deci-sion. This point will be discussed further under "Long-range Forecasting" in the next chapter. It is sufficient to note here that most studies cover a period related to the life cycles of major investment, which may be two, three or even four decades ahead. The degree of firmness with which recommendations are made will, of course, decrease the further ahead in time the strategy is pushed.

Efforts are now usually made to design strategies in such a way as to defer commitment in any direction until as late a date as possible, so that if circumstances change there is more scope for altering the strategy to meet these changes and less investment is wasted or under-used. A logical extension of this idea is the introduction of a monitoring system.

Within the plan period, the way in which items of investment are phased is important and the time lags between action taken and the effects of that action being felt may vary from one item of a plan to another. For this reason the Leicester/Leics. team give details of the way in which they expect their strategy to evolve at each 5-year stage through to 1991. The reasons for attempting this are strong ones, but more recent studies have argued that their forecasting processes are just not capable of producing staged plans with the necessary degree of accuracy, and they have opted rather for "single-shot" strategies.

Another consideration is the way in which resources flow for each item of the plan—whether allocations are made annually, quinquennially and so on. Some agencies may be able to cope with investment in 10-year gobbets of millions of pounds while others need to allocate cash, year by year, in myriads of relatively small amounts. A Sub-regional plan needs to be designed in such a way as to enable these various agencies to implement it. The Notts./Derby. Study, for example, outlines a single leap strategy to 1986 and follows this up with confidential reports giving advice and details for local areas on a year-by-year basis.

THE TOPICS
(i) *Population*

Present population structure is important for social and welfare policies and gives an indication of the potential of the area in terms of human resources. However, the techniques for presenting and analysing information about the present population structure and past and future changes are fairly well known.*[20, 21] We therefore concentrate here on a few examples of the way population forecasting has been treated by teams in different circumstances.

The major division is, of course, between Overspill/New Town studies on the one hand and Co-ordination studies on the other.

In the first group a target population may be laid down by the sponsors. The Central Borders Study, for example, looks at the possibility of accommodating 25,000 immigrants from Central Scotland by 1980 and Grangemouth/Falkirk are given a similar task with a target of 50,000. Other studies such as Severnside are asked to make their own assessment of how many people should be taken.

The second group are usually concerned with a "trend" type situation in which movement in or out of the area is only a small proportion of the total population. Once assumptions have been made about birth and death

* See, for example, The Lothians Regional Survey and Plan, discussed in Chapter 4.

rates, the natural increase of population can be calculated fairly simply, but assessing the likely scale of population movement gives rise to some problems. This may be related to forecasts of labour demand as in Teesside or Leicester/Leics., but labour demand forecasts are themselves subject to high levels of uncertainty. In Notts./Derby. the team feel that they have no basis for predicting a "trend" migration forecast because migration 1961–6 is so small as to be within the extraordinary margins of error of the 1966 sample census. In Coventry/Solihull/War. the team base estimates on information derived from consultations with the Census Office, the Department of the Environment and the West Midlands Study.

The degree of detailing of forecasts differs from area to area and with the Study purpose and its general nature. For example, Grangemouth/ Falkirk gives details of trend population and migration in 5-year age/sex groups for every 5-year period through to 2001. The uncertainty involved is acknowledged, but presumably the information is considered desirable for implementation purposes. In contrast Notts./Derby. publishes only total figures, rounded to the nearest thousand, for the terminal date of their strategy. In this case the intention to follow the Study with a monitoring procedure has reduced the pressure for more detail which might normally be expected from implementation authorities.

In no two studies was the treatment of population identical. Much of this variation was justifiable, reflecting the different problems and resources. But some was due to the predilections of the planners. This component of the variation needs careful assessment and clients should make comparisons between studies for this purpose. This is true of course for all the topics in a study and not just population analysis.

(ii) *Industry and employment*

This section is dealt with in more detail than the previous one because of the key importance of policy formulation that bears on national economic management. The relationship between the proposals of a Sub-regional plan and the economic policies of central government are widely recognised by Sub-regional planners as critical.

Economic forecasting is inevitably associated with a much higher degree of uncertainty than population forecasting, because levels are much quicker to respond to changing circumstances and may fluctuate widely even from month to month.

This point is well illustrated by Roy Gregory[22] when he describes a contest between an ironstone mining company wishing to mine unexploited reserves in Oxfordshire for the South Wales steel industry on the one hand and the County Planning Department and local conservation interests on the other. The latter argue that extensive areas of the County are already reserved for ironstone mining and, in any case, that the balance of both local and national advantage lies in favour of imported ores. During the course of the controversy, it emerges that the decision in favour of using Oxfordshire ores is backed by the Iron and Steel Board. This Board recommended some years previously that it was in the national interest that local ores should be used rather than imported ores. While this recommendation has stood for several years, however, the County is able to show that the balance of economic advantage has swung away from home ores: labour costs have risen sharply while shipping rates, high at the time the policy was laid down, have now fallen. In the end the conservationists are successful and the Oxfordshire reserves are not exploited.

Allocating resources on a grand scale in the light of purely short-term criteria can be full of pitfalls and one would normally expect to allow a very wide margin of error before taking decisions on such evidence alone. This lesson is valid in employment forecasting. Employment levels fluctuate a great deal with such factors as the season and central government policy, and forecasts are therefore subject to a high level of uncertainty. Moreover, this uncertainty is compounded when estimates of population have activity rates applied to them to produce "labour supply" which is compared with "labour demand" and the marginal difference between the two is put forward as an indication of congestion or social hardship which may be experienced in the future.

One purpose of employment analysis and forecasting is to give an indication of the economic health of the area and its parts and to identify any social and economic problems which are likely to arise. A number of well-known techniques are available for this sort of work and it is usually a question of selecting those which seem most appropriate to the team's purpose.

One which is perhaps worth singling out for discussion here is a measure of employment growth potential which has been used in the Glamorgan area[23] (see Fig. 3.1).

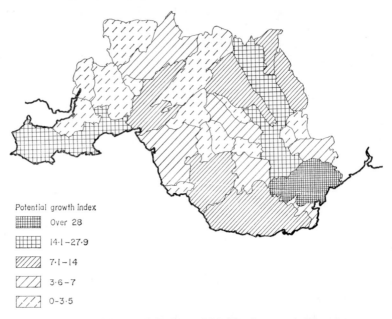

Potential growth index

▦ Over 28

▦ 14·1 – 27·9

▨ 7·1 – 14

▨ 3·6 – 7

▨ 0 – 3·5

Fig. 3.1. Potential Growth Indices—Male Employment in Manufacture, 1961. Glamorgan Area.

This index may be calculated using Employment Record II information in conjunction with a list of industries which are expected to expand their labour forces. Taking these growth industries in each local area, their employment is calculated (a) as a percentage of total employment in that area and (b) as a percentage of employment in growth industries in the Sub-region. The square root* of each is taken and the two multiplied together to give an index of growth potential.

This technique is not a substitute for rigorous analysis. It does not, for example, include any weighting according to whether fast or slow growth is expected in any particular industry. Some idea of the effects of different growth rates can, however, be obtained by producing several sets of indices based on (a) industries expected to grow 1% or more in a relevant period, (b) those likely to grow 5% or more, (c) those likely to grow 10% or more, and so on.

* Taking the square root reduces the influence of very large figures in the index.

This simple technique may be used in two ways. It can give a quick preliminary impression of the area which will serve as a background to subsequent, detailed analysis. Alternatively it may be used as a generalising technique to demonstrate the results of analysis. In the Glamorgan area it served the latter purpose and in fact proved more acceptable to lay opinion than industry by industry forecasts.

As well as indicating the economic health of the area, employment forecasting is needed to give the dimensions of the strategy in terms of total number of jobs at the terminal date and where these are likely to be located. This gives information not only about the location of land-uses, but about where people will wish to live (which is often related to where they work), the nature of movement in the area and so on.

It is useful to distinguish two different kinds of approach to employment forecasting proper, although we must emphasise that they are often used to supplement one another in practice. The first approach is more mechanical and usually far more economical in terms of cash and staff time than the second. It is the more commonly used of the two. It consists of identifying a relationship between Sub-regional and national trends in the past and extrapolating this into the future. The ratios derived in this way are then applied to national forecasts from some exogenous source to give forecasts for the Study area. However, the two national sources which have been habitually used—National Plan documents [24, 25] and Beckerman's forecasts to 1975[26]—are now outdated, and there seems to be no intention to produce any replacement, so that new methods may have to be developed in the near future. The second approach consists of a much more thorough analysis of trends and growth conditions in the area and is usually based on a survey of local industry. This is, of course, very expensive and time consuming and for this reason is less widely exploited than the first alternative.

We can now look at one or two examples of employment forecasting procedures and the role of forecasting in different studies. An example which belongs essentially to the first group is found in South Hants 1966. Here the team make use of the Base : Non-base concept although, of course, the concept itself can be used in adopting either of our two approaches. The Base : Non-base concept makes a distinction between industries and activities which are "basic" to an area in that they produce goods and services for sale in other areas, and activities which are "non-basic" in that they serve the needs of the resident population dependent on that basic industry. The South Hants team derive forecasts for basic industries from national forecasts by means of an "attraction factor", which is an equation relating past national and local employment trends. Having obtained a forecast of basic employment, dependent population is then estimated. The number of "non-basic" employees required to serve this dependent population is then calculated. These non-basic jobs support more population which in turn supports more non-basic jobs. Thus a number of iterations are necessary until the next addition of jobs/population become insignificant.

Like all forecasting methodologies the Base:Non-base approach has some serious limitations, but it can be useful in the right context. The relationship between population and non-basic employment has not remained very stable or changed at a reasonably constant rate over time, so that in areas where the level of population is fairly stable its use as a forecasting technique is not to be recommended. Where a major change in the level of population is anticipated, as in South Hants, the technique is more useful because the effect of population change on the level of non-basic employment is likely to be greater than that of unpredicted changes in the ratio.

Another example which involves relating local to national trends is Leicester/Leics.' use of the Ratio:Apportionment method. Here the ratios of regional to national employment are calculated for all of the Standard Regions over a past period and then extrapolated into the future to give ratios which may be applied to national forecasts. When the resulting forecasts for all Regions are added up, they do not equal the national total and they have to be made to do so by "apportioning" the difference between the Regions. At the end of this process, future estimates for the East Midlands Region have been achieved which are compatible both with national estimates and forecasts for other Regions. A similar exercise is then undertaken to break down the estimate for the Regions into Sub-regional totals and so produce forecasts for Leicester/Leics.

So far, however, estimates are for total employment only, whereas the Study requires a breakdown for eight groups of activities. Regional estimates for these groups are produced by means of two equations involving the above-mentioned "attraction factor" from the South Hants 1966. These equations are applied to national industry by industry forecasts from

Beckerman and South Hants 1966 and a set of forecasts are obtained for the East Midlands Region and subsequently for the Sub-region. Since these industry forecasts substantially exceed the previously obtained totals (which have been reconciled with forecasts for other parts of the country), there is another squeezing stage using a combination of pro-rata methods and the advice "of those knowledgeable about particular industries".

This approach is methodical and economical in time. It does not lead to a very rigorous examination of the local economy, but it is quite compatible with an hierarchical planning structure in which forecasts in the Sub-region must be made compatible with assumptions at regional and national levels. This is a valuable quality in demonstrating the strategy to central government departments. It is not, on the other hand, well equipped to deal with a situation where rapid change in the balance between Regions is likely to take place, or where some local change is prescribed and there is a need to find out how it should be brought about.

Neither South Hants 1966 nor Leicester/Leics. cover areas which appear to have major economic problems: the first is an area of great pressure for growth and the second appears to have quite sufficient growth potential taken as a whole. The next two examples are quite different, however: both are chosen as growth points to serve extensive economic problem areas, and it is therefore very important to assess the extent of existing growth potential and the way in which it can be exploited and built on. Both involve rigorous survey and analytical work on the existing industrial structure and use this as a basis for framing policies for the future.

The Impact on N.E. Lancs. Study has details of a very thorough survey of manufacturing industry in the area carried out by Economic Consultants Ltd. A summary of their approach to the survey is given in the following quotation:

> We interviewed firms with over 500 employees. In all cases we met either the managing director or a person responsible for the general management of the firm and in most cases the personnel manager was interviewed as well.
>
> We asked questions covering the general history of the firm, the type of products and the future policy of the firm. Where the firm was a branch of a national firm we asked about the way in which the plant fitted into the firm's national organisation, the degree of autonomy possessed by local management and the general advantages and disadvantages of North-east Lancashire as a location. If the firm had recently moved to the area the reasons for the move were discussed. Managers were also questioned on the degree to which the plant was flexible in making different products and what their future plans

were in terms of expansion or contraction of activity and diversification of products.

Personnel managers were asked about the skill composition of the labour force, the local supply of labour, and the firm's training programme amongst a large number of other questions.

All the firms interviewed were asked to fill out a copy of the questionnaire asking questions about the origin of raw materials and the destination of final output and the composition of the labour force. In addition to the firms interviewed all other manufacturing firms in the Study Area were sent a copy of the questionnaire which was produced in eight basic types with slightly varying format for different industrial groups.

This information is used to make forecasts of changes in demand for labour over the period studied, to assess the impact of the New Town on industry in the area and to suggest an industrial structure which would be appropriate to the New Town in terms of future growth potential.

Teesside report on three separate surveys of employers in their area. ES 1 covers all non-residential property and also hotels, hospitals and institutions and asks for information about products or activities of the establishment. ES 2 is a survey of all 250 manufacturing establishments with ten or more employees and involves six-page questionnaire. This covers production and employment, details of the site, services and facilities, transport and trade (including sources of supply, markets and mode of transport), expansion prospects and current problems, and recent movements by those firms who have established at their premises since 1950. Finally ES 3 covers the twenty-five largest establishments of warehousing, wholesaling and storage "surveyed in a simpler, though similar manner compared with form ES 2".

One purpose of the surveys is to establish the locational needs of industry in order that these can be catered for by urban structure policy, as part of a general policy of creating conditions in which growth can take place. The team identify three groups of industry as a result of this work, each group having quite different requirements. These three groups are described as follows:

(a) heavy capital intensive industry characteristic of the riverside, dependent on imported raw materials and reliant on rail and sea transport. Land uniquely suitable for these purposes must be reserved for their use;

(b) labour intensive industry located mainly on industrial estates, relying on road transport and employing relatively large numbers of workers, but otherwise flexible in their choice of location; and (c) storage and service industry which employ relatively small numbers and are pollution free.

Group (c) has two sub-groups, one based on heavy industry and needing to be located close to it and the other needing good road communications and a central position.

A second purpose is to establish the scale of future labour demand in the form of a set of industry by industry forecasts for the area as a whole to 1991. Here a decline of employment is predicted of some 9% taking into account two questions: firstly, the probability of individual establishments closing during the period and, secondly, predicting changes in those which remain open. The first operation is seen as the more reliable.

Thirdly, using Sub-regional control totals, estimates are produced for local areas by a very careful examination of local trends and commitments:

(a) the distribution for 1965 is measured as accurately as possible;

(b) the autonomous change in employment by 1991 whose future location is known is predicted. This includes:

  (i) changes in manufacturing and extractive employment in firms already on Teesside in 1965;

  (ii) changes in services employment associated with the redevelopment of older housing and new residential development whose location forms part of current planning policy;

(c) estimates are made of the changes in services employment likely to be associated with the additional residential development proposed as part of the urban structure policy;

(d) the future employment is forecast on industrial estates for which sites have already been selected and at least partly laid out with services, but on which industrial development had not yet started in September 1965; at Seal Sands, for central government offices and the proposed university;

(e) Finally, estimates are made of the future employment on additional industrial estates for which a location is recommended as part of urban structure policy.

Teesside was an expensive study, paid for half by central government, half by local. It was a pioneering work and some mistakes were made—promises of confidentiality to employers had the effect of depriving the team's successors of important information for example.

The limited availability of synthetic models at that time also led to collection of data on a scale which could usually be avoided nowadays.

However, these are the sorts of problems one would expect to arise when a team is breaking new ground. Teesside was a revolutionary study which has raised the whole level of Sub-regional work and the benefits derived from subsequent studies alone—Leicester/Leics., Notts./Derby., Coventry/ Solihull/War.—would probably have made the investment of well over £300,000 worth while.

Before concluding this section on employment analysis and forecasting it may be noted that while some of the most advanced and rigorous work to date has been carried out at this level, no Sub-regional examples are available of input:output analysis, which seems to the writers to have the greatest potential of all of the techniques available. This is not altogether due to a lack of data since one or two studies, at least, seem to have collected enough material to have made an attempt. More important perhaps is the possibility that no team has yet thought their area to be sufficiently self-contained for this sort of analysis to be realistic.

A lot of effort has been expended on employment forecasts by various Sub-regional teams and we have dealt with the subject at some length. We have seen how techniques used and the amount of effort involved have been related to the role of employment forecasts and their importance in the area concerned. Nevertheless this remains one of the least satisfactory areas of Sub-regional work and some problems seem insuperable. In the absence of national forecasts to draw the various Sub-regional and Local efforts together—and these do not seem to be forthcoming—the standard could even decline in future. A more promising line may simply be to accept the very high margin of uncertainty in the forecasts and concentrate more effort on using them in such a way as to minimise the adverse effects when errors materialise with the passing of time.

(iii) *Mobility of population and employment*

The extent to which both population and jobs are assumed to be mobile may be a critical factor in determining the range of land-use dispositions tested in Sub-regional planning, although jobs are usually taken as much the greater constraint. The limited degree of movement allowed by central government controls (Industrial Development Certificates) in the Coventry area, for example, has almost certainly influenced the Coventry/Solihull/ War. strategy.

Comparatively little research has been undertaken in this field and several teams have been obliged to do their own surveys. Notts./Derby., for example, recommended it as essential follow up work and a report has now been published by the Monitoring and Advisory Unit.[27] The work which has been undertaken suggests that planners' assumptions tend to be at or beyond the limit of mobility which has taken place in the past. Independent work by Barbara Smith,[28] for example, has recently cast doubts on the assumptions behind Birmingham overspill projects at places like Telford and Daventry. One wonders also how far South-east 1970 really demonstrated that sufficient mobile industry could escape the IDC net (certainly as it existed at the time) to allow dispersement on the scale recommended.

If a strategy was too optimistic in this respect the effects would depend to some extent on the location of the area and the pressure for development there. The chances of acceptance by central government would, however, be much reduced because a failure in implementation would almost certainly result in increased political pressure on the Department of Trade and Industry and IDC policy. Growing awareness of the critical nature of mobility for strategic planning will generate much more work in this field. Mobility of people and jobs has been inadequately treated in the studies examined and future clients will need to be satisfied that this defect does not persist.

(iv) *Housing*

In an established area where only a marginal change in population due to migration is expected, the treatment of housing as a topic will be quite different from a New Town study. In the former case there will be a large stock of existing housing in varying conditions and the team will probably wish to find out how much investment is needed to bring this up to a required standard and maintain it over time, as well as to cope with increasing demand for an expanding and increasingly wealthy population. In the latter case, they will be concerned mainly with new houses for incoming population and will therefore view housing primarily as a problem of obtaining and phasing new investment over time. This section therefore concentrates on examples which fall into the first category.

Housing is important because it is one of the most expensive items in a plan and because local government has a particular responsibility for maintaining an adequate supply of housing where the free market is not meeting whatever idea of need is accepted in the area. Thus when the sponsors ask what the strategy will cost, housing is likely to be one of the major items on the balance-sheet. Central government will need this information in making decisions as to how resources available for housing should be allocated between the different authorities. The authorities' own estimates are not a reliable guide, since they are compiled on the basis of widely differing standards.

Variations in the quality of the housing stock over the area may also have important implications for the strategy. For example, in the Notts./Derby. Study it is argued that persons leaving slum-clearance areas in Nottingham cannot be expected to live outside the city because their low incomes and job locations will not allow this. This has strategic implications in that these people, who are to be housed at lower densities than in the past, take up much of the land which the Study recommend for development on the north side of Nottingham. In Teesside it is found that slum-clearance areas near the river are valuable for industry and the likely date of clearance is of strategic importance.

A topic study of housing involves two different calculations: (1) to estimate housing need by looking at the structure of population and applying some accepted standard of housing provision to it; (2) to measure the size and quality of the present housing stock, the backlog of poor housing and what programmes of rehabilitation or clearance are needed. The second task is particularly time consuming if, as is usually the case, it is decided that an on-the-ground survey is needed, since even if the sample is very small it will inevitably involve many houses. These surveys, of course, vary widely in degree of detail: some teams make a detailed examination of each house in the sample using a building inspector, while others make little more than an assessment of residential environmental quality.

So far as housing need is concerned, an example which illustrates some of the problems involved is found in the Leicester/Leics. The standards on which these calculations are based lay down that all sharing households of two persons or more and a quarter of all one-person households need a separate dwelling.

The first question which arises is just how many "concealed households" exist, i.e. persons who, the standards say, should have a separate dwelling but are obliged to share at present? The ratios of actual households to all potential households are known as "headship rates" and these are essential to the calculation. Unfortunately the latest full census data available to the team (1961) gives ratios only for all population groups together, and this is not good enough because headship rates can vary widely between different groups. The team therefore go back to 1951, because for that year separate headship rates for individual age/sex/marital status groups were made available, and the ratios they derive are projected forward through 1961 to 1996.

Another problem is that the Study forecasting program gives age groups for males and females, but does not show marital status. Marital status information is, however, available for 1961 and ratios of married persons to total persons in each group are calculated and projected through to 1996.

Clearly the use of 1951 headship rates and 1961 marital status percentages for years as far ahead as 1996 builds in the possibility of a substantial error and in an attempt to overcome this problem the team introduce a "drift factor". This is produced by comparing the total number of households revealed in the 1961 census with the sum of the estimates for the various age–sex–marital status groups produced from 1951 data. A difference of $+0.9\%$ emerges for 1961. In 1951, of course, there was no discrepancy so that the calculations must have led to an error of $+0.9\%$ over a 10-year period. The error is then assumed to continue to increase at the rate of $+0.9\%$ every 10 years ($+0.45\%$ every 5 years) up to 1996 and the crude housing-demand forecasts are adjusted accordingly.

This process is carefully thought out and includes all of the factors the team consider to be really critical in determining housing need. The limited availability of statistics has imposed a certain amount of juggling with figures, but this is less serious than appears at first sight, since headship rates (based on 1951 data) have, in fact, remained remarkably stable over long periods of time.

It will have been noted that the term "housing need" has been used in the discussion and not "housing demand". This is because calculations usually include some measure of social provision: they are not so much based on a balance of market forces between those who can afford to buy their own house and the number of old and new houses being made available. Rather they reflect some generally acceptable idea of the number of people who ought to be provided with a dwelling, whether or not they can afford to buy. Such standards are, however, subject to change over time.

Acceptable minimum standards of house structures and environment also change and if surveys are not capable of disaggregation to enable estimates of obsolescent stock to be recalculated, their results may quickly become useless. Thus the Coventry/Solihull/War. team describe their approach:

> A systematic survey and analysis of the Sub-region's housing stock was required considering both the physical characteristics of dwellings and the quality of their environment. This analysis had to be framed to allow the consequences of differing and changing standards of physical and environmental fitness to be gauged, so that the survey did not become invalid as soon as there was a change in standards, in the availability of money for redevelopment, or when a new housing authority might take charge of the public building programme. The analysis was concerned with what it would make economic and social sense to retain.

An outline description of the survey and analysis of housing in the Coventry/Solihull/War. area is instructive here, since it builds on both Teesside and Leicester/Leics. experience:

> The sequence of the study was:
> (i) To survey dwellings on a sample basis looking at structural conditions and the local environment.
> (ii) To rate the surveyed dwellings on a penalty points system considering the cost of bringing both dwelling and environment up to a defined standard.
> (iii) To carry out a multiple regression analysis on the survey results in an attempt to relate condition penalty points to age of dwelling and rateable value. The ensuing simple model was then used to predict future housing conditions at the 5-year intervals of time for which clearance and rehabilitation were projected.
> (iv) To calculate the return on the cost of bringing dwellings up to the standard, and thereby gauge the point up to which rehabilitation was economic, but beyond which rebuilding would be the best investment.
> (v) To consequently produce a phased programme of clearance and rehabilitation based upon predicting housing conditions, defined standards and the financial calculation.

In this field of rehabilitation and demolition of houses there is ample scope for variation in standards. An apparently minor change in these may produce a substantial change in the number of dwellings defined as below-standard. Since changes in standards do occur over time and also with changes in political control, it is important (as the Coventry/Solihull/War. quotes imply) to so design housing surveys and store data as to enable the estimates to be recalculated easily. Changes such as the 1972 Housing Finance Act are also relevant here. So far as definition of standards is concerned, it has sometimes been found that quite minor improvements made to existing houses have produced large reductions in the number recognised as "sub-standard". Where this happens it is an indication that those who devised the standards have failed to distinguish the critical factors.

It could, perhaps, be argued that in view of the wide range of possible standards which operate between housing authorities and the fact that in any Sub-region there will be several authorities, housing surveys are unrealistic, even when they allow for alternative calculations based on different standards. Such an argument would point out that housing authorities are likely to be influenced by their own priorities as between different fields of action, their cash resources and the financial policies of central government, rather than by the condition of the housing stock in their district compared with others.

Thus it would not be possible to maintain an absolute policy in relation to housing standards at Sub-regional level. To find out how many houses will be cleared in a particular area would rather call for an examination of the decision-making complex of each housing authority, or a "black-box" approach, looking at past policies and extrapolating these into the future.

Against this it may be pointed out that where the demand for housing land in the Sub-region is substantially dependent on housing conditions, it becomes necessary for the demolition and improvement criteria adopted by the various housing authorities to be mutually acceptable. To achieve this it may prove necessary for an independent survey to be carried out by the Sub-regional team. In any case the quality of the housing stock will affect the strategy and the way land uses are disposed over the urbanised areas: whether residential land is converted to industry, whether special efforts should be made to induce growth and new wealth as a means of improving particular areas, and so on. Some idea of the cost of the options open to the sponsors must be obtained and housing is too big an item to be ignored. Also central government will require that the strategy be demonstrated to them and this will probably involve giving information about the housing stock. A Sub-regional team would also certainly wish to develop views as to how national resources should be channelled to the various housing authorities in the area. Finally, the housing authorities themselves might benefit from comparing their policies with an independent assessment of housing stock over their own and neighbouring areas.

During the decade which has seen the Sub-regional studies prepared there has been a great deal of progress in understanding housing and housing policy. At the present time new developments in understanding and techniques are occurring. It is to be expected therefore that later studies should have a different approach to the earlier ones and that all should show substantial shortcomings. Much good work has been carried out on measuring the size, quality and ageing of the housing stock, and much subtle analysis of demographic trends has led to the more realistic measurement of numbers and varieties of households. But no effective study has been mounted on the operations of the public and private housing markets. Only in Leicester/Leics. was housing information used as part of the simulation process. Perhaps work by Parry Lewis, who is currently leading the study of the Cambridge Sub-region, may make progress in these fields.[29]

(v) *Investment and resources*

Several teams have found that, for given standards of provision and population, the cost of providing infrastructure where no spare capacity exists at present does not vary substantially between outline strategies. Purely local site conditions are the critical determinants. This is argued in the following quote from Coventry/Solihull/War.:

> . . . the alternative strategies which emerged suggested that the costs and programming of education, welfare, library and similar services would not substantially differ between alternative strategies. It was not possible to prepare realistic plans for the siting of schools, clinics and other buildings for each strategy for the period up to 1991, when the cost of providing these services would be influenced primarily by local site conditions and scarcely at all by the general form of the strategy. We did not wish to present a specious evaluation of costs as between alternative strategies when within the preferred strategy they could be varied much more by moving a school, for example, from one side of a road to the other.

The way in which investment would have to flow through public and institutional agencies can have a bearing on the acceptability of particular solutions however. For example, New Towns need large units of investment in the early years and involve very long periods of deferred repayment and some spare capacity in utilities and services. Because of this a New Town appears to make a major call on national resources, rather than being a diversion of resources from alternative destinations. Harold Orlans[30] illustrates this point in relation to Stevenage, when he describes the controversy as to whether a New Town was feasible because it involved spending £2 million on a sewage works at an early stage in the development. Projects such as this are controversial because they involve large amounts of investment all at once and well in advance of a return being obtained. Incremental trend-type development, on the other hand, does not overload the system and involves much less commitment, in that it can be stopped or deferred at any time with less wasted investment. For these reasons New Town projects may be frowned upon by central government. Indeed the Notts./Derby. team were informally advised that money under the New Towns Act was most unlikely to be made available and this was taken into account in designing their strategy.

Humberside is another example of a strategy phased in the light of when investment funds might be made available, in this case for the estuary crossing. In more conventional situations, the Buchanan studies of Edinburgh, Bath and Cardiff offer high, low and no investment alternatives, because of the way financial constraints were operating at the time.

In terms of other resources, it was argued[31] at the Third London Airport inquiry that if Thurleigh were to go ahead and an airport city were planned, there would be insufficient manpower in the construction industry available in the region for this and the expansion programmes at Wellingborough, Milton Keynes, Northampton and Peterborough to proceed concurrently.

This section has touched on three different aspects of Investment and Resources: the comparison of costs of alternatives in Evaluation, the problem of channelling investment into the area in amounts which the implementation agencies can cope with, and the question of the share of the national investment cake which the Sub-region can expect to receive. This latter aspect also includes questions of the rate of growth of national resources in the future and differential rates of growth between the various headings: roads, housing, social services. These three different aspects partly account for the variety of ways in which the topic has been approached. All three have scope for further theoretical development.

(vi) *Physical constraints*

Physical constraints are tangible in the sense of being fairly easily identifiable, but they are difficult to quantify: when do we feel justified in building on grade one agricultural land for example? Attempts have been made to solve such problems in terms of value of annual production, but for most studies they remain a matter for qualitative judgement. Physical constraints may be thought of as falling into three groups:

(i) Those whose destruction would represent a serious and irreversible loss to the nation, such as sterilised mineral reserves, pollution of aquifers, building on good agricultural land, the destruction of beautiful landscape, nature reserves and land of ecological interest.

(ii) Those which would render life to people who live in the new development less pleasant than it might be elsewhere: atmospheric pollution, aircraft noise, windswept or fog-bound locations.

(iii) Those which render an area expensive to develop: floodland, watershed areas, steep slopes and the problems associated with thresholds.

Information will be readily available on many of these constraints, notably those which are resources to be protected, and this has simply to be collected from the appropriate agencies. Others are less well documented, however, and require special survey work.

Landscape quality is a useful example, because special surveys are usually necessary and these are expensive and involve value judgements which are difficult to make explicit. In order to cut down costs of landscape survey work, some teams confine themselves to analysis of Ordnance Survey map data. The East Anglia Consultative Committee,[32] for example, use 1 in.:mile O.S. maps and identify areas where (a) two, and (b) three or more of the following features coincide: hills, cliffs, dunes, heaths, woods, rivers/open water and various vertical features. The West Midlands Planning Authorities Conference have used $2\frac{1}{2}$-in. O.S. maps for: "The identification of the main physical criteria by which landscape can be judged and the definition of these. . . . The allocation of numerical ratings to the elements and components, the production of total scores to each 2 × 2-km square by computer programme and the mapping of the results of this evaluation by symap process."[33] The results of this process led to the identification of larger landscape areas with identical or very similar scores. On a much larger scale, the Landscape Research Group of Manchester University, sponsored by the Countryside Commission, are attempting to derive a National Countryside Classification Structure which can be applied over the whole country.

All such methods have a strong subjective element, if not incorporated into the survey itself, then built into the weighting of the selected variables.

Some would argue that they also make a serious omission and a classification can only be valid if it is related to demand, e.g. for leisure purposes, as well as the need to preserve. Thus in South-east 1970 an assessment of countryside resources (not a survey) from the point of view of demand and accessibility is made as follows:

> The team assessed the pressures on the region's countryside which the main population growth centres in the two strategies might be expected to exert. In addition, accessibilities between these different environmental resources were measured, although it was recognised that the results required careful interpretation in view of the conflict between the desirability of enabling as many people as possible to enjoy good environment and the need to preserve certain environments from over-crowding. The team concluded that increased pressures on the countryside were inevitable and that, in this respect, there was little to choose between the two strategies.

A study which looks at the countryside from the point of view of assessing the scope for increased exploitation is that of Donegal,[34] which is concerned with the development of tourism. This analyses prospects and potential for development of tourism and conducts surveys of natural and man-made resources to which capacities are assigned. A survey of visitors is also conducted and the varying levels of intensity of use which should be assumed in order to attract particular client groups is indicated. From this various policy options are put forward.

The majority of Sub-regional plans have been produced in what are almost "city-region" type situations, where one or more large urban settlement dominates the surrounding countryside. Some feel that in this sort of situation the needs of the countryside are given insufficient thought. For example, Gerald Smart[35] looks at the impact of urban development on the countryside in the Bournemouth/South Hampshire area and argues the need for long-term planning for the countryside:

> The countryside should not be regarded as a back cloth or a left over; its recreational resources are as important as urban leisure facilities and they require comparable management in the interests of conservation, its agriculture should be seen as a developing industry, with technological requirements which are not unlike those of urban industries, needing guidance, perhaps in the interests of its neighbours, but above all, freedom from uncertainty which can only come from long term planning.
> . . . I think it is absurd that we should still be applying widely a countryside planning philosophy which is based upon the assumption that rural areas will remain "for the most part undisturbed" and that villages will accommodate "local needs". The situation calls for positive, rather than defensive objectives which are likely to reach far beyond the traditional role of planning.

(vii) *Commitments*

A survey of existing commitments is an essential preliminary to the Sub-regional planning process and the extent to which the authorities are willing to abandon past policies must be ascertained at an early stage. The importance of this point is illustrated by the fact that the Teesside Interim Plan was substantially modified when information on committed land became available. Similarly, in terms of local feeling of commitment to long-standing policies, Hertfordshire protested strongly about the medium growth proposals for Bishops Stortford and these were later deleted from the 1970 South-east Region strategy.

Committed land may be substantial: in parts of Nottinghamshire for instance sufficient land was committed for residential development in 1968 (at the inception of the Notts./Derby. Study) for the period up to the year 2000. In the case of South-east 1970, commitment to existing development plans was such that no regional strategy proposals were acceptable for the period before 1981. This represents a serious problem for the planner: should additional land be allocated far in excess of what is required, but in accordance with the strategy, and thus make possible a mess of haphazard development, with buildings here and there as and when owners decide to sell. Alternatively, should one control supply in favour of a more "desirable" pattern of development? The policy decision which must be taken in such circumstances is one for elected representatives rather than for the planner, but this is the sort of critical implementation factor which the planner should seek to identify.

A team may find its room to manoeuvre very limited indeed. They may perhaps find no freedom of action at all in terms of alternative land-use patterns. In such circumstances they will be limited to commenting on issues like (a) priorities for development, (b) areas of special need for investment and whether this should be public or private or (c) publicity for particular problems—perhaps geared to influencing central-government distribution of industry policy or road programmes.

Central government departments have national policy commitments and these are well known, although the way in which these should be interpreted for a particular Sub-region may not be so clear. Several methods have been used to overcome this problem and in some cases joint discussion groups may be set up at which both sides can raise problems. In addition, limits are usually laid down for such things as job mobility assumptions which will be acceptable to the Department of Trade and Industry and the amount of investment which the Department of the Environment will allow for roads.

DEMONSTRATING THE STRATEGY

The team will usually have a considerable amount of planning experience at their disposal and it will be fairly clear to them what argument and data will be required by local government planning departments, to persuade them to accept the strategy and enable them to translate it into structure and local plans. The information needs of other agencies and interests may be less obvious, however, even though their co-operation may be no less vital to successful implementation. This applies particularly to central government.

Central government policies are national and recognise a need for special assistance to particular, underprivileged areas. They are concerned with the allocation of resources between different parts of the country. Thus if a team make recommendations which imply a diversion of money, jobs, etc., to their area and, by implication, away from some other place, the case must be presented in a form which is acceptable and understood by central government. Such an argument might have to be conducted in terms of discount rates, marginal costs, the gap between the strategy and what might be expected under a free-play of market forces and so on. This seems to us to be a particularly important point because, as plan generation and evaluation techniques have become more complex and to some degree more esoteric, we suspect that there may have been a widening gap between central government and Sub-regional thinking in recent years. This problem may be partially overcome if the Department of the Environment model terms of reference are followed as in Leicester/Leics. Another solution is, of course, a joint central:local government team as in the South-east 1970 and North Glos. The team may also demonstrate that their strategy does not involve calling on national resources to any greater extent than would have been necessary for the area in any event, as, for example, in Leicester/Leics.

Lastly, the team need to attune themselves to attitudes of other agencies, interest groups and the population generally in the area in order to try to identify sensitive issues which are likely to arouse strong opposition. In some cases, of course, the whole project may be doomed to failure from the outset, because of the impossibility of convincing local interests that their sacrifice is necessary and just. Of interest here are the Ipswich town-expansion proposals and the study which followed it. Neither of these were entirely successful in convincing the local farming community as to the desirability of expanding the town in the recommended direction. The Stanstead airport proposals are, of course, a further example.

CONCLUSIONS

This chapter has considered some of the more usual topic studies which are expected to be undertaken by a Sub-regional team. Topic studies as we have described them should enable the team to establish a preliminary understanding of the area, to check that their sponsors' views of its problems are well founded, and to begin to develop criteria for plan generation. They should establish the main quantities of population and employment which will determine the scale of the strategy and provide necessary input to models, and evaluation techniques.

The team will also begin to assess how much room to manoeuvre exists in devising alternative strategies for testing, in terms of physical, social and economic constraints, political and public attitudes and commitments. They will also consider the sorts of organisations concerned in implementation, to decide what sort of information they will need in order to implement the strategy and what sort of arguments must be put forward to convince them that they should do so. Much of this, of course, does not depend on formal analytical work and it is in these highly critical areas that the quality of the team leadership is so very important.

So far as the technical process is concerned, we have shown that there are a number of ways of carrying out the analysis and forecasting work involved under each topic and we have not tried to identify a "best set" of techniques appropriate for all occasions. This would be neither desirable nor realistic. We have argued, however, that the methodology should be selected in relation to the role of each topic study in the planning process as a whole and that the techniques adopted should be appropriate to the particular roles they have to play.

Much more needs to be said about "analysis", however, because so far we have looked only at individual topics. The next chapter is concerned with the way in which the urban system(s) as a whole is treated.

CHAPTER 4

The Impact of New Techniques on the Analysis Stage

SUB-REGIONAL planning has been evolving rapidly over the last few years and this is certainly true of the analysis/forecasting stage. The familiar topic analysis is still with us, but its role is changing and it is no longer seen as an adequate base, in itself, for a Sub-regional plan. New techniques have appeared as a result of the application of systems thinking and these are more powerful than the traditional methods. It is also usual to "calibrate" these computer models, i.e. to require that they demonstrate an ability to reproduce the existing situation before use for other purposes. This is a more rigorous test than has been applied to many of the traditional analytical methods. We have therefore devoted a whole chapter to discussing a few of these systems-based techniques and indicating some of the ways in which Sub-regional planning has been changed and improved as a result of their application.

The techniques we have elected to discuss have by no means been applied only at the "analysis" stage and, indeed, many will be surprised to find them in this chapter rather than in, say, "Strategy Generation". However, it seems to us that these techniques, and the systems concepts which lie behind them, are contributing much to Sub-regional understanding and the present discussion of "analysis" would be incomplete without some reference to them. We do not, of course, claim that any of the techniques receives comprehensive treatment—since we have set out to take a synoptic view of a very wide field, that would be inappropriate. In addition, it may seem to the specialist that some models of high technical merit receive scant attention while others are treated generously. This is because we have been concerned only to illustrate points which are relevant to our overall purpose. A fair and balanced evaluation of individual computer models we leave to others.

We have already discussed various topics which figure prominently in analysis. Before going on to consider changes which are now taking place, it is useful to take one example of the role these topics have played in the traditional Sub-regional planning process.

THE TRADITIONAL ROLE OF ANALYSIS

The Lothians Regional Survey and Plan is one of the most thorough surveys and analyses ever undertaken at the Sub-regional scale and it is presented as something of a demonstration study. Thus Professor Robertson writes in the first volume:

> We take the view that this Volume should, if we have done our job well, be of interest and value to those who are concerned with, or interested in regional development and the planning of areas quite apart from Central Scotland. Apart from what we have to say on each topic, we suggest that there may be interest and guidance to be found in examining our choice of topics and our method of discussion. We have provided one answer to the question—what can social scientists say in a practical way about planning problems. We have also illustrated the issues that arise in practice in implementing a policy of regional development.

The Study covers part of the Central Lowlands of Scotland lying west of Edinburgh and centred on the New Town of Livingston. Although commissioned before the publication of the 1963 White Paper,[36] it is concerned with one of the Scottish Development Department's recommended growth areas and is ratified by them.

The work is divided clearly into two parts, which are presented in separate volumes. One volume is concerned with economic and social aspects and is by a team from the University of Glasgow, headed by Professor D. J. Robertson. The other volume deals with physical planning aspects and is by a team from the University of Edinburgh led by Professor Sir Robert Matthew.

Volume I, "Economic and Social Aspects", is divided into two sections. One is concerned with analysis, technical appendices and data tables and takes up 238 of the 289 pages. The other, in which the conclusions are set out and social and economic policies put forward, takes up only 38 pages. In the analysis, a long list of topics is covered and each topic is handled by a different, named, member of the team. The diligence with which the topic analysis was persued is indicated by 182 statistical tables.

Volume II, "Physical Planning Aspects", takes target population figures derived from volume I and relates them to physical conditions in the area "so that the Regional Plan can be evolved". Again the thoroughness of the work is indicated by the length of the volume, 360 pages in all. After a preamble, there are thirteen chapters covering the following topics: geology, relief and climate; historic, architectural and scientific interests; agriculture; forestry; mining and subsidence; rehabilitation and conservation; population and housing; industry; community services; utility services; communications; recreation; urban settlements and landscape studies. Each makes policy recommendations and these are brought together at the end of the volume to form a preferred strategy.

It would now be generally accepted that topics cannot be treated in watertight compartments in this way. Action taken in one policy area can seem perfectly acceptable while having harmful side effects which prevent the achievement of more important objectives in other fields. Consequently over the last decade there has been a growing awareness of the need, at various stages, to bring topics together and consider the way they interact together. One informal way of tackling this problem is the Consensus Method.

THE CONSENSUS METHOD

This method has been exploited widely by the Economic Planning Boards and Councils in producing their Regional Economic Reviews and Strategies and in their Sub-regional work. It operates in the following way: civil servants of the Research Officer level* prepare descriptive/analytical documents on the area concerned, from the point of view of their particular specialisations (employment—Department of Employment; trade and industry—Department of Trade and Industry; population, housing and roads—Department of the Environment, and so on). These are discussed and amended by a Research Group comprising the authors of the various papers, under the chairmanship of a senior research officer who will probably be from the Department of the Environment. Thus the analysis and conclusions on each paper are subject to scrutiny by several different disciplines and interests. Gradually a consensus view of the area, its problems and likely solutions begins to emerge. The revised document(s) is then referred to a steering group which comprises civil servants of the

* This may vary somewhat from area to area and Department to Department.

senior research-officer level and a similar process of discussion and dissection ensues.

This is followed by reference upwards once again to the Economic Planning Board which comprises persons at Regional Controller level from all the interested civil service Departments in the Region. Again there is discussion and amendment and, if necessary, reference back for redrafting. The draft is then passed to the Economic Planning Council for consideration by eminent men and women of the Region with varying experience and backgrounds and once again there is discussion, amendment and redrafting until a strategy (or alternative strategies) is fully agreed. During this stage, there will be consultations with various other interested parties, particularly the statutory planning authorities, before agreement is finally reached on a document which can be published.

This procedure has distinct advantages and round-table discussions have an important part to play in planning generally. Debate gives rise to a clearer understanding of problems, enables contradictions to be ironed out and allows cross-fertilisation of ideas, including those of non-planners.

This sort of approach was adopted in the Halifax/Calder Valley, which is a study in detail of an area with problems which are typical of those confronting much of West Yorkshire and the higher Pennine Valleys. In addition to the plan-process adopted, this Study is interesting because it ends with an "Assessment and Pointers to the Future" which is in effect an evaluation of the trend situation in the area. There are four main headings in the table: (a) Human Resources, (b) Employment, (c) Environment and Building Stock, and (d) Land Availability, Urban Structure and Locational Potential. Under these are arranged twenty-nine sub-headings. Against each of these an assessment rating of high, medium/high, medium, medium/low or low is recorded. The reasons for each rating are set out in the text and the results are brought together in the form of a discussion.

The Consensus Method was well suited to the Economic Planning Boards and Councils at the time it was adopted, in terms of fully exploiting the expertise and experience available to them. On the other hand, Stafford Beer[37] points out that the striking of consensus may be a prudent technique which protects us from lunatics, but it also suppresses ideas which lie beyond the experience of the consensus and these may well be what are needed. The ability of the human mind to assess complex situations quantitatively, especially where problems of probability arise, is very limited, although we do not realise it: "It is astonishing but true that almost any scientific model, however exiguous and crude, quickly surpasses the capability of the brain to evaluate a complex situation in quantitative terms."

We get a subjective illusion of coping only by our "organisational refusal to consider more than a tiny part of the problem at once".

This introduces us to a body of theory which has demonstrated the inadequacy of topic analysis and the shortcomings of the Consensus Method of relating them together.

SYSTEMS THEORY

One of the reasons why Sub-regional planning is moving beyond topic analysis and the Consensus Method is the influence of systems thinking on the profession. The flexibility of Sub-regional planning procedures and the fact that techniques based on systems concepts were readily applied at this level brought about an earlier change here than in other areas of planning.

Systems thinking has demonstrated the unreality of looking in more or less watertight compartments at things which are mutually dependent and interacting. This point is illustrated by Jay W. Forrester[38] in his book *Urban Dynamics*, and it is useful to consider his argument here.

Forrester explains that intuition may be adequate in identifying causes of problems and suggesting solutions when dealing with very simple systems. However, in the case of complex systems, of the sort which confront the Urban and Sub-regional planner, the intuitively obvious solution is often ineffective and may be actually harmful:

> But in complex systems cause and effect are often not closely related in either time or space. . . . In the complex system the cause of a difficulty may lie far back in time from the symptoms, or in a completely different and remote part of the system. In fact, causes are usually found, not in prior events, but in the structure and policies of the system.
>
> To make matters still worse, the complex system is even more deceptive than merely hiding causes. In the complex system, when we look for a cause near in time and space to a symptom, we usually find what appears to be a plausible cause. But it is usually not the cause. The complex system presents apparent causes that are in fact coincident symptoms. The high degree of time correlation between variables in complex systems can lead us to make cause-and-effect associations between variables that are simply moving together as

part of the total dynamic behaviour of the system. Conditioned by our training in simple systems, we apply the same intuition to complex systems and are led into error. As a result we treat symptoms, not causes. The outcome lies between ineffective and detrimental.

Forrester is particularly concerned with the problems of the "inner core" of the present-day city. His book describes the operation of a computer model which starts with an area of undeveloped land and generates a life cycle of urban development on it, beginning with a period of vigorous growth over the first hundred years of the 250-year period and ending with stagnation and decline. A variation on this model starts when equilibrium is reached at the end of the century of growth and is used to explore how various changes in policy would cause the urban area to be altered in the next 50 years.

We do not necessarily imply that the assumptions on which this particular model is based are reasonable[39,40] and many would argue that the work of Hamilton *et al.*[41] on the Susquehanna River Basin project is technically more satisfactory. We do, however, find the relevance of systems thinking to community management in the planning field exciting and in this context it is useful to outline, briefly, some of Forrester's findings.

In the growth phase, industry has a high degree of intensity and employment per unit of industrial land is also high. Housing is constructed for those in the expanding and prosperous industries, at low densities. As the stock of buildings and investment ages, natural vitality declines; new industry starts up elsewhere and employment per unit of industrial land declines because, although industry is less buoyant, the stock of industrial buildings remains. At the same time as the stock of housing grows older, rent costs fall; people who can only afford to pay low rents move in and densities increase. The model is used to examine different policies which have been used to combat this kind of problem situation. The description of the effects of these policies is in terms of effects on three broad population groups: managerial-professional, labour and under-employed.

One policy is to increase the amount of low-cost housing in the area. This brings in "under-employed" people and the level of this group rises for a time and then falls back as the number of jobs decreases because industry is leaving the area. "Labour" falls substantially and the population mix is altered. The pressure on land for housebuilding makes the area less attractive for businesses, causing decline in this sector. Also, since the labour population is falling, the area becomes less attractive for industry and the number of jobs falls.

An alternative policy involves demolition of some of the housing for the under-employed and the encouragement of new business enterprise in an attempt to revitalise the area. This has the effect of inducing employment growth and attracting labour population so that the under-employed:labour ratio improves and the area becomes more attractive generally. Forrester argues that, while one might think such a policy would be detrimental to the under-employed group, this is not so because the drop in numbers under-employed is due primarily to their conversion into "labour" rather than to their exclusion from the area. Moreover, inward movement is kept in reasonable balance with the employment opportunities available.

Michael Batty[42] criticises Forrester on the grounds that he ignores the spatial component of the city and, more important, for the way in which the various hypotheses (many unverified and probably unverifiable) are linked. On the other hand Forrester does tackle the problems of time-lag.

Batty quotes Chorley and Kennedy,[43] who point out that a major feature of system behaviour is relaxation time: the time taken for a system to adapt to exogenous inputs and return to a steady state. Major problems arise where relaxation times of systems are difficult—if not impossible—to observe, and this is particularly likely with urban systems. This has led to modelling of the structure of urban systems rather than their behaviour, so that very few models exist which attempt to simulate the dynamics of urban systems. Most models simply represent the structure of urban systems at one cross-section in time, without recourse to any explanation of the changes in structure over time which constitute system behaviour.

Nevertheless static models do involve some implicit measure of system behaviour: because they attempt to explain the location of urban activities, measures of locational attraction are fundamental to them. Most of these measures in effect average the locational attraction of the system over its past history. These measures Batty considers quite unsuitable for forecasting with such models. Indeed, the truth is probably that system structure cannot be modelled separately from system behaviour.

In spite of the problems involved in developing dynamic urban models, significant advances are being made and we are likely to see practical planning applications in the fairly near future. These are to be welcomed.

Continuing the policy adopted for this book of quoting liberally from existing Sub-regional examples, however, we must now turn to the more familiar static Lowry model.

ACTIVITY ALLOCATION MODELS

We have opened the discussion on the influence of systems thinking by referring to Forrester's work, but this has not yet become a practical tool. The first methods to prove effective have been the Activity Allocation models and these have had a greater impact on planning to date. These models are steadily increasing in popularity but they are not perhaps familiar to everyone, and a brief and very simple description of how the most common, Lowry, version works may be useful here.

Activity Allocation models are based on the idea that where people live will be related to where they work and how far they are prepared to travel to work. Two kinds of employment are recognised: in basic industries which serve the needs of national and international trade and are locationally independent of the area, and in non-basic industries which serve the needs of the local resident population and whose location is determined by the distribution of that population over the area. Given a distribution of basic employment over the area and a measure of impedence (distance, travel time or cost) between the various zones, the model uses observed relationships between numbers of workers travelling and the distance they travel to allocate amongst the zones the residential population (i.e. workers and their families) who are dependent on those basic industries. Given a distribution of resident population, it then works out the numbers and locations of non-basic jobs which serve that population: some non-basic jobs located in the same zones as the population served, others are generated in various service centres. These non-basic jobs, of course, give rise to more dependent population which is allocated over the area. This population gives rise to more non-basic jobs and thus more population and so on, so that a number of iterations are necessary.

Clearly, however, it would be unrealistic to suppose that all zones can take as much population and employment as would wish to locate there—some will be fully built up, others will be protected by such planning devices as green belt. It is therefore necessary to introduce constraints into the model to prevent more than a predetermined level of new development from taking place in those zones where it is felt necessary or desirable to impose some limit. The way in which these constraints are introduced varies from model to model and this is the principal difference between the original formulation and the more sophisticated Garin–Lowry version.

Although mathematical models have only been in use, even in the United States, for a decade and a half, the way in which they are used has changed a great deal over this time and it is useful here to refer to American experience. The quote is from Alonso:[44]

> A decade ago . . . models were viewed primarily as predictors of the future. Somewhat later, stress was placed on their use as conditional predictors of the consequences of alternative policies, and efforts were made to incorporate into them policy variables which would permit such experimentation. Most recently, as experience has been gained, the practitioners of this craft have tended to play down the ability of the models to predict and to stress their value as educational instruments which serve to bring to the consciousness of those who make decisions the complex inter-relationships among the variables, including those which can be manipulated for normative purposes. . . . The large model may serve as a context or evolving background for a collection of more partial and overlapping quantitative models and for that vast reservoir of knowledge about the urban system which inhabits the heads of experienced men and which has yet to find its way into formal models.

Having set the scene, it is now appropriate to refer to an example of the way in which an Activity Allocation model has been used in this country. The example is from the South Hampshire Structure Plan, taken from a paper by I. Caulfield and T. Rhodes,[45] and although its use in this instance is not Sub-regional, the procedures adopted are very similar to those of Sub-regional teams. The Activity Allocation model is used in conjunction with a "Regional Growth Model" which projects the population and basic employment needed as input and a "Transportation Model" which estimates the likely pattern of transport movements. The role of the Activity Allocation model in the Structure planning process and the way it was used are described as follows:

> The model played two important parts; it first acted as a learning device for exploring the likely impact of particular planning proposals on the urban system; second it produced the ultimate allocations of urban activities (through an iterative process of modifications and constraints) which were used either as the basis for evaluation of alternative development strategies, or as the ultimate description of the urban system stemming from the application of the Structure Plan's policies and proposals.
>
> The use of the model in this way involvd three basic steps which are outlined below, followed by a series of examples:
>
> (i) The formulation of a sketch set of planning proposals indicating in broad

strategic terms the envisaged pattern of change in the main urban activities of the area. This sketch emerged from the interrelation (via planning criteria) of a partial set of objectives and was described in terms of the location of new "basic" jobs, the existing and proposed transport network (presented as an inter-zonal travel time matrix), major countryside recreation areas, and land unavailable for development following the application of overriding objectives. In this context, the paramount importance accorded to conservation of areas of resource value saw an embargo placed on development on for example the Downs and Grade I agricultural land.

(ii) The response of the urban system to these sketch proposals (together with commitments to future development already entered into) was then simulated through their interrelation with the framework of planning assumptions and criteria embodied in the Activities Allocation model. The reaction of the urban system was presented as a quantified set of conditional projections of urban change.

(iii) These local area projections were then evaluated against the planning criteria representing the objectives not so far embraced by the model framework. This action pinpointed the conflicts between planning objectives which were subsequently reconciled through a process of explicit compromise. As a result, the procedure was repeated to amend the strategy either *positively* through direct changes to the initial set of sketch proposals (for job location or transport links) or *negatively* through the enforcement of objectives by more widespread constraints upon land development.

South Hampshire used the Lowry model for two purposes. We would applaud its adoption as a learning device while questioning its role in forecasting. The use of the model to provide predictions of more or less precise quantities depends on its being a good model of the system, producing predictions of proven worth. But this has not yet been achieved, despite the many refinements that are sometimes used. Indeed the refinements often so modify the nature of the model that its operation becomes quite unlike that for which it was originally selected. The Lowry model is a very crude representation of reality and should not be used as though this was not so. It does some things very well, but prediction is not one of them. In our view the use of its power to relate things together should be confined to exploring the planner's understanding of the area.

POTENTIAL SURFACES

Another technique to be developed under the influence of systems theory is the Potential Surface, devised by Notts./Derby. The background to this development is given by William Murray:[46]

Strategy generation and testing developed as a learning process with major scalar shifts in thinking as it progressed. That is to say, we began with a macro analysis of the Sub-region as a whole, and refined this in terms of the level of detail of the characteristics, and in spatial terms.

The cybernetic underpinning of such an approach is Ashby's "Law of Requisite Variety" which, as Chadwick has explained, "demands that models of low variety must be tested against criteria of the same variety—high variety factors may be useful to test high variety sub-system models, but not for low variety overall regional models—only regional goals are appropriate to regional models". Stafford Beer's concept of the "cones of resolution" is perhaps easier to grasp. This suggests that the parts, or cones, of a model need only be resolved in detail, i.e. down from the vertex, to such a degree that the detail is essential to the operation of the whole model.

We therefore reviewed the strategy generation and testing process in total and found that, although several tools were available for examining the relative merits of quite high variety strategies, the initial evaluation of a serious range of region-wide alternatives was a much less-developed field, and we could find no readily available means of satisfactorily evaluating quite extreme alternatives against each other. . . .

The requirements of the (Potential Surface) were that it should incorporate dimensions of (1) within, and (2) between place characteristics over (3) time. One strength of the tool is that it incorporates many spatial characteristics, such as environmental quality, and others which are significant in assessing potential, which are as yet operationally underdeveloped in inter-actence models. A great weakness, however, is that it takes only a static view of both space and time, that is to say it does not simulate interaction in these dimensions and treats them in a snapshot rather than a dynamic process way. Model builders have successfully simulated dynamic spatial interaction and this could theoretically have been incorporated in the Potential Surface. We decided instead to use the spatially dynamic Lowry model in parallel with this static but multi-element tool and in both cases treated time as a series of incremental but static situations. In this way we hoped to examine the same problems from different angles, and thus learn from the different but overlapping advice they offered.

The construction of the tool owed much to Chadwick's Meta Procedure, which we describe in the context of Batty's Central Lancashire project in Chapter 5. The team began with the list of Study objectives expressed in very general terms, and examined these for "factors" which had land-use implications. The factors were then compared and some were considered to be related strongly, some weakly and others not at all. Taking only the strong relationships, a linear graph was produced (for Batty's, similar, linear graph see Fig. 5.1), which suggested groupings of factors and arranged these groups into an hierarchy. Not surprisingly, three very broad groupings emerged concerned with economic, social and physical factors. As one would expect, however, physical factors were found to be relevant at a different level from economic and social ones. This manifested itself particularly in a dilemma over the size of zones which should be used in applying the technique: the social and economic factors were capable of being dealt with by much coarser zones than the physical factors. Consequently, in opting for a coarse pattern of 48 units (about 100 square kilometres each), the team effectively eliminated physical factors from the index: the physical variations within any zone were so great that no significant differences between zones could be picked up. Other ways of coping with these physical factors were introduced into the plan-making process, but this was at a later stage.*

In computing index values for each zone it was not meaningful to take account only of measures within the zone itself. It was necessary also to include opportunities in nearby zones (using, of course, an appropriate decay function with distance from the zone). This was done manually because insufficient funds and time were available to develop the necessary computer programs. The method adopted was similar to the calculation of the gravity measure of population potential,[47] hence the name Potential Surface. Index values for each zone were calculated separately for each of the twelve indices listed in Table 4.1. These were also weighted and the weighted values added together to produce composite indices. Weightings "were determined largely by group consensus, although quite strenuous, but largely unsuccessful, efforts were made to find more quantitative bases for relative weightings" (Murray).

In addition to the positive indices, an inverse potential surface was derived by dividing the shortfall on the maximum possible score for each zone by the zonal population.

Index values were calculated for the base date, 1966, and for 1976 and 1986.

In setting up the potential surface it was found that variations in weightings in all but two of the factors produced similar results. This consistency aided plan generation. The two factors "population quality" and "urban and rural environment" were always inconsistent with the rest, but in order to materially affect the overall result they would have had to be

---

* Note here that the recognition of an hierarchical arrangement of factors does not necessarily imply an order of importance in terms of planning policy: decision-takers might well decide that the physical environment is more important than social and economic factors. It does, however, imply something about which factors should be considered together and which separately.

considered at least ten times more important than was thought. Nevertheless in devising strategies the team were careful to allocate some development in locations where the response of these two factors could be most satisfactorily coped with, should society's values change in this direction.

TABLE 4.1. NOTTS./DERBY. POTENTIAL SURFACE INDICES
(Extract from Record Report 38)
Method of calculation

I. *Index of Economic Potential*
   1. *Job potential.* Employment growth potential is calculated by expressing employment in growth industries in each zone as a percentage of the total employment in each zone and of the total employment in the Sub-region. The square roots of the two percentages are then multiplied together to derive an index.
   2. *Labour pool.* This is calculated by relating the population within each zone and adjoining areas with its relative distance from the zone centroid by means of a work-trip curve.
   3. *Communications.* This index is calculated by determining the relative importance of major communications facilities, e.g. motorway access points, railway stations and depots, airports, etc., in terms of the volume of traffic handled and the nature of the facility, and dividing the values thus obtained by the distance from each zone centroid.
   4. *Servicing.* This index is calculated by determining the service employment in each centre in relation to its distance from individual zone centroids.
   5. *Social potential.* This index is derived directly from the total for Section II, below.

II. *Index of Social Potential*
   6. *Population potential.* This index is calculated by applying correction factors, derived from the "PROP" Population forecasting program, to the total population for each zone.
   7. *Job pool.* This index is calculated by relating employment within each zone and adjacent areas with its distance from the zone centroid, by means of a work-trip curve.
   8. *Population quality.* This is calculated by determining the professional and managerial population of each zone as a percentage of the total zonal population.
   9. *Social interaction.* This index is calculated in the same way as Index 2 above.
   10. *Retail.* This index is calculated by determining the turnover for each centre and dividing the values thus obtained by the distance from each zone centroid.
   11. *Urban and rural environment.* The quality of the environment is determined by reference to survey work undertaken by the Unit, taking account of such elements as site, built features and identity, housing, conservation, air pollution and dereliction, areas of special landscape value, etc.
   12. *Communications.* This index is calculated in a similar way to Index 3 above.

It should be noted that the nature of the output from the Notts./Derby. Potential Surface was not dependent on the precise definition of objectives.

Any set including economic and social considerations and involving the use of Alexander's[48] decomposition techniques (as adapted by Chadwick) would have steered in a similar direction. The various factors included and the weights given to them involve hypotheses about society, of the way in which people and organisations are thought to behave in terms of being attracted or not to areas with particular economic, social and accessibility characteristics. Thus the weights are most likely to be changed as understanding of behaviour increases and as behaviour itself changes, *and in fact they were changed by Notts./Derby. for both reasons as the model was operated.* They were also varied individually and in groups to test the sensitivity and robustness of the strategy.

As with Lowry models, when this Potential Surface technique is applied, analysis, plan generation and plan evaluation become difficult to separate, since it can be adopted for any of the three purposes. It does not give ready-made answers and a great deal of interpretation is required, particularly as one progresses down from the very coarse Regional/Sub-regional scale. In Notts./Derby. it was effective in isolating a "mainstream area" within which the most favoured alternatives were likely to be found but it was not a complete and self-contained tool, in that it did not measure flows. This could not be accomplished in the time available. The team therefore regarded the parallel use of a Garin–Lowry model as essential. The tool was put together very quickly—only two years were available for the whole Study—and a number of untested assumptions are included. The use o, statistics more than once also gives an impression of double countingf although they are in fact proxies for quite different things. Despite its limitations, however, the team clearly identified a real need for such a technique and the idea of potential surfaces has certainly "caught on".

The Coventry/Solihull/War. Potential Surface is much more concerned than Notts./Derby. with physical planning and the allocation of land and much less with economic and social interaction, although measures of accessibility and opportunity are included. It is a method for bringing together study objectives with explicit weights ascribed to them, and the effects of varying these weights are thoroughly tested since the process is computerised. The technique is very fully documented in the Study volumes and this description need not be repeated in full here. A very brief summary is, however, useful.

The team start with a list of discriminatory objectives, which are defined as those whose attainment varies between strategies. (Some objectives are equally well satisfied by all strategies.) From these are developed ten factor surfaces (see Table 4.2). Factor scores are calculated for squares of 1 km and 5 km and particular care is taken to ensure that the results are not affected by the alignment of the net. Care is also taken to avoid double counting in the indices and, in this, the team probably have more success than Notts./Derby.

TABLE 4.2. COVENTRY/SOLIHULL/WAR. FACTOR SURFACES

Factor surface	Discriminatory objective
Landscape	To locate new development so as to conserve areas of high landscape value.
Agriculture	To locate new development so that the loss of good-quality farmland is kept to a minimum.
Services	To locate new development so that the costs of new utility services and land development generally are kept to a minimum.
Residential environment	To locate new residential development in areas of high environmental potential.
Annoyance	To locate new development in areas which will not be adversely affected by atmospheric and noise pollution.
Job access	To locate new population and employment so that there is the greatest possible choice of jobs available to all workers.
Labour access	To locate new population and employment so that there is the greatest possible choice of labour supply for all firms.
Shop access	To increase the potential range of shopping facilities available and to provide the greatest possible accessibility to them for all residents.
Road access	To locate new principal roads to serve the new population and employment so that there is the greatest possible benefit to all road users.
Rail access	To locate new population and employment where there is the greatest possible potential for public transport services.

Taking each square in turn, a score is awarded to each factor. These scores are then converted to a 0–100 scale and multiplied by the weight which is given to that factor. The resulting scores are then summed to give a total score for each square. This process is gone through each time the weights given to the objectives are varied, i.e. 42 times in all. Variations in weights are based on the team's own ideas, supplemented by a small public opinion survey. Analyses for 1969 are carried out on both 1 km and 5 km squares and for 1991 on 5 km. The team emphasise that the scores are only valid within the context of the Coventry/Solihull/War. Sub-region; they are not absolute values and cannot be compared with results obtained elsewhere. Neither do they allow for cumulative pay-offs where, say, six factors combined might have a potential more than six times greater than an area with only one factor.

The Coventry/Solihull/War. Potential Surface is clearly a different tool, playing a different role, from that of Notts./Derby. It is used primarily to explore the effects of varying the weights given to study objectives, on areas of land which are indicated as being suitable for development. The technique does not attempt to describe behaviour, although measures of accessibility are included. The use of a computer makes possible not only a large number of tests but the use of fine-grain land-use data and a network of small zones.

The Notts./Derby. technique has a much coarser set of zones and is concerned with aspects of economic and social behaviour. It is not put forward as a self-contained tool, however, and is operated alongside a Garin–Lowry model to give some measure of flows. Alternative methods are also used to bring into the analysis those (land-use) items which are too fine to be included in the surface, e.g. by sieve map. In the case of Coventry/Solihull/War., no adequate supplementary techniques seem to have been used to cope with economic and social interaction, which are inadequately dealt with by the surface. This is a serious omission and the result is that the question of the green belt, which lies between Birmingham and Coventry, is not rigorously examined, particularly from the point of view of pressure from the conurbation.

CORPORATE PLANNING

In the foregoing text, some of the interrelationships between "topics" which have been studied separately by planners in the past became apparent and it has been suggested that these interrelationships might be so complex as to be beyond the powers of our intuition to identify causes and solve problems. Causes of problems might often be far removed from the physical manifestations of them in both space and time.

If it is important to think in terms of interaction between population, employment, housing and so on in the planning process, it is also important to think in terms of co-ordinated government policies to tackle the problems which are identified. A greater emphasis on policy co-ordination is a logical development of the idea that solutions may not lie within the same policy area as the causes of the problems. Thus the various departments of local government need to pull together to solve problems of social welfare, clearance of slum housing and setting up industrial estates. Some of the solutions to local physical planning problems may lie in action by central government or public utility suppliers and so on. The trend in Sub-regional planning over the last few years has reflected a growing acceptance of such ideas and their influence can be seen both in the nature of processes which have become progressively more integrated and the recommendations which have been less constrained by the limits of physical planning powers. The new Development Plans Manual shows that a similar change can be hoped for at County level.

The point is illustrated in the second document of the Eastern Lowlands Study which states:

> Early in the course of the Study it became apparent that we had to concern ourselves with far more than the physical aspects of planning. If the Study was to be of practical use it would have to examine the whole spectrum of local authority services, including the financial situation. We believe it to be a logical development of the 1968 Act, in the context of present proposals for local government reorganisation, that a Sub-regional Study should become an instrument of corporate planning.
>
> We were convinced that we should properly concern ourselves with organisational factors in the Sub-regional Study. In fact, we concluded that organisational factors were of paramount importance; organisational flexibility over time was essential and a new approach and different systems would be required in differing circumstances.
>
> It follows that there is a need for the close involvement, particularly of all sections of local government (but also of other executive bodies), in the formulation of strategy; and also the close involvement of the public in the planning process.
>
> The major call is for the establishment of Sub-regional machinery for ascertaining the needs of the area; for elucidating the nature of the changes taking place and anticipating the variability of change; for implementing Sub-regional decisions; for monitoring the effects of these decisions and for redefining policies where necessary.
>
> Further to this requirement is a necessity for considerable rethinking of the role of the local authorities in the Sub-region, particularly with regard to influencing other organisations to achieve community objectives without themselves being directly involved.

LONG-RANGE FORECASTING

Earlier in this chapter we considered Forrester's work in simulating urban change over long periods of time. It is now appropriate to return to this question of forecasting secular change and consider some quite different techniques for long-range forecasting.

One way of tackling the long-term forecasting problem is to try to identify those aspects of urban and economic development which are particularly slow moving and consistent over long periods of time, where forecasts appear to be possible with an above-average degree of confidence. An interesting example of this kind of approach is found in Doxiadis' study of the Urban Detroit area,[49] where he shows that the symptoms of growth may be detected long before the effects become noticeable "on the ground". This is done using a series of maps showing the percentage of land area classed as "farmland" in grids 50×50 km in the Lake Erie–Lake Huron–Seginaw Bay area for 1900, 1920, 1940, 1950 and 1959. This shows Detroit's expansion into adjacent rural areas, where densities increase very slowly at first and then at an accelerating rate until complete urbanisation is achieved. As intensity of development of existing colonised areas increases so the frontiers expand over a wider and wider area. Because these movements are slow moving (though accelerating), it is possible to predict the way in which unimpeded growth is likely to occur to the end of the century. From a comparison between this area and the developing megalopolis in the Eastern U.S.A. between Boston, New York and Washington, Doxiadis concludes that a megalopolis is incipient in the Detroit area.

Most of the forecasting techniques currently being used involve quantitative data about the past and present, which is extrapolated to provide information about the future. There is an important school of thought, however, which argues that this procedure is inappropriate in long-range forecasting and that qualitative methods are called for. This is because society is changing at an increasingly rapid rate. Moreover, it is currently emerging from an industrial to a post-industrial age where society will undergo a revolution more fundamental than any known in the past. Under these circumstances, it is argued, the past cannot provide a basis for predicting the future. We must look rather at the sorts of changes which can be seen to be taking place, or which are about to take place, and think through their implications for the future.

These sorts of ideas are more advanced in the United States of America than in this country, where there have to date been few actual planning applications. The reader who wishes to pursue the subject a little further is therefore referred to an introduction by David Bayliss[50] and papers by Melvin Webber.[51] One practical example is in Milton Keynes, where Professor Webber acted as a consultant: the following quotation is from the Milton Keynes Interim Report.

> The 250,000 people who will live in Milton Keynes 30 years from now, when the city reaches its target size, will differ from us in many ways, some of which are known. For many the freedom of choice, the variety and the richness of life at present enjoyed only by a very few, will be established and expected as a consequence of increased incomes. For others, perhaps very few, perhaps not so few, there will be financial or other disability which prevents them from achieving what others around them have. But their hopes and expectations will be similar, and society will be concerned to close the gap.
>
> Work will be different, as jobs involved in the production and distribution of knowledge supplant those of today which are mostly in the production and distribution of goods. Many more jobs will require special skills, special training and advanced education. Purely manual labour will have almost disappeared. The production of goods will be highly automated and require very few workers. Higher income and more free time will accelerate the already rapid growth of every kind of recreation. Activities, at present the privilege of relatively few, such as golf, riding and sailing, will be available to all. Higher education standards for everyone will increase the demand for music, opera, ballet and other sophisticated forms of entertainment and recreation.
>
> These are changes which can surely be predicted; there will be many more which we cannot now foresee—perhaps more profound in their effects on people's lives. Medicine, science and technology are each likely, within the next thirty years, to make discoveries and innovations leading to dramatic changes.

The report then goes on to emphasise the important role to be taken by private enterprise and the importance attached to public participation in the planning process. A brief description of the city which is expected to develop is then given:

> What does this mean in practice? How will a city offering these freedoms look? A city with room for change will look more open; homes that can grow will have more space around them; trees and landscaping will establish the visual character of much of the city including the primary roads which could be built as parkways; locating important activities in different places and encouraging a mixed character of development throughout the city, will give a variety to all parts of Milton Keynes—as the mixing of uses does in older cities. Pedestrian paths, roads and public transport will pass the same places— separated where necessary for safety—but each allowing people to come directly to their destination. From all of these routes it will be possible to see

the important places in the city, the centres, the schools, the parks and others. Above all Milton Keynes will be built by many different people and imagination and experiment must be encouraged.

CONCLUSIONS

Systems thinking has pointed up the limitations of topic analysis, which assumes things to be in separate compartments that are in fact interacting with one another. This interaction has two implications: first problems and their causes may not lie together in either space or time and second much more powerful techniques are required, to indicate the way systems will react to particular stimuli. These techniques have applications in analysis/ forecasting, strategy generation and also evaluation and their use naturally tends to draw these three stages together, so that their boundaries become blurred and unreal.

The first simulation techniques were introduced quite recently in this country, but they have spread rapidly and are also being constantly improved. Forrester's work points to one avenue where further major developments may take place. There is also scope for sub-models to increase our understanding of topics, particularly in the economic field. Until these become available however the familiar topic forecasting will continue to take up a major part of planning effort.

The greater understanding which systems thinking and modelling allows of the way elements of an urban system interact with one another has naturally led to a demand that the various policy instruments which are designed to control those elements should be operated together, towards the same ends. Since these policy instruments are operated by different departments and agencies this naturally underlines the need for corporate planning and Sub-regional teams have made recommendations outside the powers of statutory planning departments. There is, however, a long way to go before full policy co-ordination even within local government is achieved and it remains to be seen how far the 1968 Act will be successful in this respect.

CHAPTER 5

Goals and Objectives

HAVING achieved some understanding of the area and the way it is evolving under current planning policies, a team is able to begin devising new strategies for the area. The more recent Sub-regional teams have approached this task through the definition of goals and objectives which are to be pursued by these strategies. Of course, the planner will usually have had a general idea of what he is expected to try to achieve right from the start, and for this reason the subject was introduced at the beginning of Chapter 2. At this present stage, however, he must define his criteria much more precisely, so that he can isolate the strategy with the most satisfactory performance.

For a useful introduction to our discussion of goals and objectives we refer to Sir Geoffrey Vickers[52] who compares the "political governor" with an engineer:

> The engineer watches dials, each of which displays the course of some important variable showing how closely it approximates to some desired standard or how dangerously it strays from some critical threshold. These standards and thresholds are the settings of the system; and these signals of match and mis-match alert him to the need for regulative action. The picture serves equally well for the political governor. He too watches the course of a limited number of variables—limited by his own interests in them and further limited by the number which he can usefully attempt to watch and regulate; and he too depends on signals of match and mis-match for guidance.
>
> There are differences also. The indices which a political governor watches are for the most part not mere observations of the present state of critical variables but estimates of their future course, based on his latest knowledge of them (which is usually imperfect) and worked up by a process of mental simulation. A more important difference is that half his skill consists in setting the standards which he shall try to attain. For unlike the engineer, who controls a system designed to be controllable, the politician intervenes in a system not designed by him, with the limited object of making its course even slightly more acceptable or less repugnant to his human values than it would otherwise be.

Thus the setting of standards which will serve as the basis for policy formulation is a major part of government activity. This is true of the whole planning field and there are reasons why it is particularly important at the Sub-regional level.

OBJECTIVES AND SUB-REGIONAL PLANNING

The majority of decisions in government are taken within well-established procedures, with many precedents and familiar criteria to give clear guidance as to the action to be taken. This is certainly true of much of the work of local government planning departments. In Sub-regional planning, however, the situation is far less clear.

As we have seen (Chapter 1), Sub-regional studies can cover almost any cross-boundary problem and a wide range of different procedures and techniques are adopted. The teams have no statutory responsibilities and there are no Acts of Parliament setting out the limits within which they must work, the type of process to be adopted, the form of presentation of argument required and so on. On the contrary, a deliberate attempt is often made to encourage a fresh approach to problems which may have proved intractable over the years and therefore there is often a wish to influence and constrain the team as little as possible. Moreover, the causes of the problems may not always be known, or it may be politically unacceptable to set them out in detail. In such circumstances there is a need to go back to fundamentals and think through the whole process step by step.

TERMS OF REFERENCE

Clearly the starting-point for devising goals and objectives must be the Terms of Reference, since these indicate what sort of function the Study is expected to perform, what it should cover and so on. Co-ordination studies are usually given Terms of Reference based on the model provided by the Department of the Environment, although the degree of detail may vary from area to area. For example, the Leicester/Leics. and Coventry/Solihull/War. Studies' Terms follow the model very closely and in consequence are almost identical to one another. Those of Notts./Derby. have a similar flavour but are much more brief, because it was felt that a very large and complex area with a great diversity of problems called for few constraints on the team.

The Department of the Environment model Terms are divided into two main sections: "general" and "main components" of the Study. The latter indicates what topics should be covered in the technical work. The former is of greater interest here and is worth quoting (from the Leicester/Leics. Study):

> The object of the study is to prepare proposals for the major land uses in the sub-region, having regard particularly to the development of population, employment, recreation and shopping in relation to each other and to transport. The purpose of the study is to serve as a bridge between regional considerations and the development plans of local planning authorities and to provide the authorities concerned with a common framework within which they can co-ordinate their plans and programmes.
>
> The area to be examined will have regard to the economic and social hinterlands and catchment areas of the main settlements. It should take into account economic and commercial linkages and employment and travel to work patterns.
>
> The area for which proposals are to be made will be defined having regard to the main problems arising and to the dominant linkages within the area and need not necessarily be as extensive as the area examined.
>
> The study generally should look forward towards the end of the century, although some elements may not be predictable with reasonable certainty for more than twenty years.
>
> It will be necessary to examine the relationship of the study area to adjoining areas, to assess the development potential of the various parts of the study area and to consider for what form of development, if any, they may be suited. Account must be taken of the function, structure, requirements and potential of existing towns.

There is emphasis here on providing a bridge between regional considerations and local authority development plans and a framework within which the authorities can co-ordinate their planning activities. Clearly, however, this is not the whole story: these functions could usefully be performed at Sub-regional level in nearly all parts of the country, while only a handful of authorities have felt it necessary to spend the £100,000 or so required by a Sub-regional team to conduct a full-scale exercise. Several additional reasons for undertaking a co-operative study spring to mind:

political dissent—planning authorities in adjacent areas may have a long history of discord and it may be that a joint planning exercise is the best way of establishing some degree of co-operation between them;

political change—if political changes are being considered, a study of the new government area to be established may be desirable;

'*on the ground*' problems may exist which are peculiar to the area: fear of an incipient conurbation affecting two or more authorities, decline of a major industry and so on;

political power may be gained if authorities combine to produce a joint strategy, for example, as protection against a powerful neighbour or some other agency.

Each of these considerations could be (and we suspect have been) seen as reasons for establishing a Sub-regional Study, although they hardly ever appear in the Terms of Reference. Indeed the inclusion of some of them would be positively harmful, for the simple reason that to make them explicit would reduce the prospects of ultimate success.

It is evident, then, that the Terms of Reference are by no means sufficient as a basis for formulating goals and objectives: many issues and problems are likely to be hidden and these must be uncovered by the team if they are to produce an acceptable strategy. Thus the Coventry/Solihull/War. team began their process of defining goals and objectives as follows:

> Our Terms of Reference suggested the broad scope of the Study, and from this starting-point the goals and objectives were initially developed with help from the following sources:
>
> (i) The local knowledge of policy issues already in the minds of the Members of the three authorities, including the issues which led to the establishment of the Study in the first place.
>
> (ii) Scrutiny of the Council minutes of the three authorities, particularly of the policy-planning committees and of their revenue and capital expenditure budgets.
>
> (iii) Discussions with officers of the authorities, and reference to the Development Plans and reports of the authorities.
>
> (iv) The items of local news and the editorial opinions of the newspapers circulating locally in different parts of the sub-region.
>
> (v) A professional consensus as to what the Study should be planning for and of the economic, social and physical environment which the sub-regional strategy should seek to encourage.

In the case of feasibility and impact studies the issues will usually be less clouded by political rivalries and sensitivities and will be easier to identify. The teams' instructions are likely to be derived from a well-argued regional or national study in which the important considerations are clearly set out. Thus South-east 1964 gave rise to South Hants 1966 and Northampton/Bedford/North Bucks. and the white paper on Central Scotland[53] resulted in Grangemouth/Falkirk, Tayside and Central Borders. It is interesting to follow one of these examples through, as an illustration of the way in which the conclusions of one study may provide the Terms of Reference or objectives of another. This will also throw a little light on the differences between objectives at different levels of planning.

Northampton/Bedford/North Bucks. is to assess the feasibility of large-scale overspill from London being accommodated in the area and, should this be recommended, to comment on the appropriate form of development. Four main objectives are listed and these clearly derive from South-east 1964. They relate to the location and urban form to be identified, which should be suitable for:

(a) large existing commercial centres likely to be able to attract and to provide the necessary facilities for offices on a considerable scale as soon as possible;
(b) areas with a potential for growth of existing industry in order to minimise the amount of new industry which would need to be moved to support population growth;
(c) areas able to provide for the requirements of large industrial units;
(d) a concentration of effort to make the most efficient use of manpower and resources in the planning and implementation of the South-east Study proposals.

There are further instructions which make it clear that the need to minimise congestion is also an important objective and a number of other objectives related to the nature of the desired urban form are also implied. Following the recommendations of the Sub-regional Study, a New Town Development Corporation is set up for Milton Keynes and consultants are engaged to assist in the preparation of a Master Plan.

Once the decision to establish a New Town has been taken, however, the influence of the Sub-regional Study is minimal and the Corporation rethink their goals. The way in which these are identified, using long-range forecasting, has already been discussed (see Chapter 4). The new objectives derived from long-range forecasting are concerned primarily with producing pleasant living conditions:

(1) Opportunity and freedom of choice.
(2) Easy movement and access of good communications.
(3) Balance and variety.
(4) An attractive city.
(5) Public awareness and participation.
(6) Efficient and imaginative use of resources.

These are discussed at some length in the text and the more detailed criteria which they imply are identified.

THE PLANNER'S CULTURE

So far, we have been concerned with the way in which the attitudes, opinions and results of investigations by others are passed on to the Sub-regional team. We have also noted that attitudes may not always be openly expressed (although they are none the less real for that) and may have to be sought out. But clearly the team must make a more active contribution than this, in identifying problems and objectives for themselves, and finding new solutions to situations which have proved intractable in the past. As we explained in Chapter 2, the first steps to be taken involve leaning heavily on the team's "culture" as planners: that body of knowledge and experience which tells them what information to collect, what technical specifications to lay down.

In the Tayside Study, for instance, the conclusions of the team are influenced by four "considerations":

(1) Early improvement of the existing situation in terms of redeveloping the existing urban fabric and arresting the symptoms of decline is required.
(2) Whatever the form chosen it should be as viable as possible in all aspects of city region life at any stage of its evolution.
(3) The pattern must be responsive to changes, many of which are unknown or difficult to predict at this stage, over at least the next thirty years.
(4) Any solution must pay respect to the aspirations and attributes of the existing communities.

Number (1) might be held to arise either from terms of reference or analytical work by the team; number (4) is perhaps a necessary requirement in a democratic country; numbers (2) and (3) derive from a planner's knowledge and experience—they are part of his "culture".

Another example of the derivation of objectives from technical knowledge is in Dee Crossing, which initiates what is basically an engineering exercise to appraise the practicability of a crossing of the estuary from an engineering and hydrological point of view (although the consultants rightly point out the need for a widening of the terms of reference and also of the area of study). Twenty-eight detailed criteria are listed, concerned with the impact of the crossing on traffic in the area, water catchment, reclamation of land, local fisheries, silting up of the channel, conservation of local ecology, local coalmining activities, etc.

ANALYSIS

The work involved at the analysis stage has been discussed in some detail in the previous two chapters and thus need not be repeated here. We emphasise, however, that the list of goals and objectives cannot be defined sufficiently firmly for the generation and evaluation of alternatives until the team have completed their own technical analysis. Indeed, some teams adopt the practice of setting out objectives as conclusions to each analytical chapter.

THE DISTINCTION BETWEEN ENDS AND MEANS

No clear distinction has so far been made between goals, objectives, standards, etc., and this reflects a certain amount of confusion in planning generally about the appropriate terms to use. Robert C. Young[54] suggests one solution, claiming that a goal is a direction, not a location, a value to be sought after and not an object to be achieved. An objective, on the other hand, is capable both of attainment and measurement, it is an end to be achieved and nothing need be said about why that point is aimed at. Goals are universal and lasting, objectives change with varying circumstances.

As an example of the confusion between the two, Young quotes the goal of "lowering the tax rate". An objective derived from this might be to "reduce municipal expenditure". Unfortunately this last measure, which is advocated in order to move towards the goal, tends to become an end in itself and when this happens the possibility of trade-offs in the future is lost. As long as the objective is seen clearly as a means, then the possibility of trade-off with other alternatives such as greater efficiency remains. Since trade-off between criteria is at the heart of planning, the importance of this point cannot be over-emphasised.

OBJECTIVES IN AN INTEGRATED PLAN-MAKING PROCESS

Recently Sub-regional plan generation and evaluation has been tied much more closely to goals and objectives than hitherto. There has, for example, been a swing away from evaluation in terms of monetary values on costs and benefits and in favour of ranking against weighted objectives. In the generation process, goals and objectives have been used to identify land suitable for development much more rigorously than was possible in the old sieve-map process.

We have already introduced this subject in Chapter 4, in relation to Potential Surfaces. We now return to it in order to discuss Chadwick's Meta Procedure. This was an important influence on Notts./Derby. in constructing their surface and the two might have been discussed together. We would emphasise, too, that the Meta Procedure is a complete plan generation and evaluation process and is by no means important only for its treatment of goals and objectives. However, it could logically be introduced in any one of a number of chapters. We have elected to discuss it here because it offers a particularly useful illustration of the breaking down of general statements into very specific land-use criteria and instructions as to how they may be handled in arriving at an envelope in which development should take place.

The Meta Procedure[55] accepts Young's concept of goals and objectives and it is asserted that

   (i) goals are broad indications of the general direction of planning policy in the area;

  (ii) goals and objectives are hierarchical not only as between different levels of planning (national, regional, sub-regional, local) but also at a given level. This suggests perhaps that different weights should be given to the various objectives or that they should be considered in a particular sequence;

 (iii) there will inevitably be conflict between objectives.

Chadwick sets out to provide a framework within which the planner can resolve these conflicts between objectives, recognising their hierarchical arrangement and taking those which occur at the base of the pyramid first and gradually working upwards until all conflicts between them have been resolved in a final synthesis. For a demonstration of this part of the Meta Procedure we refer to selected parts of Michael Batty's study of Central and North-east Lancashire[56] which was completed by Batty while at Manchester University, under Chadwick's direction.

To identify the envelope within which development should take place, Batty takes as his starting-point four broad directional goals: efficiency, economy, participation, habitability. From these he derives "aims", from aims "implications" and from implications "factors". Each stage elaborates on the goals and is less abstract than the last and the final sixty-two factors state explicitly what the goals imply in physical terms. They are concerned with avoiding high-altitudes and steep slopes, proximity to service institutions and large towns, solving problems of obsolescence, transport economies and so on. An attempt is also made to distinguish between the wishes of "society" and "individuals" and take these distinctions into account in mapping areas for development.

At this stage, Batty has a set of precisely defined criteria for identifying land for development and he points out that it would be possible to develop a plan directly from them. This, however, would be difficult because some are related and some are in conflict while others are completely independent. Moreover, they are not all of the same degree of importance. Use is therefore made of Alexander's decomposition techniques to clarify their relationships and arrange them in such a way that they may be combined logically in a physical plan.

A number of cycles follow in which the factors are scrutinised, grouped and regrouped. Criteria for grouping include factors which show direct causal relationships and factors which have the same spatial implications for urban development. When the final factor groupings have been achieved, these are looked at in terms of the way in which they interact with one another. Here Batty quotes Alexander, who says, "requirements interact if what you do about one of them in design necessarily makes it more difficult or easier to do anything about the other". The factors are presented in matrix form and where there is conflict he indicates its strength by -1 or -2; where the factors are complementary he has $+1$ or $+2$. Thus, for example, one which aims to prevent large-scale development in areas where the transport structure is not capable of taking it, has a strong positive interaction with the need to avoid hill land physically difficult to build on, but a strong negative interaction with the need to avoid development on first-class agricultural land.

Batty now presents these groupings in a linear graph with strong interactions ($+2$, -2) shown by thick black lines linking pairs of factors and weak ones ($+1$, -1) shown by thin lines. The weak interactions are, however, omitted after this stage. Using only the strong interactions, he draws another linear graph and from a visual inspection of this derives an hierarchy of factors (see Fig. 5.1). It is argued that the factor groupings indicated in the hierarchy represent "sub-problems" which are best solved together. Thus Specifications 21, 27, 5 and 1 are taken together and a map indicating areas suitable and unsuitable for development with reference to these is produced. Then come 15, 3, 4, 14 and 29. The two maps are then considered together and a third stage of synthesis results (stage C) and so on to the highest level of the tree (stage Q). When the apex of the pyramid is reached a complete synthesis has been achieved, and the final map therefore shows the solution space into which the activity systems are to be fitted.

So far as the activity systems are concerned these require a parallel, and equally important, process involving making forecasts of population and employment and plotting the dispositions of these with the aid of a Lowry-type gravity model. The results are then compared with the solution space. An evaluation stage then follows which involves Cost–Benefit Analysis.

As a method of synthesis the Meta Procedure has some major advantages:

(i) it provides a logical framework within which the planner may use his creative ability, although it is, of course, an essentially "static" method;

(ii) it tackles problems by focusing on "misfit" (i.e. land unsuitable for development) which is easier to identify than "fit" (land most suitable for development);

(iii) the tremendous variety is reduced and related problems are solved together, beginning at the base of the tree where conflicts are most difficult to resolve and working upwards;

(iv) the area concerned in our example of Central/N.E. Lancs. is a relatively simple one and Chadwick would claim that the Meta Procedure can cope with much more complex Regional and Sub-regional problems.

The Meta Procedure makes an advance in attempting to bring into the plan generation process the conflict between "individuals" on the one hand and "society" on the other. Traditional planning has paid little attention to the fact that plans can vary considerably in terms of their impact on different groups in society. Although some evaluation techniques have been devised which are designed to deal with this problem (see Chapter 7 on Cost–Benefit Analysis, the Planning Balance-sheet and the Goals-achievement Matrix), it has not, in general, been considered at the generation stage. Now, that goal definition is being recognised as an essential

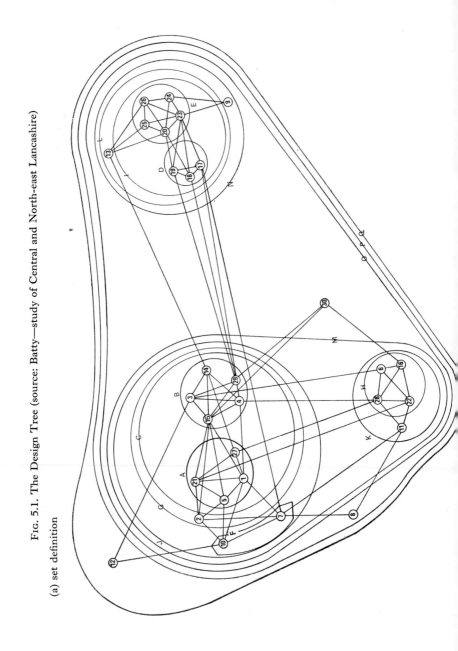

Fig. 5.1. The Design Tree (source: Batty—study of Central and North-east Lancashire)

(a) set definition

(b) the synthesis of form

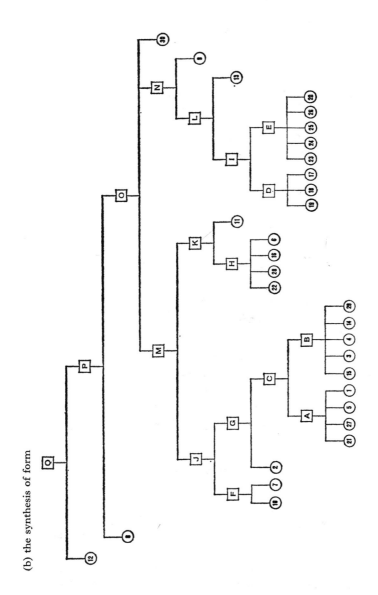

starting-point for planning, however, it seems likely that the problem will receive more attention. The advance of computer-technology should also help in increasing our capacity to deal with the related problems of measuring the impact of alternative proposals on different groups.

Another point in relation to the Meta Procedure is concerned with a weakness of the linear graph method generally: the linear graph, and hence the arrangement of the hierarchy, can vary according to the operator. It also concentrates attention on the *number* of links between factors and not on the *strength* of links and *sensitivity*. One factor group might have direct links with perhaps only two others, but through them it has indirect links with the whole of the remainder of the network. If one can envisage a situation where such a factor were highly sensitive and because of indirect links the solution of its problems determined the solution of a whole host of others, then the design method might not produce the best fit. This sensitivity would probably not be detected in a complex situation, although in a simple one a planner might recognise it instinctively. If it were not identified the critical conflict would not be considered until most of the dependent problems had already been apparently resolved.

"Aspatial" objectives

Some would assert that the planner should avoid defining and pursuing objectives which are "aspatial" in character. Whether or not this view is tenable, the fact is that few objectives have no spatial implications: for instance, if one were to try to reduce the level of unemployment in a Sub-region by one-tenth, the key to this might well be in stimulating economic activity in certain population centres.

What is important is to distinguish between lead conditions and dependent conditions and to ensure that objectives and advice are set out to cover all lead conditions. In a heavily developed area, the disposition of housing estates would represent a lead condition in determining the location of primary schools and other service facilities. In a rural area consisting of small towns and villages in a widely dispersed pattern the reverse might be true, with primary education representing a lead condition for population location. Thus a change in (aspatial) policy on class size or building structure might affect the number and size of primary schools required (compare this with the implications of comprehensive education) and this could well determine settlement structure and key village policy (spatial).

Different uses of the concept of goals and objectives

We began this chapter by showing that goals and objectives are needed to clarify what one is trying to do. This is very necessary because, without such a discipline, we are quite likely to go on doing what has always been done, or adopt methods and techniques which are available without thinking what the situation demands or whether they are really appropriate. Indeed it could be argued that because this view has not been accepted in the past Development Plan procedures have operated for many years with little or no discussion as to what success was being achieved, or whether an attempt should be made to measure the success rate.

One difficulty involved in the use of very abstract goals together with objectives in Young's sense of being simply a statement of means or intentions, is that if we are not very careful much of the value of defining goals and objectives may be lost. Goals become so abstract and all embracing as to be almost meaningless, while objectives are reduced to simply a statement of the action to be taken.

This may be overcome by setting out a number of levels in the hierarchy, as in the Batty exercise. Another example is found in the American–Yugoslav project in the Ljubljana Region. In this Study, goals are directional and are very broad indeed: "efficiency", "quality", "equity". The team go through each aspect of planning in the area and identify "problems" associated with these broad goals. Thus for the policy area concerned with provision of public utilities, the goal "efficiency" indicates one problem, namely the scarcity of capital for the construction of new capacity. This gives rise to two spatial objectives: (1) to link up urban development in order to reduce servicing costs and (2) to increase the size of future residential and employment projects. Similarly with the distribution of goods and services, "efficiency" gives rise to six problems, but some of these are not followed through: one, "lack of sectoral planning", because it is held to be non-spatial, and two others, "congestion of high-order service centres" and "inadequate parking facilities in higher-order centres" because they are not appropriate to the regional scale.

PUBLIC PARTICIPATION

There is some difference of opinion as to the value of consulting political representatives and the general public on goals and objectives (as opposed to specific proposals for land-use dispositions). Andrew Thorburn[57] expresses one view in relation to Notts./Derby.:

> Sometimes planners try to obtain public agreement to a series of stated objectives in advance of making a plan, and the Skeffington Committee supported this approach. We ourselves defined objectives in an early stage of our work with just this intention, but our Committee did not wish to discuss them. Indeed, all my experience suggests that it is extremely difficult—probably impossible—to get a group of people to commit themselves to objectives before they know what the consequences of that commitment will be, and our political processes are designed to achieve a consensus in a real action situation not an abstract one. In other words, until they know the consequences the public does not have sufficient information to decide on objectives.

Others, such as the South Hants 1972 and Coventry/Solihull/War. teams, have opted to approach the general public on goals and objectives. The South Hants 1972 team circulated a pamphlet and questionnaire setting out four alternative strategies and the "aims" of the plan to all local authorities in the area, selected representative organisations and some 3000 electors chosen by random sampling. Of the electors 62% replied.

So far as the aims of the plan are concerned, the team note that the general public's preference for any particular aim was not very strong. Economy rated highest, closely followed by conservation, environment, mobility and choice. Lower scores were given to implementation, flexibility and image, but these were not significantly poorer. Only one of the local authorities decided to give specific scores to aims, although parish councils indicated a strong (unscored) preference for conservation and City Planning committees underlined the importance of implementation. Only a few other organisations replied to the question about aims and their preferences seemed to be broadly similar to those of the general public.

Of the general public, 43% of the random sample and 68% of those who bought copies of the report suggested at least one additional aim, but:

> . . . The vast majority of replies (over 80% in each case) were found to be a restatement in new wording or a re-emphasis of specific aspects of the aims already given. Over 25% of all respondents mentioned features associated

with the aim of environment, the majority being concerned with social and community provision, both in general and with special emphasis on the need for community facilities for the young and for the old. This emphasis resulted, in part, from the apparent omission of a "social aim" from the list of defined aims. This "omission" was deliberate, as the provision of such services is related to several aims of the plan and is a subject of optimisation of the preferred strategy and not, therefore, a sub-regional aim against which the strategies might be judged. . . .

This raises the question as to how far the general public really understood the significance of the aims on which they commented. Nevertheless the team deserve credit for "perhaps the closest approach to a referendum and true participation in local affairs that has been attempted in recent years in this country". They rightly point to the relatively high response rate as an indication of a high degree of interest in planning matters amongst the general public.

We believe that the reluctance of decision-takers to express an opinion on abstract criteria until the implications of these have been made clear is well founded. The problem of presenting these criteria in public opinion surveys in such a way that they can be readily understood is even more difficult. There is, moreover, a tendency at present to compare criteria which are quite different in character and not, in fact, alternatives. In designing public surveys it would be useful to distinguish groups of criteria within which the public can reasonably be asked to make a choice. Linear graphs might, perhaps, be used for this purpose. Otherwise we may simply have to confine ourselves to asking them to select alternative plans.

CHANGING OBJECTIVES OVER TIME

Society is changing over time at an accelerating rate and it is reasonable to suppose that, as income levels, standards of education, health and so on increase, the objectives of members of society will also change. Indeed this has been a primary concern of the long-range forecasters mentioned in Chapter 4. Looking back it can be seen that for at least some major on-going projects, objectives have indeed been revised over the years.

C. J. van den Berg[58] has traced some such changes in his examination of the arguments used to justify investment in various Zuider Zee reclamation projects since the turn of the century. Initially the goal was simply to promote agriculture. Arguments then developed and widened to cover a range of regional, as well as local, planning objectives. Later still, the aim was to produce a physical master plan which would fit the project into a wider national context. Van den Berg himself argues for a further increase in the spatial frame of reference, to bring in not only national, but European goals. At a purely local level too goals and objectives changed. The completion of part of a project itself changed objectives, when an Enclosure Dam made a direct rail link between Friesland and North Holland feasible. This led to a call for more connections between the two regions, so as to make possible decentralisation of growth from the West to the North-east.

This point has implications for the kinds of plans which should be prepared. It suggests a need for some flexibility to cope with change not merely in levels of population, employment, etc., but in what people want from the plan. It has relevance for monitoring too and suggests periodic reference to the objectives which lie behind the plan rather than simply checking on progress towards the physical land use dispositions themselves. We will, however, be taking up these items later.

CONCLUSIONS

The discipline of making goals and objectives explicit is useful, especially at Sub-regional level where the guidelines from other sources allow a high degree of discretion. We hope we have demonstrated, however, that the definition of objectives can be a subtle problem. The purpose of the initial set will be to clarify the nature of the task as the team sees it. As the technical process advances, these ideas are expanded and different groups of criteria begin to emerge:

(a) aims to be pursued during a trade-off process;

(b) essential requirements for all strategies, which are not subject to trade-off; and

(c) the best ways, from an operational point of view, of completing particular tasks.

Moreover, these will be further elaborated, possibly several times, as the plan process is completed. Clearly, then, rigorous definition is of major importance at each stage.

In order to clarify the nature of objectives and their role in Sub-regional planning, we have introduced subjects here which overlap with several other chapters; the hierarchical arrangement of objectives, trade-off and the elimination of alternatives over time, and public participation in the planning process. We now go on to develop some of these in a fuller discussion of strategy generation and evaluation.

CHAPTER 6

Strategy Generation

THE previous chapter was concerned with defining criteria for plan-making; this one is concerned with identifying possible courses of action and the next (headed "Evaluation") will be concerned with isolating the preferred course of action. This seems, on the face of it, a logical sequence of dealing with goals and objectives, generating strategies and evaluating them. It does, however, over-simplify the situation somewhat.

We have seen in Chapter 4 that the simulation techniques used in generation seem to offer the best prospects of improving on our purely intuitive knowledge of how systems work. If they are used for educational purposes the boundary between "analysis" and "generation" becomes blurred. This is also true of generation and evaluation. Some studies adopt cyclical processes in which a set of alternatives is devised, examined and the conclusions embodied in a fresh set of alternatives in the next cycle when the process is repeated. Cycles go on until a preferred course of action is finally isolated. The distinction between generation and evaluation is very difficult to make here and not, perhaps, particularly helpful.

In the majority of studies, however, it is still possible to make a reasonably clear distinction between the two and some of the techniques which are used in evaluation are quite different from those used in generation. In addition the operations involved at these stages are so complex that some means of ordering the discussion is needed. A division between the two has therefore been made and the problems of evaluation will be discussed in the following chapter.

In order to simplify the discussion as far as possible, the approach adopted here is to take those generation procedures which seem to involve a narrower range of topics and problems first and progressively broaden the scope and increase the complexity towards the end of the chapter. It has also been considered desirable to examine the various concepts one by one and to discuss each fully before going on to the next. There has inevitably been some conflict between these aims: a concept may be used very narrowly and simply in one study, but be the basis for a very free ranging and complex process in another, so that the layout of this chapter is something of a compromise. It is hoped, however, that the approach which has been adopted will make the generation process reasonably easy to understand, even if the relative position of a study in the chapter does not accurately reflect its complexity or quality.

PROBLEM-SOLVING

Problem-solving studies look at existing problems and put forward policies to solve them. This is the simplest approach to plan generation: it does not usually involve looking far ahead and the problems of forecasting are played down. Halifax/Calder Valley, for example, looks only 3 years ahead in its employment forecasts. If this approach is adopted it is important to recognise its limitations: policies based on present-day problems may not be valid for very long because, without forecasting effort, changes are soon likely to occur which have not been anticipated.

Problem-solving is frequently used in conjunction with topic analysis (see Chapter 3), when each activity is looked at more or less in isolation and they are not brought together. This tends to lead to non-integrated sets of policy proposals, some of which may be incompatible because the system has not been examined as a whole.

A more sophisticated type of study, but one which still concentrates on particular problems and often takes a fairly narrow range of alternatives is the Land-use/Transportation Survey.

LAND-USE/TRANSPORTATION SURVEYS

These merit discussion in some detail, since most Sub-regional studies have a strong transport element. Indeed it is the need to control transport systems perhaps more than any other which has led to the quickening of interest in Sub-regional planning in the last decade. The following outline Land-use/Transportation Survey was given by Mitchell, one of the pioneers in this field, to a United States Presidential Committee in 1959.

The quote is from McLoughlin's[59] book. It will be noted that Mitchell describes the application of two models: one to simulate traffic movements and incorporating a modal split, the other to model changes in relative dispositions of population and employment in the metropolitan area:

> . . . using the metropolitan growth model and holding transportation considerations constant (i.e. assuming past trends to continue and commitments to be binding in road building, public transport and parking policy) a first spatial distribution of population and major employment types is made. On this "land-use" basis, alternative transportation (i.e. networks and public transport systems) schemes which vary the emphasis given to public and private means are carried out.
>
> The metropolitan growth model is again used, this time allowing the different access-opportunities embodied in the alternative transportation schemes to influence the spatial distributions of population and employment. At this point therefore we have a set of internally consistent land-use and transportation plans.
>
> But the public transport and road networks have not been tested to see in more detail what sizes and levels of service would be required to cope with the expected volumes. The traffic assignment model must now be called upon to produce this information. Study of the results may show that certain of the alternatives are not feasible. For example, one may depend upon a high degree of private vehicle usage and call for very large expenditure on new road construction. Another may demand levels of service in certain parts of the public transport system which are likely to be unattainable within the bounds of reasonable investments.
>
> The remainder should now be subjected to first-level cost/benefit analysis to help determine the most efficient "mix" of public and private transportation.
>
> At this stage a near-optimal land-use and transportation plan should have emerged "which is both desired and apparently attainable". Further refinements in land-use dispositions and transportation systems should be attempted until the best balance is attained.
>
> The remainder of the process of plan-making comprises an assessment of the capital and operating costs involved, the public powers available or desirable for accomplishing the plan, and the "long-range programming of stages of development . . . studies should be made to assure that at the obvious stages the transportation system will function effectively".

This is basically an engineering exercise. Land-use dispositions appear to be based on trend, with adjustments made to allow for different access opportunities arising from changes in the network. Mitchell is essentially concerned with working up a single Land-use/Transportation plan in a heavily constrained situation, rather than with trying to represent all of the various land use and transport combinations which might conceivably be effected.

One interesting point is that Mitchell stages his plan, as did the Leicester/ Leics. The definition of a plan for various time intervals is a means of describing a dynamic system in terms of the states through which it passes and as such is compatible with the use of computer models, which are essentially static. It is useful for examining some of the more important time lags between the application of policies and response from the urban system and the varying speed of response between activities. It is also claimed to be useful for monitoring, in that the team's intentions for any point in time are easier to divine than they are from a "single shot" plan. Unfortunately staging has a major disadvantage in that it relies heavily on the accuracy of forecasts, which must be specified in some detail. For this reason, it has been rejected by the more recent Sub-regional studies.

THRESHOLD ANALYSIS

Threshold Analysis views constraints as obstacles which may be overcome at some cost quantifiable in money terms. These may be either badly drained land, steep slopes, etc., or infrastructure with spare capacity (which represents a cost to the community if not taken up). Using this technique, Grangemouth/Falkirk isolate those areas which appear most suitable for development, by eliminating areas which are developed already and those where costs of development are excessively high. The team identify five threshold lines, which suggest both directions for development in the area and stages of development, taking the lowest-cost areas first. Thus the first threshold delimits those areas in the "main town groups" where costs are lower than £20 per new inhabitant, the second involves costs of £20– £50, the third £50 – 100 and so on.

The difficulty of obtaining accurate estimates of costs is a major obstacle. A more fundamental criticism, however, is that the approach puts too much emphasis on the cost of infrastructure and not enough on studying the systems which this infrastructure is designed to accommodate. How can one be sure that development costs saved will be greater than loss of efficiency if systems are forced into a particular envelope? On the credit side, threshold analysis does focus attention on the cost of alternatives and there is a feeling in some quarters that planners are not always sufficiently cost conscious.

STEREOTYPES

Stereotypes are model dispositions of urban development. They have usually been devised to incorporate either the experience of using urban forms in the past or thoughts about the sorts of urban forms which will be needed in the future to accommodate changing life styles. A variety of such forms are available to Sub-regional planners for testing in their own particular situation, each with its own advantages and disadvantages which can be traded off against Study objectives. Since stereotypes are very widely used as a starting point for generation in Sub-regional planning they merit lengthy discussion here.

Gerd Albers[60] shows that most of the designs for "model cities" have their origins in one or more of three basic forms: concentric cities, dispersed development and linear cities. The concentric structure, associated with an hierarchial arrangement of centre-functions, is typically found in agrarian communities where towns depend on their agricultural hinterland. Industrial societies with problems of over-concentration have recognised the advantages of dispersed development and linear arrangement. Dispersed development assumes the ubiquitous availability of energy and services which is only possible in an advanced economy. Linear cities are based on the idea that important benefits are to be had from the greater accessibility which this arrangement affords, for some activities.

It may be noted that the principal advantage of each form can be equated with particular goals and objectives: good accessibility to central areas— radial growth; flexibility to cope with future change—linear forms; maximum choice of location for residential development—dispersed forms.

In the use of stereotypes at Sub-regional level, three different approaches can be seen: the first involves selecting what appears to be the most suitable form from a number of alternatives and "bending on" to the local landscape (N.B. the choice may be made either before or after bending on has been accomplished). The second involves stereotypes which are developed by the team to crystallise the findings of their analysis in a form suitable for testing. The third approach involves sorting through the various stereotypes available and developing from these a list of criteria which can then be applied to various possible patterns of development generated in other ways.

In the first category the best-known examples are plans based on Ebeneezer Howard's garden-city design. Thus Sir Frederick J. Osborn and Arnold Whittick[61] suggest this design as the best solution to the congestion problems confronting our major cities.

> '. . . a limit on residential development is necessary if we are loyal to the fundamental aims of all personal and social effort—a satisfactory home environment. Short and quick internal communications saves leisure time and minimises traffic costs, strains and hazards; but as the phenomenon of urban sprawl everywhere proves, it is for most people a secondary consideration. The time–distance factor has been reduced by mechanical transport, and with all the troubles this has brought, it remains an astounding anomaly that speedier movement should lead to tighter packing of people in communities. . . .
> Howard's sample "cluster of cities" of from 32,000 to 58,000 shown in his diagram adds up to a total population of 250,000—by coincidence just what is proposed for several of Britain's "new cities". Given a regional arrangement permitting easy access from moderate-sized urban units to large stretches of open country, that seems to us a valid concept. But to create new continuously-built-up cities of 250,000 or more would be to repeat the mistakes of the past.

Also in the first category, the South Hants 1966 team undertake a theoretical study of urban structure and isolate three basic possibilities for their growth area:

centripetal ("radiating, not centrally focused"), an example of which is Norwich;

a linear "directional grid" after the layout of the Portsmouth area; and

a grid layout along the lines of Philadelphia.

These are discussed in relation to five main criteria which are described as follows:

(i) maximum freedom of choice, communications and association for people throughout the area;

(ii) as the structure grows, it should be possible for each phase to function efficiently and not to be dependent upon further growth taking place;

(iii) the structure should lend itself to change and renewal in its elements, once they have been brought into existence;

(iv) the versatility of the structure should not be limited by rigid standards in such matters as transport modes and housing groupings;

(v) the structure should be capable of growth without the risk of deformation or distortion.

A subjective assessment is made of each of the three alternatives in the light of these criteria and the directional grid is favoured because it is considered to have:

(a) greater flexibility to accommodate change;

(b) greater accessibility; and

(c) the advantage of enabling growth to be phased in a variety of different ways.

The Study then proceeds to the simulation of the directional grid in use in the particular conditions existing in the area and to the detailed evaluation.

In the second category the Leicester/Leics. team crystallise their ideas about the area into six basic forms. These are based on employment distribution, rather than resident population, as the lead condition in determining other land-use patterns. The forms are:

(a) Concentration (on the main city, Leicester).

(b) Dispersal.

(c) Accessibility—Trend.

(d) Accessibility—Rejuvenation.

(e) Trend—Rejuvenation.

(f) Concentration in the Soar Valley.

Alternative (b) is an attempt to direct growth to the main county towns; (c) involves the continuation of the pattern of basic employment growth since the war; (d) and (e) are both concerned to revive the industrial base of declining areas by the introduction of new basic employment; (c) and (d) aim to encourage the growth of new industrial sites near the main national road network (present and future) and near Castle Donington Airport; (f) is concerned with thresholds—some growth in the area between Leicester and Loughborough is inevitable and will necessitate extensive flood-control work. Additional growth is considered desirable to reap the full benefits of this expensive investment.

The Leicester/Leics. approach is a compromise between the use of predetermined basic forms and allowing a plan simply to emerge from analysis. It makes use of ideas which have formed the basis of models in the past, but the forms evaluated arise primarily from analysis.

In the third category, South-east 1970 sets out to make recommendations on patterns of development in the Region, starting with the strategy proposals of South-east 1967. One alternative based on the 1967 proposals is ready-made therefore, and since the team's resources allow for detailed testing of only two alternatives, one further strategy is developed. Clearly the number of possibilities is enormous. To help them narrow these down, the team begin with an examination of stereotypes moving down from the

Regional to Sub-regional and finally Urban Structure levels, taking examples which have been used in this country and various other parts of the world. None of these is accepted in its entirety and the process does not involve testing on the landscape of the South-east. The stereotypes simply serve to provide criteria with which to assess the possibilities open to the team. Since this examination of stereotypes is one of the most thorough we have encountered, a summary is useful here.

Regional stereotypes are the first to be considered, with ten alternatives involving various concentrations of growth, radial growth, scattered growth and so on. These ". . . are theoretical concepts applied in the region in order to increase the understanding of the various forces that must be reconciled in designing an alternative strategy . . .". This is followed by a chapter which indicates ways of looking at regions and methods of analysing them, in the hope that this will assist in developing hypotheses to be tested. However, the team admit that "In the event, the aspects covered . . . contributed little to the finally selected strategy".

The next step is an examination of city-region strategies including Stockholm, Copenhagen, Paris, Washington D.C., Chicago, Randstadt (Netherlands), Ruhr (Germany) and New York. Included here is a discussion of the corridor or axial form recommended by South-east 1967. The team consider it significant that, in the case of axial growth, unforeseen pressures have led to modifications of some of the earlier proposals, even in the short term. Polycentric regions, on the other hand, appear to show that this form has the potential to work well. Another important conclusion is that, however similar the conceptual thinking of different teams may be, the plan selected as most suitable will be closely related to local geographic, economic and historic circumstances and means of implementation. Thus, "The ideal solution for one metropolitan region will rarely be exportable to another".

Having concluded that there are advantages in concentrating growth rather than dispersing it, the team go on to look at examples of urban form which have been proposed at the Sub-regional level, particularly areas where rapid growth is anticipated. The Sub-regional proposals considered are from Ipswich, Central Lancs., Teesside, Leicester/Leics., Humberside, South Hants 1966 and the Northampton–Milton Keynes area. They find great variety and are again impressed by the way in which solutions are influenced by local circumstances and particularly by the need to structure partly urbanised areas into coherent urban systems. This they see as particularly relevant, since any proposals they put forward for growth areas are likely to contain some urban development rather than be "greenfield" sites.

With these ideas in mind they go on to examine recent concepts of urban growth "in order to identify the structural factors which would be important in areas of expansion". The directional grid is found to have some important advantages, but there is a feeling that, while the forms reflect recent advances in transport planning, much remains to be done in understanding land-use systems. The team therefore conclude that an optimal land-use pattern is more likely to be identified through an analysis of the activity systems rather than working backwards from a conceptual framework.

The use of stereotypes as a basis for generating alternative strategies offers a professionally acceptable, easy and time-saving solution to a major problem. Stereotypes can therefore be seen as an important part of the planners' culture. There is of course a temptation to apply ready-made solutions with too little thought about how they will function in the particular area concerned and to dismiss possibly viable alternatives out of hand. One would therefore wish to see close links between the results of analytical work and the ideal forms put forward for testing, and in particular that testing occurred after rather than before "bending on".

The South-east 1970 investigation is not seen to be closely linked with the alternative finally selected and this is a weakness. In particular their Part Four document, which sets it out, was not published for some considerable time after the preferred solution was put forward, and people were asked to form an opinion without full information about the way in which it had been developed. This is an important general problem which we shall refer to again later.

THE RANGE OF ALTERNATIVES

It is obvious that, before constraints are applied, the amount of land available in any Sub-region is likely to exceed by many times that which will be needed for development in any plan period, so that the range of alternative plans which could be developed is very wide indeed. The application of physical and other constraints apparently reduces the alternatives to a number which it is within the capacity of the team to test. However, systems theory has shown that, even within a fairly restricted area of development, the number of possibilities can be substantial and Mitchells land-use/transportation example described above has already hinted at this.

Professor Chadwick[62] makes this point succinctly using Zwicky's "morphological method". His diagram is reproduced in Fig. 6.1. The six elements, A, B, C, D, E, F, correspond to parts of the regional system, e.g. functions, activities or adapted spaces. Any set—A_2, B_3, C_1, D_2, E_4, F_3—forms an elementary morphology of the system for a given point in time, whether it be feasible or otherwise. The elements X, Y, Z, P, Q, R, are unknown but possibly existing. The sum of all possible morphologies of the system shown, discounting the unknown possibilities, is $4 \times 3 \times 5 \times 2 \times 4 \times 3 = 1440$. Chadwick notes, however, that if it is assumed a choice can be made between the alternatives for each element independently, the possibilities reduce to $4 + 3 + 5 + 2 + 4 + 3 = 21$.

Thus it is clear that the most critical stage of strategy generation is that of identifying an appropriate range of possibilities to test. If the net is cast too wide then the number of possibilities becomes so vast as to be virtually

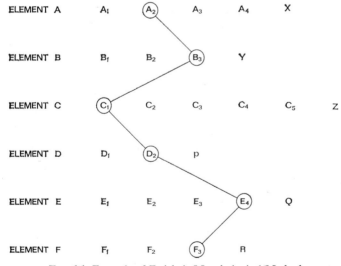

FIG. 6.1. Example of Zwicky's Morphological Method.

beyond the planner's capabilities; if it is not cast wide enough he may well fail to embrace a number of efficient and possibly superior alternatives. It is the acceptance of this fact which has led to the growing complexity of plan generation procedures in the last few years. One, Chadwick's own Meta Procedure, has already been described in Chapter 5. Three others are discussed below.

DEVELOPMENT POTENTIAL

The Coventry/Solihull/War. team reject the use of stereotypes in favour of a Development Potential Technique (mentioned in Chapter 4) as a basis for generating alternative land-use dispositions, because they consider the latter to be more sensitive to circumstances in the Sub-region. It is capable of firming up a few alternatives for testing logically and in a way which is not likely to neglect any realistic alternative. At the same time it is efficient in making use of a considerable amount of land-use data already available to the team.

Ten factor surfaces are produced related to landscape, agriculture, services and so on, each derived from a discriminatory objective and measuring the desirability or otherwise of development in local areas (grid squares). Development potential scores in a range 0–100 are produced for each of these surfaces for each grid square, and the ten sets of scores are then added together to produce total potential scores for each area. The objectives on which the ten factor surfaces are based are not all of equal importance, however, and one person might well give different weight to a given factor than another person. To cope with this problem there are discussions within the team and a small sample survey is carried out, and as a result forty-two different sets of weights for the factors are devised. Using these weights forty-two different Development Potential surfaces are produced.

The preliminary results show, of course, that land already developed is theoretically the most attractive and is often next best as well, so that the team are really concerned with areas of third or fourth grade potential. In order to accentuate these differences, the scores are weighted by the amount of land remaining undeveloped (at 1976). An analysis is then made of the highest ranking squares from the forty-two surfaces and these are graded I, II and III. Of the fifty or so squares in the area, only thirteen merit a grade in any one of the forty-two surfaces and of this thirteen only nine have at least one grade I mark. The team then assemble the forty-two surfaces into three groups, with all surfaces in a given group showing grade I potential for the same squares.

A sensitivity test is then carried out by giving greater weight to the most important factors for each of the forty-two alternatives, to see whether this would alter the overall potential, and this shows that the overall forms hold good until the ratio of the highest to the lowest weight exceeds 10:1, at which stage the most highly weighted factor begins to dominate all others. Consultations with other professionals suggest to the team that this is quite acceptable since few planners would choose ranges of weights greater than 6:1 and none greater than 10:1.

The three sets of strategies are therefore accepted as a basis for three alternatives for detailed testing and to them is added a fourth based on a "trend" situation.

In a generation process which is based on study objectives, a major problem is the relative importance to be attached to these criteria when they are brought together. The Coventry/Solihull/War. team overcame this problem by varying weights given to objectives and computerising the process. This enables a vast amount of data to be taken into account and a very large number of possibilities to be considered. Once the frame of reference has been established and the techniques developed, the various possibilities are approached without bias. All have the same tests applied to them and are examined to the same degree of detail.

The process is an interesting alternative to Chadwick's Meta Procedure (see Chapter 5) which does not involve weighting, but uses a linear graph to structure the various criteria derived from goals into a hierarchy which determines the order in which the criteria are considered. Both techniques attempt to eliminate prejudice on the part of the team and the high degree of clarity they achieve is itself useful in this respect. No process can completely eliminate the exercise of discretion, however, and this is involved in Coventry/Solihull/War. in the initial definition of objectives and the construction of the Potential Surface, and in the Meta Procedure in breaking down goals to criteria and drawing out the linear graph.

The adequacy of study objectives as the sole basis for plan generation is a critical question. We have already pointed out, in Chapter 5, that Sub-regional planning has not yet really come to grips with the question of the competing objectives of individuals, societal groups, private and government agencies. One way is to recognise the "market": to observe and simulate behaviour, on the assumption that the balancing out of objectives which this represents will continue to hold good in the future, or will change in some predictable way. We would expect to be convinced that some attempt had been made to take "market" forces into consideration. No really satisfactory techniques exist for this purpose at present, but computer models are of some value. We do, however, have some reservations about the adequacy of the Coventry/Solihull/War. potential surface for this purpose (see Chapter 4), particularly in relation to the question of interaction between the Sub-region and Birmingham.

CYCLICAL AND LEARNING PROCESSES

Boyce, Day and McDonald[63] compare two approaches to plan generation: linear and cyclical. Both start with a number of alternatives, which may be stereotypes or alternatives selected in some other way. The linear approach then goes on to test these alternatives and select from them the one which performs the best on the results of these tests. (There may be some combination of favourable aspects of more than one alternative, but this is done on a very limited scale.)

The cyclical approach also has tests and these are arranged in a series of cycles, but at the end of each cycle fresh alternatives are produced which may be quite different from those input at the beginning. Each is likely to combine characteristics from several of the original alternatives and may introduce new ones where deficiencies have been observed. This introduces greater flexibility into the process and if the original selected alternatives are inadequate to deal with the situation this is far less serious, since these deficiencies are likely to be remedied during the course of the generative cycles. Cycles have another important advantage in that they can be readily adapted as the basis of a learning process whereby the models and techniques commonly used in plan generation play a more analytical role. Cycles can be used to explore directions in which the Sub-region's urban systems might be encouraged to develop. During the course of these cycles, model output is examined for information about the ways in which systems are likely to respond to policy stimuli. It is also possible to make some assessment of the effects on the form of development of changes in critical factors such as mobility of population and jobs and willingness to travel further to work.

A Study which attempts to combine analysis, generation and evaluation is Notts./Derby. which involves four stages and since the nature of this process is not generally familiar, some lengthy but selective quotes are included at the end of this chapter.

This is more than a straightforward cyclical generation process, however, since the team set out to learn about the area and its performance under different policy assumptions, as well as to generate alternative plans.

Stage I of the Notts./Derby. process takes seven theoretical concepts (trend, potential welfare needs, constraints, utopias, etc.) and develops from these forty-seven strategies. Time constraints will not, however, allow testing of all of these so that twelve representatives only are selected. This stage is concerned with very coarse, broad scale testing and therefore uses low-variety techniques such as the Potential Surface and Garin–Lowry model. Thus the most important output is the identification of a "main stream area" within which the preferred strategy will locate most new development.

At stage II thirty-five strategic ideas are carried forward and combined into six alternatives for testing, which is now in relation to specific Sub-regional locations. These six are not, however, regarded as coherent strategies so much as assemblages of ideas, some of which will eventually form part of a preferred strategy. To the tests adopted at stage I, some more detailed ones are added, notably by using a synthetic transport model, a shopping model, and a matrix of organisational needs suggested by different patterns of development. Output from this stage includes the identification, within the main stream, of areas where growth potential is insufficient and some stimulus is required, and the areas where potential appears suffi-ciently strong to allow siphoning off should this be desired. Testing for links and associations show that some of the areas of need are linked with areas of good growth potential, others are not.

At stage III, three coherent strategies are tested, representing basically one set of dispositions under different assumptions about mobility of firms and population. These strategies again represent a combination of favoured ideas from the previous stage. Testing at this stage pays particular attention to local planning considerations, servicing problems and pilot studies of areas where substantial development is likely to be recommended.

Stage IV combines the best features of the three alternatives into a single strategy which is now subject to final adjustment in terms of detailed locations and quantities.

The Notts./Derby. approach applies the lessons of systems thinking and in particular the Law of Requisite Variety. It begins with low variety tests at the very broad scale and reserves high variety tests for more detailed work at the end of the process. It benefits from American experience of computer models and uses them to explore the performance of a wide variety of strategy elements in various sub-regional locations, rather than employing them on forecasting tasks. This brings the team up against the problem of trying to understand how urban and rural systems behave under different policy stimulii and, while their techniques cannot offer any easy solutions, at the very least the procedure has the advantage of focusing attention on the problem.

This sort of process is not likely to satisfy those who demand "proof" that a preferred strategy is the "best". We would, however, regard this as an indication of the need for a better understanding of the nature of Sub-regional planning than a criticism of the process (see our comments in Chapter 7 in this respect). Nevertheless, it is difficult to communicate such a process satisfactorily. This main problem of securing acceptance and of consulting the general public, who have not participated in, and may well not understand the learning process, remains to be tackled.

CONCLUSIONS

The nature of the strategy generation process adopted will represent a trade-off between a number of different considerations: clearly the nature of the problem will be important: New Town studies will be particularly concerned with urban form, Co-ordination studies with system control and interaction and so on. If investment funds are very scarce then thresholds will take on much greater significance; if firms cannot be assumed mobile this takes much of the point away from more free ranging exercises. The nature of the area in relation to the techniques and resources available will also be important: the South-east, for example, is so complex a problem as to be beyond the capacity of many computer models, while rural settlements may be too small for some techniques to be effective. In addition to this technical trade-off, however, the selection may also be influenced by the value systems of the team and sponsors and the political facts of life in the area.

The range of alternatives tested should be as wide as is practicable and should be representative of the more important possibilities. In satisfying himself that this is so, anyone evaluating a Sub-regional study would need to look at the team's more obvious value judgements but also at the techniques themselves, since these can effectively rule out some possibilities before the generation/evaluation process even begins.

The question of demonstrating the strategy is important: how successfully the team have described the process and presented the case for following up some possibilities and rejecting others. The extent to which this has been accomplished will have an important bearing on whether the final strategy becomes generally accepted.

APPENDIX

Excerpts from Notts./Derby. Record Report 31. "The Development of Strategy Proposals"*

Our approach involved the assumptions that the strategies would be evaluated against an hierarchy of factors. Those strategies which did not satisfy the most fundamental factors were discarded even though they might satisfy more detailed requirements. These factors resolved themselves into three broad groups, representing three levels of analysis. The first of these (Stage I) was a macro level designed to define areas for more detailed study by identifying "mainstream" ideas and eliminating those on the fringe. Stage II was concerned principally with the interactions between elements within the refined areas, and Stage III involved urban structuring and the broader aspects of specific site characteristics. A final fourth non-analytical stage defined the recommended Strategy. . . .

Basis of Stage I Strategies

The group concerned with the production of alternative strategies held a series of meetings to discuss how best to ensure that the strategies prepared were as comprehensive as possible. It was decided to devise a series of theoretical concepts on which the initial strategies should be based, and seven such concepts were suggested:

(a) Trend-led.
(b) Potential-led.
(c) Welfare, i.e. based on areas of need.
(d) Opportunity.
(e) Constraints-led, i.e. physical constraints or organisational constraints.
(f) "Utopias", i.e. spatial patterns and social systems.

* The authors' own linking text is in italics.

(g) Implementation-oriented, e.g. based on type of development with which agencies could readily cope.

The last of these was subsequently incorporated into group (e), being regarded as a form of organisational constraint.

At the same time a search through material collected in the office was made for existing ideas and propositions about the future development of the Sub-region, and the implications of existing policies and goals.

The trend-led and potential-led concepts would essentially have only one form each, designed to optimise the particular factor concerned. The strategies would be devised by on the one hand studying past trends and on the other by making use of the initial indications derived from the Potential Surface.

The remaining four concepts, on the other hand, could take many different forms, and it was decided to develop strategies from these by two processes. Initially, each member of the group would be responsible for a different concept and would devise as many strategies as possible based on this concept. The results were submitted to a "jury" for comment, and subsequently each member of the group devised a strategy for each concept which he had not previously studied. In this way it was hoped to avoid the danger of a person's mind fixing on one idea or group of ideas and being unable to envisage others.

It may be noted here that both the trend-led and potential-led strategies make use of Potential Surface output so that it would be misleading to say that this technique is used for testing purposes only and not in generation. In fact it has a major influence in determining the "mainstream area" in which later strategies are concentrated. Within the context of a cyclical process, however, most techniques used have both a generative and an evaluative role.

Content of Stage I Strategies

Welfare-based strategies investigated a variety of ideas for attempting to alleviate different sorts of problems, e.g.

(a) Diversion of growth in the southern half of Sub-region to northern areas of mining rundown and high unemployment.

(b) Diversion of growth in the southern half of Sub-region but only to the northern fringes of the prosperous area, with assumed commuting from declining areas.

(c) Sub-regional problem areas assumed to have Development Area status, and development therefore associated with good inter-regional communications as well as labour supply.

(d) Development in areas of poor environment:
   (i) based on poor housing,
   (ii) based on dereliction.

(e) Development designed to stem decline in remoter rural areas.

(f) Development in areas with high natural increase of population.

(g) Development in areas with ageing population.

(h) Development to promote new centre able to provide major services in central part of Sub-region, out of reach of Nottingham, Derby and Sheffield.

These strategies showed the strong attractions of the western exposed coalfield from the point of view of need, and pointed to the major problem of determining how far the much greater but still limited growth potential of the Nottingham–Derby belt could be harnessed to exploiting the surplus labour and alleviating the social and economic problems of the northern half of the Sub-region. They also emphasised, however, that other parts of the Sub-region had their problems, notably the distance of some parts of the agricultural fringes of the Sub-region from good service centres, and the concentration of poor housing in Derby and Nottingham.

The strategies based on opportunities tended to contrast with the welfare strategies by concentrating on the southern half of the Sub-region, where the economic opportunities clearly lay. Some examined various directions for expanding Nottingham and Derby, including taking advantage of proximity to the East Midlands Airport, linking up with the potential of Loughborough and the longer-term potential of the Burton–Swadlincote area (for accepting overspill from the West Midlands), and linking Derby and Nottingham together along the line of the closed railway line through Breadsall and Ilkeston. Opportunities in other parts of the Sub-region were also examined, including the considerable residential attractions of good landscape in various parts of the area, the communication advantages of access points to M.1, the reopening of the Nottingham–Mansfield–Worksop railway line, and the possibilities of the establishment of a new hospital and new technical college to solve part of the welfare problem of the coalfield. The ability of the rural part of the Sub-region to accept large-scale growth from outside was also investigated under this heading.

Under the heading of "utopias", all the possible theoretical patterns for urban development that could be envisaged were examined in relation to various parts of the Sub-region. At the same time an examination was made of the spatial implications of a variety of possible future patterns of social activity but it was concluded that these were adequately catered for by the various forms of urban development dealt with here. These included: Corridors of Growth, Finger growth, Linear growth, Commuter towns, New Towns, Satellite towns, Joined ring of towns, Villages, Counter-magnets, Grid-based development, "non-plan", "Scatteration". In practice it was found that the satisfaction of the unit objectives was not closely dependent on the adoption of any specific urban form. Further consideration of urban form was therefore postponed until the preparation of structure plans was undertaken.

The study of physical constraints produced strategies based on giving relative weightings to different constraints. The most restrictive situation therefore assumed all constraints to be absolute and development was limited to the comparatively small areas which were completely unaffected. The least important constraints were then removed successively to provide additional land for development. These strategies showed a strong emphasis extending north–south along the exposed coalfield from east of Chesterfield to west of Ilkeston. The "institutional constraints"—land commitments, and what information was available on spare capacity in the public utilities, such as roads, sewers, gas and electricity—tended to show a somewhat similar pattern, with constraints strongest in and around Nottingham and Derby and weakest where existing policies were proving relatively unsuccessful in attracting development.

At the end of Stage I generation, the team had forty-seven strategies, which was too great a number for their testing routines. They in fact tested ten, but made efforts to ensure that none of those rejected included any which were essentially dissimilar in spatial implication from those chosen. The tests applied at this stage include the Potential Surface, the Garin–Lowry model and physical constraints. The main conclusions drawn from this round of testing were as follows:

1. Large-scale development outside the main urbanised belt was not likely to be feasible although moderate growth in the rural areas was necessary for welfare reasons.
2. The least constrained sites for development lay on the old coalfield.
3. Development south of Nottingham and Derby towards Leicester was not desirable because of physical constraints (including the airport), administrative boundaries, and its failure to assist the areas of need. On the other hand, discussions with Leicestershire were desirable because of the possible effects of development south of the Sub-region on pressures within the Sub-region.
4. A strategy based on south Nottinghamshire only favours Loughborough, is damaging environmentally, and has no inherent advantages for Nottingham over other growth directions.
5. Possibilities for the development of urban fringes, particularly those of Nottingham and Derby, depend on the structure of the towns, and should therefore be examined at Stage II.
6. A dispersed pattern of development, which could not be tested at Stage I, must still be investigated.
7. The use of concepts as a basis of strategy formation should give way to spatial distributions, since it was found that the satisfaction of the Unit's objectives was not closely dependent on the adoption of particular theoretical concepts.
8. Stage II should examine:
   (a) precise locations on the edge of towns,
   (b) the viability of a Clay Cross–Bolsover strategy,
   (c) the importance of location and form,
   (d) the possibility of growth continuing indefinitely and its direction,
   (e) growth in smaller centres, such as Newark.

Stage II takes the mainstream area identified and the other lessons from Stage I as a starting point and dispenses with "concepts":

It was decided that the basis of the Stage II strategies should be location rather than any particular concept, and that, with one or two exceptions, the greater quantity of development should be confined to the principal urbanised zone running from Nottingham and Derby to Sheffield. The various strategic ideas therefore represent alternative locations for distributing growth within the urbanised zone.

Although Stage I had eliminated perhaps half of the whole Sub-region from the "mainstream" the options within the remaining area were still very wide. There were twenty to thirty different possibilities for different parts of the mainstream area which we wished to test, but time and money precluded testing more than about six strategies. It was therefore decided to combine several different "strategic ideas" in each strategy plan. Because these different ideas were shown on a single plan it did not mean that they were in any way related—indeed, the contrary was more likely to be the case, because in deciding which ideas to put together on one map our main aim was to couple those which would not interact with one another so that their effects could be clearly distinguished. The Stage II "strategies" are not, therefore, total strategies at all, but combinations of various ideas for testing purposes.

Regard was had to the existence of physical constraints in the distribution of population up to 1976, but the previous assumption that development up to that date would follow trends was abandoned. Instead, rough estimates of the size of the additional population which would tend to locate in different parts of the Sub-region were made, and a proportion were taken out from some of these and added to the area of need, so as to give a bias northwards. Two further refinements were to modify the resulting distributions in accordance with major commitments, where these seemed likely to be taken up, and in relation to the main areas of slum clearance and overcrowding. These Stage II strategies were designed to represent extreme situations which for testing purposes would be more useful than more evenly spread distributions, even though the latter might ultimately prove desirable.

Seven strategy plans were originally prepared for Stage II but it was found that these contained a certain amount of duplication and that one could be "cannibalized" by incorporating parts of it in the remaining six. . . .

These strategies were subjected to five sets of tests:

(a) Transportation model,
(b) Garin–Lowry (location) model,
(c) Retail Sales model,
(d) Physical constraints tests,
(e) Objective and organisational tests.

Several weeks were spent in studying the results of these tests, which are separately described in Record Reports Nos. 34, 36, 37, 39 and 40. The main conclusions were as follows:

(1) A growth zone east of Chesterfield was desirable to absorb the growth requirements of the northern part of the Sub-region in an area of need. Rapid expansion might be possible if Sheffield again becomes short of space.

(2) A growth zone was required in the Alfreton–Sutton–Mansfield–Kirby area with strong links through Hucknall to the growth potential of Nottingham.

(3) Gradual growth was required to meet the local needs of Belper, Ashbourne, Newark, Retford, Worksop, Bingham and other small towns and villages.

(4) The restrained growth of Derby was desirable probably towards the south and south-east in association with the East Midlands Airport, up to the limits imposed by physical and transportation constraints and job opportunities, on the assumption that it will develop as a centre of advanced technology. Some restructuring to strengthen neighbourhoods will be necessary to reduce pressure on its centre.

(5) The restrained growth of Nottingham on its boundaries was desirable where suitable land is available. Emphasis should be on its development as a regional capital and centre of educational health, entertainment, and cultural facilities, but with office growth also encouraged. Decentralisation of industrial and other uses should be pursued as far as necessary to avoid congestion.

(6) Land west of Ilkeston, in the Ripley–Belper–Derby area, north of Alfreton–Sutton, in the Doe Lea Valley, and at Clay Cross, was noted as having possibilities for development in either the short or the long term. In addition, it was apparent at this stage that the development of growth zones and the carrying out of necessary environmental and social improvement plans would require the establishment of special committees or agencies.

The main purpose of the Stage III strategy formulation and testing cycle was to refine the various spatial indications derived from Stage II and outlined above.

Accordingly, three strategies were devised to represent the realistic extremes of concentrated and dispersed development; more or less favourable economic growth prospects; and varying amounts of individual and industrial mobility, in relation to each of the main development areas defined at Stage II. Each Stage III strategy was designed as an entity in itself, rather than the collection of unrelated elements which had formed the Stage II strategies.

The practical difficulties of achieving a particular pattern of development at this scale are of two principal kinds: the difficulty of obtaining people and jobs in appropriate locations; and the need to avoid major physical and financial constraints. The procedures for developing the Stage III strategies were designed with these in mind. Population and jobs were allocated to each strategy, firstly according to their area of origin, subsequently according to assumptions about mobility and economic prospects, and finally according to land availability. The distributions thus created were then modified in the light of the recreational study, which had been proceeding separately, and was now able to suggest that certain areas should desirably be reserved for recreational purposes.

The Stage III strategies were tested by an application of the models and testing routines used for Stage II, but particular attention was devoted to local planning considerations. Confidential discussions were held with servicing authorities on problems likely to be associated with development in particular areas, and more detailed examinations and pilot studies were made of the parts of the area likely to be proposed for substantial development. This process is described in more detail in Record Reports 34–37, 39–40.

The main conclusions from these tests were as follows. Broadly speaking, those strategy elements which envisaged a high degree of mobility and a high level of governmental economic assistance came closest to achieving the Unit's objectives, whereas those strategy elements which were based on the opposite assumption tended to be operationally more satisfactory but at the expense of increasing problems of unemployment and long distance commuting in the Northern areas and increased congestion in Derby and Nottingham.

As a result of the long-term tests it appeared that each of the three 1986 strategies was sufficiently adaptable as to form a satisfactory basis for either of the two main alternative patterns of development which seemed likely in the longer term. It was also possible to define a single basic road system for the Sub-region which would accommodate either of these two alternative patterns of long-term development.

The conclusions reached from a consideration of the Stage III tests and studies formed the basis for a final draft strategy A21, which was evolved and tested as Stage IV of the Plan Formulation and Testing Process. This strategy was created to bring together what were judged to be the best features of the three previous strategies. A detailed explanation of the factors which led to the choice of this particular strategy, and what were the rejected alternatives, will be found in Chapter 11 of the Report. . . .

The Stage IV strategy was then evaluated against the models and testing routines employed at previous stages so that final adjustments could be made to the locations and quantities proposed and to provide the statistical information on which subsequent work would be based.

CHAPTER 7

Evaluation

THIS chapter is concerned with the way in which a Sub-regional team make their own technical evaluation of the alternative strategies they have devised. It is not to be confused with the overall purpose of this book which is to enable implementation agencies, political bodies and so on to make their own assessment, probably involving some quite different criteria, after the Study has been published. The way they may do this is indicated in Chapter 9. Here the team adopt planner's techniques to measure the advantages and disadvantages of a limited number of alternative strategies, in order that their final selection might be made.

It has become common practice to regard "generation" and "evaluation" as part of the same process, on the grounds that both are concerned with the elimination of alternatives which seem less satisfactory in relation to chosen criteria. We subscribe to this view, but nevertheless find a division useful in organising our argument. It is also true that, for the majority of studies, the techniques which have been used in detailed evaluation have differed from those of generation sufficiently to make our division an acceptable one.

Before leading into Sub-regional evaluation proper, we propose to set the scene by considering some of the problems of evaluation at Regional and National levels. This is for two reasons. Firstly, it is necessary to form an opinion as to the value of Regional and National advice where this led to the setting up of the Sub-regional Study. Secondly, detailed evaluation at Sub-regional level may be seen in a different light if the original Regional and National decision were based on very crude assumptions.

I. REGIONAL AND NATIONAL EVALUATION PROBLEMS WITH IMPLICATIONS AT SUB-REGIONAL LEVEL

It is generally accepted that National and Regional planning proposals should be broad in scale and leave the detail to be filled in at Sub-regional and local levels after further analysis and evaluation. This is to some extent unavoidable. It means, however, that the really critical decisions, involving perhaps millions of pounds, are taken at precisely those levels of planning at which evaluation is most difficult. When, at local levels, one is able to accumulate sufficient information for a fairly rigorous evaluation to take place the decisions concerned may be relatively much less important.

Cripps and Foot[64] look at South-east 1967 and point to the need for a better Regional generation/evaluation process, particularly from the point of view of internal consistency:

> The physical manifestations of these strategies appear to be largely intuitive and exhibit very little evidence of systematic evaluation of alternatives. It is also true that, by and large, these plans are non-specific in their explanation of the relationships between the main components of the regional strategy and entirely so when one looks for a disaggregation of related components by small area. There is a suspicion that the repercussions of change in the economic base of local areas on the distribution of population, etc., is over-simplified and probably obscured by a global approach to change in the region. An examination of small area change is usually left to an expression of the need to carry out sub-regional studies, particularly in Strategy for the South-east.
>
> What is needed is an overall system of analysis which is capable of explicitly defining the relationship between the various elements in the regional strategy and discovering the direct effect of change in any element in the whole or part of the region on all other elements in the system.

They suggest the appropriate techniques to deal with the problem would be a model package including an activity allocation model. This raises the question as to whether the present level of model-building technology is capable of dealing with the size and complexity of the South-east megalopolitan region. The most recent "Strategic Plan for the South-east" seems to imply that it is not. Whether or not they are correct, one would hope that such models may be developed in the not so distant future.

The models Cripps and Foot describe are capable of generating internally consistent strategies in terms of population, basic and service employment distributions and alternative transport networks. They can also assess feasibility by relating the total cost of the system to the resources available, using linear programming.

Several writers have recently pointed to the need for continuous monitoring as a means of evaluating Regional planning strategies over a long period of time. G. M. Lomas and P. A. Wood([65]) go back to the Abercrombie plans of the forties for the South-east and West Midlands and note their recommendations for monitoring and investigation of the means of controlling physical change. Ironically they then advance two decades and show the West Midlands Study asking the same questions and posing the same problems.

On a national scale, formal evaluation is in some ways even more difficult because of the greater area involved. On the other hand, the allocation of national resources between regions, and between national programmes, are problems that have exercised the minds of the Civil Service for centuries. A large body of experience and expertise exists here that planners are slow to exploit. Recent developments in this field are becoming more widely known, and there is considerable interest in central government in making more explicit use of the disciplines of evaluation. For example, Sir Richard Clarke, K.C.B., O.B.E., describes the role of P.E.S.C. (Public Expenditure Survey Committee) in his Civil Service College lectures([66]) and this bears directly on the discussion of the role of Sub-regional Planning and Corporate Planning in local government.

In some cases, however, the issues are so wide and difficult to evaluate that only the world of political debate can provide an answer (for example, the Third London Airport). In others, evaluation may only be possible over long periods of time and here the academic world may make a contribution.

The significance of this level of evaluation to the Sub-regional planner is illustrated by current discussions on the success or otherwise of the British New Towns. The arguments in favour of New Towns are well known; they are included in the syllabus of every planning school and need not be repeated here. However, academics who have looked at the original goals and objectives of the New Town movement and compared them with its actual achievements years later, have questioned the success and even the desirability of New Towns. William Peterson,([67]) for example, doubts whether the growth of London has been reduced from what it would have been anyway and points out that, whether or not this is true,

London's expansion has certainly not been halted. He questions whether the monotony of existence is any less and shows how the original "optimum size" is very unlikely to be maintained in most New Towns. The fact that a New Town "takes off" and grows is not evidence of success and he asks whether it would have been better to have invested the New Town subsidies in improving living conditions in London itself?

William Alonso[68] sees New Towns as having a limited role as a tool for experimental planning, on a relatively small scale:

> On the whole a national policy of settling millions of people in new towns is not likely to succeed, and would not advance the national welfare if it could be done. The principal flaw in new town proposals lies in an under-estimation of the social and economic integration and connectivity of a modern society, which is expressed in the complex reticulation of functional areas and the counterpoint of centres and sub-centres which constitute a metropolis. This complexity allows specialisation and complementarity; its fluidity makes it capable of producing innovations and accepting change; and its ambiguities permit it to encompass the strains and inconsistencies which inevitably accompany change. We may be vexed at the inertia of this system with respect to its many grave problems, such as pollution, massive segregation, and ugliness; but new towns, with their stress on diverse "balances" seem to fall into a deterministic fallacy which, under the guise of increasing choice, would reduce it in nearly closed subsystems of too small a scale. It is curious that an idea which has most of its roots in humanism should take such a materialistic form, basing itself largely on reducing the cost of infrastructure and on physical environmental determinism, and slight the importance of freedom under uncertainty and of communications and interaction in a society based on information.

Another area where National and Sub-regional planning meet is that of location of industry policy. Lomas and Wood[69] point to a confusion which exists here and trace this to two origins. One is a lack of monitoring and investigation by the then Board of Trade who were unable to give adequate advice on these problems, and the other is a lack of co-ordination between that department and the then Ministry of Housing and Local Government:

> In summary, the established approach has tended to break up into two streams of action, which have often run counter to one another. The Board of Trade have been taking work to the workers, by steering factories to the congested areas of the older coalfields and great estuaries of the West and North, while the Ministry of Housing and Local Government have been trying to decongest these areas by building new towns and by pursuing a general policy of "containment". The result has been an inter-departmental battle rather than a policy.

It may well be, of course, that the strains of the political situation make this problem irresolvable, particularly as between the Development Areas on one hand and of the South-east and West Midland overspill areas on the other. But more empirical knowledge is needed on the whole question of industrial mobility if evaluation of National and Regional policies is to be improved.

II. ELABORATION OF SUB-REGIONAL ALTERNATIVES

We now return to the Sub-regional level and set the scene for evaluation by considering the elaboration stage. This converts outline strategies into quantified patterns of activities, communications and land uses which are suitable for detailed evaluation. The elaboration stage is important because errors of judgement in selecting methods and deciding on the degree of detail, can be critical to the evaluation. Particular dangers to avoid are the use of a method containing assumptions that invalidate the subsequent evaluation, or one that is subsequently used for evaluation itself. For example if the derivative of the Lowry model used as an elaboration routine in Leicester/Leics. had been replicated in the evaluation stages by a similar method, there would have been problems of circular reasoning. In any event the process of elaboration is a useful step for it enables much detailed cross-checking to be done in the figuring, and reveals weaknesses and inconsistencies that might not otherwise show up until much later.

Boyce, Day and McDonald[70] discuss two methods of "elaboration": manual and computer, and list advantages and disadvantages of each. Computer programs take a long time to develop, but once operational they can quantify a large number of alternatives in a short space of time. An advantage claimed for these models is that output is more consistent than for manual methods. Investigation showed, however, that output is often freely adjusted manually to make it more "realistic" and results are mapped in a quite insensitive and misleading way. Another disadvantage is that input must be specific and models are incapable of dealing with subtle questions and issues which are normally taken into account in a manual process. Manual methods on the other hand are slow and cumbersome and the number of alternatives which may be tested when they are employed is more limited.

In this country elaboration processes are almost always basically manual, although it is possible that standard computer programs will be developed in the foreseeable future.

The Leicester/Leics. technique is relevant here. This has been described as a compromise between mathematical modelling and gaming simulation. Given a pattern of basic employment as the lead condition which determines other land uses, and a time lag of 5 years, the team predict the likely response of government, developers and other agencies. The process has two stages, the first producing dispositions of land uses for broad zones and the second breaking these down to much smaller areas of 2×2 km. The first stage makes some use of a computer, the second is entirely manual. Figures are produced for each of six strategies at 5-year intervals to 1991.

This example is easy to follow and incorporates staging. It could, if necessary, be repeated for monitoring purposes after the team has disbanded. It could also make fuller use of computing facilities, given time to develop the necessary programs. The principal trade off which the team make in developing the technique is to forgo testing certain assumptions about mobility of industry, but this is not regarded as critical in the particular context of Leicester/Leics.

Elaboration procedures should be made easy to follow so that other departments and agencies who are concerned with evaluation, structure planning and monitoring can see what has been done and, if necessary, repeat the operation with different assumptions. They should also be flexible enough to deal with sensitive local issues. Like data banks, however, elaboration can take up as much time (and more!) as the team is prepared to allow, so that it is important to remember that they are a means to an end and not an end in themselves. It is essential not to go beyond that minimum level of detail required by evaluation techniques on the one hand and implementation agencies on the other. Of course, there should also be safeguards against arithmetic errors and especially cumulative errors which occur through feeding unchecked figures from one cycle to another.

We can now go on to discuss evaluation techniques. In the following text we have not indicated a preference for any particular techniques, but have tried to set out the more important questions as we see them. We would emphasise, however, that evaluation (and, indeed, many other) techniques may not be neutral.

III. TOPIC EVALUATION

This stage is concerned with evaluating strategies in terms of particular topics taken separately—accessibility, transport, environment, economic interaction, servicing, shopping facilities and so on.

Several techniques are available for topic evaluation and some of them have been referred to already (transport models, shopping models). Unfortunately, it is impracticable, here, to assess them all rigorously. It has been decided therefore to limit the discussion to topic evaluation as an operation, discussing one selected Study in some detail.

Teesside was the first of four pioneer studies (Teesside, Leicester/Leics., Notts./Derby. and Coventry/Solihull/War.) which made major advances in Sub-regional planning in this country. It made use of transport and shopping models and was the first Study to include a separate evaluation stage. The evaluation of seven alternatives is in terms of individual topics—industry, workers' needs, housing and environment and so on—together with local sensitivity testing.

The regional background to Teesside is "The Challenge to the Changing North" published by the Economic Planning Council. This suggested Teesside as a growth area for the North-east, to encourage industrial growth and accept inward migration from other parts of the Region. Thus it is prescribed that Teesside should achieve an inward movement of jobs at the rate of 2000 per year which, the Study explains, is twice the rate achieved in the recent past.

The Study puts forward seven strategies embodying the following organising principles: linear growth (three alternatives), satellite development, dispersed development (two forms) and a compact development as close as possible to the existing built up area. Eighty per cent of population and employment location which will exist at the terminal date of 1991 is already committed, but the remainder is distributed in accordance with these principles. It is argued that these seven adequately represent a large number of possibilities. For example, the conclusions drawn from testing the satellite development are taken to be valid for new towns in other locations. Strategy generation is carried out before the results of the several detailed surveys have been received, as is the first of the two stages of evaluation. The second stage of evaluation is carried out with the benefit of survey results and is performed on one strategy only.

At the first stage of evaluation the team examine each strategy in the light of requirements which are derived from Regional and Sub-regional objectives, and a short summary of the points they make is useful here:

(a) *Industrial estates.* The ability to attract light industry is a major objective if the role of Teesside in the Northern Region is to be fulfilled. The team argue that sufficient land and labour are available, but that ease of access is an important factor which the final strategy must provide for both labour catchment and markets/linkages. The latter are likely to be with areas to the south of Teesside in the main; and although it can be argued that ease of communications are less critical than they were, the team rate good accessibility as an important psychological advantage in attracting new industry. Each alternative is therefore examined in the light of these criteria and five of the seven alternatives are found to be satisfactory.

(b) *Workers' requirements.* Another objective is that workers should be offered as wide a range of jobs as possible within reasonable commuting distance of their homes. To test this criterion, an index of job opportunity is developed. Indices are calculated for a number of zones for each strategy. They bring together workers resident in the zone, jobs there and in nearby urban zones, and the travelling distance between the zones. The higher the index value the greater the job opportunity for workers resident in the zone. The principal conclusions from this test are that the satellite development offers relatively poor job opportunity; another strategy which locates new jobs close to areas of poor job opportunity has a high rating, with the other five falling fairly close together between these two extremes.

(c) *Housing and environment.* Two criteria are identified. These concern (i) the topography of the main areas to be developed and (ii) the extent to which a *variety* of environmental types are made available (coastal, small villages, suburban). Two strategies can be dismissed on these grounds. One, involving very dispersed development, because insufficient demand is likely to arise for the type of residential environment provided, while the penalties of intrusion by building and traffic in rural areas are high. Another is abandoned because it involves large-scale development on land with poor site characteristics and few compensating advantages.

(d) and (e) Regional centre development and sewerage problems are also discussed briefly at this stage.

(f) *Land use and transport.* Data from home interviews and the survey of the existing network and land uses are not yet available. Because of this and the high cost of running a computer model for several alternatives, a simplified and mainly manual simulation procedure is devised at the first evaluation stage. This is, however, held to be sufficient to test the general principles in the seven strategies. It deals with traffic flows by public and private transport separately and compares travel costs with and without personal travel time (as opposed to travel to work). The most compact strategy is found to be the cheapest and there is spare capacity in the committed road system which is "significant in suggesting locations for the additional population".

At the end of this first stage of evaluation, the findings are drawn together into a "provisional urban plan" for more detailed testing in the second stage.

The second stage involves testing the strategy in the light of (a) local studies of critical areas and (b) survey data which has now been assembled and processed. Local evaluation studies lead to two main changes. Firstly it is found that parts of the South-east development are less suitable than originally supposed and the capacity of alternative sites in this direction is lower than the original ones. Secondly the Leavenside area to the South is seen to have potential for the creation of a suitable urban environment and there are very strong arguments in favour of this from the transport point of view. Thus more development is assumed in the South and less in the South-east.

More detailed survey data and a closer examination of forecasts and assumptions lead to some revision of estimates of likely population and employment (both upwards) but these reinforce rather than invalidate the general conclusions drawn. In addition a much more precise and detailed testing of transport implications now becomes possible. Although this second stage involves one strategy only, it covers three different networks, three alternative public transport systems and then three combined·road networks/public transport systems. Following this, the strategy is further elaborated by recommendations for other land uses, including open space, the countryside, etc. At this stage, too, a shopping model is used to assess the consequences of the proposed land-use distributions on regional, major and district centres.

In the Teesside Study one can trace the progression from Regional–Sub-regional to Local level. The problems of link up between the Sub-regional and Local planning should be easier than in many studies. The large amount of detailed local survey work means that Teesside are better able to comment on local implications than other teams. Unfortunately, to save time (by evaluating before the results of surveys are received) and money (in computer runs), evaluation of all but the "provisional urban plan" is largely unquantified. On the whole, computerised models tend to be used by Teesside for elaboration of the favoured strategy rather than for evaluation of alternatives.

The strategy is not staged, but this is seen as a follow-up task. Cost estimates for the strategy as a whole, as opposed to transport costs, are given only for the recommended strategy and not seen as a vehicle for evaluation, some would feel rightly so.

One criticism is that there appear to be no specific tests for feasibility, even though the optimistic assumption made at the outset of doubling the inflow of jobs to the area is quite likely not to be achieved. It is true that the team recommend a monitoring procedure, but its implications could have been examined more thoroughly during evaluation and in particular whether uniformly lower rates or fluctuating rates of inward movement have implications for the shape and form of the recommended strategy. On the other hand, the team might argue that to question the terms of reference would have served little purpose in this particular case and would have been unacceptable to the sponsors.

Teesside represented a major advance in Sub-regional planning in having a separate evaluation stage and basing that evaluation on clearly stated objectives. It also consolidated earlier work on transport and shopping. On these foundations subsequent studies were to build. Perhaps one of the most important subsequent developments has been the trend towards composite evaluation.

IV. COMPOSITE EVALUATION

By composite evaluation we mean that stage where two or more strategies are compared, taking all of their various characteristics together, as opposed to considering each characteristic separately and more or less in isolation. In practice, the difference between composite and topic evaluation is usually a question of degree, as reflection on Teesside and the following Ljubljana examples will show. Nevertheless, the distinction is a useful one and helps to structure this discussion.

Composite evaluation techniques are now coming to be regarded as an essential part of the Sub-regional process. However, composite evaluation has not enjoyed the esteem that topic evaluation has amongst Civil Servants, interested experts and academics. The types of logical proof employed in topic studies can be readily related to scientific method and scrutiny, and are familiar. At its best composite evaluation develops its arguments from the relatively new fields of complex systems. The methods and characteristics of logical proof these employ are unfamiliar (but not unscientific) and are not often used by topic experts. It may well take some time to gain widespread acceptance for these new and better methods.

Informal methods of composite evaluation

Informal methods of evaluation are the least demanding in technical resources and also, arguably, in staff time, so that they are the oldest established and most familiar. A particularly interesting example which might be held to fall into this category is the American–Yugoslav Demonstration Study of the Ljubljana Region. The team evaluate four alternative spatial patterns as they might exist in 1981 and 2001. They consider a number of formal methods, which are rejected as inappropriate to their own particular view of their planning function. They do not, therefore, produce a formal plan or strategy, but rather a policy discussion and set of recommendations which are sufficient to initiate a process in which policies are continuously monitored, revised and developed over time. The evaluation is therefore simple and informal:

> The technique of our composite evaluation is simply to organise the relevant material from each sector evaluation by policy area, then to list and discuss policies and policy instruments. In the discussion particular attention is paid to departures from existing policies and to the creation or use of new policy instruments.

An extract from the evaluation tables reproduced in the text is given in Table 7.1.

This is well adapted to the area of study and the particular circumstances of the team, with limited resources and data availability on the one hand and a study area containing large tracts of under-developed rural landscape on the other. The way in which performance measures are related to goals and spatial objectives is also impressive. A more complex area might,

TABLE 7.1. EXTRACT FROM "SPATIAL POLICIES FOR REGIONAL DEVELOPMENT—A DEMONSTRATION STUDY OF THE LJUBLJANA REGION"

Statement of goals, problems, objectives, indicators and measures for utility systems

Broad goals	Associated problems	Spatial objectives	Performance indicators	Proxy measures	Year	Real measures Alternative patterns			
						A	B	B	C
Efficiency	Scarcity of capital for the construction and operation of utilities	Connect urban development	Increase residential and industrial density or project sizes	% of additional population living in zones with the communal housing construction rate of over 100 dwellings p.a. and with density over 100 people per hectare	1981	35·5	38·5	35·7	41·8
					2001	35·9	47·8	49·4	49·0
		Increase residential and employment project size	Increase residential and industrial density or project sizes	Number of zones having more than 3000 non-population serving employees	1981	1·3	14	15	15
					2001	16	17	19	18
Quality	Impure water supply	Building housing at a density high enough to justify eliminating septic tanks	No. of people above X persons per acre	Same as performance indicators					
		Protect water catchment areas from development	No. of people forecast to be living in catchment area	Same as performance indicators					

TABLE 7.1 (*continued*)

Broad goals	Associated problems	Spatial objectives	Performance indicators	Proxy measures	Year	Real measures Alternative patterns		
						A	B	C
	Inadequate water supply	Non-spatial						
	Inadequate service levels (pressure and volume) of the water distribution system	Non-spatial						
	Inadequate capacity for sewerage collection and treatment	Non-spatial						

however, demand a more powerful technology, even as a starting-point to continuous monitoring.

Formal methods of composite evaluation

A considerable number of techniques are available for formal composite evaluation and since the majority are very sophisticated instruments space limitations require that we be very selective here. Even so, only a brief discussion of each technique selected is possible. We have tried, however, to recommend a number of sources from which more detail may be obtained.

To simplify the discussion, we have accepted Boyce, Day and McDonald's[71] division of formal composite evaluation techniques into efficiency and effectiveness methods.

Efficiency methods

These involve comparing the costs and benefits accruing from each alternative in terms of money units, which means not only estimating costs of investment projects but often putting a cash value on things which do not have a market price, such as travel time and ancient monuments. The most sophisticated technique in this category is Cost–Benefit Analysis.

Cost–Benefit Analysis. Although there have been some examples of Cost–Benefit Analysis at the Sub-regional/Regional scale, its use here has perhaps been less frequent than on smaller-scale engineering projects. It is, however, strongly proposed for strategic planning by Professor Lichfield,[72] who sets out ten criteria for selecting an evaluation technique for regional planning. This should:

1. Have regard to the stated or implied objective (ends, values) of the decision makers (which may or may not be the objectives of those for whom they are planning).
2. Cover all systems of urban and regional facilities which are encompassed in the plan.
3. Cover all sectors of the community which are affected, that is which should be included within the decision maker's concern.
4. Subdivide the sectors into producers/operators of the plan output and its consumers so that all "transactions" implicit in the plan are considered.

5. Take account of all costs to all sectors including externalities.
6. Take account of all benefits to all sectors including externalities.
7. Measure all the costs and benefits in money terms.
8. Facilitate the adoption of a satisfactory criterion for choice.
9. Show the incidence of the costs and benefits in all sectors of the community.
10. Be usable as an optimising tool with a view to ensuring the best solution.

He discusses a number of evaluation methodologies and finds that none meet all of his requirements fully. Most nearly satisfying them, however, are the Planning Balance-sheet (which is discussed later in this chapter) and the Roskill Cost–Benefit Analysis.

Roskill[73] is perhaps the most detailed and comprehensive planning evaluation exercise ever undertaken in this country. At the same time it has given rise to controversy which has brought out many interesting ideas. We have already seen that Cost–Benefit Analysis is claimed to be the most comprehensive and exhaustive evaluation technique available. On the debit side some relevant points are made by Professor Peter Self[74] who criticises this application of the technique, on the grounds that it is pseudo-scientific and diverts attention from some of the issues of major importance:

> In the first place the framework of analysis becomes distorted by the grotesque attempt to place all factors on the same monetary basis. The Roskill balance-sheet, for example, places side by side on an apparently equal footing such diverse items as "capital construction costs" and "passenger surface travelling costs". The former represents expenditure which will definitely and necessarily be incurred for the construction of the airport itself and its surface transport links, and which can be estimated within tolerable limits. The latter item—which is so enormous as to swamp the whole Roskill equation and far outweigh differences in capital costs—is based upon an enormous chain of speculative analysis.
>
> First, the volume, origins and destinations of air traffic at distant dates must be estimated. Then this traffic must be allocated between possible airport sites according to assumptions about their accessibility (airport accessibility model). Then average journey times to the possible sites are calculated. This first stage of calculating the crude data is enormously speculative, depending as it must upon all sorts of assumptions about how and where traffic will grow, which airports should be included in the model, what transport improvements will actually have occurred by various dates—not to mention the relevance of possibly dramatic technological developments.
>
> But now, as a further exercise, these speculative savings of x minutes' time must be put in monetary terms. There is no market in marginal time-savings, and no objective way of deciding the absolute or relative worth of the time of a

businessman or tourist, of a national or a foreigner. A wide range of opinions upon these matters is therefore included, described as "sensitivity analysis".

The ultimate point of this procedure is to be able to aggregate such items as capital costs and passenger travelling costs, within the same global equation. To put it mildly, the latter figures are so vastly more speculative and tendentious that the final result, once the procedure is understood, could hardly inspire confidence. But in the process attention has been diverted from the concrete issues involved in the first part of the analysis to artificial arguments about monetarisation. For example, the airport accessibility model includes Manchester (Ringway) but not any midlands airport, although the choice of Foulness rather than Cublington would plainly be a major incentive to the development of an international airport serving the Birmingham area.

Self goes on to argue that the whole exercise is also basically undemocratic:

> . . . one of the meanings of civilisation is that direct clashes of values, where these occur, should be directly resolved and not sidestepped with the aid of magic incantations. Such is the function of politics in a democratic society. . . .
>
> Ultimately decisions about such matters as airport location can only be taken through a series of policy judgements, which should be as open and explicit as possible, and supported by relevant information which can never itself be conclusive. Greater rationality in the final decision is not helped, but hindered, by the use of notional monetary figures which either conceal relevant policy judgements or else simply involve unrealistic and even artificial degrees of precision.

In defence of Cost–Benefit we should point out that the political decision processes had in fact broken down over the selection of an airport site. The exercise was intended as a means of breaking that deadlock, so that the failure here was on the political rather than the planning side. In an atmosphere of controversy and emotion an acceptable solution had not been found. Even in a situation of general apathy, a cynic might question the superiority of political processes over Cost–Benefit, on the grounds that (a) there is a good reason to doubt whether political representatives are capable of tracing through all of the consequences of their decisions subjectively and any assistance which planners can give may be welcomed, and (b) there is a growing feeling in some quarters (see Lisa Peattie[75]) that politicians represent only limited interests and that the wishes of large but non-vocal sections of the community are frequently overlooked or ignored when planning decisions are taken.

One is left with the feeling, however, that much of Self's argument is justified and that a wider consensus needs to be established on the valuation of benefits and costs if cost–benefit exercises on a large scale are to be convincing.[76] Even assuming such a body of agreement on valuation can be built up, however, there remain some major difficulties. In particular, Cost–Benefit assumes that proposals are specified in a very high degree of detail and that the behaviour of the public under the influence of these proposals can be predicted very precisely. The climate of opinion in Regional/Sub-regional planning seems, to us, to be moving in the opposite direction, and the need for flexibility and monitoring to replace the old "single shot" plans is becoming accepted. Perhaps one should therefore seek to be less demanding and more flexible in evaluation procedures. In this respect the Planning Balance-sheet is preferable, although a fairly high degree of precision is assumed here too.

The Planning Balance-sheet. This technique was devised by Professor Lichfield[77] who classes it as a variety of cost–benefit analysis. The general approach is similar to that of Cost–Benefit proper, but it is less ambitious in its quantification of costs and benefits.

A recent example of the application of this technique is set out in Lichfield and Chapman's case study of Ipswich.[78] It must again be emphasised that our description is only sufficient for the purpose in hand and is not intended as a comprehensive assessment of the Ipswich exercise.

This exercise followed recommendations by consultants that, to cope with 70,000 overspill population from London, the town should be expanded westwards onto good agricultural land. Agricultural interests and the County Council questioned this and suggested expansion to the East, where the land is of poor quality. The special evaluative exercise was therefore commissioned.

For the Planning Balance-sheet, the community is divided into homogeneous sectors distinguished by the kind of operations they wish to perform. Thus the initial breakdown is into producers/operators and consumers, and beneath these headings several sub-groups are recognised. Many people, of course, appear under two or more headings. For each alternative strategy, the advantages (benefits) and disadvantages (costs) accruing to each sub-group are then listed. It is recognised that some of these cannot be quantified in money terms and others cannot be quantified at all, only ranked. A ranking system is therefore used and the rankings are added algebraically, to produce net totals for each sector and ultimately for the whole community.

This method retains what we consider to be the principal advantage of Cost–Benefit proper, in tracing through the effects of the Plan on the various elements of the community. It also goes some way to meet Self's objections to Cost–Benefit, particularly in avoiding much of the mystique of a complicated accounting framework and being more readily understood by the intelligent layman.

In this example, the method is effective in isolating the preferred alternative from the second choice. The other three alternatives have total recorded scores which are too close to allow discrimination between them, but the way in which costs and benefits fall on particular sections of the community is different and a change of weighting would emphasise these differences.

Some critics of the Planning Balance-sheet have suggested that, as an "efficiency" method, it still places too much emphasis on reducing money-costs and is insufficiently related to study objectives. Thus Morris Hill([79]) writes:

> . . . a major criticism of "the development balance sheet" is that it does not appear to recognise that benefits and costs have only instrumental value. Benefits and costs have meaning only in relation to a well-defined objective. A criterion for maximising net benefits in the abstract is therefore meaningless. Whereas benefits can be computed referring to different planning objectives, the benefits and costs are not necessarily additive or comparable. It is meaningful to add and compare benefits only if they refer to a common objective.

This brings us to the other major group of formal methods of composite evaluation: effectiveness methods.

Effectiveness methods

Effectiveness methods concentrate on the extent to which alternatives satisfy study objectives and are measured in relation to these by scores and ranks, rather than by money costs. Comparison of scores is made within the context of the particular area of concern. This rules out comparison with other areas, which is implicit in the use of money units having a universal value. The units of measure involved are also usually much coarser than in efficiency methods in general and Cost–Benefit in particular.

Our first example in this group is from the Milwaukee Study as described by Boyce, Day and McDonald.([80]) This makes use of Schlager's rank-based expected value method.

Rank-based expected value. The Milwaukee Study recognises nine general development objectives, eight land-use development objectives and seven transport objectives. These are broken down to give detailed planning standards and the extent to which the standards are met by each of three alternative strategies is considered and set out in a table. The table shows "met", "partially met", "could be met", etc., with more specific quantities shown where these are available. Each table is supplemented by verbal descriptions of the reasons for each group of entries. Overall scores are obtained in an independent staff evaluation. Next, separate analyses are prepared for each land-use plan and each transport plan. Objectives are then grouped into three major categories, ranked in order of importance. The three alternatives are then ranked against the three groups of objectives in order of their increasing ability to meet them. Thus the most important of the three groups of objectives is given the rank of three, and the best of the three alternatives is given the score of three. For each alternative the score against each category of objectives is multiplied by the rank order of the objective group and the results are summed to produce an overall score.

This overall score is again weighted by an index of "probability of implementation" which represents a trade-off between feasibility and desirability. Boyce, Day and McDonald criticise this index firstly as being too conservative, because the difficulty of modifying public and private institutions to implement any plan which diverges significantly from existing trends is heavily weighted and has a substantial effect on the overall assessment. Secondly, they point out that one cannot see that the impact on particular societal groups is considered, except in so far as they may be referred to in the objectives, and thirdly, the threefold grouping is very coarse and a lot of subjective weighting must take place which may not be made clear to the reader.

Goals achievement matrix. This technique was devised by Morris Hill[81] in the United States, but has recently been used in this country by the Coventry/Solihull/War. team and it is their exercise which we take as an example here. (N.B. The reader will recall that we are looking here at only a part of the Study evaluation process which began with the use of their Potential Surface.)

The Objective Achievement Matrix (which term is preferred in the Study) begins with sixteen objectives, concerned with a wide range of physical planning factors—landscape, choice of location for homes and jobs, private and public transport and so on—but excluding flexibility, which is the subject of a separate test. Two sets of weights only are involved at this stage (in contrast to forty-seven sets for their Potential Surface): one of these is derived from within the team and the other from a small public survey. The four alternatives to be tested are regarded as representing an area of doubt about weights which is to be removed.

Performance scores are given for each alternative against each objective and normalised to a 0–100 scale. They are then weighted. Taking each strategy in turn as the preferred one, the numerical advantage it has over the other three is calculated. Disadvantages are also calculated in a similar fashion. The scores are then added up and the alternative with the most favourable overall score is identified. The favoured strategy has the highest total score from both team and public weightings and from the unweighted table. It is most effective, not because it comes out top against many objectives (it is first against only 2 of the 16), but because it scores consistently well in all tests.

The process gives an unequivocal result which proved acceptable in the area and it can therefore be judged to have been successful. One valid point made at a C.E.S. Conference on the Study,[82] which relates to this technique but is in part a general one, is that while the technique gives results which are valid within the context of the Study objectives, these are not necessarily shared by other agencies and particularly central government. If schemes were proposed requiring major participation by agencies operating outside the confines of the Sub-region's local government structure, reference to national objectives and the market mechanism might well be necessary.

V. FLEXIBILITY

The techniques of topic and composite evaluation, which we have discussed in the previous sections, are usually applied to strategies designed to deal with the "most likely" set of circumstances at the end of the plan period. We must now consider attempts to build into strategies the capacity to deal with the unexpected.

For our first example we quote ourselves[83] on the Notts./Derby. process Stage 3, in which three alternatives are considered, incorporating maximum, minimum and median assumptions about mobility of population and employment:

> Now that the (three) strategies were integrated and not merely a collection of propositions under test, examining their evolution over time and specifying the relations between activities and places became important tests of feasibility. . . .
>
> The tests over time were used comparatively, to note the incidence of thresholds and the way they varied between strategies, looking always at sequences of events that were constant, and isolating items that were critical in limiting the opportunity for strategy changes. With the room for manoeuvre constrained up to 1986—by the inertial character of change, and having regard to behavioural uncertainty in the distant future the criteria for the evaluation of the 2001 results changed in emphasis. It was thought appropriate to interpret them as "feedback" and so to arrange the advice for the 1986 period that it kept open the options for the long term, and did not lead—if consistently followed—to conditions whose solution was not already possible. For each of the two extreme strategies the policies advocated for 1986 were assumed to continue unchanged until 2001—except in respect of accessibility. Each result was then examined to determine the extent to which it could have been achieved if its commencing situation had been the alternative extreme. In this way responsiveness to policy and behavioural change was examined, and in many respects seen to be feasible.

The second example is from Coventry/Solihull War., where tests were developed in conjunction with the Local Government Operational Research Unit. This follows on from the Objective Achievement Matrix tests described in the previous section and displays flexibility tests in terms of numerical indices rather than in the form of written argument. Four objectives relating to flexibility are defined as follows:

Objective 17: To be able to adapt to changes within a possible range of departures from "most likely" forecasts.

Objective 18: To be able to cope with sudden and unexpected events.

Objective 19: To be able to respond to changes in social values. . . .

Objective 20: To retain as far as possible the option of switching from any preferred strategy to one of any of the strategies examined, once implementation had begun.

Each strategy is examined in the light of performance criteria and assumptions derived from these objectives, scored and ranked. Ranks under all four tests are then added for each strategy and the strategy which achieves the lowest total is held to be the most flexible. This is in fact the strategy which is also preferred on other objectives.

VI. NEW DIRECTIONS IN EVALUATION

One of the problems of evaluation is the initial decision as to what it is that is being evaluated. Usually alternative plans are the obvious objects, but this is not always so. For some purposes it is more important to translate the plans into a different format so that they are displayed as sequences of decisions appropriate for various implementation agencies. Each step in a sequence then becomes the object of an evaluation, especially in terms of the marginal "costs" of the action to which the decision refers. When more than one plan is the subject of evaluation, each plan having its own decision sequence, the comparative evaluation of the sequences of marginal "costs" is fraught with difficulties. This, however, is not sufficient reason for choosing simpler methods, because evaluation by decision sequence more nearly reflects the procedures adopted by the Civil Service and the "market" than do the normal comparative methods hitherto adopted by planners. This approach bears directly on the characteristics of a Monitoring System. The growing interest in this methodology stems from the impact on the profession of decision theory and management systems.

An aspect of composite evaluation that is often not made explicit is the "trade off" or bargaining between conflicting objectives. Weighting methods do not deal adequately with this nor, many would suggest, does political confrontation. Cost–Benefit Analysis can often obscure the conflict of values implied, and methods such as the Planning Balance-sheet and the Goals Achievement Matrix display but do not resolve the conflicts. We are inclined to the view that the Sub-regional planner needs to select a balance between the displays that the last two methods make available and the political (participation) involvement of the main interest groups.

Whether to evaluate a plan in terms of its state upon completion or whether to evaluate in terms of its significance for present decisions is a key issue. It is customary in the studies we have examined for the alternative plans to be compared upon completion. For example, the 1991 network of several alternatives are compared for their cost effectiveness, their impact on environment, their contribution to accessibility conditions, and so on as at 1991. The planner is, however, concerned with providing advice about the probabilities of the future for the present decisions. Consequently in his evaluation he needs to compare the discounted values of the alternative plans in much the same way as an accountant would compare the present values of the terminal sums of life insurance policies. In Holland, whenever the benefits of land reclamation are under discussion, a discount rate for future benefits is specially devised. The market rate is deemed inappropriate and a social discount rate of about 2% is used. This is done so that the long-term benefits of major projects can stand comparison with the short-term benefits that accrue under current market conditions. There is a case for Sub-regional planning in this country similarly devising a social discount rate for use when evaluating the present benefits of future probabilities. (This does, of course, raise questions on social values, and rightly so.) We referred earlier to the evaluation of plans by defining their decision sequence. The role of discounting is especially important for this. In none of the Sub-regional plans we have studied has this approach been adopted (except as part of some of the Cost–Benefit calculations on new topics), but developments along these lines are necessary if Sub-regional planning and corporate planning are to move closer together.

CHAPTER 8

Monitoring and Implementation

THIS chapter is concerned primarily with advising on the way in which the selected strategy should be implemented and how its progress should be measured and revisions made over the years. This activity is not always considered to be a part of the process of making a plan. More often it is relegated to some time after a strategy has been adopted. In our view it has such important implications for the design of the whole process, its technical content, and the nature of its output that no Sub-regional study should in future exclude it. As support for our view it seems appropriate to quote Chadwick's[84] account of the planning process and use it as an introduction to our discussion.

> The initial process is to set up overall programmes which allocate resources to the planning process, and provide for its review . . . then the stages of problem statement, consideration of the value system . . . and a system description will follow as the first major level of enquiry. These lead, via system modelling, design method, and exploratory and normative forecasting, towards the generation of alternatives. The alternatives are expressed as programmes, i.e. networks of actions, at a strategic level, and selected programmes are then simulated using Forrester type dynamic simulation, with appropriate feed back to earlier stages. . . . Pre-implementation programming and review whilst implementation takes place follows. . . .

This chapter is divided into three sections: Consultations, Implementation and Monitoring. "Consultations" are closely associated with implementation in that the strategy will have been devised by a team isolated from the general public and with only infrequent contact with some of the agencies whose co-operation is essential to the achievement of its objectives. Thus consultations and the enlisting of their support becomes an important first step in implementation. Under the general heading "Implementation" we consider briefly the nature of the inputs required from the Sub-regional team to the County planning organisations and other implementation agencies and discuss some characteristics of the machinery and the political and human elements involved. This prepares the ground for the final section headed "Monitoring" and our argument that, because of the nature of Sub-regional planning and the way in which strategies are implemented, monitoring at this level is quite different from County or New Town monitoring where much of the existing development work has been undertaken.

CONSULTATIONS

Information on consultations by Sub-regional teams is not easy to come by and is not usually published, for obvious reasons. However, the writers have had access to Notts./Derby. files and have compiled Table 8.1 which shows the kinds of agencies who were specifically asked to comment on the strategy, the number of written approaches made and written replies received. The constituent authorities and central government departments are not shown in the table, because consultations with these bodies were more or less continuous throughout the two and a half years of the Study. Utility operators' responses are shown in the table, but these too are probably under-represented for a similar reason.

TABLE 8.1. CONSULTATIONS BY NOTTS./DERBY. AFTER PUBLICATION OF THE STRATEGY

Agencies	Number contacted	Number of written replies received
Economic Planning Boards and Councils	8	6
Regional Development Conferences	4	2
Planning authorities in adjacent areas	8	6
Boroughs and districts in the Sub-region	43	25
Transport undertakings	5	3
Water Boards and River Authorities	9	5
Gas and electricity producers/suppliers	7	2
Countryside and rural interests	10	7
Further education and sport	2	2
Employers organisations and trades unions	5	1
Chambers of trade, chambers of commerce, trades councils	39	6
Other bodies	9	4

The list of agencies consists of:

(a) bodies set up specifically to consider strategic planning problems;

(b) local government bodies likely to be indirectly affected by the strategy;

(c) utility operators and transport undertakings whose co-operation is necessary if the strategy is to succeed; and

(d) representatives of major interest groups in the area.

In addition the published document, taking its cue from the Skeffington Report,[85] canvassed the views of any other interested persons or bodies.

The table shows that the response rate varied considerably. Those bodies who one might have expected to think in strategic terms and make a useful and constructive contribution to the debate showed response rates well above average. On the other hand, some of those who, one would suppose, were approached because they might wish to be heard rather than for the value of any strategic ideas they might have, showed much lower response rates. The response to the open invitation to the general public to participate in a discussion of the strategy was virtually nil.

The second example of Sub-regional consultations, by the South Hants 1972 team, has already been mentioned in Chapter 5. This involved a questionnaire survey of a scientifically selected sample of 3000 electors in the area, of whom 62% responded. We have already discussed the objectives questions and noted that the response to questions about the "Four Possibilities" (i.e. alternative strategies) was considered by the team to be more significant than the comments about "Aims" (objectives). The main results of the alternatives questions were as follows:

> A clearer preference emerged, however, in the choice of one of the Four Possibilities. Replies from the random sample indicated a preference for Strategy D, with the individual results in the following order: D—33 per cent, A—26 per cent, B—21 per cent and C—19 per cent. Among local authorities, both the City Councils indicated a preliminary preference for C and of the eight district councils who replied, three preferred B, two D, two C and one A. In general the organisations replying preferred C followed by A, but in particular tended to suggest a combination of strategies.

The team enlarge upon these findings and then indicate the way in which the results were used in the evaluation process:

> While the response to this publication of the Four Possibilities provided valuable guidance on the views of the Local Authorities, organisations and general public, any strategy preference was inevitably based on an assessment

of the outline descriptions presented in the blue pamphlet. A far more detailed technical examination of the future possible locations of activities, land-uses and networks was made for the purposes of the complex evaluation carried out by the Advisory Committee.

In the event a combination of strategies C and D was adopted for Structure Plan purposes.

A survey of this scale and thoroughness is a significant step forward in planning and most planners would probably agree with confining the results to background information to the evaluation process. In fact this had to be so, because the results from different groups and agencies were not the same and the team had no basis for weighting to put them together. In addition, it was not practicable to give the public a full and detailed explanation of all of the relevant facts, so that their evaluation is inevitably less comprehensive than that of the Advisory Committee with whom the final decision lies.

These two examples represent genuine attempts to follow the spirit of the Skeffington Report, but they raise enough problems to suggest that the question of consultations at Sub-regional level needs putting on a firmer footing than at present. There has been widespread disenchantment with consultation processes in the past, because people have felt that it made little difference to the plan whatever they might say. This is particularly likely to happen at Sub-regional level because you can no longer rely on simple consultation processes: the issues involved in consultation are not simple and readily identified, like building a school on plot A or plot B. They are community decisions and bargains between several communities and groups of interest. To cope with consultations at Sub-regional level we need to think about the democratic process itself and the planner's training does not necessarily equip him for this task.

Sub-regional planners have copied statutory consultation processes and taken the Skeffington recommendations, which may be quite suitable for local planning, and inflated these to the Sub-regional level. A Sub-regional consultation process has not been conceived in its own right. The latest Planning Act, however, is changing the nature of Inquiries into Strategic Plans: even in a parliamentary democracy it has been found desirable to decide who should make representations on what subjects and to indicate the level at which the criteria and issues should be considered. Decisions will include a mixture of some professional and some government interests, and not be simply a question of the constitutional rights of the individual.

If there is a lack of success in terms of low response rates, is this because people do not believe Sub-regional plans to be relevant to their daily lives? Do agencies feel that they can ignore Sub-regional plans with impunity? It seems more likely that the fault lies with planners who have yet to learn how to consult. We have, for example, put questions in a form whereby electors were asked about points of principle when they can only think of points of fact. Perhaps we need to consult each particular interest group in terms of its own interest. The issues raised at present are not those which inspire the body politic: an unemployed man may not be interested in water resources and perhaps some other body should be consulted about this. If the questions seem irrelevant in terms of their own priorities, people will not respond with enthusiasm.

If consultations are to be framed in this way, so that the general public are consulted in terms of the more concrete issues which they can understand while agencies are approached on specialist problems, this puts more responsibility on the planner in identifying and weighting objectives and social values to ensure that the interests of community groups are taken into account. Market objectives need also to be included and perhaps this may be achieved through systems modelling, demand and supply and trend analysis.

We would suggest that:

decision systems should be displayed so that agencies and individuals at various levels in the decision-making hierarchy know what their interest in the strategy is and where it lies in relation to others;

specialists could usefully be retained to advise on the appropriate forms and channels of communication in consultations;

deviations from expectations which the plan involves should be made clear;

implications of the plan for societal groups, particularly the disadvantaged, should be made clear.

IMPLEMENTATION

The major role in implementation will be played by the constituent authorities themselves, with the support of central government. The principal vehicles will be Structure and Local plans, which will guide and stimulate development in the light of Sub-regional advice. Thus the first three sub-headings of this section are concerned essentially with physical development and the powers of agencies to control and stimulate building. The fourth section is concerned with the implementation of a strategy which has social and economic objectives which would ideally involve a corporate plan, and with the need to influence agencies other than those concerned with physical development.

1. *Some characteristics and limitations of the implementation system for physical plans*

The discussion in this section is mainly in terms of the pre-Local Government reform situation because it is not possible to predict at this stage with any accuracy how the balance of power in planning will change with reform. The best we can do is to pick out those lessons from past experience which seem to have validity for both the old and new situations, leaving aside those problems which are likely to disappear.

After the 1947 Act, in most areas quite long periods elapsed before Development plans were produced and much more time went by before they were approved by the Minister. Although Town Maps were pushed through fairly quickly in some cases and development policies were drawn up for the interim period, it was fairly clear that the Development Control machine was capable of rolling along without formal policy documents for long periods of time. Officers seem to have used a combination of old policies developed under previous legislation, local traditions built into a sort of unwritten "case law" and an instinctive knowledge as to what was acceptable to the local and national authorities. The climate of opinion in the planning profession generally encouraged this purely pragmatic approach, for their was a high level of consensus that plans should be based on slow growth and only marginal change—a legacy of the thirties. This climate of opinion no longer persists, but the ability of the Development Control juggernaut to roll on whether or not a current Development plan is available remains, because the long delays involved in drawing up plans and getting them accepted by national government have not been eliminated. It is to be hoped that the new procedures will have success in cutting down these delays.

Thus a self-sustaining machinery exists which will carry on doing what has been found acceptable or effective in the past. Its reactions are slow and, since forecasts of population, employment and other elements basic to the plan are constantly being revised, there is a tendency for those concerned with implementation to take running averages, smoothing out fluctuations and avoiding the need for violent changes in policy.

This has been found over long years of experience to be a workable and acceptable solution to the major problem of framing decisions about very long-life investment in the light of information which may have only short-term validity. It does, however, have important implications for the Sub-regional planner. He needs particularly to identify those policy areas where major changes are necessary and a concerted effort must be made to bring about changes in direction. If the machine is incapable of responding sufficiently quickly, then it may be that alternative agencies must be identified or created. For instance, an inertial machine with a time lag of seven years would clearly be inappropriate for social policies able to tolerate a maximum lag of one year. On the other hand, in some policy areas it may be acceptable to recommend no change in the existing situation and to allow the machine to continue to balance out the various forces as it is accustomed to doing.

Another important factor in implementation is the pressures for development which exist in the area and how strong these are. In the centre of an expanding town or city these pressures may be such that the development control officer can achieve a very high degree of control over developers, who will be willing to accept planning regulation in seeking the substantial profits which they believe are to be made. In an economically stagnant or declining area, where the prospects of profits from speculative development are much less favourable, the local authorities will be much less inclined to impose restrictions on those few developers who may be interested, so that controls will be much weaker. In most areas, of course, the situation lies somewhere between these two extremes and a certain amount of trading takes place between the two sides.

The problem of trying to impose the community will in place of market decisions has been the concern of planners at all levels since the time of the Uthwatt Committee and before. It is certainly not restricted to the Sub-regional level, but is important here. This is not necessarily to say that one should always opt for the alternative nearest to the "expected" situation: some strategies are intended to be frankly promotional and indeed most will seek to promote some change. What is essential is awareness of the extent of this variation from the expected and the problems which will arise in implementation.

2. *Co-operation by planning agencies*

When the evaluation process has been completed and the results are submitted to the Study sponsors and others, the team are unlikely to find that all aspects of the preferred strategy find favour with everyone. Most of the outstanding problems, however, will be thrashed out during consultations and some sort of compromise will be worked out before the final proposals are published. However, after this stage is past, there may remain some reluctance to promote and enforce the provisions of the strategy on the part of various bodies and individuals. Within Local Government these problems are likely to arise at the professional level, the political level, or both.

Large administrative organisations have their own natural conservatism and resistance to change and the planning implementation system is no exception to the rule. It is therefore important to explain the proposals carefully and to justify them to officers at all levels who will be concerned with implementing them, if the available powers and controls are to be used with maximum effect.

At the political level, Sub-regional planning inevitably involves sacrifices on the part of the constituent authorities and the costs and benefits will not always be evenly distributed, when radical solutions are necessary. This means that even if no one voices open opposition, some bodies will be more enthusiastic than others in supporting the proposals. An evangelising activity is likely to be needed of converting everyone to a new level of consciousness and behaviour. Sub-regional teams have no statutory powers and no means of enforcing their will: they have to rely on voluntary co-operation and in the long run the extent to which they can stimulate and encourage this may be even more important than the nature of the proposals contained in their strategies.

3. *Sub-regional advice on implementation and follow-up studies*

The Sub-regional team's responsibility is not usually confined to explaining the strategy and winning support for it from the resident population and implementation agencies. More information is usually needed by the local planners as to further research work which needs to be done, what priorities should be recognised in deploying their limited staff resources, what powers are to be used and so on.

The period between acceptance of the Study proposals and the time when they actually begin to be implemented may be protracted, or changes may be taking place in the area so quickly that even if there is no undue delay the strategy is eroded. Therefore interim policies, which can be put into effect quickly, may be recommended to cover this period. On Deeside, for example, the announcement of a proposed crossing of the estuary was sufficient to create pressure for housing in anticipation of a bridge and the impact study therefore recommends a restrictive development control policy until the bridge is completed so as to ensure that population growth does not outrun employment growth and that "long-term opportunities are not prejudiced by interim developments". It is suggested, too, that the activities of the local planning authorities and the Land Commission* should be co-ordinated, since good management is essential to keep down land and house prices and also to permit lower densities if these are desired. Dealing with the actual implementation of the strategy, the Deeside Study indicates the sequence of development which should take place in the area, culminating in the completion of a new urban complex in the third stage.

Usually, however, the situation will be less predictable than this and a similar purpose is served by recommending priorities for the completion of plans for particular areas and of particular kinds of plans. Thus Notts./ Derby. indicate that the follow-up work to the Study will take 7 or 8 years and that initially resources should be concentrated on six particular tasks including the preparation of Structure plans and arranging ways of managing and carrying out implementation of the Mansfield–Alfreton growth zone. Teesside also indicate the most urgent tasks and they go further and carry out some of the local planning work themselves, which also serves the useful function of assessing feasibility of the strategy in local terms.

Some studies indicate special problems which have been identified at Sub-regional level although their solution may be essentially a local matter. Thus Coventry/Solihull/War. recommend special studies of employment

---

* Abolished in 1971 and partly replaced by *ad hoc* encouragement to Local lanning Authorities by Central Government to acquire and dispose of land.

growth in central Leamington and central Stratford in order that these towns' capacity to absorb increasing pressure can be assessed and detailed plans can be drawn up to preserve their character. They also make recommendations as to co-operation with other planning bodies, suggesting that Warwickshire County Council should associate with the West Midlands Conurbation Structure Plan Authorities regarding the transport and employment aspects of the Structure Plan for Sutton Coldfield.

Other problems which are more extensive geographically may require policies of a special kind to solve them. Thus the Coventry/Solihull/War. team recommend that an early start be made on a plan and programme for environmental improvement of the north side of Coventry and for Bedworth and Atherstone, and Notts./Derby. recommend an improvement plan for the Erewash Valley.

Powers available for implementation are set out by the West Midlands Reginal Study as follows:

   (i) The New Towns Acts, which relate to the setting up of New Towns Corporations;

  (ii) The Town Development Act 1952 which is concerned with the expansion of existing towns;

 (iii) The use of statutory powers by the local authority for development within or outside its own area;

 (iv) Comprehensive development under the terms of the Town and Country Planning Acts;

  (v) Powers contained in the Highways Acts, particularly for inter-urban roads; and

 (vi) Development carried out by the private sector following the granting of planning permission.

These powers are judged adequate to permit the strategy to be put into effect, although it is emphasised that a corporate act of government is required by Central Government, the Regional Conference and the individual local authorities in the Region. This is needed not only on policy items but on executive and financial decisions. On the financial aspects of the strategy the Study quotes a report by the Treasurers of the Administration Group of the West Midlands Planning Authorities Conference, which shows that the strategy is indeed feasible in financial terms both at the Regional level and the individual local authority level. It does, however, make two important points in respect of those authorities who are intended to receive substantial numbers of overspill population. Under the current arrangements these areas should not have excessive financial difficulties, but the control of capital expenditure which is exercised by central government varies from time to time and a situation should be avoided where receiving authorities with big financial programmes are put into difficulties by this. In addition the report notes that some legislative changes could be made to ease the short-term problems of these authorities.

In some areas, uncertainty is increased for Sub-regional and Local planners by lack of knowledge about policies of other agencies, particularly central government. Thus the Coventry/Solihull/War. team recommend that their constituent authorities ". . . should seek a statement from the Government as to the long term national distribution of population and the place of the West Midlands and the sub-region in this National Strategy".

Most studies are subject to serious limitations of time and manpower and therefore have to recommend further Sub-regional work, after their strategy has been published. This commonly involves investigation into assumptions embodied in the strategy, thus the Notts./Derby. team recommended a study into mobility of industry and jobs. It may also involve testing of assumptions about capacity of particular areas to accommodate population or jobs, about capacity of the local road network and so on. An example here is the North Glos. recommendation that a detailed traffic model be run for the Gloucester–Cheltenham area because, if excessive congestion was indicated in these towns, this would have important implications for the whole of the recommended strategy.

4. *Social and economic objectives*

To most people, the word implementation in a planning context involves physical development—building roads, creating country parks, giving planning permissions—but if a plan includes quasi-social or economic objectives implementation needs to be more comprehensive. There are only weak links between physical planning controls and human behaviour and these controls need to be supplemented with other measures, which might involve setting up policy working parties, sending deputations to ministries and so on.

Thus we distinguish between (a) getting things done, such as building roads and schools, which are essentially means to an end, and (b) achieving objectives, which ends are likely to involve a variety of other means besides physical development. The first implies a programme and powers to do things and planners are well accustomed to this sort of thing. The second would ideally involve a corporate agency and the elaboration of a series of related programmes.

However, Sub-regional planners cannot reorganise their commissioning agencies as political and managerial entities, this would take years. They therefore have to fall back on implementing their plans by influencing those various departments and agencies who do have the necessary powers. Unfortunately these agencies often do not publish, and may not even formulate, coherent plans and programmes which can be measured against the actions which the Sub-regional team would wish to be taken. If this is so, the only way of discovering their (implicit) intentions may be to observe their behaviour over time.

MONITORING

The need for some sort of monitoring has long been accepted, but it is only recently that planners have begun to think seriously about establishing formal monitoring procedures for their plans. This springs from a change in concept of planning and the activities which planning is trying to control, which is being brought about as a result of progress in systems thinking and operational research. The effects of these ideas are only now being felt at a grass-roots level and it is not yet completely clear what the full implications are likely to be, but they have been given some official recognition in the new procedures and the Development Plans Manual. One of the innovations is that counties are now specifically requested to look out for changes which may have implications for their structure plans and revise policies in the light of these findings.

It is not difficult to see that many of the forecasts and assumptions on which a plan is based are likely to prove inaccurate or invalid over the 10 or 20 years which it is intended to cover, but it is useful here, as a background to the following discussion, to set out some of the reasons why this is so. They can be grouped into four as follows:

1. Forecasts of future population, employment, recreation habits, income levels and patterns of expenditure, car ownership and level of usage and so on, involve making many assumptions about all sorts of things, some quantifiable, others not and these may or may not be moving in the same direction. For example, the numbers of people likely to be seeking work in

the future are derived from applying assumed activity rates to forecasts of population between certain ages. These future activity rates are in turn derived by making assumptions about the future in the light of past changes and whatever is known about factors believed to influence them: the tendency of teenagers to remain in full-time education, income levels, social attitudes, new inventions, age of retirement and so on. The chain of assumptions, one following another, in this one example alone could be continued almost *ad infinitum*. It is simply not possible to take all of the many considerations specifically into account in projecting activity rates and we usually have to hope that, by examining past changes and assuming that the complex relationships will not change over-much, the forecasts will be somewhere near the mark.

In planning for recreation, even if there are sufficient resources to under-take regression analysis to identify and weight those factors which seem to determine recreation demand at the present time, there is usually no hope of examining changes in their relative importance over time and the weights given to each have to be assumed constant, with only the quantities being changed. For transport planning there may be little or no information available about the area, either for the past or the present, and relationships derived in other parts of the country may have to be assumed in a synthetic model.

It would be easy to go on, but unnecessary perhaps for most of the examples are well known. It is clear, however, that, on this ground alone, there is reason for keeping track of changes as they occur and comparing them with the strategy. However, although these problems are well known, for a variety of practical reasons which are equally well known, they have not proved sufficient in themselves for the setting up of formal monitoring procedures. It was necessary for them to be reinforced by theoretical argument derived from systems thinking before the present changing climate could be brought about.

2. Systems thinking is bringing about changes in plan-making processes. At the same time, it has highlighted the limitation of the planner's controls in relation to the problems they are designed to treat. This has increased our sense of uncertainty of the future and forced us to recognise what may not have been denied in the past, but was usually put aside on grounds of cost or insufficient manpower in practice, namely the need to monitor the effectiveness of these controls over time.

3. As we have pointed out in the section on implementation, with increased interest in social and economic planning, there has been a tendency to use physical planning controls to try to achieve additional objectives, outside the field of physical development and the environment. This use of controls to deal with problems which they are not specifically designed to treat, naturally increases uncertainty about their ultimate effectiveness. There are also other problems associated with time lags and the fact that planning controls are slow to take effect while social and economic change may take place very quickly.

4. Finally there is the fact that the values and attitudes of society can be seen to be changing over time, so that some of the objectives formulated 20 years ago might be considered quite irrelevant and even undesirable today. This is true of the objectives themselves, it is even more so of the way in which the various objectives are balanced in a particular strategy. We therefore need some procedure for checking that what the planner is aiming for is indeed what the various interest groups in the community seem to want and for changing the strategy if this is not so.

For these reasons we cannot expect all parts of a given strategy to remain valid indefinitely: there will eventually be a need to reconsider some of the assumptions, forecasts and policies, and this will be increasingly true as time goes by. Finally, a point will be reached at which a full-scale revision is necessary and this may well be before the period which the strategy is designed to cover has ended. A monitoring system should be designed to keep track of these changes and be linked with an advisory service to suggest remedial action when deviations have been observed.

Having sketched out the background it is now appropriate to consider some of the proposals for monitoring which have been put forward recently. Shortage of space dictates that only a limited number may be selected and we will therefore discuss only three documents, concerned specifically with the problems of monitoring at Sub-regional level. We have thus had to rule out some interesting pioneering work being done by other planning bodies, particularly the New Town corporations. Similarly we have considered it important to focus on those broad principles which, we feel, should be covered in a Sub-regional study and to leave aside detailed technical problems of selecting indices, organising files for automatic data processing and so on which would form part of the follow-up work to a study rather than be included in the study itself.

The documents selected for discussion are the Leicester/Leics., the Notts./Derby. work on "The Implementation Process" and a report by ISCOL Ltd.([86]) (a company wholly owned by the University of Lancaster). The latter followed on from the Notts./Derby. document and set out a basic design for a monitoring and advisory system for the Sub-region.

1. *Leicester and Leicestershire monitoring proposals*

Leicester/Leics. is particularly important because it was the first Sub-regional study in the country to set out in some detail the way in which changes in the area should be monitored and related to the study proposals.

To facilitate monitoring, the plan is presented in terms of states through which it is intended the area should pass at 5-year intervals: 1971, 1976, 1981, 1986 and 1991, and a key measure of success is seen as comparing the actual states in the area with those intended in the plan. It is therefore necessary for the authorities concerned to keep watch on certain indicators to see if the area is on course. The main elements in this job are:

(1) A series of statistics relating to the Sub-region as a whole including total population, households, persons of school age, total employment in various sectors, private motor cars, average *per capita* income and expenditure and so forth.

(2) The distribution of several of these aspects between the various parts of the Sub-region, especially those which form the basis of the strategy—population distribution, employment distribution, size of main shopping centres, the transport networks and traffic volumes, etc.

The object of (1) is seen as checking on growth in total employment and population to compare with forecasts embodied in the plan and to provide a basis for reworking of these where necessary.

The object of (2) is to provide a subject by subject and area by area check on the way the Sub-region is changing and compare the plan's intentions with actuality. It is also anticipated that the procedures will provide early warnings of localised changes which threaten to drive the Sub-region off course and guides to the treatment of single substantial development proposals or groups of smaller applications. It is envisaged too that the simulation techniques used by the Study team or any such improved techniques as may become available will be used in predicting the effects of major developments.

From time to time it is anticipated that there will be substantial deviations between the plan's intentions and the actual state of the area and when this happens a thorough review of the plan may be called for, including a reappraisal of public aims and objectives. This may in turn lead to forecasts of new growth rates for the Sub-region and changed distributions of its main components.

The report specifies that there must be consistency in the data collected, in interpretation, in assumptions and in purpose and action. It points out that it is quite possible, in the absence of the right sort of framework for co-operation, that two authorities could act quite inconsistently with respect to implementing a plan covering their areas, even though each were acting with the best intentions. In order to achieve this essential consistency, the team recommend the establishment of a permanent joint planning group consisting of the City Planning Officer and the County Planning Officer and able to co-opt other officers from time to time, including representatives of passenger transport undertakings.

These proposals and the recognition that "An information and intelligence service is the vital element in successful implementation of the plan for the Sub-region" were an important advance in Sub-regional thinking. The procedures themselves are very much concerned with statistical measures and checking ". . . on the way in which the social and economic geography of the Sub-region is changing, comparing intentions with actuality . . .". The report does recognise the need for co-ordination of both development plan preparation and implementation work and suggests machinery whereby this might be achieved, but it goes less far in this direction than later work in the Notts./Derby. Sub-region.

2. *Notts./Derby. proposals for monitoring*

Some weeks after the main volume outlining the recommended strategy was published, the Notts./Derby. team produced additional reports giving advice on implementation and further studies to be undertaken and setting out some preliminary ideas on monitoring which, it was hoped, would be developed at a later stage with specialist help.

The monitoring of the strategy is described in the document as "a continuous review of the situation" for which a separate monitoring and advisory unit should be set up with its own staff and budget and able to operate independently of the four planning departments. The purpose of this continuous review is described as checking whether or not the adopted policies are being carried out, whether they are succeeding in the task of achieving Sub-regional objectives and, if not, recommending what remedial action should be taken. The review work is seen as involving, primarily, the collection and processing of statistical information on certain key issues and comparing the results with the proposals in the strategy.

It is basic to the Notts./Derby. team's philosophy that precise forecasts of population, employment, etc., cannot be devised for any strategy for as far ahead as two decades and it follows from this that the strategy cannot be seen as involving a steady progress towards precise quantities of these basic elements. A need is therefore identified for some other quantifiable form for the strategy for monitoring purposes. This leads to the concept of balances and levels, indicating limits within which the authorities should try to steer, in order to accord with Sub-regional objectives. These quantities are intended to be independent of forecasts of growth or change and therefore independent of the uncertainties of forecasting, but they are held to be very sensitive to critical imbalances between different parts of the Sub-region. Selected examples of balances and levels are given in Table 8.2.

If the continuous review indicates that no progress is being made towards achieving the objectives, then policies will need to be changed and it may be that the whole strategy should be revised. In order to define new policies under such circumstances, the planning process developed by the Sub-regional team will need to be reworked either in part or as a whole. For this purpose a data base is to be maintained and arrangements are made with the consultants to rerun the computer models if necessary.

A review of the objectives on which the strategy is based will also be necessary from time to time, although this is seen as a matter for political and public discussion rather than technical calculation. It is nevertheless recognised that such discussion will need to be stimulated, and as a means of achieving this the team recommend that the monitoring leader should prepare an annual report to the planning authorities. The monitoring system itself could influence and perhaps distort the results and will need to be examined at regular intervals to see that it is performing its functions effectively and without bias and this again might be the subject of an annual report.

TABLE 8.2. NOTTS./DERBY. SUB-REGIONAL STUDY—THE STRATEGIC BALANCES

Balance number	Nature of balance	Geographical area to which balance applies	Reason for balance
2	Net outward migration should not exceed half the natural increase	Each of zones 1, 5, 7, 8, 15, 16, 17, 18 and 23—i.e. zones where economic prospects are uncertain	To avoid local hardship, to secure social variety in communities and assist supply of minority facilities and to maintain and improve availability of skills of all kinds needed for economic progress
4	Availability of separate dwelling units to potential household heads should be 1·05:1	Each zone and Sub-region as a whole	To avoid housing shortages, and allow adequate mobility of population
5	The mean national standard of housing quality should be achieved and maintained	Sub-region as a whole. Each of zones 1, 3, 5, 6, 7, 8, 10, 15, 18, 19, 20 and 23. Also sub-divisions of zones 3 and 10, i.e. areas having substantial unsatisfactory housing	To maintain the relative attractiveness of the Sub-region's housing and to improve and maintain the well-being of the population
11	Average journey speeds in Nottingham and Derby should not be less than 10 m.p.h.	Within outer ring roads of Nottingham and Derby	To allow the efficient functioning of the major centres by minimising congestion

These Notts./Derby. monitoring proposals contain a number of ideas which were recognised in Leicester/Leics., with some additions. The most important addition is, perhaps, the acknowledgement of a need to check that Sub-regional recommendations are in fact being put into development plans, a requirement which leads naturally to the idea of an independent unit with its own staff and resources. The conceptual differences between the two teams are also underlined in their monitoring proposals: Leicester/Leics. monitoring is to compare on the ground changes with a plan which is staged for this purpose, while Notts./Derby. monitoring is not intended to relate to a plan so much as to objectives.

The Notts./Derby. team recognise that in the limited time available they can do little more than set out a few needs and directions and a lengthy period would be necessary to solve the major conceptual and practical problems involved. Specialist advice is therefore required from the academic world. The Institute of Local Government Studies (INLOGOV) of the University of Birmingham were first approached for advice as to how to integrate the proposed Monitoring and Advisory Unit into the local government structure. INLOGOV recommended that the further conceptual work on the monitoring system should be undertaken first and, on their recommendation, ISCOL of the University of Lancaster were approached. The ISCOL report, produced after 5 months' work by B. Riera and M. Jackson is worth examining at some length, although we must confine ourselves here to outlining the system in broad terms; anyone interested in the more detailed flow diagrams and processes must consult the report itself.

3. *The ISCOL report*

The report divides the agencies for change in the Sub-region into two groups:

(1) Local Authorities, whose actions are described as "controlled" actions, used to influence change in the Sub-region, and

(2) other agencies, whose actions are described as "uncontrolled" actions because they are not under direct control, although local authorities do try to influence them.

These agencies operate in the Sub-region in what is conveniently thought of as a "transformation process", which converts their decisions and acts into "dependent outcomes" in a process which involves many complex interactions of which our understanding is only limited. These "dependent outcomes" include changes in housing, employment, journey times and so on.

Objectives are usually framed in terms of dependent outcomes and most monitoring procedures concentrate on reviewing changes in these. In addition to such reviews, however, the report points out the need to monitor inputs to the transformation process, namely the decisions and acts of the agencies identified above.

One reason for this is the fact that there are time lags between the taking of a decision and the effects becoming noticeable "on the ground", so that by the time statistical measures reveal a change it may be too late for preventative or remedial action. It is therefore important to *anticipate* changes in dependent outcomes by monitoring the decisions and actions from which they spring.

The other reason why decisions and actions should be monitored arises from the need to give advice as to the appropriate action to take when departures from the strategy are detected. As we have already explained, our understanding of the "transformation process" and our ability to simulate it is very rudimentary, and it is very difficult to predict how it will react to particular policy measures. However, a continuous and close scrutiny of the inputs and outputs of the process over a period of time should improve understanding and lead to better advice as to the actions necessary to achieve desired outcomes.

The absolute test of effectiveness in Sub-regional planning is the extent to which the objectives can be achieved. One of the problems of the monitoring and advisory system will be to obtain satisfactory measures of objective achievement. With this in mind, various standard sources of data which might be used are listed in the report.

So far as Local Authority decisions and actions are concerned, the main sources of information recommended are Council and Committee Minutes and Reports, the Statutory Register and notifications from the Local Authorities themselves of items of possible Sub-regional significance. For other agency decisions and actions, the available sources are more diverse and less satisfactory; they include local housing statistics, development applications, company reports, press reports and so on.

The monitoring and advisory system which the report recommends is divided into four conceptual sub-systems: the first concerned with monitoring changes in the area, the second with the giving of advice, the third with the technical processes required and the fourth with developing and improving the system as a whole. The diagram and summary of the system that follow are taken from the ISCOL Report.

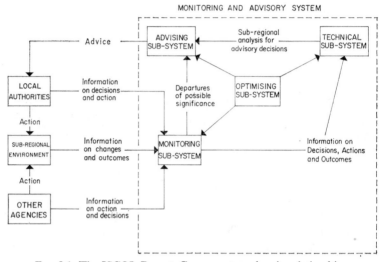

Fig. 8.1. The ISCOL Report. Components and main relationships of the monitoring and advisory system.

(1) *The Monitoring Sub-system*
The activities included in the monitoring sub-system are:
(a) The collection of information on actions by Local Authorities and other agencies and, where possible, the decisions being made which may lead to action.
(b) The measurement of changes in the Sub-regional environment.
(c) The selection of decisions, actions and changes which might have significance for the achievement of the Sub-regional objectives.

(2) *The Advisory Sub-system*
The activities included in the advisory sub-system are:
(a) The determination of departures from the provisions, or predicted outcomes of the strategy, which have significance for the achievement of Sub-regional objectives and hence require the provision of advice.
(b) The updating of the objectives and the determination of the specific nature of the necessary advice.
(c) The appropriate communication of advice.

(3) *The Technical Sub-system*
The activities included in the technical sub-system are:
(a) The analysis of departures and changes for their effect on the achievement of Sub-regional objectives.
(b) Examination of alternative courses of action to eliminate or reduce the effect of a significant departure.
(c) The examination of alternatives in the process of continually updating the strategy.
(d) The improvement of the understanding of Sub-regional behaviour.

(4) *The Optimising Sub-system*
The activities included in the optimising sub-system are:
(a) The objective appraisal of the performance of all sub-systems and activities.
(b) The consideration of changing situations which require changes in the method of operation of the Unit.
(c) The generation, selection and development of improvements to the overall system.

The purpose of Sub-regional advice is to stimulate decision-making in the Sub-regional interest and to enable the Sub-regional interest to be taken into account in all relevant decision-making. It is emphasised that Sub-regional planning depends on the willingness of the constituent authorities to act together. The Unit is not therefore seen as a policing agency but rather as a catalyst: "The Monitoring and Advisory Unit has a crucial role to play as a catalyst which encourages and enables corporate action. If the Unit is to be successful in its role, it is essential that acceptability and credibility with the Local Authorities is maintained by the Unit." This is of basic importance in Sub-regional monitoring—if one or more of the authorities feel it is not in their interests to participate, and argument and persuasion fails to convince them otherwise, nothing further can be done. The strategy must therefore be sufficiently flexible to allow for this or must be revised accordingly. It is very important, however, that a sense of commitment to corporate action should be encouraged, and in this respect the act of contributing funds to an independent monitoring unit is itself valuable.

The report goes on to set out some principles and ideas about the nature and significance of different kinds of decisions and policies and the way in which advice should be communicated by the Unit to the authorities. This is followed by a detailing of the proposals for the system in terms of activities which the Unit should perform, routines developed to cover these activities and analytical guides to be used in the routines, information flows which the Unit should initially monitor, the organisation of the Unit, staff needed to implement the system and the way in which the system should be developed over time.

The report emphasises the importance of implementing its recommendations immediately. One reason for this is, of course, the danger that if undue delay occurs substantial parts of the strategy could be affected by unforeseen changes before monitoring even begins. In addition to this, however, there is the fact that the system is a revolutionary one and for this reason there is very little background knowledge available which can be used by such a monitoring system—knowledge and experience must be gained "on the job".

A great deal of important follow-up work is indicated for the Unit. This includes making sure that all of the various committees of the four authorities who are likely to be making decisions of Sub-regional significance are brought within the scope of the system. Decisions which are of Sub-regional importance must then be distinguished. This is a formidable task, because they will not always be obviously major decisions—small ones can have a cumulative effect and major decisions can be committed by a variety of smaller ones taken before the major question has been discussed. There is also the problem of identifying those decisions which are taken within local government but not in the formal framework, at meetings of political parties or by officers who establish precedents which may become accepted policy within their own departments.

It is impossible to predict at this very early stage how successful the ISCOL proposals will be. However, it makes an important contribution to thinking about Sub-regional monitoring and clarifies, develops and puts into a logical framework many of the ideas found in earlier reports. If it is successful it should lead to an increase in knowledge of how systems respond to the various policy instruments available to planners and provide valuable feedback to earlier stages of the planning process. While the process is specifically designed for the Notts./Derby. strategy and the particular circumstances pertaining in that area, it also suggests ideas which, no doubt, could have much more general application.

CONCLUSIONS

We would suggest that the plan-making process is appropriately seen as a special case of monitoring, of looking at problems, testing and taking action. The recording and analysis of change begins when a Sub-regional team is appointed, and plan-making is merely the preliminary to a continuous monitoring and review process. This has implications at all stages of plan-making: data collection, plan generation and evaluation, documentation and consultations.

So far as the recommended strategy is concerned, part of it may be robust and resistant to unexpected changes and these will call for less attention than those parts which are not very robust and likely to be upset by errors in forecasts and assumptions. As an aid to those responsible for monitoring, therefore, the study report should contain some indication of the relative vulnerability of the various elements of the strategy.

In Sub-regional situations there is a particularly high level of uncertainty, so that we see the detailing of the strategy as less important and the role of monitoring more important than in, say, a pre-reform County situation. Not only may technical assumptions and forecasts prove to be wrong, but the willingness of the constituent authorities to participate may change. In this sort of situation a process of "partisan mutual adjustment"[87] may prove the answer. This has implications both for the nature of the strategy itself and for the monitoring process. The strategy may best be so designed that there is some balance of benefits and contributions for each of the constituent authorities and if any one of them wishes to withdraw it can only do so at the risk of losing some benefit. In addition the monitoring framework should make possible the sort of bargaining between the authorities which partisan mutual adjustment requires, since this bargaining will have to take place at various times over the years if permanent ruptures are to be avoided.

CHAPTER 9

A Procedure for Evaluating Sub-regional Studies

WHEN the need for a procedure for evaluating Sub-regional studies first arose, we combed the literature for useful ideas. We were able to find only one suggestion which was directly relevant. This was by Boyce, Day and McDonald[88] and involved devising some arithmetic measure of the range of difference between the various land-use dispositions tested during generation/evaluation. There were several important reasons why such a test would be inadequate for our purposes and these led us to develop our own procedure. These could be summarised as follows:

First, while, in some ways, the test would cope reasonably well with the type of study where a few well-defined alternatives were generated, say from stereotypes, it seemed ill equipped to deal with a Notts./Derby. or a Coventry/Solihull/War. process.

Second, there was a problem of constraints: the test had been conceived in the United States and it might have validity in the planning climate existing there. In this country, however, the existence of a variety of constraints on a team's freedom of action—which we discussed in Chapter 3 —could make the results of such a test quite meaningless here.

Third, as we hope the foregoing chapters have demonstrated, the Sub-regional planning process was a much more complex problem than the test would imply. It was quite possible to envisage situations where the range of land-use dispositions tested, whether constrained or not, would not be the critical issue. Moreover, we would not always wish our comments to be as neutral as possible: there were certain aspects of Sub-regional planning which we would, on occasion, feel free to promote and these were the very ones which Boyce, Day and McDonald's test tended to ignore.

MATRICES

In seeking our own procedure, we first considered the possibility of devising some other quantified method of evaluation, which would set out grouped criteria, or, alternatively, questions against which numerical scores could be awarded. These scores might then be aggregated in some way to produce an overall score. The most promising techniques which we identified along these lines involved the use of matrices.

The initial matrix showed various topics—terms of reference, data handling, analysis, forecasting, etc.—along one axis and a number of groups of criteria along the other. The criteria would be derived from the discussion in Chapters 1 to 8 and arranged into groups using Alexander's decomposition techniques described in Chapter 5. Not all groups of criteria would be relevant to each topic and where they were not, the square in the matrix would be blanked off at the outset. A "score" would be given against each relevant set of criteria for each topic and these scores would be normalised to, say, 0–100 before being summed. Before aggregation the scores might be weighted according to the importance of the topic concerned, using weights derived from looking at the nature of the Study and its purpose.

Initially there were some doubts about the validity of aggregating scores for different sets of data, but it was felt that this would be acceptable in a clearly defined framework. It was felt, however, that the matrix focused too much attention on crude overall scores when a "mark" for a single study in isolation was meaningless: some standard would have to be established against which it might be compared. But so few studies had been produced in similar circumstances that little confidence could be placed in any standard which might emerge. Indeed, techniques had developed very rapidly and seemed likely to continue to do, so that there was little prospect of deriving a stable standard in the foreseeable future. Reference back to our purpose also suggested that to achieve an overall rating for each study was not essential.

A modified matrix form was therefore produced which dispensed with overall scores. It followed Batty's approach described in Chapter 5, with $+2$ and $+1$ indicating degrees of favourable achievement of topics against sets of criteria and -1, -2 indicating degrees of failure. Where there was no particular achievement against a set of criteria, no score was indicated, which had the effect of giving emphasis to significant achievements and failures. Weighting could also be incorporated at a second stage.

We were also dissatisfied with this matrix, however, because it seemed to focus too much attention on the purely technical process. Moreover, one of the principal advantages we had hoped to gain through adopting a formal method was greater objectivity, but it became apparent that this was not being achieved. We favoured varying weights between studies to deal with the wide variety which we had found to exist, but introducing weights placed a heavy burden of responsibility on the operator. While these judgements would have to be made under any evaluation procedure, we preferred that they should be openly acknowledged and not partially hidden as formal methods tended to do.

TRADE-OFF

A more fundamental question was involved, however, and this was the extent to which we should attempt to take account of the existence of "trade-off" and the bargaining process in evaluation. Our experience certainly suggested this was a major factor in Sub-regional planning and since we were particularly concerned to promote *understanding* of the *whole* process, we decided that it must receive recognition in our procedure.

This point is illustrated in Friend and Yewlett's[89] paper on the organisational structure set up to control the Droitwich expansion. This project has some important features in common with Sub-regional planning because it involves control by a joint committee of the County Council and the local Borough Council. The authors argue that in this situation of divided control the normal master-plan procedures are not sufficient, and new skills and processes of mutual adjustment have to be developed:

> ... it was evident both to the officers concerned and to ourselves as observers that, in a many-sided development programme impinging closely on a variety of existing community interests, the processes of planning were necessarily complex, continuous and intrinsically multi-organisational in nature. In consequence, the officers of the Development Group had had to cultivate skills which differed significantly in character from those which are conventionally associated with the preparation of an initial master plan, its translation into a capital investment programme, and the subsequent implementation of a set of well-defined development projects. Furthermore, these skills could not be seen simply in terms of an ability to control the processes of implementation through

occasional adjustments to previously agreed plans; rather they required judgements of what kind of strategy to adopt in contending with a continually shifting pattern of uncertainties, arising from an economic, political and social environment which was not merely uncertain but often turbulent. . . .

Meanwhile we were aware of a persistent sense among many members of the Borough Council—and particularly among those not serving on the joint Development Committee—that the exercise of shared rather than exclusive control over the skills of the Development Group was depriving them of a role in decision-making which was commensurate with their direct accountability to existing residents. Justifiably or otherwise, it could be suspected that the proposals formulated by the experts might sometimes conceal debateable value judgements behind arguments which it was difficult to challenge on technical grounds. As in local government generally, it was not easy for the member to ascertain how fully the professionals had explored the range of available options; and sometimes the suspicion would arise that courses of action which had become more or less irrevocable could and should have been challenged at an earlier stage of the decision-making process.

Despite the persistence of such tensions in certain areas where interests were most clearly in conflict, there was also much evidence of a gradual and largely successful process of adjustment in the attitudes and mutual relationships of the individuals participating in the Droitwich "multi-organisation" during the first seven years of its existence. Lindblom, in "The Intelligence of Democracy",([90]) explores the concept of co-ordination, through various modes of *partisan mutual adjustment* between decision-makers who do not necessarily subscribe to a shared set of values or objectives, as opposed to more conventional concepts of co-ordination which place their emphasis on the role of some central source of authority or arbitration, through which commonly accepted values may emerge and any sectional conflicts can where necessary be resolved.

They argue that the situation calls for the skills of Dr. John Power's "reticulist" profession, which Power([91]) describes in the following way:

> . . . the "contact man" who "supplies political and ideological intelligence the leader needs in order to find his way around modern society; he mediates the relations of the organisation and the outside world. . . . He is valued for his knowledge of the political and social topography of the containing society—the kind of realistic political intelligence that tells him who can make what decisions or who has what information and how and when to reach him; for his 'contacts', which are so well developed that they become non-transferable; and for his skills in exploiting these contacts—skills in private inquiry, consultation, negotiation, mediation."

We feel that the ideal Sub-regional team-leader would have many of the qualities of a reticulist. In addition to organising and planning the technical work of his team, he must be very concerned with sounding out opinion in his sponsoring organisations, implementation agencies and interest groups and putting forward possible solutions which will enable partisan mutual adjustment to take place between them. In the long run, his success in accomplishing these tasks may well be of greater importance in the area than the quality of the purely technical processes performed by the team.

THE EVALUATORS' PURPOSE

Clearly, therefore, any evaluation which aimed to be comprehensive could not be simply a measurement of the technical process. There was also the different purposes with which evaluators approached their task to consider. In order to structure our thoughts, we tried to recognise groups of individuals and agencies who might possibly evaluate in a similar way and with a similar purpose. We were aware that this involved making some very broad generalisations, but it was nevertheless valuable in developing our procedure. We specified four groups, which were as follows:

Firstly, people who lived in the area, and others directly affected by the strategy in their role as citizens, would assess how the proposals might affect their daily lives. Their evaluative process would be quite different from that of the Sub-regional team themselves as we described it in Chapter 7 and would make reference to highly personal goals and objectives. It would probably compare the strategy with the present situation or with vague impressions about the future based on an extrapolation of current trends rather than coherent strategies. To gain an idea of the kind of issues which might be raised, we examined the results of the South Hants 1972 public survey (although our findings here were based on comments by representative organisations rather than individuals). These were concerned with preservation of the countryside, agricultural land and green belts; the form of development proposed; effects on existing communities and the need to maintain and create balanced communities and communications and congestion. Questions of implementation difficulties and costs, flexibility and servicing, received some limited attention, but were naturally of much less concern to the general public than to government organisations. (It was clear that, in the South Hants example, virtually all of those questioned had accepted the plan as being of a high degree of professional competence.)

The second group included government organisations, public utility operators, private developers and certain other agencies. These would have to decide whether or not to implement the plan and commit investment in the expectation that it would succeed, at least so far as to ensure that the resources which they might dispose were not wasted. These agencies would be much more concerned with the professional competence of the plan, since many of the things which particularly concerned them would be specifically included in the team's own evaluation procedures: flexibility to cope with unexpected change, satisfactory performance in relation to expected change, the ability of the existing implementation machinery to cope with its proposals and so on. They would also be particularly concerned with whether or not other implementation agencies were likely to formally accept the plan and, more important, commit their resources to it.

The third group included politicians and elected representatives. Their approach lay somewhere between the first and the second, in that they would both assess the plan as decision-takers concerned with resource allocation and judge it as might the electorate (to whom it would have to be explained). They would be very concerned with trade-off, with the extent to which each interest group received benefits and were asked to make sacrifices.

The fourth kind of evaluation was a technical and professional one by planners, other professions, book reviews, and so on. These evaluators would be concerned to safeguard the standards of the profession, assess the achievements of the team and consider to what extent they had added to the stock of knowledge and experience of planners in general. Also included were a numerically small, but very important, sub-group embarking on Sub-regional work of their own, who would wish to benefit from the experience of others.

It was clear from our reflections on these four groups that the weight given to the various factors involved would vary considerably according to the purposes of the evaluator and that his final assessment was likely, in most cases, to be highly coloured by his own value judgements. It seemed to us, however, that all evaluators would have a general need for a technical background: whatever standpoint one adopted a major consideration was the professional respectability and technical excellence of the work under consideration.* In particular this would influence the reaction of

---

* Each age has its own views on the nature of proof. The use for this purpose of the opinions of those with social power has been suffering a decline over the last century as various versions of "scientific logic" have been adopted. Currently "systems thinking" is modifying the acceptability of "simple logic" in favour of the logic of "complexes". There is no doubt, however, that many groups in our society place great weight on technical excellence.

important implementation agencies and decision takers. The nature of the recommended strategy would also be of great concern to most evaluators and would need to be included in our procedure. Indeed, it was our opinion that neither the technical process nor the strategy could safely be considered in isolation from the other.

This speculative exercise was of some value in suggesting criteria for an evaluation procedure, but we were well aware of its superficiality. In our examination of the various Sub-regional processes, we had not attempted to develop theories of Sub-regional planning although we believed—and we hope this is evident from our text—that there was a close relationship between our views and the Mixed Programming Strategy of Chadwick.[92] Compared against the millions which Chadwick discusses in the final chapter of his book, our four groups were indeed a gross over-simplification:

> . . . for only a system of (say) a million decision-makers (the public) is likely to have a variety requisite to that of a system of a million people (the same public). This is not to reject the normal democratic processes of decision-making where responsibility is delegated to groups or individuals, but to stress that social choices in day-to-day life are made by individuals and family groups, that is, incrementally, rather than being controlled exogenously. Social choices are made, not by dictation from without, but by systems of individuals perceiving changes in their environment (i.e. their social and economic, as well as physical spaces), and making images and plans from these changes, and resetting courses of action in response. If planning really is about people, this is the first thing which it must recognise: even the most authoritarian regimes cannot suppress social choice, for they, too, are subject to the laws of variety and feedback-behaviour.

Not only would each evaluator have different attitudes and objectives, but his perception of the environment and how it related to the plan was likely to be highly individual.

THE PROCEDURE

We decided that our evaluation procedure should cover technical problems, the strategy itself, and also attempt to identify some of the more subtle "political" issues and problems which might lie behind it. Only by doing all of this could we enable the operator to achieve some understanding of the way the strategy had been evolved and also allow him to focus on those particular parts of the process which were of concern to him. This fitted in well with our own purposes.

We wished to avoid the view of a Sub-regional study as simply a once and for all exercise ending in a printed booklet which could be admired and filed away. In our view it was one part—neither beginning nor end—of a continuous planning process and should be evaluated against this background. Thus the procedure we adopted focused on wider issues before delving into technical detail. This presented the operator with a difficult task because it raised some questions he might feel unable to answer, without participating in the Study process himself, since the team might have been prevented, for one reason or another, from discussing some issues publicly. We sympathised with this problem. Indeed, our own text had been affected by these constraints to some degree. It was, however, a point which could be over-emphasised and we felt most political issues in an area would be well known. In any case it was important to acknowledge the existence of any areas of doubt which might reduce the validity of the evaluator's conclusions.

The procedure is basically an interrogation process which draws the attention of the evaluator to a series of important points in a logical sequence. It is set out at two levels, the first being concerned with the wider issues and the second looking specifically at technical operations. It would be unsafe, however, to make final judgements at either level without first having gone through the whole procedure.

The operator will not award "marks" at each stage and the relevance of some of the observations he makes at early stages will not become apparent until later. The procedure is intended to impose a certain amount of discipline on him and the further he departs from the sequence, the more difficult it will be to ensure that all points have been covered. However, the inexperienced will probably find it necessary to go into the technical process before feeling able to tackle some of the questions in the upper level. In any case, one would expect a strong feedback from the lower to the upper level and the revision of some of the earlier judgements as technical factors behind the team's decisions emerge.

The procedure summarises points made in the previous eight chapters and it cannot be divorced from them. It is intended to promote understanding of Sub-regional planning and this cannot be accomplished in just a few pages. The points we list should therefore be regarded simply as an aide-memoire to help the operator recall the detailed facts and judgements set out in more balanced form earlier in this book.

The headings of the various stages are set out below and these are followed by the stages themselves. Since the procedure is basically a list of points which the evaluator will wish to consider carefully, and is not intended as general reading, the style is quite different from the remainder of our text. It is therefore set out in a contrasting typeface.

Upper level	*Lower level*
(1) The operator's purpose	(i) Data collection and processing
(2) The purpose of the Study	(ii) Analysis and forecasts
(3) The nature of the area	(iii) Goals and objectives
(4) Resources of the team	(iv) Generation
(5) The technical process	(v) Elaboration and evaluation
(6) The quality of the advice	(vi) Consultations
(7) Acceptability and consultations	(vii) Monitoring
(8) Implementation and monitoring	

The first-level stages are as follows:

(1) *The Operator's Purpose*—what he is trying to achieve from his evaluation. He may be completely disinterested and wish to ascertain whether the work is well executed and fair, what are its prospects of having a real and beneficial effect on the area over the plan period and of making a contribution to the stock of knowledge and techniques in planning generally. At the other extreme he may be personally involved in the area and anxious to develop arguments which will suit his own interests. It would be unrealistic to suppose that each operator will be in the first group, and asking him to honestly examine his own motives will, hopefully, make his judgements more fair. Whether disinterested or not, however, to clarify his purpose at the outset is a valuable discipline.

(2) *The Purpose of the Study*. Here the operator ascertains why the work was initiated and asks what it was intended to cover and what not to cover. This question will first be raised by the Terms of Reference but a number of issues, major and minor, will occur which have been given greater or less prominence than they appear to deserve, because they are sensitive issues in the area.

The extent to which both sponsors and team are clear about their purposes will be relevant. This is also true of the origins of a Study: if it arose from the recommendations in a previous work, the quality of that work will be a matter of concern.

In the past, Co-ordination Studies have been produced to increase co-operation between planning bodies; to build a bridge between vertical levels of planning; secure co-ordination in order to achieve greater political "weight" in approaching other agencies (usually central government); solve problems caused by increasing personal mobility; prepare the way for political and/or administrative reorganisation; co-ordinate response to some major exogenous change; and so on. Studies may be concerned with very long-term investment or short-term economic and social problems or both; they may be speculative or concerned with developments which can be confidently predicted. Allocation Studies have been concerned with the feasibility and desirability of major investment projects and the large-scale movement of population, jobs and services.

(3) *The Nature of the Area.* How far the evaluator goes in passing judgement on the strategy will depend on how well he feels he knows the area and has understood the many pressures on the team. He must, however, form some opinions, either from his personal knowledge or from a careful reading of the text, on problems in the area and how these are affected by its topography, climate, location, pressures for development and so on. This is important in reflecting on the purpose of the Study, the team's selection of techniques and methodology and how appropriate they are in the circumstances, as well as on the final strategy itself. He will also think about the area in a wider regional and national context and compare its conditions with those existing elsewhere.

(4) *Resources of the Team*—how well equipped were the team to carry out the tasks indicated under (2) and (3). Here it is necessary to take account of the following: staff directly employed and available on secondment, facilities available to them in terms of computing power, data from survey work previously undertaken in the area, experience existing in planning departments and elsewhere which they could draw on, consultants who might help on critical problems, and so on. Time available is a major factor and will usually impose serious restrictions on what the team can do. Bearing this in mind, the operator will weigh what has been done against those possibilities which it was decided not to follow through.

(5) *The Technical Process.* Here the operator will consider how the team's resources have been divided between the various stages of the plan-making process and whether this division represents a reasonable balance of effort. The first question will be whether the techniques and procedures adopted are appropriate to the task in hand, compatible with one another and do not involve circular reasoning. The criterion should be relevance rather than availability—there has been an over-emphasis on transport and topic analysis/evaluation in the past, simply because techniques and expertise were readily available to cope with these problems. The extent of any major technical innovation will also be an important factor to consider.

The management of the process is important, meeting deadlines and using resources to the maximum effect. Relevant here are survey data already held by other agencies, available techniques, computing facilities, consulting services, etc., as well as such questions as accuracy of data and confidence which is or is not inspired in the results from technical routines. Time will be a major constraint and the evaluator will need to consider the pay-off from any long periods of time spent developing and setting up techniques and carrying out surveys. Finally the design of a process which can be repeated, if necessary by planners other than members of the team, with fresh data and different assumptions will be useful if monitoring is intended.

(6) *The Quality of the Advice.* This stage is concerned with how far the technical process, plus the team's experience, has thrown up a sound strategy which looks as though it could be successful if implemented and makes a positive contribution to the planning of the area; also with the extent to which that strategy is "better" than the alternative possibilities. The operator will ask whether the team cover all the strategic issues relevant at Sub-regional level (both spatial and non-spatial). This also implies avoiding purely local issues, although the team may be required by their sponsors to form judgements on some of these. The operator will consider the range of alternatives tested and whether these fully represented all of the main possibilities. The nature of the team's evaluation process will also be important, including whether it tests for flexibility, phasing problems and the ability of the various agencies to implement it. Similarly, the operator will ask whether the team have identified policy areas where a major effort is necessary to bring about change, and consider the extent to which the proposals match the time scale necessary for the lags in the inertial machine. Within the team's framework for evaluation, he will ask whether the choice clearly follows from the tests. He will also question the framework itself and consider the extent to which it may be biased in favour of some possibilities, away from others.

(7) *Acceptability and Consultations*—steps the team have taken to find out what the various agencies and members of the public hope for from the strategy and to secure acceptance of it; also the reaction to the strategy after publication. The operator will first look at the technical process and consider whether it is clear and the arguments put forward to explain and justify the preferred strategy are convincing. In doing this he will bear in mind that arguments suitable for the sponsors may not be acceptable to other agencies and individuals. Consultation procedures can play any or all of three different roles: (1) giving people a chance to be heard before the preferred strategy

has been finally selected, (2) obtaining technical advice which is essential to drawing up the strategy and (3) securing full co-operation from implementation agencies. Which have been adopted and who consulted will be relevant here. In the strategy itself, the evaluator will look for concessions made to the various interests involved to induce them to accept it, and the ability of the team leader will be important here, in conducting this trade-off process. An important test will be whether the strategy is being incorporated into structure plans. Another obvious one is the extent to which approval or disapproval is voiced in the area. These are not necessarily conclusive, however: an absence of criticism does not necessarily indicate willingness to co-operate. If the strategy has proved definitely unacceptable, the reasons why this is so will clearly be important.

(8) *Implementation and Monitoring.* This section is concerned with bridging the gap between the Sub-regional Strategy and Structure and Local planning (and, of course, the implementation activities of various other agencies). It also covers any proposals which may be made for monitoring the strategy over future years.

The main role in implementation will be played by the statutory planning authorities with assistance and backing from central government, and the principal instruments used to put the strategy into affect are likely to be structure and local plans. Much of the advice on implementation will therefore be in this direction. Advice about priorities for action in terms of both geographical and policy areas will be needed. There will probably be important areas where further technical investigation is necessary. So far as strength and urgency of action is concerned, questions such as the extent of departures from existing trends envisaged in the strategy, and pressure for development before and after publication of the plan will be relevant. The question of corporate action involving departments and agencies outside the field of physical planning will need to be considered.

So far as monitoring is concerned the question whether a system is envisaged at all will have to be asked and, if one is, whether it will be Sub-regional or one disaggregated between the statutory authorities. The operator must form his own opinions as to the adequacy of the arrangements, although his judgement of the team will, of course, need to be tempered by reflections on what might have been politically (and financially) acceptable. If monitoring arrangements in some form are not proposed, this raises a question as to the future of Sub-regional co-operation.

A second level of criteria are set out below which are concerned with the technical process in rather more detail.

As with the first level, the criteria have been derived from Chapters 1 to 8 above, and are matched against the level of understanding we have aimed at in the text. The specialist might well wish to delve deeper and list many more criteria. We have resisted this temptation because of the overriding need, as we see it, to maintain a sense of proportion and not to be over concerned with matters of detail at the expense of broader and more important problems.

(i) *Data Collection and Processing.* The nature of the area and the purpose of the Study will, of course, be important in deciding on the kind of information to collect. In designing a data system, the main criterion will be the extent to which it aids and does not constrain other processes. The use of a computer gives greater power in analysis and computing resources may be more readily available than manpower, but an overall strategy is needed to keep data collection within reasonable bounds. Since many of the systems to be examined are spatial, information needs to be capable of being examined on maps and also compared with other kinds of data, which argues in favour of common areal units. Point referencing of data can be very time-consuming and time spent on it will reduce effort at some other stage. Similarly there is a problem of deciding how far to go in collecting data beyond the boundary of the area for detailed study and systems concepts are useful here. Confidentiality is a major problem in both obtaining data for use and presenting findings to clients and others and the operator will ask whether the team have negotiated for all useful information which might have been available.

(ii) *Analysis and Forecasts.* The objects of this stage, as we have defined it, is to understand the area as it exists and is changing over time, to decide what kind of planning intervention is needed, ascertain how much room to manoeuvre exists in putting forward fresh policies, provide forecasts which will give the dimensions of the final strategy and provide input data to generation/evaluation.

The team will design the stage bearing in mind the nature of the area, the purpose of the Study, the time period it covers, the sort of overall process which is envisaged and the nature of the techniques (and their data requirements) which will be used at later stages. Who the Study is intended to convince will also influence selection of techniques and subjects to be studied. Within the analysis stage, new facts will be discovered which may change the emphasis and the team must pick out critical questions early enough for more detailed investigation to take place. Mobility of jobs and population, the operation of the housing market and investment resources are all subjects where existing knowledge is inadequate. In some topics a high degree of uncertainty is unavoidable—employment forecasting for instance—and this has implications for the final strategy.

Topics cannot reasonably be studied and incorporated into a plan in isolation; some attempt must be made to bring them together and consider how they interact with one another before plan generation begins (as well as in the generation/evaluation stages themselves). The consensus method is the oldest and least demanding way of achieving this but is limited to the experience of the consensus and is not free from bias. Simulation techniques are now being introduced and these have great potential and are rapidly being improved. They are useful for learning about the area and the impact of different policies but not for making precise forecasts for local areas.

Where new techniques are introduced (at any stage) the team deserve full credit for this: Sub-regional planning has been a fertile ground for innovation in the past, which is one reason for the high degree of interest in the subject. There is a temptation, of course, to use new techniques beyond their limitations and this will be discovered earlier if they are fully documented. How the technique was constructed and operated, what assumptions were incorporated into it, what parts of the model were sensitive (in the sense that, if they were varied, a significant change could be observed in the output), what parts of the Sub-region were sensitive, will all be relevant here. The operator will look at the role of any new technique in the Study process and its capacity to fill that role.

(iii) *Goals and Objectives.* Sub-regional planning does not operate within well-established procedures and goals and objectives are important initially to establish and maintain a consistent direction and inform others what the team are about. The Terms of Reference are a starting point but the planner draws substantially on his own experience and the results of his analysis of the area.

As the process advances different groups of objectives appear:

(a) aims to be pursued in a trade-off process,
(b) essential requirements for all strategies, which are not subject to trade-off, and
(c) the best ways, from an operational point of view, of completing particular tasks.

Confusion between these three can occur. Also some are likely to be further broken down or elaborated as the process goes on, so that clear definitions at each stage are important. The bridge between very broad goals and detailed criteria for selecting land uses is difficult to build and worthy of the operator's close attention. Similarly the adequacy of the objectives for the role they play in strategy generation/evaluation. Different objectives held by different societal groups is an area where there is room for further development.

(iv) *Generation.* This stage is very important, because the way it is designed, and the nature of the input to it, determines the breadth and intensity of search for a preferred strategy. Some important possibilities may be excluded from consideration altogether, so that the process is biased however exhaustive the testing at later stages. The nature of the Study and the area is important: New Town Studies clearly have different requirements from Co-ordination Studies, and a megalopolitan area will call for different techniques from a sparsely populated rural area.

Generation processes are now becoming highly sophisticated and difficult to summarise. As an aid to memory, however, some of the most striking characteristics and weaknesses of different approaches which we have observed in the past are as follows: "Problem Solving" can cope with only a short time horizon and tends to lead to non-integrated policies which may be incompatible. Land-use/transportation surveys are now tending to be replaced by more broadly based planning studies because they focus over-much on a single aspect of planning. Threshold analysis also focuses strongly on a single problem—cost of infrastructure. "Stereotypes" are professionally acceptable as a basis for generation and can be chosen so as to represent the achievement, in urban form, of particular objectives. One cannot assume, however, that forms which have been successful in one area over one period of time will necessarily be successful in another. In particular, the need to consider the structure of existing settlements before and after the plan will influence the form adopted. Objectives-based techniques tend to be easily demonstrated, although they are based on assumptions and criteria which may not necessarily be accepted outside the area. A cyclical generation process gives opportunities for developing strategies as lessons are learned from each cycle, and it is well equipped to exploit computer models, although all strategies are not tested with the same rigour.

(v) *Elaboration and Evaluation.* The techniques adopted at this stage should focus attention on the really important issues and be effective in isolating a preferred strategy. The strategy should be seen to follow from the tests and the process should be understood by the public and be convincing.

Elaboration is a useful discipline of quantifying the alternatives. Its design is important because errors in arithmetic and circular reasoning can bias the process.

We have pointed, several times, to the difficulty of distinguishing clearly between generation and evaluation, and some of the points made in section (iv) are relevant here, particularly that alternatives representative of all the main possibilities should be tested at some stage. The degree of detail which should be applied to this full range is a question where opinions differ.

The nature of the area and problem is again important: some techniques, for example, focus strongly on cost of fixed investment and may be preferred in some circumstances. Perhaps the main division, however, springs more from the personal preferences of team and sponsors than anything else, and is between efficiency and effectiveness methods. Putting money values on things for which there can be no market price is repellent to some, as is the idea of adding costs which can be estimated fairly confidently to those which are very speculative, particularly if the latter are the biggest item in the equation. On the other hand, evaluation based on criteria which have meaning only in the context of the particular Sub-region may have less impact on central government who must allocate resources between Sub-regions.

The problem of different objectives held by different societal groups is one where there is room for development in the future.

There has recently been interest in designing strategies which allow for changing circumstances, and we would expect flexibility tests to form a part of any evaluation stage.

(vi) *Consultations*. Most of the work under this heading (as with "Implementation") will not involve the application of techniques, but will rather be questions of experience, judgement and "political" ability. As such it is more relevant at the upper stage of our procedure. The operator will, however, wish to look at the mechanics of consultations and ask who were consulted and who were not approached, what they were consulted about and how the answers were fed into the technical process. The design of questionnaires and how fully those consulted understood the questions and had a grasp of the problems will be relevant.

(vii) *Monitoring*. Monitoring is a subject where, no doubt, evaluation of the techniques and procedures used will be possible in the future. We therefore allow for this in a separate stage here. At the time of writing, however, very little experience has been gained of Sub-regional monitoring and we are unable to suggest many criteria. Since continuous monitoring involves a more or less permanent financial commitment, the question whether it is undertaken will not be entirely a technical one. If a procedure is adopted, the operator will ask: whether it is concerned with monitoring progress towards a set of land-use dispositions, or the objectives which lie behind the plan; the extent to which it involves monitoring decisions as well as collecting statistics; whether it is geared to giving advice about action to be taken when departures are observed from what is anticipated in the Study.

USING THE PROCEDURE

The Procedure is not a mechanical one which is amenable to the straightforward awarding of "marks" at clearly defined stages. We make no apology for this, because we do not feel it is the main issue. We prefer to try to increase the operator's awareness of the various influences on a Sub-regional team and help him understand the problems they are confronted with, the choices they must make. Nevertheless, those who prefer to obtain some quantified assessment will, no doubt, record marks against some of the headings we have suggested. The question of formal weighting then arises.

Weights will vary with the operator's purpose and with the nature of the Study. A New Town study, as we have noted above, will be much more concerned with technical excellence and less with trade-off and compromise than will a co-ordination study and this will obviously suggest something about weighting.

Another question will be his idea of the nature of Sub-regional planning in general. We have covered as many facets of Sub-regional planning as was expedient in this book, and while we have tried to set out arguments for and against with impartiality, the final listing of criteria, their arrangement under headings and even the inclusion of some of them in any form, represent decisions which some will question. To some extent this is unavoidable, but it has also been our desire to promote interest in certain things. If the operator objects to these he will, no doubt, take this into consideration in weighting.

CONTINUING EVALUATION

We have referred elsewhere to our views that a Sub-regional plan is not a once-and-for-all document, but part of an on-going process of decision-making at a strategic level. For people and planners in the area, therefore, a once-and-for-all evaluation is not enough. Circumstances change very quickly and soon questions will arise which were not anticipated in the Study. These must be judged in relation to the strategy and, as time goes by, the relevance of the strategy itself will be assessed against the new situations which have arisen. This is the sort of evaluation which continuous monitoring is intended to facilitate.

In terms of the purpose of this book we recognise, therefore, that a comprehensive evaluation of a Sub-regional study can only really be made after the plan period has elapsed. Unfortunately, because interest in monitoring is only now being translated into action, we have not been able to draw on sufficient experience of evaluating plans over time to give advice in this direction. There is a need for such evaluation in general terms, as well as for specific areas, to assess the relative effectiveness of the various techniques and policy instruments available to the planner and feed back this information into the plan-making process. It is to be hoped that the monitoring systems which are now being set up will eventually make a further book possible alone these lines.

CONCLUDING REMARKS

Sub-regional plans can be thought of as advice for sets of co-operative/ joint decisions—some sets necessarily in sequence and some not. We have also noted that these decisions relate to issues and events that interact strongly with one another and upon which many local planning decisions are dependent. It seems to us that the processes of making these plans, of evaluating them and of monitoring them, are so closely bound up together that new forms of Sub-regional planning are emerging.

Many people in Britain expect these to be "structure plans" because they are designed to deal comprehensively with the major strategic issues for areas that are supposed to have planning significance. Others suggest that the corporate management of local authorities is a more fruitful form despite its limitation to an administrative area and to a set of local government functions. We think that neither of these will suffice though each is capable of development along the lines we envisage. We can discern a possible outcome by looking at the activities that followed on the studies we have reviewed.

Several of the Sub-regional studies have been followed by structure plan preparation; some by master plans and some by nothing at all. In Coventry the planning activity of the early and mid-60s has been followed by first steps in corporate management. Teesside may well claim both structure planning and corporate planning; but all of these have been seen as follow-on activities and not as new forms or developments of Sub-regional planning itself.

The sequence in Notts./Derby. has some interesting features to show; features which suggest that some form of Sub-regional planning may persist and evolve.

We have already recorded that Notts./Derby. was succeeded by a series of studies into some critical issues that warranted further investigation. In addition, advice on the detailing of the strategy and its implementation was prepared. These studies and activities are properly called follow-up studies. We have also recorded how a monitoring system was recommended and how this has been initiated as an important decision-making activity at the Sub-regional level. In addition, each of the four constituent authorities in the Sub-region has taken steps to institute a monitoring system for its own local and structure planning as well as in some instances other activities of the authority. Moreover, a programme of co-ordinated structure planning has been prepared and special studies associated with this, and arising from the findings of the Sub-regional Study, have been initiated. An example is the Transport Study for a Nottingham and Environs area. The political, technical and administrative co-ordination of all these activities is a complex task, but one which is being grappled with. It is the desire for such co-ordination together with the continuing provision of the sort of technical advice that has been available over the last few years that has contributed to the initiation of the next step in the exciting sequence of events that has taken place in the Sub-region. The community management process developed in Toronto in association with the Decision Sciences Corporation is now undergoing experimental test applications in the Nottingham County and Nottingham City combined area. The two Authorities, in examining this method for its relevance to the management of their combined area after reorganisation, have, we believe, identified strategic planning for all local government activities at the Sub-regional scale, as an essential component of their decision-making activities.

This system, designed, marketed and operated by the Decision Sciences Corporation, is essentially a series of linked models (familiar on the one hand to planners and their professional colleagues and on the other hand to financial and administrative experts), arranged so that the output is presented in terms of the criteria habitually used for major strategic decisions, and in terms of the impact of proposals and trends on the operations and activities of the existing communities. Full details of this process are given elsewhere.[93] The important point for us to note, however, is the way in which the techniques of planning and the techniques of decision-making are brought together so that a framework exists for politicians and senior officers to be directly involved in the process of plan-making, evaluation and monitoring. At this stage the process is necessarily crude, but it is not without significance that it is in Notts./Derby. that these experiments are being tried.

References

1. COLIN COOPER, contribution to "Regional planning and implementation", *T.P.I. Journal*, Sept./Oct. 1970.
2. *Proceedings of the Nottingham Symposium on Sub-regional Studies*, Regional Studies Association, 1969.
3. Quoted by J. BRIAN MCLOUGHLIN in *Urban and Regional Planning—a Systems Approach*, Faber & Faber, 1969.
4. Ministry of Housing and Local Government, *Development Plans—a Manual on Form and Content*, H.M.S.O., 1970.
5. GEOFFREY STEELEY, The Evaluation Process, *Papers from the Seminar on the Process of the Notts./Derby. Sub-Regional Study*, CES IP 11.
6. AMITAI ETZIONI, *A Comparative Analysis of Complex Organisations*, Free Press, 1961.
7. AMITAI ETZIONI, *The Active Society*, Collier–Macmillan, 1972.
8. CHARLES E. LINDBLOM, *The Intelligence of Democracy*, Collier–Macmillan, 1965.
9. *Challenge of the Changing North*, H.M.S.O., 1967.
10. *East Midlands Regional Document Part I*, East Midlands Regional Development Conference, 1971.
11. DEREK SENIOR, Raw deal for England, *Municipal and Public Services Journal*, 26 Mar. 1971.
12. GEOFFREY VICKERS, *Value Systems and Social Process*, Penguin Books, 1970.
13. M. STEPHENSON and K. YOUNGER, Problems of Introducing a Point-referenced data system in an Urban Authority, paper in *PTRC-Datum CIUT Symposium Proceedings, Urban Data Management*, 11–14 April 1972, London.
14. ERLET A. CATER, *Information Needs of Planners—a Survey*, USRU-WP-4, University of Reading.
15. F. STUART CHAPIN (Jr.), *Urban Land Use Planning*, Urbana, Illinois, 1965.
16. E. L. CRIPPS, *An Introduction to the Study of Information for Urban and Regional Planning*. Working note USRU-WN-1, Urban Systems Research Unit, Dept. of Geography, University of Reading.
17. HARVEY S. PERLOFF, Key features of regional planning, *Journal of the American Institute of Planners*, May 1968.
18. Record Report No. 9, *Analysis of Employment Structure and Trends*, Notts./ Derby. Sub-regional Planning Unit, 1970.
19. MARGARET ROBERTS, series of articles published in *Official Architecture & Planning*, 1970–71.
20. JEFFREY WILLIS, *Population Growth and Movement*, CES WP 12.

191

21. *Population Projection Manual*, West Sussex County Council, 1971.
22. ROY GREGORY, *The Price of Amenity—Five Studies in Conservation and Government*, Macmillan, 1971.
23. *Glamorgan, A Planning Study*, Glamorgan County Planning Department, 1964.
24. *The National Plan*, H.M.S.O., 1966.
25. *The Task Ahead*, H.M.S.O., 1969.
26. W. BECKERMAN and Associates, *The British Economy in 1975*, National Institute of Economic and Social Research, Cambridge University Press, 1965.
27. *Mobility of Firms—The Study Findings*, Notts./Derby. Sub-regional Monitoring and Advisory Unit, 1972.
28. BARBARA SMITH, *Industrial Movement in and out of Birmingham*, Industrial Location Working Paper No. 39, Centre for Urban and Regional Studies, University of Birmingham.
29. Centre for Urban and Regional Research, University of Manchester, 1971.
30. H. ORLANS, *Stevenage: a Sociological Survey of a New Town*, Routledge & Kegan Paul, 1952.
31. Commission on the Third London Airport, Ref. 5016: Stage V Submission—Thurleigh. Evidence of the County Councils of Bedfordshire, Northamptonshire, Huntingdon and Peterborough and Buckinghamshire.
32. *East Anglia—a Regional Appraisal*, East Anglia Consultative Committee.
33. Listed in Countryside Commission, *Research Register No. 3*.
34. P. E. MCCARTHY and MICHAEL DOWER, Planning for conservation and development, *T.P.I. Journal*, Mar. 1967.
35. GERALD SMART, Rural Planning on the Context of the City Region, paper presented to T.P.I. Summer School, 1968.
36. SCOTTISH DEVELOPMENT DEPARTMENT, *Central Scotland: a Programme for Development and Growth*, H.M.S.O. Cmnd. 2188, 1963.
37. STAFFORD BEER, Operational research as revelation. Inaugural Address by the President, *Operational Research Quarterly*, Mar. 1970.
38. JAY W. FORRESTER, *Urban Dynamics*, M.I.T. Press, 1969.
39. G. K. INGRAM, review article on Urban Dynamics, *A.I.P. Journal*, May 1970.
40. G. F. CHADWICK, *A Systems View of Planning*, Pergamon, 1971.
41. H. R. HAMILTON, S. E. GOLDSTONE, J. W. MILLMAN, A. L. PUGH III, E. B. ROBERTS and A. ZELLNER, *Systems Simulation for Regional Analysis. An Application to River Basin Planning*, M.I.T. Press, 1969.
42. MICHAEL BATTY, An Experimental Model of Urban Dynamics, paper presented to the P.T.R.C. Conference on Urban Growth Models, 1971.
43. R. J. CHORLEY and B. A. KENNEDY, *Physical Geography: a Systems Approach*, Prentic-eHall International, 1971.
44. WILLIAM ALONSO, Predicting best with imperfect data, *A.I.P.*, July 1968.
45. I. CAULFIELD and T. RHODES, The Use of an Activities Allocation Model in the Preparation of a Structure Plan for South Hampshire, paper presented to the P.T.R.C. Seminar on Urban Growth Models, London, 1971.
46. WILLIAM MURRAY, *Analysis by the Potential Surface Method, Papers from the Seminar on the Process of the Notts./Derby. Sub-Regional Study* CES IP 11.
47. J. Q. STEWART, Empirical mathematical rules concerning the distribution and equilibrium of population, *Geographical Review*, Vol. 37 (New York, 1947), quoted by F. J. MONKHOUSE and H. R. WILKINSON, *Maps and Diagrams*, Methuen, 1952.

48. CHRISTOPHER ALEXANDER, *Some Notes on the Synthesis of Form*, Harvard University Press, 1964.
49. DOXIADIS ASSOCIATES, *The Emergence and Growth of an Urban Region—the Developing Urban Detroit Area.* A project of the Detroit Edison Company, Wayne State University, Doxiadis Associates, 1966–70.
50. D. BAYLISS, *Some Recent Trends in Forecasting*, CES WP 17.
51. M. M. WEBBER, *Beyond the Industrial Age and Permissive Planning*, CES WP 18.
52. See ref. 12.
53. *Central Scotland: a Programme for Development and Growth*, H.M.S.O., 1963.
54. ROBERT C. YOUNG, Goals and goal setting, *A.I.P. Journal*, Mar. 1966.
55. G. F. CHADWICK, *A Method for Regional Planning*, University of Manchester, 1969.
56. MICHAEL BATTY, extracts from project reproduced in *Planning Education at the University of Manchester*, University of Manchester, 1969.
57. ANDREW THORBURN, The Decision Oriented Framework for the Study, *Papers from the Seminar on the Process of the Notts./Derby. Sub-Regional Study*, CES IP 11.
58. C. J. VAN DEN BERG, *Changing Regional Planning Goals in a Changing Country*, Report of Proceedings, T.P.I. Summer School, 1966.
59. J. B. MCLOUGHLIN, *Urban and Regional Planning—a Systems Approach*, Faber & Faber, 1969.
60. GERD ALBERS, Toward a Theory of Urban Structure, paper given to the T.P.I. Summer School, 1968.
61. F. J. OSBORN and A. WHITTICK, *The New Towns: the Answer to Megalopolis*, Leonard Hill, 1969.
62. See ref. 55.
63. DAVID E. BOYCE, NORMAN D. DAY and CHRIS MCDONALD, *Metropolitan Plan Making—An analysis of experience with the preparation and evaluation of alternative land use and transportation plans*, Regional Science Research Institute, Monograph Series Number Four, 1970.
64. E. L. CRIPPS and D. H. S. FOOT, Strategy for the South East—5: Evaluating alternative strategies, *OAP*, July 1968.
65. G. M. LOMAS and P. A. WOOD, *Employment Location in Regional Planning—a Case Study of the West Midlands*, Frank Cass & Co., 1970.
66. SIR RICHARD CLARKE, *New Trends in Government*, Civil Service College Studies 1, H.M.S.O., 1971.
67. WILLIAM PETERSON, On some meanings of planning, *A.I.P. Journal*, May 1966.
68. WILLIAM ALONSO, What are new towns for?, *Urban Studies*, Feb. 1970.
69. See ref. 65.
70. See ref. 63.
71. See ref. 63.
72. N. LICHFIELD, Evaluation methodology of urban and regional plans: a review, *Regional Studies*, Aug. 1970.
73. Commission on the Third London Airport, *Report: Papers and Proceedings*, H.M.S.O., 1971.
74. PETER SELF, Nonsense on stilts: the futility of Roskill, *Political Quarterly*, July 1970, also published in *New Society*, 2 July 1970

75. LISA PEATTIE, Community drama and advocacy planning, *A.I.P. Journal,* Nov. 1970.
76. See ref. 37.
77. See ref. 72.
78. NATHANIAL LICHFIELD and HONOR CHAPMAN, Cost–benefit analysis in urban expansion: a case study of Ipswich, *Urban Studies,* June 1970.
79. MORRIS HILL, A goals achievement matrix for evaluating alternative plans, *A.I.P. Journal,* Jan. 1968.
80. *Op. cit.*
81. See ref. 79.
82. The Next Stages in Sub-regional Planning, Conference organised by the Centre for Environmental Studies, London, 7 Dec. 1971.
83. See ref. 5.
84. See ref. 40.
85. *People and Planning,* H.M.S.O., 1969.
86. A Study by ISCOL Ltd., *The Design of a Monitoring and Advisory System for Sub-regional Planning,* Notts./Derby. Sub-Regional Management Committee, 1972.
87. CHARLES E. LINDBLOM, *The Intelligence of Democracy,* Collier–Macmillan, 1965, and J. K. FRIEND and C. J. L. YEWLETT, Inter agency decision processes: practice and prospect, published in *Beyond Local Government Reform: Some Prospects for Evolution in Public Policy Networks,* Institute for Operational Research, 1972.
88. See ref. 63.
89. See ref. 87.
90. See ref. 87.
91. J. M. POWER, Planning: Magic and techniques, published in *Beyond Local Government Reform: Some Prospects for Evolution in Public Policy Networks,* Institute for Operational Research, 1972.
92. See ref. 40.
93. Requirements for Local Authority Planning and Systems—unpublished report prepared for the City of Nottingham and Nottinghamshire County Council by the Decision Sciences Corporation, Dec. 1971.

Author Index

Studies Index

Subject Index